By Tessa Bailey

Secretly Yours

BELLINGER SISTERS
It Happened One Summer • *Hook, Line, and Sinker*

HOT & HAMMERED
Fix Her Up • *Love Her or Lose Her* • *Tools of Engagement*

THE ACADEMY
Disorderly Conduct • *Indecent Exposure* • *Disturbing His Peace*

BROKE AND BEAUTIFUL
Chase Me • *Need Me* • *Make Me*

ROMANCING THE CLARKSONS
Too Hot to Handle • *Too Wild to Tame* • *Too Hard to Forget*
Too Close to Call (novella) • *Too Beautiful to Break*

MADE IN JERSEY
Crashed Out • *Rough Rhythm* (novella)
Thrown Down • *Worked Up* • *Wound Tight*

CROSSING THE LINE
Riskier Business (novella) • *Risking It All*
Up in Smoke • *Boiling Point* • *Raw Redemption*

LINE OF DUTY
Protecting What's His • *Protecting What's Theirs* (novella)
His Risk to Take • *Officer Off Limits*
Asking for Trouble • *Staking His Claim*

SERVE
Owned by Fate • *Exposed by Fate* • *Driven by Fate*

BEACH KINGDOM
Mouth to Mouth • *Heat Stroke* • *Sink or Swim*

STANDALONE BOOKS
Unfixable • *Baiting the Maid of Honor* • *Off Base* (with Sophie Jordan)
Captivated (with Eve Dangerfield) • *Getaway Girl* • *Runaway Girl*

Secretly Yours

a novel

TESSA BAILEY

AVON

An Imprint of HarperCollinsPublishers

SECRETLY YOURS. Copyright © 2023 by Tessa Bailey. Excerpt from UNFOR-TUNATELY YOURS © 2023 by Tessa Bailey. All rights reserved. Printed in the United States of America. No part of this book may be used or reproduced in any manner whatsoever without written permission except in the case of brief quotations embodied in critical articles and reviews. For information, address HarperCollins Publishers, 195 Broadway, New York, NY 10007.

HarperCollins books may be purchased for educational, business, or sales promotional use. For information, please email the Special Markets Depart-ment at SPsales@harpercollins.com.

FIRST EDITION

Designed by Diahann Sturge

Chapter opener illustrations © baza178/Shutterstock

Library of Congress Cataloging-in-Publication Data has been applied for.

ISBN 978-0-06-323898-5 (paperback)
ISBN 978-0-06-323902-9 (hardcover library edition)

22 23 24 25 26 LBC 5 4 3 2 1

For Kristy
A genuine friend, longtime encourager, and powerful advocate.
Thanks for the decade of laughs and truth telling.
I'm down for another one.

Acknowledgments

They say to write what you know. And if I know two things, it's wine and an identity crisis, so *Secretly Yours* is well within my wheelhouse. This book is best paired with whatever makes *you* happy, whether it's a perfectly aged Cabernet or a milkshake. Speaking of milkshakes, I'm going to try and not lay this on too thick, but you, reader, are the thing that makes *me* happy. I appreciate your voices, emails, and social media posts. I appreciate you even if you're one of the quiet ones. Thank you for giving me the confidence to keep doing this. Thank you, as well, to my steadfast and talented editor, Nicole Fischer at Avon, Holly Rice-Baturin—publicist of my dreams and perpetual ray of sunshine—and the wonderful and valued Naureen Nashid. Much gratitude to my agent, Laura Bradford. Eternal love to my husband, Patrick, and daughter, Mac.

Secretly Yours

Chapter One

$\mathscr{H}$allie Welch tipped down one corner of the comics section and peered across Grapevine Way, her stomach sinking when yet another group of locals bypassed Corked, her favorite, sleepy little wineshop, in favor of UNCORKED—the new, flashy monstrosity next door that advertised hot sauce and wine pairings in the window. The exterior of UNCORKED was painted a metallic gold that caught the sun and blinded passersby, giving them no choice but to stumble inside or risk vision loss. From Hallie's position on the bench, she could see through the front window to their state-of-the-art wine fountains and wall of stinky cheeses, the cash register lighting up like a pinball machine.

Meanwhile, the peeling white wrought-iron tables in the front courtyard of Corked sat empty and forgotten. Hallie could still see her grandmother at the far-right table, a modest glass of Cabernet sitting in front of her. Everyone would stop to say hello to Rebecca as they passed. They would ask her what flowers were in season and which bulbs were best to bury in the soil a particular month. And even though she was always reading a bestseller, she would carefully lay her silk-tasseled bookmark in the crease and give them her undivided attention.

The newspaper in Hallie's hands sunk lower, crumpling slowly at the vivid memory and eventually landing in her lap.

On the front patio of UNCORKED was a literal dance floor and a disco ball hanging from the eaves. It spun all day long, casting light refractions all over the sidewalk and turning people into apparent zombies who preferred wine out of a vending machine. At night, that ten-by-ten square patch of wood was packed to the gills with tipsy tourists, their purses full of overly pungent Rochefort, no one sparing a thought for Corked next door. Or outraged at the mockery of their very name by the overzealous newcomers.

When the shop opened a month ago, Hallie almost felt sorry for the young couple from downstate. Poor dears, sinking their hard-earned money into a gimmick. It would never attract the loyal Napa locals who honored tradition and routine. She'd been wrong.

UNCORKED was thriving. Meanwhile, Lorna, the sweet elderly owner of Corked, didn't even emerge at sunset anymore to light the candles on her outside tables.

Hallie looked down at the shatterproof wineglass in her purse. She'd been bringing it into Corked for tastings every day this week in an attempt to support the failing institution, but she needed a better game plan. Continuous day drinking had started off fun, but the days were beginning to blur together, and she'd found her car keys in the microwave this morning. Supporting Corked with only the help of a couple friends wasn't going to keep her grandmother's favorite table from vanishing off the sidewalk. And it needed to stay there. Far too many pieces of her grandmother seemed to float away into the wind lately, but not that table. Not the place Hallie had gone with Rebecca every single Sunday evening since high school and learned the art of gardening. It had to stay.

So, all right. Time to play offense.

Very carefully, Hallie folded up the funnies and tucked them beneath her arm. She scanned the sidewalk for any friends or clients, then walked briskly across the street toward UNCORKED. They'd added two potted ficuses on either side of their door, beautifully pruned into the shape of an ice cream cone, but there would be no brownie points awarded to the UNCORKED crew for proper plant maintenance. Not even for lush, well-loved greenery. And if Hallie Welch, proprietor of Becca's Blooms and St. Helena's premier gardener, didn't warm up to someone for diligent care of a plant, that's when they'd really pissed her off.

Besides, the plants weren't her current focus.

She paused outside of UNCORKED and eyed the disco ball, shifting in her rubber slip-ons.

Here comes trouble, said her grandmother's voice, drifting in somewhere from the great beyond. How many times had Rebecca taken a look at Hallie and said those words? Hundreds? Thousands? Now, in the reflective window of UNCORKED, she could see how her grandmother might make that prediction based on her facial activity.

Two round spots of color on her cheeks.

A firm set to her chin.

Expression . . . diabolical?

Let's go with "driven."

Mrs. Cross, owner of the coffee shop across the street, walked out of UNCORKED with a bottle of some celebrity's wine in hand and a paper bib around her neck that read *Sip Sip Hooray* on the front. She skidded to a stop and bowed her head guiltily upon spotting Hallie. "I don't know what happened," started Mrs. Cross, quickly tearing off the bib. "I let them add me to their text alerts just to be polite and this morning . . . I woke up to a message about wineglass rims dipped in chocolate and my feet just sort of brought me here for the three o'clock session."

"How was the wine?" Hallie asked, feeling winded. *Another one bites the dust.* "Robust, with a betrayal aftertaste, I'm guessing."

Mrs. Cross winced—and had the nerve to lick some chocolate from the corner of her mouth. "Sorry, hon." She slunk past Hallie and into the crosswalk, clutching her bottle of duplicity. "Have to run. I'm working the evening shift . . ."

Hallie swallowed and turned back to the disco ball, the glaring light forcing her to squint.

After a too-short second of debate, she retrieved a piece of bark that had been used to pot the nearest ficus—and reached up, jamming it into the top motor of the disco ball, halting the eyesore's next revolution. Then she bolted.

Okay, maybe "bolted" was an exaggeration. She jogged.

And she quickly realized she was not dressed for fleeing the scene of her first act of vandalism.

Rubber shoes were for plodding around in soil and grass, not for potentially being chased by the 5-0. Her colorful woven cross-body purse slapped against her hip with every step, her array of mismatched necklaces bouncing up and down in solidarity with her boobs. She had a teal scrunchie in her pocket, which she'd planned to use later to fashion a blond knot on top of her head while working. Should she stop and put her hair up *now* to make running easier? Curls were flying into her face, fast and furious, her gardening shoes making an embarrassing *squawk* with every step. Crime clearly didn't pay.

When a familiar face stepped into her path on the sidewalk, Hallie almost collapsed with relief. "Without asking me any follow-up questions, can I hide in your kitchen?"

"Fuck sake, what have you done now?" asked her friend Lavinia, donut artist and British transplant. She was just about to light a cigarette, a sight that wasn't all that common on Grapevine Way in St. Helena, but lowered the lighter to her thigh when she saw Hallie rushing toward her in a flurry of necklaces, curls, and frayed jean shorts. "Behind the standing mixer. Be quick about it."

"Thank you," Hallie squeaked, catapulting herself into the air-conditioned donut shop, Fudge Judy, speed walking past a group of gaping customers, and pushing through the swinging door into the kitchen. As advised, Hallie took a spot behind the standing mixer and embraced the opportunity to finally pull her curls up into a bun. "Hello, Jerome," she called to Lavinia's husband. "Those bear claws look beautiful."

Jerome tipped his head down to observe Hallie over the rim of his glasses and offered a slightly judgmental hum under his breath before going back to glazing donuts. "Whatever this is, don't drag my wife into it this time," he drawled.

Well used to Jerome's gruff, no-nonsense demeanor, Hallie saluted the former detective from Los Angeles. "No dragging. Message received."

Lavinia blasted into the kitchen, the smell of Parliaments trailing after her. "Care to explain yourself, missus?"

"Oh, nothing, I just sabotaged a certain disco ball outside of a certain wineshop." Hallie slumped sideways against the wall. "We had another defector. Mrs. Cross."

Lavinia looked disgusted, and Hallie loved her for it. "The one who owns the coffee shop? These hoes ain't loyal." She mimicked Hallie's posture, only she leaned against her husband's back, instead. "Well, I know where I *won't* be buying my afternoon coffee."

"The one you pour half into the garbage and replace with whiskey?" Jerome inserted, earning himself an elbow in the ribs.

"I knew you would understand," Hallie said, reaching a hand toward Lavinia.

"Oy. 'Course I do." The other woman grimaced. "But even I can't do any more daily wine tastings at Corked. Yesterday I gave away three dozen free donuts and told the postman I love him thanks to a Beaujolais buzz."

"Yes." Hallie replayed the whine of the disco ball grinding to a halt and her subsequent getaway jog. "I'm starting to think the daytime alcohol consumption might be affecting my behavior in a negative way."

Jerome coughed—his version of a laugh. "What's the excuse for your behavior *before* you started attending daily wine tastings?" he wanted to know. He'd turned from the glazing station and leaned back against the metal table, his deep-brown arms crossed over his barrel chest. "When I was on the force, we would have called this an escalation."

"No," Hallie whispered in horror, gripping the strap of her bag.

"Leave her be, Jerome," Lavinia scolded, swatting her husband on the arm. "You know what our Hallie has been through lately. And it is distressing to watch everyone migrate over to

UNCORKED like a big lot of lemmings. Too much change, all at once, innit, babe?"

Lavinia's sympathy caused a pang in Hallie's chest. God, she loved her friends. Even Jerome and his brutal honesty. But their kindness also made Hallie feel like the sole upside-down crayon in a box of Crayolas. She was a twenty-nine-year-old woman hiding behind a standing mixer after committing disco ball sabotage and interrupting the workday of two *normally* functioning people. Her phone buzzed incessantly in her purse, her three thirty appointment, no doubt, wanting an explanation for her tardiness.

It took her a full minute to fish the buzzing device out of her packed purse. "Hello?"

"Hallie! This is Veronica over on Hollis Lane. Are you still planning on landscaping my walkway this afternoon? It's past four o'clock now and I have early dinner plans."

Four o'clock? How long had she been brooding across the street from UNCORKED, pretending to read the same Nancy and Sluggo comic strip over and over? "That's fine. Go ahead and take off. I'll be over to get started soon."

"But I won't be home to let you in," explained Veronica.

Hallie opened her mouth and closed it. "Your garden is outside, right?"

"Yes, but . . . well, I should be here to *greet* you, at least. The neighbors should witness me acknowledging your arrival, so they don't think you're trespassing. And—oh fine, maybe I wouldn't mind supervising a little. I'm very particular."

There it was. Hallie's personal kiss of death.

A client wanting to control the flower narrative.

Her grandmother had been patient with that sort of thing, listening carefully to a customer's demands and gently guiding them over to her camp. Hallie didn't own a pair of kid gloves. She could produce beautiful gardens bursting with color and life—and she did. All over St. Helena. Keeping the name Becca's Blooms alive in the spirit of the grandmother who had raised her from age fourteen. But she didn't have a method to her madness. It was all gut feelings and mood planting.

Chaotic, like the rest of her life.

That's what worked for her. The madness kept her busy and distracted. When she sat down and tried to get organized, that's when the future seemed too overwhelming.

"Hallie?" chirped Veronica into her ear. "Are you coming?"

"Veronica, I'm so sorry for the inconvenience," she said, swallowing, hoping her grandmother couldn't hear her from heaven. "With it being late June and all, I'm afraid my schedule is bursting at the seams a little. But I have a colleague in town who I know could do a fabulous job on your garden—and he's much better at interpreting a specific vision than I am. I'm sure you've heard of Owen Stark, seen his name around town. I'm going to call him as soon as I hang up and have him give you a ring."

Hallie ended the call a moment later. "Well, my evening is free now. Maybe I'll go knock over a convenience store."

"Do steal me a pack of smokes while you're at it, babe," Lavinia requested without missing a beat. "And some antacids for our Jerome."

"Anything for my accomplices."

Jerome snorted. "I'd turn you in to the police in a heartbeat," he said, turning back to his bear claws, dusting them with powdered sugar.

He doesn't mean that, Lavinia mouthed at Hallie.

Hallie gave her friend a wry look. Truthfully, she didn't blame Jerome for being annoyed with her. This wasn't the first time she'd hidden behind the standing mixer. Come to think of it . . . had it even been a full month since the last time? On opening day at UNCORKED, she might have pilfered a few of the flyers being circulated around town. And by a few, she meant she'd canceled all of her appointments and snuck around, taking them out of store windows. On the final leg of her quest, she'd been caught by an overdressed manager in a tweed suit and little round glasses. He'd chased her half a block.

She should stop worrying so much about things she couldn't change. If she'd learned anything growing up with a vagabond for a mother, it's that change was inevitable. Things and people and even traditions were often there one minute and replaced the next. But her grandmother wasn't going to be one of them. Rebecca was the ship's rudder of her life. In which direction would Hallie go without her?

Hallie forced a smile onto her face. "All right, I'll leave you to it. Thanks for harboring me." Because she knew herself too well, she crossed her fingers behind her back. "I promise it's the last time."

Lavinia doubled over laughing. "My God, Hallie. I can see your crossed fingers in the stainless steel fridge."

"Oh." Face heating, she sidestepped toward the rear exit. "I'll just see myself out—"

"Wait! I forgot. I have news," Lavinia said abruptly, speed walking in Hallie's direction. She slung their arms together and pulled her into the small parking lot that ran behind the donut shop, as well as the rest of the stores on Grapevine Way. As soon as the screen door of Fudge Judy slapped shut behind them, Lavinia lit another cigarette and hit Hallie with the kind of eye contact that screamed *this is big news.* Exactly the kind of distraction Hallie needed to stall her self-reflective mood. "Remember that tasting you dragged me to a few months back at Vos Vineyard?"

Hallie's breath hitched at the name Vos. "Yes."

"And remember you got sloshed and told me you've been in love with Julian Vos, the son, since you were a freshman in high school?"

"Shhhh." Hallie's face had to be the color of beet juice now. "Keep your voice down. Everyone knows who they are in this town, Lavinia!"

"Would you stop? It's just you and me here." Squinting one eye, she took a long pull of her cigarette and blew the smoke sideways. "He's back in town. Heard it straight from his mum."

The parking lot seemed to shrink in around Hallie, the ground rising up like a wave of asphalt. "What? I . . . *Julian?*" The amount of reverence she packed into the whisper of his name would have been embarrassing if she hadn't hidden behind this woman's standing mixer twice in one month. "Are you sure? He lives near Stanford."

"Yes, yes, he's a brilliant professor. A scholar with a case of the tall, dark, and broodies. Nearly your first snog. I remember everything—and yes, I'm sure. According to his mum, the hot prodigal son is living in the guesthouse at the vineyard for the next several months to write a historical fiction novel."

A zap of electricity went through Hallie, straight down to her feet.

An image of Julian Vos was always, always on standby, and it shot to the forefront of her mind now, vivid and glorious. His black hair whipping right and left in the wind, his family vineyard like an endless maze on all sides of him, the sky burning with bright purples and oranges, his mouth descending toward hers and stopping right at the last second. He'd been so close she could taste the alcohol on his breath. So close she could have counted the black flecks in his bourbon-brown eyes if only the sun hadn't set.

She could also feel the way he'd snagged her wrist and dragged her back to the party, muttering about her being a freshman. The greatest tragedy of her life, right up until she'd lost her grandmother, was not landing that kiss from Julian Vos. For the last fifteen years, she'd been spinning alternate endings in her mind, occasionally even going so far as watching his history lectures on YouTube—and responding to his rhetorical questions out loud, like some kind of psychotic, one-sided conversationalist. Though she would take that humiliating practice to the grave.

Not to mention the wedding scrapbook she'd made for them in ninth grade.

"Well?" prompted Lavinia.

Hallie shook herself. "Well what?"

Lavinia waved her smoking hand around. "You might bump into the old crush around St. Helena soon enough. Isn't that exciting?"

"Yes," Hallie said slowly, begging the wheels in her head to stop spinning. "It is."

"Do you know if he's single?"

"I think so," Hallie murmured. "He doesn't update his Facebook very often. When he does, it's usually with a news article about space exploration or an archaeological discovery—"

"You are literally leaching my vagina of moisture."

"But his status is still single," Hallie laughed. "Last time I checked."

"And when was that, if you don't mind me asking?"

"A year, perhaps?"

More like a month, but no one was counting.

"Wouldn't it be something to get a second chance at that kiss?" Lavinia poked her in the ribs. "Though it'll be far from your first at this stage of your life, hey?"

"Oh yeah, it'll be at least my . . ."

Her friend squinted an eye, prodding the air with a finger. "Eleventh? Fifteenth?"

"Fifteenth. You got it." Hallie coughed. "Minus thirteen."

Lavinia stared at her for an extended moment, letting out a low whistle. "Well, Jesus. No wonder you have so much unspent energy." She stubbed out her cigarette. "Okay, forget what I said about bumping into him, you two-kiss pony. Happenstance isn't going to work. We must arrange some kind of sly meeting." She thought for a second, then landed on something. "Ooh! Maybe check the Web and see if Vos Vineyard is having another event soon. He's bound to be there."

"Yes. Yes, I could do that." Hallie continued to nod. "Or I could just check in with Mrs. Vos and see if her guesthouse needs some new landscaping. My waxed begonias would add a nice pop of red to any front yard. And who could turn down lantanas? They stay green all year."

". . . Hallie."

"And of course, there's that late-June discount I'm offering."

"You can never do anything the easy way, can you?" Lavinia sighed.

"I'm much better at speaking to men when I'm busy doing something with my hands."

Her friend raised an eyebrow. "You heard yourself, right?"

"Yes, pervert, I heard," she muttered, already lifting the phone to her ear, excitement beginning to skip around in her belly when the line started to ring. "Rebecca always said to look for signs. I just canceled that biweekly job with Veronica on Hollis Lane for a reason. So I'd be open for this one. Potentially. I might have Napa running in my blood, but wine tastings aren't my element. This is better. I'll have my flowers as a buffer."

"I suppose that's fair enough. You're just having a little look at him."

"Yes! A tiny baby of a look. For nostalgia's sake."

Lavinia was beginning to nod along with her. "Fuck me, I'm actually getting a little excited about this, Hal. It's not every day a girl gets a second shot at kissing her lifelong crush."

Exactly. That's why she wasn't going to overthink this. *Act first, reflect later.* Her credo worked out at least half the time. A lot of things had far worse odds. Like . . . the lottery. Or cracking open a double-yolked egg. No matter what happened, though, she'd be laying her eyes on Julian Vos again. In the flesh. And soon.

Obviously, this course of action could backfire. Righteously.

What if he didn't even remember her or that night in the vineyard?

After all, fifteen years had passed and her feelings for Julian in high school were woefully one-sided. Before the night of the almost-kiss, he'd been blissfully unaware of her existence. And immediately afterward, she'd been pulled from school by her mother for an extended road trip to Tacoma. He'd graduated soon after, and she'd never seen him again in real life.

A blank look from the man who starred in her fantasies could be a crushing disappointment. But her impulsivity had gotten worse since the loss of Rebecca in January, and it was too tempting to throw herself into one of her unknowns now. To let the chips fall where they may without reasoning through her actions first. A little niggle beneath her collar warned her to stop and slow down, take some time to think, but she ignored it, her spine snapping straight when Corinne Vos's crisp, almost amused-sounding voice curled in her ear. "Hello?"

"Mrs. Vos, hello. It's Hallie Welch from Becca's Blooms. I do the landscaping around your pool and refresh your porch every season."

The slightest pause. "Yes. Hello, Miss Welch. What can I do for you?"

Hallie held the phone away so she could gulp down a breath for courage, then settled the screen once more against the side of her face. "Actually, I was hoping I could do something for you. My waxed begonias are just stunning this year, and I thought some of them might look beautiful around your property..."

Chapter Two

Julian Vos forced his fingers to move across the keyboard, even though the plot was going off the rails. He'd set aside thirty minutes to write without stopping. Therefore, thirty minutes needed to be completed. His hero, Wexler, who had time traveled to the past, was now musing over how much he missed fast food and indoor plumbing of the future. All of this would be deleted, but he had to keep writing for another thirty seconds.

Twenty-nine. Twenty-eight.

The front door of the guesthouse opened and closed. Julian kept his eyes glued to the cursor, though he frowned. On the screen of his desktop, Wexler now turned to his colleague and said, "No one is scheduled to be here this afternoon."

His timer went off.

Julian slowly sat back in the leather executive chair and allowed his hands to drift away from the keyboard to rest on his thighs. "Hello?" he called without turning around.

"It's your mother." Her crisp footsteps moved from the entryway to the hall beneath the stairs, which led to the back office overlooking the yard. "I knocked several times, Julian," she said, coming to a stop in the doorway behind him. "Whatever you're writing must be quite engrossing."

"Yes." Since she didn't specifically ask *what* he was writing, he assumed she wasn't interested and didn't bother elaborating. He turned the chair around and stood. "Sorry for the wait. I was completing a thirty-minute cycle."

Corinne Vos cracked a small smile, briefly unearthing the lines around her eyes and sides of her mouth. "Still sticking to your tight schedules, I see."

Julian nodded once. "All I have in the fridge is sparkling water," he said, gesturing for her to precede him out of the office. Deleting words was part of the writing process—he'd read extensively about drafting methods in *Structuring Your Novel*— but his mother didn't need to see Wexler waxing poetic about cheeseburgers and toilets. The fact that Julian was taking a break from teaching history to write fiction was already providing her with more than enough amusement. He didn't need to add fuel to the fire. "Have a glass with me?"

She inclined her head, her gaze ticking briefly over his shoulder to the computer screen. "Yes, please. Sparkling water sounds fine."

They relocated to the kitchen in silence, Julian removing two slim glasses from the cabinet and filling them up, handing one to his mother, who hadn't taken a seat. Not wanting to be impolite, Julian remained standing, too.

"How is this place?" Corinne asked, tapping her row of Sacramento-green nails on the glass. They were always painted the same shade, to match the Vos Vineyard logo. "Comfortable?"

"Very."

"Are you sure you wouldn't rather stay up in the main house?" With a bemused smile, she swept the kitchen with a look. "We have food there. A staff to prepare it. Without those things to worry about, you could focus more on writing."

"I appreciate the offer, but I'd rather have the quiet." They sipped in silence. The watch on his wrist ticked. Not audibly, but he could feel the gentle drift of the second hand as it rounded the midnight-blue face. "Operations are running smoothly at Vos?"

"Of course. Why wouldn't they be?" Corinne set her glass on the counter with a touch too much force and folded her hands at her waist, pinning him with a look that made him oddly sentimental. It called to mind the times his sister, Natalie, got them into trouble around the vineyard as kids. They would return home to find Corinne waiting at the back door with a pinched forehead and instructions to clean themselves up for dinner immediately. By no means could his family be termed close. They were simply related. They carried the weight of the same last name. But there were instances in the past, like showing up at the back door just before dark covered in mud and sticks, when he could pretend they were like every other family. "There is something I want to speak with you about, Julian, if you have a moment."

Mentally, he deducted fifteen minutes from his next writing sprint and added it to the final one of the day, bringing him up even. Right on schedule. "Yes, of course."

Corinne turned her head and looked out at the acres sitting between the guesthouse and the main one. Land filled with row after row of Vos grapes. Lush green vines wrapped around wooden posts, pops of deep-purple fruit warmed and nurtured by the Napa sunlight. More than half of those support posts had been there since his great-grandfather founded the vineyard and the distribution side of Vos Vineyard in the late fifties.

The other half of those pillars had been replaced after the wildfire four years prior.

Also known as the last time he'd been home.

As if he'd recalled that hellish week out loud, Corinne's attention snapped back to him. "It's summer in Napa. You know what that means."

Julian cleared his throat. "Enough wine tastings to turn St. Helena into drunk Disneyland?"

"Yes. And I know you're busy here and I'm not trying to interrupt. But there is a festival coming up in just under two weeks. Wine Down Napa. It's a ridiculous name, but it draws a lot of attention from the media, not to mention a crowd. Naturally, Vos will have a significant presence there, and it would look good, in the eyes of the press—and the Valley as a whole—if you were there. Supporting the family business." She seemed fascinated by the crown molding. "If you could be there from seven to nine in the evening, that should suffice."

The request gave him pause. Namely, because it was a request from his mother, and Corinne didn't make those. Not unless there was a very good reason—especially with favors pertaining to the vineyard. She took great pride in managing the operation solo. Still, he couldn't shake the feeling something was off. "Does the family business *need* some additional support?"

"I suppose it wouldn't hurt." Her expression didn't change, but there was a flicker in the depths of her eyes. "Nothing to be alarmed about, of course, but there is a lot of competition in the Valley. A lot of new flash."

In Corinne terms, that was tantamount to admitting to trouble. What degree of trouble, though? Julian didn't know, but the subject of the winery had been closed to him four years ago. Forcefully. By his father. Still, he couldn't very well *ignore* the buried note of distress in his mother's tone, could he? "What can I . . ." He cleared his throat hard. "Can I do anything to help?"

"You can be present at the festival," she said without missing a beat, a smile returning to her face.

Given no choice but to back away from the subject for now, Julian dipped his chin. "Of course."

If Corinne was relieved, she showed it only briefly by dropping her clasped hands and shaking them out. "Wonderful. I would tell you to mark it on your calendar, but I suspect it's the first thing you'll do when I leave."

Julian smiled tightly. "You're not wrong."

Maybe the one thing the Vos family could be counted on to know about each other was their individual quirks. Their faults. Corinne hated relying on anyone but herself. Julian needed an airtight schedule. His father, though gone now, had been obsessed with cultivating the perfect grape to the point that everything else fell to the wayside. And his sister, Natalie, was never not scheming or planning a prank. Good thing she was off terrorizing the population of New York City, three thousand miles from Napa.

Leaving his glass on the counter, Julian followed his mother to the door.

"I'll let you get back to it," she said briskly, turning the knob and stepping into a wash of sunshine. "Oh, before I go, there may be a small commotion outside later today, but it's nothing to concern yourself with."

Julian drew up short, a vision of his stopwatch app vanishing like mist. "What do you mean by a *small* commotion? There is no such thing."

"I suppose you're right." She pursed her lips. "It'll just be a commotion."

"What sort?"

"The gardener. She'll be dropping by to plant some begonias."

Julian couldn't hide his perplexity. "Why?"

Brown eyes, very similar to his own, flashed. "Because I hired her to do so."

His laugh was short. More like a scoffing exhale. "I couldn't care less about flowers, and I'm the only one here to look at them."

They both stopped and visibly straightened themselves. Arguing was beneath them. They were civilized. They had been taught to grin and bear their way through anger, to not give in to the urge to win. Victory meant everyone walked away half satisfied, relieved to get back to their own separate world.

"What time is she arriving?"

Did the corner of Corinne's mouth jump a little? "Three o'clock." She smiled and stepped onto the porch, descending one step. Two. "Approximately."

Julian's eye twitched.

He loathed the word "approximately." If he could remove one word from the dictionary, it would be "approximately," followed by "nearly" and "somewhat." If this gardener gave only ballpark arrival times, they were not going to get along. Best to stay inside and ignore her.

Should be easy enough.

THE GARDENER ARRIVED with five minutes left in his writing sprint.

What sounded like a truck crunched to a stop in the pebbled driveway, the rumbling engine falling silent. A squealing door slammed. Two dogs started to bark.

Sorry, make that *three* dogs.

Jesus. Christ.

Well, if they needed something from him, they would all have to damn well wait.

He wasn't even going to break concentration to look at the time.

But considering he'd started this thirty-minute writing session at four o'clock, he assumed it was nearing four thirty—and that made this gardener a grand total of an hour and a half late. That was so late, it didn't even constitute late. It was a full-blown absence.

He would be letting her know it. Just as soon as his timer went off.

"Hello?" called an extremely cheerful voice from the driveway, followed by a chorus of excited barking. "Mr. Vos?"

Julian's fingers almost stopped on the keyboard at being called Mr. Vos. At Stanford, he was Professor Vos. Or simply Professor.

Mr. Vos was his father.

For the breath of a second, the motions of his fingers grew stiff.

He typed faster to make up for the stutter. And he kept right on going when the front door of the house opened. "Hello? Is

everyone decent?" Something about the voice of this gardener—
and apparent trespasser—tugged at his memory, but he couldn't
quite land on the face that matched. Why the hell did she need
to enter the home when his garden was outside? Had his mother
hired this person as payback for not coming home for four years?
If so, the torture was effective. His blood pressure rose with every creak of her footsteps down the hallway. "I'm here to plant
your begonias . . . *Boys! Heel!*"

If Julian wasn't mistaken, that was a pair of paws resting on
his shoulders. The cold, wet muzzle of another canine snuffled
at his thigh, then tried to dislodge his fingers from the keyboard.

Briefly, Julian's gaze fell to his stopwatch. Three more minutes.

If he didn't finish the session, he wouldn't relax all night. But
it was hard to concentrate when he could see the reflection of
a yellow lab in the computer monitor. As if sensing Julian's attention, the animal rolled over onto his back on the rug, tongue
lolling out.

"I'm so sorry to interrupt . . ." came the bright, almost musical
voice behind him. "Oh, you're just going to keep going. Okay." A
shadow fell over a portion of his desk. "I see. This is some kind of
timed session." She shivered, as if she'd just found out he was a
phantom haunting the premises, rather than someone who simply valued minutes and their many uses. Perhaps she should take
note. "You cannot stop . . ." she said slowly, her presence warming his right upper back. "Until the stopwatch runs out, or you
won't earn your glass of whiskey."

Wait.

What?

Oh, Jesus. Wexler was voicing the thoughts inside of Julian's
head again.

And the gardener was reading over his shoulder.

Finally, the timer went off, sending the dogs into a howling competition.

Julian pinned his phone's red timer button with his index finger, took a deep breath, and turned slowly in the executive chair, preparing the rebuke of the century. In the history department at Stanford, he was known for being particular. Exacting. Rigorous. But when it came to censuring students, he let his grades do the talking. He didn't have time for *extra* lectures after hours. When a student requested a meeting, he accommodated them, of course. As long as they scheduled in advance. God help the ones who showed up unannounced.

"If there is some reason you've decided to enter my home without permission, I would love to hear it . . ."

He finished turning.

Right there in front of Julian was the single most incredible pair of breasts he'd ever seen. Julian wasn't the type to gawk at women. But these breasts were just below his eyeline, mere inches from his face. There was simply no looking away. God help him, they were spectacular. Big, to put it bluntly. They were big. And displayed rather prominently in a baby blue T-shirt, through which he could make out the polka dot pattern of the gardener's bra.

"Is it true?" asked the breasts. "That you won't let yourself have a drink at the end of the day unless you write for the full thirty minutes?"

Julian shook himself, searching desperately for the irritation he'd felt pre-breasts, but he couldn't seem to locate it very easily. Especially when he looked up and finally met the gardener's sparkling dove-gray eyes and something, very unexpectedly, jolted in his midsection.

God. That's a smile.

And a whole lot of chaos.

Blond corkscrew curls rioted down to her shoulders, but a lot of them stood on end, pointing east or west, like broken couch springs. She had three necklaces on, and none of them matched. Gold, wooden, silver. The pockets stuck out of the bottom of her jean shorts and . . . yeah, he really needed to keep his attention above her neck, because her bold curves were demanding to be acknowledged and he had *not* been invited to do so. A lot like she hadn't been invited into the guesthouse.

Still. She was full-figured and hiding none of said figure.

There was something about the enthusiastic enjoyment of her body that made his own start to harden. Julian's realization that he was becoming aroused caused him to sit up straighter and cough into a fist, searching for a way to regain control of this insane situation. Three dogs were now licking themselves on the rug of his office and . . .

Something about this young woman was very familiar. *Very.*

Had they gone to school together? That was the likely explanation. Napa Valley might be large, but the inhabitants of St. Helena were a close-knit bunch. Around here, vintners and their employees tended to remain local forever. They passed on their practices to future generations. Just this afternoon, while on his daily run, he'd come across Manuel, the current vineyard manager whose father emigrated from Spain when Julian was in elementary school. Manuel's son was only twelve, but already he was learning the trade so he could take over for his father one day. Once wine seeped into the lifeblood of a family, it tended to stay there. Similarly, wine ran in the veins of most locals. With the exception of newly minted tech millionaires purchasing vineyards for bragging rights, there wasn't a lot of turnover in residents.

Certainly, however, if he'd gone to school with this now-gardener, he would remember.

She was nothing if not memorable.

Why was the sensation in his belly telling him he should know her *well*, though?

It would be better to proceed as if this was their first meeting, just in case his perception was off, right? Weren't men always trying to pick up women by claiming to know them from somewhere? Or was that just his colleague Garth?

Julian stood and extended his hand. "I'm Julian Vos. Nice to meet you."

The light in her eyes dimmed distinctively, and he suspected, in that moment, that he'd already fucked up their acquaintance. His stomach soured at the way she blinked rapidly and renewed her smile, as if putting on a brave face. Before he could claw his way back and ask why she struck him as so familiar, she spoke. "I'm Hallie. Here to plant your begonias."

"Right." She was short. Several inches shorter than him. With a sunburned nose that he couldn't seem to stop staring at. More appropriate than her incredible breasts, he supposed. *Stick with the nose.* "Did you need something from me?"

"Yes. I do." Now she seemed to be shaking herself free of whatever was happening in her head. Why did he feel as if he'd disappointed her? Furthermore, why did he want to discern her thoughts so badly? This unpunctual woman and her hounds were interrupting his work, and he still had one more thirty-minute session before his workday ended. "The water that leads to the hose outside is turned off, since no one has been living here. I'll need it to water the begonias after they're planted. You know? To really welcome them home? There should be a handle in the cellar or maybe in a laundry room ... ?"

He watched her hand mimic the motion of twisting a knob, noting the abundance of rings. The dirt under her nails was from gardening, no doubt. "I have no idea."

She flicked a curl out of her eye and beamed a smile up at him. "I'll go have a look."

"Please. Be my guest."

A beat passed before she turned, as if expecting more from him. When he didn't deliver, she whistled at the dogs, bringing the trio of them to their feet. "Come on, boys. Come on." She coaxed them down the hallway with vigorous scratches behind their ears.

Without realizing right away what he was doing, Julian followed them.

Everything about her movements drew the eye. They were harried and controlled all at once. She was a walking whirlwind, knocking into her dogs, apologizing to them, and turning in circles, searching for the handle of this faucet. In and out of rooms she went, muttering to herself, surrounded by her pack of animals.

He couldn't look away.

Before Julian knew it, he'd followed Hallie into the laundry room, finding her on hands and knees, trying to wrench a circular piece of metal to the left, her dogs barking as though delivering encouragement or possibly instructions.

Had this house really been dead silent five minutes ago?

"I've almost got it, boys, hold on." She groaned, strained, her hips tilting up, and the blood in his head rushed south so quickly, he nearly saw double.

One of the dogs turned and barked at him.

As if to say, *Why are you just standing there, asshole? Help her.*

His only excuse was being thoroughly distracted by the lightning jolt of energy she'd delivered to his space in a matter of moments. And yes, also by her attractiveness—an odd cross between radiant pinup girl and unkempt earth mother—and being distracted by her appearance wasn't appropriate at all. "Please get off the floor," Julian said briskly, unfastening the buttons on the wrists of his dress shirt and rolling up the sleeves. "I'll turn it on."

When she scooted back and stood, her hair was even more disarrayed than before and she had to tug down her ridden-up jean shorts. "Thanks," she breathed.

Was she staring at his forearms?

"Of course," he said slowly, taking her spot on the floor.

In the reflection of the handle, he could have sworn she was smiling at his bent-over form, specifically his ass, but the image was probably just inverted.

Unless it wasn't?

Shaking his head over the whole odd situation, Julian gripped the handle and wrenched it left, turning until it stopped. "Done. Do you want to check it out?"

"I am," she said throatily. "Oh, the hose? I—I'm sure the water is on now. Thank you."

Julian came to his feet just in time to watch Hallie tornado her way out of the house, her canine admirers following her with utter devotion in their eyes, their nails clicking over his hardwood floor until they disappeared outside. Silence descended hard.

Thank God.

Still, he followed Hallie.

No idea why. His work was waiting.

Maybe because he felt this oddly unsettled feeling, like he'd failed a test.

Or perhaps because he'd never answered her question.

Is it true? That you won't let yourself have a drink at the end of the day unless you write for the full thirty minutes?

If this young woman was blunt enough to ask a stranger about his habits, there was a good chance she would have several uncomfortable follow-ups, which he didn't have the time or inclination to answer. Yet he continued to the porch, anyway, watching as she lowered the gate on her white pickup truck and started to unload pallets of red flowers. The tiny woman who barely reached his chin staggered under the weight of the first load of flowers, and Julian lurched forward without thinking, the dogs yipping at his approach. "I'll carry the flowers. Just tell me where you want them."

"I'm not sure yet! Just set them down on the lawn. Where that line of shrubs begins."

Lifting a pallet of flowers, Julian frowned. "You're not sure where they're going?"

Hallie smiled over her shoulder. "Not yet."

"When will you decide where they should go?"

The gardener dropped to her knees, leaned forward, and smoothed her hands over the turned brown soil. "The flowers more or less decide for themselves. I'll move them around in their individual containers until they look just right."

Julian didn't exactly love the sound of that. He stopped a few feet away, trying and failing not to notice the strands of frayed, white denim lying on the backs of her thighs. "They will be an equal distance apart, I assume."

"Maybe on accident?"

That did it. His mother was definitely punishing him. She'd sent him this curvaceous gardener to throw off his concentration and flaunt his need for organization. Detailed plans. A schedule. Relative sanity.

She laughed at his expression, stood, and chewed her lip a moment. Brushed her hands down the worn-in lap of her shorts. Was she blushing now? Back in the house, he could have sworn she was cataloguing his physique. Now, however, she ducked past him, almost as if too shy to look him in the eye. The mini blond hurricane returned to the truck for a canvas bag full of tools, then picked her way back across the yard in his direction. "So," she started on her way past him. "You took a break from teaching to write a book. That's so exciting. What made you decide to do that?"

Finally, he set down the tray of flowers. "How did you know?"

Trowel in hand, she paused. "Your mother told me."

"Right." He didn't know what to do with his hands now. They were too dirty to put in his pockets, so he just kind of stood there looking at them. "It's something I'd always planned to do. Write the book. Though the occasion came sooner than I expected."

"Oh. Why?"

Hallie knelt straight down into the dirt, and his stomach turned sideways. "Can I not get you a towel or something?" She threw him an amused glance but didn't answer. And, in a way, Julian supposed he was stalling. He didn't know how to answer her question. Why was he back in Napa, writing the book sooner than expected? His answer was personal, and he'd spoken it out loud to no one. For some reason, though, the idea of telling Hallie didn't make him feel uncomfortable. After all, she was casually digging away in the dirt, instead of waiting on his answer as if it would be some monumental revelation. "I changed the order of my ten-year plan slightly after . . . well, my colleague at Stanford, Garth, had something of a mental breakdown."

She set down the trowel. Twisted her butt around in the dirt to face him, cross-legged.

But her undivided attention didn't throw him off or make him wish he hadn't started down this path. Her knees were caked in soil. This was as low pressure as it got.

"Normally I would be teaching through the summer. I've been going year-round for some time now. I wouldn't . . . know what the hell to do with a break."

Hallie's gaze flickered past him to the sprawling vineyard, and he knew what she was thinking. He could come home to his family's nationally renowned vineyard on a break. No. It wasn't quite as easy as that. But that was a far different conversation.

"Anyway, toward the end of the spring semester, there was a commotion during one of my lectures. A student ran down the hall and interrupted my lesson on the geographical conceptions of time. They asked me for assistance. Garth had . . ." The difficult memory had him rubbing at the back of his neck, remembering too late that his hands were dirty. "He'd locked himself in his office. And he wouldn't come out."

"Oh no. Poor guy," Hallie murmured.

Julian gave a brief nod. "He had some personal issues I wasn't aware of. Instead of dealing with them head-on, he'd taken on a heavy course load and . . ."

"It was too much."

"Yes."

One of the dogs approached Hallie, nuzzling her face. She received the lick, absently patting the animal on the head. "Is he doing better now?"

Julian thought of the relaxed phone conversation he'd had with his colleague three days prior. Garth had even laughed, which had relieved Julian, while at the same time filling him with a certain envy. If only he were as resilient and quick to get on the road to recovery as his friend. "He's taking some much-needed time off."

"And . . ." She picked up her trowel again and started creating a completely new hole. As far as he could tell, she wasn't even finished with the first one. "The situation with Garth made *you* want to take a break as well?"

A rock formed in his throat. "We've been teaching the same length of time," he said briskly, leaving out the fact that he wasn't without his own—unacknowledged—personal issues. Many of which had to do with their current surroundings. Memories of the tendons in his throat constricting, a weight pressing down on his chest. The dizziness and inability to find roots in his current surroundings. Julian determinedly shuffled aside those thoughts, returning to the matter of Garth. "We had the same course load with very little leeway. Stepping back just seemed like the wise thing to do. Thankfully, I'd left some flexibility in my schedule."

"Your ten-year plan."

"That's right." He looked back at her truck, noting the bright blue-and-purple script reading *Becca's Blooms*. "As a business owner, surely you have one."

She rolled her lips inward and gave him a sheepish look from her position in the dirt. "Would you settle for a one-hour plan?" Her hands paused. "Actually, scratch that. I still haven't decided if I'm picking up dinner from the diner or Francesco's on the way home. I guess I have a ten-minute plan. Or I would if I knew where these flowers were going. Boys!"

The dogs descended on her, snuffing happily into her neck. Almost like she'd called them over with the express purpose of derailing her train of thought.

"Who is Becca?" Julian asked, wincing at the slobber left behind on her shoulder. "Your truck says Becca's Blooms," he explained a little too loudly, trying to drown out the odd pounding of his pulse. He'd never seen anyone so casually muddled in his life. In the dirt with her flowers and dogs and no plan.

"Rebecca was my grandmother. Becca's Blooms was established before I was born. She taught me how to garden." She tilted her head a little, didn't meet his eyes. "She's been gone since January. Just . . . heart failure. In her sleep." A shadow moved across her features, but she brightened again quickly. "Now *she* would have put your flowers an equal distance apart."

"I'm very sorry," he said, stopping when he realized she'd planted three big gatherings of red blooms and their accompanying greenery. It had happened so quickly and organically as they spoke, he didn't even notice. Stepping back, Julian framed up the plantings with the house and found she'd sort of . . . anchored the empty spaces in between the windows with flowers. Like filling in gaps. Did she do it unconsciously? There seemed to be a method here that he couldn't decipher. Still, the spacing was way off-kilter and already she was positioning the next one *way* off to the left, prompting a throbbing behind his eyes. "Would you mind just putting it closer to the others? You're right on the brink of a semicircle. If I tilt my head. And squint."

A lot like in their initial meeting in his office, he sensed her

disappointment even though she kept right on smiling. "Oh."
She bobbed her blond curls. "Sure."

"Never mind."

The words were out of his mouth before he realized he'd spoken.
But she'd already put the flowers closer to their counterparts.
Patted the dirt around them and turned on the hose to give them
some water. And now she was gathering her things, sliding the
trowel into a pocket it hadn't been in earlier, if he recalled correctly. The dogs were circling her, sensing their imminent departure, dancing on their paws.

Yes, they were leaving.

Thank God. Right? Now he could get back to work.

What time was it, anyway?

Had he actually *lost track* of the minutes since Hallie's arrival?

Julian was so startled by the rare possibility that Hallie was
halfway to the truck with her fan club before he realized it. "Bye,
Julian," she called, tossing her tool bag into the open cab of the
truck and prying open the creaking driver's-side door, stepping
back so her dogs could pile in. "Good luck with the book. It was
really nice to see you again."

"Wait." He froze. "Again?"

She started the truck and drove right out of his driveway
without answering.

They'd met before. He knew it. Where? How?

The stillness that fell in the wake of Hallie's hectic presence
eventually reminded Julian that he had a purpose for being
in Napa. The cursor was blinking on his screen inside. Time
marched forward. And he couldn't spare any more thoughts on
the pinup earth mother or the fact that she was extremely pretty.
She'd caused a disruption to his routine, and now it was over.

He should be grateful.

No, he *was*.

Perhaps he'd been momentarily fascinated by someone so wildly different from him, but on a regular basis? That kind of disorder in another person would drive him up the wall.

"No, thank you," Julian said to himself on the way back inside. "Not happening."

Chapter Three

Hallie pushed her cart down the outdoor aisle of the nursery, tapping the skip button on the music app with her thumb. Next song. Next song. She'd gone through everything from Glass Animals to her nineties hip-hop mix and couldn't seem to settle on anything today. After seeing Julian Vos again the afternoon before, she was caught between songs about unrequited crushes, letting go of the past, and hot tub orgies. In other words, she was a tad confused.

She stopped pushing the cart and stooped down to pick up a bag of potting soil, adding it to her cart with a grunt and continuing on. Oh, fifteen years later, Julian Vos was still gorgeous. *Beyond* gorgeous, really, with his ropey forearms and perfectly groomed black hair. Those same bourbon-brown eyes she remembered, in all their intensity and intelligence. She'd actually forgotten how much he towered over her five-foot-three-inch frame.

And that *butt*.

That butt had aged like a Cabernet. Full-bodied and—she assumed—delicious.

Neither Julian nor his backside had remembered her, however.

It surprised Hallie how much him forgetting that night crushed her. Sure, she'd always carried a torch for him. But until yesterday, she wasn't aware of exactly how bright it burned. Or how much it would suck to have it snuffed out by his foggy memory.

And his exact oppositeness.

Yes, he'd always been studious and structured. She should not have been surprised when he asked her to relocate the begonias. But apparently she'd created some idea of Julian Vos in her mind that wasn't technically real. The man from her dreams who connected with her on a molecular level and could read her mind? He didn't exist in reality. She'd built him up into a fantasy that would never play out. Had she been measuring men with the Julian Vos yardstick for fifteen years? Who could measure up to a figment of her imagination?

Although, some stubborn part of her brain refused to accept that he was flat-out stodgy with a side of arrogance. There was a reason she'd crushed so hard on him during freshman year of high school, right? Yes. As a senior, he'd been nothing short of brilliant. A shoo-in for valedictorian. A track-and-field star. A local celebrity, by virtue of his last name. But those weren't the only qualities that had attracted Hallie.

No, on more than one occasion, she'd witnessed him being *good*.

At the one and only track meet she'd ever attended, he'd stopped running during a four-hundred-meter dash to help up an opponent who'd fallen and twisted his ankle, thus sacrificing his own opportunity to win. As she'd held her breath in the stands, he'd done it the same way she'd observed him doing everything else. With quiet intensity. Practical movements.

That was Julian's way. He broke up fights with a simple line of logic. He'd have his head buried in a book while the senior girls swooned over him from a distance.

Hallie had traveled all over the West Coast by that point. On the road, traveling from gig to gig with her mother. She'd met thousands of strangers, and she'd never encountered anyone like Julian Vos. So at ease in his good looks and rich with character. Unless her fourteen-year-old mind had truly embellished the finer points of his personality? If she was asking herself that question, it was probably time to let the crush go.

Later tonight, she'd remove the bookmark of his YouTube lectures. She'd smooth out the dog-eared page containing his senior yearbook photo. In order to blot out the memory of their almost-kiss, she'd probably require hypnosis, but the recollection of his head dipping toward her, the fiery sky blazing all around them, had already begun receding at the edges. Her chest hurt over the loss of something that had been her companion for so long. The only constant besides her grandmother. But feeling stupid for nursing a crush on someone who didn't even remember her?

Yeah, that stung a lot worse.

She knelt down and admired a flock of honeydew-green zinnias. No way she could pass them up. Later today—she couldn't remember what time—she was landscaping the front yard of a summer home, preparing it for the arrival of the owners who lived in Los Angeles the rest of the year. They'd requested lots of unique colors—and that was an ask she didn't mind in the slightest—

"Well, if it isn't the talented Hallie Welch."

The familiar voice brought Hallie to her feet, and she smiled warmly at the young man with ginger hair approaching her from the opposite direction. "Owen Stark. What on earth are you doing in the nursery buying flowers out from under me? It's like you own a competing landscaping business or something."

"Oh, you haven't heard? So sorry you have to find out this way. I am your competition. We are mortal enemies."

She narrowed her eyes at him. "Pistols at dawn, Stark!"

He slapped a hand across his chest. "I'll alert my second."

They broke into mutual laughter and traded places so they could see what the other had picked up. "Oooh, I'll have to grab some of those succulents. Their popularity refuses to wane, doesn't it? I like them for window boxes."

"I've got a client requesting them along his walkway. White stone."

"Low-maintenance special. Table for one."

Owen chuckled and fell silent. Hallie gave him a smile on her way back to her own cart, trying not to notice the way he catalogued her features, the piercing blue of his eyes softening along with his expression. She liked Owen, a lot.

Surely a better match for Hallie didn't exist anywhere in the world. On paper, at least. They were both gardeners. They could talk flora and fauna until they were blue in the face. He was kind, the same age, good-looking.

There was nothing *not* to like.

But she might as well admit that Owen Stark had fallen victim to the Julian Vos barometer. *That* and . . . Owen would fit into her life seamlessly. He'd make perfect sense in a way that was too perfect. A relationship with Owen would be natural. Expected. The person who coined the term "settling down" probably had this exact kind of partnership in mind. And settling down meant . . . this was it.

She'd be a gardener from St. Helena and would remain one for the rest of her life.

Did she want that? Her heart said yes. But could she trust that feeling?

When Hallie came to live with Rebecca, she had taken a deep breath for the first time ever, her grandmother's routine grounding her. Giving her a firm place to settle her feet. To stop spinning like a top. Without Rebecca's anchoring presence, though, she was picking up speed again. Whirling. Worrying she'd only belonged in St. Helena because of Rebecca and now . . .

Owen cleared his throat, alerting Hallie to the fact that she'd drifted.

"Sorry," she muttered, attempting to focus on him. Consider him.

Maybe next time he asked her out, she would say yes. And she would wear a dress and perfume, hire a dog sitter, and take it seriously this time. She could see it was coming, too. Owen popped a tablet of gum into his mouth, chewed a moment, and exhaled at the ceiling. Oh, this was serious. He was going to go for a steak house.

Why had she left the dogs at home? They were always the perfect excuse to bolt.

"Hallie," Owen started, red infusing his cheeks. "Since it's Friday and all, I was wondering if you had plans for—"

Her phone rang.

She sucked in a thankful breath and snatched it up, frowning down at the screen. Unknown number. So what? She'd even take a telemarketer over agreeing to a steak house date and hours of personal conversation with Owen.

"Hello?" Hallie chirped into the phone.

"Hallie."

Her stomach dropped to the ground like a sandbag. Julian Vos? Julian was calling her?

"Yes. It's me." Did her voice sound unnatural? She couldn't decipher her tone over the sudden babble of white noise in her ears. "How did you get my number?"

"I googled 'Becca's Blooms in Napa' and there it was."

"Oh right." She wet her dry lips, searching desperately for something witty to say. "So important to have that internet presence."

Nope. That wasn't witty.

"Who is that?" Owen asked, not so quietly.

"Who is that?" Julian asked, too, after a beat.

Client, she mouthed to Owen, who gave her an understanding thumbs-up. To Julian, she said, "I'm at the nursery buying materials for a project later today. I ran into my friend Owen."

"I see."

Seconds ticked by.

She checked the phone to see if they'd gotten disconnected. "Are you still there?"

"Yes. Sorry." He cleared his throat, but the sound was muffled, as if he'd briefly placed a hand over the receiver. "I'm distracted by the gopher holes in my yard."

Her blood pressure spiked at the utterance of a gardener's least favorite words. Except for maybe "weeds" or "crabgrass" or "do you take personal checks." "Gopher holes?"

Owen winced with sympathy, turning away to peruse a plastic shelf of mini cactuses.

"Yes, at least three." She could hear footsteps, as if he'd walked to the window to look out over the green expanse of lawn and the sun-drenched vineyard beyond. "One of them is right in the middle of the flowers you planted yesterday, which made me think you'd dealt with something of this nature before. Do you have a way of convincing gophers to move on? Or should I call pest control?"

"No need for that, I have a mixture I can use to . . ." The seal busted on her laughter. "Convince them."

He made a considering sound. "You're taking issue with my word choice?"

"Not at all. I'm picturing a formal negotiation. Once the contracts are signed, we'll shake his little paw. He'll pack his tiny suitcase and promise to write—"

"You're very entertaining, Hallie." Briefly, she heard a ticking, as if he'd lifted his watch closer to his face. "I'm sorry, I only have five minutes for this phone call. Are you able to make it over or should I just try and flush him out with the hose?"

"God, no. Don't do that." She cut a hand across her neck, even though he couldn't see her. "You're only softening the soil and making it easier for him to dig."

Owen shot her a horrified glance over his shoulder. *Amateur,* he mouthed.

"I have a job this afternoon, but I can swing by afterward," she said to Julian.

"At what time?"

"Whenever I finish."

Julian's breath released in her ear. "That's extremely vague."

How could it be so painfully obvious that someone was all wrong for her, yet his deep voice, and the very fact that he'd called her at all, was causing a mudslide in her stomach? It made little to no sense. Her lingering crush made her feel like a silly, naive teenager. While at the same time, the anticipation of seeing him again made Hallie almost light-headed.

So she would let herself go to the vineyard once more, even at the risk of extending this infatuation longer than it should have ever gone. But she wasn't going to jump over hurdles for him. Oh no. At this point, her pride was on the line with this non-remembering fool.

"Vague is all I've got, I'm afraid." She stared into the eye of an iris for moral support. "Take it or leave it."

He was going to tell her to shove it. She convinced herself of that distinct possibility as the silence stretched. The Vos family had money coming out of their ears. They could find someone else to resolve their gopher issue at a moment's notice. Julian didn't necessarily need her.

"I'll see you later, Hallie," he sighed. "God knows when."

"Why?" she blurted.

"Excuse me?"

Why couldn't she just have said good-bye and hung up the phone like a regular person? Owen was looking at her strangely. As if maybe he realized this wasn't a normal client call and was growing more curious by the moment. "Why do you want *me* there, specifically, for gopher negotiations? It obviously bothers you that I can't give a formal time."

"That's a very straightforward question for someone so committed to being vague."

"I'm not . . . committed to . . ." Was she committed to being vague? "Please just satisfy my curiosity."

"Is your friend Owen still there?"

Was he? She glanced up, passing a tight smile to Owen, who was definitely attempting to eavesdrop. "Yes, he is. Why?"

"Just satisfying my curiosity." She could almost hear the ticking of his jaw. Was he . . . annoyed at her being somewhere with another man? No. No way. That didn't track—not even in the slightest. "Very well. Yes, I want you, specifically, to come back and intervene with the gopher. When you left yesterday, you said, 'It was really nice to see you again,' and the fact that I can't remember how or where we met has shot my concentration to hell."

"Oh." Well. She hadn't been expecting that. In fact, she'd been under the impression he was relieved to see her go and couldn't care less about greetings and salutations. "I'm sorry. I didn't realize it was going to be such a big deal."

"I'm sure it wouldn't be. To most people."

Hallie thought of the meticulous way he stacked his lecture notes. How precisely he rolled up his shirtsleeves. The way he couldn't stop writing until the time ran out. "But you need things organized and tidy. Don't you?"

He expelled a breath. "That's right."

That's all this was. Julian didn't want to see her again because of an attraction or because he enjoyed her company. He simply needed their acquaintance tied up in a neat little bow so he could go back to his manic typing sprees.

Maybe she needed their relationship, however casual, tied up, too.

The gopher wasn't the only one who needed moving on.

"All right." She swallowed the object in her throat. "Maybe I'll tell you how we know each other later."

"Vague."

"Bye, Julian."

When she hung up the phone, Owen gave her a questioning look. "That was a weird conversation," he chuckled.

"Right?" She pushed her cart past him slowly. "Gophers put everyone on edge."

Metal rattled behind Hallie, signaling that Owen had turned his cart around so they could walk in the same direction. Normally that wouldn't bother her. Not at the nursery, anyway, where colorful flowers shot up out of the dirt everywhere she looked, acting as bright little buffers. But before the call from Julian, Owen had been on the verge of asking her out. And she'd been resigned to saying yes. Now, though? Now she hesitated. Once again, because of Julian Vos.

Man, she really needed to get Professor Forearms out of her head, once and for all. She wasn't being fair to herself. Or to Owen, for that matter.

"Owen." Hallie stopped the cart abruptly and turned, looking him right in the eye. Which seemed to stun him. "I know you want to ask me to dinner. On an actual date. And I want to say yes. But I need a little time." Julian's intense bourbon eyes blinked in her mind, but instead of stalling her speech, they gave her the impetus to push forward. "That's asking a lot, considering how much space you've given me already. If you say no, I'll understand."

"I'm not going to say no." He scrubbed at the back of his head. "Of course I'm not. You take your time." A beat passed as he sobered. "I'm just asking you to take me seriously."

His words hit her like stones. "I will," she said, meaning it.

Chapter Four

$\mathcal{H}$allie may have been vague about her timing, but her arrival resounded like a fireworks show. The growl of her truck engine cut out, followed by the slam of her rusted door. One dog started woofing and his buddies joined in solidarity, announcing the entrance of their queen.

Julian sat at the desk in his office printing out an article about a sundial that had recently been unearthed in Egypt. He planned on reading it tonight before bed for research purposes. His hand paused on the way to the printer, and he slowly leaned sideways, looking past his computer monitor to the yard beyond. And when her blond corkscrews—tied up in a white scrunchie this time—came into view, his mouth went bone-dry. A very disconcerting reaction to someone who played fast and loose with arrival times had caused him stress all goddamn day. Coupled with the fact that he'd lost hours of sleep last night trying to figure out how they knew each other? Suffice it to say, his attraction to her was an irritant.

One he hoped to forget about after tonight.

He just needed this one little loose end knotted, and he'd get back to sleeping and working and concentrating as usual.

According to his mother, as a child, he'd suffered from anxiety. *Nervous episodes*, Corinne had called them, the one and only time they'd had a discussion on the topic. No one had a clue if his anxiety was precipitated by a certain event or if he'd just been born with dread in his bones, but at age six he'd started seeing a therapist.

Doctor Patel gave Julian the gift of schedules. To this day, an organized list of times and activities was the tool he used to control his anxiety. Simply put, it worked.

Right up until the vineyard fire four years ago, anyway. For the first time since childhood, he'd lost his grip on structure, because time meant nothing in a fire. Since that weekend, he'd kept the schedules even tighter than before, refusing to have another slipup. Another leak through the cracks. Garth's mental break was a wake-up call, the impetus to take a rare step back and reassess.

Prior to the fire, Julian had returned to St. Helena every August at the outset of grape harvesting season, staying at the vineyard for a month and making sure the annual process ran smoothly, after which he'd return to Stanford in the fall to teach. Even from a distance, he consulted on matters pertaining to the winery. But no longer. Maybe if Julian had taken a breather at some point, he could have avoided what happened after the damage was wrought by the flames. His father might have continued to trust him to help run the vineyard, instead of dropping it all on his mother and hightailing it to Italy.

A bone seemed to grow sideways in his throat.

Focus on the problem at hand.

This young woman whom he'd apparently met at some point in the past was poking at the careful net he'd constructed around himself. He probably shouldn't have called her back here. It had been a risk. He'd weighed the threat to his sanity against the reward of knowledge—and fine, the damn urge to see her again—and surprisingly, the risk column had lost.

He was paying the price now.

The howling dogs were distracting enough, but nowhere near as sidetracking as her. Even though early evening had arrived, the sun was still going strong in the Napa sky. Orange rays settled on her like loving spotlights, giving her cheeks a youthful glow. Did she *ever* stop smiling? Her lips always seemed curved, as if she were holding on to a secret—and she was, he reminded himself. That's primarily why he'd called her over, instead of just making the homemade gopher-repelling mixture himself (really, the information was one quick internet search away). Not to lust over the silhouette of Hallie's curves.

"Jesus Christ, pull it together," he groaned, dragging a hand down his face and pushing away from his desk. He tucked in his chair and straightened the wireless keyboard before turning and striding for the front of the house. Yes, he'd lost sleep last night for more than one reason. Trying to unearth a forgotten memory was how it started. But all that thinking about the bubbly blonde and her tight T-shirt had led to something very different. Twice.

When was the last time he'd masturbated *twice* in one night? Had to be in high school. And even back then, he couldn't remember being so . . . vigorous about it. While lying facedown on his stomach, no less. He'd been forced to throw the sheets into the washing machine in the middle of the night and move to one of the other bedrooms. A humiliating turn of events if he'd ever heard one. Really, calling her back here was incredibly stupid.

What if this visit didn't give him closure? Would he try to see her *again*?

Back in Palo Alto, he purposefully dated women who *didn't* occupy too much headspace. Women who kept tight schedules and didn't have a problem coordinating them for things like dinner or sex or a work function. Hallie wouldn't even ballpark her ETA. If they spent significant time together, they'd be fitting him for a straitjacket within a week. So yes, get the closure and go back to work. The plan was firm.

A lot like he'd been last night.

Disgusted with himself, Julian pried open the front door, closed it behind him, and descended the steps onto the driveway. Then he hooked a right to the yard, where Hallie sat cross-legged in front of the freshest gopher hole, shaking up something in a large plastic bottle. "Hello there, Professor," she called, her voice echoing slightly through the vineyard.

The dogs ran over to greet him, yipping and snarfing at the air. He patted their heads, one by one, watching helplessly as they slobbered all over his pant leg. "Hello, Hallie." One of the dogs nudged Julian's hand until he scratched him properly. "What are their names?"

"The yellow lab is Petey. My grandmother was a big fan of the original *Little Rascals*." She pointed at the schnauzer. "That's the General. Not General. *The* General, because he bosses everyone around. And the boxer is Todd. I can't explain it—he just looks like a Todd."

Julian leaned back to study the boxer. "That's eerily accurate."

She breathed a laugh, as if relieved to be in agreement. He liked it, as well. Too much.

Stick to business.

He nodded at the plastic bottle. "What's in the formula?" As if he didn't already know.

"Peppermint and castor oil. They hate the smell."

She shifted onto her knees and dug some cotton balls out of the pocket of her jean shorts. They were lighter today. More faded. Meaning the material clung like underpants to her backside, while the sun stroked the worn denim in burnished gold. Her top wasn't quite as tight today—fortunately or unfortunately—but finger streaks of dirt were directly over her breasts, as if she'd wiped her hands off on them, palms chafing right over her nipples. Up and down. Feeling herself up in the front yard of some suburban hamlet, knees twisting in the dirt.

This is getting embarrassing.

While watching Hallie soak the cotton balls, he tamped down his attraction as much as possible, attempting to focus on more practical matters. Like getting himself untangled with this person. "Tell me how we know each other, Hallie."

She'd started nodding halfway through his demand, obviously expecting it—which he didn't love. Being predictable to her made him itchy. "I never said we knew each other. I just said it was nice to see you again."

Yes. That was correct. They didn't know each other at all. And they wouldn't.

Why did that only intensify the itch?

"Where have we seen each other, then?"

A blush rode up the side of her face. For a moment, he thought the sunset was responsible, but no. The gardener was blushing. And involuntarily, he held his breath.

"Okay, do you remember—" she started.

Hell broke loose before she could finish.

As soon as Hallie dropped those fragrant cotton balls into the gopher hole, the sucker peeked his head out the other end. Just like that. A real-life game of whack-a-mole, only with a gopher. And the dogs lost their ever-loving minds. If Julian thought they were loud before, their excited barking was nothing compared to the screeches and yelps of alarm as they dashed toward the emerging gopher—who, wisely, took off running for his very life.

"Boys! No!" Hallie jumped to her feet and sprinted after all three dogs. "Come back here! Now!"

Julian watched it all happen in a semi-trance, wondering how his plan to have a bowl of soup and read the Smithsonian article he'd printed out had been so spectacularly derailed. He'd anticipated having a clear head for the rest of his stay in Napa, this blip from the past having been resolved. But, instead, he was now running toward this loud explosion of mayhem, worried Hallie might get in between dog and gopher and accidentally get bitten for her trouble.

Wow.

He really didn't like the idea of her being bitten.

Or slipping. In the mud. Risking an injury.

Because that's what was happening. In slow motion, she turned into a pinwheel of limbs and corkscrews, and then her butt landed soundly in the bank of dirt that skirted the front lawn.

"*Hallie*," Julian barked—great, now he was barking, too—and scooped her up from behind by the armpits. "Christ, you can't just take off half-cocked like that. What were you going to do if you caught them?"

It took him a few seconds to realize her entire body was shaking with laughter. "Of course this is when I choose to have the most embarrassing fall of my life. Of course it is."

Frowning at that odd statement, he turned her around.

Big. Mistake.

The sun on her face made everything surrounding them—the

endless sky, the rambling vineyard, and the streaks of clouds, all of it—seem inadequate. Something tugged inside of him like a thread. The shape of her mouth . . . their height difference. Was there even something familiar about her earthy scent?

A heavy object rammed into Julian's leg, followed by a second one. Todd inserted himself between Julian and Hallie, barking in quick succession. A crunching sound came from behind Hallie—and there went the gopher again, followed by Petey and the General.

"Boys!" Hallie shouted, running after them.

They chased the damn gopher right back into the hole.

Hallie groaned and threw her hands up in the air. "He'll probably leave sometime during the night when my beasts have gone. No way he'll be able to stand the smell for long."

He could still feel the smooth skin of her arms in his palms, so it took him a moment to recover enough to respond. "I'm sure you're right . . ." he started, curling his fingers inward to capture the sensation before it fled.

But she didn't hear him, because she was busy wrangling her three frantic dogs. In shorts caked with mud. One of her feet was slipping dangerously toward the gopher hole. If an ankle sprain wasn't imminent, then something else anarchic would probably take its place. His whole evening would be off now. She'd done this to him for a second time, and he needed to take it as a sign to keep away. Strict schedules stopped the floor from rising up and swallowing him whole.

He wouldn't survive the shame of that downward spiral again. The night of the fire, he'd held on to his mettle long enough to do what was necessary, but what followed had been enough to drive his family to four different corners of the earth, hadn't it?

Julian required order. Hallie was *dis*order in the flesh. She seemed to shun the very method he used to cope with anxiety. Yes, she was beautiful and lively. Clever. Fascinating.

Also? So completely wrong for him that a sitcom writer couldn't make it up.

Why was he so interested in her thoughts and actions, then?

Or if this Owen character was really just a friend or a boyfriend of some description.

It made little fucking sense.

A vein throbbed behind his eye. He longed for pencil and blank paper, something simple that he could focus on, because being near Hallie was like staring through a kaleidoscope while someone twisted it really fast.

"Julian, is everything okay?"

He opened his eyes. When had he closed them? "Yes." He noticed the awkward way she stood, as if the mud on her shorts was beginning to harden. "Come on." He moved past her toward the house. "We'll get you something clean to wear."

"Oh, no, it's fine," she called to his retreating back. "I more or less go home in this condition every day. I usually strip in the backyard and hose myself down." Then, to herself, "Don't overshare or anything, Hallie."

Don't think about rivulets of water coasting down her ripe body. Don't do it.

Setting his jaw, Julian held the door for Hallie, who ambled past awkwardly, attempting to hold the denim away from her thighs. When the dogs tried to follow her into the guesthouse with paws that looked chocolate-dipped in mud, Julian pointed a stern finger at the General. "*Sit.*"

The schnauzer's butt hit the ground, tail wagging in a blur. The boxer and the lab followed their buddy's lead, plopping down at the base of the stairs and waiting.

"How did you do that?" Hallie whispered behind him.

"Dogs crave leadership, just like humans. It's in their DNA to obey."

"No." She wrinkled her nose at him. "They want to eat snails and howl at fire trucks."

"They can be trained *not* to do those things, Hallie."

"But you're forcing them to deny their natural urges."

"No, I'm preventing mud from being tracked into the house."

They looked down simultaneously to find she'd left four footprints just inside the door. With a tinge of pink in her cheeks, she toed off her rubber shoes and nudged them as close as possible to the door, leaving her barefoot on his clean hardwood floor. She had sky-blue nail polish on her toes, daisies painted onto the biggest nails. "If you tell me to sit, Julian Vos, I will kick you in the shin."

A strange lightness rose upward in his sternum, stopping just beneath his throat. A twitch of his lips caught him off guard. Did he . . . want to laugh? She seemed to think so, didn't she? The way she watched his mouth, a sparkle appearing in her eyes at his rare show of humor. Suddenly he was a lot more aware of their location—inches apart in a house glowing with late-afternoon sun—and again he encountered a tug of recognition but couldn't find the source.

God help him, he was too distracted, unable to look at her without his attention straying to her mouth, wondering if she kissed as wildly and without rhythm as she did everything else.

Probably.

No. Definitely. And he would hate the unpredictability of it. Of her.

Right.

"I'll get you that shirt," he said, turning on a heel. Though he didn't see her move farther into the house, he sensed that she would meet him in the kitchen, the heart and focal point of a home, not that he used it for much besides preparing turkey on whole wheat, soup, and coffee. Inside the bedroom, he hesitated for a moment at the dresser, observing himself in the mirror. Hair in disarray from his fingers, tightness surrounding his eyes and mouth. He took a long breath and looked down at his watch.

6:18 P.M.

The back of his neck clenched, so he filled his lungs one more time and mapped out a new schedule. At six thirty, he would eat and read his sundial article. At seven, *Jeopardy!* Seven thirty, shower. Then he would make some notes about tomorrow's writing plan, have them ready to go on his desk in the morning. If he kept to this schedule, he'd let himself have a glass of whiskey.

Feeling more in control, Julian took a folded gray shirt out of the top drawer. One with the Stanford logo silk-screened onto the pocket. As predicted, thank God, he found Hallie in the kitchen. But she didn't lift her head when he walked in because she was frowning down at something on the granite island in the center of the room. What did she find so offensive about his stack of mail? He'd had his correspondence forwarded to the vineyard for the summer, but the postal service was slow to begin the switch, meaning he was mostly receiving junk at this point.

She pinched one such advertisement between her finger and thumb, turning it over, letting out a distressed sound at whatever was on the back. "Wild Wine Wednesday . . ." she muttered. "'Let us blindfold your party and ply you with wine. Guess the vintage correctly and win a trip to the cheese wall.' I *hate* how fun that sounds."

"Beg pardon?"

"UNCORKED." She blinked rapidly, as if to keep moisture from forming in her eyes, and Julian experienced an uncomfortable pinch in his chest. "The newest wine bar sensation in town."

He set the Stanford shirt in front of her, an offering he hoped would prevent whatever was happening to her emotionally. "You don't like this new place," he guessed.

And then he died a little, because she used the Stanford shirt to dab at her eyes.

When there were perfectly good napkins within reach.

"Well. I've never been inside. I don't know the owners *personally* or anything. They might be lovely people who don't realize they are robbing a sweet old lady of her livelihood."

"Explain what you mean."

"Corked is right next door. A quiet little wine bar owned by Lorna. It has been there since the late fifties. My grandmother and I used to spend hours sitting at the white wrought-iron table outside. It was our spot. Lorna would give me a wineglass full of grape juice, and my grandmother and I would solve crossword puzzle clues or we'd plan gardens together." She looked down at her fingers for a few seconds. "Anyway, the whole shop is empty now because UNCORKED moved in beside it. They have a twenty-four-hour disco ball outside and endless stunts to attract tourists. The worst part is they *specifically* named their shop as a play on Lorna's bar and made a mockery of it. No one seems to mind, though. Lorna has quiet, intimate tastings without the fanfare. How is she supposed to compete with Adult Spin the Bottle?"

Her eyes took on a sheen that worried him, so he reached for a napkin and handed it to her, sighing when she used the shirt again, instead. "You're very upset about this. Are you close with Lorna or something?"

"She was closer to my grandmother, but yes, we're friends. And we've gotten a lot more friendly since I started attending daily wine tastings to offset the UNCORKED effect."

The corner of his mouth tugged. "Day drinking is always the solution."

"Said no one ever. Even in Napa." For a beat, she appeared almost thoughtful. "It has definitely made me more prone to committing petty crimes."

He waited for her to say she was joking. She didn't.

With a big inhale, she let the shirt unfurl down onto her lap. "I'm just going to change into this outside before I hop into the truck, so I don't get mud anywhere." With one last glance at the wineshop advertisement, she backed out of his kitchen. "Any *more* mud, I should say."

His plan had been to get Hallie out the door quickly, so he could start checking things off his to-do list for the night, but when she started to edge out of his kitchen, an anxious ripple in his stomach surprised him into saying, "Do you want a drink?" Totally normal to offer. He was just being a gracious host. "I have wine, obviously. Or whiskey."

He might even need two whiskeys himself tonight.

Could he drop the strict limits he placed on himself enough to allow that indulgence?

The offer of a drink had visibly surprised her, too. "Oh. I don't know." She considered him a moment. A long moment. As if she was trying to make some important decision. About him? What was it? "I better not," she said softly. "I'm driving."

"Right," he said, finding his throat was going dry. "Responsible of you."

She hummed, nodding at the mostly full bottle of Woodford Reserve whiskey sitting by the stove. "You should have one, though. A gopher in residence might even earn you two." She hesitated on the threshold of his kitchen, this wild-haired gardener with muddy shorts and a vendetta against a wineshop. "What would you have to do to earn two?"

His head came up quickly.

Because he'd been wondering that exact same thing.

How did she . . .

And then he remembered. Yesterday. When she'd walked into his office and read over his shoulder and asked afterward, *Is it true? That you won't let yourself have a drink at the end of the day unless you write for the full thirty minutes?* He'd never answered her question, but she'd held on to it. Was she that curious about his habits?

Julian had never told anyone about his goal-setting system. It would probably sound completely idiotic out loud. But he got the sense . . . well, he couldn't help but feel as if she were leaving for good, never to return, so what harm would it do to reveal this part of himself? She'd slipped onto her butt and cried in front of him in the space of twenty minutes. Maybe a part of him hoped admitting to his peculiar behavior would make them even. Make her . . . feel better.

Which was troublingly important to him.

"I only have two drinks at the end of a semester. The rest of the

year, I allow myself the whiskey if I've checked the day's boxes."
He'd been right. It did sound idiotic out loud, but it was how
he remained glued together. Time had always been the stitches
running through the fabric of his life, and he had nothing but
gratitude for the structure it afforded him. "For instance, if I arrived everywhere on time. To class, to meetings. If I completed
my workload and planned for the following day. Cleared my in-
box. Showered. Then I have the drink."

She stared at him. Not judgmentally. Just taking it all in.

"I've adjusted my routine for the summer . . ." he added unnecessarily, just to fill the silence. "I guess you could say I'm in
vacation mode."

An abrupt giggle snuck out of her mouth.

And satisfaction plunged from his neck down deep into his
belly.

He'd made her laugh. Yes, but now she just looked a little . . . sad?

"Julian, I don't think there are two more different people in
this whole world." Again, she didn't say those words as a judgment. More of a musing. Or an observation. "Do you?"

"No," he felt forced to admit. "I don't."

Oddly, that didn't mean he wanted her to leave.

His gaze ticked between Hallie and the UNCORKED advertisement. "They really named their store UNCORKED and
moved in right beside a shop called Corked?"

She threw up her hands, as if relieved to finally have someone's attention regarding the matter. "Yes."

"I'm surprised the local business association allowed that."

"I've emailed them on seven separate occasions. My last one
was in all caps!"

He hummed, not totally surprised to find his fingers twitching.

"What are you thinking about?" she asked slowly, turning slightly to glance over her shoulder. "You look like you're trying to visualize a new backsplash."

He almost said nothing and walked her to the door. But he'd already outlined the mind games he played with himself. What was the sense in holding back now? After all, he weirdly, confusingly, wasn't quite ready to let her leave. "I don't like when things are out of order like this. A shop moving in and presenting a direct threat to the business next door should not have been allowed to happen."

"I agree."

He *especially* didn't like the whole situation making Hallie cry, but he'd leave that part out. "When things are unfair or disordered, I tend to . . ."

"What?"

"I have something of a competitive streak. A small one. For instance, last year a *Jeopardy!* contestant gave their answer after the buzzer and was given credit. It didn't seem like a big deal at the time, but he went on to win Final Jeopardy with a margin of one hundred dollars. You see, a small breach in fairness can cause a snowball effect." He paused to gauge her reaction, deciding she looked more curious than judgmental. "A lot of us contacted the show and suggested . . . rather strongly that the other contestant be allowed to compete again. They relented."

"Oh my gosh." She rocked back on her heels. "You're a *Jeopardy!* groupie. I always wondered, who are these people? Who feels so passionate about holding this game show accountable? It's you."

He scoffed. "There are thousands of us." Seconds ticked by. "Hundreds, at least."

She very visibly bit down on a smile. "What does this have to do with UNCORKED?"

The offer to help sat right on his tongue, but he couldn't do that. Helping would mean spending more time with her, and he'd already decided that was not a good idea, despite the fact that he couldn't seem to stop prolonging their acquaintance. Hadn't she been on her way out the door a few minutes ago? He'd been the one to stop her. "You might not be able to stop UNCORKED from operating, but you can help the underdog compete."

"You're saying that jamming bark into their disco ball isn't a solution?"

"What?"

She pressed her lips together, eyes twinkling. "Prank calls are out, too?"

"Hallie, my God. Have you been prank calling this new wine store?"

"Yes," she whispered. "You are the type to sit down with Lorna and find ways to save money. Or revamp her brand. My approach is less logical, more reactionary. Like I said, we are the two most opposite people in the world."

"You don't think I could prank call someone?"

What in the actual hell was coming out of his mouth now? His competitive streak was humming, sure. But Hallie obviously thought he was stodgy and boring, and for some reason, he couldn't let her leave with that impression of him. Even if it was true.

He'd never placed a prank call in his life.

"No, I don't think you could," she responded, studying her nails. "Julian Vos, St. Helena wine royalty, prank calling a local vendor? Unheard of."

That did it. Now he had no choice. "Very well." He unearthed his phone from his back pocket, smirking when she slid the advertisement across the island in his direction, propping her chin on a bent wrist and pursing her lips, clearly skeptical that he would go through with it. And really. Why *was* he engaging in this behavior? To impress this woman he had no business spending time with? Or was it actually just to make her feel better after she'd cried?

Because even minutes later, the knot underneath his collar remained very opposed to her crying. She was too . . . jubilant. Too bright for that.

This woman should be happy at all times. He was intelligent enough to know that one person could not be responsible for another's happiness. Not completely. But he found himself wondering what it might be like to fill that role for Hallie. In another life, obviously.

A full-time giver of Hallie Smiles.

Suddenly he valued his teaching tenure a lot less.

Stop being ridiculous.

"Put it on speaker," she said, her doubtfulness beginning to lose ground.

Doing as she asked, he raised an eyebrow at her and dialed the number.

Her mouth fell open.

A young man answered after the fifth ring. "Hello, this is UNCORKED." Music blared in the background. "We'll get you drunk and tell you you're pretty."

Julian and Hallie traded a withering look. It struck him that this one little act of rebellion had turned them into teammates of sorts. Temporarily, of course. "Yes, hello," he said briskly. "This is the health department. I'm afraid I have some very bad news."

A pause dragged itself out. "The health department? Why . . ." Sputtering. "Bad news?"

"Yes, we're going to have to shut you down."

It appeared Hallie's legs were no longer working. Hands slapped over her mouth, and the upper half of her body fell across the island for support. "Oh my God," she wheezed.

"What are we being shut down for?" whined the gentleman.

"It's the disco ball." Hallie's sides started to shake with laughter, making it nearly impossible to keep a straight face. Or his cold, dead heart from doing the cancan. "According to section fifty-three dash M of the health code manual, you're in direct violation of the public's right to avoid bad dancing."

A sharp curse. "Another prank call? Are you working with that woman—"

"Yes." Julian hung up, neatly setting down his phone. "And that's how it's done."

Still unable to subdue her laughter, Hallie laid a hand across her chest. "That was . . . like . . . the Cadillac of prank calls." Pushing off the island, she looked at him as if through fresh eyes, before shaking herself slightly. "Thank you. With the exception of the friends I've dragged into this rivalry, I've felt pretty alone in my outrage."

He'd made her feel less alone. On top of provoking one of her Hallie Smiles.

It feels like Christmas morning. People were always saying that, but he could never relate, because opening presents with the Vos family had been a quiet and hurried affair.

He could understand that phrase better now.

"It's no problem," he said succinctly.

They nodded at each other for an extended moment. "Well,

you have my word that I will never again make fun of the *Jeopardy!* message board warriors."

His lips jumped. "Then I suppose my work here is done."

As soon as he said the words, he sort of wanted to take them back. Because she appeared to interpret them in a way he hadn't intended. As in, *time to go.*

With a nod, she said, "Bye, Julian." She passed him on the way out of the kitchen, leaving soil and sunlight lingering in the air. "Have those drinks. You definitely earned them."

All he could do was incline his head stiffly, turn, and follow her to the front door.

He watched through the screen as she reunited with the howling and yipping dogs, who celebrated her existence all the way to her truck. He traded a long look with her through the windshield when she climbed into the driver's side and slowly realized she'd never told him how they knew each other. Or where they'd met.

The tick of Julian's watch reached his ears, distracting him, and his chest grew tight enough to make his vision narrow. How awry had his schedule gone since she showed up? He had no clue. In an attempt to center himself, he pressed his ear to the ticking watch on his wrist and forced himself to concentrate on minutes. The next few hours in front of him. He couldn't change the ones behind him.

And he didn't want to, either. Wouldn't take back a second he'd spent with Hallie. Unfortunately, starting now, he wasn't sure it would be wise to spend any more.

But maybe, in the name of closure, he'd take one more look at the Becca's Blooms website before bed . . .

Chapter Five

$\mathcal{H}$allie stared across the table at Lavinia without really seeing her.

Around them, conversations swelled in the dining room of
Othello, her favorite St. Helena bistro. They'd already done serious damage to the breadbasket and were awaiting a family-style
plate of spicy butter garlic shrimp with linguine. Naturally, they'd
gone with a white wine pairing, and, Lord, it was never a good
sign when they ordered a second bottle before the main course
made an appearance. They may have cut back on day drinking,
but they obviously had no qualms with doing so at night.

For the life of Hallie, however, she couldn't stop lifting the
glass to her mouth. She'd crafted a new state of being. Bewil-
dered drunkenness. In turn, Lavinia's current state of being was
more like irritated anticipation with a side of sloshiness, but
she'd imbibed far less than Hallie. So, clearly, there was a first
time for everything. Such as drinking a Brit (who'd once been a
Gorillaz roadie) under the table.

Or getting a glimpse at the real, adult version of her teenage
crush . . . and liking that peek way too much.

Hallie forced herself out of a trance and looked around. Once upon a time, being a regular at a restaurant had been a new experience. She'd enjoyed the process of becoming one. Loved walking into the candlelit Italian bistro and having everyone know her name. Lavinia always sat with her back facing the kitchen; Hallie took the wall. But her grandmother had been around to make normalcy seem . . . well, normal. Now the repetition of coming here made Hallie feel jumpy in the absence of her grandmother's anchoring presence.

With a long, steadying breath, Hallie fell back in her chair, taking the glass of wine with her. She downed half and pushed aside her one-third life crisis for now. It had been twenty-four hours since she last saw Julian, and she still hadn't recounted the impromptu hang to her best friend, despite a serious amount of pestering and prodding.

"Come clean, Hallie Welch, goddamn you." Lavinia leaned in over the candlelight. Close enough to feel the heat on her chin, yip, and flinch away. Maybe they'd both had too much wine. Was this their second bottle or third? "I'll start smashing dishes. Don't think I won't."

"Okay, okay, okay." Hallie set the glass down on the table, holding up a finger when the waiter set the massive steaming bowl of pasta between them. Both women sighed as the savory aroma hit them like culinary crack. "Pasta presentation never gets old."

Lavinia threw an exaggerated chef's kiss at the swinging kitchen door. "Our deep and undying admiration to the chef."

"I'll let him know," the amused waiter said, skating away.

"Oy, don't forget that second bottle. Or third?" Lavinia called after him. Loudly.

"They love us here."

Hallie used the provided silver tongs to settle a heaping portion of pasta onto Lavinia's plate, laughing when she rolled her finger for more.

"Go on, then. Didn't have a single donut all day so I'd have extra room for this."

"You got it." Hallie forked up some more, sighing as a waft of fragrant steam hit her in the face. "Okay, before this pasta coma collides with my wine coma, I'll spill." She took a centering breath, as if preparing to impart very sensitive information. It was obvious Lavinia was expecting juicy news. And that left her wide open to be messed with. "Me and Julian did something pretty . . . intimate."

"You shagged him." She put her arms up in the shape of a V, whooping at the ceiling mid-chew. "Jerome owes me twenty bucks. I *knew* you had it in you, Hallie."

Hallie's mouth opened and closed on a sputter. Was *she* the one being messed with now? "You placed bets with your husband? On whether or not I would . . . would . . ."

"And I won." An eyebrow waggle from Lavinia. "You and I both did, from the sounds of it."

"You didn't let me finish." Indignation warred with amusement, leading to Hallie giving Lavinia a very pointed look that didn't quite stick. "We engaged in the intimate act of *prank calling*."

Lavinia's face lost any trace of mirth. She pretended to signal the waiter. "Excuse me. Garçon? I'd like to order a new best friend." Her eyelids punched shut. "Prank calling? *Really?*"

"Yes." Hallie fanned herself. "Best I've ever had."

"There wasn't even a grazed tit? Or an itty-bitty peck?"

Hallie dug into her pasta with more gusto than necessary, thanks to her overwrought and underserviced hormones. "Nope."

"But did you *want* a little bit of action from him?"

No use in pretending. "Since I was fourteen."

"Then why didn't you make a move, babe? I raised you better than this!"

It was a totally valid question. Women *had* to make moves on men these days, or everyone on planet earth would be single. Her attraction to Julian Vos had always been off the charts, and yesterday . . . well, she'd sensed interest. Right? The way he sort of regulated his breathing in her presence wasn't a figment of her imagination. More than once she'd definitely noticed his attention dip to lower parts of her anatomy. Mainly, her mouth. Like maybe he was thinking of kissing her. But nothing. And she had an inkling as to why.

"We are extremely different people. I think I might even unnerve him a little?"

"Hallie." Lavinia pushed aside her plate and leaned forward. "A history professor doesn't sound like a man who operates carelessly or without a lot of thought."

"Meaning?"

"Meaning the attraction can't be one-sided or he wouldn't have created an excuse for you to return to the house."

She gestured with her fork. "There was a gopher—"

Lavinia interrupted her with a groan. "Men don't ask for assistance without being under extreme duress. *Unless* they are setting aside that pride in the name of a woman."

Hallie considered that. She thought of the way Julian had called her to handle the gopher issue when he absolutely could have created the mixture himself. The way he watched her with an almost reluctant fascination. How he'd followed her from the house and down the stairs, like he was barely aware his feet were moving. It all added up to attraction, didn't it?

Maybe she *should* have made a move?

Lavinia regarded Hallie, drumming her nails on the table-cloth. "You're still carrying that torch. Either extinguish it or fan the flame."

"Fan it? To what end?"

"To *your* end, if you're feeling adventurous."

"Someone needs to cut you off." Hallie realized she was squinting in order to keep the image of her friend from doubling. Probably because she'd been punctuating the end of every sentence with a gulp of wine. "Imagine *me* dating a history professor. Ridiculous."

Lavinia pushed out her bottom lip. "You've still got a mad crush, don't you, babe?"

"Yes." Remembering those intensely curious bourbon eyes and how they sparked with rare humor during the prank call, Hallie's chest squeezed. "It's a hard fascination to explain, but . . . ugh, Lavinia, I wish you could have seen him in high school. He once tutored one of our classmates—Carter Doherty—who'd been struggling to pass physics. I suspect some difficulties were happening at home, but whatever the case, he'd decided to drop out. But Julian wouldn't let him. Tutored him all the way from a failing grade to a B. And never took any credit. The only reason I knew about it is my grandmother gardened for Carter's family and witnessed Julian showing up on their doorstep every Tuesday." She'd swooned right there on the kitchen floor when Rebecca told her, refusing to budge until dinnertime. "Spending time with him last night made the crush worse, even while it forced me to see we're completely different."

"You're horny *and* pragmatic now."

"Yes. Does that officially make me a grown-up?"

"Afraid so. That's what the wine is for."

Hallie slumped. Took a deep breath. "All right. Well, he's only here to write the book, and he'll be leaving again. I'll just brazen my way through any future encounters. And when he's gone, I'll force myself to stop comparing everyone to him—"

"You mean comparing Owen, yeah?" Lavinia popped a shrimp into her mouth. "Give him the green light and you'll be a fall bride, if that's what you want. The man is lovestruck for you."

Guilt flip-flopped in Hallie's belly. "That's why I owe it to him—or any other man who I might see in the future—to not be hung up on a ridiculous crush. It's gone on way too long."

Lavinia pursed her lips, twirled her pasta. "Then again . . ."

"Oh no. Don't give me 'then again.'"

"Then again, you owe it to yourself to really make sure there is nothing there. Between you and Mr. Vos. You're in heat over a prank call. Imagine if you actually kissed the son of a bitch."

Hallie sighed. "Believe me, I've thought about it."

Lavinia fell back into her chair and settled her wineglass on her pasta-filled belly. "You should write him secret admirer letters or something. Get all this angst off your chest before you end up walking down the aisle toward Owen with a bridal bouquet of regrets."

Hallie laughed, trying not to let it show how thickly her heart was beating over those three little words. *Secret admirer letters.* The romantic inside of her sat up, stars twinkling in her eyes. God, what a unique chance to express the feelings she'd been carrying around half her life without the risk of embarrassment. "Where would I leave the letters?"

Lavinia hummed. "He runs through town every afternoon. He passes the donut shop at two eleven, like clockwork. And he cuts down the trail on the corner of Grapevine and Cannon. No one else uses that path because it leads to Vos property. You could find a tree stump or something to . . ." Her friend straightened in her chair. "You're not taking this *seriously,* are you?"

"No." Hallie shook her head so hard, a few curls fell across her eyes, forcing her to shove them back into place. "Of course not."

"Me and my big mouth." Lavinia sighed. "You don't have to make this complicated. Just tell the man you like him and see what happens. Or is that *too* easy?"

"You think baring fifteen years' worth of feelings would be easier in person?"

"All right, no. Not technically, but . . ." Slowly, Lavinia set down her glass, visibly taking time to gather her thoughts. "Look, I know I encouraged you to see him again. But I want you to stop and think before getting yourself into a tangle, Hallie. You know I love you to death, but . . ." She paused. "Since we lost Rebecca, you've been a little more quick to wreak havoc where none is necessary."

Hallie nodded. Kept right on nodding until the back of her neck was too tight to continue.

While on the road with her mother growing up, Hallie had felt like a slot machine. Drop in a coin, pull the lever, and pick a new adventure. A new persona. Clean the slate. Her mother was as ever-changing as the wind, and she took Hallie with her, inventing new stories, new identities in the name of fun.

Hallie recalled that itchy feeling right before her mother pulled the metaphoric lever, and it felt suspiciously like her current, restless state. The state she'd been in since January. And constant, restriction-free movement was the only way to smother it these days. Or ignore it, rather. "Thanks for being honest," she said, finally, to her expectant friend.

Lavinia reached across the table to lay her hand on top of Hallie's. "Let's put the ol' letter-writing nonsense to bed, shall we?"

"I've read it a story and tucked it in," Hallie said, firmly ignoring the excited static licking at her nerve endings. "Good night, bad idea."

"Thank fuck," Lavinia said, raising her wineglass.

Hallie reached for her own glass and found it empty. Blinking away the increasing blur, she poured herself another glass. A final one, she vowed.

Absently, she wondered how late the stationery shop stayed open these days.

Wouldn't hurt to check on the way home, right?

Surely her Uber driver wouldn't mind a detour.

BARBED WIRE WRAPPED around Hallie's skull and it appeared to be tightening with a full twist every five to eight seconds. She walked into Corked, which hadn't yet opened for the day, and draped herself over the dusty, timeworn counter, burying her head in folded arms.

Knowing laughter approached, and then Lorna patted her forearm with beautifully aged fingers, her cinnamon-and-dish-detergent scent drifting down to Hallie and providing her with a small sense of comfort. Quite a feat considering the circumstances.

"One cure for cobwebs coming right up," sang the elderly woman, her footsteps carrying her behind the counter. "Overextended yourself last night at dinner with Lavinia, did you?"

"It was a special occasion."

"What were you celebrating?"

"Saturday night." She tried to smile at the older woman, but the action juiced her brain like an orange. "Please, Lorna. My Advil is lost somewhere in the wilds of my house. Either that or the dogs buried it in the backyard. I come begging for mercy."

Lorna clucked her tongue, hummed to herself. "You don't have to beg." She fiddled in the cabinet beneath the register a moment, before setting down twin blue pills on the counter in front of Hallie. "You should be right as rain in forty-five minutes."

"That's ambitious, but I will attempt to manifest that outcome." Pills dry swallowed, Hallie stood up a little straighter and focused on the sweetly smiling woman beside the antique brass register. One of her grandmother's best friends. If she closed her eyes, she could see them sitting together, heads bent over a crossword, giggling like teenagers over a whispered joke. "How . . ." She cleared the emotion from her throat, glancing around the quiet, dusty shop. "Has business been any better?"

Lorna's smile remained in place, her head ticking slightly to the right.

She said nothing.

Hallie swallowed, shifting in her seat. "Well, have no fear. I'm sure this hangover will be cleared up by the two thirty tasting. And it's well past time to restock my whites—"

"The last thing you need is more wine, dear. I'm a big girl. I can handle no one showing up for a tasting." Chuckling, Lorna reached out and squeezed Hallie's hand. "Would I like to see this place packed like the old days? Of course. But I'm not filling the register with your hard-earned money, Hallie. I'm just not doing it." She gave Hallie a final pat. "Rebecca would be proud of you for trying to help."

Tears pricked the backs of Hallie's eyelids. Didn't Lorna realize she was being partially selfish? Not only did this place hold a million special memories for her, but . . . Hallie needed it to *remain*, this piece of her grandmother. The more Rebecca faded into the past, the more anxious and rudderless Hallie started to feel. This place, her routine, *everything* felt foreign without Rebecca's stalwart presence. Like her life belonged to someone else.

"Will you at least bag me up a Pinot—" The bell over the entrance dinged, and Hallie's heart leapt hopefully in her chest. "Oh! A customer . . ." Her excitement faded when she saw the man who entered. The tweed-suited, round-glassed manager from UNCORKED sporting a very brisk, very harried smile on his face. She recognized him from the afternoon she'd gone around town removing their grand opening flyers and he'd chased her half a block.

"Hello." Just inside the door, he clasped his hands together at his waist and threw a pitying glance at the sparsely stocked shelves. "I'm from UNCORKED next door. And I hate to do this, but we have two bachelorette parties coming to the afternoon tasting and our supply delivery truck was delayed. We are low on wineglasses, if you can believe it. The party got a little out of control last night, and there was some unfortunate breakage. Would you happen to have a dozen or so we could borrow until tomorrow?"

Lorna was already rising from her seat, eager to help. "Of course. I'm sure I can spare a few." She crouched down to survey her supplies behind the counter. Hallie hopped up to assist before Lorna could lift something too heavy, helping her settle a box of rattling glass onto the counter. "I have two dozen here. You're welcome to half."

The young man in tweed sauntered forward, peeling back the cardboard flaps and extracting one of the glasses, holding it up to the light. "These must be the emergency stash. Not exactly high quality, are they?"

Lorna wrung her hands. "Sorry about that."

"No, no. Don't apologize," laughed Tweed Twit, the disingenuous nature of it causing acid to climb the walls of Hallie's throat. "Well, I guess I have no choice. I'll take whatever you can give me." The manager wasn't even looking at them. He was craning his neck to observe the line forming in front of UNCORKED. "Are you able to spare the full two dozen? It looks like we need the glasses a tad more than Corked," he said absently.

"Oh. O-of course." Hastily, Lorna slid the box across the counter. Hallie was too stunned by the sheer audacity of Tweed Twit to offer assistance. And she remained open-mouthed in shock as the manager lifted the glasses with a hurried thank-you and scurried back out the door.

Hallie's entire body was racked by hot tingles and second-hand embarrassment. Her face was hotter than the sun's surface, and her throat? Good Lord. Was she transforming into a werewolf or something?

"That . . ." She could barely speak around the cluster of sticks in her throat. "He cannot get away with that."

"Hallie—"

"I'm going over there."

"Oh dear."

This was bad. She knew it the moment she stepped onto the sidewalk and cool air practically sizzled on her skin. This was not a disco-ball-sabotaging level of righteous indignation. It was far worse. This was Hulk-level irritation, and it needed an outlet. A dear, sweet old lady, an institution of the community, had been brazenly belittled to her face by Tweed Twit, and Hallie's anger demanded satisfaction. What form would it take? She had no idea. Which should have been a signal to return to the safety of Lorna's shop and regroup, but instead, she found herself ignoring the protests of people in line and yanking open the front door of UNCORKED, the scent of blue cheese and chocolate hitting her in the face.

"Why don't you wine about it?" sang the robotic automatic door greeting.

"Shut up," she said through her teeth, seeing UNCORKED for the first time from behind enemy lines. Unlike the soft, homey feel of Corked, this place was a study in bad lighting. Neon signs that said HELLO GORGEOUS and GOOD VIBES ONLY cast a tacky glow on the endless rows of wine bottles that appeared to be purchased based on the aesthetic of their labels, rather than the quality of the contents. Unfortunately, there were cushy ottomans begging people to sit and lounge for an afternoon and polish off forty-dollar cheese plates. It was clean and new, and she hated it.

What exactly are you doing in here?

At the moment, she was kind of hovering between the door and the counter, the customers who'd made it inside staring at her curiously, along with the register person. A bead of sweat rolled down her spine. She should go—

Tweed Twit's voice reached her then. He strode behind the counter with Lorna's box, giving the register person an exasperated smile. "Scrounged up some glasses from the old folks' home next door. I should probably take them in back and clean them first. There's probably a decade of dust caked on the rims."

Hallie's adrenaline spiked back up, and she glanced around through the red haze, attention landing on the cheese wall. Each block had its own shelf, backlit by pink lighting. Little silver dishes extended out with samples arranged in neat rows, sort of like human feeding troughs. And she was already moving toward it, turning her shirt into a makeshift apron and piling the cheese samples into it by the handful.

This was it.

Grand Theft Gouda would be the crime that finally brought her down.

"Hey!" That was Tweed Twit. "What are you doing?"

Focused on her mission, whatever the hell it was, Hallie didn't answer. She just needed some sort of compensation for the chunk the manager had taken out of Lorna's pride. Was it silly? Probably. Would Hallie regret this? Almost definitely, but only because it wouldn't help Lorna in any way. Not really.

She ran out of room in her shirt apron and started stuffing cheese samples into her pockets.

"*Hey!*" The manager came to a stop beside her and started slapping at her hands, but she blocked him with her back. "Call the police!" he shouted over his shoulder. "This . . . Oh my God, it's the same girl who stole the flyers a few weeks ago!"

Uh-oh.

Jerome was right. This was textbook escalation.

Hallie made a break for it.

Tweed Twit was faster. He blocked the exit. She turned, searching for a back door. All of these places had them. It would empty into the alley, just like Fudge Judy. And then she would . . .

what? Hide behind the standing mixer again? Would she even be able to avoid the fallout this time? Her temples started to pound, the sounds of the wineshop turning muffled. Her face stung. Some of the cheese chunks plunked to the ground.

And then the craziest thing happened.

She locked eyes with Julian Vos through the glass window of UNCORKED.

He had a brown paper bag in one sculpted arm, and she recognized the convenience store logo. He'd gone grocery shopping. Julian Vos: *He's just like us!* The professor's attention dropped from her face to the mountain of assorted cheese blocks in her shirt apron, and he popped out his AirPod, a single black eyebrow winging up.

Slowly, Julian's gaze drifted over to the manager—who was simultaneously yelling at her and shouting orders to the person behind the counter—and his expression darkened. One long stride and he was inside UNCORKED. Leaving a chorus of complaints in his wake from people in line, he very effortlessly took command of the whole establishment without saying a single word. Everyone stopped and looked at him, somehow knowing his arrival was important. This man was a bystander of nothing.

The only person who didn't notice Julian entering UNCORKED was Tweed Twit, who continued to demand she pay for the ruined cheese, listing the crimes she'd committed against the wineshop like broken commandments.

But his mouth snapped shut when Julian stepped in front of Hallie.

"You're finished yelling at her now." Hallie couldn't see his face, but based on the clipped delivery of his words, she imagined his features were tense. "Don't ever do it again." He turned and glanced at her over his shoulder. Indeed, with his Very Serious eyebrows and jawline, he resembled a gallant duke come to rescue a damsel in distress. Well, call her Princess Peach Toadstool, because she welcomed his services. "Hallie, please go outside where this man can't shout at you anymore."

"I'm fine right here," she whispered, her belief in chivalry rising like the dead in an old zombie movie. Not even the threat of being bitten by a walking corpse could have convinced her to miss what was happening here. Julian defending her. Taking her side without getting both sides of the story first. Just being all-around wonderful. *God*, he was wonderful.

Tweet Twit sputtered. "She stole our cheese!"

"I can see that," Julian said with forced calm, turning back to the red-faced man. He lowered his voice to such a level that Hallie almost didn't hear his next clipped words to the manager. "You're still not going to yell at her anymore. If she's upset, I'm upset. I don't think you want that."

Hallie . . . was finding religion. Is that what was happening? *Am I ascending to a higher plane?*

Whatever was happening on his face must have convinced the manager that ticking Julian off should be eliminated from his chore chart. "Fine, I'm done yelling, but we're calling the police," the manager said, snapping at the counter person.

"You're going to call the police over cheese samples?" Julian asked slowly. Hallie looked down at his butt—she couldn't help it, not when he was using the snobbish professor tone of voice—and, God, the way it tested the seam of his jeans almost made her drop the hunk of Parmesan that she'd been secretly planning to keep for herself. "I don't think that would be wise. Number one, that would upset her, too, and we've already established I'm not a fan of that. And two, you'd have to press charges. Over cheese. Against a local. I don't think the other locals—your customers—would like that very much, do you? We both know I wouldn't."

Heaven looked suspiciously like a cheese shop, but surely her personal cloud was around here somewhere. Could she book an angel-guided tour, perhaps?

"She stole our flyers out of shop windows and . . . yeah, I think she might have broken our disco ball?" Uh-oh. Hallie's stupor popped like a bubble, and she peeked around Julian in time to see the manager throw up his hands. "She's a menace!"

Hallie gasped.

"You're probably right," Julian drawled.

She gasped a second time.

"But if you say another word about her, I'll break a lot more than your disco ball."

Tweed Twit blew a raspberry in his outrage. "I can't believe this—" He stopped cold and squinted up at Julian. "Wait a minute, you look familiar."

Julian sighed, transferring the paper bag to his other arm. "Yes." He kept his voice low. "You must be familiar with Vos Vineyard."

"Vos Vineyard? Not really. We don't stock anything from those dusty-ass has-beens."

Hallie almost threw the block of Parmesan at the store manager—and it was definitely a big enough chunk to deliver a concussion. Did he really just say that out loud to Julian? The secondhand embarrassment she'd experienced for Lorna roared back now in his honor, flushing her skin and making her wish she'd stayed in bed this morning, like a good little hungover soldier. For Julian's part, his reaction was not what she might have expected. Instead of getting angry over the insult to his family business, he merely looked . . . perplexed. Curious.

"Dusty-ass has-beens?" he repeated, brow furrowing. "Why would you call—"

The manager cut him off with a finger snap. "No, wait. I know why you're familiar. You were in that alien documentary! What was it called . . ."

Julian was already turning on a heel, ushering Hallie out of the store with his free hand. "And that's our cue."

"Wait!" called the overdressed twentysomething. "Can we take a selfie?"

"No," Julian said flatly.

"What alien documentary is he talking about?" Hallie whispered up at Julian's set chin.

"Quiet, cheese thief."

"That's fair," she muttered, plucking the Parmesan out of her apron and taking a bite.

As soon as they were outside the shop and moving at a brisk pace down the sidewalk, Julian asked a question Hallie really didn't want to field. "Why did he speak that way about the vineyard? Was it an unpopular opinion or the consensus?"

Hallie gulped. "If I answer, will you explain the alien documentary?"

His sigh could have withered an oak tree. "Deal."

Chapter 6

They were the adult version of Hansel and Gretel. Except, instead of bread crumbs, they were leaving crumbles of Manchego in their wake. Somehow Julian wasn't surprised by this turn of events. Of course he'd stumbled upon this captivating, lunatic woman who inspired him to make prank calls stealing cheese from a local establishment. What *else* would she be doing?

He couldn't quite locate the wherewithal to be exasperated with her, however. Who could be upset over anything when she was smiling? Not him. Especially when two very prominent emotions were crowding everything else out.

Number one? He was pissed the hell off. Wanted to go back into UNCORKED and knock some teeth out of the manager's head, which was unlike him in every way. He wasn't a violent man. He'd been in a few scrapes as a teenager, but he'd never experienced that hot surge from his belly to his throat before, like he'd felt when he'd seen Hallie being yelled at through the window. Who could shout at this . . . human sunflower? *None of my business*, his head tried to tell him. But his gut compelled him to storm inside and stand between her and any sort of negativity. *Not on my watch.*

Number two? An encroaching sense of dread tightened his arm around the sack of groceries. *Dusty-ass has-beens.* Those words cycled from one corner of his brain to the other, back and forth, so unlike the phrasing he was used to hearing describe Vos Vineyard.

Institution. Legendary. A cornerstone of the industry.

They stopped at a trash can, where Hallie rid herself of countless cheese samples, though she stubbornly held on to the Parmesan. "Before I tell you anything," she started, squaring her shoulders and taking a deep breath that did nothing to settle his nerves. "I want you to know that I, personally, do not share any negative opinions about your family's vineyard. Case in point, I just knocked over that cringey wine nightclub because it's stepping on the toes of my beloved old stomping grounds. I value tradition and history—those are both words I would use to describe Vos. It's part of St. Helena. But it, um . . . well, in recent years, some might say . . ."

The dread deepened. "Don't soften the blow, Hallie. Let's have it."

She nodded once. "The fire was a setback to a lot of established wineries. They tried to recover, but the pandemic came along and knocked them out. Now there is a flood of competition from the buyers of those turnkey wineries. They've come along and modernized their operations, found new ways to lure in the crowds. And Vos . . ." She wet her lips. "According to what I've heard, it's still in recovery mode, while all the new kids are expanding, bringing in celebrity spokesmen, and conquering social media."

Bolts twisted on either side of his jugular. He'd found his mother's request that he attend the Wine Down Napa festival a little odd, but he didn't anticipate this. How bad were things? And . . . was he still so unwanted in the family business that she wouldn't even ask for his help in a desperate situation? Yes, his father had made it very clear he didn't want Julian's influence on the vineyard. But his mother? Maybe she had even less faith in him than he'd realized. After his humiliating behavior after the fire, could he blame her?

"My mother mentioned none of this," he managed.

"I'm sorry." Hallie offered him the Parmesan, lowering it back down to her side when he declined with a curt head shake.

"I'm more of a goat cheese type."

She did a double take. "Okay, Satan." She nudged him in the ribs to let him know she was joking, and he barely resisted catching her wrist, keeping her hand there. *Near.* "If it makes you feel any better, I got extremely drunk last night on a bottle of Vos Sauvignon Bl . . ."

She trailed off, her face losing some of its rosy color.

"What's wrong?" he asked, concerned. Just how much had that scrawny manager upset her? "I'm going back in there," he growled, wheeling back toward the shop.

"No!" She caught his elbow, stopping him. "I'm . . . I'm okay."

Clearly that wasn't true. "Too much Parmesan?"

"No, I just . . ." Suddenly she seemed unable to look him in the eye. "I just remembered I forgot to tip my Uber driver from last night. And he was really good. He even waited for me while I made a stop."

Why did she sound almost winded by the oversight?

"You can tip after the fact."

"Yes." She looked right through him, glassy-eyed, her color high. "Yes. I can. I will."

"Does this hangover have anything to do with the decision to burgle cheese?"

"No." She visibly shook herself, but her color was slow to return, voice slightly unnatural. "Maybe a little. But it didn't help matters when the Tweed Twit walked into Corked like an entitled troll and made off with two dozen wineglasses, claiming UNCORKED needed them more."

"Ah." Irritation snaked through him all over again. "I'm extra glad I didn't give him a selfie."

"Speaking of which." They walked down the sidewalk while Hallie tried and failed to tuck the cheese block into the front pocket of her jeans. Honestly, she was a constant jumble. And he couldn't seem to take his damn eyes off her nonetheless. "What alien documentary?"

"It's nothing," he responded briskly.

"No way it's nothing." She laughed, and he was relieved to see her looking less pale than a moment ago. "Also, you promised an explanation, Vos. I demand satisfaction."

A corner of his lips tugged. "Yes, I'm aware. I just don't like to talk about it."

"You just caught me committing a robbery. Give me something."

He grew momentarily fascinated by her cajoling smile. Hungover or not, she still had her glow, didn't she? Her brand of discombobulated beauty. And a lot like the first two times he'd been in the presence of Hallie, the pressure of his schedule seemed to have receded. But it tried to roar back into focus now, demanding he regroup. His watch became heavier on his wrist, minutes flying by without being accounted for. "Right, I'll explain. But I have writing to do . . ."

She blinked at him, and he nearly leaned in to get a better look at the black circle around her irises. Is that what made their color so . . . distracting? He could take half an hour, couldn't he?

Might as well face facts. Hallie was a stick of dynamite to his peace of mind, and he couldn't seem to adhere to his plans when she was around. Especially when she tilted her head one way and squint-smiled up at him, the sun basking in that crease in the middle of her bottom lip. And the fact that he was noticing these details in lieu of the ticking clock meant something was seriously wrong with him.

"Why are you looking at me like that?" he asked.

"I was just thinking the morning could have turned out a lot different," she said. "If you hadn't intervened, that is. Thank you. That was pretty heroic."

What was the odd feeling in his middle? Heroic he was not. Yet he couldn't help but covet Hallie thinking of him that way. To have this woman smile at him was some sort of celestial reward he didn't know he'd been missing. When was he going to get enough of it? Soon, hopefully. This couldn't very well be *sustained.* "No one should ever yell at you."

She blinked. Was she breathing faster now? He wanted to know. Wanted to get close and study her and mentally file away the patterns of her behavior. The pathways to her Hallie Smiles.

"Th-thank you," she responded, finally. Quietly. As if she couldn't get the breath for much more—and it was little wonder why after her altercation with the manager.

He should really go back in there.

Would have. If she didn't beam a grin at him and turn in the direction of the path that would lead to Vos Vineyard. The path he *would* have already gone down if this unruly woman hadn't dragged him from his routines in such an adorable—no, criminal—way.

"I still want to know about the alien documentary."

"I suspected as much," he muttered, ignoring his watch. "A few years ago, I was asked to be part of an untitled documentary film. A *student* film. I assumed it was a semester project, something they would be turning in for a grade, so I didn't read the fine print on the release form." He shook his head over such uncharacteristic negligence on his part. "They asked me to speak on camera about the timekeeping methods of the ancient Egyptians. I was not aware that my theories would, in a roundabout way, support their belief that aliens are responsible for influencing certain time-measuring devices. They got a B minus on the film, but somehow it was picked up by Netflix, and now I'm an unwitting participant in an alien documentary. My students find it all very amusing."

"And you clearly do not."

"Correct." Reluctantly, he added, "It's called *Time Martians On*."

She slapped a hand over her mouth, then let it drop, giving him a sympathetic look. "Sorry, but that's extremely clever."

"I suppose it is," he admitted. "Unfortunately, I was not. And now I'm on film talking about a very important subject and they've edited it in such a way that I appear to be . . . *very* passionate about the existence of aliens."

Looking ahead, she said something under her breath. It sounded like *How did I not know about this?* He must have heard her wrong. And then he got distracted by the way a dimple appeared in her cheek when she tried to bury a smile. It was adorable, really, and he had the insane impulse to fit his thumb into it.

"You're lucky I don't have Netflix or I'd be watching that sucker tonight with a bowl of popcorn."

"Don't have Netflix?" He couldn't hide his shock. "Their documentary section alone is worth the membership, *Time Martians On* notwithstanding."

"Oh no," she deadpanned. "I can't believe I'm missing out on all that excitement." Whatever his expression—he guessed it was affronted—it made her giggle, the sound making him swallow thickly. "Oh, come on. There are worse things to be passionate about," she said. "At least it wasn't a Bigfoot biopic."

The giggling was over, then? "That's the only silver lining."

"Oh, I don't know." Amusement spread across her face, and a corresponding ripple went straight through him. "It was kind of nice watching Tweed Twit get starstruck in the midst of his tirade against me."

They'd reached the beginning of the trail leading to the vineyard. He needed to wish her a good rest of the weekend and be on his damn merry way. But he hesitated. The full half an hour hadn't passed yet. Changing his plan of action twice in one morning would throw him off even more, wouldn't it? Yes. So he might as well keep talking to her. And ignore the relief sinking into his gut.

"Where did you go to high school?" He asked the question without thinking about it. Because he was genuinely curious, not just making the necessary small talk as he tended to do with women. He needed to know where a woman like Hallie sprang from.

A few beats of silence dragged out. Very briefly, her smile dimmed, and his stomach dropped with it. "Napa High," she said, continuing on without giving him a chance to process that bombshell information. "You would have been three years ahead of me, I believe. A cool senior." Her shoulder jerked. "I'm sure our paths didn't cross very often."

But they obviously had.

And he'd forgotten? *How?*

Who wouldn't remember every detail of Hallie?

This was why she'd been disappointed in him the first time they'd met. Now he'd made the blunder twice. He'd be terrible at the job of full-time provider of smiles for this woman.

"I'm sorry, I didn't realize—"

"Stop." Cheeks red, she waved off the apology. "It's fine!"

Uh-oh. Not fine. Definitely not fine. He needed to get that smile back on her face by the time they parted ways, or he wouldn't sleep tonight.

"Let me guess," he said, equally determined to find out more about her. For reasons that couldn't possibly be wise. "You were in drama club."

"Yes. But only for a week. Then I tried playing the trombone in the marching band. For a month. Then I got a pair of nonprescription horn-rim glasses and joined the newspaper. And that was only sophomore year." She looked into the distance at the rows of grapes on his family's property, the sun bathing the earth in gold. Bathing her in gold. Her cheeks, her nose, the wild ringlets buried among the bigger curls on her head. "By junior year, my grandmother had gotten ahold of me. Helped me settle down."

"I can't imagine you ever settling down, Hallie."

Her eyes shot to his. Probably because of the way he said her name. Like they were in bed together, tangled up in damp sheets. He could visualize them there so easily. Could feel himself liking what they did there. Loving it. To such a point that coming back down would be difficult. His *reaction* to her was flat-out difficult. It was too much.

"Um . . ." She wet her lips. "Well, she had a way of reining me in. Or maybe I just felt at home with her and I could relax. Focus. I'm a little untethered without her around. If she was there this morning for the cheese show, she would have said something like, 'Hallie, all that glitters is not gold' or 'an empty vessel makes much noise,' and I would have sighed or maybe even argued with her, because not every situation can be summed up with a proverb. But I probably wouldn't have felt the need to steal cheese in the name of justice, either. Maybe I've been wrong all along and those proverbs are golden. Or at least a way of saving bail money." She took a much-needed breath. Interested as he was in what she was saying, he'd actually started to get worried. "It's terrible how you only realize these things when it's too late."

"It is. My father . . . he hasn't passed or anything and God knows our relationship was never perfect. But I often find myself discovering meaning in something he told me, right out of the blue. It'll just be relevant." He went on speaking without considering his words. Odd behavior for him. Normally everything he said out loud was weighed and measured beforehand. "Your grandmother sounds like someone worth missing."

He didn't realize he'd stopped breathing regularly until a smile formed on her mouth again. Again, he had the sudden urge to touch, to stroke her cheek, so he slipped his hand into the pocket of his shorts.

"Thank you. I like that. And she is."

They just kind of looked at each other, her face turned up to the sun in deference of his height. Maybe he should stoop down slightly so she didn't get a crick in her neck?

"She never quite pushed me as far as she'd hoped. Or she left before she could. The library . . . you know the town library? They'd been asking her to landscape their courtyard for years. She kept saying no. She asked *me* to do it, instead. It would be the biggest project I've ever taken on. The one that required the most commitment. I think . . . I don't know, she wanted me to realize my potential to knuckle down and nurture something. The topper on her master-plan cake." She shook herself as if embarrassed she'd been speaking for so long. As if he wasn't praying she'd continue. "Wow, I've definitely taken up enough of your time. You came into town for a quick stop at the store and ended up sympathizing with a burglar." Abruptly, she held out her hand to him for a shake. "Friends, Julian?" When he didn't take her hand right away, she shifted right to left. "I appreciate what you did for me this morning, but wow . . . it really did make it obvious that we should probably be the kind of acquaintances that wave at each other in the store, right?"

Yes. That was true. Totally true. That didn't mean he enjoyed parting ways with her. Didn't like it last time, either. But if it had to be done—and since it did—he definitely preferred it happening as friends. Unfortunately, she was a friend he suspected he'd be thinking about to the point of distraction for a long time. "Right . . ."

Finally, he took her hand.

"Would it make you smile if I gave you my Netflix login?" He was actually saying this out loud. "So you could watch *Time Martians On* with popcorn?"

The slow grin that spread across her face made the entire world feel brighter.

"I think that would elevate you from friend to hero. Twice in one day."

How in God's name did he forget being in the same place at the same time as her?

She must have been dressed up for Halloween at the time. Or been wearing a potato sack that covered her head to toe. Those were the only explanations he could muster.

"Then I'll text it to you," he said, shaking her hand. "Enjoy."

Hands dropping to their sides, they hesitated a moment, then turned and walked away. And Julian continued down the path, not glancing at his watch even once. He was too busy (a) texting Hallie his login and password, double- and triple-checking his punctuation and briefly considering a flower emoji, because it reminded him of her. And (b) replaying the last hour of his life and trying to figure out how the whole Hallie business had been so completely peculiar and off-beat, while also . . . dangerously exhilarating.

However, when he saw the white envelope sticking out of a tree stump ahead—an envelope with *his name* looping across the front—he had a feeling the day was about to get even more peculiar.

And he was right.

"OH JESUS!" HALLIE cried into the phone. "Oh *Jesus*. You're not going to believe this."

"Quiet down. Someone has stabbed me through the fuckin'

eye with a high heel," Lavinia screeched back, clearly neck-deep in her own hangover. "What has you in a state?"

"Lavinia, I want to die."

"Me too, currently." Her friend's voice was now muffled by a pillow. "I'm suspecting for a different reason. State your business or I'm hanging up."

"I wrote the letter," Hallie scream-whispered into the phone, just as she reached her truck. She threw herself inside and slammed the door, her pulse frenetic, stomach roiling. "I wrote Julian a secret admirer letter last night after dinner and I left it for him to find. I wrote it in the back of an Uber. I'm pretty sure I even asked the driver for advice and he said don't do it. Don't do it, crazy passenger. But I did. I left it for him on the jogging path, and unless it blew away, he's in the process of finding it *right now*."

"I can't believe you did that. You swore you wouldn't."

"I can't be expected to make promises under the influence of pasta and wine!"

"You're right. I shouldn't have trusted your word." A couch groaned in the background. Lavinia's voice was clearer when she spoke again. "There's no way to do damage control?"

"No. I mean, I didn't sign my name, obviously. I think, anyway?"

"That would seriously defeat the purpose of a secret admirer letter."

Her phone dinged to signal a text message. Julian's Netflix login.

He'd saved her from a troll in tweed, rekindled her belief in good deeds and noble men, made her heart beat like it had finally remembered how, *and* given her his Netflix password—which was "calendar," by the way—and in return, she'd word-vomited her admiration of him in a torrent of compulsiveness.

"I can't even remember what I wrote!" Hallie dropped her forehead onto the steering wheel. "Please tell me the morning dew blurred the ink or the whole thing blew away. Please tell me that's possible and Julian Vos isn't reading my drunken ramblings right now."

Lavinia's pause lasted a beat too long. "I'm sure it blew away, babe."

"No way I'm that lucky, huh?"

"Doubt it." There was a muffled voice in the background. "Got to go. Jerome needs help with the rush. Keep me posted, Shakespeare!"

Hallie took a deep breath and let the disconnected phone drop to her lap, staring into a void. What was she going to do?

Nothing. That's what. Sit tight and hope. That if the letter didn't get caught in the wind, nothing she said in those paragraphs could identify her. For all she remembered, she might have actually labeled the envelope with her home address. *God.*

Okay. Tomorrow she was scheduled to be back at the Vos guesthouse to do some planting. She'd just have to remain in the dark until then—and then she'd either be granted a reprieve. Or her feelings for Julian would no longer be her innocent little secret.

Chapter Seven

Julian stared down at the letter, his eyebrows dangerously close to being swallowed up by his hairline.

Dear Julian Vos,

Oh my God. I can't believe I'm really doing this.

You get one shot at life, though, right? Have to pull that trigger!

Okay. Seriously, though. I think you're wonderful. Really, truly wonderful. I've been dying to get that off my chest for a very long time, but I didn't have the guts. You've always been so quietly kind, never lording your name over anyone or acting superior, you know what I mean? Just a real down-to-earth fellow with brains to burn and a big, secret heart.

I wish I'd told you all of this a million years ago, because when you feel something, you should just say it! You know? I don't want you to think I'm creepy (of course you're going to think I'm creepy, I mean, look what I'm doing), but way back when, in days of yore, I witnessed your character when you didn't think anyone was watching and it really inspired how I've treated other people throughout my life. Mostly! I'm not perfect. Sometimes I hang up on telemarketers. But I hope you're happy and healthy and headed for the kind of happy future you deserve. I used the word "happy" twice there, sorry, but you get up what I'm putting down.

Okay! This was great. Let's do it again sometime. Maybe you'll write back? You're never too old for a pen pal. I'm sure that's the generally held belief on the subject.

Secretly Yours

Julian lifted his head. "What the fuck?"

A secret admirer letter?

He turned the envelope over in his hands, searched the back of the paper for some sign of the prankster's identity—because that's definitely what this was. A prank. But there were no clues to point him in the direction of the person apparently trying to mess with him.

Who the hell had written it?

Who knew about his habit of taking this shortcut between home and town?

A lot of people, he supposed. Anyone he jogged past on Grapevine Way in the afternoon. Shop owners. Or people who lived in the residential houses closer to the top of the path. It could be any number of women. Or men.

He shook his head, scanning the lines one more time. Nobody wrote secret admirer letters these days. Contact was made through social media, almost exclusively, right? This had to be some kind of joke at his expense, but why? Who would go to so much trouble?

As soon as Julian arrived at the guesthouse to find his sister loitering in the driveway, the mystery solved itself. "Wow. How long have you been in town? An hour?" He waved the letter. "Barely made it off the plane before kicking off the psychological warfare?"

He didn't buy her confused expression. Not for a second.

"Uh. Thanks for the warm welcome," Natalie said, skirting the bumper of her hatchback. Rented, based on the window sticker. "Tone down the emotion before this family reunion gets embarrassing." Sauntering toward Julian, she eyed his letter as if she'd never seen it before. "Yes. It is I, the prodigal daughter. I would give you a hug, but we don't do that sort of thing . . ." Her smile was tight-lipped. "Hi, Julian. You look well."

The way she said it, with a hint of measuring concern in her eyes, made the back of his neck feel tight. The last time they'd been together in St. Helena, on the soil of Vos Vineyard, was never far from his mind. The smoke and ash and shouting and flames. The worry that he wouldn't do what needed to be done in time. He could taste the acrid burn in the back of his throat, could feel the grit that seared the backs of his eye sockets. The hundred-ton weight pressing down on his chest, making it impossible for him to breathe in the smoky air.

Natalie scanned his face and looked away quickly, obviously remembering, too. How he'd lost his composure in a way that was so physical, he could only remember it happening in snatches of sound and movement. One moment he'd been capable of thinking critically, helping his family, and the next, when he knew Natalie was safe, he'd simply gone dark. He'd retreated into the sooty house, closed himself in a back bedroom, and gone to a place where he was comfortable. Work. Lessons. Lecture notes. When he came up for air, days had passed while he'd been in a state of numbness. Leaving his parents and Natalie to deal with the fallout from the fire. Unacceptable. He'd never go to that place again.

"What are you doing here?" he asked, a little too sharply.

Her chin snapped up. Fast. Defensive. With her face to the morning sun, he catalogued the differences since the last time they saw each other. Natalie was younger than him by three and a half years, making her thirty now. She had his mother's ageless complexion, black hair down past her shoulders, messy from the wind constantly moving through the valley, although she continuously tried to smooth it with impatient palms. She'd arrived dressed for New York City, where she'd moved after attending Cornell. In black dress pants, heels, and a ruffled blazer, she could have walked straight off Madison Avenue into the front yard.

As for *why* Natalie was in St. Helena, Julian expected a practical explanation. She was in town on business. Or here to attend the wedding of a colleague. He definitely wasn't expecting the reason she gave him instead.

"I'm taking a break from work. A *voluntary* one," she rushed to add, picking lint from the sleeve of her jacket. "And if I have to stay in the main house with our mother, I'm pretty sure we'll fight enough to invoke the apocalypse, so I'll be crashing here with you."

The muscle directly behind his right eye had begun to spasm. "Natalie, I am writing a book. I came here for peace and quiet."

"Really?" Genuine, surprised pleasure crossed her face before she hid it behind amusement. "My brother, a novelist? Very impressive." She studied him for a moment, visibly evaluating the information. "Who says I'm going to mess with your process?" She pressed her lips into a line, seemingly to suppress a laugh. "You call it your process. Don't you?"

"That's what it's called." He folded up the prank letter, already planning on tossing it into the trash can as soon as he walked inside. "And it's your track record that says you'd mess with it."

Natalie rolled her eyes. "I'm a grown woman now, Julian. I'm not going to throw a kegger on your front lawn. At least not until I lull you into a false sense of security." When a rumbling sound started coming from his throat, she reached for the rolling suitcase waiting behind her on the driveway. "Oh, come on, that was a joke."

He watched in disbelief as she dragged the suitcase up the stairs, letting it smack loudly into each wooden step. "Natalie, there has to be somewhere else you can take a break."

"Nope."

The screen door snicked shut behind his sister, her heels tapping toward the kitchen.

Julian followed her, nearly wrenching the door off its hinges in the process. This couldn't be happening. Fate was determined to fuck him over. This guesthouse had been sitting empty for four years, and suddenly *both* of them were back? And at the very same time, it had also been imperative to plant begonias? The women in his life were dead set on derailing his goals. At this very moment, he was supposed to be in the shower, preparing for the second half of his writing day.

Julian arrived in the kitchen and watched his sister remove her jacket, hanging it neatly on the back of a chair. Thank God, at the very least, they had tidiness in common. Their father hadn't tolerated anything less growing up. When Natalie and Julian were younger, the driving force in Dalton Vos's life had been crafting wine better than his father. To make the vineyard twice as successful and rub it in the face of his estranged old man. And when Dalton succeeded, when he'd been showered in accolades and become the toast of Napa, being better than his father wasn't as satisfying as he'd hoped. Nor did he have a son he found capable of bestowing his legacy upon. The fire was the final blow to Dalton's invincibility, so he'd signed over Vos Vineyard to his ex-wife as a parting gift in the divorce and moved on to the next project, leaving this one behind for Corinne to assume.

As badly as Julian wanted to believe himself nothing like Dalton, there were similarities, and he'd stopped trying to fight them. Did he resent anyone who interfered with his plans? Yes. Was he competitive? Perhaps not as much as Dalton, but they both craved perfection in every one of their undertakings. In a way, he'd even followed in Dalton's footsteps and abandoned the vineyard for the last four years.

Just for a very different reason.

Clearing the discomfort from his throat, Julian moved to the coffeepot and pressed the on button, the sounds of it warming up filling the quiet kitchen. "Afternoon caffeine boost?"

"Count me in."

While removing mugs from the cabinet, he observed his sister, taking note of the bare ring finger on her left hand and raising an eyebrow. At Christmas, she'd emailed him and Corinne to inform them of her engagement to "the Tom Brady of investing."

Had it been called off?

Natalie caught him noticing her lack of hardware and glared. "Don't ask."

"I'm going to ask."

"Fine." She hopped up onto a stool and crossed her arms, mimicking his earlier posture. "There's no law that says I have to answer."

"No, there isn't," he agreed, getting the milk out of the fridge and trying desperately not to panic over the minutes as they slipped away, one by one, right through his fingers. As soon as he drank this cup of coffee and squared the Natalie situation away, he would tackle his afternoon schedule. In fact, he would add extra writing time to put himself ahead. Julian's shoulders relaxed at that reassurance. "I don't know a lot about the financial sector, but I know it's too competitive in New York to simply take a break."

"Yes, it's part of the doctrine. You don't leave New York City finance unless you die or get fired, right?" She gestured to herself. "Unless you're a unicorn like me and you're valuable enough to earn some leeway. I'm a partner at my firm, Julian. Stop hunting. I just wanted a vacation."

"And you came *here*." He paused for emphasis. "To relax."

"Is that not what people do here? In the land of endless wine?"

"Other people, maybe."

Her arms dropped heavily to her sides. "Just make the coffee and shut up."

Julian gave her a dubious look before turning back around and doctoring the mugs with milk, plus one sugar for Natalie. Unless she'd changed her order in the last four years, that's how she took it. When he set it down in front of her and she sipped without comment, flicking him a reluctantly grateful glance, he guessed her ideal formula remained the same.

It surprised Julian that he experienced a tug of comfort in that. Knowing the way his sister took her coffee. They weren't close. Twice a year, they exchanged emails to wish each other a happy birthday and a merry Christmas. Unless his mother needed to inform them of the death of a relative, their line of communication was pretty inactive. Shouldn't she have contacted them about her engagement being called off? With three thousand miles between them, he never stopped to wonder about his sister's personal relationships. But now, as she sat in front of him clearly trying to outrun something, the lack of knowledge was a hole in his gut.

"How long are you staying?"

The mug paused on the way to her mouth. "I don't know yet." Her attention slipped over him. "Sorry. I know unquantified time gives you heartburn."

"It's fine," he said stiffly.

"Is it?" She stared into her coffee. "Last time we were here—"

"I said it's fine, Natalie."

His sister's mouth snapped shut, but she recovered quickly. Even faster than he could begin to feel guilty for being harsh. "So . . ." She took a deep breath and exhaled, somewhat unevenly. "Have you had any heartwarming encounters with our mother yet?"

"Perhaps not heartwarming," Corinne said from the kitchen entrance, arrival unannounced. "But positive and productive. That's what we aim for here, isn't it?"

Julian noticed the barest flash of hurt in Corinne's eyes. Over his sister arriving without warning? Or her offhanded sarcasm about their heartwarming relationship? It wasn't like his mother to be, or at least appear to be, upset over anything. Natalie and Julian's stiff upper lips were genetic, after all. After his conversation with Hallie this morning, it was easier to notice a chink in Corinne's armor, however. Not only now, but the last time she'd stopped by, too.

Was the vineyard in trouble? Would Corinne let the family business fade into obscurity, rather than request a helping hand? He was almost afraid to ask. To find out if she had the same use for him as Dalton. Namely, none. Sure, she'd asked him to participate in a festival, but that was far from hands-on. That was merely for the cameras.

"Since you're here, Natalie, I'll extend the same invitation I made to Julian. Wine Down Napa takes place in a week. A little Vos representation won't hurt. Will you be in St. Helena long enough to attend?"

No movement from Natalie, save a thick swallow. "Probably."

Corinne processed that information with a tight nod. "Lovely. I'll make sure you're issued a badge." She folded her hands at her waist. "Please try and remember the wine at these events is mainly for the paying attendees, Natalie."

"There it is." Natalie laughed, sliding off her stool and batting at the wrinkles in her pants. "It only took you forty-five seconds to put me in my place." Julian's sister split a venomous look between him and his mother. "I'm thirty now. Can we all get past the fact that I rebelled a little bit as a teenager?"

"A little bit?" With a bemused expression, Corinne tucked

some hair into the bun at the nape of her neck. "A little rebelling doesn't land you in rehab at seventeen."

Color infused Natalie's cheeks. "Yes, well, I landed on my feet at Cornell, didn't I?"

"Not without some strategic maneuvering."

"I'm . . ." Natalie's head of steam was diminishing quickly. "I made partner last fall."

Corinne eyed the suitcase. "And how is that going?"

"That's enough," Julian said firmly, his coffee mug hitting the island. "Natalie shouldn't have to explain her presence in her own home. I'm . . . sorry I made her do that. It ends now."

Natalie's head swiveled toward him, but he didn't meet her eyes. For some reason, he didn't want to see her surprise that he'd defended her. Once upon a time, it would have been a given. They might not be confidants or the closest of siblings, but he'd offered quiet support for his sister. At school, at home. Hadn't he?

When had he let that part of their relationship fall by the wayside?

His sister was obviously going through something serious, and he found it impossible to turn a blind eye to that now, as he'd been doing more and more since they'd each left St. Helena. Hadn't he been so wrapped up in his world that he'd missed the warning signs with his colleague Garth? One day they were discussing quantum theory in the hall, and the next, Garth was locked in his office and refusing to communicate with anyone outside. It didn't appear that Natalie was on the verge of a breakdown, but he should pay attention.

Be more present. More empathetic.

I witnessed your character when you didn't think anyone was watching and it really inspired how I've treated other people throughout my life.

Unexpectedly, that line from the secret letter popped into his head, and he mentally scoffed it away. The whole thing was a prank—and he wouldn't think about it a second more. It wasn't the letter that had inspired him to step up for Natalie.

Was it Hallie and the way she staunchly defended the owner of Corked, by fair means or foul?

Thinking of the gardener, he immediately caught a whiff of her soil and sunshine scent. Had it been lingering in the kitchen since Friday night or was that his imagination? What had that impulsive, curly-haired bundle of energy done to him?

Why couldn't he stop thinking about her?

Julian ordered himself back to the present, where his mother and sister were eyeballing each other across the kitchen. Yes, the Vos family had their share of issues—and he was far from the exception.

"Was there anything else either of you needed?" Julian asked, tight-lipped. "I need to shower and get to work." He glanced at his watch and felt his pulse accelerate. "I'm already forty minutes behind schedule."

Natalie staggered dramatically, gripping the handle of her suitcase. "The keeper of time hath spoken! To be idle is to smite his holy name."

Julian gave her a dead-eyed stare. His sister smiled back, which was odd and unexpected. All because he'd intervened with their mother?

Corinne cleared her throat. "I only came down to let Julian know the gardener will be back tomorrow."

The dueling spikes of relief and alarm in his chest were disturbing to say the least. "She's coming back here, then."

"Yes, I spoke with her on my walk over." Oblivious to his imminent coronary, Corinne gestured to the side of the house facing the vineyard. "I like what she did with the begonias. The guesthouse is visible on the vineyard walking tour, you know. I should have made more of an effort to give it some exterior charm before now."

"Is there no one else you can hire to plant some flowers?" Even as Julian posed the question, he wanted to take it back. Badly. Didn't they agree to be friends, despite the sour taste the word put in his mouth? Someone else digging in the front yard would just be . . . wrong. Very wrong. But the thought of Hallie coming back and taking a Weedwacker to his itinerary unnerved him a great deal. Unnerved *and* excited him. Made tomorrow seem far away.

In other words, nothing made sense anymore.

"There is one other gardener in St. Helena. Owen something, I believe?" Corinne checked the screen of her phone. "But I've already hired the girl."

So Owen was *also* a gardener?

Someone with her exact interests. Were they really friends? Or friends with benefits? Or had Hallie simply referred to Owen as her friend to be professional, when the man was actually her boyfriend?

Jesus Christ.

A few brief meetings and she'd already put him in a tailspin.

"Fine. I'll deal with her," he growled, a surprising wave of jealousy curdling the coffee in his stomach. "Is there anything else?

Would you perhaps like to send the high school marching band over to practice outside my window?"

"That's all," Corinne said simply. Then to Natalie, "Welcome home."

Natalie inspected her nails. "Thank you." She wheeled her suitcase out of the room toward the guest room on the opposite side of the kitchen from Julian's. "See you two around."

"Good-bye," Corinne called breezily on her way out of the house.

Leaving Julian standing alone at the counter with a ruined schedule and another visit from the ultimate distraction on the horizon. Why couldn't he wait? "Fuck."

Chapter Eight

$\mathcal{H}$allie shifted the truck into park in Julian's driveway, heartbeat wild as a jackrabbit's. There he was, stretching in the front yard. Deep, long movements that had her head tilting to the right unconsciously before she realized it. Wow. She'd never seen those kind of shorts before. They were gray. Loose sweatpants material that stopped just above the knee, a drawstring hanging down over the crotch. Which had to be why her eye was continually drawn there. Among other places. He could have cracked walnuts with those thigh muscles. Squeezed grapes in those butt cheeks. They were on a vineyard, after all.

"You should be locked up," Hallie muttered, forcibly closing her eyes.

A full day had passed since she'd last seen him and—good news—she hadn't been slapped with a restraining order yet. Which was generous of Julian, assuming he'd even found the letter in the first place. But that was the thing—*she had no idea.* And as the queen of avoidance, she would rather not know. Sneaking around for the rest of her life sounded so much easier.

Why did he have to be standing outside? She'd timed her

arrival with the end of his run, hoping she could do her planting while he was in the shower and skedaddle again before he ever knew she was there. Now he was watching her through the windshield with that impeccably raised eyebrow. Because he knew she'd written the letter and found her cutely pathetic, like a puppy? Because he couldn't believe the audacity of her, to show up after such a humiliating display of drunken affection? Or had the Napa winds been in her favor yesterday morning and the letter was halfway to Mexico by now?

Act natural.

Stop smiling like you just got your tax return.

You're still waving. It's been, like, fifteen seconds of gesticulation.

In her defense, Julian was sweaty—and that would turn a nun's head. His white shirt was sodden, straight down the middle, plastering the material to his chest. With the sun beating down on him, she could see through the white cotton to his black chest hair and the hills and valleys of muscles it decorated. God almighty, celibacy was no longer working out for her. At all. A virgin in heat is what she'd become.

She could no longer delay getting out of the truck to face her fate. The dogs were in doggy daycare today, so she couldn't even use them as a diversion. A few words out of his mouth and she would know whether or not he'd found and read the letter, right? Maybe he was even accustomed to women professing their admiration of him and this would be no big deal. They could laugh about it! And then she could go home, curl up, and die.

Hallie alighted from the truck on shaky legs, lowering the rear gate.

"Need some help?" he called.

Did he mean the psychiatric kind? If so, that would indicate he'd read her confession.

Hallie peeked over her shoulder to find him coming toward her with his usual commanding grace, expression inscrutable. Even in her nervous state, every step this man took in her direction turned a screw in a different location. Deep, deep in her belly. Between her legs. Just above the notch at the center of her collarbone. Was her distress obvious to the naked eye? It didn't appear so, since he continued to come closer instead of calling an ambulance.

As soon as she was alone with her phone, she would google, *How Horny is Too Horny?* Those search results ought to be interesting.

"Hi, Julian," she sang. Too loudly.

"Hello, Hallie," Julian said seriously, scrutinizing her closely. Wondering if she was the secret admirer? Or perhaps being fully aware of it already? For all she knew, she'd signed her actual name at the bottom. "What are you planting today?"

Oh. Oh, sweet relief. The wind blew the letter away.

Either that or he was being extremely kind.

Those were the only two options. Obviously he wasn't *interested* in her now, thanks to the sloppy admission. This man would only respond to a sophisticated approach to romance. A colleague introducing him to a young professional at a gala. Something like that. Not a spewing of infatuation scrawled in the back of a spiral notebook. And that was fine, because they'd agreed to be friends, right? Yes. Friends. So thank God for the Napa winds.

"Your mother asked for color, so we're going with some flannel bush," Hallie said. "Those are the yellow flowered plants you see in the bed of my truck. I'm going to come back tomorrow with some Blackbeard Penstemon, too."

"This is going to be an ongoing, long-term project." He nodded once. "I see."

"Yes." The tightness at the corners of his mouth made her heart sink down to her knees. "I know you're working. I won't make a lot of noise."

He nodded again. The wind tripped around them, blowing a curl across her mouth, and he surprised Hallie by reaching for it. She held her breath, lungs seizing almost painfully, but he stopped, drawing his hand back at the last second and shoving it into his pocket with a low curse. "And what are we going to do about you?"

Breathe before you pass out. "Me?"

"Yes." That word hung so long in the air, she swore she could see the outline of those three letters. Y-E-S. "You're more . . . disruptive to me than the dogs," he said, almost so quietly that she didn't hear him. "Hallie."

That grinding snap of her name was the equivalent of fingertips raking downward over her breasts. Was he admitting to being attracted to her? Like, out loud? Between that and him almost touching one of her curls, she was in imminent danger of passing out from sheer shock and happiness. "I can't do anything about that. Sorry," she whispered. "However, I am not sorry that I spent last night watching *Time Martians On.* So, you really believe the government is hiding an entire extraterrestrial colony in New Mexico?"

"I do *not* believe any such thing," he murmured, leaning closer. So close she was beginning to grow dizzy. "As I said, they were very liberal with the editing button."

"You're definitely on a watch list, nonetheless," she breathed.

He hummed in his throat. "Did it . . . make you smile? Watching the documentary?"

How could one man be so magnetic? "So much that my face hurt afterward."

A muscle popped in the history professor's cheek. His right hand flexed at his side. And then he forcibly withdrew from the intimacy of their conversation. So abruptly that she almost staggered under the sudden absence of it. "Good." He looked back toward the house, speaking after a few beats of silence. "I apologize for my mood. My sister, Natalie, has become my new roommate. At this rate, maybe it would be better if I rented office space in town."

She swallowed her disappointment. "Maybe it would be."

His attention slid down to her mouth and away, leaving her pulse rapping in her temples. Drunk or not, she'd meant every word of her letter. Her attraction to Julian Vos was twice as potent as before, when he'd been just a memory. A two-dimensional person on the internet. Then he'd gone and delivered a top-notch prank call and saved her from the Tweed Twit. Now she couldn't stop wondering what else he was hiding under the surface.

She *wanted* to know.

Unfortunately, he found her presence disruptive.

Where was the lie? But did he find her distracting in a sexy way? If so, he clearly didn't *want* the distraction. Or perhaps . . . the temptation.

Lord, to be a temptation to Julian Vos. She'd throw out her entire bucket list.

As soon as she got around to making one.

Was it possible she *did* tempt him? The way he continued to catalogue different regions of her body, seeming to get stuck on the area just above her knees, made her wonder if the answer was yes. Unless this burdensome horniness was playing tricks on her. Entirely possible. Lately she'd been finding the angles of her gardening hoe more and more charming.

Flirtatious, even.

A gardening tool could never make her heart race like this, though. The way it had done when he stood up for her at the scene of her—totally justified—UNCORKED crime.

If she's upset, I'm upset.

Hallie found herself staring into space at the oddest times, repeating those words. Wondering how seriously he'd meant them or if he'd just been trying to defuse the situation as quickly as possible. It scared her how much she wished for the former. Wished for a man this good and honest and valiant to care about her feelings. Enough to not want them hurt.

She waited for Julian to leave, to go back into the house—and he seemed on the verge of doing so at any second, but he never made the move. Simply continuing to study her as if she were a riddle. "So . . ." Hallie cleared the rust from her throat. "Natalie's visit wasn't planned?"

He scoffed, crossed his wrists at his back. "No. God forbid anyone have a plan."

Ouch. She was definitely not a sexy distraction to him.

"Hey, look at me," she said with determined sunniness. "Here before the kickoff of your fanatical writing sessions."

His eyes narrowed slightly. "Did you plan that?"

"Uh . . . no." That would mean she'd been paying way too close attention. Heh. "My day just kind of started . . . earlier than usual. A squirrel in the backyard set off a howling event before the crack of dawn, and I figured since I was already awake, might as well plant some things."

"And so," he said in a very professorial tone, "without the squirrel's intervention . . ."

"I'd have been here around dinnertime." She hefted one of the larger bushes, taking a moment to smell a yellow bloom. "Between noon and seven, at least."

"You're a menace." He took the bush from her hands, jerked his chin at the rest of the lot, as if to say, *I can take another one.* "No, Natalie showed up out of the blue. We didn't know she was coming in from New York." Grooves formed on either side of his mouth as he glanced back toward the house. "*She* didn't seem to know she was coming."

"Didn't say why?"

"A break from work. No further details."

Hallie hid a smile, but he caught it and raised a questioning eyebrow. "Is it gnawing at you?" she asked. "The vagueness of it all."

"That smile suggests you've answered your own question." Again, his gaze dipped to her mouth, but this time it lingered twice as long. "Then again, you're usually smiling."

He'd noticed her smile?

"Unless I'm masterminding a cheese heist," she responded, breathless.

"Yes, unless that," he said quietly, brows pulling together. "That man hasn't gone near you again, has he?"

His dangerous—almost protective?—tone of voice made her fingers dig into her palms. In a way, he'd claimed her as a responsibility. Someone to look out for. Because that was just so totally Julian Vos, wasn't it? Everyone's hero. Champion of men. "No. I haven't seen him."

"Good."

Trying and failing not to feel flustered, Hallie picked up the other bush, and they walked toward the front yard, side by side, their shadows stretching on the grass to highlight their difference in height. The companionable feeling of carrying plants with Julian made fizz pop in Hallie's bloodstream. Man, oh man, she had it so bad. For a split second, she even felt a niggle of regret that he wouldn't see the letter. God knew she'd never have the courage to say those words in person.

"Um." She swallowed. "Your mother must be thrilled to have both of her children home, though."

A humorless laugh. "I guess you could say it's complicated."

"I know a little about complicated relationships with mothers."

Her gait faltered slightly. Did she just bring up her mother? Out loud? Maybe because she'd been having digital, one-sided conversations with Julian's face on YouTube for so long, she'd forgotten this one was real? Or perhaps talking to him in person seemed surprisingly easier than it was when she fantasized about them riding through a misty vineyard on horseback. Whatever the cause, she'd said the words. It was done. And she certainly didn't expect him to turn with such rapt attention. As if she'd shocked him with something less than teasing or small talk about flowers.

"How do you know?" he asked, setting down the bushes. He took hers and put it on the ground, as well. "Does your mother live in St. Helena?"

"She grew up here. After high school, she ran away to Los Angeles. That's where I was . . ." Her face heated, definitely turned red, and he watched it all happen with a small, fascinated smile. "I was conceived there. Apparently. No further details."

"The vagueness of it all," he said, echoing her earlier words.

"Yes," she said on a big breath. "She tried raising me on her own. We came here, from time to time, when she needed to recharge. Or long enough to soften up my grandmother into loaning her some money. Then we'd be off again. But by the time I reached high school, she finally admitted I would be better off here. I still see her every couple of years. And I love her." Hallie wished she could rub at the discomfort in her throat but didn't want him interpreting the action. Or chalking it up to pain that had been building over a lifetime. "But it's complicated."

A low grunt from Julian. "Why do I get the feeling you've given me the CliffsNotes?"

"Maybe I have. Maybe I haven't." Hallie tried to smile, but it wobbled. "The vagueness of it all," she tacked on in an almost whisper.

Julian stared at her long enough that she started to fidget.

"What?" she finally prompted.

He shifted, drawing those long fingers through his hair, still sweaty and windswept from his run. "I was thinking, in order to make this an even exchange, maybe I should give you the Cliffs-Notes version of why the Vos family, or what's left of it in Napa, is complicated."

"What's stopping you?"

Mystified eyes flickered over her face, her hair. "The fact that I've completely lost track of time. And I don't do that. Not around anyone but you, apparently."

Hallie had no idea how to respond. Could only stand there and savor the information that she made this man forget the most important component of his world. And how . . . that could either be a great thing or literally the worst possible thing.

"Makes me wonder how long you could make me . . ." He dragged that bottom lip through his teeth while seemingly transfixed by the pulse on her neck. "Lose track of time."

That pulse sped up like a sports car on an open road. "I have no idea," she murmured.

He took a step closer, then another, a muscle bunching in his cheek. "Hours, Hallie? Days?" A raw sound ground up from his throat, one hand lifting to run a single finger down the side of her neck. "*Weeks.*"

Do I just jump him now? What was the alternate option? Because her thighs were actually trembling under the onslaught of his full intensity. That exploring gaze. His deep, frustrated tone of voice. Before she could fully convince herself they were talking about the same thing—sex, right?—behind her, a shout went up from the vineyard and they both turned, watching the tops of several heads move down the horizontal rows, all gathering in one place.

She turned back to Julian and found him frowning, his chest lifting and falling a lot faster than usual. "Looks like they're having a problem," he said hoarsely, clearing his throat. After that, he seemed to hesitate, those long fingers flexing. "I should see if they need help."

Nothing happened. He didn't move. The shouting continued.

Hallie shook herself free of the lingering need to get up close and personal with the apparent game-changing invention of sweatpants shorts. Did he seem uncertain about walking into his own family vineyard? Why? "I can come with you," she offered, not sure why. Only that it felt like the right thing to do.

Those eyes cut to hers, held, as he inclined his head. "Thank you."

When Hallie and Julian approached the group of men—and one woman—among the vines, every head swiveled in their direction. Conversation ceased for several seconds.

"Mr. Vos," blurted one of the men, the tan of his cheeks deepening. "Sorry. Were we being too loud?"

"Not at all, Manuel," Julian said quickly, flashing him a reassuring smile. Silence fell again. So long that Hallie looked up at Julian and found his jaw in a bunch, his eyes wandering over the rows of grapes. "It just sounded like something was wrong. Can I do anything to help?"

Manuel looked horrified at Julian's offer. "Oh no. No, we have it under control."

"The destemmer is broken again," the woman said, giving Manuel an exasperated look. "Damn thing breaks once a week." Manuel buried his head in his hands. "What? It does!"

"Does Corinne know about this?" Julian asked, frowning.

"Yes." Manuel hedged. "I can fix the destemmer, but we're already short-staffed. We can't lose one more person out here. These grapes need to come off the vine today or we won't stay on schedule."

"Corinne is stressed enough," said the woman, whipping a handkerchief from her pocket and swiping sweat from her brow. "We don't need another delay."

"My mother is stressed," Julian responded tightly. "That's news to me."

Just like yesterday, when she'd informed Julian of the slow decline of Vos Vineyard, Hallie could see that he truly had no idea. He'd been kept completely in the dark. Why?

"I can call my son home from summer school—" started Manuel.

"No, don't do that," Julian broke in. "I'll pick the grapes. Just show me where to start." No one moved for long moments. Until Julian prompted Manuel, the apparent vineyard manager. "Manuel?"

"Uh . . . sure. Thank you, sir." He stumbled in a circle, making a hasty gesture at one of the other men. "What are you waiting for? Get Mr. Vos a bucket."

"I'll take one, too," Hallie piped up automatically, shrugging when Julian gave her a measuring look. "I was going to spend the day in the dirt anyway, right?"

His attention flickered down to her knees. "I think you mean every day."

"Careful," she returned. "Or I'll pinch your grapes."

Manuel coughed. The woman laughed.

It was tempting to go on staring into Julian's eyes all day, especially now, when they were sparkling with that elusive humor, but Manuel gestured for them to follow, and they did, trailing behind him several yards into the vines. "This is where we left off," Manuel said, gesturing to a half-picked section. "Thank you. We'll have the destemmer up and running in time for the grapes to come in."

"No need to thank us," Julian said, hunkering down in front of the vines. He stared at them thoughtfully for a moment, then glanced back at Manuel. "Maybe we could sit down later and you could let me know what else around the vineyard needs attention."

Manuel nodded, his shoulders drooping slightly with relief. "That would be great, Mr. Vos."

The manager left, and they got to work, which she would have done much faster if Julian Vos wasn't kneeling beside her in sweaty clothing, with a bristly jaw, his long, incredible fingers wrapping around each grape and tugging. Lord, did she experience that tug everywhere.

Hide your gardening tools.

"The quality of these grapes is not what it should be. They've overcropped," Julian said, removing a cluster of grapes from the vine and holding it out to Hallie. "See the lack of maturation in the cane? They weren't given room to breathe."

His professor voice sounded so different out in the open like this, as opposed to pumping from her laptop speakers. "Hey, I just drink the wine," she murmured, wetting her lips. "I don't know the intimate details." He had the nerve to smirk at her while adding the grape cluster to his bucket. "You are one of those professors who gives a test review that covers nothing that ends up being on the actual test, aren't you?"

His gaze zipped to her, with something close to surprised amusement. "The entire body of material should be studied."

"I thought so," she drawled, trying not to let it show how flushed and sensitive his attention made her skin. "Classic *Jeopardy!* enthusiast move."

He chuckled, and she couldn't help but marvel at how different he looked in this setting. At first, he'd been tense, but he relaxed the longer they moved down the row in tandem, plucking grapes from their homes. "What did you do after high school?" he asked her.

"Stayed right here. Went to Napa Valley College. By then, my grandmother had already made me a co-owner of Becca's Blooms, so I needed to stay close."

He hummed. "And did you have professors like me in school?"

"I doubt there are any professors *exactly* like you. But I could usually tell on the first day of a semester which classes I would be dropping."

"Really. How?"

Hallie sat back on her haunches. "Cryptic comments about *being prepared.* Or understanding the *full scope* of the course material. That's how I knew their tests would try to trick us. Also that they were most likely sadists in their spare time."

His laughter was so unexpected, Hallie's mouth fell open.

She'd never heard him laugh before—not like that. So rich and resonant and deep. It appeared he'd startled himself, too, because he cleared his throat and quickly returned his attention to the vine. "It's safe to say you would have dropped my class."

She shifted on her knees beside him, still awash in the sound of his laughter. "Probably."

Yeah, right. She'd have sat front and center in the first row.

"More likely, I would have dropped you the tenth time you showed up late."

Now it was her turn to smirk. "Actually, I managed to make it to most of my classes on time, obviously with some exceptions. It was . . . easier back then. My grandmother wasn't a strict person, but she'd cross her arms and look stern while I set my alarm. I made the effort because I couldn't stand disappointing her."

The rest of her explanation hung unspoken in the air between them.

Showing up on time no longer mattered, because she had no one to disappoint.

No one but herself.

That thought made her frown.

"It helps me to write my schedule down, too," he said. "I would have liked her."

"What happens when you don't write down your plans?" she asked, surprised to see his fingers pause midair, the line of his jaw turning brittle. "Do you still . . . keep them as usual? Or does not seeing them on paper throw you completely off track?"

"Well, I definitely didn't have picking grapes on my schedule today and I seem to be doing fine." In one fluid motion, they crab walked to the right and continued picking. The action was so seamless, they traded a fleeting look of surprise, but neither one of them addressed their apparent grape-harvesting chemistry. "Schedules are vital to me," he continued a moment later. "But I'm not totally thrown off by a deviation. It's more when things sort of . . . move beyond the bounds of my control that I don't . . . maintain the course."

"I hope you're not revealing your rage-control problem while we're alone in the middle of this vineyard."

"Rage control," he scoffed. "It's not like that. It's more of an attack of nerves. Followed by sort of the opposite. I just . . . check out. In this case, I did it when my family needed me most."

Panic attacks. That's what Julian was getting at. And it was telling that he couldn't call them by their proper name. Was he simply irritated by something he saw as a weakness or was he in denial?

"That must be why your colleague's breakdown affected you so much," she said, worried she was overstepping, but unable to help it. Not when they were side by side like this, hidden from the rest of the world by six-foot vines, and she wanted so badly to know the inner workings of his mind, this man she'd been fascinated by for so long. He was nothing like she expected, either, but his flaws didn't disappoint her at all. They actually made her less self-conscious. Less . . . alone in her own shortcomings.

"Yes, I suppose so," he said, finally. Just when she thought the subject was closed, he continued, though the words didn't seem to come naturally. "My father's head would explode if he knew I had my hands on these grapes," he muttered. "He doesn't want me anywhere near the operation of the winery. Because of what I just told you."

It took her a full ten seconds to grasp his meaning. "Because of . . . anxiety?"

He cleared his throat loudly by way of answering.

"Julian . . ." Her hands dropped to her bent thighs. "That's the single most ridiculous thing I've ever heard in my life."

"You didn't see me. That night. The fire. What came after." He used his shoulder to wipe away a bead of sweat, remaining silent for a moment. "He's well within his rights to ask me to keep a distance. This morning, the destemmer breaks down, tomorrow there will be a lost shipment and an angry vendor pulling out. This is not for someone with my temperament, and he did the hard thing by pointing it out."

"What happened the night of the fire?"

"I'd rather not, Hallie."

She tamped down her disappointment. "That's fine. You don't have to tell me. But, look, you handled the broken destemmer just fine. You filled the need as efficiently as you do everything else." Okay, it sounded like she'd been paying way too much attention. Sort of like a secret admirer might? "Or, at least, that's how you seem to me. Efficient. Thoughtful." She swallowed the wild flutter in her throat. "Heroic, even."

Thankfully, he didn't appear to pick up on the notes of swooning admiration in her voice. Instead, a trench formed between his eyebrows. "I think my mother might need help. If she does, she's not going to ask for it." He pulled down a grape cluster, studying it with what she could only assume was an expert eye. "But my father . . ."

"Isn't here." She nudged the bucket toward him. "You are."

He scrutinized Hallie. And went right on looking until she felt her color rising. He seemed almost surprised that getting the worry off his chest hadn't been a waste of time.

When the quiet had stretched too long, Hallie searched for a way to fill it. "It's funny, you know? We're both shackled by these parental expectations, but we're dealing with them in totally opposite ways. You plan everything down to the minute. The very *peak* of adult responsibility. Meanwhile I . . ."

"You what?" he prompted, watching her closely.

Hallie opened her mouth to offer an explanation, but it got stuck. Like one of those king-sized gumballs, trapped behind her jugular. "I, um . . ." She coughed into the back of her wrist. "Well, I guess unlike you, I'm kind of self-destructive, aren't I? I calmed down a lot for Rebecca. *Because* of her. Don't get me wrong, I've never been well organized. Never owned a planner in my life. But lately, I think maybe I've been *intentionally* getting myself into messes . . ."

Seconds passed. "Why?"

"So I don't have to slow down and think about . . ." *Who I am now. Without Rebecca. Which version of myself is the real one.* "Which style of necklace to wear," she said on a laughing exhale, gesturing to the eclectic collection around her neck. There was no chance he was buying the way she made light of their discussion, but thankfully, he just studied her in that quiet, discerning way, instead of prodding her to elaborate. She couldn't even if she wanted to. Not with these troubling revelations still so fresh in her head. "I guess we better finish up," she muttered. "I have a few other appointments today that I'm considering keeping."

"There you go. Already turning over a new leaf," he said quietly, humor flickering in his eyes—and something more. Something that had his lids growing heavy, his focus sinking to her mouth. The notch of her throat. Her breasts. She would normally take offense to that, except when this very disciplined man checked her out inappropriately, as if he couldn't help it to save his life, her vagina was the opposite of offended.

If she leaned a few inches to the left, they would? Could? Kiss? Weren't they about to kiss when they were interrupted? Or had she imagined it?

Despite her sad lack of make-out partners throughout her life, she could tell he was considering it. Very. Strongly. They'd given up any pretense of harvesting grapes, and he'd wet his lips. Holy shit. This had to be a fever dream, right?

She'd had plenty of those starring this man.

"If I regret one thing about not having a direct hand in making wine at this vineyard . . ." He leaned in, letting out a long, heavy breath into her hair. "It's that I can't watch you drink a glass of Vos wine and know my efforts are sitting on that tongue."

Oh my God. Oh my God. Goose bumps made their presence known on every inch of her skin, her blood turning hot and languid. Definitely not a dream. She couldn't have come up with that line to save her life. "I mean . . ." Her voice wobbled. "We could pretend."

"As friends, right, Hallie?" His lips brushed her ear. "Is that what you suggested to me?"

"Yes. Technically."

"My friend who I think about at night in her polka dot bra. That friend?"

Wow. New fave undergarment.

Focus. Don't get pulled under. There was a reason she'd suggested friendship, right? Yes. "You need control and punctuality." His teeth closed around her ear, bit lightly and licked the spot, leaving her moaning, her fingers itching to rub her sensitive nipples through the front of her shirt. "I'm like a leaf blower to those things."

"Oh, I'm well aware. I wish I could remember that when I look at you."

Hallie's ears echoed with the beats of her twisting heart. How could she do anything but kiss this man who was equally incredible in the past and present? How?

She turned her head slightly to the left, and his mouth skated across her cheek, getting closer. This was it. Finally. She was going to kiss Julian Vos, and he was even better than her memory. But there was something about the setting that tugged hard at her memory. The last time they'd almost kissed was right here in this very vineyard—a moment that had ruined her forever. And he didn't even recall it. *Still.*

Didn't she have more pride than to pucker up after he'd implied without words that she was so forgettable? Yes. She did. Not to mention . . . she was reeling a little bit after her trip down Self-Discovery Lane. Her frame of mind was scattered. Enough to act in character and do something she might possibly regret. Like give in to her attraction to Julian while her disappointment over his lack of memory still jabbed sharply upward beneath her skin. After acknowledging the root of her recent behavior, she was too aware of those faults to indulge them now. If he just *remembered* her, maybe she could justify turning her head that final inch.

Meeting his parted lips with her own.

But while he regarded her with enough lust to power Canada, there wasn't any of the recognition she needed to make this okay. Furthermore . . . she didn't know if she wanted to be this man's leaf blower. Any kind of relationship with her would be bad for him, wouldn't it? Even if it was strictly physical. Did she want to be bad for him?

"I better go," she said, questioning her decision more with every passing second, especially when the fingers of his left hand curled in the dirt. As if restraining himself from reaching for her. "See you soon, Julian."

"Yes," he rasped, visibly shaking himself. "Thank you for the help."

"Of course." Hallie started to pick her way down the row, but hesitated, looking back to find the professor watching her from beneath two drawn brows. The last thing she wanted was to walk away and leave things awkward or heavy, when talking to him had unlocked something big. When he'd shared so much with her in return. "Hey, Julian?"

"Yes?"

She hesitated for a beat, before blurting, "Abraham Lincoln had anxiety. Panic attacks ran in his family."

His expression didn't change, but he shifted slightly. "Where did you learn that?"

"*Jeopardy!*," she answered, smirking.

A laugh crashed out of him. That was two in the space of one afternoon. She held it to her chest like a cozy sweater, sort of wishing she'd let go of her pride and kissed him after all. What was she going to do about her feelings for this man? "You watch?" he asked.

She turned and walked away, calling over her shoulder, "I've caught it once or twice."

His chuckle was lower this time, but she could feel his gaze on her back, following her out of the vines.

JULIAN FELT DIFFERENT when he walked into the guest room bathroom late that afternoon. Not bothering to turn on the light, he stopped in front of the mirror and observed himself streaked in dirt and sweat from hours spent harvesting grapes. The sun's muffled shine through the frosted glass window backlit his body, so he could barely see his own shadowed expression. Only enough to know it was unfamiliar. A cross between satisfied at having sunk his fingers into the soil of the family land for the first time in years . . . and haggard with hunger.

"Hallie," he said, floating her name into the silent bathroom.

He thickened so fast in his briefs that his dirt-caked hands curled into fists on the sink. Squeezed. With a jerky motion, he turned on the faucet, and after adding several pumps of soap, he scrubbed the earth from his palms, knuckles, forearms. But even watching the soil circle the drain reminded him of the gardener and her dirty knees. Hands that always looked fresh from planting something. The polka dot bra that remained pristine and protected inside of her shirt . . . and how she'd look stripping it off after a long day.

"Fuck. Not again."

Even as he issued that denial, his teeth were clenched, his

breaths coming faster and fogging up the mirror. His brain didn't issue an order to shove down the waistband of his filthy sweatpants shorts, his hands simply knew beating off was inevitable when the polka dot bra came into play. God, the irony that something so frivolous could literally make him pant was galling—but his dick didn't care. It strained free of his waistband, and he gripped it hard, biting off a moan.

Apparently Julian wasn't half as evolved as he'd believed himself to be, because his fantasies about Hallie were increasingly sexist. In a way that was unforgivable. This time, she was stranded on the side of the road with a flat tire and no idea how to change it. She almost definitely had that knowledge in real life. Did his dick want to hear it? Hell no.

It just wanted that reward of Hallie sighing in relief as he wrestled the spare tire out of her trunk and jacked up her vehicle, dogs and all.

No, wait, the dogs are at home. It's quiet, except for the sound of him tightening the lug nuts. She leans against the truck in nothing but that polka dot bra and jean shorts, watching him work and smiling.

Christ, yes. She's smiling.

Julian groaned while mentally picturing those unbelievable lips spreading into her cheerful grin, propping a forearm against the mirror and burying his face in the crook of his elbow, his opposite hand moving in hard strokes, the base of his spine already beginning to gather and jolt. It wasn't even funny how hard he was going to come. How hard he climaxed *every* time he gave in to his infatuation with Hallie.

Infatuation.

That's what this was.

Infatuation was why, in his fantasy, *he imagined her running to him, throwing her arms around his neck and thanking him breathlessly, her tits barely contained inside the bra now. Just bare and bouncy against his chest, her hand exploring the front of his pants, her eyes widening with appreciation at the length of him, her frilly bra just kind of disintegrating into the ether of his daydream. Along with the jean shorts. Still smiling.*

She was still smiling as he took those generous tits in his hands and guided them to his mouth, one at a time, sucking her hardening nipples and listening to her whimper his name, her fingers clumsily yanking down his zipper.

"Please, Julian," she purred, jacking him off, mimicking his increasingly frantic movements over the bathroom sink. "Don't make me wait for this."

"As long as this isn't out of gratitude for changing your tire," he rasped back, making a pitiful attempt to prevent his fantasy self from ditching ethics altogether. "Only because you're hot for it. Only because you want it."

"I want it," she moaned, arching her back against the truck. "No, I need you."

"I give you what you need, do I?"

"Yes," she whispered, twisting a blond curl around her finger. "You make me happy."

Lights out. No matter where the fantasies started, he knew only precious seconds were left when she said those words. *You make me happy.* His harsh inhales and exhales filling the bathroom, he mentally *stooped down, lifted her naked body against the side of the truck, and entered her with a grunt, watching her face transform with total euphoria—this was his dream, after all—her pussy pulsing, gripping him nice and tight. Slippery. Heaven.* "Such a good girl. So fucking wet," *he praised in her ear, because even the imaginary version of this woman deserved worship, especially when he was driving into her so hard, the encroaching orgasm putting him on that desperate edge.* "If this was real life, sweetheart, I'd take better care of you than this."

"I know," *she gasped, her curls and tits and necklaces shaking, moving with her, part of her.* "But it's a dream, so be as rough as you want."

"As if I could help it when you make me feel like I'm going to fucking die at any second. Unless I'm inside you. Unless I'm as close as possible to that smile, that voice, your . . . sunlight."

Julian choked on that truth into the crook of his elbow, stroking fast enough to break the sound barrier, picturing Hallie's legs around his hips, her head thrown back in a throaty call of his name, her pussy cinching up with an orgasm, their mouths latched together while he joined her with a final ram of his hips, impaling her maddening body to the truck.

"I'd make you come just like this. Hard and wild. That's not a fucking dream, do you understand me?"

"Yes," *she said on a shaky rush of breath, still trembling against him, even while she blinked up at him with a sweep of eyelashes.* "Just like I'm making you come right now."

A sizzle in his loins was followed by a trap door opening, all of the pressure and sexual frustration escaping. He dug his teeth into the muscle of his forearm, the tension that had been coiling leaving him in sharp waves while he still thought of her. Those eyes and breasts and filthy knees.

Julian couldn't stop thinking of her when it was over, either—

and he was beginning to wonder if a moment's peace from the captivating gardener was nothing more than wishful thinking.

THAT EVENING, HALLIE walked into her house and stopped just inside the door, seeing the mess through fresh eyes. It hadn't always been like this. Not when Rebecca was alive. Not even immediately following her death. Sure, Hallie's heartbeat naturally spelled out the word "clutter" in Morse code, but the disorganization was nearly a hazard now. Precarious stacks of mail and paperwork. Laundry that would never see the inside of her dresser. Dog paraphernalia galore.

Her mind was still stuck in the vineyard with Julian, replaying their conversation over and over.

I'm kind of self-destructive, aren't I?

I think maybe I've been intentionally *getting myself into messes...*

So I don't have to slow down and think about...

Anything, really. Wasn't that the truth? As long as the whirlwind of trouble continued to spin, she wouldn't have to figure out how to move forward. And as who? As Hallie, the dutiful granddaughter? As one of the many personalities crafted by her mother? Or was she a version of herself she hadn't truly gotten to know yet?

Only one thing was for certain. When she was talking to Julian in the vineyard, she didn't feel as alone. In fact, everything inside of her had quieted and she'd seen the source of her problem, even if she had no earthly clue how to solve it. The strict control Julian kept on himself had grounded her, too, in those stolen moments . . . and she wanted more of them.

It took Hallie a good fifteen minutes to find the notebook

she'd purchased in the stationery shop, thanks to the General partially burying it in the backyard. And another ten minutes to locate a pen that wasn't out of ink. She started off writing a to-do list, but stalled out almost immediately after writing *Clean Out Refrigerator* and *Cancel Subscriptions for Phone Apps You Are No Longer Using.* What she really wanted was to be back in the vineyard, talking to Julian. There was something about his directness, the intent way he listened, and his own willingness to admit his flaws, that made it so easy to dig into her own. To see them clearly.

After today, she was pretty sure Julian was attracted to her. They could talk about personal things like they'd been having heart-to-hearts their entire lives. But she'd been living with her feelings for Julian so long, it was almost hard to be around him knowing his couldn't measure up. It was so impossible, she'd actually suggested they be friends only, just to avoid that potentially painful speech from him.

But here, in her letters, she could let her admiration pour out, almost in a therapeutic way.

And so, instead of being responsible and outlining a way out of #thatclutterlife, she found herself turning to a fresh page.

Dear Julian...

Chapter Nine

Julian ran extra hard the next afternoon.

He'd woken with purpose that morning. Plowed through four writing sprints, made himself a protein shake, and now he was focused on beating yesterday's running time.

Yes, that was the plan—and he'd be sticking to it.

Unfortunately, his feet had other ideas. When Julian spied the line outside of UNCORKED, the loitering mass of people blocking the entrance to Corked, he jogged to a stop and frowned. At them. At himself for once again being unable to stay on schedule.

Initially, the unfairness of UNCORKED's success had gotten under his skin. They were making a mockery of the long-standing shop next door and, frankly, insulting the whole process of wine tasting by turning it into a stunt. A thumbing of the nose at the wine industry wouldn't normally bother Julian, except that *everything* these assholes did bothered him now.

Because they upset Hallie.

He loathed her being upset. The real version of her *and* the fantasy version.

She should always be smiling. Simple as that.

Was there something he could do about this?

Back in high school and even slightly beyond, he'd been more inclined to reach out a helping hand to those who needed it. He'd gotten involved. Tried to make himself useful. Somewhere along the line, he'd become focused on his own agenda, never glancing right or left.

Hallie's passionate defense of Corked had really brought that into focus, and he couldn't seem to continue on his merry way this afternoon. If Hallie could burgle hundreds of dollars' worth of cheese, he could certainly make his presence known.

In the process, perhaps he could help Corinne. And Lorna.

After he'd finished picking grapes yesterday, he'd invited Manuel into the guesthouse for coffee and . . . yeah. Suffice it to say, the manager had pulled off Julian's blinders. Corinne was doing an admirable job of maintaining the winery, but quality had begun to fall by the wayside in favor of expediency. Vos Vineyard needed money, so they churned out wine, but the superiority they once claimed had been slowly waning.

His mother had not asked him for help. Maybe that was in deference to his father's wishes or perhaps she didn't have any faith in Julian, either. Whatever the reason, he couldn't stay on the sidelines and watch his family legacy fade into obscurity. Nor did he want his mother carrying this load by herself when he was willing and able to pitch in. Was Hallie's refusal to let UNCORKED bully her friend's shop responsible for this head of steam?

Yes. In a way, perhaps it had reminded him that legacy was important.

Maybe there was a way to give Vos Vineyard a boost *and* make Hallie happy in the process. The possibility of a Hallie Smile over something he did made his pulse knock around.

Refusing to let himself hesitate any longer, Julian made his way through the line of tipsy tourists who would probably benefit from sitting out their next tasting, and walked into Corked. He was greeted by soft music and lighting, and a woman with a lined, smiling face behind the register. She couldn't quite manage to hide the fact that he'd startled her by simply walking in.

"Hello," sang the woman, who had to be Lorna. "Are you . . . here for the tasting?"

"Yes," he lied briskly, perusing the shelves, relieved and maybe even slightly prideful to see a wide selection of Vos wines for sale. "What is on deck today . . . ?"

"Lorna. This is my shop." She emerged from behind the counter, fussing with her hair. "To be totally honest with you, I didn't think anyone was showing up, so I haven't even set up glasses." She rushed to the back of the store, clearly excited to have some life within the shop's walls. "Choose any bottle you want and we'll crack it open. How about that?"

Julian nodded after her, continuing his trip up and down the aisles, circling back to the front of the store. Behind the register was a black-and-white picture of Lorna as a young woman holding hands with a man outside on the sidewalk, the Corked storefront in the background. The man was her husband, most likely. Both of them looked so optimistic. Proud. Ready to take on the future. No inkling that someday a disco ball would be stealing their business. No wonder Hallie was fighting the decline of Corked so fiercely.

That sealed it. He was going to be the best customer this woman ever had.

As he waited for the older woman to set up two glasses and produce a corkscrew from her apron, Julian selected a Vos Vineyard

Cab from 2019. Ideas to aid Lorna formed, one after the other. Some bigger than others. But he thought it best not to overwhelm the woman all at once.

She poured him a half glass of wine, and he took a brief moment to mourn his productivity for the rest of the day. "Thank you. Are you joining me?"

"Don't mind if I do," she said, eyes twinkling.

Yes, it was becoming quite clear why Hallie felt the need to rob and vandalize in this woman's honor. Kindness rolled off her in waves. "Great." He sipped the wine, holding it on his tongue for several counts before swallowing. "Wonderful. I'll take three cases."

She almost spat out her wine. "*Three cases?*"

"Yes, please." He grinned. "I'll pay now and pick them up later, if that's all right." Seemingly in a daze, she took the American Express he handed over, but like any smart businesswoman, she beelined for the register before he could change his mind. "With an established shop like this, you must have local regulars."

"Lately, everyone seems so busy. And it has become increasingly easy to order wine online." Her tone retained its pep, but he could see wilting beneath the surface. "I do have some loyal customers, though, that refuse to let me down."

"Oh? Who might those be?" Good God, he was fishing. "Maybe I know them."

"Well, there's Boris and Suki. A lovely couple that come in every other day for a bottle of their favorite Shiraz. There's Lavinia and Jerome—they own and operate Fudge Judy and make the most *delicious* Boston cream pie donuts. But I'd have to say my most loyal regular is the granddaughter of one of my dearest friends, God rest her soul. A local gardener named Hallie."

Lorna brightened. "Actually, she's close to your age. A bit younger, maybe."

Yeah. No mistaking that his heart had picked up speed. "Hallie Welch?"

Lorna ripped the credit card receipt with a flourish. "That's her! Did you go to school with Hallie, then?"

Sore spot prodded, he hid a grimace. Why could he not *remember*?

"Yes. High school." He took a casual sip of his wine, set it down, twisted the stem. "She's doing some gardening work for my family at the moment, actually. Small world."

"Oh my, isn't that a coincidence?" laughed Lorna over the register, her lips turning down at the corners after a beat. "Poor girl took it very hard when Rebecca passed. I don't think she knew up from down. Came to the funeral in two different shoes and everything."

The sensation of having his chest stomped on was so visceral, he actually looked down to make sure nothing was there. Hallie in mismatched shoes at a funeral, not knowing up from down, made him feel very helpless. Was she better now? Or just better at hiding her grief?

"Of course, she does have some very good friends to see her through. She's joined at the hip with Lavinia. And of course there's that lovely Owen—but I doubt you know him, he moved here about—"

"Owen. And Hallie. Have they . . ." He relaxed his grip before he could snap the stem of the wineglass. "Dated?"

The older woman went right on smiling, clearly unaware there was a shiv to his throat. "Yes, I think they have. Casually, though." She spoke in an exaggerated whisper out of the corner of her mouth. "Although I think Hallie is the one who keeps putting on the brakes."

"Oh." Tension escaped him like air leaving a balloon. "Interesting." He barely restrained himself from asking Lorna *why* Hallie continued to put on the brakes. Did Owen have any annoying habits? Did he double dip, perhaps? Any reason to validate Julian's irrational dislike of the man would be welcome. But he'd gone far enough with this line of questioning. Going any further would be considered stalking in at least twenty states.

No more inquiries about Hallie. But . . . the whole making-her-smile thing was still on the table, wasn't it?

"Lorna, do you happen to have business cards of any kind?"

"I'm afraid not. I've always relied on foot traffic. It used to be enough to have a sign outside that said 'free wine tasting.'"

"As it should be." He twisted the glass right to left. "I would be happy to make you up some cards. Maybe . . ." It had always been rare for him to drop the Vos name, but there was no way around it in this instance. "My family owns a vineyard here in St. Helena. Maybe we could give cards for Corked out to our visitors. If they bring in the card, ten percent off their first bottle? Does something like that sound agreeable to you?"

"Your family owns a vineyard?" She handed him back the credit card, along with his receipt to sign. A blue pen. "Isn't that nice. Which one?"

He coughed into a fist. "Vos Vineyard."

Lorna lurched against the tasting table, nearly upsetting the open wine bottle. "Vos . . . Are you the son? Julian?" Her mouth opened and closed. "I haven't seen you in years. Forgive these old eyes, I didn't recognize you." She shook her head a moment. "And you would really offer to hand out cards for me?"

Julian nodded, grateful she didn't seem inclined to make a huge deal out of his last name. "Of course." She chewed her lip as if waffling. Perhaps scared to be hopeful? So he added, "Your shop is a landmark. If you haven't been here, you haven't been to St. Helena."

The older woman's eyes sparkled at him. "You're damn right."

That competitive streak of his was ticking like a metronome. "Actually, I'll take a few bottles to go now." He winked at her. "In case I get thirsty on the walk home."

Which is how Julian found himself in the neighboring yoga studio eight minutes later, handing bottles to the men and women emerging from class. "Lorna sent these," he explained to the sweaty and confused people.

They traded perplexed glances. "Who?"

"Lorna," he said again, as if they should know. "From Corked. Next door. The longest-standing wine store in St. Helena. No trip to Napa is complete without it." He smiled at the girl behind the counter. "I'll drop off some business cards for you to hand out."

When Julian left the yoga studio and restarted his watch, his shoulders were lighter. He continued down Grapevine Way for a while, past the health spa and several cafés. As he got farther from the center of town, the shops he passed were more for the locals. Pizzerias and a dance school for children. A car wash and a donut shop named after Judge Judy, which he could not find fault with. And that's where he turned right and cut down the wooded path leading to Vos Vineyard. Another three-quarters of a mile and he'd be at the guesthouse. Sure, he had a slight wine buzz, but he wouldn't let it postpone his shower, and then it would be straight to work—

Up ahead, a square, white object, totally out of place among the greenery, snagged his attention. Julian stopped so abruptly, his sneakers kicked up a dust cloud.

No way. Not again.

Another envelope. With his name on it. Stuck in the crack of a tree stump.

Standing in the center of the path, he looked around, positive he'd find Natalie hiding and snickering behind a bush. Apparently she hadn't gotten the prank out of her system yet. But she must have come and gone a while ago, because he was quite obviously alone there, no sound save the afternoon breeze sweeping down off the mountain. What kind of bullshit had his sister written this time?

Shaking his head, Julian plucked the letter out of the stump— and immediately noticed the handwriting was the same as last time, but more controlled. And the further he got into the correspondence, the more it became clear Natalie had *not* written it.

Dear Julian,

There is something so easy about an anonymous letter. It puts less pressure on both of us. There is less fear of rejection. I can be totally honest, and if you never write back, at least I let out the words that have been trapped in my head.

They're your problem now—sorry.

(Forget what I said about less pressure.)

When you run down Grapevine Way in the afternoons, a solitary figure on a mission, I wonder how you feel about your solitude. If it's the same way I feel about being alone. There's so much space to think. To consider where I've been and where I'm going. I wonder if I'm who I'm meant to be or if I'm just too distracted to keep evolving. Sometimes it's overwhelming. Do you ever get overwhelmed with the silence or are you as content in the solitude as you seem?

What would it be like to know you completely?

Does <u>anyone</u> know you completely?

I've been loved by someone for all my faults. It's a wonderful feeling. Maybe you want that for yourself. Or maybe you don't. But you're worthy of it, in case you're wondering.

This is getting too personal coming from a stranger. It's just that I don't truly know you. So I can only be honest and hope something inside you . . . hears me.

I'm sorry if you found this letter strange or even terrifying. If so, please know that I meant the opposite. And if nothing comes from this, your main takeaway should be that someone out here thinks about you, in the best way possible, even on your worst day.

Secretly Yours

Julian finished the letter and immediately read it again, the tempo of his pulse increasing steadily. This letter was nothing like the last. It was more serious in tone. Earnest. And despite the oddness of finding a letter on his jogging path, he couldn't help but respond to the wistful tone woven into the words. No way Natalie wrote this, right? He couldn't imagine his sister taking an emotional deep dive like this, even for a joke.

The envelope was bone-dry, meaning it hadn't been there since last night. The morning dew would have dampened it, at the very least. Although noon had come and gone, Natalie was asleep when he left for the run, plus there had been two empty wine bottles on the kitchen counter, neither of which he'd had a single glass from. He supposed his sister might have battled through a hangover to prank him—she'd never lacked dedication. And she would have had opportunity, since he'd run for nearly half an hour, plus his pit stop at Corked.

Maybe he just *hoped* Natalie hadn't been the one to write the letter, because the damn thing had unexpectedly struck a chord with him. It was written by the same person who penned the last letter, meaning their interest was romantic in nature.

What would it be like to know you completely?

The closer he got to home, the more that question circled his head.

I wonder if I'm who I'm meant to be or if I'm just too distracted to keep evolving.

Four years had passed since he'd been home, and he'd barely registered the length of time. Not until he'd arrived in St. Helena to find his mother keeping the winery's troubles a secret. His sister going through a crisis, and he didn't even know the barest details. What if his coping mechanisms weren't helping him anymore?

What if keeping rigid schedules was harming him . . . and his relationships, instead?

Julian entered the house and immediately strode toward his sister's room.

She was asleep. Sprawled out, an empty wineglass on the floor near her dangling hand.

When the scent of alcohol hit him, he closed the door again with a wince.

If she'd left the house this afternoon with all of the alcohol in her system, she would have either burst into flames or passed out somewhere along the trail.

Which meant he actually had a secret admirer in town. The first letter had been real. Should he write back?

Jesus.

He should forget about the letters. Cast them aside as a disruption. But he continued to think about the questions she'd posed in the second one. He'd read the letter only twice, and he could already mentally recite it, word for word.

How odd.

What if Hallie is my secret admirer?

No. Impossible. She was not a serious romantic interest, despite the amount of time he spent fantasizing about her, leading to an embarrassing amount of breaks being taken from work to relieve himself of sexual frustration.

Julian, I don't think there are two more different people in this whole world.

Hadn't she said those very words? Not to mention, she'd been the one to suggest a relationship based purely on friendship. He'd never met a more bluntly honest person. If she was his admirer, she would simply tell him, wouldn't she? She didn't lie about her faults—no, she practically bragged about showing up late and flying by the seat of her pants.

Or her annoyingly tight cutoffs, as it were.

Whoever was on the other side of these letters, there would be no writing back, despite his being reluctantly intrigued. Something about establishing communication with this person didn't sit quite right—but exploring that too deeply could come only at his own peril, so Julian quickly stuffed the letter back into his pocket with the intention of forgetting about it.

Again.

Chapter Ten

If Hallie leaned just so to the right and stretched, she could see Julian through his office window. Working diligently, with his ticking stopwatch and rigid shoulders. The sky was clouded today, so the lamplight from the house spilled across the grass, highlighting the mist in the air. It was definitely getting ready to rain. She should absolutely get going. But she wouldn't have this view of Julian Vos and his cleft chin from home, so she risked the inclement weather by planting extra slowly, spreading the soil with slow-motion hands.

Their eyes met through the glass, and she quickly looked away, pretending to be enthralled by the blooming stem of a snapdragon, while her belly continued to take one long skydive. Had he found the second, decidedly more coherent letter? She'd been working in the guesthouse garden for two days and they hadn't spoken, so she couldn't get a read. But he definitely hadn't written back. She'd checked. And that couldn't be a good sign, right?

Maybe he'd marched her letter directly to the police and asked them to handle it. Maybe they were forming a task force right now. Find and eliminate the rogue secret admirer before any more men were forced to read about feelings.

Thunder rolled loudly overhead.

Once again, their gazes danced toward each other through the mist-covered window, and he raised a very sharp eyebrow. As if to say, *Do you not have a weather app on your phone?*

Or eyeballs?

Finally, he lifted a phone to his ear. She assumed he had to take a call until her own phone started vibrating in her back pocket. "You're calling me from inside?"

He hummed, and the low sound was like a soft shock down her spine. "Shouldn't you be wearing a jacket? Or maybe calling it a day altogether, considering it's about to pour?"

"I'm almost done. These lilacs just can't decide where they want to be." Julian's head fell back on his shoulders, eyes imploring the ceiling for sanity. "You know I can see you, right?"

Despite Julian's frustration, his lips tugged. "Maybe you could try something new and space out the flowers evenly—"

"This just in: they want to be directly behind the daisies."

His laugh was like the sizzle of water on a hot stove. There was something intimate about it. About the storm and his lamplit window. "Are you enjoying yourself?"

"Maybe a little." She fell forward on hands and knees, securing the lilacs in place and patting the earth around the edges. "I don't mind working in the rain, actually. The one responsible thing I've done recently is buy a waterproof phone case. Did you know there is no dog slobber damage clause in the Apple contract?" The raindrops on the window didn't quite obscure the twitch of his lips. "If you need to get back to writing, we can hang up."

"No," he answered, as if involuntarily. "How is Corked doing these days?"

Hallie paused and studied Julian. Was he really not going to take credit for buying three cases of his own family's wine? Apparently not. He was frowning at the computer screen, no sign of the good deed visible in his expression.

She'd skidded into Corked for the afternoon tasting, only to find that Julian had not only stopped in and had a glass of wine with a thoroughly charmed Lorna, but he'd dropped enough cash to pay this month's rent. As if she needed another reason to send him love letters—of which there would be only two. Two, tops.

Unless he answered.

Which he definitely didn't seem inclined to do.

Maybe a third would nudge him?

"Corked is doing slightly better than usual, actually. Lorna has more of a spring in her step the last couple of days, which is nice to see," she said breathily, her hands working the earth. "I'm not sure why, though. She's been very tight-lipped. Maybe she landed an investor. Either that or she's got a boyfriend."

He studied her through the window, trying to either determine if she was joking or perhaps deduce whether or not she'd been made aware of his generosity. When she only kept her features schooled, he cleared his throat. "And this makes you . . . happy? Lorna having more spring in her step?"

Did he appear hopeful, or was that her imagination? "Yes. It does."

"Hmm." Apparently the topic was dismissed, because he leaned forward to look up at the sky and shifted in his chair. "There is going to be a downpour any second now, Hallie. Come inside," he said, without thinking. "I don't want you cold."

Her hands paused slightly at his deeper tone.

She looked up, their eyes latched, and her oxygen grew scarce. Did he have any idea how his caring affected her? It was a glimpse at the man beneath. The man she'd always known was there, but who had been buried in his adulthood. Not so deep that she couldn't see it. Couldn't wish to dig and dig and wrap herself in his uniquely refined kindness.

"Do I need to come out there and get you?" he prompted.

Mother Nature sent thunderheads rolling across the sky above them. Or maybe that turbulence was moving straight through her, reverberating in her bent thighs and tightened tummy muscles. She was the human version of a plucked tuning fork. Bottom line, if she stood up right now, her arousal might not be visible . . . but she couldn't guarantee it. Who could hide *this* potent a feeling? Better to stay crouched, maybe drown in a flash flood.

"Very well," he clipped, hanging up before she could . . . what? Tell him not to bother coming to collect her? Was she really going to pretend that she didn't want to go inside his house to wait out this romantic rainstorm?

A screen door opened in the distance, and her heart accelerated, beating even faster when Julian came into view. Just in time for the sky to make an ominous tearing sound and condensation to begin falling in a spiky deluge.

"Come on," he said, reaching down to take her hand, his warm palm sliding against hers, his fingers compressing around hers, leading to what felt like an electrical charge straight to her hormones. Leaving her tools to fall where they may, she allowed herself to be pulled along the front path and into the cool, dry interior of the house.

Julian guided her into the kitchen and stopped, looking down at their joined hands, his thumb ever-so-slightly brushing over the pulse at the small of her wrist. Could he feel it pounding like McConaughey on a pair of bongos? Did she want him to? Ultimately, a muscle popped in his cheek and he let her go, retreating to the opposite side of the island like last time, with his hands propped wide, dress sleeves rolled up to his elbows. Oh Lord, the forearms. There they were. In her fifteen years of fantasizing about this man, she'd definitely neglected one of his best features. Going forward, she needed to do better.

She opened her mouth to make a joke about Californians never being prepared for rain. But she stopped short, a flash of cold running up her arms. There on the marble counter sat the envelope containing the secret admirer letter.

No.

Both of them.

They were in a neat stack, naturally, with a brass duck paperweight on top.

Oh Lord. He'd gotten them. Both letters. Read them with his eyes and brain and forearms. They sat between them like an accusation. Was she too blindsided by her crush to realize she'd just walked into a confrontation? Her pulse picked up. She needed to figure out what was going on here and fast.

"Is Natalie home?" she asked, glancing toward the back of the house.

"No. On a date, I believe."

"Really? Good for her. In the rain and everything."

"Yes." He seemed to blink himself out of a trance. "She met someone at the gas station of all places. I don't understand how that happens. I've never had a conversation with anyone while filling my tank, but she seems to have built-in . . . what do my students call it? Tinder?"

"Her sixth sense is locating single people. That's an enviable skill."

His left eye twitched. "You wish you were better at asking out men?"

"Sure." Were they having the most ironic conversation possible considering the letters sitting beneath the mallard? Or had he intentionally led them here in preparation for a secret admirer intervention? "Don't you?" she managed through her dry throat. "Wish you were better at coming right out and telling someone that you're interested?"

He considered her from across the island.

Thunder boomed outside.

Though she couldn't see the lightning that came a few moments later, she imagined it zigzagging across the sky. Much like the veins in his forearms.

My God, pull yourself together.

"I don't usually have a problem with that," he said, narrowing his eyes.

There you have it, folks. Julian Vos didn't have any issues telling the opposite sex he was interested. Was this a gentle letdown? *Nice letters, but I'm into scholars who like to attend astronomy lectures instead of getting drunk and eating linguine.*

"My problem mostly comes later in the acquaintance," he continued. "When it's time to state my intentions. I worry they'll become attached when I have no intention of doing the same. I don't want to promise something and not deliver. That's worse than being..."

"Being what?"

"I don't know. Disconnected." He was beginning to look troubled. "I tend to remain disconnected with people, because it's easier to focus. On work. On keeping time. It's never bothered me until now. I never meant to become so unattached in all my relationships. Only romantic ones. But my sister. I don't know what's going on with her and . . ." He caught himself with a hard headshake. "Sorry, I shouldn't be bothering you with this."

"I don't mind." In fact, with his halting revelation still hanging in the air, she could barely stand the pressure in her chest. "You're worried about Natalie?"

"Yes," he answered succinctly. "She's always been so good about taking care of herself. Coming home would be a last resort for her."

"Have you tried talking to her about it?"

After a moment, he shook his head, those bourbon eyes finding her from across the island. "What would *you* say? To make her comfortable enough for that?"

It meant something that Julian was asking her this. The tentative manner in which he posed the question told her exactly how often he requested advice. Next to never. "I would tell her you're glad she's here with you."

Julian's spine straightened more than it already was. "That's it?"

"Yeah." Hallie nodded, folding her hands in front of her. "But before you say it, make sure you mean it. She'll be able to tell the difference."

His lips moved slightly, as if repeating her advice to himself. This man. She'd been right about him. All along.

He was heroic.

Somewhere along the line, had he convinced himself of the opposite?

It took all of her self-control not to cross to the other side of the kitchen, go up on her tiptoes, and press their mouths together.

But . . . would that be unethical now? He was opening up to her without knowing she'd written him those letters. Letters he'd obviously read and kept.

His gaze shifted down to the letters briefly, then away. "Someone recently asked me how I feel about my solitude. They said, 'There's so much space to think. To consider where I've been and where I'm going. I wonder if I'm who I'm meant to be or if I'm just too distracted to keep evolving.'" A wild rush of butterflies carried through Hallie, winging up into her shoulders and throat. Did he just quote her letter from *memory*? "That made sense to me."

Oh dear. This wasn't an intervention.

He'd read the letters . . . and liked them. They'd resonated with him.

Hallie's first reaction to that was a burst of joy. And relief. This distant bond she'd always felt with Julian . . . maybe it wasn't a figment of her imagination after all.

"That makes sense to me, too," Hallie rasped into the kitchen, the sound of rain almost drowning her out. Wait. Now she was having a full conversation with him about the contents of her letter. That wasn't good. She'd never intended this, and she needed to come clean right now—

"Lately I've been wondering if I'm so trapped inside this need for structure that it's ceased to have any meaning at all," Julian said, looking just beyond her shoulder. "I haven't used minutes or hours on anything besides my job, and does that mean I've essentially . . . wasted some, if not all of it?" His attention fell to the note. "Maybe I haven't evolved, as this person says. Maybe I've been too distracted to grow, when I thought I was being so productive."

She related to that so hard, she almost reached across the island for a high five. "Sort of like, as you get older, you start taking on myriad responsibilities that make you an adult. But really, they're just distracting you from the things that matter. And then you've misspent your time, but there's no way to get it back."

"Exactly."

"When your colleague had his breakdown, you started to wonder about this?"

"Almost immediately. He should have been somewhere else. A healthier place for him. With his family. And then I thought, is this where I'm supposed to be?" He tucked his tongue against the inside of his cheek, examined her. "Do you ever lose sleep wondering if you're in the wrong place or timeline?"

You have no idea. "Sure," she whispered, wondering if he could read her mind. Maybe he could. After all, there was something magical charging the air in that moment, in the nearly dark kitchen with a thunderstorm rioting outside. Standing with this staid and private man while he confessed his inner turmoil. There was nothing she could do to stop herself from leaning into the intimacy. Going after it with both hands.

Not even her conscience, apparently.

"The first fourteen years of my life, I was on the road with my mother. We were never in the same place longer than a week. And my mom . . . she's kind of this beautiful chameleon. She likes to say midnight transforms her back into a blank canvas, like Cinderella and the pumpkin. She became whatever her current love interest wanted. If she changed bands, went from soul to country, she'd go from a lounge act to a cowgirl. She evolved constantly, and she . . . took me with her. On the road *and* on these makeovers. She redesigned me over and over. I was punk,

I was girly, an artist. She'd kind of impress these different identities on me, and now . . . sometimes I don't know if this is the right one, if this is actually *me*. It felt right when my grandmother was here."

Julian's gaze dipped to her multitude of necklaces. None of them made sense together, but she could never decide which ones to wear. Throwing them all on got her out of the house and away from the mirror fastest. The simple act of picking a piece of jewelry or restricting flowers to certain beds of soil felt like major decisions.

So she flaunted them, committing to everything and, thus, to nothing.

"Anyway," she said quickly. "For what it's worth, I think you're in the right timeline. You were there to help your colleague in a moment of need and it propelled you here at the same time as your sister, who also needs help. Not to mention the vineyard. That can't be an accident." A smile stretched her lips. "If you weren't in this timeline, who would the perpetually late, unsystematic gardener be driving crazy these days?"

For some reason, that drew his brows together.

And he started around the island. Toward Hallie.

Her breath came out in a short burst, and she couldn't seem to replace the expelled oxygen. Not with Julian looking at her like that, his jaw locked, each step purposeful, his gorgeous features arranged in a near scowl. He reached the closest corner of the island and turned. Continued. Then, oh Lord, he moved in close enough to Hallie that her head tipped back automatically to maintain their searing eye contact.

"I don't like being driven crazy, Hallie."

"I sort of noticed."

He propped his hands on either side of her on the island. Stepped closer. Enough that his body heat warmed her breasts, his jagged exhale stirring her hair. "I also spend a lot of time wondering who else you're driving crazy."

Hallie melted back against the island. In theory, she wasn't a woman who found jealousy attractive. At least, she didn't think so. No one had ever displayed envy where she was concerned. That she *knew* about, anyway. Still, she shouldn't like it. She also shouldn't like the smell of gasoline. Or cold pizza crust dipped in barbeque sauce, but explain the word "shouldn't" to her taste-buds. Explain "shouldn't" to the hormones that went absolutely wild at the knowledge that he'd spent his precious minutes and hours thinking about where she was.

And with whom.

You can like it. Just don't reward him for it.

"Keep wondering, I guess."

His right eyebrow went up so fast, it nearly made a *whoosh*ing sound. "Keep wondering?" A blast of lightning briefly turned the kitchen white. "That's what you're . . . giving me . . ."

When he didn't continue, she prompted him. "What's wrong?"

Several seconds passed. His chest started to move faster, up and down, his head ticking slightly to the right. Recognition slowly registered in his eyes, and he cursed low and sharp under his breath. "Your hair wasn't curly back then."

What was he talking about? She had no idea, although her pulse was beginning to zigzag, as if it knew something was coming. "Back when?"

"That's how we know each other." He eagerly traced her features with his gaze. "We went for a walk together in the vineyard. The night my sister threw that party."

She blinked rapidly, pulse kicking into an even faster gallop. "Wait, you . . . remember?"

Julian nodded slowly, perusing Hallie as if seeing her for the first time.

This decade, at least.

"My friend straightened my hair that night. She thought it made me look older." A corner of her lips jumped. "It fooled you. Until I fessed up to being in your sister's grade."

"Right." His mouth opened and closed. "I thought you had to be from a different school. I never saw you in the halls after that. Anywhere."

"My mother took me back on the road." God, she sounded like she'd been running on a hamster wheel. "It wasn't until you'd left for college that I settled into St. Helena permanently with my grandmother."

"I see." A shadow crossed his face. "I'm sorry I didn't remember. My sister threw that party without permission. Without planning or telling me first. I tend to . . ."

"What?"

This appeared hard for him to say out loud. "I've been known to check out after I lose control of a situation. It makes my memory spotty. Not to mention the alcohol I drank . . ."

Knowing what she did about him now, that made sense, though she suspected there was a much more elaborate explanation behind *checking out*. "You're forgiven."

A handful of heavy seconds ticked by.

"Am I?" Slowly, he crowded her closer to the island. Their chests pressing together, her head tipping back. Rain pounded the windows. "I'd like to be one hundred percent sure that you don't hold my cloudy memory against me." His breath stirred her hair. "I want to feel you forgive me. I want to taste it in your mouth."

Mother Mary, he had a way with words. "Maybe that's a good idea," she managed, legs almost losing strength completely. "For the sake of closure and all."

"Right," he rasped. "Closure."

And then his fingers were sliding into her hair. He rubbed her curls between the pads of his thumb and index finger, as if fascinated. His warm breath accelerated so close to her mouth, and it was a heady thing, their inhales and exhales matching, quickening, their gazes linking. Holding. His was glazed. Heavy. He looked at her mouth as though it would anchor him in a storm, and he went for it desperately.

Hallie's lower back flattened against the island, and he quickly moved with her, rubbing his thumb against her cheek, as if apologizing for coming on so strong. But he didn't seem capable of slowing down, either. He took rough pulls of her mouth, tilting her head sideways and taking deep tastes. Thorough and savoring. *My God.*

Their tongues plunged and collided, causing her to whimper and Julian to groan, and that sound raced in her blood like rocket fuel. In seconds, this had gotten completely out of control, and Hallie loved being punted straight out of reality. Craved the unpredictability of his mouth and the unexpected courses taken by his hands. His right one left her curls to scrub down her spine, just like he'd done in the vineyard fifteen years earlier, but now the man gripped fabric and pulled her body closer. Their bodies just kind of melted, like liquefied metal being poured into a mold. Curves fit into peaks, muscle flexed against softness.

"I like it when you're standing in one place," he growled,

breaking the kiss so they could suck down heavy pulls of air. "When you hold still."

"Don't get used to it," she whispered breathily.

"No?" His mouth opened on her hairline. "Would you like me to unzip these shorts so you can move better, Hallie?" She found herself nodding before he even finished posing the question. At the mere suggestion they get rid of the denim barrier between them, her shorts became unbearable. An offense. Looking her right in the eye, he lowered her zipper and shoved them down her hips, a *whoosh* followed by the material hitting the floor, the buttons making a metallic clink. After several breaths lost among the thunder, his hand curled around Hallie's wrist, guiding her own hand to her upper thigh. Higher, until her fingertips almost met her panties.

Sensations bombarded her. Julian's rain-and-spice scent. His quickening breaths near her ear. The chafe of his dress shirt on the cotton of hers. When his chest shifted to one side, then the other, it rubbed her nipples to life and electricity snapped out into her limbs.

"If you can't hold still . . ." He brought her fingertips another inch higher—and flush with her sex, her wetness evident through the material of her panties. "Make it count."

The ground rippled beneath her feet. "You want me to—"

"Touch yourself. Yes." His open mouth raked over her ear. "It's only fair, since I've been fucking my hand on a regular basis since you started working outside my window."

Was this *real life*?

How many times had she brought herself to orgasm while thinking about this man? Having him not only watch but *order* her to do it made her knees shake. Sensory overload. She kind of wished she'd imagined this scenario sooner. Wished she'd known long before now what it would feel like to have Julian slide a finger into the waistband of her panties and tug them down, slowly, to the tops of her thighs, exposing her sex to the storm-lit kitchen, then re-brace his hands on the island where he had her body pressed. Waiting.

Hallie bit her lip, fingers twitching—and that alone made him groan. Yes, this buttoned-up professor groaned even before she started tracing the damp seam of her flesh with her middle finger, raking that digit up and down until her folds parted organically. In need of more. She all but bloomed for him on a rush of wetness, her fingers gathering the moisture and spreading it over her clit, her gasp mingling with the sounds of rumbling thunder.

"Fuck me," he muttered into her ear. "You do this in your bed at home."

Not a question. A statement. So she didn't answer. Couldn't.

Her head fell back, neck strength depleted, fingers rubbing eagerly.

"Do you ever go to bed with those dirty knees, Hallie? Do you climb onto the mattress facedown and open those filthy knees wide in your sheets, like you do on the front lawn? God, I'd fucking pay to see it."

Holy mother of . . .

The words this man gritted out like a modern-day barbarian into her ear were not what she'd expected. Not what she'd imagined him saying for years and years while feverishly writhing in her bed. In her fantasies, Julian usually told her she was beautiful—and that had been enough to bring her to climax? God, how boring. He was giving her dirty *knees* talk. He'd pulled down her underwear and asked her to masturbate in his kitchen.

In the future, her spank bank was going to be lit.

But she didn't want to consider the future right now. There was only this man's harsh pants in her ear, those intense eyes locked on the actions of her fingers. Two of them now that speared wetly through her flesh to stimulate her clit and, really, it was *beyond* stimulated. If she gave it three seconds of concentration, she could peak, no questions asked.

Something else continued to circulate in her mind, though, preventing her from giving her pleasure full concentration. What he'd said. *It's only fair, since I've been fucking my hand on a regular basis since you started working outside my window.*

Okay, she'd fantasized about Julian going solo.

Her imaginary sex life hadn't been *that* boring.

Would she ever get another chance to see it live? This storm, the happenstance of being in his front yard when it started to rain and having this forced intimacy . . . there was a high chance it would never occur again. Her desire to watch Julian touch himself was more than just a desperate need to satisfy her curiosity or gather fantasy fodder for the future. She felt a bone-deep welling of responsibility, of need, for him to find satisfaction, too. If he didn't come with her where she was going, it wouldn't be as fulfilling.

"You, too," Hallie managed, moaning when his mouth stamped over hers. Not kissing. Just magnetized. Drawn instantly by the fact that she'd spoken. "Please."

A beat passed. Then, lips still clinging, he reached down and unfastened his belt, lowering his zipper. She saw none of it, but the metal zing alone was enough to make the muscles in her tummy tighten, her bare toes curling on the floor.

"I had to put this on my schedule. Right there on my notepad.

Beating off to Hallie." His tongue traced her bottom lip. "I've already done it once today."

"You wrote those words down?" she said, gasping when he nipped at her jaw.

"No, I just wrote your name. My cock knew what it meant."

Leaning back slightly, Julian looked Hallie right in the eye and reached into the opening of his pants, grunting through his teeth, eyelids drooping over the first stroke—

And Hallie's orgasm blew in without warning. Like a door flying open during a hurricane. She whimpered, legs turning to jelly, and very nearly dropped into a heap on the floor. But Julian moved fast, supporting her with his upper body, his mouth heating her neck while his hand never stopped moving. Hallie had never wished more fervently for better camera angles in her life, because she couldn't see the way Julian guided his erection up into the juncture of her thighs. Not touching her. Just stroking himself faster, faster, into the opening between her legs, just above her tugged-down panties, their aroused parts never meeting. But she felt him *everywhere* nonetheless.

"Jesus Christ, this is out of control," he rasped into her hair. "I'm not in control."

"That's okay."

"Is it?"

She nodded, but he couldn't see the way she bobbed her head, not with his face buried in her neck. And then his free hand slid around to palm her backside, massaging it roughly in his hand—and her fingers turned slippery again. She began stroking her too-sensitive flesh, because there was no help for it. No stopping. No easing the twist of those deep, deep knots growing more complicated beneath her belly button, twining and snaring, urging her fingers to increase their pace. Their pressure. *Oh God, oh God.*

"Good, Hallie," he muttered thickly. "Is that pussy going to give it up twice?"

"Yes," she gasped.

He pressed his mouth to her ear. "God. The way you lost it when I wrapped my hand around my cock. I'll be thinking about it for years. Decades. How many times do you need to be on the schedule per day? Three? Four?" The swollen head of his arousal pressed flush to her mound and they both moaned, body jolting against body. Shaking. And when he ground himself there, against her fingers and, in turn, her clit, a second climax drew all of her muscles tight and let them go rapidly, leaving pulsations in its wake. The *throb throb throb* of release. "Jesus. You had to be so fucking sweet."

Julian crushed her against the island, his muscles coiling, his big shoulder pressing to her open mouth—and he jerked, groaning as he left warm moisture on her inner thigh. Two, three, four stripes of liquid heat, until he slumped against her, the sounds of the storm roaring back in along with the pounding of hearts.

For long moments, she could only stare off into space. In utter wonder.

Her first sexual experience with a man, beyond kissing, and it had blown her preconceived notions out of the water. She'd been right to be picky. Even without a lot of experience, Hallie somehow knew not all men would turn her on like Julian had just done. Nor would their pleasure make her own so much fuller.

And yet, as breathless and exhilarated as she felt, there was something in the air.

Something stirring.

Julian's hard body stiffened a little more with every passing minute, but he hadn't quite caught his breath. Not the way she had. And when he finally pulled away from her, it was more of a ripping apart than anything. Like a Band-Aid being torn from skin, it took a piece of her along with it. She caught a flash of thickly rooted flesh as he rearranged himself back in his pants, and then he paced to the other end of the kitchen, plowing a hand through his hair.

Several seconds ticked by while he said nothing.

It didn't take a genius to know he had immediate regrets.

For his hasty behavior. For letting his body make decisions for itself.

For engaging in something unplanned and spontaneous . . . when that was something he never did.

They'd agreed from the start that he was control and she was chaos—and he was obviously feeling the impact of that now, unable to look at her while fixing his clothes, that groove between his brows deeper than ever before.

Not only had she caused him to lose the control he needed so badly . . . she'd discussed the letters with him. Openly. As if she hadn't written them. Sure, the fact that he was quoting from *actual* correspondence was never said out loud, but she'd known. She'd lied by omission, hadn't she? She was given every opportunity to stop, too, and she didn't take it. Even now, when she had the chance to confess, she couldn't bring herself to do it, because he was visibly shaken by what they'd done. How would it help to tell him she was his secret admirer?

"I have to get home to walk the dogs," she said, sidestepping to yank the shorts up her legs and buttoning them with unsteady fingers. "The next phase of planting shouldn't be for a few days. Next week, most likely—"

"Hallie."

His hard tone propelled her toward the front door. "I really have to go."

Julian caught up with her at the door, curling a hand around her elbow and slowing her to a stop. They faced each other in the darkness of the entryway. "Listen to me for a second." His eyes went right to left, as if searching for an explanation. "I go from zero to a hundred in three seconds flat with you. I'm not used to it. Somehow I go from having boundaries for everything to burning them down. Something about you brings me to the edge of my comfort zone. In the past . . . look, my experience going beyond that boundary hasn't been positive."

"I'm messing with your inner compass and you want to keep it pointed north. It's fine. I totally understand." It *wasn't* fine. He was ripping her heart out. Why did she say that? "I really have to go."

As she spoke, he'd started pinching the bridge of his nose between his thumb and index finger. "Goddammit. Maybe that was too honest. But that's my other problem around you, isn't it? I talk to you in ways I don't talk to anyone else."

"I'm glad you're honest with me," she said with a catch in her throat. How did he say the exact right thing while simultaneously breaking her in two? "But sometimes the truth is just the truth and we have to accept it. We're too different."

Julian dropped his hand away, braced it on the doorjamb. He shook his head as if to deny it, but didn't. How could he? Facts were facts. "It's still raining pretty hard. You shouldn't drive." He started patting his pockets, coming up empty in an obvious search for his keys. "Please let me get you home safely."

She almost laughed. Like this wasn't awkward enough? "Look,

I can talk to my friend Owen about taking over the garden out front—"

"I'll have no one but you."

Hallie waited a beat for him to clarify that confusing statement, which seemed to indicate the opposite of what was happening here—a good-bye of sorts?—but he added nothing to that stern denial, the confusing, complicated man. Not wanting to give Julian a chance to find his car keys, she spun on a heel and jogged out into the rain. "Good-bye, Julian. I'll be fine."

As much as she wanted to leave without looking back, her gaze was drawn to him while backing down the driveway. *I'm sorry,* he mouthed to her. And she replayed his silent apology over and over on the way home, deciding to accept it and move on. Which would be a lot more difficult now that he'd exceeded her fantasies, both physically and emotionally, by about several hundred miles.

Unfortunately, their differences had never been more obvious. *I go from zero to a hundred in three seconds flat with you. I'm not used to it. Somehow I go from having boundaries for everything to burning them down.*

Something about you.

Julian needed planning and predictability, and she bucked those qualities like a rodeo bull. And she couldn't, in good conscience, continue to play Julian's imaginary girlfriend now that she'd missed her opportunity to reveal herself as the secret admirer. It wouldn't be right. Even she didn't have that much anarchy inside of her.

Time to put this crush behind her once and for all. Before she caused any more trouble.

Chapter Eleven

Julian stood in the low-lit kitchen, drumming his fingers on the island, the sound weaving together with the tick of the clock to create a pattern of sorts. Even by his own punctual standards, he'd gotten dressed too early for the Wine Down Napa event this evening. Anything to avoid the blinking cursor on his computer screen. And memories of a certain energetic gardener gasping for air against his mouth. *Jesus.* He couldn't get the fucking taste of her out of his head. It stayed with him day, night, and every second in between.

Turned out, he'd almost kissed her once before. Fifteen years ago. That night, he'd drunk too much out of pure irritation with his sister. Vodka and anxiety had blurred the details of the evening. But ever since the memory resurfaced, details were returning. Vivid ones that made him question how he could have ever forgotten in the first place—even after checking out for a brief window of time afterward. Now? Julian remembered the fading light on her hair and the overwhelming urge to kiss her. The smooth skin of her back.

And the realization that she was a freshman, after which Julian was fairly certain he'd hustled her back to the party with his face on fire.

How did he misplace a memory that had the power to rock him now?

Julian didn't know, but it appeared that Hallie was determined to turn up once every decade and put cracks in his concentration. He couldn't fit his regular thoughts in between the ones of her moaning, thighs shaking with her orgasm. And what happened afterward.

What *had* happened afterward?

Still unclear. He'd been thrown the hell off, he knew that much. Normally, with a woman, there was an orderly physical progression from kissing to more. With Hallie, he'd operated on blind instinct, his body in total control, not his mind. Yeah, he'd been off-kilter when the fever cooled, trying to put his head back together. By the time he'd succeeded, she was halfway to the door.

Which was for the best, right? He'd been trying to convince himself of that for two days.

Obviously she was a danger to his control. Control he relied upon so he wouldn't aggravate his anxiety. With Hallie, he'd lost any sense of self-preservation and . . . took. Gave. Got lost. With her breath on his mouth and her green-thumb scent infiltrating his brain, he'd moved without conscious thought. If he'd wanted to keep touching her, if he'd wanted release, he'd had no choice. But coming down had been like crashing into a wall. His mind wasn't supposed to go offline like that. His impulses were meant to be . . .

Subdued.

Funny, he'd never thought of them that way.

Julian jerked his chin to the side, setting loose a series of cracks in his neck. Tension that continued to build with the passage of time since Hallie's hasty departure. Now Saturday night had arrived, and his mood was not the kind he should be unleashing on the general population, especially when representing Vos Vineyard, but what choice did he have? At least he could get away from the blank page taunting him in the office for a few hours.

Natalie trudged into the kitchen in stoic silence, dressed in all black, oversized mirrored sunglasses hiding her eyes. One might think they were on their way to a funeral, instead of an outdoor wine event on a fine summer evening in Napa. And Natalie could easily be the grieving widow, considering she'd only gotten out of bed for the day an hour earlier.

What *was* going on with his sister? Despite a rebellious phase in her youth, Natalie had turned into a Grade A overachiever once she'd gotten it out of her system. Once, after not hearing from her for a while, he'd checked her Facebook page and found she'd posted a Forbes article in which she'd been touted as a rising star in the world of investing. Add in her missing engagement ring and things had obviously taken a turn. But the Vos family operated on a need-to-know basis. They didn't exactly shoot the shit. Information was given out as needed and, more often than not, kept to oneself.

Why was that?

Growing up, he'd more or less assumed that sucking it up and handling a crisis alone, so as not to disappoint or inconvenience anyone, was normal. In college, he'd been shocked by his roommate's semiweekly phone call to his parents, during which he told them every piece of information under the sun, from his

cafeteria meals to the girls he dated. Then, as a history professor, he'd witnessed the close relationships his students had with
their parents, as well. On Family Weekend at Stanford, they
showed up in droves wearing red sweatshirts and bearing care
packages. They . . . gave a shit.

Perhaps not every family was close, sharing trials and triumphs as a matter of course. But based on the real-world data
he'd witnessed with his very own eyes, families that cared
about one another were more commonplace—and healthier—
than his.

*I would tell her you're glad she's here with you. But before you say
it, make sure you mean it. She'll be able to tell the difference.*

He cut Natalie a speculative glance, hearing Hallie's words in
his head—far from the first time today. In fact, since she'd left
Thursday night, braving a storm to get away from him, he'd been
hearing the gardener's voice in his fucking sleep.

Natalie removed a flask from her purse, unscrewed the cap lazily, and tipped it to her lips. After a second gulp, she offered him
the metal container.

"No, thank you," he said automatically. Why, though? Didn't
he *want* a belt of whatever was in that flask? Yes. Obviously. He
hadn't slept since Thursday night due to his brain's insistence on
replaying every second of his interaction with Hallie on a torturous loop. "Actually . . . yes, I'll have some."

Natalie's eyebrows shot up behind her sunglasses, but she
passed him the flask without comment. "Rough going on the
book, big brother?"

He studied the opening of the container for a moment, trying
not to make a mental list of all the reasons he shouldn't imbibe
hard liquor at five o'clock. For one, he'd have to interact with the

public on behalf of the family business—which might be in more trouble than anyone realized. And two, he desperately needed to get back to his book at some point. But if he had a drink this early, he would almost certainly have two, which would lead to lethargic thoughts tomorrow.

Hallie running away from him into the rain, feelings hurt.

"The hell with it," he muttered, tilting the flask to nearly a ninety degree angle, letting the river of whiskey warm a path down his throat and hit his empty stomach like a boulder. "I can already tell that was a terrible decision," he said, handing the whiskey back to Natalie.

She took another rip of the drink, then stuffed it back into her purse. "Evidently I'm rubbing off on you."

Normally, he would let that cryptic statement go without comment. Letting someone's bad mood go unaddressed was the standard. None of his business. Only, it was, wasn't it? "Why do you say that? Have you . . . made any bad decisions lately?"

"What?" Natalie did a double take. "Why are you asking me that?"

Apparently communing with one's family was harder than he thought. "For one, you slept until four o'clock in the afternoon. Now you're dressed like you're going to deliver a eulogy instead of shaking hands at something called Wine Down Napa."

"Maybe I'm eulogizing the grapes. Do you know how many of them had to die so people from Oklahoma can pretend they're getting an oaky aftertaste?"

She would get along great with Hallie.

That thought came out of nowhere and stuck like an arrow in his jugular.

Well, he might as well let that possibility go right now. Natalie and Hallie would probably never spend time together, unless one of these days Natalie actually went outside and introduced herself in the yard. After all, Hallie probably never wanted to see him again—and rightly so. How could one woman draw him in so intensely, while throwing him so far outside his comfort zone?

He rubbed at the throb in the center of his forehead. "I just wish you would tell me what has brought you back to St. Helena, Natalie."

"You go first."

Julian frowned. "I'm writing a book."

"'I'm writing a book,'" she mimicked. "If all you wanted was to write a book, you could have done it back at Stanford." Her fingers fiddled with the air. "Subtract two hours of gym time per week, eat your meals five minutes faster. There's your writing time. You didn't have to come to Napa to write Wexler's adventures."

He blinked. Shifted against the island. "How did you know my hero's name is Wexler? Have you been reading my manuscript?"

Did her color deepen? "I might have skimmed a page or two." She looked like she was considering reaching for her flask again. Instead, she threw out a frustrated hand. "How long are you going to leave him dangling over that stupid cliff?"

"You seem oddly invested," he sputtered, kind of . . . touched that his sister seemed concerned about old Wexler?

"I'm not," she said, waving him off. "Just, like . . . he has a grappling hook attached to his belt. In case you forgot."

He'd totally forgotten. "I didn't."

"No, of course not." She sighed, pursing her lips. Then: "Why did you make him blond?" His expression must have betrayed his utter puzzlement, because she elaborated. "Blond men are unrelatable."

A laugh came very close to sneaking out of him. That was happening more and more frequently lately, wasn't it? He couldn't remember his chest ever having felt this loose. But then why, around Hallie, did it get so tight again? "That sounds like theory, not fact."

"Nope. It's fact. Have you ever stood there talking to a man with white-blond hair and not speculated on his lifestyle? You can't *not* do it. It's impossible. You don't hear a single word coming out of his mouth."

"So you're saying I should make Wexler a brunette."

"Obviously, yes. Look. Blond men say things like 'hot tubbing' and they go hiking in Yosemite with the cool girl. I want to root for a guy who is unlikely to go on an adventure." She gave him a wry look. "Like you."

Julian made a sound. "I'll take the hair-color change under advisement."

"Great." She waited a beat. "So you are just going to own the unadventurous label?"

"No arguments there," he said briskly, nudging the brass mallard on the kitchen island. "Unless you count having a secret admirer as adventurous."

"*What?*" Natalie slapped a hand down on the marble. "No way. What? You are lying."

"Nope. They've been sitting right here. Maybe if I'd kept them in the wine refrigerator, you'd have found them." He grinned at her middle finger. "At first I thought you wrote it as a prank, but they're too ..."

"There's sex stuff in them?"

"No. Nothing like that." Lines from the second letter drifted through his head. "They're just . . . more personal than one would get when pulling a prank, I suppose."

She raked both hands down her face, dragging the skin beneath her eyes farther than seemed wise. "Oh my God. I need to know everything."

"There is nothing important to share." Saying that made his stomach sour. Why did he have such a loyalty to this unknown person? Perhaps because, although he knew Hallie hadn't written those letters, some part of him secretly wished she had. Out of sheer masochism, he'd imagined her penning those words on the pages, and he'd sort of gotten stuck picturing her as the admirer. Which was nothing short of ridiculous and yet another way for the gardener to occupy his brain day and night. "I'm not going to write back."

"Fuck that. Yes, you are, Julian." She clasped her hands together beneath her chin. "Please let me help? I am so *bored*."

"No." He shook his head, the bitterness in his stomach turning even more acidic. "I'm here to work. I don't have time for some sort of ridiculous pen pal."

Natalie's shoulders slumped. "I officially hate your guts."

Guilt trickled in slowly. Why was he denying his sister something that might serve as a distraction from whatever was causing her to drink too much and hibernate in her dark bedroom? Anyway, maybe he *should* write back to the admirer. If for no other reason than to satisfy his curiosity. Obviously at some point he would have to put the gardener out of his mind. He could either do it now or when he inevitably returned to Stanford. If he could stop picturing Hallie when he read those words, moving on eventually would be a lot easier.

Still didn't feel right, no matter which way he sliced it. Damn, she'd gotten to him.

Although, writing the return letter didn't necessarily mean he had to *send* it. But having a mutual project might create an opening for Natalie to confide in him. He wanted that, didn't he? "All right, since we have some time to kill before we leave, you can help me write a response," he said grudgingly, already regretting the decision. At least until his sister started fist pumping her way around the kitchen, more animated than he'd seen her since she'd come home.

FORTY-FIVE MINUTES LATER, Julian and Natalie trudged up the path to the main house. Natalie walked to his right, freshly written letter in hand, rows of grapes extending out past her like outstretched arms into the evening. Light from his mother's windows beckoned ahead, crickets chirped in the near distance, and that elusive vineyard smell hung in the air. Kind of like a three-day-old floral arrangement. He'd forgotten how familiar it could be.

"Where are we supposed to leave the letter again?"

Julian bit back a sigh and pointed at the tree stump about twenty yards away, shaking his head when Natalie skipped toward it gleefully. He didn't have the heart to tell her he would come out later tonight and take it back. Nor could he regret the time they'd spent together writing the response. Such a simple activity had loosened something between him and his sister. Enough for him to pry?

"You mentioned that you're bored in St. Helena," he said slowly. "So why aren't you back in New York, Natalie?"

She finished tucking the letter into the stump, turned, and rolled her eyes. "I know. I'm intruding on your solitude."

"No, I'm . . . I'm glad you're here with me." Her step faltered as they started up the path again, side by side. And Julian must have meant what he said about being glad, because she didn't call him a liar. In that moment, he had the most pressing urge to tell Hallie what was happening. To call her right in the middle of it, although she probably wouldn't even answer.

"I guess you could say that I'm . . . worried," he tacked on around the goose egg in his throat. "About you. That's all."

Several seconds ticked past before she laughed, turned, and carried on up the path. "You're worried about me? You haven't called me in a year."

His stomach sank. "Has it really been that long?"

"Give or take."

"Well." Following her, he clasped his hands behind his back. Unclasped them. "I'm sorry. I shouldn't have let so much time pass."

He felt her considering him from the corner of her eye. "I guess it's not that hard to understand why. After everything that happened . . ."

"I'd rather . . ." He avoided looking at the vineyard. "Do we have to talk about the fire?"

"Do we have to talk about the fact that you were a total hero and saved my life?" She let out an exasperated laugh. "No, I guess not. I guess we can ignore the fact that you were incredible that night, but our father only saw what happened afterward. He had no right to judge you like that, Julian. To call you unfit to be involved with your family vineyard. He was *wrong*."

Julian couldn't unclench his jaw to respond. He could only

see images from that night. The nighttime sky lit up like something from the apocalypse, putting the people he loved in danger. People he was supposed to protect. Needles digging into his chest. His fingers curling into his palms and remaining that way. Stuck. Everyone watching him come apart.

That slow slide into nothingness afterward that he couldn't break free from, no matter how much he commanded himself to focus, to pull it together. No, instead, he'd gone dark. Left everyone else to sort out the mess while he navigated his mental fallout.

"It's my fault," Natalie said quietly.

That broke Julian out of his haze of discomfort, his attention whipping to the right. "What are you talking about?"

Even in the muted light, he could see the red staining her face. "If you didn't have to save me, if I hadn't put you through that, you wouldn't have lost it in front of him. I shouldn't even have gone into the shed. The fire was moving too fast—"

"Natalie. Don't be ridiculous." Realizing how harsh he sounded, he softened his tone. "You didn't do anything wrong. *Nothing* is your fault."

She made a sound, kept her face averted. "Could have fooled me. I mean, we weren't exactly the Tanner family to begin with, but we've barely spoken at *all* since then."

"I take responsibility for that. I should have been better about . . . being in your life. Obviously you've needed some—"

Natalie stopped walking abruptly, a glint in her eye that he could only interpret as dangerous. "Some what? Guidance? Advice?"

"I'm going to go with 'support.'"

A few degrees of tension left his sister, but her expression remained suspicious. She opened her mouth and closed it again.

Turned in a circle and looked out at the vineyard. "Okay, since you're so *deeply* concerned, Julian. I . . ." The corners of her mouth turned down. "I made a play on an investment and it tanked. Hard. Like . . ." Her tone turned choppy. "A billion dollars hard. I was asked—forced, really—to step down at the firm. And my fiancé . . . ex-fiancé . . . broke our engagement to save face." A lump moved up and down in her throat. "Morrison Talbot the *third* was too humiliated to be associated with me. And, of course, since I am no longer being paid, I was the one who moved out of the apartment." She splayed her hands. "So here I am. Half-drunk, talking shit about blond men and writing love letters with my brother. Wow, that really doesn't sound good out loud."

Julian couldn't hide his shock. She'd just been quietly living with this baggage since arriving in St. Helena? He didn't have a clue where to begin . . . what? Comforting her? He really should have clarified his goal before he started to question her. "Your ex-fiancé's name is Morrison Talbot the third and you're calling blond men unrelatable?"

Natalie stared at him blankly for long moments, but it only took Julian half of one of those moments to know he was not good at this. At least, until his sister burst into laughter. The loud kind that rang out across the vineyard and loosened that elusive something inside of him a little more. He started to think maybe—maybe—he would join her in laughing, but a voice sliced abruptly through the evening and cut off the sound.

"I had a feeling you weren't just home for a visit," his mother said, coming down the porch steps of the main house. Her features were backlit by the flickering lanterns hanging on either side of the front door and mostly hidden, but Julian swore a flash of hurt crossed his mother's face before she replaced it with a mask of indifference. "Well." She ran a hand along the loop of her silk scarf. "How long were you planning to wait before asking for money?"

His sister's spine snapped straight. Julian waited for her to issue a denial, to say that she wouldn't be asking for money—if for no other reason than pride—but she didn't. In the end, she looked their mother square in the eye and took a king-size pull from her flask.

"Lovely," muttered Corinne.

It wasn't lost on Julian that they were standing in the same spot—or close to, anyway—where the Vos family had been informed the fire was moving faster than originally predicted. Of course, they were minus one member. His father was in Europe racing Formula One cars. But *they* were here. They had problems to solve. Was he going to let an absent presence dictate how and when that was done?

No. Julian didn't think he would. What had four years of silence yielded, except for the three of them suffering alone, stubbornly refusing to turn to one another for support or solutions? "Corinne." He coughed into his fist. "Mother. Natalie isn't the only one who has been hiding something."

"What are you talking about?" Corinne snapped, quickly. Too quickly.

When he noticed the layer of panic in her eyes, he softened his tone. "The vineyard. We haven't quite made it back after the fire. Sales are down. Competition is fierce. And we can't afford to implement the changes that will make us viable again."

Natalie dropped the flask to her hip. "The vineyard . . . isn't doing well?"

"We are doing *fine*," Corinne stressed, letting out a forced laugh. "Your brother was probably speaking to Manuel. Our manager is a worrier, always has been."

"Our equipment is malfunctioning and outdated. I've seen it with my own eyes. The public relations team is on permanent leave. We're behind on production—"

"I'm doing the best I can," Corinne hissed. "You think it was easy to be handed a burned-out vineyard along with divorce papers? It wasn't. I'm sorry it's not up to your standards, Julian."

He started to argue that he wasn't blaming anyone, let alone her, but his mother wasn't finished. "Do you know I have to attend a luncheon next week in his honor? It's the twentieth anniversary of the Napa Valley Association of Vintners being formed, which I'll admit has done a lot of good in the region. He might be their founding father, but he's not even here! This place is falling into *disrepair,* and yet they want to celebrate the glory days. Your father trailblazed a path to them lining their pockets. They don't care that he abandoned this place and his family. He's still their hero. And I'm . . . ."

"You're the one that kept the doors open, despite it all. I'm not blaming you for the decline. Please, I wouldn't do that. I'm asking . . ."

In the back of his mind, he could hear his father's voice echoing through the vines. *You've always been a fucking head case, haven't you? Jesus Christ. Look at you. Pull yourself together. Stick to teaching and just . . . stay away from what I've built, all right?*

Stay away from the vineyard.

Whether his father's assessments were true or not, he wasn't leaving his family to carry their burdens alone anymore. His father was gone. Julian was there. He could *do* something. "I'm asking to help, Mother. I know I'm not necessarily welcome—"

"Not welcome?" Corinne shook her head. "You're my son."

His throat muscles felt stiff. "I'm referring to what happened. And I understand if my input makes you uncomfortable, but frankly, that's too bad. You're getting it, anyway."

Corinne made a small sound, burying her face in her hands a moment. Just when Julian assumed she was working up the courage to ask him to remain detached from the business, she came forward with open arms and embraced him. For several seconds, he could only stare dumbfounded at his sister before she, too, came forward and wrapped her arms around both him and Corinne. "I did not have this on today's bingo card," Natalie sniffed.

"I'm sorry. To both of you." Apparently having reached her capacity for emotional displays, Corinne shifted free of the group hug. "It has been a long four years. I just . . . I never wanted either of you to feel unwelcome in your own home. You might have noticed I have a hard time admitting I need help. Or even . . . company."

"Well, you've got it now," Natalie crowed, hoisting her flask. "I'm never leaving!"

"Let's not get carried away," Corinne said, smoothing the sleeve of her dress.

Julian needed more time to process the revelations of the last five minutes. For now, he needed a distraction from the growing notch in his sternum. Remembering the small box stuffed into his jacket pocket, Julian removed the object, holding it out to Corinne. "This is only a small start, but I thought we could hand these out tonight at our table."

Corinne shied away from the white box like it might contain a garter snake. "What is it?"

"Business cards. For Corked on Grapevine Way." The two

women stared at him in expectant silence. "There is a new wine-shop next door giving the owner, Lorna, some competition. I thought we could send some business her way. In the process, we're giving people an incentive to buy our wine. Here, look." He flipped open the top. "It's a small discount on Vos wine. Nothing major. But it's a first step toward selling the stock currently on shelves and making way for the new vintage. Wholesale orders will remain low until we clear what's already there—and there's a lot. Let's get the money we need to make this place whole again. It won't be restored overnight, but we have the framework, and that's half the battle."

His mother and sister traded an eyebrow raise.

"What brought this on?" asked Corinne while examining a business card. "Have you secretly been wanting to help all this time?"

Hallie. Making her happier. "Obviously, I don't have a stake in the situation. I just . . ." *Breathe easier when there is less of a chance of our gardener crying.* "Thought it could look good for the vineyard. You know, one local business helping another."

Though visibly skeptical, Corinne finally took the box and removed the top, sighing at what she revealed. "Well, at least they're not tacky."

"Thank you," said Julian, briskly.

"Wait. Did *you* design business cards for a local retail shop?" He nodded, prompting his sister to continue. "*And* you're getting secret admirer letters." Natalie looked down at the metal container in her hand. "I need to get out more."

"You *are* looking quite pale," his mother commented.

Natalie turned and let out a strangled scream over the rows of grapes.

Yes. Things certainly wouldn't change overnight. With them or the vineyard. But hell if they weren't at least pointed in the right direction now.

"We should go," Julian said, heading for the courtyard and driveway of the main house. "Wouldn't want to be late to Wine Down."

"You don't have to say it like that," his mother complained in a withering tone. "Sarcastically."

"He's not," Natalie interjected. "The name itself is doing all of the sarcasm heavy lifting. Do I have a minute to run inside and pee?"

Julian and Corinne groaned.

"Shut up," Natalie called over her shoulder, trotting back toward the house. Despite his exasperation, the night didn't feel like a total chore anymore. If he'd spent tonight working, he would have missed the revelation from his sister. Or these awkward family moments with Corinne that were semi-painful, but also . . . them. For so long, he'd been focused on making every minute productive. But perhaps his definition of "productive" was beginning to shift.

Chapter Twelve

*H*allie loved crowds.

Being able to hear everyone speaking at once but not make out a single word. The fact that all these people had dressed up and driven to the same location, all at once, for a special purpose. Crowds were a celebration of movement and color and trying new things.

For the second year in a row, she'd agreed to help Lavinia and Jerome behind the counter at Wine Down Napa. Convincing the festival committee to agree to allow a donut shop to display at the event had taken some fancy footwork, but the gooey baked goods were a huge hit the year prior, leading to a lot of stuffy connoisseurs walking around the massive tent with chocolate wings extending out from the corners of their mouths. Looking around the buzzing aisles of vendors, Hallie was pleased to see an even more eclectic mix this year.

Most of the displays were for local vineyards, and they were elaborate. Tasteful. Wine Down Napa didn't have the feeling of a typical indoor market. In true Napa style, the booths were constructed of polished wood. There was a step and repeat behind each one splashed with the vineyard's logo. Romantic lighting had been angled throughout the tent to create a dreamlike atmosphere, fairy lights twinkling on the ceiling, turning wineglasses into enchanted goblets. But in addition to Fudge Judy breaching the boundaries of wine world, there was an exhibit for gourmet dog treats and another for CBD gummies. They'd cast a wide net.

Ticket holders were beginning to arrive, journalists in press badges snapping pictures of people enjoying their first glasses of wine, angling the shots to capture the sprawling courtyard of the Meadowood hotel in the background. The air was sultry; orchestra music drifted down the mountain and through the tent on a light June breeze. And she couldn't help but remember her grandmother roaming the aisles slowly last year, saying hello to old friends and new, accepting pamphlets for vineyard tours to be polite.

Lavinia came up beside Hallie and gave her a gentle hip bump. "After weeks of designing the new, ultrarefined Merlot cruller, the Lucky Charms donut holes will probably be our biggest seller. Not even wine snobs can resist an artificially flavored marshmallow."

Hallie dropped her head to Lavinia's shoulder. "Especially when the CBD kicks in and they relax. Hopefully not enough to mistake the dog biscuits for donuts."

"Oh, I don't know. Could be entertaining."

They laughed, watching more and more people arrive in the tent, various levels of VIP access displayed around their necks. "So," Lavinia prompted. "We were in such a mad rush to get set up, I haven't had a chance to ask. What is the latest with our illustrious professor?"

Hallie blew out a breath, her gaze drifting over to the Vos Vineyard booth. No one had arrived yet, though they'd most likely tapped their in-house sommelier to represent them tonight. And even if Corinne Vos made an appearance, Julian definitely wouldn't be there. She'd assured herself of that for the last two days and still couldn't prevent the low sink of disappointment in her belly. "Oh, um . . ." She adjusted her Fudge Judy apron, heat creeping up the sides of her face. "The latest isn't really up for discussion. Not in polite company."

Lavinia reared back with raised eyebrows. "Good thing I'm not polite."

Hallie threw a pointed look at Jerome. "Later."

"Oh, come on, we both know I'm going to tell him, anyway."

"Good to know." They stopped to smile at two guests who wandered past looking down their noses at the donuts. They would definitely come crawling back after a few glasses of wine, though. "There might have been some . . . further intimacy. Not the whole enchilada. More like, I don't know, jalapeño poppers."

"You are speaking to a British woman in Mexican food terminology. Does not translate."

"Sorry. It's just that . . . honestly, I'm not really sure *what* happened in Julian's kitchen." She only knew her entire body started to tingle thinking about it. His breath on her neck, their mouths interlocked and panting. "Or if it was a-a . . . normal thing to do?"

Lavinia was agog. "Fuck off. He tried anal?"

"No!" Her cheeks were hot enough now to be fresh from the oven. "Not that."

"Oh, thank God." Lavinia briefly doubled over. "I was going to need a cigarette for this."

"It was more like . . ." Hallie looked around to make sure nobody was within earshot, then dropped her voice to a whisper. "The internet calls it mutual masturbation."

"Bloody hell, I do need that cigarette." Lavinia stared at her for a beat. *"What?"*

"I know."

Jerome approached his wife from behind, his default suspicious expression in full swing. "What's going on here?"

"I'll tell you later," Lavinia said quickly. "But in brief: it involves wanking." Without missing a beat, Jerome turned and moseyed to the other side of the booth. Lavinia shrugged defensively in the face of Hallie's sputtering shock. "I had to get rid of him so I can hear the rest of it, didn't I?"

Hallie slumped. "There is no rest of it. This time I'm really, *really* sure it was the last occasion we . . . do something both confusing and . . ." She tried to swallow, but her mouth was too dry, thanks to the sensual memories bombarding her. The way he'd ground his hardness there, the movements of his hand speeding up, his grunt of her name. ". . . arousing. Together."

"Yes, yes," Lavinia said, peering at her thoughtfully. "I can see you are definitely capable of saying no. Your nips aren't hard or anything."

"What?" Hallie looked down and saw the apron was definitely low enough to make out the outline of her nipples—and they were indeed bullet-shaped. Had they been anything but puckered and uncomfortable for the last two days? With a hasty yank, she tugged up the neck of the apron to cover the evidence. "No, really." She hesitated a moment, then blurted, "I wrote him a second secret admirer letter. Sober this time."

Lavinia rocked back on her heels. "No. You didn't."

"Lavinia, note my track record of complicating things. You know I did." She bit her lip. "And they were right there, in plain view in his Food Network–worthy kitchen. He *quoted* them at me, and I couldn't bring myself to tell him I'm the author."

Her best friend crossed herself. "Only God can save you now, Hallie Welch."

"That's a little dramatic." Nervous energy snapped in her veins. "Right?"

"What's a little dramatic?"

They both turned to find Owen standing at the front of the booth. At first, Hallie wondered if maybe the man was an evil twin. Or a doppelgänger. Since she'd only ever seen Owen in jeans and a T-shirt. Or shorts and gardening shoes. But tonight he wore pressed slacks and a tucked-in polo shirt, hair styled. And was that cologne?

"Owen. Darling." Lavinia recovered from the interruption first, leaning across the table to kiss Owen on both cheeks. "You look fabulous."

"Thanks." Rather adorably, he scrubbed at the back of his neck. "Same to you." His attention drifted to Hallie and stuck. "You look great tonight, too, Hallie. Really great."

She looked down at her outfit of choice, most of which was covered by the apron. Probably a good thing, considering she'd found it impossible to settle on an ensemble, so she'd ended up with a low-cut floral shirt tucked into a plaid, high-waisted skirt. At least her hair was in order tonight, curls tamed and loose around her shoulders. "Thanks, Owen—"

Her words cut themselves off. Because when she glanced up from her schizophrenic getup, there he was, directly over Owen's shoulder.

Julian Vos had entered the tent.

It was shocking to find out that she'd almost *slightly* gotten used to his presence—but only when it was just the two of them. In public like this? He was a Van Gogh in a gallery of children's finger paintings. He was quite simply incomparable. Tall and intense and handsome and attention-grabbing. Kind of impatient-looking, on top of it all. Every head turned at his arrival, as if they'd sensed a shift in the atmospheric balance.

He wore a starched white shirt totally devoid of wrinkles and navy blue slacks. A burgundy tie. Cuff links. He looked like the type of man who would wear those old-fashioned sock garters below the knee. And she'd touched herself in front of him. He'd done the same. They'd been completely weak in front of each other while the storm rampaged outside, and seeing him now, so composed and in charge, made the whole thing feel like a dream.

"Bet you'd have done anal," Lavinia said out of the corner of her mouth.

Thankfully, Jerome and Owen were engaged in a conversation about golf and didn't overhear. "Could you please never bring that up again?" Hallie implored.

"He'll be the one bringing it *up,* if you catch my meaning."

"Oh, don't worry. I do. You're as subtle as a chain saw."

Hallie ordered herself to stop staring at Julian, who was now crossing the tent with his mother and sister. And she failed. Everyone in the tent did. Vos Vineyard might be in need of an upgrade, but the first family of St. Helena moved like royalty and looked the part, too. Meanwhile here she stood in mixed patterns talking about butt sex.

She wouldn't change a thing. But the contrast only brought it home how utterly unalike they were.

None of that seemed to matter when Julian glanced over sharply, slowing to a stop when he saw her behind the Fudge Judy counter. *Oh my God*, her heart was going to beat right out of her body. It was magic, having this gallant, thoughtful man notice her from across a crowded room and stop dead in the middle of it all. Those times she'd opened up to him about her grief and one-third life crisis, she'd felt so utterly safe sharing with him. Did she imagine that bond?

No. She couldn't have.

In addition to the magic of being pinned by those whiskey eyes across the tent . . . was now lust. The urgent, frustrating kind she'd never experienced with anyone else. The kind she'd only half understood while mooning at him on YouTube, before his return to St. Helena. Beneath those lusty layers, though, was the wistfulness of regret.

Every time they connected, the *dis*connect between their personalities became a little more obvious, and what could be done about that?

"Hallie?"

Owen laid a hand on her arm, and she caught the barest change in Julian's expression. It clouded over, a groove fashioning itself between his brows. A muscle had begun to tick in his jaw when she finally managed to wrestle her attention away from Julian and focus on Owen. Who, apparently, had been addressing her to no avail for quite some time.

"I'm sorry. All this excitement . . ." Her laugh sounded strained. "I think I have wine envy."

Owen quickly set down the donut he'd picked up with the provided pair of silver tongs. "I'll get you a glass. What are you in the mood for?"

She could not let this man run around fetching her a drink when she was remembering how Julian's abdomen felt flexing against hers. "No, that's really okay, Owen—"

He was already off like a shot.

Hallie traded a guilty look with Lavinia, but they didn't have time to talk. The tent was quickly filling up and people wanted donuts. Mainly because, unlike last year, a lot of guests seemed to have brought their children. In the past, no one under the age of twenty-one had been admitted to wine-tasting events in Napa, but since the fire that damaged so much of the region, followed by the economic wrecking ball of the pandemic, St. Helena had slowly adopted more of a family-friendly image in the hopes of appealing to new visitors.

Apparently kids were the newest caveat.

And, in the case of Wine Down, the pitfalls of that decision quickly became obvious.

Children ran figure eights around the older clientele, their mothers receiving more than their fair share of judgment. The hosts of the event might have allowed children, but being that the beverage of choice was alcohol, there was nothing for the youngsters to drink or eat.

Except for the donuts.

That's how Hallie became the official babysitter of Wine Down Napa.

It started off with a single offer to watch the toddler of an overstressed mother while she went off and indulged in a glass of wine. Then a second family approached, inquiring about the professional childcare services, to which Hallie saluted them with her wineglass—and they left their child, anyway. Although Lavinia needed Hallie as an extra set of hands, the parents were buying donuts in gratitude, so they took the trade-off and booted Hallie in favor of the extra sales. Half an hour later, she had a football team of kids under the age of eight playing red rover on the field outside the tent and chomping on chocolate crullers.

She actually lost track of which one had eaten what. Or how many.

Now that, out of everything, turned out to be the biggest mistake.

Hopped up on an obscene amount of sugar, the kids decided they were thirsty.

"I want water!" announced one of the dinosaur-obsessed twins while picking a wedgie.

What was his name? Shiloh?

"Oh, okay," Hallie said, looking back toward the tent. There had to be water in there somewhere, right? "Um, everyone hold hands and let's go inside quietly and check—"

"MOM!" Shiloh screamed, running toward the tent, barreling through the flap—followed by the rest of the children, all shouting for their mothers.

"Wait. Guys, wait."

Hallie hurried after them with two empty donut boxes under her arms—whoa, empty?—but it was too late to prevent what happened next. She entered the tent just in time to watch the sugar-hyped kids fly around like pinballs. Wineglasses sloshed in the hands of VIP guests, and in two cases, tables were bumped, glass shattering and the hum of conversation grinding to a halt. Hallie stood just inside the entrance in a sort of trance, her gaze moving unerringly to Julian, who stood on the other side of the flabbergasted crowd, a glass of wine poised halfway to his mouth.

She could practically hear his thoughts out loud, they were so plain on his face.

Here was Hallie, once again proving herself a purveyor of chaos.

Barely fit to be among adults. And patently incapable of managing children.

Destruction in the flesh—now available for parties.

Julian lowered his glass, set it down, and just managed to steady a row of wine flutes on the Vos Vineyard display before they were knocked over.

Hallie winced and began chasing the wayward children. She was quickly joined by Owen, who gave her a sympathetic smile, which was a lot more comforting than Julian's steely-eyed judgment.

Like most times she was faced with an unpleasant truth about herself, she dodged it—and what else could that look in Julian's eyes mean except for exasperation?

Forget about him and fix your mess.

Chapter Thirteen

Owen has to go.

There was already a crowd assembled, wanting to be entertained for the night. Why not make it a murder mystery? Everyone could take turns guessing who killed the redhead for continuously putting his hand on Hallie's arm. They'd eventually figure out it was Julian, or would perhaps take one look at his face and know straight off the bat.

God, he did not like the way they were laughing together. The way they sort of matched each other step for step, two very alike people on the same mission. Tame the maniacs who were currently blowing like miniature cyclones through the event, chocolate and sprinkles smeared across their chins and cheeks. The people sipping wine in front of the Vos table were complaining about the shoddy childcare—and he liked that criticism of Hallie even less than the sight of Owen staring at her curls as if eternally fascinated by their shape.

Actually, scratch that. He didn't like it less.

He simply liked none of this. Whatsoever.

Having her so close, looking so fucking beautiful, and feeling as if he wasn't allowed to speak with her. Had their last encounter been so bad that they weren't even on speaking terms anymore?

Her halting laugh reached Julian, and a tug started behind his collar. He'd missed that laugh. Had it really only been two days? Was he just supposed to never hear it again, even if embarking on any sort of relationship together would end in disaster?

No. That didn't work for him.

Julian didn't realize he was walking toward the emcee booth in the corner of the tent until he arrived there and held out his hand. "May I borrow the microphone for a moment?"

The emcee juggled the mike, clearly caught off guard by Julian's abrupt approach. He was thrown off, as well. What the hell was he doing?

Joining the fray. Just because she's there.

Refusing to question that disconcerting certainty, Julian raised the microphone to his mouth. "If I might have your attention, please?" He couldn't see anything but Hallie's blond head popping up from the floor, where she'd been trying to coax a crying child out from under a table—with *more sugar*, for the love of God. "I'm beginning children's story time now out on the lawn." He checked his watch automatically to register the time. "Please send them outside now. Pick them up at eight oh five. Thank you."

"Are we sure CBD doesn't get people at least buzzed?" Natalie asked as he passed. "I could have sworn you just said you were conducting a children's story time."

A bead of sweat trickled down his spine. "I did say that."

"Why?" she said, visibly astonished.

Julian started to brush off the question or give an unsatisfactory answer, such as, "I don't know," but he didn't want to take a step backward with Natalie. They'd formed a tenuous bond tonight. If he'd learned anything in that brief window of time, it was that having a relationship with his sister meant sharing potentially embarrassing things with her. "It's because of a woman."

Natalie's mouth dropped open. "*Another* woman?"

Jesus, when she said it like that, it sounded awful. "Well, yes. But . . ."

There was simply no way to explain that he'd cast the net of his interest in Hallie so far and wide that it had swallowed up his secret admirer. He'd wished them to be one and the same. Now they were inseparable entities.

"I don't get it." His sister sounded almost dazed. "You barely leave the house and there are two women on deck."

Julian scoffed. "That is hardly the case." She waited, saying nothing. More sweat slid down his spine. "It's complicated with Hallie. We aren't seeing each other. Nothing can come of it and we're agreed on the matter." Damn. Saying *that* out loud felt far worse than his sister's claim about him juggling two women. "It's just that when she's in trouble or experiencing any kind of distress, I feel somewhat . . . upset about it."

Natalie stared.

"That is to say, I feel as if I'm going to explode if the situation isn't fixed for her. When she isn't smiling, the world becomes a terrible place."

Several seconds passed. "Do you think what you're saying is normal?"

"Forget it," Julian growled. "Please continue to pass out the damn business cards for Corked. I'll be back in a while."

He strode out of the tent while unfastening his cuff links and tucking them into his pants pocket in order to roll up his sleeves.

It seemed like a best practice when dealing with kids. Wouldn't want to appear intimidating.

Brisk mountain air dried the layer of perspiration on Julian's forehead as he walked out of the tent. He stopped short when he found Hallie hustling a dozen youngsters into a half circle on the lawn—while Owen watched, his devotion to her clearer than a freshly washed windowpane. The other man turned at his approach, cautiously sizing him up.

Julian's sleeve-rolling movements became increasingly hasty. "Hello."

"Hi," Owen said back, taking a quick sip from his wineglass. "I'm Owen Stark."

Julian held out his hand. They shook. Quite firmly. He'd never really considered his height an advantage until the other man had to crane his neck slightly. "Julian Vos."

"Yes, I know." The redhead's smile didn't reach his eyes. "It's nice to meet you."

"Likewise." *State your intentions toward her, motherfucker.* "How do you know Hallie?"

Was it his imagination or did the bastard look a little smug? Yes, he was definitely the kind of man who would make a perfect guest of honor at a murder mystery. "We own competing gardening businesses in St. Helena." Of course, Julian had already known the answer to that. Apparently, he just wanted to torture himself by hearing this man speak with familiarity about the woman who occupied his every thought these days. "Someday, I'm hoping to convince her to join forces."

Now that was news. Or was it?

Owen's emphasis on *join forces* made it sound as if he meant something else—not business related. As in, a personal relationship with Hallie. Marriage, even. How close *were* they, exactly? And truly, what business was it of Julian's, when she appeared to want nothing to do with him anymore? He didn't know. But the gravelly grind in his chest was so unpleasant, it took him a moment to speak. "Maybe she doesn't want to be convinced or it would have happened by now."

"Maybe she needs to know a man is willing to play the long game."

I guess I'm going to kill him. Julian stepped closer. "Oh, is it a game to you?"

Hallie slid in between Julian and Owen, splitting a startled glance between them that quickly turned nonplussed. "Oh dear." Her hip brushed Julian's groin, and he had the most pressing urge to drag her up against him like a fucking caveman. "M-maybe we can continue this later? When we aren't under threat of mutiny?"

"That works for me," Owen said with a big, dumb smile, saluting with his wine.

"Absolutely," Julian agreed, keeping his eye on the other man as he went to the front of the semicircle. And then all he could do was stand there and absorb the absolute disarray that lay at his feet. Several children were sprawled out on the grass, coming down from their sugar highs with glazed eyes and twitching limbs. Sprinkles were trapped beneath fingernails and plastered to the corners of mouths. One of them was actually licking the grass, another trying to balance a small Nike sneaker on his head. Two girls fought over an iPad with twin expressions of violence. "Well, aren't you all just a mess? Your parents will have to hose you down before putting you in the car tonight."

A dozen pairs of eyes snapped in his direction, some of them startled.

Including Hallie's.

Maybe his greeting had been a little harsh—

One of the children—a girl—giggled. And then they *all* started to giggle.

"Our moms aren't going to spray us with a hose," she shouted, unnecessarily.

"Why not? You're all disgusting."

More laughing. One of them even pitched sideways onto the lawn. Was he doing all right at this? He'd spent exactly zero time around kids this young, but his college students definitely never laughed at him. They could barely be bothered to crack a smile. Not that he ever joked during a lecture. Time was a serious matter. Somehow he didn't think these kids would appreciate a talk on the impact of capitalism on the value of time.

"Why don't we talk about time travel?"

"I thought you were going to read us a story."

Julian pointed a finger at the interjector. "Disgusting *and* impatient. I'm getting to the story. But first I want to hear where you would go on a time-traveling mission."

"Japan!"

He nodded. "Japan now? Or a hundred years ago? If you hopped in your time-traveling machine and arrived in Japan in the year 1923, you might land in the middle of the great earthquake." They blinked up at him. "You see, all the events of the past are still . . . active. They remain in order of occurrence, existing in a linear path, beginning at a starting point and reaching all the way to this moment. Everything you're doing in this moment is being recorded by time, whether you realize it or not."

"Even this?" A boy in a San Diego Zoo shirt attempted a handstand, landing at an awkward angle in the grass.

"Yes, even that. Would anyone else like to tell us where they would go if they time traveled?" Several hands went up. As Julian got ready to call on someone, he happened to look up and catch the most fleeting expression on Hallie's face. One he wasn't sure he'd seen before and couldn't really describe.

What was it? Certainly not . . . adoration. He wasn't doing *that* well up here.

Still, it was hard to put any other description to her soft, dreamlike expression. The way she looked as if she were being held up only by a string.

He had to be misinterpreting the whole thing.

Or worse, what if that adoration was for Owen? Not him?

When Julian cleared his throat, it sounded like he'd just guzzled a handful of broken walnut shells. "All right, in keeping with the time-travel theme, on to the story." He clasped his hands behind his back. "There was once a man named Doc Brown, who built a time-traveling machine out of a DeLorean. Does anyone know what a DeLorean is?"

Silence.

Thankfully, the quiet carried over into the story, and the children remained seated on the grass, listening with only the occasional outburst of giggles or interruptions, until Julian finished. When he finally glanced up from his rapt audience, their parents were standing behind them holding little coats. And he was pleased to see that many of them were carrying the discount cards for Corked. Natalie must have worked overtime to put them in everyone's hands.

He watched Hallie slowly notice them, too, her gaze bouncing around to all the green-and-white cards. Then over at him. *That's right, sweetheart. I deliver for you.*

I can't help it.

"Okay, then. Story time has ended." He shooed the children away. "Go get hosed off."

They climbed to their feet in a way that reminded him of newborn giraffes. Most of them went straight to their parents. Julian was startled, however, when a pair of twins ran full speed in his direction and wrapped their skinny arms around his thighs. Hugging him.

"You're getting me dirty," he pointed out, surprised when his throat tugged. "Fine." He patted their backs. "Very good, thank you."

"Isn't that the guy from that alien documentary?" one of the parents mused out loud.

Julian sighed.

Finally, it was over. Thank God.

When the kids left, he didn't miss them at all.

Right.

Slowly, Hallie approached him, the beginnings of sunset creating a halo on top of her blond head. Over the course of his story time, she'd taken off her shoes, and her toes sunk into the grass now, tipped in all different colors. Red, green, pink. He could envision her sitting on the floor of a living room, trying to choose a shade, giving up and deciding a rainbow would give her the best of all worlds. When had that kind of indecisiveness started to come across as tremendously charming to him?

That mysterious look from earlier was no longer in her eye, and he wanted it back, wanted her to adore him again. How could he crave something that he'd obviously imagined?

"Thank you for doing that," she said to him, her soft voice mingling with the crickets, the music still coming from the wine tent. "You were great. I guess I shouldn't be surprised. They say kids are drawn to authenticity. You really nailed the genuine vibe, calling them disgusting and all."

"Yes." In the distance, he heard the grass-licker relating *Back to the Future* to his parents, and a weird clunk happened in his chest. "People say this all the time, and I never believe them. But did you notice the children were also kind of . . . cute?"

She pressed her lips together, clearly suppressing a laugh. "Yes, I noticed. Why do you think I was compelled to ply them with chocolate? I needed them to like me."

"I understand now," he admitted.

Hallie spent the next few moments staring down at her feet. Why? He had to stuff both hands in his pockets to keep from lifting her chin. Owen was watching them from the shadow of the tent, too, and, Christ, was Julian so selfish that he would sabotage her potential relationship with the gardener when he wasn't in a position to offer her one himself? No.

"Yes," he countered himself. Out loud.

Hallie's head came up. There. There were her beautiful eyes. "Yes, what?"

Pulse firing, he shook his head. "Nothing."

She hummed, narrowing her gaze. "Do you happen to know anything about those promotional cards for Corked that everyone was holding?"

He kept his expression neutral. If he informed her of their origin, he'd probably have to tell her about the new awning he'd ordered for Corked, too, and he didn't need to be told he'd gone overboard. He was well aware. And while a relationship with Lorna could help the vineyard, the true reason he'd intervened was standing right in front of him, with that perfect little crease that ran down the center of her bottom lip. That dimple in her cheek. "Promotional cards for Corked? I didn't notice."

"Really." She folded her arms across her tits, drawing his attention downward, and God almighty, the way the material of her shirt stretched over those generous mounds would keep him awake tonight. Already, he was mentally uncapping his bottle of lube, pressing his open mouth to the center of the pillow, and imagining her beneath him, naked, legs thrown over his shoulders. "How odd. I wonder where they came from."

If Julian told her, maybe she would kiss him. Or even come home with him. And fuck, that was tempting. But would he be leading her on? Yes, he wanted to make her happy. Yes, he wanted to eviscerate everything that caused her to worry and put an eternal Hallie Smile on her face. Every time he let himself indulge in Hallie, though, that out-of-control feeling threatened to topple him. He didn't know how to allow himself to . . . let go like that. It unnerved him. And he'd ultimately hurt her feelings—which was the exact opposite of what he wanted.

They were cut from different cloth. He craved order, and she was human pandemonium. Yet why was he beginning to have such a hard time remembering that? Maybe because those gray eyes were on him, her soft, round face brushed in sunset, her mouth so goddamn close, he could taste it.

"I thought of you earlier tonight," he said, without thinking, distracted by the dip of her dimple. "You were right about what to say to Natalie."

"Was I?" She searched his eyes. "You two had a heart-to-heart?"

"Of sorts, I suppose. The Vos version." There was no denying how good it felt to speak to Hallie like this. Just the two of them. He'd met women throughout his life who were logical and concise and regimented. Like him. Shouldn't it have been easier to open up to someone who operated the same way? "We . . . I guess you could say we bonded."

"That's amazing, Julian," she whispered. "Over what?"

Hallie wanted to be kissed. She was standing too close for him to draw any other conclusion. And when she snagged that full, creased bottom lip between her teeth and dropped her gaze to his mouth, he had to suppress a groan. Fuck it. There was no stopping himself. Two days without her taste and it was like being starved to death. "She helped me with a letter I've been meaning to write," he muttered, dipping his head—

Hallie straightened. "Oh." She blinked down at her hands. "Natalie helped you write a letter?"

Julian replayed his thoughtless words. What in the hell had he been thinking bringing up the secret admirer letter? He *wasn't* thinking. He couldn't keep his head on straight around Hallie. That was the problem. Why was he suddenly more desperate than before to go retrieve the letter from the stump before anyone could accidentally find it? Especially his admirer.

Jesus. As he stood there looking down into Hallie's face, the fact that he'd even temporarily left correspondence for someone else made him ill. But Hallie was waiting for an explanation, and he couldn't bring himself to lie. Not to her. "Yes," he said, praying the matter would be dropped immediately. "A secret admirer, if you can believe it. Writing back seemed like the polite thing to do, although it was more a way for me and Natalie to—"

"That's wonderful, Julian," she blurted. "Wow. A secret admirer. That's so old-school. Um . . ."

Wait. She wasn't letting him finish. He wasn't going to let the letter be found. It was important she understood that—

"I'm glad things turned a corner with your sister. I'm sure the fact that you're making an effort means the most of all. Not what I suggested you do." She took a step backward, away from him. "I better get back inside to see if Lavinia needs me."

"Yes," he clipped out, already missing her. Again. "But, Hallie—"

"Good night."

Why did he have a mounting sense of guilt over writing that letter? He and Hallie weren't dating. In fact, they'd specifically agreed *not* to form any kind of personal relationship. So why did he feel like he'd fucking betrayed her? No matter that he'd pictured Hallie's face while writing back to the secret admirer—the guilt remained.

"Hallie . . ." he called to her again, no clue what to follow up with.

Jesus Christ, he was nauseous.

"I'll be over sometime tomorrow to plant some dusty miller to really accentuate the lavender," she sang on her way back into the tent, thanking Owen for holding the flap open for her. "Thanks again for leading story time."

With a smirk for Julian, Owen followed in Hallie's wake.

Julian stared after the swinging canvas, winded. What the hell just happened?

And would anyone actually *miss* Owen if he disappeared?

When Julian reentered the tent, it took every ounce of his self-control not to pluck Hallie out from behind the donut booth and carry her back outside. To finish their discussion in a way that would end in her smiling. Why? It would only confuse this *thing* between them more. But it was a hell of a lot more preferable than leaving . . . their *thing* unsettled. This mental bedlam came part and parcel with Hallie, and yet, he couldn't stop going back for another helping.

Julian was just about to approach the donut booth when he spotted Natalie across the room. Since he'd gone outside for story time an hour earlier, his sister had clearly put the pedal to the metal on wine consumption and was now flirting with one of the wine vendors, a giant linebacker of a man in a *Kiss the Vintner* apron. As Julian watched, she made an attempt to boost herself onto the man's table in what she no doubt believed to be the ultimate seductive move. Until she slipped off—and would have landed on her ass if the linebacker's arm didn't shoot out from behind the table to steady her.

In Julian's periphery, he watched a photographer weave her way through the thinning crowd, her expression one of single-minded focus. The last thing the winery needed was a picture of drunk Natalie ending up in the gossip section of some wine blog. With a final frustrated glance toward Hallie, he hastened his way across the room, hoping to intercept his sister before she became internet fodder. But apparently his worry was all for nothing. The vintner noticed the photographer, too. At the last second, he maneuvered Natalie so his gigantic self was blocking the journalist from getting a decent shot.

"I'm telling you, August, it's impossible to hum while you hold your nose," Natalie was slurring when Julian reached them. "Try it."

Julian assumed this man would say something to humor or distract her, so he was surprised when the man actually pinched his nose and attempted the feat, flashing a navy tattoo in the process. "Son of a bitch," he rumbled. "Can't hum a note."

Natalie laughed long and loud. "You will remember this moment the rest of your life, August Cates."

"Yeah." Lopsided smile from the navy man. "Pretty sure I will."

His sister stared up at the man for an awkward length of time. "Are we going to make out?"

A flash of white teeth. "Cancel all my calls," he shouted over his shoulder to an imaginary secretary.

When Natalie took a step in the vintner's direction and the photographer finally found a better vantage point, that was Julian's cue. "Time to go, Natalie."

"Yep," she agreed without missing a beat, allowing herself to be dragged away by her brother. Although, Julian lost count of the number of times she looked back over her shoulder at her would-be make-out partner. "Forget gas-station guy. *That* man is the perfect rebound."

"Make that decision when you're clearheaded."

"I don't make good decisions when I'm clearheaded. That's why I'm in Napa, remember?" She pulled him to a stop while they were still out of Corinne's earshot. "How did things go with Hallie, for whom you would sacrifice your life but will not date?"

"Not well, if you must know."

She mimicked him, employing a British accent while doing it. Then she just kind of deflated all at once. "God. We are dysfunctional people, aren't we? Who unleashed us on the world?"

With perfect timing, their mother's most diplomatic laugh rang out while she raised a wineglass to the couple standing at the Vos booth. As soon as they departed, her smile dropped like an anvil from a ten-story building.

Natalie snorted. "I guess we have our answer."

Julian watched his sister rejoin Corinne behind the table, his attention straying back to the other side of the tent before he could stop it.

We are dysfunctional people, aren't we?

Perhaps Hallie was a wrench in the engine of his mental well-being, but was Julian the same to her? Or worse? He thought of the first afternoon they met, when he criticized her placement of the flowers and she'd lost some of her glow. Just minutes ago, she'd been soft and flirtatious, and he'd somehow ruined it. Again. Maybe he should be staying away from her because of the damage *he* could inflict. Because as much as she drove him crazy with her lack of plans and organization, he liked her. A lot. Definitely too much to be leaving letters for someone else.

With a spike in his throat, Julian rejoined his family behind the table, where they were preparing to leave. Logical or not, he needed to get that letter and destroy it. Tonight.

Chapter Fourteen

It was well after midnight when Hallie, Lavinia, and Jerome drove down Grapevine Way, having packed up their Wine Down display and carpooled back to town. Shops were shuttered, though a few wine bars remained open, probably nearing last call. Along the road, ornate rooftop cornices were silhouetted by silver moonlit sky. Through the open back seat window of Jerome and Lavinia's catering van, she could hear the chirp of crickets carrying down the mountain and from nearby valleys and vineyards.

Jerome and Lavinia dropped Hallie off at her parked truck, and with an exchange of exhausted waves, they continued down the block to where they would unpack the catering equipment at Fudge Judy before heading home.

Hallie got into her truck and let her head loll back against the headrest. She should go home and climb into bed right now, surrounded by snoring dogs, but she made no move to start the engine. Julian had written back to his admirer, and try as she might, she couldn't seem to let it go. There was no way around it—she had to collect that letter. Now. Tonight. Under the cover of darkness, like a certified weirdo.

Teeth gritted, she pushed open the driver's-side door and hopped out, pulling her jacket tighter to her body to ward off the cool, misty air. She stole across the silent road, intending to cut through Fudge Judy's to their back alley, then down the road to Julian's jogging path. Having helped Lavinia and Jerome with catering events in the past, she knew they would be busy shelving items in the giant walk-in storage closet and would be none the wiser that she'd used the shortcut. Furthermore, any potential witnesses would assume she'd remained in the donut shop the whole time.

"Any witnesses? Listen to yourself," she muttered.

This whole activity was pointless—

Hallie stopped short in front of Corked.

Was that . . . a new awning?

Gone was the old, faded red-and-white-striped one. It had been replaced by a bold green one with scripted lettering. *Corked Wine Store. A St. Helena institution since 1957.*

Where did it come from? Between the rainstorm yesterday and preparing for Wine Down today, two afternoons had passed since the last time she'd stopped into Corked to visit Lorna. Apparently she'd missed the store getting a face-lift? Who was responsible for this?

Intuition poked and prodded at Hallie, but she didn't want to acknowledge it. Earlier as Wine Down . . . wound down . . . she'd gone on a mission to find the origin of the business cards, and lo and behold, everyone she spoke to claimed they'd been given out at the Vos Vineyard table. She'd already caught Julian buying pity cases of wine from Lorna. Then came the cards. And now this. A beautiful, crisp green awning that updated the struggling shop by several decades.

He'd done this, hadn't he? Bought Lorna an awning. Driven business her way. Put money in the register. What did all of it mean, and why, oh, why, did it have to make her heart pound like steel drums on a cruise ship?

This was not for her.

There was a *reason* he hadn't taken credit for any of this. He didn't want her to get the wrong idea. He was merely helping out a local business owner, not making some kind of dramatic romantic gesture, so the swooning had to stop. She should be ashamed of the fact that her knees were wobbling like chocolate pudding. If Julian wanted her as more than a onetime accidental hookup, he would have said so by now. God knew he was blunter than a baseball bat about everything else.

And he'd written back to the secret admirer.

Hello. Those were not the actions of an interested man.

Those were the actions of a man who'd perused the grocery aisle and said, *I think I'll take this reliable cauliflower, instead of the mixed bag of root vegetables I can't name.* She needed to get his lack of interest through her thick skull, collect his letter, and read it out of pure curiosity, then be done with this whole confusing mess with the professor.

With a final yearning look up at the awning, Hallie jogged down Grapevine Way toward Fudge Judy. She peeked in through the window, making sure her friends were nowhere in sight before she slipped in through the front door and went into the kitchen. Lavinia appeared from behind the stainless steel workstation and threw up her hands at Hallie's entrance, then slumped forward onto the waist-high table, clutching at her chest through a pink apron. "Fucking hell, I thought we were being robbed. What in the bloody hell are you at?"

Trapped, cursing herself for not taking the long way, Hallie shifted onto the balls of her feet. "I just thought I would go for a little moonlight stroll."

"What? *Where?*"

Why did her ideas always sound worse when they were spoken aloud? Like, every single one. "Down Julian's jogging path," she mumbled.

After a moment, Lavinia banged a fist down on the table. "He's written you, hasn't he?"

"Everything all right in there?" Jerome called through the door of the storage closet.

Hallie pressed a finger to her lips.

"All's well, love. Just bumped my elbow!" Lavinia reached back to untie her apron, a somewhat maniacal look in her eyes. "I'm coming with you."

There would be no stopping her. Apron removal meant business. "I'm not reading you the letter. It's private."

Lavinia rocked back on her heels, considering those parameters. "You don't have to read it to me word for word, but I want the general temperature."

"Fine."

"Going out for a smoke, love," Lavinia shouted, the door banging behind the two women on their way out into the alley. "How do you know he's written back?"

"He told me."

"He told you . . ." Lavinia drew out.

"Yes." She hugged her elbows tight, then realized she looked defensive, so she let them drop. "And yes, I realize that means he isn't interested in real-life Hallie. Only the Hallie from the letter. I'm just going to read his answer to satisfy my curiosity. That's all."

"I might trust you on that." Lavinia jogged to keep up. "If you hadn't sworn to me you wouldn't write these letters in the first place."

"Did you see the new awning on Corked?"

"Your ability to distract us from an actual problem is unparalleled, but I'll bite." Lavinia tilted her head. "A new awning? What happened to the red one covered in pigeon shite?"

"It's gone. And I think it was Julian who arranged it." Hallie snagged Lavinia's wrist and guided her down the private path leading to Vos Vineyard. "I traced those promo business cards for Corked to their table at Wine Down. That has him all over it, too, right? I realize this is all beginning to sound very Scooby-Doo."

"Ooh. I'm Daphne. She gets to shag Fred."

"You can have him. I have a healthy distrust of blond men."

"I don't want to trust him, I want to bang him. Where am I losing you?"

Hallie covered her mouth to muffle a laugh. "You aren't. The fact that we're sneaking around in the dark discussing sexual relations with a cartoon character—one who wears a sailor suit, no less—is exactly why we're friends."

They traded a wry smile in the moonlight. "Back to the case of the mystery awning, then. We think Julian is responsible."

"Yes." Hallie sighed, despairing over the zero-gravity sensation in her breast. "I could have walked away mostly unscathed if he wasn't prank call champion of the universe. If he didn't keep making these . . . these gestures that remind me why I was infatuated with him in the first place. Why I spent so long hung up on him."

Lavinia made a sound of understanding. "He's got you dangling from a fishing hook, all gape-mouthed and wiggly."

"Thank you for that flattering comparison." Hallie laughed, stopping in front of the tree stump, frowning. "This is where the letter should be. Wedged in between the crack."

"What a coincidence. That's right where you'd like Julian to be."

Hallie overcame her blush. "You're not totally wrong."

They each took out their phones and turned on the flashlights, searching the ground around the stump. "Could he have taken it back?"

Why was she dizzy with hope over that possibility? "No. Why would he do that?"

"Maybe he realized you're his dream girl—" Lavinia's beam of light landed on something white behind a brambleberry bush. "Ah, no. Sorry. Found it. Must have blown over."

"Oh," Hallie said, too brightly. "Okay."

She approached the envelope the way one might approach a lit puddle of kerosene and picked it up, commanding her stomach to stop pitching. "All right, so I'll just bring this home and read it."

Several seconds ticked by in the foggy stillness.

Hallie tore open the envelope.

"Exactly," Lavinia said, sitting down on the tree stump. "I'll be right here, awaiting any bread crumbs you choose to throw me."

She barely heard her friend's quip over the pounding in her ears. Pacing a few steps away, she shined her flashlight down at the letter and read.

Hello.

I don't know where to begin. Obviously this is all quite unusual. After all, we are communicating as two people who know each

other, but we have never met. It feels like we have, doesn't it? I apologize for talking in circles. It's not easy to expose oneself on paper and leave it out in a field where it could fall into the wrong hands. You were brave to go first.

In your letter, you mentioned having too much space to think. I always thought I wanted that. Lots of space. Silence. But lately it has become more of a force field to keep ~~you~~ people out. I've had it activated so long that anyone brave enough to come inside feels like an intruder, rather than what ~~you~~ they really are. An anomaly. A fork in the road of time. The thing that pulls me from distraction and forces me to become the next version of myself. And isn't it ironic that I teach the meaning of time for a living and, yet, I am staunchly fighting the passage of it? Time is change. But letting it move you forward is hard.

Enough about me. I am nowhere near as interesting as you are. I'll say this. I believe that if you're brave enough to write a secret admirer letter to someone, you're brave enough to evolve, if that's what you want. Maybe writing back will inspire me to do the same.

Sincerely,
Julian

"Well?" Lavinia called from her stump. "What is the temperature?"

Hallie had no earthly clue. He'd gone way more in-depth than she was expecting. It reminded her of the conversation they'd had in the kitchen. Emotional. Honest. Only, this time, he'd had it with someone else. On one hand, his words had spread a balm over a wound inside of her. *You're brave enough to evolve.* On the other, it felt worse than if he'd asked to meet the mystery person. Or expressed serious romantic interest.

Tears pricked against the backs of her eyelids. "Um." She quickly folded the letter up and stowed it in the pocket of her hoodie. "I would say he's cautiously interested. Complimentary but not flirtatious. He leaves it open-ended for more correspondence."

When Lavinia didn't respond right away, Hallie knew her friend had picked up on the hurt in her tone. "Are you going to write him again?" Lavinia finally asked, quietly.

"I don't know." Hallie tried to laugh, but it sounded forced. "None of my impulsive decisions have resulted in actual pain before. Maybe that's a good sign to stop."

"I have a lighter in my pocket. Shall we go burn him at the stake?"

"Nah." Hallie turned, giving her friend a grateful look. "I hear they don't even have shrimp and garlic linguine in prison."

"I guess we'll let the lucky prick live," Lavinia muttered, pushing to her feet. Coming to stand beside Hallie, she put an arm around her shoulder, and they both stared out over the top of the vines. "You did something sort of brash, babe, but I have to tell you, I fucking admire you for taking a shot and doing something a little wild. Once in a while, a good thing comes from a shot of sudden bravery."

"Just not this time."

Lavinia didn't answer. Just squeezed Hallie's shoulders.

"This is a good thing," Hallie said slowly, watching her breath turn into fog. "I needed a wake-up call. Since Rebecca left us, I've fallen into this pattern of disorganized commotion. I don't want to acknowledge how bad it hurts to be alone now. And I don't know what happens next in my life. So I just . . . kept finding ways to avoid making decisions. To avoid being the Hallie I was when she was around, because it's too hard to do it alone." She closed her eyes and squared her shoulders. "But I can. I'm ready. I need to grow up now and stop making these . . ." She gestured to the stump. "Ridiculous choices. Starting tomorrow, I'm turning over a new leaf."

"Why not start tonight?"

"I need closure." Again, her gaze rested on the stump. "I need to tell him good-bye first."

THE LETTER WAS already gone.

Julian stared down at the stump with a pit in his stomach.

It was nearing one o'clock in the morning. They'd been home for an hour, but he'd spent it convincing Natalie to go to bed, instead of cracking open a bottle of champagne and playing an old version of Yahtzee she'd found in the hallway closet. As soon as he'd heard his sister sawing logs through her bedroom door, he'd booked it up the path to take back the piece of communication, but obviously he'd been too late. His secret admirer had retrieved the envelope while he was at the party. And he supposed that eliminated everyone who was there tonight. Why did that surprise him? Had he been holding out a small amount of dumb hope that his admirer was Hallie?

Idiot.

Why would she admire someone who was a rainstorm compared to her sunshine?

She'd been the one to point out they were too different and should only be friends.

He agreed, of course. Of course. He did.

Still. God, why did he feel so slimy? Despite the dropping temperature, the back of his neck was covered in sweat. He had no choice but to return home, carrying mounting senses of dread and shame behind him like chains, knowing he'd written back to a stranger while he was—let's face it—infatuated with someone else.

What the hell was he going to do now?

Chapter Fifteen

Julian jogged down Grapevine Way that afternoon, his pace slowing when he spied the lazy-Sunday line of people on the sidewalk. But this time, they weren't waiting outside UNCORKED. They were patiently waiting their turn to get inside Corked. Others were emerging with bottles of his family's wine in their hands, tied up in ribbons.

He made a sound in his throat, nodded once, and moved at a faster clip to make up for lost time. After running more than a block, he finally allowed himself to smile. Finally acknowledged the somewhat unsettling flip in the dead center of his chest. Now that Lorna's shop was on an upswing, Hallie wouldn't worry anymore, right? She'd be happy.

Perhaps it wouldn't hurt to update some of Lorna's indoor displays. Have the floor buffed. That line of people might be there because of the deal on the business cards he'd handed out, but what about a long-term plan? For Corked and Vos Vineyard? Instead of working on Wexler's book this morning, he'd had a meeting with the bookkeeper and, with Corinne's approval, had shifted some of their financial priorities. This year would be less about producing stock and more about selling what was already on shelves. Once they had the revenue in place, they could make the necessary improvements to come back better than ever.

Julian was busy making calculations in his head when he ran past the stump.

He stopped so quickly, dirt kicked up in the air.

A new letter?

His immediate instinct was to keep jogging. *Don't pick it up. Don't open it.* Hallie was not on the other end of these notes. After last night, they seemed to be at even more distinct odds than before. Just two people who'd traded heavy personal secrets in a vineyard. Two people who'd completely lost their minds one night and pleasured themselves together in his kitchen. Who couldn't seem to stop colliding. He would almost certainly return to Stanford with the sense that he'd left behind unfinished business, but that couldn't be helped, could it?

He'd have to simply . . . live with it.

How?

They would never again have a conversation like the one they'd had the night of the storm. Or while picking grapes on his family's land. Exchanges he continued to replay over and over in his head, trying to make sense out of them being so different while finding it so easy to understand each other. So much so that when he'd written his letter back to the secret admirer, his words were almost a period on the end of his conversations with Hallie. It was hard not to crave a response to that, even if it wasn't coming from her.

The letter was in his hand before he realized he'd picked it up.

"Fuck."

Julian started running again, through the cool, twisting haze escaping down off the mountain. The sun broke through the mist in fragments and cracks, a rolling spotlight over different sections of the vines. Beneath his feet, the earth was solid, and Julian was grateful for that, because holding the letter caused anticipation and dread to war in his middle all the way back to the house. On the off chance Natalie was awake before two P.M. on a weekend, he tucked the envelope into his pocket on the way to his bedroom, making it there without incident.

After closing the door behind him, he stripped off his sweaty shirt and placed it in the hamper. Toed off his running shoes and paced the floor beside the king-size bed. Finally, he couldn't stand the unknown anymore. He took the letter out of his pocket and broke the seal.

Dear Julian,

There was one part of your response that stuck out to me. That there are events or people in our lives that force us to become the next version of ourselves. Are we all constantly fighting that change to something new and unfamiliar? Is that why, no matter what we do in our personal or professional lives, somehow it's never done with full confidence? There's always the fear of being wrong. Or maybe we're afraid to be <u>right</u> and make progress, because that means change. And moving forward is hard, like you said. Scary. Lately, I think moving forward as an adult means accepting that bad things happen and there's not always something you can do to avoid or fix it. Is having that knowledge the final change? If so, what is beyond *that* bitter pill? No wonder we're digging in our heels.

As I'm writing this, I'm starting to wonder if the longer we fight change in ourselves, the less time we have to live as better people. Or at least more self-aware people.

I propose that we both do something that scares us this week.

Secretly Yours

"Fuck," Julian said again, finding himself on the edge of the bed, without remembering exactly when he'd sat down. Once again, he was completely and utterly intrigued by this person's letter, and yet, he wanted to tear it up and burn it in the fireplace. Not only because he alternated between hearing the words in Hallie's voice and feeling immense guilt for reading it in the first place. But more so because the letter challenged him. He hadn't accepted or denied the challenge yet. Still, his veins felt like they'd been pumped full of static.

Something that scares us.

Julian left the letter on his bed, but mentally carried it into the shower. Then into his office, where he once again sat in front of the blinking cursor for hours. At some point, he heard Natalie stumble out of her room for sustenance, before going straight back in. Finally, he gave up attempting to concentrate on anything else and returned to his bedroom, picking up the letter and trying to find some sort of clue in the handwriting, something about the basic stationery and ink color that might identify the author. Maybe if he could just meet this person face-to-face, he could confirm whether or not that attraction ran both ways. For some reason, he hoped it wouldn't. But nonetheless, they could be friends, right?

Even though they'd only exchanged letters, he couldn't help feeling a sort of kinship with this person who was capable of identifying the worries he'd never been able to speak aloud.

Except with Hallie.

Maybe rather than writing back, he should go talk to *her*, instead.

Anticipation swelled so rapidly at the thought of seeing her, hearing her voice, that he dropped the letter. From a person he'd now willingly corresponded with. A person who was *not* Hallie. What the hell had he gotten himself into?

"I'M SORRY TO drag you away from your fan club," Hallie teased Lorna, smiling at her grandmother's best friend across the console of her truck. They drove through town Sunday afternoon, yielding for buzzed pedestrians every fifty yards or so, Phoebe Bridgers playing gently on the radio. "Are you sure about taking a lunch break?"

"Of course I am, dear. These old feet need a rest." Lorna smoothed the silk patterned scarf around her neck. "Besides, Nina has it under control." Before she even finished her sentence, she'd started laughing. "Can you believe I have an employee now? A couple of weeks ago, I barely had customers. Now I've hired part-time help just to keep up with them all!"

Hallie's chest expanded with relief. With gratitude. When she'd pulled up outside of Corked, patrons were gathered around her grandmother's white wrought-iron table with glasses of wine in hand, bringing it to life. Giving it purpose again. Keeping Rebecca's memory alive, at least for Hallie. And she owed most of this to Julian.

His name in her head was a simultaneous shot of adrenaline and a punch to the gut.

Was he writing back to his admirer again at that very moment? *I propose that we both do something that scares us this week.*

Was he in the process of figuring out what scared him? At the very least, Hallie was in the process of checking that box today. Doing something uncomfortable. Fulfilling the challenge she'd laid down for herself and Julian by moving forward. She'd called Lorna about her trip to the library this morning and the wineshop owner had insisted upon coming along for moral support, despite the crowds that were now descending on Corked with Vos Vineyard discount cards and unquenchable thirsts.

"Lorna, I couldn't be happier for you." One of Hallie's hands left the wheel to rub at the euphoric pressure in her chest. "I could just burst."

"I didn't see it coming," breathed the older woman, staring unseeing out the windshield of the truck. "Then again, some of the best things in life happen when you least expect them."

Sort of like Julian suddenly showing back up in St. Helena to write a book? Or the professor somehow being the chivalrous hero that lived rent free in her memory, while also being completely different than she'd imagined for the last fifteen years? Yes, he might be the quietly studious man of her imagination, but he was also intense. A keeper of painful secrets. Funny and quick to find solutions. Protective. A million times more engrossing than the person she'd crafted in her mind, and she had no choice but to leave him with some final food for thought and move on. Which is what she should have done in the beginning, before getting in too deep. "What if you spend your whole life expecting one thing . . . and get another entirely?"

"I'd say the one thing you can expect in life are thwarted plans," said Lorna. "Fate keeps its own schedule. But sometimes fate drops a present in our lap, and we realize that if everything we'd arranged ourselves had gone according to plan, the gift from fate never would have arrived. Like you coming to live with Rebecca in St. Helena. All those attempts to get your mother on the right path didn't work out, but in the end, those struggles are what brought you here. Rebecca was always saying that. 'Lorna, what's meant to be will always find a way.'"

"She loved a good saying."

"That she did."

Hallie shifted in the driver's seat but couldn't get comfortable. "What if I only belonged here in St. Helena while Rebecca was alive? That's how it feels. Like I don't . . . know how to be in this place anymore. As just myself."

Lorna was quiet for a moment. Hallie could feel the shop owner gathering herself before she eventually reached out and laid a hand on Hallie's shoulder. "When you came here, this place changed, along with Rebecca. It rearranged itself to fit you, and now . . . Hallie, you are part of the landscape. A beautiful part of it. St. Helena will always be better for having you here."

When Hallie shook her head, a tear came loose and she swiped it away. "I'm a disaster. I'm flighty and disorganized and I don't know how to control my impulses. She was always around to help me do that. To know who I am. I was Rebecca's granddaughter."

"You still are. Always will be. But you're also Hallie—and Hallie is beautiful for all her flaws. Because the good things about you far outweigh the bad."

Until Lorna said those words to Hallie, she didn't know how badly she needed to hear them. Some of the density in her chest lessened, her grip loosening on the steering wheel. "Thank you, Lorna."

"I'm happy to tell you the truth any time you want to hear it." Lorna patted her shoulder one more time before taking her hand back. "What made you decide to approach the library today about the landscaping job?"

Hallie hummed. Took a deep breath. "I want to do something she would be proud of. But . . . I think, more importantly, I have to do something I'm proud of. I have to start . . . taking pride, period. In myself and my work. It has to be for me now."

Hallie pulled her truck up against the curb across the street from the white, U-shaped building, also known as the St. Helena Library. It stood by itself at the end of a cul-de-sac, sun-soaked vineyard vines spreading out behind the structure in endless rows.

This morning, while pondering the trip, she'd bitten her nails down to the quick.

It had been a long time coming. Some part of her never really expected to get there.

The courtyard of the library definitely needed greenery and color and warmth. As of now, it had none of those things. Just overgrown indigenous plants that would have been beautiful with a little maintaining and the addition of some perennials. It did have a big lawn in front, shaded by an oak tree. Two children sat on that lawn now, blowing bubbles with very little success, suds dripping off their wrists onto the grass. A smaller toddler nodded off in her mother's lap, their library books spread out around them.

Hallie couldn't help but think the library could be thriving, with a little care. If people drove past, the flowers would call to them like an invitation. Marigolds and sunflowers and water fixtures. But in order to do this particular job, she would have to come up with an exact blueprint, have it approved by the library manager, Ms. Hume, and *stick* to it.

With Rebecca there to guide her, Hallie would have had no problem with a plan. But she was a dress pinned to a laundry line in a windstorm these days, waving in every direction. Had the years she'd spent under her grandmother's wing been a waste, though?

No.

As soon as Rebecca left, Hallie had gone back to being indecisive and jumbled. But it didn't have to continue that way. She could do something spectacular, all by herself. She could be proud of herself, discombobulated chaos and all. She was the granddaughter of a community staple—a gloriously kind woman who loved routine and simple pleasures, like wind chimes on the back porch and teach-yourself-calligraphy kits. Hallie had settled down as much as she was capable, because it was important to her grandmother. She appreciated when Hallie tried, when she reined in her scattered focus and applied it to schoolwork or carried out a specific landscaping strategy. There was no one around now to appreciate those efforts.

No one but herself. That would have to be enough.

I propose that we both do something that scares us this week.

Taking on a huge project like this definitely qualified as scary. It was a job that would require structure, diligence, and a very particular librarian looking over her shoulder the entire time.

Was she up for it?

Yes.

Something had to give. Putting her anxieties on paper, writing letters to Julian, had been therapeutic. She could be totally honest about her fears and feelings. That honesty felt good. Authentic. But now she needed to be truthful with herself. To admit she'd been avoiding the library job, because she didn't believe herself capable of the focus it would take to complete a task so large. Rebecca believed in her, though. So did Lorna. It was time to take that faith and turn it inward.

Lorna nudged her in the ribs from the passenger seat. "Go ahead, dear. You can do it. I'll be waiting right here."

She turned to her. "Are you sure you don't want bottomless champagne brunch, instead?"

"Maybe next week." Lorna laughed, shooing her into opening the driver's-side door. "For now, I want to watch my best friend's wild-child granddaughter learn a lesson. That she doesn't have to change to suit anyone. Unless that anyone is herself."

They held hands for a moment; then Hallie blew out a slow breath, climbed out of the truck, and crossed the street.

The cool brass doorknob slid against her palm, and she opened the heavy library door. Just as she remembered, the place was bright and inviting on the inside. Stained glass windows lit the stacks in reds and blues, hushed conversations took place over laptops at the tables, and the distinctive scent of old leather and floor polish drifted out to greet her.

Ms. Hume's head popped up from behind the reception desk, her slender, deep-brown fingers pausing on the keys. She removed her glasses, letting them drop to where they were caught by a long, beaded necklace, and stood. "Hallie Welch. Rebecca told me you would show up sooner or later," she said, a smile tugging at her lips. "Are you here to apply for a library card or finally fix our garden?"

Hallie took a moment to reconnect with her grandmother. Like a whispered hello from somewhere beyond. Then she centered herself and approached the desk. "Maybe both. You wouldn't happen to have any self-help books on staying organized, would you?"

"I'm sure I can pull a few."

"They're for a friend, obviously," Hallie joked, matching the librarian's knowing smile. "As for the garden . . . yes, I'm ready. I thought we could discuss layout today and I could get started soon."

Ms. Hume arched an eyebrow. "*When* exactly?"

"Soon," Hallie said firmly, in that moment accepting that there were some things about her she could never change.

And that . . . maybe she didn't need to.

Chapter Sixteen

The familiar rumble of Hallie's truck grew louder as it made its way down the driveway, and Julian stood, crossing his bedroom to the window. Sunset was beginning to deepen the Sunday evening sky to orange.

How long had he been sitting there, contemplating the letter on the floor?

And thinking of Hallie.

Not long enough to reach his limit, apparently, because he stared through the glass now, starved for the sight of her. The dogs dove free of the truck first, moving in streaks of fur toward the trees at the back of the house. Hallie didn't follow right away. She sat in the driver's seat chewing her lip, unaware that he could see her. That he could witness her indecision or nerves. About... seeing him? He hated that possibility as much as he could relate to it. Being around her always left him in a state of hunger and confusion. Regret, too, because he couldn't seem to stop fucking up and either leading her on or pushing her away.

Finally, Hallie hopped down from the truck, went around to the rear, and lowered the tailgate. Sunset spilled across her shoulders, turning her cheeks gold. She tipped her face toward the sky and closed her eyes to let the fading light kiss her features, and yearning plowed into his stomach. Hard.

Something that scares us.

Hallie would definitely be at the top of that list, but a man didn't scale Kilimanjaro on his first hike. And would he now be betraying the letter writer if he used the challenge as an excuse to go after what he—might as well admit it—wanted so goddamn bad, he was being tortured day and night by the thought of it? Her? Also known as the beautiful gardener trudging toward his garden in rubber boots, cutoff shorts, and a navy blue hoodie that hung off one shoulder.

In her arms, she carried a pot of what Julian assumed was the dusty miller she'd referred to at the Wine Down event. The dogs trotted over to escort her, sniffing at her elbows and knees. She greeted each of them by name, her voice fading into the evening light as she disappeared around the side of the house. And he moved like an apparition to his office so he could pick up the sound again, hear it in full effect. The silly baby-talk way she spoke to her pets that was beginning to sound totally normal to him. The soft expulsions of breath when she exerted herself or dropped to her knees in the soil. Her voice seemed to fill the entire house, warm and sultry and singularly hers.

Jesus, was he starting to sweat?

Julian was on the verge of returning to the bedroom out of pure necessity, to handle the situation arising in his pants, when his sister's voice joined Hallie's outside the office window.

He felt as if ice water were spilling from the crown of his head to his toes.

This wasn't good.

He didn't know *why* exactly it wasn't good, but it was decidedly not.

Last night at Wine Down, he'd been distracted by Hallie. Too distracted to be careful with his words. It was only after he'd said those revealing things to Natalie about his unyielding drive to make Hallie happy that he wished he could go back in time and cram a cork in his mouth. There'd been more than enough of the bottle stoppers around, after all.

He might have made progress with Natalie last night—they were working their way back to a better sibling relationship, slowly but surely—but unfortunately, she wouldn't know discretion if it bit her on the ass.

Julian moved at a fast clip toward the front of the house and blew down the steps, only slowing to a sedate walk when the two women came into view. They were smiling, Hallie introducing Petey, Todd, and the General to Natalie, who was still in night shorts and a Cornell T-shirt. "Aren't you all just the sweetest gentlemen? Yes, you are! Yes. You. Are."

What was it about dogs that made people talk like that?

The animals were eating it up, too, tails whipping like chopper blades.

They shocked the hell out of Julian by bounding over to him next, reacting with—dare he say—*triple* the enthusiasm they'd displayed for Natalie? He was oddly pleased by that. Did he have an undiscovered way with animals? He always assumed pets were for *other* people. People who chose to devote hours of their lives to caring for an animal instead of useful endeavors. Now, looking down at the guileless eyes of Todd, he wondered if being loved unconditionally wasn't useful after all. "Hello," he greeted them in a normal voice, patting them each on the head. They weren't satisfied with that, however, weaving through his legs until he scratched them behind the ears. "Yes, okay, you're very good boys."

"They are slobbering on your socks, Julian," Natalie said, looking at him curiously. "Hey, you . . . forgot to put shoes on? You?"

"Did I?" he murmured, looking down with a pinch of alarm. He'd never gone outside without his shoes before. There was a process to going outdoors, and he'd forgone it completely. The dogs were indeed getting strings of saliva all over the no-nonsense white cotton tube socks, and he would need to change them, but that delay didn't gut him like it might have before.

How odd.

He looked up to find Hallie watching him with a curious expression. "Evening," she said, bringing the dogs tangling back in her direction.

"Good evening, Hallie," he said, his tone deep and formal. And he had no idea why. Only that he wanted to reestablish their footing somehow. Everything between them felt off-kilter, and he was getting really tired of analyzing why their being in balance was so important to him.

Natalie, however, was only getting started.

She split a gleeful look between Julian and Hallie, rocking side to side on the balls of her feet, as if waiting for the starting gun of a race. "So, Hallie. I didn't put it together last night, but we went to St. Helena High together." She narrowed an eye. "You were the cool new kid for a while. At least until someone else's parents decided to move here and open a vineyard."

Hallie tore her eyes from Julian and beamed at his sister,

and his chest crunched like cans in a trash compactor. Jealousy brewed inside of him like a pot of dark roast.

Damn, did he want that smile directed at him, instead.

"That was me. Although I challenge your assessment that I was cool." Absently, she scratched the General under his chin, still smiling that delighted smile. If she could just glance at him once while it was on her face . . . "You were the one throwing the parties. I had the pleasure of attending one or two."

"So you've seen me topless," Natalie said conversationally, producing a withering sigh from her brother. "Good to know."

"They still hold up," Hallie commented, giving her chest an impressed nod.

"Thank you," Natalie returned, pressing a hand to her throat.

Julian, for his part, was dumbfounded. "For all intents and purposes, you've just met and you're already discussing your . . ."

"Oh boy, do you think he's going to say it out loud?" Hallie murmured out of the corner of her mouth. "Ten bucks says he doesn't."

"I can't bet against you. I'd lose and I'm too broke to pay up." She faced Hallie fully. "You wouldn't happen to need a firmly titted assistant by any chance?"

Julian slashed a hand through the air. "You are not working together."

Both female heads swiveled in his direction. One startled. One looking like a cat who was on her way to snuff out the family canary. "Why not?" Natalie drawled. "Are you worried we'd talk about you?" She propped her chin on her wrist. "What could there possibly be to discuss?"

Silence ticked by along with the pulse in his temple.

Hallie looked at him.

In reality, only three seconds passed while he tried to come up with the right words for his inconvenient fixation on Hallie, but it was long enough.

"Nothing to discuss," Hallie answered for him. For them. With color in her cheeks, she slid her attention back to Natalie. "And, sorry. You're overqualified, Cornell."

His sister shook a fist at the sky. "Dammit. Foiled once again by my sharp intellect."

They shared a fond laugh, visibly considering each other. "Listen, there is a rebound in this town that still needs to be bounded, and he has my name on him. Would you want to attend a tasting with me on Tuesday night? Wine crafted by a former Navy SEAL," she cajoled, waggling her eyebrows. "I'm sure he's got a friend. Or two, if you're into that sort of thing. Or maybe you already have a boyfriend you can bring? I don't mind being the third wheel—"

"Natalie," Julian said through teeth that could not be unclenched to save the world. "That's enough."

"Says who?" Hallie asked, pivoting to face him.

"Says me." *Idiot.*

For once, the dogs were silent.

His sister had the expression of an Olympian holding up a bouquet of roses.

"I didn't realize you spoke for me." Hallie laughed, her eyes bright.

"My sister is making trouble out of sheer boredom, Hallie. I'm just trying to prevent you from getting wrapped up in it."

Natalie reared back a little, looking genuinely hurt. "Is that what I'm doing?"

Hallie laid a hand on Natalie's arm, squeezing. The look of reproach she gave him was like a line drive to the gut. "Friends don't let friends go to tastings alone. Someone has to talk you out of buying in discounted bulk. Count me in. But . . ." She avoided his stare. "No plus one. Just me."

He battled the urge to drop to his knees and worship her.

"Are you sure?" Natalie cut her a sideways glance. "You're not just saying yes because my brother is being a tool?"

This time she looked him square in the eye. "I'd be lying if I said that wasn't a good forty percent of the reason."

Natalie nodded, impressed. "I respect your honesty."

What the fuck was going on? He'd lost his grip on this situation entirely. In the blink of an eye, his sister had become friends with Hallie. Friends who went drinking together in the company of Navy SEALs. Somehow *he* was the bad guy. But the real problem, the reality he did not want to admit to himself, was that he liked Natalie and Hallie forming a bond. It reminded him of the moment Hallie turned her face to the orange sky and he could hear the dogs barking in the yard, and it hit him like a wave of preemptive melancholia. He'd think of this someday. He'd think of all of it. A lot.

With a rough clearing of his throat, Julian walked on dirty socks back into the house, which really took the dignity out of it all, and stripped the soggy things off before setting foot on the hardwood floor. He threw them into the hamper, on top of his running clothes, and paced back to the kitchen, pouring himself a third of a glass of whiskey, cursing, and adding another inch. He slugged it back, then stood there staring down into his empty glass until the rumble of Hallie's truck engine brought his head up, just in time for his sister to storm into the kitchen.

"Are you a whole-ass moron, Julian?"

No one had ever asked him a question like that. Perhaps it had been implied by his father, but in a far more aggressive format. "Excuse me?"

Natalie threw up her hands. "Why did you let me let you write back to that secret admirer?"

A mallet swung and connected with his temple. "Hallie told you she knew?"

"In passing. Yes."

He came as close as he ever would to smashing a glass on the ground. "How does something like that get mentioned in passing? Couldn't you talk about the weather instead of swapping life stories after a five-minute acquaintance? *Jesus!*" he shouted. "I told you I didn't want to do it."

"You didn't tell me why!" She raked her fingers through her dark hair. "Oh my God, the way you spoke about her last night and now the chemistry and the angst." She threw herself backward into the pantry door, rattling it loudly. "*I'm going to die.*"

It was not good for whatever peace of mind he had left to have someone recognize the connection between himself and Hallie and say it out loud. Why was he suddenly winded? "You think I should pursue Hallie. Is that what I'm getting from your theatrics?"

Her eyes flashed with accusation. "I don't know if you have a chance with her now, secret-admirer-letter returner."

Was there a pickax buried in his chest? "You *begged* me to write that letter!"

She made a disgusted face, flashing him a middle finger. "You want to get tangled up in semantics, fine, but the point is, you blew it. She's a rare spot of sunshine, and you're committed to huddling in the shade." She paused. "Maybe I should write a book, instead of you. That was a sick metaphor."

Julian started to leave the kitchen. "Speaking of which, I'm going to work."

"You haven't written in a week. It's because of her, isn't it? You're all . . . tied in knots and full of woe like a T-Bird in love with a Scorpion. *Grease* is my comfort movie. Okay?" Her voice rose. "What is the issue with pursuing her?"

He spun around at the mouth of the hall. "She makes me feel out of fucking control," he snapped. "You've been that way your whole life, so maybe you don't understand why that would be undesirable to someone. She leaves things to chance, she's flighty, she doesn't think her course of action through from beginning to end, and chaos is the result. She comes with dirty footprints, and corralling dogs and sticky children, and tolerating lateness. I'm too rigid for that. For her." A low, distant ringing started in his ears. "I'd dim her glow. I'd change her, and I would hate myself for it."

Natalie's throat worked for a series of heavy moments, the room lightening and darkening with a passing cloud. "Learn to let go, Julian. *Learn.*"

He scoffed, making his throat burn worse. "You say that like it's easy."

"It's not. I know, because I've done it in reverse."

That gave Julian pause, drawing him out of his own misery. In reverse? Natalie had gone from free spirit to . . . dimmed down? Fine, she'd quit her antics, buckled down, and gone to a prestigious college, worked her way up to partner at a major investment firm. But she wasn't anything like him. Was she? She was full of humor and spontaneity and life.

Unless there was a lot more happening under the surface. A lot he couldn't see.

She diverted her gaze before he could search for it.

"Come with us Tuesday night, Julian. Don't live with regrets."

Julian stared at the empty archway long after Natalie had vacated it, trying to remember how he'd gotten to this point, this edge of the cliff where leaping was necessary. He hadn't asked for this. Never wanted it. But now?

I'm too rigid for that. For her.

Learn to let go.

That advice had come across as flippant at first. It made sense to him, though. If he knew how to do anything, it was learn. Expand his way of thinking. He'd just never done so in the name of romance. With the intent of . . . what? Was he going after Hallie now? Pursuing her?

The very idea was absurd. Wasn't it?

They lived an hour and a half away from each other, leading extremely different lives. The fact that they were polar opposites hadn't changed one iota. Hallie still brought disorder with her wherever she went. And he . . . would dull all of that. He'd squash it. When they first met, he thought she needed to change. Learn to be punctual. More organized. He'd even been so arrogant as to critique her as a gardener and decide she could do with some symmetry training. Now the idea that she would change, even in the slightest, on his account made Julian feel seasick.

Then learn.

It would have to be him that changed.

Pursuing Hallie meant easing his grip on time management. It meant learning to exist without the constraints of minutes and hours. Living with paw prints on his pants and understanding that she would do inconceivable things like volunteer to babysit thirty children and stuff them with donuts. Or steal cheese in broad daylight.

Why was he smiling, dammit?

He was. He could see his reflection in the microwave.

I propose that we both do something that scares us this week.

Was it in bad taste to take the advice from his secret admirer and use it to suit his purposes with Hallie? Probably. But, Jesus, now that he'd given himself permission to go get her, a rush of anticipation started in the crown of his head, blasting down to his feet so swiftly, he had to lean against the wall.

Okay, then.

My goal is to date her. My goal is to be her boyfriend.

He could barely hear his own thoughts over the ruckus his heart was making.

And yes, he was going to try his damndest to stop stuffing everything in life into the parameters of a plan and a schedule. But not when it came to this. To her. He needed a plan for winning her, because something deep in the recesses of his chest told him this was too important to be left up to chance.

Chapter Seventeen

Tuesday night Hallie stood in front of her full-length mirror in two different shoes, trying to decide which one looked better. She snapped a quick picture with her phone and fired it off to Lavinia, who promptly responded with: Wear the heels. But if you replace me as your best friend tonight, be warned that I will stab you with one.

Never, Hallie texted back, snorting.

She kicked aside some of the clothes and beauty products on her floor and found the lint roller, dragging the stickiness down her snug black dress to rid it of three varieties of dog hair. She stepped over the pile of rejected shoes and entered her en suite bathroom, leaving the lint roller in a place she probably wouldn't find it next time and—

Hallie straightened, her fingers pausing in the act of rooting through lipsticks to find the right shade of golden peach. Watching her actions as if they were being performed by someone else, she removed the sticky strip of dog hair from the roller, threw it in the trash, and replaced the essential tool for dog owners in the drawer, where she used to keep it.

She stepped back from the mirror and looked around, wincing at the clutter.

Now that she'd taken a big step in her professional life, tomorrow she needed to take a leap in her personal one—and rein in this house jungle. Or at least get a running start.

But first, she'd get through tonight.

Going to a wine tasting with Julian's sister was a terrible idea considering she'd resolved to move on. For real this time. Especially after the awkward scene that had played out in his front yard. He'd made it clear that they were incompatible and written a letter to someone else, so what gave him the right to decide what she did with her time? Or whom she spent it with?

The guesthouse garden was almost complete. She hadn't quite decided what she would use to fill the final spaces, but it would come to her. Hopefully on her next trip to the nursery—and then she could wrap up her responsibilities to the Vos family, bill the matriarch, and move on. No more secret admirer letters, either. They were just another ill-conceived part of her life. She'd acted on impulse, and where did it lead her?

To having him validate all of her feelings. The ones she'd held on to for so long. And those things were not good, because Julian remained unavailable to her. Nothing had changed. If she revealed herself to him as the author of those letters, he would probably be disappointed that she wasn't some like-minded scholar with a home filing system.

Maybe she would write the letters to herself from now on, instead of to Julian. They'd led her somewhere useful, hadn't they? She'd finally admitted that avoidance through chaos was harming her livelihood. Even her friendship with Lavinia, who had begun looking at her in that worried, measuring way. Hallie needed to turn onto a new path. A healthy one.

Hallie shuffled a few lipsticks into her makeup case and snapped it shut, suddenly looking forward to a cleaning spree in the morning. A fresh start. Maybe she would even pick a new wall color for the living room and do some painting. Peony pink or peacock blue. Something vivid that would serve as a reminder that she was not only capable of admitting her self-destructive habits, but of finding a way to correct her course while remaining true to herself.

With a nod, Hallie requested an Uber and spent the ten-minute wait saying good-bye to the boys, which led to another harried trip to the lint roller, but the snuffling snuggles were well worth it. She'd taken them to the dog park after dinner so they could run off any excess energy that might lead to her coming home to couch stuffing all over the floor. Now she put some extra food in their bowls and walked out the front door, clutch purse in hand, sinking into the back seat of the black Prius.

Julian must have given his sister Hallie's phone number, because Natalie had texted her that afternoon with an address to the apparently SEAL-owned winery, Zelnick Cellar. The place had a website, but it was under construction, and she'd never heard of it from anyone in town. She was curious, even if spending the evening with a Vos wasn't the wisest step on her road to separating herself from all things Julian.

Ten minutes later, the Uber stopped in front of a medium-size barn surrounded by wooden fencing. Flickering light shone from within, and she could see a small crowd standing around. She had to imagine they were locals, since she hadn't been able to find the tasting advertised anywhere on the Web. Was it entirely through word of mouth?

Tossing a thank-you to the driver, Hallie climbed out of the back seat and stood, tugging down the snug hem of her dress. She opened the flashlight app on her phone—getting a lot of use out of it lately, huh?—and did her best to navigate the dirt path leading to the barn while wearing skinny three-inch heels. The closer she got to the music and the crowd, the more well-lit the path became, and she slipped her phone back into her purse. Glowing white bulbs bounced up and down in the breeze, strung from high points of the barn. Was that the Beach Boys playing? This had to be the most casual wine tasting she'd ever attended. No doubt she'd overdressed—

Julian stepped into the barn entrance.

In a sharp, charcoal-gray suit.

Holding a bouquet of wildflowers in his hand.

Time slowed down, allowing her to feel and experience the over-the-top response of her hormones. They sang like tone-deaf preteens in the shower, screeching the high notes with misplaced confidence. Wow. Oh wow. He looked like he'd walked out of an advertisement for an expensive watch with too many dials. Or Gucci cologne.

Good. Lord.

Wait. Wildflowers were her favorite. How had he known?

Honestly, it tracked that they would be. But still.

She recognized the pink cellophane wrapping. He'd gone all the way to the nursery for that colorful spray. Who were they for?

Why was he here in the first place?

Close your mouth before you start drooling.

Salivating became even more of a possibility when Julian closed the distance between them, striding forward in that purposeful way of his. And when his head blocked the light coming from the barn, she saw determination and focus in the set of his jaw, the intensity of his eyes, the deep line of concentration between his eyebrows.

"Hello, Hallie."

The sheer depth of his voice, like the belly of a submarine scraping the ocean floor, almost had her backing away. Just dropping her purse and running.

Because what was happening here?

Without breaking eye contact, Julian picked up her free hand and wrapped it around the bouquet of wildflowers. "For you."

She shook her head. "I don't understand."

He seemed to be expecting that, because his expression didn't shift at all. He merely seemed torn over which part of her face to study. Nose, mouth, cheeks. "I'll explain. But first, I want to apologize for my behavior on Sunday. I acted like a jackass."

Hallie nodded dazedly. Was she accepting that apology?

Hard to say, when she was watching Julian slowly drag his tongue from right to left along his bottom lip, an answering clench taking place between her thighs. Something was different about him. He never failed to be entirely magnetic, but this was on a whole other level. It was almost *intentional*. Like he'd forgotten his filter at home.

"I'd like the opportunity to spend time with you, Hallie." His attention traveled downward, stopping at the hemline of her dress, that bump in his throat traveling high, then low, along with the register of his voice. When he reached out a single finger and traced the location where her skin met the hem, the air vanished from her lungs. "I want to . . . *date* you."

He packed so much bite into the word "date," there was no pretending it didn't have more than one meaning. Especially when his finger was just inside the hem now, teasing side to side to side, setting her legs trembling.

"You want to date me?"

"Yes."

"I still don't understand. What changed?"

Julian hooked his finger and dragged her close by the hem of her dress. Breathless, her head fell back so she wouldn't have to break eye contact. God, he was tall. Did he grow in the moonlight or did he just seem larger now that he'd apparently stopped withholding himself?

"Truthfully?" he asked.

"Yes, truthfully," she whispered.

Acute distress flickered briefly in his gaze. "I felt you slipping away from me. On Sunday in the yard." He paused, visibly searching for an explanation. "We'd left things up in the air before, but this was different, Hallie. And I didn't like it." He studied her closely. "Was I right? Have you slipped away from me?"

Under such intense scrutiny, there was no point in providing anything but the truth. "Yes. I have."

His chest rose sharply, shuddering back down. "Let me try and reverse that decision."

"No." She ignored how sexy he looked with that single professor's eyebrow hoisting into the air and let the word hang between them. Maybe the longer she left it there, the better chance she would have of actually *keeping* her resolve. Panicked by her slim odds, Hallie reminded herself that he'd written back to the other woman. Or what he *assumed* was another woman. He'd told a stranger deep, important things about himself, and that hurt, because he'd made Hallie feel like his confidant. Then he'd given that confidence to someone else.

Oh, she was the furthest thing from blameless here. Writing those letters had been deceptive and shortsighted. Part of the reason for distancing herself now was to leave her folly behind her, pretend she hadn't acted so impulsively, and enjoy the clean slate she planned to start writing on tomorrow. She could admit that. However, the sting of him leaving a letter on that stump continued to linger.

And last, but definitely not least, hadn't she proposed in her last letter that they both do something that scared them? For her, it was walking into the library and taking the landscaping job. For Julian, obviously it was her. She—this—scared him.

Hallie bit back the sudden need to knee him in the jewels.

"No?" he echoed Hallie, his fingertip pausing in its sensual travels beneath her hem, misery etching itself on his features. "I really have behaved poorly, haven't I?"

In all honesty, they both had.

So she couldn't answer with a yes. Not without being a hypocrite.

"What happened to us being wrong for each other?" she asked instead. "We decided that pretty early on, didn't we?"

"Yes," he said, moving his hand away from her with a visible effort, curling his fingers into a fist, and shoving it into his pants pocket. "It's come to my attention that I am far more wrong for you than the other way around, Hallie. You're nothing short of breathtaking. Unique and beautiful and bold. And I'm a goddamn idiot if I ever made you feel otherwise." She could feel in her bones how badly he wanted to reach for her in that moment. "I'm sorry. Every second we've spent together, I've been restraining myself. Trying to keep . . . to stay controlled."

"And that's not important to you anymore?"

"Not as important as you."

"Wow," she whispered, breathless. "Hard to fault any of these answers."

That fist came out of his pocket, and he shook it out, flexed his fingers and stepped forward to cup her cheek, his thumb tracing the cupid's bow of her upper lip. "I want to learn you, Hallie." His voice was low, imploring. "Let me learn."

Oh my.

A tremor coursed from her belly down to her knees, almost causing her to lose her balance. She might have, if the magnetism of his gaze wasn't holding her steady. Of course, when this man decided to be romantic, decided to try and woo a woman, the results were deadly. She'd just underestimated *how* potent his full effort and attention would be.

Also, if this was an inappropriate time to be turned on, someone needed to tell her vagina, because while standing with Julian in the swirling mist of the moonlit night, his breath bathing her mouth, belt buckle grazing her stomach, it took serious effort not to lick him. Just lick him anywhere she could reach. Maybe those cords in his neck or the forearms he was hiding underneath the sleeves of his suit—

"Everything you're thinking is right there on your face," he said, battling a smile.

Hallie took a step backward, losing the warmth of his hand, his breath. "I'm thinking about the wine I'm going to drink."

"Liar." He tossed a glance toward the barn. "And don't get your hopes up. It's terrible. If my sister wasn't in there, I'd suggest we make a run for it."

"Terrible wine?" She grimaced. "How badly does anyone *need* a sister?"

He laughed. A rich, rumbling sound that made the air feel lighter. "Come on." He held out his hand to her. "We'll spill it out under the table while his back is turned."

"That sounds like the kind of plan I would come up with."

His eyes flickered with determination. Affection. "I'm learning you already."

Lord help her, she couldn't do anything but twine her fingers through his after that. She watched with a grapefruit in her throat as he kissed her knuckles gratefully, pulling her at his side toward the barn. Then . . . she was walking into a wine tasting holding Julian's hand. Like a couple. He led her through a light-strung barn, through a gathering of about two dozen people, the scent of fermented grapes and straw heavy in the air. Guests stood in groups around candlelit high-top tables, their glasses of wine remaining noticeably full.

The waiter who'd obviously been hired to refill glasses and prod attendees to buy bottles to go looked stressed, unsure of what to do with himself. And his boss, the Navy SEAL turned Napa vintner, was too busy staring deep into Natalie's eyes to advise him.

"Oh boy," Hallie muttered.

"Uh-huh. Ask me how glad I was when your Uber pulled up."

"Maybe we should help." Julian slid a full glass of red wine in front of her, looked at it pointedly. She picked it up and took a sip, bitterness oozing down her throat. "Dear God," she croaked. "There's no way to salvage this."

"None," Julian agreed.

Someone a few tables over called Hallie's name—a recurring client—and she waved, smiling and exchanging some predictions about what would be blooming soon. When she turned back to Julian, he was watching her closely, that deep groove taking up real estate between his brows. All she could do was stare in return, sighing shakily when he rested a big hand on her hip, tugging her closer. Closer. Until she was in the circle of his heat, head tilted back. "You're dangerous like this," she murmured.

That thumb dug into her hip bone, ever so slightly. "Like what?"

Tingles ran all the way down to her toes, hair follicles prickling on the crown of her head. "Are you going to pretend like you're not trying to seduce me?"

His focus fell to her mouth. "Oh, I am one hundred percent trying to seduce you."

A long, hot clenching took place between her thighs, tummy muscles coiling, skin temperature skyrocketing. With a trembling laugh, she glanced over her shoulder and quickly scanned the room. "At least three of my regular clients are here. It wouldn't be very professional to be seduced where they can see me."

Was he looking at the pulse in her neck? It started beating faster, as if preening under the attention. "Then I suggest we go for a walk."

She pursed her lips at him and hummed. "I don't know about that. The last time we went for a walk in a vineyard, I only came back disappointed."

The corner of his mouth jumped with humor, but his eyes were serious. "Not this time, Hallie."

A promise. A confident one.

"What does that mean, exactly?" Hallie asked softly, haltingly.

He hesitated a moment, tongue tucked into his cheek. Then he dropped his mouth to her ear and said, "It means, this time I'm not finishing on your thighs."

Holy mother of God.

Images bombarded her mind. Those wires in Julian's neck straining, hands roaming desperately in the darkness, her knees in his big hands.

If she didn't know any better, she would have thought that one sip of terrible wine had gone to her head, the giddy lift of lust was so magnificent. Letting herself get carried off on Julian's current could be a really bad idea. Not only did she have a secret—that *she* was his secret admirer—but there was no evidence that a relationship would work. In fact, it was a total long shot. People couldn't change so drastically, could they?

But weren't moments like this why she'd finagled her way into fixing the guesthouse garden in the first place? She'd wanted her dose of magic with Julian Vos. Now that she knew him, now that she'd fallen for the real man, being happy with a single moment was impossible. She didn't have to think about that tonight, though. She could just let herself be taken for the ride. The one she'd dreamed about since high school. The one that was so much more powerful now that she'd gotten to know him, this man who bought awnings for failing wineshops. Or jumped in to host children's story time and saved her from being arrested.

Lost in her thoughts, she swayed forward involuntarily, and her breasts grazed his upper abdomen, the suggestive rasp of their clothing making her want to moan. Rub against him like a cat. Especially when his eyes went smoky, lids heavy.

"Hallie," he half growled. "Take the walk with me."

With the word "yes" on the tip of her tongue, her conscience made a last-minute attempt to throw up a barrier, talk her out of taking something she needed and wanted. *Tell him the truth first, or you'll regret it.* But apparently she'd need more time to become a reasonable, non-reckless person. Because all she said was "Yes."

Chapter Eighteen

If he didn't kiss her soon, the world was going to end. Julian was convinced of this beyond any shadow of a doubt. He was so starved for the taste he'd been denying himself that he hustled her out of the barn like they were escaping its imminent collapse. Nothing was collapsing, however, except his self-control where Hallie was concerned. How the fuck had he kept his distance from this woman? When he walked out of the barn and saw her teetering up the path, so familiar and so unforgivably unknown at the same time, he'd wanted to crawl to her on his hands and knees.

This was not the way he'd planned for the evening to go.

He was supposed to apologize. They were supposed to sit down and talk, sort through the obstacles between them and devise a mutual plan for moving forward together. As two adults with a common goal: a healthy, communicative relationship. Maybe if she hadn't worn that tight black dress, his chances for success would have been more realistic. Maybe if she didn't make him feel animalistic, he wouldn't be dragging her out into the darkness right now, his cock halfway to erect, a bead of sweat trickling down his spine.

And maybe if he didn't feel himself falling irreversibly in love with her, he might have already dragged her into the shadows by now and satisfied his craving for her perfect mouth. But he felt what was happening. Acutely. Thus, he couldn't ignore the sore weight of his heart where it sat in his chest, wondering why it hadn't been used until now. Couldn't ignore the way his throat seemed to be jammed through with pins every time she blinked at him.

Jesus Christ. Love was pain, apparently.

Love was being stripped down to the bones. Being more than willing to beg for more.

And because he wanted more than just one night, because he wanted to try his fucking hardest for more than a sweaty encounter with this woman, he slowed his step and breathed deeply in through his nose, out through his mouth.

"Everything you're thinking is right there on your face," she said to his left, echoing the words he'd said to her earlier. Because she was absolutely incredible. And he'd been denying himself due to his fear of the unknown. He was in the exact right place when they were together, and he couldn't fight that feeling anymore. More important, he needed to make sure she felt right being with him, too. As if they were standing in the exact same spot in this big fucking universe, not a single inch apart, physically or emotionally.

Was that utterly terrifying? Yeah. It was. As he'd known from the beginning, this woman threw him off-center, dashed his plans, and flaunted time like it was a suggestion. She could very well drive him completely insane. But while holding her hand and leading her into the vineyard, between the rows of fragrant nighttime vines, no other choices existed. Tomorrow no other choices would exist. Or the day or the year after that. There was only being with Hallie. He'd have to let something other than himself determine the course of his time going forward.

Chance. Possibilities he didn't control.

That realization was so heavy, so hard for a man like him to grasp, that he slowed to a stop about a hundred yards into one of the rows. As if they'd been made specifically to lock together, she walked right into his arms, her nose flattening against the side of his neck in such an endearing way, such a trustful way, it took him a moment to speak.

"Being in the vines reminded me of the fire. Until we went picking together. Now when I look out at them, I just think of you," he said, watching, fascinated by the way one of her curls looped around his finger. "Were you in St. Helena when it happened?"

His stomach was already plummeting like an elevator with a snapped cable in anticipation of her answer. He'd barely be able to stand it if she'd been scared, let alone in danger. Especially knowing he had been in town at the time.

"My grandmother and I drove south. We stayed in a motel and watched the news for five days straight." She pulled back and searched his face. "You stayed behind."

He nodded, hearing the distant crackling of burning wood. "My father and I did what we could to prepare. Evacuated everyone, moved equipment. But they said . . . fire officials told us we had six hours before the fire reached us. And it happened in one. One hour instead of six." He could still remember the way that stolen time had choked him, the way denial unzipped him straight down the middle. Time was supposed to be absolute. A foundation for everything. For the first time, it had betrayed him.

"My sister was in one of the larger sheds when it happened—she'd been loading wine stock into a truck. Just an ember carrying on the wind, they said. The whole thing was up in flames in a matter of minutes. I was acres away when it started. By the time I'd run to the building, it was engulfed. We were the only ones here, so no one heard her screaming. I almost didn't get her out." He didn't want to think about that, so he moved on briskly. "I'd never had an—"

"Wait. Go back." Was she *shaking*? "How did you get her out?"

"I went in," he explained.

"You went into a burning building to rescue your sister. I'm just clarifying."

"I . . . Yes. She needed help."

"You saved her life and she still brought you to this terrible wine tasting," Hallie murmured, shaking her head. Despite the joke, however, she appeared almost shaken by the story. "I interrupted what you were going to say. You'd never had a what?"

He rarely said the term out loud, but this was Hallie. "An anxiety episode. As a child, I had them, but not since then. Not as an adult. My schedules didn't make sense in the context of the fire. We were supposed to have six hours, and, suddenly, we're driving through smoke just hoping to escape with our lives. Time wasn't safe anymore. My sister wasn't safe. I didn't do well with it." He paused to gather his thoughts, wiping the perspiration from his palms down the sides of his pants. "I hated that feeling. That locked-up feeling. And you might think the fire would have acted as some kind of immersion therapy and I'd loosen my grip on time, realizing it can't be controlled, but I doubled down instead. I lost time. Completely. I just sort of went numb, Hallie. For days. My family was trying to salvage the winery, and mentally, I wasn't there. I did nothing to help them. All I could do was sit in a dark room and write lesson plans. Lectures. I remember almost nothing from the days after the fire.

"That's why I've been trying so hard to stay away from you. Anything that threatens this control I have . . . I've been seeing it as the enemy. When it gets ahold of me, I don't recover quickly like Garth. It's something to avoid at all costs. But I can't do that with you anymore, because you're worth burning for. You're worth turning and driving straight into the fire."

"Whoa," she whispered, the gray of her eyes swimming and starlit. "I don't know which part of that to address first. The part that maybe you're a hero for saving your sister, but you can only focus on a dark moment or—or . . ."

He stripped off his jacket and tossed it behind her onto the ground, only sparing a fleeting thought for the dry cleaning. "The part when I said I'd drive through fire for you?"

She nodded, her eyes locked on his fingers where they were unknotting his tie, then shoving the balled-up material into the right front pocket of his dress pants. "Yeah, that part."

"What about it?" he asked.

Her eyes lifted hesitantly. "What if I said I would do the same for you?"

This is what it meant to be choked up. To have his sanity in the hands of another person to do with what they wanted. "I'd be fucking grateful." He caught her by the hips and dragged her close, hissing a breath when her belly finally, finally met his aching length. "But I'd also lose my mind if you were ever in that kind of danger, so please don't ever say that out loud again."

"It was your analogy," Hallie teased, going up on her toes, a slow raking of tits and belly and hips up the front of his primed body, and he groaned loudly, there in the middle of the vineyard. "Thank you for telling me that."

Oh Jesus, he couldn't take her whispered gratitude on top of his dick being so hard. Who had sent this woman to kill him? He was hungry and desperate and ready to give up years of his life to get his hands on those breasts. "I'll tell you anything you want, just let me kiss that goddamn mouth. Let me get on top of you."

With a small sound of shock—did she not understand he was dying?—Hallie lurched higher onto her toes and gave up her mouth, letting him come from above and wreck it, broken and starved and needy, his hands trying to clutch and smooth every part of her at once, experience every inch. They tunneled through her hair and raked down her back, yanking her by the ass into the cradle of his lap, both of them gasping into the kiss over the miraculous friction they created. The chafe they kept alive with rubs and pushes and grinds.

"Tell me we're fucking tonight, Hallie," he gritted out, teeth pressed to her ear.

"Was your mouth always this dirty?" she gasped.

"No." He urged her down onto the ground, and she went, landing flat on her back on top of his spread-out jacket, her curls bouncing out in ninety directions, a sight that made his hands shake, it was so *her*. "And you can blame my colorful vocabulary on the fact that you've been bent over on your knees outside of my office window for weeks." He let his weight settle on top of her incredible curves, slowly, his breath escaping like air from a tire puncture, his balls throbbing like a son of a bitch. "*Weeks.*"

"That is the standard flower-planting position."

He reached down, gathered the hem of her dress in his hand,

and worked it up to her hips, immediately rocking into the space between her thighs, deprived at never having been there before. Being like this, with her, was where he belonged. And God, the way she moaned and arched her back, covered in moonlight and a flush, was the closest he'd ever come to magic. "Flowers are the last thing on my mind when you're on all fours," he gritted out, rocking again, gratification thick in his stomach when she pressed her knees open, grabbed the sides of his waistband, and pulled, urged, lifted. "I'm thinking of your bare ass slapping against my stomach."

"G-great," she stammered in between hot rakes of their open mouths. "I'll never be able to do my job again without blushing."

"Speaking of this blush." Christ, he could barely make out his own words, they were so slurred with lust, muffled into her neck as he traced a line downward with his tongue, over the smooth patch behind her ear, the curve of her collarbone, the sweet-smelling hollow of her throat. "How far down does it go?"

"I don't know," she breathed. "I've never checked."

"We better find out." Julian watched her face closely as he licked a path over the hills of her cleavage, needing to know they were together in this. Continuing. "Hallie. Are you wearing that goddamn polka dot bra?"

"I . . . Yes. How did you—"

Groaning, he kissed her stiff nipples through the material of her dress, the fact that she'd worn that tormenting underwear turning his dick to stone. "Let me take it off and suck them, sweetheart."

She struggled to pull in a breath. "Oh, wow. Key moment to pull out the endearment."

He opened his mouth over the stiff bud, raking his lips side to side, groaning when it swelled, grew sharper. "I've been calling you that in my head for much longer."

"Just pull my top down already," she said in a rushing laugh that got his chest so heavily involved in the moment, even more than it already was, he had to press his face between her breasts and steady himself with her rapid-fire heartbeat. Inhaling through his nose and out through his mouth until the squeeze turned bearable. Mostly. "Julian . . ."

"I know." He had no idea what that exchange meant, only that Hallie's use of his name anchored him even more, made his mouth eager for the taste of her tongue again. And he gave in to it, traveling back up to her mouth for more kissing, more wild drawing of suction and wetness, then back down to her heaving tits. At some point, they'd started working down the neckline of her dress together, or maybe the drag of his chest up and down had done it, because her breasts were almost free of her bodice and polka dot bra, so big and lush and sweet, he whispered a prayer before his first lick across her bare nipples. "First part of you I saw up close," he muttered thickly. "Last thing I want to see before I die."

She giggled, and Julian accepted that he'd be going to hell someday, because Hallie giggling while he sucked her nipples, the polka dot bra pushing them up for his attention, his hands molding those pretty mounds thoroughly, was the hottest moment of his life. Nothing would ever top it. Although he was proven wrong a few seconds later when she started to whimper, her fingernails digging into his scalp, hips restless on the ground.

"*Julian.*"

"That getting you wet?"

She nodded jaggedly, bottom lip clamped between her teeth.

"You going to let me check?" His fingertips were already trailing down her inner thigh, massaging the inside of her knee, then tracing up, up, toward the heat. "I want you more than ready, Hallie. I'll play with them until the zipper of my pants is your worst enemy."

"Oh my God."

The way she kind of melted into the ground and writhed her hips every time he said something dirty made it clear she loved it. And Julian loved it, too, the freedom to say whatever came to his mind, wanting her to know what he was thinking, down to the letter. He'd never cared before. Never spoken much at all during the act. Now he couldn't seem to keep his mouth shut, craving connection with her on every level available. Verbal, physical, emotional.

His fingers found her then, massaging through the thin nylon of her panties, dampness soaking through to meet him. *Yes. Jesus Christ, yes.* So much of it that he dropped his face between her tits and moaned, parting the folds of her flesh with a gently sawing knuckle and teasing her clit. When her hips reared up off the ground and she sobbed, he moved on instinct, capturing her mouth in a rough kiss, knuckling that sensitive little bud over and over again. The wild way she gave herself over to the kiss made him wonder if . . . was she already close?

Julian paused with his mouth on top of hers. They inhaled and exhaled together. Fast. Faster. Anticipation so real he could feel it pressing down on his spine. "You come easy, don't you, Hallie?" Looking her in the eye, he pulled down her panties, just below her pussy, trapped around the tops of her thighs. "I remember in the kitchen how sweet you got off. How quick." He parted her folds with his thumb, stroked the full length of her sex, and watched her eyes roll into the back of her head. "You're not just beautiful and sexy and—Jesus—the fucking *curves*." With a nip and tug of her earlobe, Julian pushed his middle finger inside of her. "You are a horny little thing, aren't you?"

"*Julian*."

She was saying his name, but he could only sort of hear it through the ringing in his ears. Tight. God, she was *really* tight. And the way her thighs jerked in around his hand, like the sensation of his finger was foreign? No . . . But when he looked down into her face and saw she was holding her breath, visibly waiting for him to catch up, he knew. "Hallie, you're a virgin."

A brief silence passed. "Yes."

Why wasn't he shocked? He should have been, right? This vital, spontaneous woman had somehow made it to age twentynine without exploring a sensual side of herself that was very much alive and well. The woman was practically vibrating beneath him, every single part of her engaged in what they were doing. Maybe he was just too overcome with hunger for Hallie to dwell on something so useless as surprise. His focus remained locked on the fact that she had needs *right now*. She'd decided to let him handle them and that was good enough.

If anything, he just needed to be extra sure. Before he took her virginity.

I'm her first.

Did the crowding of pride in his throat make him a caveman?

No. No, who wouldn't be fucking proud that a woman like Hallie had decided he was worthy of her first time? A man who didn't treasure this position didn't deserve it—and that was the last time he thought of men in general and Hallie in the same context, because his teeth were snapping at her neck as a result. *Mine.*

Calm the hell down.

Julian tried to inhale a steadying breath, but it brought her scent along with it and only succeeded in making him salivate. Press his finger a little deeper inside of her, just to watch the pulse jump at the base of her neck. "Hallie." Lord, he sounded like the big bad wolf. "Be one hundred percent honest with me now. Are you sure about this?"

Fingers flexing on his shoulders, she nodded vigorously. "Yes. Positive."

Thank God. "Why do you sound relieved?"

"I thought you were going to be responsible and call a stop to everything."

"That *would* be the responsible thing to do," he agreed, even while biting a path down the center of her body, nipping at her tits, her belly, her thighs, before bringing the flat of his tongue up firmly between the folds of her sex. "Your first time should be in a soft bed. Somewhere familiar. Comfortable." He pressed the V of his fingers over her flesh and strip of blond hair, opening her up to him, and he could only wish for sunlight to see her better. To memorize every ripple and shadow. "And here I am, getting ready to fuck you on the hard ground. Flat on your back with your dress up around your waist. Aren't I, sweetheart?"

Before she could answer, he drew the tip of his tongue up the center of her pussy and left it poised on top of her clit for long seconds, before wiggling it roughly. And God help him, she came. The proof of it met his tongue unexpectedly, and he didn't think, just followed instinct by lapping at her, pushing her thighs as wide as he could get them, and going for broke, licking that swollen pleasure source until she whimpered at him to stop.

"Please!"

Out of his fucking mind, horny beyond belief, he rose up over her flushed body while fumbling with his belt, his wallet, and the condom, ripping the foil packet open. She tried to help him, their hands knocking together, their mouths seeking each other for wet, illicit kisses that went straight to his head. Both of them.

"I'm putting on a condom, but I'm going to blow where it's so deep and tight, it'll feel like I'm wearing nothing—"

"Oh God, oh God."

"If I don't get inside you soon—"

"Don't even joke like that."

And so they were laughing in pure pain when he pressed his cock into her, the sound of amusement dying on a long, guttural groan from Julian. "Oh my fucking *God*," he barked into her neck, easing his hips closer, closer, meeting the resistance of untried flesh and stopping, panting, inwardly calling himself a bastard for taking something so perfect, but her fingers fisted in the elastic sides of his briefs and pulled him deep, *so motherfucking deep*, her mouth moaning, hips lifting, the insides of her knees grazing his rib cage, her eyelids fluttering.

Fuck oh fuck. That was when he started to spin out.

Out of control. He was out of control.

He thought he could do this, throw himself headfirst into everything Hallie made him feel, but he'd been foolish to underestimate the magnitude of it. With her flesh stretching around him, her gaze locked on his for comfort, affection and gratitude and—God forgive him—possessiveness almost buckled his heart. There was no schedule to fall back on. No pen and paper to take notes. There was nothing to do but lean into what she made him feel, damn the outcome or consequences. He didn't have any tools available to build a dam. With each stroke of her fingers on his face, every kiss of his jaw and shoulders, she was stripping him of every last one of them.

"Hallie," he growled into her neck, starting to move, fisting her hair, and starting to fuck her. He couldn't do anything else with her clutching at him like that, mewling every time he went deep. Was her virginity obvious? Yes. God yes. He could barely get in and out, she was so fucking snug. But it was equally obvious that she was enjoying herself. Enjoying him. Her eyes were glazed over, her lips chanting his name, and those silky soft thighs, they hugged him like they never wanted him to leave. Or stop. In fact, they urged him faster, and he went, burying his tongue in her sweet mouth and kicking his hips into a gallop. "You've been doing such bad things to my dick, sweetheart. Just bouncing around with those curls in your tight shorts, not a care in the world, huh? Well, you've got to deal with me now. You've got to let those beautiful tits out and deal with me, don't you?"

"Yes," she gasped, her flesh tightening up around him, her hips impatient. A cue, permission to go harder, faster, and he did, pressing their moaning mouths together and increasing his pace, a shudder racking him in the exact moment she learned her power. Learned that she could flex her pussy and turn him into an animal. "You like that," she whispered.

"Yes, yes, I fucking like it," he panted hoarsely. "I *love* it. Again."

And really, it was a reckless request, because he forgot his own name after that. Forgot it was her first time and they weren't all *that* far from a public gathering. When she constricted her already too-tight flesh around him, her eyes flashing with excitement over his desperate response, that was it. His fingers dug into the earth, and he went blind, fucking to relieve the ache between his thighs. Fucking to claim her as his own—no help for that. No rationalizing it.

"Mine, sweetheart, *mine*," he grunted in her ear, scoring his teeth down the side of her neck.

Who am I? He had no idea, only that this was right where he was supposed to be. With her. Even as his head spun and panic over the unknown threatened, he couldn't stop. There would never be any stopping. She was salvation and homecoming and lust and woman.

"Hallie. *Hallie.*"

"Yes."

What was he asking? No idea. But she knew. She knew and her body understood, her back arching so her clit could rub against his thrusting cock, this incredible virgin who'd learned her own body in advance and he praised her for it, bathing her neck with his tongue and scooping his hands beneath her ass, anchoring them so he could angle down and stroke where she needed, exultant when she whimpered brokenly in response and shook into another orgasm, her pussy clamping around him, making it impossible for him to do anything but pump deep and follow, the two of them shaking in the dirt together, mouths frantic, hands squeezing, trying to get through to the other side.

Relief like Julian felt shouldn't even exist. It was too potent. Too powerful. How would he go about his daily life ever again knowing this collision of power and weakness was available to him? To them?

He tried not to collapse on top of her and failed, his body utterly replete of tension. But she welcomed him, their tongues moving together lazily in each other's mouths, her hands molding his ass like clay inside his loosened pants. With . . . a sort of ownership that he couldn't bestow fast enough. "I'm yours, too," he said, still regaining his breath. Would he ever catch it again? "In case I forgot to mention that."

"I read between the lines," she murmured drowsily.

There was nothing to do but kiss her, savor the catch in her throat. For him. When she needed to breathe he pulled back, studying her, still unable to break the connection of their bodies, though he needed to soon. "I love you like this. Drowsy and pinned to the ground where you can't make trouble."

Those tiny, feminine muscles jumped along with the corner of her mouth. "Are you sure?"

"I take it back," he said in a gruff rush, his shaft swelling back to life. In a matter of minutes, he'd be capable of taking her again. Unbelievably, he *needed* to. More than he could remember needing anything. Even with his sweat still drying from the last time. This was love. This was infatuation. There was no way out, and he wasn't looking for an exit. No, he was sealing all of them shut. But was he going to fuck her again on the hard ground in the rapidly dropping temperature instead of caring for her like she deserved? Also no. As much as this was going to kill him. With a wince, Julian pulled out, took care of the condom. "Come home with me," he said, watching as she fixed her dress, covering love-bitten breasts and thighs chafed from the material of his pants. *Mine.* "Let me do this better."

"Wait." She blinked at him. "There's a better?"

His hearty laugh echoed across the vineyard.

WHEN THEY REACHED the lighted area surrounding the barn, he took stock of Hallie's appearance, pulling pieces of straw and mulch from her hair, dusting dirt off her calves and elbows. She did the same for him, though he'd sustained far less damage. He pulled her close and whispered in the shadow of the barn about how she should wear her hair to cover the love bite on her neck, their fingers tangling together, mouths unable to stop connecting, lips brushing, kisses deepening.

Finally, they managed to muster some decent behavior, holding hands on their way back into the barn, which was now . . . empty.

They stopped short.

Well, not entirely empty.

Natalie and the SEAL—August, right?—were toe to toe, their noses inches apart. But this time, they weren't flirting. No, he knew his sister's "pissed off" posture when he saw it.

"Uh-oh," Hallie murmured.

"I was only making a suggestion," Natalie said, very succinctly, up at the hulking military man. "I grew up on a vineyard— fermentation is in my blood."

"Only problem with that, baby, is I didn't ask."

"Well, you should have asked someone. Because your wine tastes like demon piss."

"Didn't stop you from drinking a gallon of it," he pointed out calmly.

"Maybe I needed to be drunk to consider sleeping with you!"

The man grinned. Or bared his teeth. Hard to tell from this distance. "Offer is still open, Natalie. As long as you promise to stop talking."

With that, Natalie threw wine in August's face.

Julian shot forward, no idea how the SEAL was going to react. But he worried for nothing, because the man didn't even flinch. Instead, he licked the wine off his own chin and winked at her. "Tastes fine to me."

"I hate you."

"The feeling is mutual."

Angling her face toward the rafters, she shrieked through her teeth. "I can't believe the things I was going to let you *do* to me."

That gave August pause. He gave Natalie a very distinct once-over that Julian immediately wished he could erase from his brain. "Just out of curiosity," August started, "those things were . . . ?"

"All right." Julian cleared his throat. "I'll stop you both there."

"Where have you been?" Natalie cried out, throwing up her hands at her brother's approach. "You left me here with this *Neanderthal* and—" She spied Hallie over his shoulder, and her lips twitched with humor. "Oh. I see. Well, at least one of us got laid."

The back of Julian's neck heated. "Time to go, Nat."

She'd already started in his direction, but her steps slowed now. "You haven't called me that since we were in high school."

Natalie shook herself and kept walking, past Julian and out of the barn, to where Hallie waited. She didn't turn around once, so she didn't see August's regretful expression, but Julian did. It significantly turned down the volume on what he'd been *planning* to say, though not completely. "Talk to my sister like that again and I'll break your jaw."

August's eyebrows shot up, as if unexpectedly impressed, and Julian left the barn. He found Natalie and Hallie leaning up against the side of his rental where he'd parked it along the main road. Hallie was making Natalie laugh, but he still spied a fair amount of tension bracketing his sister's mouth.

"Hey . . ." Hallie rubbed his sister's shoulder and came toward him, tightening everything south of his chin. God, she was beautiful. "You should go take care of your sister. Anyway, I've never left the dogs overnight. I'm not sure if it would be a popular move."

"Jesus," he muttered.

"What?"

"When you spend nights at my house, you'll have to bring them, won't you?"

She peered up at him. "Worth it?"

"Bring a whole circus, Hallie."

Even after everything they'd done tonight, a breathless sort of surprise danced across her features. "It wouldn't be that far off." Worry cut through the surprise, but she tried to hide it with a smile. "Are you sure you're ready for that?"

"Yes."

That's what he said. And he damn well meant it. Because he was ready for Hallie in his life. In fact, her being there felt long past due. If there was a whisper of self-doubt lingering, drifting to the present from that night four years ago, he was more than willing to ignore it in favor of kissing his girlfriend good night.

Chapter Nineteen

Hallie stood in the moonlight reading through her final secret admirer letter.

And, yes, this would definitely be the last one. She was coming clean.

After the wine tasting, she'd gone straight home and confessed everything to a piece of lined notebook paper and walked right back out the door with it, refusing to give herself a chance to back out. But *God*, did her actions sound stupid in black-and-white.

Dear Julian,

This is Hallie. I'm the one who has been writing you the letters. You're welcome to hire a handwriting analysis expert, but I think once you've read through the full contents, you'll agree no sane person would own up to something so completely asinine unless it was true.

I had a massive crush on you in high school. Like, planning weddings in homeroom massive. Meeting you as an adult, it seemed obvious that I'd imagined the spark between us. Or that we'd grown too far in opposite directions to ever meet in the middle. Now I realize that love between adults means embracing flaws as well as the sparkly stuff.

You are a river that flows in one direction. There is some turbulence under the surface, but your current keeps you moving, positive you're going the right way. Meanwhile I'm a swirling eddy, unable to choose a course. But whirlpools have a surface, too. They have an underneath. I just wanted to expose it to you and see if we could relate. I wanted to relate to you, because everything I said in those letters was true. I do admire you. I always have. You're so much more than you give yourself credit for. You're thoughtful and heroic and fair. The kind of person who wants to be better and sees their own faults is someone I want to spend time with. They'll complement mine if we want it bad enough.

I'm sorry I lied to you. I hope I haven't ruined everything, because while I thought I was in love with high school Julian, I didn't know him. I know the man, though. And now I understand the difference between love and infatuation. I've felt both for you, fifteen years apart. Please forgive me. I'm trying to change.

Hallie

That last line had been erased and rewritten several times. Something about that vow didn't sit quite right with Hallie. She *was* trying to make decisions with more confidence and to take a moment to think before making potentially disastrous ones. She'd even sat down and started a color-coded diagram of her plans for the library garden this morning. But there would always be an element of chaos inside of her. It had been there since she could remember, and even her grandmother hadn't been able to contain it. Not entirely.

Did she want to change for a man?

Nope.

Except he'd already started to change for *her*.

It's come to my attention that I am far more wrong for you than the other way around, Hallie. You're nothing short of breathtaking. Unique and beautiful and bold. And I'm a goddamn idiot if I ever made you feel otherwise.

Let me learn.

Did it qualify as changing for a man if the man was rearranging himself at the same time? Or was that simply the nature of compromise?

There was only one way to find out, and that was . . . trying. Giving their relationship a chance, up close and personal. No more hiding behind letters. No more hiding, period. They were vulnerable around each other. Had been since the beginning. And that was scary for people like them, but there was also a breath of possibility whispering in her ear, telling her that complete vulnerability could be glorious. It could be totally right. With Julian.

A chance to grow alongside someone, to adjust together until they met in the middle.

Emotionally, they had places to go. Physically?

They had that part down. Real well.

She'd dropped her defenses in the vineyard tonight like a bad habit.

Thinking about what they'd done, about breathless words spoken in chokes and rushes, not even the cold breeze could cool her cheeks. In all of her fantasies, she'd never imagined intimacy like Julian had shown her tonight. That desperate, down-in-the-dirt slaking of needs. She'd never expected to relinquish herself so totally to lust. To sensation. Or to have the wild feelings in her chest play such a part in what her body craved.

Standing there on the darkness of the path, she wanted him again. Not just the release of tension he'd give her, but the press of his weight. The scent of salt and wine and cologne, their fingers intertwining, his hips twisting and bucking between her thighs. She'd never been more honest in her life than she'd been underneath him, no critical thoughts for herself or second guesses. Just letting go. Just flying.

Hallie squinted into the distance toward Vos Vineyard and could just make out the silver outline of the guesthouse. She could go there now. Knock on his door and hand deliver the letter. Maybe she owed him that. Especially after he'd shown up tonight at the tasting with flowers and an apology. She could do the same, couldn't she? Face the music in person? And the last thing she wanted was to start down the road toward a relationship with a lie. She felt the increasing strain of that deception with every passing moment.

Hallie took a few steps in the direction of the guesthouse, her bravery slipping away like pebbles falling from a hole in her pocket. Eventually she stopped, the breeze blowing curls across her line of vision. Julian might read the letter and need time to process everything. To really consider her words. Would she be putting him on the spot by standing over his shoulder while he read it? Wouldn't it be better to end this journey how it started—with a letter? At least he'd have space to think. To consider what he wanted.

Decision made, Hallie tucked the letter as securely as possible into the designated stump crack and jogged up the path, trying to put as much distance as possible between her and the confession before she changed her mind and took it back. What if the admirer just sort of . . . vanished? Stopped writing? Julian would never know what she'd done.

Nope. You're not getting off that easy.

In a matter of hours, her craziest idea yet would be revealed to Julian and she'd just have to hope . . .

She'd have to hope he still wanted the circus.

AFTER RETURNING HOME from her letter-drop mission, Hallie had slept fitfully, the dogs seeming to judge her from the end of the bed. She'd woken up to find she'd overslept well into the afternoon, her stomach gathering like wool at the numbers on the clock. Julian would be getting ready for his run. Mere minutes from discovering her secret.

She got up and walked the dogs. Fed them.

Brewed coffee and sat in her backyard among the periwinkle hydrangeas, legs curled up beneath her on the patio furniture. Her fingers drummed on the side of her mug, a rapid-fire heartbeat in her chest. Julian must have found the letter by now. He was probably back home reading through it for the eighth time, wondering how he'd mistaken psychosis for charm. Any second now, her phone would ring and he would very curtly attempt to end things—and while she wouldn't blame him, she *would* try to change his mind.

That was one item she'd managed to resolve in the middle of her sleepless night.

Would she fight him if he tried to break up with her?

Yes. Of course. She was worth a little vexing, right? She was a slightly frazzled, often muddied gardener who could laugh easily, even while carrying around a lake of hurt inside of her. There was often no rhyme or reason to her professional ideas, but didn't they turn out beautiful enough? Likewise, when she did something ridiculous like steal cheese or begin a secret-admirer-letter-writing campaign, didn't she mean well?

Yes.

She liked her place. She loved her people.

She just needed to find a better way to channel her inherited impulses. She would, too, because sitting there in her backyard and waiting for the man she loved to discover her lies was torturous, and she never wanted to feel that way again.

When noon rolled around and there was no call or front-door arrival from Julian, Hallie set down her stone-cold cup of coffee and dialed Lavinia.

"Afternoon, love," Lavinia sang, the cash register dinging in the background. "How was the tasting last night?"

She heard a distant echo of Julian groaning her name. "Great," she responded throatily. "It was great. Listen . . . has Julian jogged past the shop yet?"

"Yes, ma'am. He was early today, actually." Someone ordered a box of assorted donuts. "Coming right up," Lavinia said, before dropping her voice. "Your man ran past the window shirtless at eleven fifteen. I remember the exact time, because that was the moment I forgot my wedding vows. Pretended to adjust the angle of the specials board on the sidewalk, but really I was watching the professor's sweaty back muscles flex in the sunshine. There's no reason you should have all the fun."

"Couldn't agree more." She paused in the middle of her pacing. "He was . . . shirtless?"

"Utterly. Beautifully. That will be thirteen fifty."

"You ogled my boyfriend, and I'm supposed to pay you?"

"I was talking to the customer. And who are you calling 'boyfriend'?" Her tone grew more and more excited. "Is that official, then?"

"Well . . ."

Lavinia groaned. "Fuck sake, woman. What now?"

"I confessed everything. In a final, no-holds-barred secret admirer letter. If he went jogging almost an hour ago, he should have found it by now. In which case, I might no longer be his girlfriend. At least during the estrangement period wherein I wiggle my way back into his good graces and we all have a big laugh about this at Thanksgiving."

"You've thought this through, which is unusual."

Pacing again, Hallie pressed a palm to her churning stomach. "I deserve that."

Her friend told the customer to have a good day. "Well, I might be able to shed some light on why your momentary boyfriend hasn't called yet cursing you to eternal damnation." She paused, sounding a little smug. "He took a different route."

Hallie skidded to a stop. "What do you mean he took a different route?"

"On his run. He didn't turn down the usual path."

"Let me get this straight. He was shirtless *and* he deviated? He shirtless deviated?"

"That is correct. Which leads me to my next question . . ." In the background, a door slapped shut and Hallie heard the flicker of a lighter. "How good was the sex?"

Halle sputtered. "What?"

"Babe. I have experience in these man matters. I left London to find a husband because I had effectively exhausted the search, if you know what I mean. No *stones* left unturned."

"Well, that needs to be on a T-shirt."

"Point is," Lavinia plowed on, undeterred, "I know a man who's been laid and laid well when I spot one. He stirred my pheromones from two blocks away."

"Okay, you're planning to leave *Julian's* stones unturned, right?"

"Oh, shut up. I'm a happily married woman. Just having a peek." Hallie heard the crackle of the end of Lavinia's cigarette as she inhaled. "Again, my point. You inspired him not only to run about town like a lion who just mated the lioness. But you inspired him to take a different path."

Pleasure warred with distress just below Hallie's collarbone. "But he won't find my letter that way."

"You'll have to tell him in person."

Not two seconds later, Hallie's doorbell rang.

OF COURSE, THE dogs lost their minds.

It wasn't very often that someone rang her doorbell. Even UPS had wised up and started dropping off packages unannounced to avoid the canine drama that ensued at the press of a button.

This time, however, as the dog sirens went off around her, they were no match for the explosives going off in her belly.

Julian.

Somehow she knew Julian stood on her stoop.

She confirmed it a moment later when she looked through the peephole, getting a magnified eyeful of Adam's apple and stubble that made her fingers twitch, her inner thighs growing ticklish at the memory of having his five o'clock shadow there.

"Julian?" she asked, unnecessarily. Stalling, perhaps, in an attempt to find out if he'd doubled back, gone his typical route, and found the letter?

"Yeah. It's me." He chuckled warmly, a sound that reached through the door and made her tingly. "Sorry for setting off the alarm."

Having recognized Julian's voice, the boys' tone had changed from defensive to excited. Why did that make her heart swell to the size of a balloon? They liked him. She loved him.

And he definitely, definitely hadn't found the letter.

Which meant she'd have to tell him in person. As in, right now. Before what was happening between them got any more serious. *Oh man oh man oh man.* Should she open with a joke? Unlocking the door, she cracked it an inch and found the most devastatingly handsome man in existence staring down at her. "Just remember that no matter what happens when you come inside, I have a lint roller."

"Consider me warned."

Biting her lip, she opened the door the remaining distance and stepped back, gesturing for him to come inside. He had to duck slightly to get beneath the doorframe, like a giant being welcomed into a dollhouse—and that theme continued as he stepped closer to Hallie, looking over her head and slowly scanning her cottage from left to right.

"It's exactly what I thought it would look like," he said, finally, voice pitched low. "Colorful and homey . . . and slightly cluttered."

Her mouth fell open on a gasp. "Are you serious? I just performed the biggest clean of my lifetime!"

Julian was laughing, lines fanning out around his eyes. "That wasn't a criticism." The smile on his mouth dropped in degrees, and he reached up to thread his fingers through her hair. "How could it be when it reminds me of you?"

The organ in her chest flopped over with all the grace of a cinder block. "Y-you're calling me cluttered, and I'm expected to find that romantic?"

He grazed their lips together, those long fingers spearing farther into her hair until he cradled her scalp, controlling the angle of her neck. Gently, he tugged, pulling her head back, and then—*oh Lord*—he ran his open mouth up the front of her throat. "If the clutter is yours, I want it," he whispered against her mouth. "If you're late, I don't care. Just fucking show up."

Hallie's knees, ankles, and hips nearly gave out, all at the same time. Especially when his grip tightened in her hair, angling her one way and his mouth another, devouring her like a meal. The kiss was leashed, but Hallie could feel the physical vibrations and knew it cost him a heaping dose of willpower to hold back. And she didn't want that. With his stubble rasping against her chin and his minty tongue licking into her mouth, she wanted more of what they'd done last night. Badly. But he ended the kiss with a growl before she could shed her robe and demand to be taken, his forehead pressing down on hers.

"I took your virginity on the ground last night, Hallie."

"Objection. I *gave* you my virginity on the ground last night, Julian."

"Fair enough." He seemed to be performing a serious study of the curls on the top of her head, that deep valley present between his brows. "But I didn't use as much care as I would have . . ."

"As you would have normally?"

"What do you mean 'normally'?" He frowned. "That implies that there is even the remotest comparison between you and anyone else."

Oh.

Okay, then.

"So I'm abnormal now?" she breathed, rearranging her entire definition of romance.

Apparently it was not wine and roses. It was this man telling her she was cluttered, perpetually late, and unusual.

"Definitely that." He took a long sampling of Hallie's mouth, until she was weaving drunkenly on her feet. "I meant to say, I didn't use as much care as I would have liked." The heel of his hand scrubbed down her spine, fisting the material of her robe. "If I hadn't let what I feel for you build until it was out of control."

Hallie stared deliriously up at the ceiling, her brilliant, beautiful lover speaking a uniquely blunt version of poetry into her ear. And she was supposed to tell him about the letters? That they'd come from her? Right now? She was just supposed to shatter this perfect bond of intimacy and honesty they'd formed? This sense that everything was right in the world when they were skin to skin, mouth to mouth?

But you haven't been honest. Not entirely.

Sure, every word of those letters had come straight from the heart. But she'd misrepresented herself. Let him believe he was writing to a perfect stranger. And worse, when he'd quoted her exact words, she'd let the opportunity to be truthful pass. Well, she couldn't regret it more than she did in this moment, when he held her so tightly, she had to limit her breaths.

"I loved what we did last night," she whispered, because at least it was the truth. And, since it felt so good to tell him the truth, she gave him more. "I want to do it again."

"We will," he said quickly, snaking a forearm beneath her butt and drawing Hallie onto her toes, aligning their laps, tilting his hips, their breaths accelerating like twin engines between them. "We damn well will, Hallie. But I'm taking you out first."

"You are?" She felt him thicken between them. "You have a plan, don't you?"

He bit off a curse and eased his hips back, holding hers away in a crushing grip. "Yes. I'm setting the tone." His mouth swooped down and caught her lips, delivering a dizzying onslaught of strokes from his tongue. "And the tone is, you're my girlfriend, not a girl I hook up with in a field and send home in an Uber, all right? I couldn't sleep last night. It felt like I'd left everything undone with you."

Last night.

When she'd been dropping off her confession letter at the stump.

Tell him.

He was being so honest, and she needed to do the same. But would telling him the truth only ruin everything? At the very least, she could bank a few more kisses before dropping the bomb.

"I didn't feel undone," she said, dazed from the prolonged contact, the shape of him, the heat they were generating. "I felt . . . done."

His rich laugh against her mouth sent a warm shiver down her spine. "Damn."

"Damn?"

"I don't want to leave you." He wound a curl around his index finger and let it spring free, watching it happen in fascination. "But there is a luncheon this afternoon in Calistoga. It's the twentieth anniversary of my father forming the Napa Valley Association of Vintners."

"I thought your father was in Italy."

"He is. Natalie and I are accepting the honor on his behalf, I'm making a speech . . ." That trench between his eyebrows now was accompanied by two more. "I told my mother I would."

"What's bothering you about doing it?"

A gruff sound came from his throat. He took his time, as if trying to pinpoint the exact source of his irritation. "Napa likes reminders of tradition. My father and grandfather were a huge part of establishing St. Helena as a wine destination—I'm not denying that. They're not the ones who kept it running when it barely had a pulse, though."

She searched his eyes. "You're talking about your mother."

"Hmm. She should be recognized, just as much as Dalton. More, possibly, at this stage." For a moment, he remained deep in thought, then cleared his throat. Looked at her, expression suddenly formal. "Would you come with us?"

"To the luncheon?"

"Yes."

"I . . . Are you sure?"

He brushed his thumb across her bottom lip, appearing riveted by the crease that ran down the middle. "If I've learned anything since we met for a second time, Hallie, it's that I'm much, much happier when you're with me."

Oh. Mama. He meant every word of that, too, didn't he? His honesty was so arresting, all she could do for long moments was stare. Obviously, after that admission, she was going to the luncheon come hell or high water. If she could be there to help him through a difficult task, she wanted that responsibility.

That privilege.

She did a mental inventory of her closet. "How long do I have to get ready?"

Visibly eager to calculate time, Julian looked at his watch. "Twenty-one minutes."

"Oh my God," she said, pushing away from him.

Todd picked up on her nervous energy and started to howl.

"Can you choose something out of my closet while I take a shower?" She shouted the second half of the question through her en suite bathroom door. "Whatever is appropriate for the dress code."

A moment later, there was a thud on the floor of her bedroom. "Hallie, are you aware that half of your possessions have been stuffed into this closet?"

Quickly, she flipped on the shower spray. "What? I can't hear you."

Muffled grumbling.

With a smile on her face, she pinned up her hair, showered, dried off, and applied some quick makeup. Her favorite black bra was hanging on the back of the door in the bathroom, and she put it on, wrapping a towel around the rest of her. She hesitated with her hand on the knob, wondering if it was too soon to walk around in front of him in a towel. With time constraints being what they were, did she have a choice? Blowing out a breath, she pushed into the bedroom. And there was Julian Vos, sitting on her bed, with a flower-print cocktail dress draped across his lap, as if he'd walked right out of her fantasies. Tall and dark and serious against the girlish white comforter.

"I have no idea if . . ."

He trailed off, the lump in his throat moving up and down, fingers curling into fists on the edge of her bed.

"You have no idea if what?" she asked.

"If this dress passes as business casual." He watched her move to the dresser and tug open her top drawer, selecting a pair of thin, nude-colored hipsters that would work for the outfit he'd picked. "I just want to see you in it."

Hallie gasped.

That last part was said against her bare shoulder.

When did he cross the room?

"I love that dress," she said with an effort. "I—it's a good choice."

His hand closed around the knot of her towel, gripped, and twisted, his mouth skating down the slope of her neck. "Can I see you without this on?"

Self-consciousness tried to ruin the party. Of course it did. She'd never been totally naked in front of a man before. Not in the light, especially. And while she loved her body, she loved it clothed more than she loved it unclothed. When she could control what and how much people saw of her thighs and stomach and butt. Could control how material sat against her curves. If he removed the towel, everything would be on display, down to her last dimple.

"Hallie, you can say no."

"It's stupid to be nervous. After last night . . ."

"It's not stupid." He kissed the area behind her ear, biting the spot gently. "Does it blow my mind that you're hesitant to show me your naked body when I would swim across a lake of fire for it? A little."

Her face warmed. "You might be picturing something else, though."

She felt him frown against her shoulder. "Would it help if you knew what I'm picturing?"

"I don't know. Maybe?"

His mouth settled in the hair above her ear. "I think you're soft. No, I *know* you're soft. I think you work hard in the sun and the dirt . . . and it shows in your hands and calves and shoulders. But the fact that you're a woman is also very . . . fucking . . . obvious. You have these incredible tits." He slid his hand up the front of her towel and slowly squeezed each mound, bringing her nipples to attention. "You've got hips. The kind that let me be a little extra rough last night." Her vision started to double, then triple, the perfume bottles on top of her dresser multiplying into an army. "I can still feel my sweaty stomach sliding up and down on top of your belly. I already love every inch of it. I probably left some chafing behind to prove it, huh?"

She managed a dazed nod.

"You show me when you're ready, sweetheart." His hand dropped, fingertips trailing up the inside of her thigh. Toward her wetness. *This* she wasn't afraid for him to know. To see and feel. They were past the point of pretending they didn't turn each other on, and, right now, she was so far over the borderline of turned on, she needed a passport. "In the meantime, can I leave you with a final thought?"

"Yes," she whispered.

His huge hand closed around her sex. The whole thing. He just swallowed it up in his grip and held it. Hard. "I know every little jiggle of this body. They've taken turns making my cock hard. One by one by fucking one." He clutched firmly enough to make her whimper. "Your curves shake when I'm packing this thing tight. I know it for a fact now. The parts you're nervous to show me are actually what make me hard, Hallie." Slowly, so slowly, he parted her flesh with his middle finger and dragged that digit through her soaked valley. "You think about that until tonight."

Secret admirer who?

Involuntarily, the letters were pushed to the back of her mind. To be thought about again . . . tomorrow.

Definitely tomorrow.

Chapter Twenty

When Julian woke up that morning, he thought his biggest challenge would be the speech he was about to deliver. He'd put together some acknowledgments for the association recognizing Dalton Vos, their founding member—people Julian didn't know, who greatly admired his father. He was accustomed to that. To smiling and agreeing with admirers who spoke of Dalton's ingenuity, his revolutionary techniques and dedication to quality.

But as an adult man who knew a lot more now about responsibility, it had grown harder to grin and bear the compliments about his father. On the way through the lobby of the resort-winery, he'd shaken hands with winemakers and critics who spoke Dalton's name as if they were conferring about a saint.

But it turned out trying to navigate the current moods of the three extremely different women in his life was even more difficult. His mother sat to his left, a smile glued so securely to her face, she looked almost maniacal. Natalie was already on her second helping of Cabernet and appeared to be looking very intently for the meaning of life in the bottom of the glass.

And then there was Hallie.

She was on his right, her eyes on the speaker at the front of the ballroom. But there was a very distinct pinkness scaling the back of her neck, probably because *his* eyes were most definitely not on the speaker. Nowhere in the vicinity whatsoever. They were on those little curls at the nape of her neck, and she obviously felt him staring. Before they'd left her cottage, she'd worked her hair up into some sort of twist on the top of her head, and he'd never seen those extra-small ringlets of blonde up close before. If they were not sitting at the very front of a watchful audience, he would press his face to the spot from which they sprung and inhale the hell out of her.

To say she looked good in the dress he'd picked would be an unforgivable understatement. Did she realize the pink and green flowers splashed across the front of her dress corresponded with the exact parts his hands were dying to touch? Although he suspected the flowers could be in any location and he would want to touch that exact place, because every inch of her consumed and fascinated him.

Julian's fingers twitched in his lap, and he tamped down the urge to wind one of those curls around the same finger he'd touched her with earlier. Christ, they were going to call him up onstage any minute to make a speech and he had a semi— because of *ringlets*—so he needed to stop thinking of Hallie in that towel. With no panties on.

Feeling as if he had some sort of fever, Julian removed his suit jacket and hung it on the back of Hallie's chair, liking the way it looked there a little too much. A man didn't hang his jacket on the back of a woman's chair unless they were together, and now the room knew—and that satisfied something in Julian he'd never known existed.

Mine.

He'd said that to her last night in the vineyard, and it rang in his head now until he forced a swallow and tore his eyes from the nape of her flushed neck.

Later.

Julian let out a slow breath and turned his attention to Natalie and Corinne. His sister was now building a fort out of sugar packets and cocktail napkins. And he could see her nervous actions weren't lost on Hallie, who sent him a look of concern over her shoulder. Nor had they gone unnoticed by his mother, whose pasted-on smile had dimmed somewhat during the introductory speech. And if this moment, this few seconds in time, were taking place a month ago, he might have been thinking of nothing but the pacing of his prepared words. The schedule of the luncheon and how it fit into his day, the routine he would need to complete upon arriving back at the guesthouse later.

But this string of seconds wasn't happening a month ago. They were right now.

And he wouldn't trade this moment for any other. Background noise and movement in the ballroom blurred everything except for the women surrounding him. He reached for Hallie's hand beneath the table; then, deciding it wasn't enough to have only that one connection with her, he moved his chair closer until her scent was stronger and inhaled deeply.

All moments were not equal.

Every second was not a grain of sand in an hourglass.

Time was bigger than him.

Maybe time wasn't something that could be controlled at all; it was about making time matter with the people he cared about.

The speaker called Julian's name from the podium, and he

stood, took a few steps before realizing he was still holding on to Hallie's hand. He'd nearly dragged her off the seat.

"Sorry." He bent his head over her knuckles and kissed them, viewing the rapid intake of her breath and parting of her lips with the clarity of a man who'd just thrown out the script. Or had it been thrown out for him—he wasn't totally sure, and, ironically, he didn't have time to figure it out.

Julian accepted a plaque from the speaker. They stood shoulder to shoulder and posed for a flurry of photographs before he found himself in front of the microphone. He angled it higher to accommodate his height and set the plaque down on the podium. That's when he realized the note cards containing bullet points for his speech were in the pocket of the jacket hanging on the back of Hallie's chair. That really should have thrown him off, but he only found himself looking down at the table of women with a sense of . . . freedom.

The hell with the speech.

"Thank you very much for this honor. My father is grateful to the NVAV for recognizing his early contribution to the association after twenty years of success. He sends his appreciation from Italy." Julian paused, traced a finger over the gold engraving. "I'm not going to accept this recognition on his behalf, though. I'm going to accept it on behalf of my mother."

Some murmuring started around the ballroom, heads ducking toward each other, whispers ensuing behind hands. Julian didn't really see any of it, because he was busy watching Hallie and Natalie and Corinne. People. His people.

Corinne appeared to be shell-shocked, but there was a distinct sheen in her eyes that, in turn, created an odd prickle in his throat. Natalie's house of sugar packets had lost the battle with gravity, and finally, Hallie—God, he was so glad she was there—was smiling at him, her knuckles white in her lap. She was outshining the entire room, so beautiful he stumbled over his words and simply stared. What the hell had he been about to say?

Focus.

"My mother picked up the pieces after the fire four years ago," he continued. "It might not be her family name on the label, but her fingerprints are on every bottle that leaves the vineyard, I can promise you that. Along with the hard work of our manager, Manuel, and the grounds crew that cultivate the grapes as if their last name were Vos, too. The vineyard only thrives because of them, because of Corinne Vos, and as much as we appreciate this honor, she should be acknowledged here today. And every day. Thank you."

"I'M JUST SAYING, it would have added to the drama if you'd thrown the plaque across the ballroom into that wineglass pyramid," Natalie said from the other side of the table, all while signaling the waiter for another round of drinks. Instead of staying for the free luncheon, they'd sensed the chill in the air and decided to find a local restaurant instead. "You offended the wine gods today, bro. They are going to demand a sacrifice as payment. Anyone know any virgins?"

At that, Hallie promptly choked on her Sauvignon Blanc.

Doing his best to remain expressionless, Julian squeezed her leg under the table. "Not a single one—you?"

"Not since our mother made me go to band camp in tenth grade. And I'm pretty sure the virgins were no longer innocent once it ended." His sister fell back in her seat a little. "Band camp: an orgy with flutes."

"Lower your voice, Natalie," Corinne hissed, but there was a sparkle in her eyes that hadn't been there prior to the luncheon. "And that was a very reputable band program. You must be exaggerating."

"We secretly called it *bang* camp, Mother."

Corinne spat out her sip of wine, only managing to catch the tail end of spray with her napkin. "Jesus Christ," she choked out. "Please spare me the knowledge that you participated in any kind of . . . banging."

"Unless it was drum related," Hallie qualified, making Natalie laugh.

Julian tugged her closer in the booth until their thighs were pressed together, her shoulder tucked beneath his armpit, curls close enough to count. *There.*

"What you said today, Julian . . ." Corinne said abruptly, some light color staining her cheeks. "You didn't have to do that. My work at the winery has been hard, but it was never a burden. It's very rewarding."

"Rewarding work can still be acknowledged," Julian said.

"Yes." His mother shifted in her seat. "But I didn't *need* it to be pointed out publicly."

Julian shook his head. "No, of course not."

"That being said, it was very . . . nice." She reached for the breadbasket, then seemingly decided against it. Fussed with her hair instead. "I didn't mind it."

Natalie buried her face in a cloth napkin. "Your son makes a dramatic speech in your honor in front of the foofiest winos in Napa and all you can say is 'It was nice.'"

"I believe I said '*very* nice.'"

"Why are we the way that we are?" Natalie mused at the ceiling.

Corinne rolled her eyes at Natalie's dramatics. "Would you rather we hugged constantly and had things like movie night?"

"I don't know," Natalie muttered. "Maybe? Just to experiment."

Surprisingly, his mother didn't seem inclined to drop the subject of togetherness right away. "Well, I'd need my children to stick around awhile for that. If they are so inclined." She folded her hands on the table, her gaze fixing on Julian. "Julian, your fresh set of eyes on the vineyard is already making a difference. We have a plan—and I can't remember the last time I could say that. I hope we can put your father's harsh words where they belong. In the past. Forgotten. You aren't merely welcome to help manage the winery . . . I would really like that. I hope it's not temporary."

Julian could feel Hallie's questioning eyes on the side of his face. She was likely wondering what exactly his father had said to him. After the fire. After he'd pulled Natalie out of the shed where she'd been cornered by flames. That's when the second half of the anxiety hit, making up for lost time, the adrenaline wearing off and the numbness stealing in. Rendering him useless to everyone when they needed him most.

It had all happened, right there in front of his family.

You've always been a fucking head case, haven't you? Jesus Christ. Look at you. Pull yourself together. Stick to teaching and just . . . stay away from what I've built, all right? Stay away from the vineyard.

Yes, he now was determined to help revitalize the winery with or without the approval of his father, but would that niggle of doubt in his abilities ever truly go away? Maybe. Maybe not. But his independent mother was openly asking for help. She really needed it—and he *wanted* to give it. Wanted to bring the land of his legacy back from the brink of failure and help it thrive. For so long, he hadn't allowed himself to miss the place. The process. But just like Natalie said to the SEAL last night, fermentation was in his blood.

And yeah, last but certainly far from least, *Hallie was here.*

"I'm not going anywhere," he said, looking down at the woman herself.

Letting her know. *I'm staying. We're doing this.*

God, she was beautiful. He couldn't stop staring—

Natalie coughed into her fist, effectively breaking the spell between them. "Let's circle back to my days in bang camp."

Julian shook his head at Natalie. "Let's not. It was bad enough watching my sister's attempts at flirting this week. Not once but twice."

Natalie sat up straighter. "*Attempts?*"

Julian's mouth twitched. "I'll let the end result speak for itself."

"Oh you're the *expert*, are you?" His sister sputtered a moment, before her attention zipped to Hallie. "Since my brother seems to be implying that he's an expert at flirting, please tell us about his masterful technique."

Hallie dove in without a single hesitation, flattening a hand to her chest. "Well, first, he forgot we knew each other in high school. That *really* got the ball rolling. But then . . ." She fanned her face. "He criticized my gardening technique and called me chaotic. That really sealed the deal."

Memories stomped to the forefront of his mind, his stomach roiling. He turned to Hallie to apologize, but she spoke again before he could get there.

"Unfortunately, he foiled my plan to ignore him, when he bought three cases of wine from my favorite shop on Grapevine Way. Corked. They've been in danger of closing down for a while and it was my grandmother's favorite place. I told him that, never knowing he would have business cards made for Lorna and finagle you all into passing them out at Wine Down. *And then* have a brand-new awning installed, giving the place a much-needed face-lift that would triple her business overnight."

Julian realized his jaw was in his lap and snapped his mouth shut. "You knew?"

"I knew."

He grunted, finding it difficult to look at her in public with that shy gratitude on her gorgeous face. He didn't need credit for his deeds, but the proof that they'd served their purpose and made her happy? God, he'd choose her smile over oxygen, right here and now. Any day of the week. And if she thought she was happy now, tonight could not come fast enough. "Why didn't you say anything?"

"I was holding out for Corked's new line of merch, of course."

"T-shirts and corkscrews would be a good start," he said gruffly.

When did he get close enough to kiss her? With a hard clearing of his throat, Julian put an appropriate distance between them. But that distance didn't last very long, because his sister, wine drunk as usual, said something next that made Hallie scoot closer. "Don't forget about how he masterminded children's story time at Wine Down, Hallie." She dropped her voice to a baritone. "'I don't like it when Hallie is in distress. I will explode if I don't fix it for her.'"

All right. Now he was starting to sweat. "Enough, Natalie."

"Did you really . . . you said that?"

"Perhaps some version of it," he answered briskly. "Are we ready to order?"

"I'll have one of you, please," Hallie said, for his ears alone. In a way that was clearly meant to be spoken *inside* of her head, not out.

A hard object flipped in Julian's chest, and he pressed his mouth to her temple, inhaling the paradise scent of her hair. Skin. *Hallie.* "You've already got me, sweetheart."

Chapter Twenty-One

Okay. Change of plans.

Come clean. In real life. Face-to-face.

Hallie could *not* let him find that letter.

That approach was too impersonal after he'd eaten lunch with one arm around her waist, that thumb occasionally digging into her hip like a promise. Not after she'd caught him looking at her so often between appetizers and dessert, as if he were seeing her over and over again for the first time. Not when they were kissing against the front door of her cottage, her keys having clattered to the ground five minutes earlier, neither of them making a move to pick them up.

His knuckles had traced her cheekbones as if they were made of porcelain. When they broke for air and locked eyes, they were in their very own solar system, the real world light-years away. His hard frame pressed her against the door securely, his hands familiarizing themselves with her breasts and hips and even her knees—he seemed particularly interested in those. Squeezing and circling his thumb around the cap. Dragging one of them high around his hip and keeping it there while he worked her up and down against the wooden barrier, his lower body rolling, surging. Bringing her up onto her toes over and over again with hoarse gasps.

God, she had goose bumps everywhere.

An escalating warmth between her legs.

She was a body of sensations and nerve endings and needs. And the more Julian kissed her, feeding her his tongue with licks she felt down to her toes, the sexier she became in her own skin. How could she feel anything but incredibly desirable when every reverent scrape of his fingertips on her waist made her breasts feel fuller, more tempting. He was so aroused, he seemed to be in pain, and now his hands were climbing the backs of her thighs to palm her butt, his huge body crowding her into the doorway with a guttural sound. *Oh Lord.*

"D-do you want to come in for coffee?" she half laughed, half moaned.

"Hallie, I need to take you to bed," he growled, momentarily breaking their frantic kiss. "This is not a joke."

His teeth raked down her neck, his mouth racing back up into her hair, messing it up. Messing every part of her up, inside and out. But especially her conscience—how could she bring this man inside and make love to him knowing full well she had a secret that might make him second-guess the decision to be with her in the first place?

Tell him. Tell him now. "Julian—"

"The problem is, I can't stop thinking about you having an orgasm." That confession was spoken directly on top of her mouth, her lips moving with his, as if they were forming the words together. "It was a problem before last night. But now . . . Hallie. Now?" His fingers moved between her thighs, massaging her through the thin material of her panties. Pulling the undergarment down hastily to the tops of her thighs and rubbing slowly, slowly—right *there*—with the heel of his hand. "Now I can't go a full minute without feeling the way this thing fucking *gripped* me at the end." His middle finger pressed deep, her mouth falling open on a silent moan. *God, oh God.* "I'm going to put you on my lap tonight. Your bra is going to be off. Gone. Burned, for all I care. And you're going to ride cock." Another finger joined the first, pumping in and out slowly, her breathy whimpers caught by nips of his lips. "I want to know how you feel from every single angle by tomorrow morning."

Maybe . . . she should reveal herself as the secret admirer in the morning, then?

Breaths rasping together, he shoved her panties down another inch, fingers pushing deep, their bodies rattling the door in an attempt to get closer.

Wow, they really needed to get inside.

Her house was surrounded by trees and her nearest neighbor wasn't close enough to witness her getting mauled on her porch, but it wasn't unusual for Lavinia to drop by for a visit. Also, the mailman happening upon them was a very real possibility.

"Inside," she sobbed when his teeth sunk into her earlobe.

"Yes." He stooped down to pick up her keys, shoving one of them into the lock, cursing. Picking another one. And then finally they were stumbling into the dark of the cottage, the dogs going absolutely nuts at their heels, their barks happy at first, before turning sort of outraged over being ignored. "Hold on," Julian said, drawing back and reaching into his pocket. He took out a balled-up napkin and unfolded it, revealing pieces of steak he hadn't finished at lunch. "Here, boys."

Hallie blinked as he laid down the strips of beef on the floor, replaced the napkin in his pocket, and captured her hand once again. "Did you plan that doggy bag diversion?"

"Yes. Believe me, I wanted to finish the whole steak." His gaze raked over her face. "But I wanted a distraction more."

"Diabolical," she whispered. "We should get out of here before they finish. We have about four seconds."

"Jesus."

Julian started to drag her toward the bedroom, but she tugged him toward her backyard instead. Maybe since she couldn't give him total honesty—not tonight, not when everything was so utterly perfect—she could give him this intimacy. Her personal garden. Her most private, intimate place. Even more so than the bedroom. On the way outside, she flipped the light switch and held her breath. Watching his face transform with awe when he stepped out through the screen door made Hallie's pulse go haywire.

"This is where I spend most of my time," she said, trying to see the space through his eyes. Wondering if it looked as magical to Julian as it always felt to her. Or if he viewed the towering greenery, jewel-toned lights, and wildflowers as an unplanned hodgepodge.

He circled the yard with narrowed eyes, as though taking the time to make a sound judgment. Hallie had a premonition that she would remember this moment for a long time, maybe forever. Julian Vos touring her backyard with a serious expression, professorial hands clasped behind his back, surrounded by rioting blooms and hanging vines while removing his coat, the sunset loving his bristly jaw and playing over the hill-and-shadow patterns of his muscles.

"What do you do out here with your time?"

Now she understood. When she'd informed him this was where she spent most of her time, that wire in his brain had lit up. The one that dissected minutes and hours and years, turned them into something scientific. "I have my meals out here. I read and garden and talk on the phone and play with the dogs." She thought of the way he'd been exposed at lunch, his behind-the-scenes care of her revealed—and her lips started to tingle. "I think of you."

His steps slowed. "Is that so?"

She gave a brief hum.

Jaw ticking, he went back to surveying the backyard, but he was moving in her direction now. With such brisk purpose, she couldn't breathe. *Touch me.*

"If I'd known you were in this perfect, hidden garden thinking of me, Hallie," he said, frowning at her mouth. "I'm afraid I would have ripped your door off the hinges to get to you."

"I wouldn't have minded."

Admissions. Truth. She would give him as much as she could to make up for the one thing she was too scared to tell him. *Yet.* They were finding middle ground. He'd taken a few steps into her chaos, and she'd started serious planning of the library job. Booking more appointments, committing, doing her best to arrive on time. And it felt good. She couldn't screw this up by revealing how absolutely harebrained she'd been.

What if the revelation was his tipping point and he walked away?

They looked at each other for so long, the sky darkened a degree with the onset of evening, turning from pink to burnt orange, the bourbon of his eyes rich and smoky. She was tempted to give him more truth but could only bring herself to act on the impulse with her body. She could open herself up and be vulnerable in this way—and, God, she wanted to. Needed to. Didn't want to hold back a single thing from this man.

That's how she found herself stepping forward, kissing the underside of his chin, her fingers working to unbuckle his belt.

Immediately, he started to breathe hard, his nostrils flaring, but he never stopped looking her in the eye. Not until she eased the zipper down past his thickened shaft and reached into his pants, stroking the full length of him through the opening. Then his lids locked down like shutters, squeezing tight. *"Hallie,"* he choked. "What are you . . . oh Christ. Oh shit."

She wasn't sure what led her to kneel. To guide him to her mouth and take him inside so eagerly. Maybe because she'd fantasized about this countless times, although, in her fantasies, they were usually in one of his lecture halls at Stanford—a fact which she'd take to the grave. Or maybe she just wanted to do good with a mouth that was holding on to a lie. She closed her eyes and worshiped the smooth steel of him, her hand growing more and more confident in its newfound skill as it pumped top to bottom, increasing the hard swell of him with every fisted stroke.

"Can't . . ." he heaved, fingers tangling in her curls. "Can't be your first time sucking . . . ?" Moaning around him, she nodded, and his breath caught, followed by the taste of warm salt in her mouth. *"Fuck.* I shouldn't have asked. I shouldn't have—I'm going to finish. Stop. You have to stop."

Oh, right. Like that was going to happen. Did he have any idea what it was like to watch the straitlaced professor of her dreams lose the grip on his self-control, to know she was the cause? At some point, he must have plowed a hand through his usually perfect hair, because it stood on end in places. His jaw was clamped down, throat flexed, and the flesh in her mouth was painfully erect. She remembered him like this last night. At the end. How he'd been at his stiffest right before the fall, and she cherished this knowledge about him now. His telltale signs. His weakness—her. *I'm his weakness.* There was so much strength and power in that knowledge that her confidence ticked up another notch, and she popped him out of her mouth. While maintaining her hold on his erection, she found his balls with her lips and blew a gentle raspberry onto one of them, before drawing it into her mouth on a groan.

"No, no, no, no. Hallie. Get up. No more of that. Goddamn, sweetheart." His fingers twisted in her hair involuntarily, a violent shudder passing through his powerful body. "Wait. Don't stop stroking," he heaved thickly. "Hard. While you're sucking them . . . *shit.*"

Using his hold on her curls, Julian hauled her face away, and as she gulped down oxygen, she savored the sight in front of her. The shine she'd left behind on his aroused flesh, the hair she'd never seen on his upper thighs and low on his muscular belly. All of him. All of him was so startlingly raw and beautiful. But then he was dropping to his knees and slamming their mouths together, angling her head to the right and invading her mouth with an animal sound.

Lust inundated Hallie, burning and wild, and she kissed him back, distantly aware of Julian searching for something in his wallet. Protection. Putting it on in a hurry while they raked every corner of each other's mouth with long strokes, hips pressing, grinding.

He must have finished applying the condom—thank God,

thank God—because he gripped her jaw and tilted her face up to meet his scrutiny. "How long have you been wanting to fuck me with this pretty mouth?"

"A long time," she admitted haltingly, barely recognizing her own voice.

She could see he wanted to question that too-revealing piece of truth further—and maybe he would later—but right now, the urgency was so great. The fire on high. "As long as we're working fantasies out of our system, how about you turn around and bury those knees in the dirt?"

Lord. Oh Lord. "Yes."

As soon as the word slipped out of her mouth, the next move was taken out of her hands. Julian turned her around and used his big body to press her forward. "Slide them around," he panted in her ear. "Get them filthy."

Hallie's eyes nearly crossed, her heart beating so fast and furious, she could feel it in her throat. Never in her life had she felt as sexy as she did while twisting her knees down into the garden soil, Julian's mouth raking up and down her neck, encouraging her with groans, his hands working the dress up her thighs.

"Are you ready to show me this body, Hallie?" His voice was a scrape of flint. "All of it?"

Knowing she wouldn't be able to speak above a wheeze, she nodded vigorously.

"No, I need the words." He palmed her backside through the dress, his hand dragging up her spine to tangle in her hair, drawing her head back in a way that made her feel utterly and welcomingly possessed. "I need you to say, *Julian, get me naked. Look at every hot inch of me.*"

The ground spun in front of her face, her inner thigh muscles turning to the consistency of microwaved butter, the slow slicking of liquid heat making it uncomfortable to be wearing underwear at all. *Just say it. Say it.* "Julian, get me naked. Look at every hot inch of me."

"That's my girl," he praised, jerking the panties down to her knees, then off. Tossed away. Bent forward on hands and knees, she battled to breathe through the rough lowering of her dress zipper, the soft material being stripped down her body, over her right arm, then left, the entire thing sent in the direction of her panties. *Oh God. Oh God.* Nothing but a bra left. And did it even matter at this point? She was bent over, knees covered in dirt, wearing nothing but moonlight, and nothing, not a single thing, was left to his imagination. "Jesus, Hallie." In one deft movement, he shucked her bra and dropped his clothed chest down onto her bare back, his hands sliding up her rib cage to take firm hold of her breasts. "You have no idea how gorgeous you are, do you? I'm stalling right now. I'm stalling, because I know as soon as I put it in, I'm going to come, you're so fucking *beautiful*. I can't deal with how tight you are on top of everything else. God, this *ass*." The last part was said through his teeth, followed by a shaky exhale in her ear. "You're going to get so comfortable with me looking and touching and tasting every part of your naked body that you'll learn to bend over with your butt in the air, just like this, and ask me to eat it whole."

With that, he thrust into her from behind, and she screamed behind her teeth at the perfection of it. How he filled and stretched her, how the blast of sensation chased away the lingering soreness from her first time. And then there was nothing save the way he groaned in her ear, thrusting into her slowly, slowly at first, then with more and more force, the expensive material of his shirt rasping up and down her back.

"You like that?"

"*Yes.*"

He collected her hips in a bruising grip, straightened in his kneeling position, and seemed to indulge himself for several sweaty moments, pounding into her quickly, hard enough that the heels of her hands slid forward in the grass, her knees burrowing deeper into the earth. She could feel the willpower it took for him to slow down. The way he bit off a frustrated sound and dug his fingertips into her waist, easing his thrusts into deep grinds that made lights twinkle in front of her eyes, her intimate muscles seizing around him like an omen. Welcoming him, wetter each time, a throb escalating in the deep recesses of her womanhood.

His tongue licked up her spine, his fingers dropping down between her legs, pressing and rubbing right where she needed it. And she wanted to tell him faster, faster, but her vocal cords seemed to have been rendered useless, so she reached for his hand instead and moved it in the right rhythm. He hummed into his next lick of her back and kept the pace she'd asked for, and his grateful acceptance of her expressed needs turned her on more than anything. So much that she couldn't stem the compulsion to reward him with pulsing constrictions of her inner walls, one after the other, until he gave a strangled yell and drove deeper, faster, with rough smacks of his lap against her backside.

"Look at that fucking shake," he growled through his teeth. "God, I love it."

Whatever self-consciousness of her body or her flaws that remained had already fled, and now beauty and exhilaration and boldness bloomed where it had once been. "I want to see you shirtless," she panted, positive he wasn't going to hear her, but the confession blew out of her nonetheless. Where had that come from? She sounded almost irritated.

"What's that, Hallie?" he said into her neck, never ceasing the rough forward momentum of his hips. "Shirtless?"

Why are you like this? "You j-jogged through town shirtless today. In front of people. And I . . . I mean, *I* haven't even seen you that way and . . ."

He slowed to a stop, and without his movements inside of her, she could marvel over how truly large and hard he was. How much space he occupied. "Are you . . ." He labored to breathe. "You're not jealous."

"I think I'm a little jealous," she muttered haltingly.

A heavy beat passed, full with the sound of crickets and mountain breeze and short, punctuated breaths. Then, with a pained grunt, he pulled out of Hallie and gently rolled her over onto her back . . . where she had a front-row seat to his disbelief. But he didn't question her. He didn't tell her she was nuts or debate how she should be feeling. Instead, he just found her mouth with his own, winding their tongues together while unbuttoning his dress shirt. He tugged it off hastily, ripping the remaining buttons free, sending them arcing into the grass. She kissed him with her glazed eyes open, watching all of it, seeing how tightly he closed his own while devastating her with the skilled journey of his tongue, deep and smooth.

Then he was shirtless, looming above her in the moonlight with a heaving chest. And wow, oh wow. She'd expected the lean lines of a runner's body, and there *was* definition where she thought to find it, but in between, the roundness of muscle and man and flesh was incredible. Human. His natural body type was not that of a runner. No, the huskiness, the thickness shone through regardless of his strict regimen. It was there in the fullness of his stomach and the meaty breadth of his shoulders. If he stopped running, he probably wouldn't fit into his suits before long, and why that should turn her on so much, she had no idea.

"Christ, Hallie. The way you're looking at me . . ." He shook his head slowly, laughter strained. "Just come and get it, already, you gorgeous woman."

As she rose to her knees and went forward, straddling his lap, she couldn't remember a single time she'd been anything but this—desired and cherished and locked in swelling heat with this man. With her butt cheeks clutched in his hands, he guided her down onto his shaft, his eyes turning glassy as she went, jaw falling open on a moan. She felt her power and flexed it, holding on to his bare shoulders and rolling her hips. On the very first one, his head fell back, teeth digging into his bottom lip, his left hand fumbling to become an anchor in the dirt, his right thumb finding the bud at the juncture of her thighs, moving in that fast, firm rhythm she'd shown him, and yes, yes, she'd be rewarding him for paying attention.

"Oh shit. Oh Jesus. Don't stop," he gritted out, strumming her, lifting his hips to meet the increasingly frantic bucks of hers. Their mouths collided in fast, wet kisses, and in between, he scrutinized her movements, her body, with a gaze that could have melted steel. "Hallie, I've got about thirty seconds of watching your tits bounce while you grind that tight thing down on my cock, all right? Please, sweetheart. Come on my fucking lap. *Christ, come on.*"

He didn't have to encourage her, it was already happening, but the way he looked at her, the way he spoke to her in that desperate rasp, propelled her closer to the edge. "More," she said through numb lips. And without her elaborating, his thumb pressed tight to her clit and rubbed deeply, deeply enough that she wailed his name, the dam finally bursting inside of her.

Hallie wrapped herself around him as the tumult washed over her, nerve endings snapping like blue fire, the terrible, wonderful pulling and releasing of her core, so intense it was almost too much to stand, but the rush . . . God, the rush on the tail end of it was blistering and beautiful and left her awestruck. Left her clinging to Julian's bucking body, before he went very still beneath her. Then he barked a curse and started to shudder, over and over again. Both of his hands were on her backside now, yanking her up and back in disjointed pulls and pushes, with a sharp, involuntary slap of his palm that she liked very much, thank you.

And then they both tumbled sideways into the grass, struggling for air, the sunset having faded to serene blue above them. Drowsy eyes met through the tall blades of green, and they smiled, tangling their fingers together between them, gravitating closer, closer until their naked bodies were pressed tightly against each other.

It would have been perfect if it weren't for the one black spot of deception that grew inkier and denser between them as her skin cooled.

But Hallie was the only one who could see it. And now that she'd allowed even more time to elapse with the secret between them, she started to get scared. What if he stopped looking at her like a goddess . . . and more like a girl who wrote intoxicated love letters in the back of an Uber?

Maybe they just needed a little more time to establish their relationship, to prove it could last before she threw a new test into its path?

Yes. That had to be for the best, didn't it?

She'd take back the confession letter and tell him later, once they were more solid.

However long it took to gain the courage, she *would* tell him.

Later that night, when they were asleep in her bed, Julian's arm curled around her waist, she carefully slipped free of his embrace, left a pile of treats for the dogs, and slipped out into the night.

Chapter Twenty-Two

Julian woke up in stages, which was unusual for him.

Normally, his alarm sounded and he went from a dead sleep to fully awake, already on the clock, mentally prepared to dig into his schedule. For the last couple of weeks, he'd woken up praying he could adhere to *some* semblance of structure, though he'd started to find it hopeless these past few days. Now, in Hallie's bed, he regained consciousness totally devoid of any motivation to do anything but lie there in her warmth, in this room that smelled like flowers and detergent and dogs and sex. Because, yes, he'd gotten painfully hard watching her go through her nighttime routine of putting on lotions and short, silky pajamas and blowing kisses to the dogs. The mattress had creaked for another half hour before they fell into an exhausted spooning position, her amazing butt tucked into his lap like it was made for him.

Thank Christ he'd pulled his head out of his ass before doing something stupid, like going back to Stanford and leaving Hallie behind in St. Helena.

He loved teaching. A lot. He would look into sporadic guest speaking engagements, and, truth be told, he was even more eager to lecture about the meaning of time now that he had a new perspective. Before, he'd been concerned with passing on information. Facts. Now he wondered if he might make a difference in the lives of the students who came to listen to him. Maybe he could prevent them from making the same mistakes as him, taking for granted that the important things in his life would still be there when he was ready. More time would never yield itself unless he made it.

It didn't even require as much effort as he thought to picture himself here, in St. Helena, using his time to make his mother's days easier. His father might not be happy about it, but Dalton wasn't here. Julian was prepared to embrace the sense of ownership of the land that bore his name.

His sister's future remained to be seen, but he could help there, too, when she was ready to ask for it.

Then there was Hallie.

His heart woke up in his chest, firing so suddenly, he sucked in a breath.

Automatically, his hand smoothed across to her side of the bed, hoping for curls. Or skin. That smooth skin of hers that made him feel like sandpaper, roughing up and reddening her, leaving imprints of fingertips and teeth behind. He'd catalogue the damage right now. Kiss every mark he'd left behind . . .

His eyes opened, head turning.

No Hallie at all. No blond curls on her big, fluffy yellow pillow. Where was she?

He sat up and listened, heard nothing except the dogs snoring in various places around the bedroom. Todd had taken edge-of-the-bed honors while the other two were sprawled on the dog beds in the corner. Other than that, there was no audible movement in the cottage. No lights on, either. Though maybe she'd gone into the en suite bathroom and left the light off so she wouldn't wake him up?

"Hallie," Julian called, annoyed by the finger of cold that traced up the back of his neck. There was no reason to be worried or alarmed. It's not like she'd disappeared into thin air.

Still, when there was no response from the other side of the bathroom door, he threw off the covers, his feet already carrying him across the angled area rug. He checked in the bathroom just to be sure, then left the bedroom with added purpose in his step. Kitchen or backyard. She'd be in one of those two places. They didn't discuss her sleeping habits, but didn't it stand to reason that Hallie's should be irregular?

A fond smile curved his mouth.

Had her off-the-wall, unscheduled lifestyle really annoyed him before? Because now the challenge of pinning her down excited the shit out of him. Like he'd said yesterday afternoon, she could show up late as long as she kept showing up. Period. Right about now, he liked the idea of carrying Hallie to bed and showing her there was no set schedule in terms of when he needed her. It was all the time. Every minute of every day . . .

Where the hell was she, though?

The living room sat eerily silent, the other, smaller bathroom empty. No one in the kitchen. No sign of anyone having passed through to get a drink of water or fix a snack. And the lights were off in the backyard. He went to check, anyway, opening the glass double doors and doing a turn around the unoccupied garden.

"Hallie."

She'd gone out. At . . .

He turned on a light to check his watch, before remembering it was on the nightstand. Glancing back over his shoulder toward the kitchen, he spied the time on the microwave.

2:40 A.M.

She'd left the house at 2:40 A.M. There was no reasonable explanation for that. Not even for Hallie. People didn't go for walks in the middle of the night, and if she did, she would have taken the dogs, right? Nothing in town was open. Not even the bars. She had a friend . . . Lavinia? But he had no phone number for her, and anyway, regardless of where she'd gone or with whom, why wouldn't she wake him up? What the fuck was going on?

She couldn't have been . . . taken against her will somewhere, right?

The idea of that was ludicrous.

Was she a sleepwalker and failed to tell him?

What was that sound?

He listened for several long seconds before realizing it was his own wheezing.

Fuck. Fuck. Okay, take a breath.

But he couldn't. And in some weird, parallel universe, he could hear sirens and smell the cloying scent of smoke. There was no fire. No one was in danger. But he couldn't convince himself of that. Because Hallie could be somewhere out on the road in her pajamas or trapped somewhere. Was she trapped?

Now the dogs had gotten up to follow him around the house, their tails wagging, heads butting up against his knees. When did his pulse start ricocheting around the inside of his skull? He could hear the pumping of blood in his veins like there was a microphone inside of his chest. The kitchen, which he couldn't even remember entering, was smaller suddenly, and he couldn't remember the way back to the bedroom.

"Hallie," he called, a lot more sharply this time—and the dogs started to bark.

Goddammit, he didn't feel good. The closing of his throat and blurring of the immediate area, the stiffness in his fingers—he remembered it well. Too well. He'd spent four years trying to avoid this happening again, this helplessness running into him like a cruise liner splintering a rowboat. And before that, before the fire, he'd worked his whole life around not ending up here. So he wouldn't. He wouldn't.

"It's fine," he told the dogs, but his voice sounded unnatural, his gait stiff as he moved through the dark living room to the front door, throwing it open, only vaguely aware that he wore nothing but briefs. The blast of cold night air on Julian's skin alerted him to the fact that he was sweating. A lot. It poured down his chest and the sides of his face.

Panic attack. Acknowledge what it is.

He could hear Dr. Patel's voice drifting forward from the past. From those sessions a hundred years ago, when they'd worked on emergency coping strategies.

Name the objects around you.

Couch, picture frame, dogs. Howling dogs.

Then what?

He couldn't remember what the hell was supposed to come next, because Hallie was missing. This wasn't a dream, it was too vivid. Nausea didn't come in sleep like this. Nor did his jaw lock up, his hands useless and fumbling as he tried to get outside to go find her.

"Hallie," he shouted, walking stiff-legged down the path toward the street, searching right and left for her figure in the darkness. No truck. It wasn't parked in the driveway. Why didn't he think to look for that? Why hadn't he tried calling her? His brain wasn't functioning the way it was supposed to, and that scared the shit out of him. "Dammit," he huffed, rubbing at the concrete pouring down his throat. "Dammit . . ."

He needed to get back into the house to try calling her.

Focus. Focus.

The sound of tires on gravel stopped Julian short, just before he walked into the cottage. He spun around quickly, too quickly, to find Hallie running across the lawn, white as a ghost. Relief almost knocked him out cold, his hand gripping the doorframe to keep him on his feet. *She's okay, she's okay, she's okay.*

But she wasn't? Not really.

Her mouth was moving, but no sound was coming out.

He didn't like that, didn't like seeing her upset, and he needed to find out where the hell she'd been. If she'd gone out in the middle of the night, something had to be very wrong.

"Is there a fire?" he slurred.

"What? No." She stumbled back, hands on her cheeks. "Oh God."

"You're shaking," he forced out, jaw refusing to loosen.

"I'm okay, I'm okay." Despite her assurances, she started to sob, and the sound dug into his gut like a shovel. "Let's get you into the house. Everything is fine, I promise."

You've always been a fucking head case.

The final blow landed in the form of humiliation. His legs weren't working correctly and he sounded like an idiot and he was scaring her. Scaring Hallie. That fact scored his insides like a razor blade. On top of the unsteady feeling in his limbs and dulled cognizance, he was already anticipating the numbness that would follow. He wouldn't be able to comfort her then.

Wouldn't be able to do anything. He couldn't let Hallie see him like that. The way his father had witnessed him in the back bedroom of the main house. When Julian couldn't mentally surface enough to help. To act. To be a useful member of the family in the most trying of times.

Stay away from the vineyard.

In her effort to get Julian back on his feet, the corner of something white peeked out of the pocket of Hallie's windbreaker. He stared at it through the blur, through the blazing-hot mortification, not sure why it was triggering something in his memory. Something about the color and shape was familiar. If he wasn't so disoriented, he might have asked to see the object in her pocket, but in this state, where nothing seemed normal or typical, he reached for it without asking and drew it out.

And stared down at a . . . letter from his secret admirer?

What was Hallie doing with it?

"Where . . ." He shook his head hard, trying to clear the debris. "Is this where you went? To go get this letter? Why?"

Now Hallie's breathing matched his own. Scattered and wheezing and not making sense, as they were both sitting down on the steps of her porch, though he couldn't remember when they'd taken a seat. "I'm sorry," she said, hiccupping. "I'm so sorry."

The truth hit him like the spray from an ice-cold hose.

Hallie had left in the middle of the night to get this letter.

Which meant she'd known it was there . . . and didn't want him to find it.

Didn't want him to read the contents. Because she already knew what they were?

With a swallow stuck in his throat, Julian tore open the envelope and read the letter, his concentration returning to him in that moment, like the blunt swing of a bat. It was hard to decide in that moment how he felt.

"I pictured you as the admirer the whole time," he said, sounding foggy, words running together. "Should have listened to my gut, I guess ..."

Hallie reared back, stricken. He tried to reach out and stroke her face, but his arm wouldn't lift. Was he angry? No. Not exactly. He really didn't know how to be angry with this woman. Was it humanly possible to be anything but grateful that she'd returned his feelings so strongly that she'd written letters to him? Grateful that she'd found a way to reach him when he'd had his head up his ass?

No, despite the fact that she'd lied, he'd honestly be a fool to be mad about this. Their connection, however it came about, was a gift. But now, the residual fear he'd woken up with—fear that she was hurt or in danger—threatened to choke him.

Julian lurched to his feet and entered the house, dead set on getting out of there immediately. It had happened again. Right in front of her. He'd just shown the woman he loved his greatest weakness. One that he'd done everything in his power to hide, to deal with, to overcome. And if he had to look at her sympathy for another second, he was going to die.

"Julian, can you please stop walking away from me? Say something, please?" She was panicking, crying, shredding the letter in her hands, and there was nothing he could do about it. Comfort her? He wasn't capable. Not in this state—and not when he already knew what was coming next. At least she was safe. *Thank God* she was safe. "I'm sorry. I thought you would find it earlier today. The letter. I wanted you to know everything, but then ...

Please, everything was just so perfect, so perfect that I couldn't mess it up."

No, he'd been the one to do that.

The sweat was still clinging to his skin like an accusation.

His stomach burned. He couldn't even look her in the eye. It only added to the humiliation that he couldn't get his voice to work.

On legs he couldn't even feel, he went back to the bedroom and dressed, shoving his watch, his phone, his keys into his pockets.

"No, Julian. No. Where are you going?"

All he could do was walk past her out of the house, away from what had just happened. Just like he'd done four years ago. But this time—and he could feel this in the marrow of his bones— the price was much higher.

Chapter Twenty-Three

Hallie walked down one of the residential blocks adjacent to Grapevine Way, hoping once again to avoid seeing . . . well, anyone really. Even Lavinia and Lorna. Talking and smiling like a normal person only made her feel fraudulent and exhausted.

Two weeks had passed since she came home and found Julian in her front yard looking like death. How long was she going to be dazed and sick to her stomach?

When would the hole in her chest suture itself closed?

She was beginning to think the answer was . . . indefinitely. Recovering from the consequences of being reckless and irresponsible didn't seem like an option. She'd be living with the reverberations of that night for a long time. Maybe forever. At least as long as she'd be living with this broken heart.

If she could go back in time and just be honest with Julian, instead of sneaking off in the middle of the night like a moron, she would jump inside the time machine and buckle up. Because he might have wanted nothing to do with her after she revealed the truth about the letters, but at least she could have spared him the fear and anxiety that had embodied him, sealed him up in a vacuum pack where she couldn't reach him for long, agonizing minutes. The fact that she'd been responsible for that . . . like he'd feared she'd be all along? It was unbearable.

The tendons in Hallie's chest and throat knit together and pulled. Her body had been maneuvering in all sorts of new, torturous ways for the last two weeks. Food made her queasy, but she forced herself to eat, anyway, because the emptiness inside of her was already winning and she couldn't give it another victory by withholding sustenance. All day long, she walked around feeling sick, her skin hot and cold at the same time. She was too embarrassed and guilty and regretful to face her own reflection in the mirror.

And she totally deserved this.

Her actions had caught up with her in an irreversible way. Julian had been right to drive away and never look back. She'd called him three times since that night to apologize again, but he'd never answered the phone. Not once. Three days later, she'd gone to the guesthouse and knocked on the door. No response. She'd planted the flowers she'd brought in the back of her truck and gone. There was a chance he'd gone into that same numb state he'd told her about. The one he'd landed in after the fire, the low that followed his panic attack.

But, God, didn't that explanation make everything worse?

After a week passed with no returned calls, she'd woken up with grim acceptance. Julian wouldn't be calling. Or showing up at her cottage. He'd dealt with her messy disorganized lifestyle, her doggy circus, a citizen's arrest, and chocolate-fueled toddlers in a wine tent, but this lie and its consequences were insurmountable. She'd lost him.

She'd truly lost the man she loved. Not just loved, but admired and cared about and needed. She *needed* him. Not for self-worth or success. Just because, when they were together, the air felt clear. Her heart beat differently. Someone saw her, she saw them in return, and they both said, yes, despite the flaws in this plan, let's execute it. Because she was worth it to him.

Right up until she wasn't.

Hallie reached the end of the block and hesitated before turning down Grapevine Way. She had no choice but to buy milk. After a cup of black coffee this morning and cereal mixed with water, she'd forced herself into real clothing and out the door.

Please don't let me run into anyone.

Lavinia had hounded her for a few days, then allowed her to suffer in peace, leaving the occasional box of donuts and wine on her doorstep. Hallie was grateful to her friend for not including a note that said *I told you so,* which would have been well within her rights. She'd canceled her jobs for a few days before resuming them. But she couldn't bring herself to go to the library. She'd driven by once, intending to cultivate the soil and prepare it for planting, but she couldn't get out of the truck.

Who am I to take on a job this size?

Did she really think she could landscape a town landmark? The woman who'd been stupidly impressed by her color-coding system of pink, light pink, and lightest pink? Because now she just wanted to laugh. *I am such a fraud. Look at the destruction I cause.*

With a permanent knot in her throat, Hallie put her head down and barreled into the small convenience store, hurtling herself toward the refrigerated aisle. She was being ridiculous, of course. The world wasn't going to end if she ran into someone she knew. She'd gone through months of grieving for her grandmother, so she knew it was possible to act normal under bad circumstances. The reason she didn't want to see or interact with anyone this time had more to do with self-loathing.

I can't believe you did that.

I can't believe you hurt him that way.

Hallie opened the glass door and took out a half gallon of milk, closing it again with a *schnick*. She move back up the aisle as quickly as she'd come, doubling back once to snag an unplanned jar of peanut butter—but she stopped on a dime about ten feet from the self-checkout register. Really? *Really?* She should have driven to the next town over to buy milk and impromptu peanut butter. Why did this town have to be so small?

Not one but two people that she knew were inside this shop. At eight o'clock in the morning on a Thursday, no less. What were the chances?

Natalie was leaning her hip against a shelf on the other side of the store, frowning down at the ingredients on the back of a cracker box. Despite liking Julian's sister so much, the woman was literally one of the very last people Hallie wanted to see. Not after what she'd done to Julian, dredging up traumatic memories from a fire. And then there was Owen. He was inside the store, too, hunkered down in front of the candy display selecting a pack of gum. He'd called her a few days ago asking where she'd been and she'd texted back claiming to have a cold. She couldn't avoid him forever, but was a few years of being antisocial and drowning her sorrow in Golden Grahams so much to ask?

"Hallie!" Owen said brightly, straightening so quickly, he almost knocked over the cardboard candy display. He steadied it with a sheepish eye roll before coming in her direction. Stopping a few feet away and raking his palms up and down the sides of his jeans. Grass-stained ones he obviously used for gardening. Over his shoulder, Natalie turned her head and surveyed the two of them sharply, her expression unreadable.

Drop the milk and run.

That's what Hallie wanted to do, but she didn't deserve to avoid this awkward situation. She'd made her bed and now she had to lie in it.

"Wow, must have been a hell of a cold," Owen chuckled, before catching himself. "Dammit, I . . . I didn't mean that how it sounded. You always look beautiful. I can just tell you've been sick, you know? Been through a few sleepless nights. No offense."

Behind Owen, Natalie was listening intently.

God save me.

"No offense taken." She forced a smile and sidled toward the register. "I'm sorry, I have to get home and walk the dogs—"

"Hey, I was thinking." Owen moved with her. "Why don't you take another few days to recover, then come with me to the home and garden show in Sacramento this weekend? I figured we could get an early start on Saturday and make a day out of it."

Natalie crossed her arms and got more comfortable in her lean against the shelves, as if to say, *Oh, I'm staying for the whole-ass show now.* Hallie gulped. And she couldn't help but search Julian's sister's face for some sign as to how Julian was doing. Was he totally recovered from his flashback? Was he writing again? Angry? Had he maybe even gone back to Stanford?

That last possibility had heat burning the backs of her eyes.

Oh God, she wasn't ready to be in town. She should have stayed home.

Cereal with water was fine. More than she deserved.

"Um, Owen . . . I don't think I can make it."

He drew back, his smile tightening in a way she hadn't seen

before. "I've given you a lot of space, Hallie. Either put me out of my misery or . . . try." The tips of his ears were turning red as a tomato. "I'm just asking you to try and see if we could be something. If we could work."

"I know. I know that."

Hallie was sweating under the fluorescent lights, black coffee burning laps around her stomach. Natalie, arms still crossed, was tapping a finger against her opposite elbow, shadows in her eyes. How many people had Hallie affected with her impulsiveness? First, her grandmother had rearranged her priorities to help manage Hallie's. Lavinia had been dragged along into her nonsense, although she *did* seem to enjoy the mayhem on occasion, even if she disapproved. Hallie's clients were always exasperated with her lack of reliability. She'd somehow managed to convince Julian she was worth all of the trouble she caused, but she'd blown even that. Lost him. Lost the man who made her heart tick correctly.

And now she stood, staring back at Owen. Here she was, once again presented with the consequences of acting on impulse, avoiding plans and sowing discontent, instead of just definitively saying *I'm not interested* in the beginning.

She couldn't do this for the rest of her life.

"I'll go with you," she said, her lips barely moving. "But just as friends, Owen. We're only ever going to be friends. If that's acceptable to you, I'll go. Otherwise, I understand if you'd rather go alone or with someone else."

Her fellow gardener and longtime friend looked down at his feet. "Sort of had a feeling that would be your eventual answer."

Briefly, she laid a hand on his arm. "I'm sorry if it's not the one you want. But it's not going to change."

"Well." He blew out a disappointed breath. "Thanks for being honest. I'll give you a call about Saturday. Sound good?"

"Sounds great," she called to Owen on his way out the door.

Now she only had to face Natalie.

"This was not worth a half gallon of milk," Hallie mused out loud.

Natalie smirked, pushing off the shelves to saunter in Hallie's direction. A full ten seconds passed without Julian's sister saying anything. She squinted at Hallie, instead, circling around the back of her, a cop interviewing a perpetrator.

Finally, she said, "What the hell was that?"

Hallie started. "What the hell was what?"

"That awkward redhead asking you out. Doesn't he know you're seeing my brother?"

Huh? All right, that was the last thing she'd expected the other woman to say. "Um . . . are you still living in the guesthouse with Julian?"

"Yes."

"And he didn't tell you that we broke up?"

Saying those words out loud made Hallie's eyes fill up with tears, so she tilted her head back and blinked up at the ceiling.

"Uh, I know he said some kind of bullshit about you both needing space. And then he locked himself in his office to finish his book. He hasn't come out for two weeks. Unless he emerges when I'm passed out, which is more and more often these days."

"You need to handle that."

"I know. I have a plan. I just need a little more courage before I enact it." A shadow danced across Natalie's features; then she was back to being steely-eyed. "Look, I don't know what happened between you two, but feelings don't just—poof—go away.

Not the kind you have for each other. Now, my ex-fiancé and I? Yeah, in hindsight, the success of that relationship was riding on money and image. I can see that now. You and Julian, though . . ." She gave Hallie a pleading look. "Don't be each other's one who got away. You can fix it."

"I wrote him secret admirer letters and deceived him about it."

"*That was you?*" Natalie sputtered. Gaped. "Why the hell did you do that, you crazy idiot?"

Hallie groaned. "It all sounds ridiculous now."

"Well, *yeah.*"

"It started off with me wanting to get this . . . crush off my chest. But then, talking to him made me feel so much better about where I am. Who I am. Our discussions made my thoughts clearer. So I wrote my feelings to him in letters, hoping . . . to know myself *and* him better in the process. I didn't think it all the way through, and that's the problem. I *never* do. He was right to leave and stop taking my calls. He should forget all about me."

Natalie scrutinized her for a breath, then patted her awkwardly on the shoulder. "All right, let's not get dramatic."

"This is nothing if not dramatic!" Julian's sister was starting to look sympathetic, probably because of the tears that insisted on escaping her eyes, but Hallie didn't want that sympathy. Not until she'd suffered for at least another decade. "I should go."

"Wait." Natalie stepped into her path, visibly uncomfortable with Hallie's overwrought emotions. "Listen, I . . . get this. My brother barely talked to me for four years after rescuing me from a fire. It had the nerve to scare our stoic asses. We never learned how to express ourselves in a healthy way, so we lean on avoidance." She gestured to herself. "See? Hello, I'm three thousand miles from the broken pieces of my life right now. Nice to meet you."

Despite her misery, Hallie gave a watery laugh. "I see where you're coming from, but . . ." *He's better off without me.* "We're better off apart."

Hallie got the distinct impression that Natalie wanted to stomp a foot. "No, you're not. Me and that arrogant Navy SEAL, August whatever, are better off apart." She paused, looked far away for a moment, before shaking herself. "You and Julian are suffering right now, and one of you needs to stop being stubborn and fix it. Yes, I realize this is a pot-meet-kettle situation, but I'm not the one who wrote fake love letters, so I'm claiming the moral high ground for the purposes of this situation. If you go on a date with that dorky redhead, even as friends, I'm going to slash your tires."

"You really would, wouldn't you?"

"I carry a switchblade in my purse."

Hallie shook her head. "Dammit. I really like you."

She watched in confused awe as a flush took over Natalie's cheeks. "Oh. Well." She scratched at the dark wing of her eyebrow. "Who doesn't, right?"

They looked at each other in silence.

"It was bad, Natalie. What happened with us." A memory of him sweating in the doorway of her bedroom popped up. She had to breathe through it. "I can't even bring myself to tell you how badly I messed up. You'd slash my tires *and* break my windows."

"Maybe." Natalie sighed, searching for the right words. "Julian gets lost in his head sometimes, Hallie. Just give him a little while to find his way out."

She nodded as if agreeing to that, even though she wasn't.

If anything, the conversation with Natalie made her even more determined to move on and not allow herself to look back and hope.

She'd wreaked more than enough havoc on the universe already.

Chapter Twenty-Four

Julian typed *THE END* in his manuscript, and his hands fell away from the keyboard. The outline of those two words thinned until they were swallowed up in white, disappearing completely. All that was left in the absence of typing was the electronic hum of his computer, the low ringing in his ears that had been there for . . . however long it had been since it happened again. He jolted at the reminder of why he'd locked himself in this room in the first place, desperate to have his distraction back.

All he had now was silence.

A bunch of words on the screen. Clammy sweat on his skin. Still. Or again. He didn't know.

Where was the almighty satisfaction that came from finishing a novel? It would sweep in any second now, surely. The triumph, the relief, the sense of satisfaction. He'd been chasing those things, needing them. Requiring *something* to be louder than the noise in his head. But there was nothing. There was nothing but his stiff joints and aching molars and bloodshot eyes, and that was fucking unacceptable.

He cleared his throat, but a hoarse sound came out instead.

He dug his fingertips into his eye sockets. Jesus, it hurt to lift his arms, his joints sore from being locked up so tight. He probably hadn't noticed, because none of it could compete with the spikes raking through his insides, and it was so much worse now that he'd stopped typing.

The light on his desk had gone out God knew when. The blinds were pulled down tight, but he could see around the edges that it was bright out. Birds were chirping, and dust motes danced in the slivers of light that he hadn't managed to keep out.

Dread weighed down his shoulders so severely that they were beginning to protest the strain, and he knew why. He knew what he was dreading, but as soon as he acknowledged it, the final stage of numbness would wear off. So he fought to keep that final veil from lifting. Fought against the outline of her head and the sound of her voice with clenched teeth and every drop of will-power he had.

Julian's hand shot out unexpectedly and sent the wireless keyboard flying across the room. He'd just finished a book. Wasn't something supposed to happen now? Wasn't there supposed to be more than an empty room and stale air and the cursor that was *still blinking*?

Wexler had done exactly what he was supposed to do. He'd braved the elements, he'd fought the enemy, solved the riddles left by his comrades from the past, and triumphed. Returned the artifact to its rightful owner. Now the hero stood in a valley, looking out, and there was no fulfillment. Only emptiness. Wexler was alone. He was alone, and he was . . .

Flawless. He didn't have a single thing wrong with him. Apart from being briefly captured by his rival, he'd made no mistakes. Not one throughout the single book. He'd been rigorous and brave and uncompromising. And Julian found that he could not care less that Wexler had won. Of course this protagonist without a single bad characteristic won in the end. He hadn't stumbled once. Hadn't questioned himself or been doubted. Hadn't recognized his own shortcomings and done anything to fix them. He'd just won. Wasn't that the dream? Didn't people want to read about someone they aspired to be? Julian did.

Normally.

But the ending left him totally empty.

Julian had been writing the man he *wanted* to be. A brave man. But there was no satisfaction in winning without the losses that came first. There was no bravery when victory was a given.

A hero with serious flaws and even weaknesses . . . could still be a hero. A person could only be brave if failing was a possibility.

And that night of the fire . . . did he fail? He'd always thought yes: *Yes, I let myself get overwhelmed, I let the screws tighten until my exterior cracked.* In reality, though, he was still here. He'd come back. The people he loved were safe. Time marched on, and he would do it all over again, even knowing the outcome. He'd run into the fire knowing the anxiety would crush him afterward, and maybe . . . maybe Wexler needed some of that. Fear. Fear of failing. Fear of weaknesses. Didn't that only make being strong more rewarding?

The screen of his computer faded to black from inactivity, and Julian surged to his feet, noting the time on the clock. Seven forty in the morning. He would sleep until noon, shower until ten after twelve . . .

Why?

Why schedule himself so ruthlessly? It didn't seem as necessary as it had before. Nothing seemed necessary, except for . . .

His focus drifted, and he found himself walking down the front steps of the house. He moved without conscious thought, knowing on some level he was moving toward the garden, but not being really sure why. Not until he stood in front of it.

The absolute . . . masterpiece of it.

The air was sucked straight out of his lungs.

She'd finished the garden.

It was a riot of color, just like her. It was wild and joyful and without structure, but, standing back as he was, it made sense. Blooms filled spaces and locked together like joints. They reached for the sky in some spots, crawling on the ground in others, creating a pattern that he hadn't been able to detect until now. When it was a finished work.

The journey hadn't been pretty, but the result was fucking spectacular.

Like this garden, she was chaos. But she was *good*, and he'd known this. He'd reached for her with both hands and asked to keep her, mayhem and all—but he hadn't accepted his *own* flaws yet. He'd recognized hers as beautiful while believing his were still hideous, and *that's* where he'd gone wrong.

He hadn't been fully right, fully ready for her. Not when he couldn't accept his own imperfections . . . and realize those imperfections were what made victory worthwhile.

And she was the victory. Hallie.

Her name in his head tore away that final layer of numbness, and, as he'd known it would, the panic ripped through him like a knife. The sound of her voice begging him not to leave, the soft but persistent pull of her hands on his elbow. The letter. The words from her letter.

The kind of person who wants to be better and sees their own faults is someone I want to spend time with. They'll complement mine if we want it bad enough.

Not really seeing the ground in front of him, he lurched toward the house. And then he started to run. Car keys. He just needed to get his car keys. Christ, he needed to see her *now*.

I'm sorry I lied to you. I hope I haven't ruined everything, because while I thought I was in love with high school Julian, I didn't <u>know</u> him. I know the man, though. And now I understand the difference between love and infatuation. I've felt both for you, fifteen years apart. Please forgive me. I'm trying to change.

They didn't even talk about her letter.

She'd had a crush on him in high school? He wanted every detail. He wanted to know everything. He wanted to laugh about it with her in her magical little garden and make up for being a stupid teenager and not knowing her and loving her for fifteen years. Where the fuck had his head *been* for fifteen years?

His mind was wide open now, free of the imprisonment of minutes and hours. They were nothing if he didn't spend them with her, that's all he knew.

Natalie emerged from her bedroom as he ran by, eye mask pushed up on her forehead. "Julian. You're out."

"Where are my keys?" He pointed at the console table that ran between the living room and the kitchen. If he didn't see a Hallie Smile immediately, he was going to split down the fucking middle. "They were right here."

"Uh, they *were* there. Now they're in my purse. I returned my rental, and I've been driving your car for weeks."

"Weeks." The clamp around his windpipe tightened. "What are you talking about?"

"You've been writing nonstop for two and a half weeks. You

showered once or twice. Ate a sandwich every once in a while. Slept here and there. I stayed out of your way so I didn't interrupt your"—air quotes—"'process.' But I'm not handing over the keys until you clean yourself up. I believe the scientific term for your condition is 'nasty.'"

Julian had only half heard everything Natalie said after "two and a half weeks." *Two and a half weeks?* No. Not again. *Please tell me I didn't do this again.* There were foggy memories of leaving the office, falling numbly into bed, watching through the grit in his eyes as his hands prepared food, words appearing on the screen. It was a blur, but he couldn't possibly have been away from Hallie that long.

He wouldn't survive it.

You have barely survived it.

His body was in horrible pain from being in a sitting position too long, but the cavern in his chest was the worst pain of all. And it stretched wider and wider now, as he realized all the important conversations that were never had. The forgiveness he'd never given. The time he'd wasted on a book that had been on the wrong trajectory since the beginning. When he could have been with her.

"Take a shower before you go see her."

"I can't. Two and a half weeks."

Natalie yawned, reaching into her room for her purse and dropping it outside the door. "Yeah—and you might want to catch her before she leaves for the home and garden show with the redhead. They are just friends, but, you know, I still don't think he's deleting his wedding playlist anytime soon."

His intestines just sort of melted into his socks. This was peak misery. How he felt didn't mean jack shit right now, though. He'd walked out on Hallie while she was crying, too bogged down in his own self-disgust that he'd neglected to take care of her. To reassure her that he wasn't upset over the secret she'd been keeping. He was *grateful* for it. Those letters were the first step in the journey to where he was now. To seeing the world differently. Seeing himself differently.

"How is she?" He rifled through his sister's purse for the car keys. Fuck the shower. "I didn't mean to leave her so long. She must hate me."

"Hate you? No." Natalie's tone of voice turned Julian around. "Julian, I don't know what happened between you two, but she's taking the blame. If she hates anyone, she hates herself."

No. No, no, no.

A pounding started in the dead center of his forehead, his stomach pitching, nausea picking up speed like a rogue wave. Driving to her house and apologizing wasn't enough. No, she needed more. A lot more. The most unique, loving woman on the planet had been writing him love letters, and he needed to show her what they'd meant to him. What *she* meant to him.

Everything.

Would she want him when he had the ability to go silent for weeks?

"The last time this happened, I . . . couldn't be there when my family needed me. Now I've done the same thing to her. She's been hurting for weeks, and I've been lost in my own head. Brought down by this fucking weakness. I was just . . ." He searched for the right explanation. "I woke up alone, and she was gone. I thought she was hurt. Or worse. And then I couldn't calm myself down . . ."

"Julian." He found Natalie looking at him with a thoughtful frown. "This has only happened to you twice," she said slowly.

"Once when I was in danger. And again, when you thought something might have happened to Hallie."

All he could think about now was getting to her. Holding her. "I don't follow."

Natalie didn't speak right away, her eyes turning slightly damp. "You're a protector. A solver of problems. Always have been, since we were kids. If your supposed weakness is caring too much about the people you love, to the point of *panic,* then that is a *strength,* not a weakness. It's just one that needs to be managed correctly."

His sister's words finally broke through. Was she right?

Did the worst of his panic stem from people he loved being in danger?

"When I check out like this, I leave everyone to pick up the pieces alone. I couldn't help with damage control after the fire. I've left Hallie for two and a half *weeks.* My God—"

"I don't have a way to solve that part, Julian. But there *is* a way to cope with it. I know there is." She tilted her head slightly, her expression sympathetic and understanding. "Maybe it's time to stop trying to do that on your own."

"Yeah." His voice was raw. "Okay. I know you're right." As soon as he didn't feel like dying for being away from his girl so long, he'd make the calls. He'd schedule the necessary appointments to get healthier. For himself. For everyone. But right now? None of that was happening without Hallie being healed first. "Natalie, please. I need your help."

HALLIE SAT IN her backyard, leaning up against the fence, surrounded by dozing dogs. She had a sketchpad in her lap, a pencil still rolling back and forth where it had fallen from her fingers. She'd finished it. The idea for the library garden was complete—and it was glorious. A plan that didn't necessarily look like one. A Hallie-style buffet of sunflowers and dogwood and native wildflowers. Shaded benches and water babbling over stones and a swing hanging from the oak tree. It was a plan Rebecca would have been proud of.

Hallie was proud of it, too.

Weird how the worst scenarios coming true could pull everything into perspective. She'd been thriving on distractions and disorder so that she wouldn't have to decide who to be. But the truth was, she'd already been the exact right person. She just needed to stop waving and shouting and listen. Feel. Center herself now in the stillness and sunshine. She was a survivor. A friend. Someone who brought the color in unconventional ways, but tried her best. She had a broken heart in more ways than one, but she was still standing, and that made her strong. She was stronger than she ever knew possible.

A car horn blared from the front yard.

Hallie's nose wrinkled. Who was that? Owen had stood her up via text this morning, claiming a work emergency—and anyway, it was late afternoon now and they'd missed the whole home and garden show.

The horn went off again, and the dogs all got up at once, howling at the sky and trotting in circles. "Okay, guys." Hallie used the fence to stand on legs that were half-asleep from sitting too long. "No need to get worked up."

Hallie padded through the house on bare feet, moving aside a curtain in the front window to determine who was causing the ruckus.

Lavinia?

Her best friend spied her peeking through the curtains and rolled down the passenger-side window. "Get in, loser."

Sketchpad still in hand, Hallie unlocked the front door of her house and went down the path, accompanied by three very harried canines. "What is happening here?"

"Get in the car."

"But . . . What? Why? Is something wrong?"

"No. Well, yes. But hopefully not much longer." Lavinia snapped her fingers and pointed at the passenger seat. "Get in this bloody Prius, Hallie Welch. I'm a terrible secret keeper, and I've got about five minutes before it just bursts out of me."

Hallie herded the dogs back toward the house, sputtering, "At least let me put on some shoes and lock the door!"

"You're pushing it!" Lavinia shouted, honking the horn.

Less than a minute later, Hallie was diving into the car in her flip-flops, still holding her sketchpad. She'd forgotten her phone and was pretty sure she'd locked herself out of the house, but at least the honking had ceased.

"What is going on?" She scrutinized Lavinia, but the donut maker remained stubbornly tight-lipped. Literally. She was pressing her lips together so tightly, they were turning white. And that's when Hallie noticed the necklaces.

Lavinia usually wore a simple chain with a small onyx pendant. Today, there were so many layers of jewelry around Lavinia's neck, Hallie couldn't even figure out how many necklaces she was wearing. Silvers and golds and chunky wooden costume pieces.

"Why are you—"

Lavinia cut her off with a middle finger, shaking her head.

All right. She was a hostage. Going sixty miles an hour in a

Prius, possibly being mocked for her taste in jewelry, and there was nothing she could do about it, apparently. Hallie leaned back in the seat, fingers wrapped around her sketchbook, staring out through the windshield and trying to determine where Lavinia was taking her. It only took about three minutes for their destination to become obvious.

Hallie lurched forward, very nearly reaching for the steering wheel to prevent Lavinia from turning down the well-manicured road that led to Vos Vineyard. "Oh God. No. Lavinia." For a beat, she seriously contemplated throwing open the passenger door and casting herself out of the moving vehicle. "I know you think you're helping, but he doesn't want to see me."

"Almost there," Lavinia gasped. "Almost there. Don't look at me. I can do this."

"You're scaring me."

The brakes screeched, and Lavinia shut off the car, making a shooing motion at Hallie. "Get out. Go. I'm right behind you."

"I'm not getting out . . ."

Hallie's protest died on her lips when three people climbed out of the Jeep beside them . . . laden with necklaces. Like, dozens upon dozens of mismatched ones. Hallie looked down at her own collection, displayed in the V of her white T-shirt, and felt a tug in her rib cage. For the last few days, she'd tried to whittle down her selection to one necklace, but she could never manage it. She liked them all. They represented different parts of her personality and experiences. The pearls were an ode to her romantic side, the gold cross a reminder that she'd been a good granddaughter—the best one she could manage. The pink choker with the bright, pretty flowers once represented the part of her that liked to avoid unwanted conversations, but now it was a reminder to stop using flowers as a distraction and have the tough talks. Especially with herself.

Although, she missed talking to Julian most of all.

The necklaces blurred together, thanks to the moisture in her eyes, and when she looked up and out the windshield again, it took a moment for the figure in front of the Prius to come into focus.

Natalie. Covered in necklaces.

"Seriously, what is going on?"

Lavinia got out of the Prius and lit a cigarette. "She's in the mood to be stubborn. You get one side, I'll take the other."

Natalie nodded and put on her sunglasses. "Let's do this."

Hallie watched in horror as both women converged on the passenger side, clearly intending to drag her out of the car. She was so stunned and confused that she didn't manage to lock the door in time, and truly, she didn't stand a chance. Each woman reached for an arm and pulled Hallie from the vehicle despite her protests, the sketchbook dangling from her right hand uselessly. "Please!" Hallie dug in her heels. "I don't know what this is, but . . ."

But what?

She wanted to avoid confronting her mistakes in person? She wanted to hide in her house for another two and a half weeks eating cereal?

No. If she'd learned anything from her time with Julian, it was that growing meant getting through the hard stuff, and coming out stronger on the other side. The sketchpad was proof she could confront her fears and tackle things she never thought herself capable of. So she could do this, too.

Whatever "this" was.

Hallie stopped struggling and walked between Natalie and Lavinia like a normal woman without avoidance issues. Obviously her friends had staged some kind of Hallie-themed cheer-up session, and they were welcome to try. Julian probably wouldn't even *be* there.

That assumption popped like a tire rolling over glass when she heard his voice ahead.

He was . . . shouting?

"Anywhere you want," boomed his deep voice, just as they rounded the corner of the welcome center. There was Julian. In jeans and a T-shirt. Messier than she'd ever seen him. Standing in the back of a flatbed truck that appeared to be transporting an entire nursery worth of flowers and shrubs and various wooden trellises.

A large crowd of people had congregated around the truck, and Hallie immediately recognized several faces. Lorna was there. Owen. Several of her clients. August, the SEAL turned vintner. Jerome. The waitstaff from Othello. Mrs. Cross, who owned the coffee shop across the street from Corked. Mrs. Vos. Two giant groups of tourists holding half-empty disposable wineglasses. Julian was handing down random pallets of flowers and potted shrubbery to the assembled mass, his hands almost black with soil.

He wore dozens of necklaces around his neck.

"Find a place for them. Anywhere in the vineyard. And plant them."

"Anywhere?" Jerome asked, skeptically.

"Yes." Hallie watched in disbelief as Julian swiped a filthy hand through his hair, leaving it standing on end. "No rules. Anywhere it feels right."

What was this?

Hallie was still piecing it all together, but her legs were rapidly turning into cake batter. Was this a dream? Or had Julian organized a planting party at his family vineyard . . . in her honor? What else could the necklaces symbolize? Why else would he be instructing people to use the signature Hallie Welch method of having no method at all?

Julian's head turned sharply to the right, meeting Hallie's gaze. They could hear the thump of her heart on Jupiter.

Looking into his eyes again, even from this distance, was so powerful that she almost turned and ran for the car. But then Julian was jumping down from the back of the truck and striding toward her, not debonaire and determined as he'd been the night of August's wine tasting. No, this was a haunted version of Julian that was hanging on by a thread.

"Hallie," he rasped, stopping a few feet away. Natalie and Lavinia let her go suddenly, which was not a good thing, because apparently they'd been propping her up in the face of this reunion. Hallie's knees buckled, and Julian shot forward, catching her in his arms before she could hit the dirt. "Okay, I've got you," he said gruffly, eyes racing over her face. "It's okay. My legs want to give out, too, from seeing you again."

She allowed him to steady her, but she couldn't find the breath to say a word.

People were fanning out into the vineyard with bright, beautiful flowers in their hands, preparing to plant them at random—at Julian's behest—and that meant something. It meant such a wonderful something that she couldn't articulate it out loud just yet. But maybe . . . had he found it in his heart to forgive her?

"Hallie . . ." Julian's big hands closed around her arms, fingers flexing. Head bowed forward, he released an unsteady breath. "I'm sorry. I'm so sorry."

Surprise jerked her chin up a notch.

What? Had she heard him correctly?

"You're sorry?"

"I know that's not enough after disappearing for seventeen days, but it's just a start—"

"You have no reason to be sorry," she blurted, still reeling in her disbelief that he was taking responsibility for *anything* that went wrong. "*I'm* sorry, Julian. I lied by omission. I let you believe you were writing back to someone else when I had every opportunity to be truthful. I pushed you into feeling a way you never wanted to feel again because I couldn't help making a mess, like always, and I won't let you claim responsibility for any of it."

She tried to pull away from Julian, but he gathered her close, instead, bringing their foreheads together. "Hallie, listen to me. You don't make messes. You follow your heart, and your heart is so beautiful, I can't believe it was mine." He seemed to brace himself. "Put me out of my misery and tell me it's still mine. Please."

She forgot how to speak. All she could do was stare. Was she dreaming this?

"It's all right, I can wait," he said, swallowing audibly. "I have so much I want to tell you. I finished my book and it's terrible."

Hallie was already shaking her head. "I'm sure that's not true."

"No, it's one hundred percent true. But I needed to finish the first horrible draft in order to know how to fix it. No one gets anything worthwhile right on the first try. That's why we evolve. That's why we change. I never would have learned that without you. Without those letters." He paused, visibly searching for the right words. "Bumpier journeys lead to better destinations. You. Me. We're the best destination of all."

Hallie's eyes started to burn, heart in a slingshot. "How can you feel that way about me after I made you panic like that?"

"Hallie." His filthy fingers sank into her hair, his eyes imploring her to understand. "I panicked like that *because* I love you." He didn't even pause long enough to let those incredible words sink in. "For so long, I thought I needed this strict control to keep the anxiety at bay, and maybe in a way, I do need structure. I'm going to find out. But that true panic only happens when someone I love is threatened. I realize that now. When I woke up and couldn't find you . . . all I could think was the worst. Hallie." He cradled her face in adoring hands. "If something happened to you, it would end me. But that fear is only an indication that my heart belongs to you, all right? It's right here. Please just take it."

Her breath left her in a great rush. But not all of it. She held on to just enough to whisper the words that had been etched on her soul in different handwriting and for different reasons over the course of fifteen years. "I love you, too," she whispered. "One bumpy ride, reporting for duty, if you're sure. If you're—"

"If I'm sure?" Foreheads pressed together, they breathed hard against each other's mouths for long moments. "All time is not created equal. I know that now. Time with you is the most substantial of all. I'll probably never be able to stop counting the minutes that we're apart, but the ones when we're together, I'm leaving room for anything. Whatever happens. Gopher holes, rainstorms . . ."

"Robberies, drunken love letters . . ."

"Drunken? The first one?" She confirmed with a nod, and he laughed. "It did have a noticeably different tone." His hands dropped from her hair, capturing her wrists and bringing them up to encircle his neck. Bodies meeting and molding together, they moved left to right in a slow dance to the sound of their heartbeats. "Promise you'll keep writing me letters."

Was she floating? "I'll write them for as long as you want."

He looked her in the eye. "That's going to be pretty damn long, Hallie Welch." His mouth slanted over hers and coaxed her into a dizzying kiss. "I'm going to write you back, too. One for every day I missed out on for fifteen years."

This was what swooning felt like. "That's a lot of letters," she managed.

His grin spread against her mouth. "We've got time."

LATER THAT NIGHT, after all of the flowers had been planted, the laughter fading into the starlit, fragrant Napa night, Hallie and Julian stood in front of the closed library, side by side.

She handed him her sketchbook and he looked it over with serious professor eyes.

"I don't know where to start," she admitted.

And he seemed to know exactly what she meant. Because he nodded once and returned to his car in that brisk, determined way of his. He opened the back door, the top half of his body disappearing into the vehicle. The muscles of his back flexed and her fingers stretched in response, missing the texture of his skin—but all thoughts of debauchery fled when she spotted the object Julian was hauling out of the car. It had been covered in a blanket before, and she'd assumed it was more supplies he'd purchased at the nursery. But no.

It was her grandmother's table.

The one that had sat outside of Corked since the fifties.

It was right there, thrown over Julian's shoulder, as he carried it across the street. The world seemed to tilt beneath Hallie, on all sides, her throat squeezing so tight it was a wonder she was still breathing. She said his name but no words came out. All she could do was run her fingers over the intricate swirls, the chipped white paint. Julian was already back at the car, taking the wrought-iron chairs from the trunk. He carried one in each hand and set them down beside the table, looking at her, chest rising and falling.

"Lorna needs triple the amount of outdoor seating now. We went ahead and ordered new tables. Chairs. None of them matched this one, though. Nothing could ever match it." He leaned over and rested his lips on the crown of her head. "Maybe it's time to give it a new home."

"I knew my plans were missing something." Through her tears, she smiled down at the familiar dips and plumes of the wrought-iron pattern. "It needed that piece of her. You brought me the heart."

His arms encircled her, wrapping her in warmth. "I'd have brought you mine, but I already gave you the whole damn thing, Hallie."

After the day he'd planned at the winery, she'd assumed her own heart was fully healed. But there must have been one missing component, because a final stitch threaded into place now and it beat like a lion's. Who could have anything less than a fiercely functioning heart when there was someone in the world who would do this for her?

Julian held out his hand, and they walked into the library courtyard together.

And they stayed late into the evening getting messy in the dirt, planting flowers and smiling at each other in the moonlight. Because their journey was only getting started.

THE END

How does a down-on-her-luck Napa heiress
end up married to an infuriating former
Navy SEAL turned clueless winemaker?
Read on for a sneak peek at Natalie's story . . .

Chapter One

*F*or as long as August Cates could remember, his dick had ruined everything.

In seventh grade, he'd gotten a hard-on during a pep rally while standing in front of the entire school in football pants. Since his classmates couldn't openly call him Woody in the presence of their teachers, they'd called him Tom Hanks, instead. It stuck all through high school. To this day, he cringed at the very mention of *Toy Story*.

Trust your gut, son.

His navy commander father had always said that to him. In fact, that was pretty much all he'd ever said, by way of advice. Everything else constituted a direct order. Problem was, August tended to need a little more instruction. A diagram, if possible. He wasn't a get-it-right-on-the-first-try type of man. Which is probably why he'd mistaken his "gut" for his dick.

Meaning, he'd translated his father's advice into . . .

Trust your dick, son.

August straightened the wineglass in front of him in order to forgo adjusting the appendage in question. The glass sat on a silver tray, seconds from being carried to the panel of judges.

Currently, the three smug elitists were sipping a Cabernet offering that had been entered into the Bouquets and Beginners competition by another local vintner. The crowd of Napa Valley wine snobs leaned forward in their folding chairs to hear the critique from one judge in particular.

Natalie Vos.

The daughter of a legendary winemaker.

Vos Vineyard heiress and all-around plague on his fucking sanity.

August watched her full lips perch on the edge of the glass. They were painted a kind of lush plum color today. They matched the silk blouse she wore tucked into a leather skirt and he swore to God, he could feel the crush of that leather in his palms. Could feel his fingertips raking down her bare legs to remove those high heels with spikes on the toes. Not for the first time—no, incredibly far from the first time—he mentally kicked himself in the ass for sabotaging his chances of taking Natalie Vos to bed. She wouldn't touch him now through a hazmat suit and she'd told him as much umpteen times.

His chances of winning this contest didn't bode well.

Not only because he and Natalie Vos were enemies, but because his wine sucked big sweaty donkey balls. Everyone knew it. Hell, August knew it. The only one to call him out on it, however, was preparing to deliver her verdict to the audience.

"Color is rich, if a bit light. Notes of tobacco in front. Citrus aftertaste. Veering toward acidic, but . . ." She held the wine up to the sun and studied it through the glass. "Overall very enjoyable. Admirable for a two-year-old winery."

Murmurs and golf claps all around from the audience.

The winemaker thanked the judges. He actually bowed to

Natalie while retrieving his glass and August couldn't stifle the eye roll to save his life. Unfortunately, Natalie caught the action and raised a perfect black brow, signaling August forward for his turn at the judging table, like a princess summons a commoner—and didn't that fit their roles to a T?

August didn't belong in this sunny five-star resort and spa courtyard on a Saturday afternoon ferrying wine on a silver tray to these wealthy birdbrains who overinflated the importance of wine so much it felt like satire. He didn't belong in sophisticated St. Helena. Wasn't cut out to select the best bunch of grapes at the grocery store, let alone cultivate their soil and grow them from scratch to make his very own brand of wine.

I tried, Sammy.

He'd really fucking tried. This contest had a grand prize of ten thousand dollars and that money was August's last hope to keep the operation alive. If given another chance, he would be more hands-on during the fermentation process. He'd learned the hard way that "set it and forget it" didn't work for shit with wine. It required constant tasting, correcting, and rebalancing to prevent spoilage. He might do better with another season to prove himself.

For that, he needed money. And he had a better chance of getting Natalie in the sack than winning this competition—which was to say, he had no chance whatsoever—because yeah. His wine blew chunks. He'd be lucky if they managed to let it rest on their palates for three seconds, let alone declare him the winner. But August would try to the bitter end, so he would never look back and wonder if he could have done more to bring this secondhand dream to life.

August strode to the judges' table and set the glasses of wine in front of Natalie with a lot less ceremony than his competitors, sniffed, and stepped back, crossing his arms. Disdain stared back at him in the form of the two most annoyingly beautiful eyes he'd ever seen. Sort of a whiskey gold, ringed in a darker brown. He could still remember the moment the expression in those eyes had gone from *take-me-to-bed-daddy* to *please-drink-poison*.

Witch.

This was her domain, however. Not his. At six foot three with a body still honed for the battles of his past life as a SEAL, he fit into this panorama about as well as Rambo at a bake sale. The shirt he'd been asked to wear for the competition didn't fit, so it hung from the back pocket of his jeans. Maybe he could use it to clean up the wine when they spit it out.

"August Cates of Zelnick Cellar," Natalie said smoothly, handing glasses of wine to her fellow judges. Outwardly, she appeared cool as ever, her unflappable New York demeanor on full display, but he could see her breath coming faster as she geared herself up to drink what amounted to sludge in a glass. Of the three judges, Natalie was the only one who knew what was coming, because she'd tasted his wine once before—and promptly compared it to demon piss. Also known as the night he'd blown his one and only chance to sweat up the sheets with Princess Vos herself.

Since that ill-fated evening, their relationship had been nothing short of contentious. If they happened to see each other on Grapevine Way or at a local wine event, she liked to discreetly scratch her eyebrow with a middle finger, while August usually inquired how many glasses of wine she'd plowed through since nine A.M.

In theory, he hated her. They hated each other.

Dammit, though, he couldn't seem to *actually* do it. Not all the way.

It all went back to August mistaking his gut for his dick as a youngster.

As in, *trust your dick, son.*

And that part of his anatomy might as well be married to Natalie Vos. Married with seven kids and living in the Viennese countryside wearing matching play clothes fashioned out of curtains, à la *The Sound of Music.* If it were up to August's downstairs brain, he would have apologized the night of their first argument and asked for another shot to supply her with wall-to-wall orgasms. But it was too late now. He had no choice but to return the loathing she radiated at him, because his upstairs brain knew all too well why their relationship would never have gone past a single night.

Natalie Vos had privilege and polish—not to mention money—coming out of her ears.

At thirty-five, August was broker than a fingerless mime.

He'd dumped all of his life savings into opening a winery, with no experience or guidance, and losing this contest would be the death blow to Zelnick Cellar.

August's chest tightened like he was being strapped to a gurney, but he refused to break eye contact with the heiress. The growing ache below his throat must have been visible on his face because, slowly, Natalie's smug expression melted away and she frowned at him. Leaned in and whispered for his ears alone, "What's going on with you? Are you missing WrestleMania to be here or something?"

"I wouldn't miss WrestleMania for my own funeral," he snorted. "Just taste the wine, compare it to moldy garbage, and get it over with, princess."

"Actually, I was going to ordain it as something like . . . rat bathwater." She gestured at him with fluttery fingers. "Seriously, what's up? You have more asshole energy than usual."

He sighed, looking out at the rows of expectant spectators who were either in tennis whites or leisure wear that probably cost more than his truck. "Maybe because I'm trapped in an episode of *Succession*." Time to change the channel. Not that he had a choice. "Do your worst, Natalie."

She wrinkled her nose at his wine. "But you're already so good at being the worst."

August huffed a laugh. "Too bad they're not giving out a prize for sharpest fangs. You'd be unmatched."

"Are you comparing me to a vampire? Because your *wine* is the one that sucks."

"Just down the whole glass without tasting it, like you usually do."

Was that hurt that flashed in her eyes before she hid it?

Certainly not. "You are an—" she started.

"Ready to begin, Miss Vos?" asked one of the other judges, a silver-haired man in his fifties who wrote for *Wine Enthusiast* magazine.

"Y-yes. Ready." She shook herself and pulled back, regaining her poise and sliding her fingers around the stem of the wineglass containing August's most recent Cabernet. A groove remained between her brows as she swirled the glass clockwise and lifted it to her nose to inhale the bouquet. The other judges were already coughing, looking at each other in confusion. Had they accidentally been served vinegar?

They spat it out into the provided silver buckets almost in tandem.

Natalie, however, seemed determined to hold off as long as possible.

Her face turned red, tears forming in her eyes.

But to his shock, the swallow went down her throat, followed by a gasp for air.

"I'm afraid . . ." began one of the judges, visibly flustered. The crowd whispered behind August. "I'm afraid something must have gone terribly wrong during your process."

"Yes . . ." The other judge laughed behind his wrist. "Or a step was left out entirely."

The rows of people behind him chuckled and Natalie's attention strayed in that direction. She opened her mouth to say something and closed it again. Normally, she wouldn't hesitate to cut him off at the knees, so what was this? Pity? She'd chosen *this* moment? This moment, when he needed to walk out of here with some semblance of pride, to go easy on him?

Nah. Not having it.

He didn't need this spoiled, trust-fund brat to pull her punches. He'd seen shit during combat that people on this well-manicured lawn couldn't even fathom in their wildest dreams. He'd jumped out of planes into pitch-black skies. Existed on pure stubbornness for weeks on end in the desert. Suffered losses that still felt as though they'd happened yesterday.

And yet you couldn't even make decent wine.

He'd failed Sam.

Again.

A fact that hurt a damn sight more than this rich girl judging him harshly in front of these people he'd probably never see again after today. In fact, he needed Natalie to just drop the hammer already, so he could show her how little he cared about her opinion. It was his friend's dream never being realized that should hurt. Not her verdict.

August propped his hands on the judging table, seeing nothing but the beautiful, black-haired dream haunter, watching her golden eyes go wide at his audacity. "You're not waiting for a bribe, are you? Not with a last name like Vos." He winked at her, leaned down until only Natalie could hear the way he dropped his voice. "Unless you're hoping for a different kind of bribe, princess, because that can be arranged."

She threw wine in his face.

For the second time.

Honestly, he couldn't even blame her.

He was lashing out over his failure and Natalie was a convenient target. But he wasn't going to apologize. What good would it do? She already hated him and he'd just found a way to strengthen that feeling. The best thing he could do to make up the insult to Natalie was to leave town—and that's exactly what he planned to do. He'd been given no choice.

With wine dripping from his five o'clock shadow, August pushed off the table, swiped a sleeve over his damp face, and stormed across the lawn to the parking lot, failure like a thorn stuck dead in the center of his chest. He was almost to his truck when a familiar voice called out behind him. Natalie. Was she actually *following* him after the shit he'd said?

"Wait!"

Fully expecting to turn around and find a twelve-gauge shotgun leveled at his head, August turned on a booted heel and watched warily as the gorgeous witch approached. Why did he have the ridiculous urge to move at a fast clip back in her direction and catch her up in a kiss? She'd break his fucking jaw if he tried, but God help him, his dick/gut insisted it was the right thing to do. "Yeah? You got something else you want to throw in my face?"

"My fist. Among other, sharper objects. But . . ." She jerked a shoulder, appearing to search for the right words. "Look, we're not friends, August. I get that. I insulted your wine the night we were going to hook up and you've resented me ever since, but what you said back there? Implying my last name makes me superior? You're wrong." She took a step closer, her heels leaving the grass and stepping onto the asphalt of the parking lot. "You don't know *anything* about me."

He chuckled. "Go ahead, tell me all about your pain and suffering, rich girl."

She threw him a withering sigh. "I didn't say I've suffered. But I haven't exactly coasted along on my last name, as you seem to believe. I've only been back in St. Helena for a few months. The last name Vos means nothing in New York."

August leaned against the hood of his truck and crossed his arms. "I bet the money that comes with it does."

She gave August a look. One that suggested he was truly in the dark—and he didn't like that. Didn't like the possibility that he was wrong about this woman. Mainly because it was too late to change his actions now. He'd always have to wonder what the hell he could have done differently about Natalie Vos. But at least he could walk away from this phase of his life knowing he did his best for Sam. That's all he had.

"Did you ever want to get to know me? Or was it just . . ." Her attention dropped fleetingly to his zipper, then away, but it was enough to make him feel like he was back in that middle school pep rally trying not to get excited. "Just about sex?"

What the hell was he supposed to say?

That he'd seen her across the room at that stupid Wine Down event and felt like he'd had an arrow shot into his chest by a flying baby? That his palms sweat because of a woman for the first time ever that night? He'd already been on that Viennese countryside holding a picnic basket in one hand, an acoustic guitar in the other. God, she was so beautiful and interesting and fucking hilarious. Where had she been all his life?

Oh, but then somehow it all went to shit. He'd let his pride get in the way of . . . what? What would have happened if he'd just taken her verbal disapproval of his wine on the chin and moved forward? What if he hadn't equated it to disapproval of his best friend's aspirations? Was there any use wondering about any of this shit now?

No.

He'd run out of capital. The winery was an unmitigated disaster. He was the laughingstock of St. Helena and he'd dragged his best friend's name with him through the mud.

Time to go, man.

"Oh, Natalie." He slapped a hand over his chest. "Obviously I wanted to twirl you around on a mountaintop in Vienna while our children frolicked and harmonized in curtain clothes. Didn't you know?"

She blinked a few times and her expression flattened as she stepped back into the grass. August had to fist his hands to prevent himself from reaching for her.

"Well," she said, her voice sounding a little rusty. *Dammit.* "Have a lovely evening at home with your *Sound of Music* references and cozy nest of wine rats. I hope you're paying them a living wage."

"It won't be my home much longer." He threw a hand toward the event that was still in full swing behind them, the judges taking pictures with the audience members, more wine being served on silver trays. "This contest was it for me. I'm moving on."

She laughed as if he was joking, sobering slightly when he just stared back. "Wow. You really can't take a little constructive criticism, can you?"

August scoffed. "Is that what it was? Constructive?"

"I thought SEALs were supposed to be tough. You're letting winemaking take you down?"

"I don't have a bottomless bank account like some people in this town. In case it wasn't clear, I'm talking about you."

For some reason, that made her laugh. A beat of silence passed, then, "You've got me all figured out, August. Congratulations." She turned on the toe of her high heel and breezed away, moving that leather skirt side to side in the world's cruelest parting shot. "My sincere condolences to the town where you end up next," she called back over her shoulder. "Especially to the women."

"You wouldn't be saying that if you dropped the disgusted act and came home with me." For some reason, every step she took in the opposite direction made his stomach lurch with more and more severity. "It's not too late, Natalie."

She stopped walking and he held his breath, not fully aware until this very moment how badly he actually wanted her. Maybe even needed. The continued flow of his blood seemed to hinge on her response. "You're right, it's not too late," she said, turning, chewing her lip, eyes vulnerable in a manner that stuck a swallow in his throat. *I'll never be mean to her again.* "It's *way* too late," she concluded with a pinkie wave, her expression going from defenseless to venomous. "Go to hell, August Cates."

His stomach bottomed out, leaving him almost too winded for a reply. "Hell, huh? Your old stomping grounds, right?"

"Yup!" She didn't even bother turning around. "That's where I met your mom. She said she'd rather live in hell than drink your wine."

A crank turned in his rib cage as she moved out of earshot. Too far to hear him over the event music that had started up. Definitely too far to touch, so why were his fingers itching for her skin? His chances with Natalie were subzero now. Just like his chance at succeeding as a vintner. With a final long look at the one who got away, August cursed, climbed into his truck, and tore out of the parking lot, ignoring the strong sense of leaving something undone.

Chapter Two

*N*atalie searched blindly in the dark for the button on her sound machine, cranking the symphony of rain and bullfrogs to the maximum level. Julian and Hallie tried to be quiet. They really did. But springs only creak at four o'clock in the morning for one reason—and creak they did. Natalie covered her face with a pillow for good measure and rolled back into the sheets, employing what she called the State Capitals Method. On the occasions her brother and his new girlfriend decided to make love down the hallway in the guesthouse they all shared, Natalie avoided that troubling imagery by naming state capitals.

Montgomery, Juneau, Phoenix . . .

Creak creak creak.

That was it.

Natalie sat up in bed and pushed off her sleep mask, giving the wine dizziness a moment to dissipate. No more excuses. It was time to bite the bullet and go talk to her mother. It was time to get the hell out of Napa. She'd been licking her wounds far too long, and while she was happy beyond words for Julian to have found the love of his life, she didn't need to witness it in surround sound.

She threw off the covers and stood, her hip bumping into the nightstand and knocking over an empty wineglass. One of *four*—as if she needed another sign that she'd turned into a lush in the name of avoiding her problems.

Life had ground to a standstill.

Looking out the window of the back bedroom, she could see the main house where she'd grown up and Corinne, her mother, currently lived. That was her destination in the morning. Asking her mother for money was going to sting like a thousand wasps, but what choice did she have? If she was going to return to New York and open her own investment firm, she needed capital.

Her mother wasn't going to make it easy. No, she was probably waiting right now in front of a roaring fire, dressed in all her finery, having sensed Natalie was on the verge of humbling herself. Sure, they'd had a few softer moments since Natalie's return to St. Helena, but just under the surface, she'd always be The Embarrassment to Corinne.

Natalie tossed her eye mask in the direction of the sad, empty wineglass quartet and plodded into the en suite bathroom. Might as well get the talk over with early, right? That way if Corinne said no to Natalie's proposal, at least she'd have the whole day to wallow. And this was Napa, so wallowing could be made very fashionable. She'd find a wine tasting and charm everyone in attendance. People who had no idea she'd been asked to step down as a partner of her finance firm for a wildly massive trade blunder that cost, oh, a cool billion.

Nor would they know she'd been kicked to the curb by her fiancé, who was too embarrassed to meet her at the altar.

Back in New York? Pariah.

In St. Helena? Royalty.

Snort. Natalie shed her sleep shirt and stepped beneath the hot shower spray. And if she thought her brother doing the deed constituted an unwanted image, it had nothing on the memory of August Cates yesterday afternoon in all his beefcake glory.

I don't have a bottomless bank account like some people in this town.

If only.

Natalie didn't have anything to complain about. She was living in a beautiful guesthouse on the grounds of a vineyard, for God's sake. But she'd been living off her savings for over a month now and she couldn't open a lemonade stand, let alone launch a firm, with the amount left over. She had privilege, but financial freedom presented a challenge. One she could hopefully overcome this morning. All it would cost was her pride.

The fact that August Cates planned to leave St. Helena imminently had nothing to do with her sudden urgency to leave, too. Nothing whatsoever. That big, incompetent buffoon and his decisions had no bearing on her life. So why the pit in her stomach? It had been there since he approached the table to have his wine judged yesterday. The man had a chip the size of Denver on his shoulder, but he always had kind of a . . . softness in his eyes. A relaxed, observant quality that said *I've seen everything. I can handle anything.*

But it was missing yesterday.

And it caught Natalie off guard how much it threw her.

He'd looked resigned. Closed off.

Now, drying her hair in front of the foggy bathroom mirror, she couldn't pretend that hole in her belly wasn't yawning wider. Where would August go? What would he do now that winemaking was off the table?

Who *was* August Cates?

Part of her—a part she would never admit to out loud—had always wondered if she would find out eventually. In a weak moment. Or by accident.

Had she been looking forward to that?

Natalie turned off the dryer with a snappy movement, ran the brush one final time through her long, black hair, and left the bathroom, crossing to her closet. She put on a sleeveless black sweater dress and leather loafers, added a swipe of nude lipstick and some gold earrings. By the time she was finished, she could see through the guest room window that lights were on in the main house and she took a long breath, banishing the jitters.

All Corinne could say was no, Natalie reminded herself on the way up the path that ran alongside the fragrant vineyard. The sun hadn't risen yet, but the barest rim of gold outlined Mount St. Helena. She could almost feel the grapes waking up and turning toward the promise of warmth from above. Part of her truly loved this place. It was impossible not to. The smell of fertile earth, the tradition, the magic, the intricate process. Thousands of years ago, some industrious—and probably bored—people had buried bottles of grape juice underground for the winter and invented wine, which proved Natalie's theory: where there is a will to get drunk, dammit, there is a way.

She paused at the bottom of the porch steps leading to the estate. Old-world charm oozed from every inch of her childhood home. Greenery spilled over flower boxes beneath every window, rocking chairs urged people to sit and relax, and the trickle of the pool's water feature could be heard from the front of the house, even though it was located behind. A gorgeous estate that never failed to make winery visitors swoon. The place was incredible. But she had more affection for the guesthouse than the manor where she'd lived from birth to college. And right now, all it represented was the obstacle ahead.

A moment later, she knocked on the door and heard the sound of footsteps approaching on the other side. The peephole darkened, the lock turned—and then she was looking at Corinne.

"Seriously?" Natalie sighed, giving her stately mother a once-over, taking in the smoothed black-gray hair and perfect posture. Even her wrinkles were artful, allowed onto her face by invitation only. "You're fully dressed at five o'clock in the morning?"

"I could say the same about you," Corinne replied without missing a beat.

"True," Natalie said, sliding into the house without an invitation. "But I don't live here. Do you even own a bathrobe?"

"Did you come here to discuss sleepwear?"

"Nope. Humor me."

Corinne closed the door firmly, then locked it. "Of course I own a robe. Normally, I would be wearing it until at least seven, but I have virtual meetings this morning." In an uncharacteristic move, her mother let a smile peek through before it was quickly quelled. "Your brother has negotiated a deal making us the official wine of several wedding venues down the California coast. He is really helping turn things around for us."

"Yeah, he is." Natalie couldn't help but feel a spark of pride in her brother. After all, he'd overcome his own baggage pertaining to this place and landed on the other side much better off. At the same time, however, Natalie couldn't ignore the wistfulness drifting through her breast. God, just once, she'd love someone to talk about her like Corinne spoke about Julian. Like she was vital. Valued. Wanted *and* needed. "It's hard to tell him no when he's speaking in his stern professor voice. Takes people right back to seventh grade."

"Whatever he's doing, it's working." Corinne squared her shoulders and came farther into the foyer, gesturing for Natalie to precede her into the living space and to the right, overlooking the rambling vineyard, the mountains beyond. They took seats on opposite ends of the hard couch that had been there since Natalie's childhood and almost never used. Voses didn't *gather*.

They kept moving.

So in the interest of family tradition, Natalie turned toward Corinne and folded her hands on one knee. "Mother." If she'd learned one thing from phase one in the finance industry, it was to look a person in the eye when asking for money, and she did so now. "I know you will agree—it's time for me to go back to New York. I've been in contact with Claudia, one of my previous analysts, and she's agreed to come on board with my new company. We're going to be small, more of a boutique firm, but both of us have enough connections to facilitate steady growth. With a couple of smart plays—"

"Wow." Corinne framed her jaw with a thumb and index finger. "You've been making important phone calls in between wine binges. I had no idea."

Clang. A ding in the armor.

Okay.

She'd expected that and was prepared for it. *Just keep going.*

Natalie kept her features composed in an attempt to disguise how fast her heart was now beating. Why was it that she could make million-dollar trades without her pulse skipping, but one barb from Corinne and she might as well be dangling from the side of a skyscraper by a pinkie, cold sweat breaking out beneath her dress? Parents. *Man*, they messed up their kids.

"Yes, I have been making calls," Natalie replied calmly. She didn't deny the wine binges, because, yeah. She'd definitely done that. "Claudia is working on lining up an investor right now, but before anyone in their right mind gives us money, we'll need to register a new business name. We need an office and some skin in the investment game, however light." She tried not to be obvious about taking a bracing breath. "Bottom line, I need capital."

Not even the slightest reaction from her mother. She'd seen this coming and it burned, even though they'd both been aware this talk was on the horizon.

"Surely you saved *some* money," Corinne said smoothly, a gray-black eyebrow lifting gracefully toward her hairline. "You were a partner in a very lucrative investment fund."

"Yes. I was. Unfortunately, there is a certain lifestyle that has to be maintained for people to trust financiers with their money."

"That is a fancy way of saying you lived above your means."

"Perhaps. Yes." Oh boy, keeping her irritation at bay was going to be even harder than she thought. Corinne had come locked and loaded for this conversation. "The excess is necessary, however. Parties and designer clothing and vacations and expensive rounds of golf with clients. Morrison and I had an apartment on Park Avenue. Not to mention, we'd put down a nonrefundable deposit on our wedding venue."

That last part burned. Of course it did.

She'd been offloaded by a man who claimed to love her.

But for some reason, Morrison's face didn't materialize. No, instead she saw August. Wondered what he would say about a six-figure deposit on Tribeca Rooftop. He would look so out of place among the wedding guests. He'd probably show up in jeans, a ball cap, and that faded gray navy T-shirt. He would crush her ex in an arm-wrestling match, too. Why did that make her feel better enough to continue?

"In short, yes, I do have some money. If I was simply going back to New York, I could afford to find an apartment and live comfortably for a few months. But that is not what I want to do." The kick of adrenaline in her bloodstream felt good. It had been a long time. Or maybe while getting lit to mourn the loss of everything she'd worked for, she'd accidentally numbed her ambition, too. Right now, in this moment, she had it back. She was the woman who used to look down at rows of analysts from her glass office and feel prepared to kick ass and take names. "I want to return better than ever. I want them to realize they made a mistake . . ."

"You want to rub it in their faces," Corinne supplied.

"Maybe a little," Natalie admitted. "I might have made one huge mistake, but I know if Morrison Talbot the third had made that bad call, instead of me, excuses would have been made. He probably would have been given a promotion for being a risk taker. They met in secret and voted to oust me. My partners. My *fiancé*." She closed her eyes briefly to beat back the memory of her shock. Betrayal. "If you were me, Mother, you would want a shot to go back and prove yourself."

Corinne stared at her for several beats. "Perhaps I would."

Natalie released a breath.

"Unfortunately, I don't have the money to loan you," Corinne continued, her face deepening ever so slightly with color. "As you are aware, the vineyard has been declining in profitability.

With your brother's unexpected help, we're turning it around, but it could be years before we're back in the black. All I have is this house, Natalie."

"My trust fund," Natalie said firmly, forcing it out into the open. "I'm asking for my trust fund to be released."

"My, times have changed," Corinne said with a laugh. "When you graduated from Cornell, what was it that you said at your post-ceremony dinner? You would never take a dime from us as long as you lived?"

"I'm thirty years old now. Please don't throw something in my face that I said when I was twenty-two."

Corinne sighed, refolded her hands in her lap. "You are well aware of the terms of your trust fund, Natalie. Your father might be racing cars in Italy and parading around with women half his age like a fool, but he set forth the language of the trust and as far as the bank is concerned, he's still in control."

Natalie lunged to her feet. "The language in that contract is archaic. How can it even be legal in this day and age? There has to be something you can do."

Her mother let a breath seep out. "Naturally, I agree with you. But your father would have to sign off on the change."

"I am *not* going groveling to that man. Not after he just blew us off and pretends like we don't exist. Not when he left you to do damage control after the fire four years ago."

Corinne's attention shot to the vineyard, which was lightening in the path of the sun. "I wasn't aware you cared."

"Of course I care. *You* asked *me* to leave."

"I most certainly did not," her mother scoffed.

Really. She didn't even remember? Natalie would digest that later. Getting into the semantics of the last time she'd been in

St. Helena wouldn't do her cause any good now. "We'll have to agree to disagree on that."

Corinne appeared poised to argue, but visibly changed course. "My hands are tied, Natalie. The terms of the trust are set in stone. The recipient must be gainfully employed *and* married for the money to be released. I realize that sounds like something out of Regency England, not modern-day California, but your father is old-school Italian. His parents' marriage was arranged. It's glamorous to him. It's tradition."

"It's sexist."

"Normally I would agree, but the terms of Julian's trust are the same. When the contract was set forth, your father had some grand vision in his mind. You and Julian with your flourishing families taking over the winery. Grandchildren everywhere. Success." She made an absent gesture. "When you both left without any intention of joining the family business, it broke something inside of him. The fire was the final straw. I'm not making excuses for him, I'm just trying to give you a different perspective."

Natalie lowered herself back down to the couch and implored her mother with a look. "Please, there has to be something we can do. I can't stay here forever."

"Oh, I'm so sorry that staying in your family home feels like exile."

"You try waking up every morning to the sound of Julian and Hallie trying and failing to stifle their sex noises down the hall."

"Jesus Christ."

"They call for him, too, sometimes when they think I'm not home."

With a withering eye roll, Corinne pushed to her feet and strode to the front window. "You would think your father's hasty departure would bruise the loyalty of his local friends and associates, but I assure you, it has not. They still have him up on a pedestal—and that includes Ingram Meyer."

"Who?"

"Ingram Meyer, an old friend of your father's. He's the loan officer at the St. Helena Credit Union, but more importantly, he's the trustee of yours and Julian's trust funds. Believe me, he will follow your father's instructions to the letter."

Natalie's jaw had to be touching the floor. "Some man I've never heard of—or met—holds my future in his hands?"

"I'm sorry, Natalie. The bottom line is that . . . short of convincing your father to amend the terms, there is nothing I can do."

"I wouldn't ask you to do that," Natalie sighed. "Not after how he left."

Corinne was silent a moment. "Thank you."

That was it. The end of the conversation. There was nothing more to be said. Currently, Natalie was the furthest thing from gainfully employed. And even further from being married. The patriarchy wins again. She'd have to return to New York with her tail between her legs and ask for a low-level position at one of the firms she once called rivals. They would eat up her humility with a spoon and she'd . . . take it on the chin. Pulling together enough money to open her own business would probably take a decade, because God knew nobody would invest in her after a billion-dollar mistake. But she would do it. She'd do it on her own.

"Okay." Resigned, hollow, Natalie stood on shaky legs and smoothed the skirt of her dress. "Good luck with your meetings this morning."

Corinne said nothing as Natalie left the house, closing the

door behind her and descending the steps with her chin up. This morning, she would head into town, get her hair and nails done. At the very least, she could look good when she landed back in New York, right?

But everything changed on the way to get that balayage— and like some weird nursery rhyme from hell, it involved a cat, a rat . . . and a SEAL.

About the Author

#1 *New York Times* bestselling author Tessa Bailey can solve all problems except her own, so she focuses her efforts on fictional stubborn blue-collar men and loyal, lovable heroines. She lives on Long Island, avoids the sun and social interactions, then wonders why no one has called. Dubbed the "Michelangelo of dirty talk" by *Entertainment Weekly*, Tessa writes with spice, spirit, swoon, and a guaranteed happily ever after. Catch her on TikTok @authortessabailey or check out tessabailey.com for a complete list of her books.

HOOK, LINE, AND SINKER

By Tessa Bailey

BELLINGER SISTERS
It Happened One Summer • *Hook, Line, and Sinker*

HOT & HAMMERED
Fix Her Up • *Love Her or Lose Her* • *Tools of Engagement*

THE ACADEMY
Disorderly Conduct • *Indecent Exposure* • *Disturbing His Peace*

BROKE AND BEAUTIFUL
Chase Me • *Need Me* • *Make Me*

ROMANCING THE CLARKSONS
Too Hot to Handle • *Too Wild to Tame* • *Too Hard to Forget*
Too Close to Call (novella) • *Too Beautiful to Break*

MADE IN JERSEY
Crashed Out • *Rough Rhythm* (novella)
Thrown Down • *Worked Up* • *Wound Tight*

CROSSING THE LINE
Riskier Business (novella) • *Risking It All*
Up in Smoke • *Boiling Point* • *Raw Redemption*

LINE OF DUTY
Protecting What's His • *Protecting What's Theirs* (novella)
His Risk to Take • *Officer Off Limits*
Asking for Trouble • *Staking His Claim*

SERVE
Owned by Fate • *Exposed by Fate* • *Driven by Fate*

BEACH KINGDOM
Mouth to Mouth • *Heat Stroke* • *Sink or Swim*

STANDALONE BOOKS
Unfixable • *Baiting the Maid of Honor*
Off Base (with Sophie Jordan)
Captivated (with Eve Dangerfield)
Getaway Girl • *Runaway Girl*

Tessa Bailey

HOOK, LINE, AND SINKER

a novel

AVON

An Imprint of HarperCollinsPublishers

HOOK, LINE, AND SINKER. Copyright © 2022 by Tessa Bailey. Excerpt from IT HAPPENED ONE SUMMER © 2021 by Tessa Bailey. All rights reserved. Printed in the United States of America. No part of this book may be used or reproduced in any manner whatsoever without written permission except in the case of brief quotations embodied in critical articles and reviews. For information, address HarperCollins Publishers, 195 Broadway, New York, NY 10007.

HarperCollins books may be purchased for educational, business, or sales promotional use. For information, please email the Special Markets Department at SPsales@harpercollins.com.

FIRST EDITION

Designed by Diahann Sturge
Woman-dancing emoji © streptococcus / Adobe Stock
Other emojis throughout © Giuseppe_R; Valentina Vectors; weberjake; TMvectorart / Shutterstock

Library of Congress Cataloging-in-Publication Data has been applied for.

ISBN 978-0-06-304569-9 (paperback)
ISBN 978-0-06-321274-9 (hardcover library edition)

22 23 24 25 26 LBC 36 35 34 33 32

To the nurses and doctors of NYU Langone Health—
particularly 15 West, Tisch Building, Manhattan

Acknowledgments

I really don't know where to begin thanking people for this book! This one was delayed, writing-wise, because my husband had the absolute nerve to get sick and spend three months in the ICU. If we hadn't received a miracle and gotten him back home, I'm not sure this book would have ever gotten written, let alone any others. So I truly have modern medicine, doctors, nurses, science, friends, and faith to thank for boosting me back to this place where I can write a madly touching love story and escape back into Westport with my beloved Hannah and Fox.

Thank you to Floral Park, Long Island, for rallying around me in my time of need. I didn't know the meaning of friendship until I was huddled out in my backyard in ten-degree weather, surrounded by frozen-solid friends in masks determined to give me moral support no matter their discomfort. For *months.* They went above and beyond. I'll be forever grateful.

Thank you to the romance community, authors and readers alike, for sending me love and support and gifts meant to comfort. Thank you to my (thankfully alive!) husband for making me love so many different kinds of music (even, maybe especially, Meat Loaf), as well as fostering my appreciation for record collecting. It really helped when writing Hannah to understand how particular one can be about vinyl. I'll never set my drink on one of your sleeves—especially the Floyd. Promise.

Thank you to my editor, Nicole Fischer, for really understanding the vibe and vision of the Bellinger Sisters series and for helping to give it so much life. This marks eleven books together, and I've loved every single finished product we've worked on. Thank you to everyone at Avon Books, including cover designers, publicists, and marketing gurus. You make all this possible!

Lastly, thank you to everyone who fell in love with this series. This one was straight from the heart, and I'm honored you came with me on the journey! Here's to many more.

HOOK, LINE, AND SINKER

Prologue

September 15

HANNAH (6:00 PM): Hey. Fox?

FOX (10:20 PM): Yeah.

H (10:22 PM): It's Hannah. Bellinger? I got your number from Brendan.

F (10:22 PM): Hannah. Shit. Sorry, I would have answered sooner.

H (10:23 PM): No, it's fine. Is it weird of me to text you?

F (10:23 PM): Not weird at all, Freckles. You make it back to LA safely?

H (10:26 PM): Not a scratch on me. Missing that signature Westport fish aroma already (only half kidding). Anyway, I just wanted to say thank you for the Fleetwood Mac record you left on my sister's doorstep. You really didn't have to do that.

F (10:27 PM): No big deal. I could tell you wanted it.

H (10:29 PM): How could you tell? Was it me openly sobbing when I left it behind at the expo? 😞

F (10:30 PM): Kind of tipped me off. 😉

H (10:38 PM): Ah. Well. I wish you could hear it play in person. It's magic.

F (10:42 PM): Maybe someday.

H (10:43 PM): Maybe. Thanks again.

F (11:01 PM): You didn't have to tell me your last name. There's only one Hannah.

H (11:02 PM): Sorry, can't say the same. I know several Fox's. 🎶

October 3

FOX (4:03 PM): Hey Hannah

HANNAH (4:15 PM): Hey! What's up?

F (4:16 PM): Just pulled back into the harbor after 3 days out.

F (4:18 PM): This is stupid, but you're okay, right?

H (4:19 PM): I mean, my therapist would probably say that's debatable. Physically I'm in one piece tho. Why?

F (4:20 PM): Just a weird dream. IDK . . . I dreamed you were missing. Or lost?

H (4:25 PM): That wasn't a dream. Send a chopper. 🚁✕

F (4:25 PM): 😵

F (4:26 PM): Fishermen don't ignore the dreams they have on water. Sometimes they're nothing, other times they're a premonition.

H (4:30 PM): If anyone worries in this friendship, it should be me. I've seen the Perfect Storm.

F (4:32 PM): That makes me Wahlberg in this scenario?

H (4:33 PM): Depends. Can you pull off white boxer briefs?

F (4:34 PM): And then some, babe.

F (4:40 PM): So this is a friendship?

H (4:45 PM): Yeah. Are you on board? (fishing puns, they are happening) 🎣

F (4:48 PM): I'm . . . yeah. So I can just text you whenever?

H (4:50 PM): Yeah.

F (4:55 PM): Okay then.

H (4:56 PM): Okay then.

October 22

FOX (10:30 PM): Hey, Freckles. What are you up to?

HANNAH (10:33 PM): Hey. Not much. How can you tell if you have a "flat" tire?

F (10:33 PM): Why what's going on??

H (10:35 PM): My car was making a weird noise, so I pulled over. I'm going to go check if it popped.

F (10:35 PM): Hannah it's past ten o'clock at night. Stay in the car. LOCK THE DOORS and call a tow truck.

H (10:36 PM): Yeah . . . I won't know how to describe where I am to them. One of the makeup artists at work had a séance. I think I'm in Los Feliz?

F (10:37 PM): You don't know where you are?

F (10:38 PM): This is my dream. It's happening. Premonition.

H (10:39 PM): Come on. No way.

F (10:40 PM): You were just at a séance and don't get to be skeptical.

H (10:41 PM): You know what? That's fair.

F (10:42 PM): Map your location on your phone and call a tow truck.

F (10:43 PM): Please?

H (10:45 PM): Are you this protective of all your female friends?

F (10:48 PM): You're the only one I've got.

H (10:49 PM): Fine. I'm calling a tow truck.

F (10:49 PM): 🙏

November 22

HANNAH (12:36 AM): Are you awake?

FOX (12:37 AM): Wide.

H (12:38 AM): Are you alone?

F (12:38 AM): Yes, Hannah. I'm alone.

H (12:40 AM): Let's start "Leaving on a Jet Plane" at the exact same time and listen to it together.

F (12:41 AM): Hang on. I have to download it.

H (12:42 AM): You're killing me.

F (12:42 AM): Sry my phone isn't a music encyclopedia like yours. Why this song?

H (12:44 AM): IDK. I miss my sister. A little in my feelings about it. Have you seen her around town?

F (12:45 AM): I've seen her lipstick on Brendan's collar. That count?

H (12:47 AM): That's why I'm bugging you, instead of her. I don't want to burst their bliss bubble.

F (12:48 AM): You're not bugging me, Freckles. Ok ready?

H (12:48 AM): Yup. Go.

F (12:51 AM): It's crazy how much better this song is than I remember. Why am I not listening to this all the time?

H (12:52 AM): Now you can. Isn't it amazing?

F (12:53 AM): Uh-huh. Do I get to pick next?

H (12:55 AM): Oooh. Okay. Whatcha got for me, Peacock?

F (12:57 AM): Something to cheer you up. You have the Scissor Sisters in that encyclopedia phone?

H (12:58 AM): Studio albums or live? Yes to both.

F (12:59 AM): Jesus, should have known. Start "I Don't Feel Like Dancin'" in 3 . . . 2 . . . 1 . . .

January 1

FOX (12:01 AM): Happy New Year.

HANNAH (12:02 AM): Same to you!
May it bring you crabs.

F (12:03 AM): 🙂 Any resolutions?

H (12:07 AM): Normally I would say no. But I want to take more risks this year. Put myself out there a little more workwise, you know? Don't copy me. You are AT CAPACITY on workplace risks.

F (12:09 AM): How else am I going to get crabs?

H (12:10 AM): At a restaurant, like a normal person.

F (12:10 AM): I always order the steak.

H (12:11 AM): That's irony for you.

February 5

FOX (9:10 AM): It's raining here. Give me something moody to listen to.

HANNAH (9:12 AM): Hmm. The National.
Start with "Fake Empire."

F (9:14 AM): On it. Got any plans for this weekend?

H (9:17 AM): Not really. My parents are in Aspen, so I have the house to myself. I have it to myself a lot lately. I keep expecting Piper to walk around the corner in a charcoal mask.

F (9:18 AM): Women put charcoal on their faces?

H (9:20 AM): That's tame. There is such a thing as a snail facial. 🐌

F (9:21 AM): Jesus. I'm just going to pretend I never heard that.

H (9:28 AM): Do you have plans this weekend? Heading to Seattle?

F (9:35 AM): That's always a possibility.

F (9:36 AM): But it's my mother's birthday. Might just run her over some flowers and say hey.

H (9:38 AM): You're a good son. Does she ever come see you in Westport?

F (9:45 AM): No. She doesn't.

F (9:46 AM): Thanks for the music rec, Freckles. Text you later.

February 14

HANNAH (6:03 PM): Happy Valentine's Day! Doing anything special?

FOX (6:05 PM): God no. I'd rather light myself on 🔥

F (6:09 PM): Are you? Doing something special?

H (6:11 PM): Yes, sir. I'm on a date.

F (6:11 PM): With who??

H (6:15 PM): Myself. Very charming. Might be the one.

F (6:16 PM): Lock that girl down. She's the kind you bring home to mom.

F (6:20 PM): Do you want to be on a date? With someone besides yourself?

H (6:23 PM): IDK. It wouldn't suck? Unfortunately, my type would probably define this whole holiday as a commercial gimmick. Or he'd buy me dead roses to represent the evils of consumerism. 😕

F (6:26 PM): That's a pretty specific type. Are we talking about your director crush? Sergei, right?

H (6:28 PM): Yes. My sister likes to tease me about pining for starving artists.

F (6:29 PM): You like them dark and dramatic, huh?

H (6:30 PM): Careful! You're going to give me an orgasm.

F (6:30 PM): If that was the plan, babe, you'd have had two already.

F (6:33 PM): Shit, Hannah. Sorry. I shouldn't have gone there.

H (6:34 PM): No, I went there first. Blame it on the single glass of wine I've had. #lightweight 😅

F (6:40 PM): Apart from being dark and dramatic . . . what makes a man your type? What is eventually going to make a man The One?

H (6:43 PM): I think . . . if they can find a reason to laugh with me on the worst day.

F (6:44 PM): That sounds like the opposite of your type.

H (6:45 PM): It does, doesn't it? Must be the wine.

H (6:48 PM): He'll need to have a cabinet full of records and something to play them on, of course.

F (6:51 PM): Well obviously.

February 28

FOX (7:15 PM): How was your day?

HANNAH (7:17 PM): It had sort of a "Fast Car" by Tracy Chapman feeling to it.

F (7:18 PM): Like . . . nostalgic?

H (7:20 PM): Yeah. A little blue. I think I miss Westport?

F (7:20 PM): Come here.

F (7:23 PM): If you want.

H (7:25 PM): I wish! We just started casting a new movie. Not a great time.

F (7:27 PM): Have you kept your resolution? To take more risks at work?

H (7:28 PM): Not yet. I'm working up to it, tho.

H (7:29 PM): Seriously. Aaaany minute now. (crickets)

F (7:32 PM): This is where I remind you that the first time we met, you were facing off with a boat captain twice your size, ready to tear his limbs off for shouting at your sister. You're a badass. 💪

H (7:35 PM): Thanks for the reminder. I'll get there. It's just . . . imposter syndrome, I guess. Like, what makes me think I'm qualified to make movie soundtracks?

F (7:37 PM): I get imposter syndrome.

H (7:37 PM): You do?

F (7:38 PM): If you could only hear me laughing.

H (7:39 PM): I . . . wish I could. Hear you laughing.

F (7:40 PM): Yeah. Wouldn't mind hearing your laugh, either.

H (7:45 PM): How was your day, Peacock?

F (7:47 PM): Worked on the boat with Sanders, so a shit ton of Springsteen.

H (7:49 PM): Blue collar boys. Making money! Sweating in jeans! Bandanas in pockets! 😍

F (7:50 PM): It's like you were right there with us.

March 8

HANNAH (8:45 AM): Hey. I think you're out on the boat.

H (8:46 AM): Hope you're being safe.

H (9:02 AM): When you're out on the water and can't text back, I really notice it.

H (9:03 AM): The lack of you.

H (9:10 AM): So I'm glad we're friends. That's all I'm awkwardly trying to say.

H (9:18 AM): If you dream of me this time, try dreaming I can fly or turn invisible. Or that my best friend is Cher. That's way cooler than a flat tire.

H (9:19 AM): Not that I'm assuming you regularly dream of me.

H (9:26 AM): I don't dream of you that often, of course. So.

H (9:39 AM): Anyway. Talk soon!

Chapter One

𝓗annah Bellinger had always been more of a supporting actress than a leading lady. The hype girl. If she'd lived in Regency England, she would be the second at every duel, but never wield the pistol. That distinction was never more obvious than now, as she sat in the dark audition room watching a girl with pure leading-lady material emote like her life depended on it.

Hannah's hands disappeared into the sleeves of her sweatshirt like twin turtles ducking into their shells, her hidden fingers curling around the clipboard in her lap. Here it came. The big finale. Across the Storm Born production studio, their lead actor ran through a scene with their final actress hopeful of the day. Since eight A.M., the studio had been a revolving door of wide-eyed ingénues, and didn't it figure that not a single one of them would click with Christian until Hannah was past the point of starving, her mouth tasting like stale coffee?

Such was the life of a production assistant.

"You forgot to trust me," the redhead whispered brokenly, tears creating trails of mascara down her cheeks. Dang, this girl was fire. Even Sergei, the writer and director of the project, was held in a rare thrall, the tip of his glasses inserted between his full, dreamy lips, that ankle crossed over the opposite knee, jiggling, jiggling. That was his *I'm impressed* posture. After two years of working as his production assistant—and nursing a long-unrequited crush on the man—Hannah knew all his tells. And this redhead could bet the rent on getting cast in *Glory Daze*.

Sergei turned to Hannah where she huddled in the corner of the freezing conference room and raised an excited black eyebrow. The shared moment of triumph was so unexpected, the clipboard slid off her lap and clattered to the ground. Flustered, she reached for it but didn't want to lose the moment with the director, so she jackknifed and gave Sergei a thumbs-up. Only to remember her thumb was trapped inside the sleeve of her sweatshirt, creating a weird, starfish-looking gesture that he missed, anyway, because he'd turned back around.

You absolute turnip, you.

Hannah replaced the clipboard in her lap and pretended to write Very Serious notes. Thank God it was dark in the rear of the studio. No one could see the tomato-colored tidal wave surging up her neck.

"End scene!" Sergei crowed, standing up from the table of producers that faced the audition area to deliver a slow clap. "Extraordinary. Simply extraordinary."

The redhead, Maxine, beamed while simultaneously trying to wipe away her dripping mascara with the hem of her black T-shirt. "Oh wow. Thank you."

"That felt fine." Christian sighed, signaling Hannah for his cold brew.

I have been summoned.

She rose from her chair and set the clipboard down, retrieving the actor's beverage from inside the mini-fridge along the wall and bringing it to him. When she held out the metal travel tumbler and he made no move to take it, she gritted her teeth and held the straw to his lips. When he had the nerve to look her in the eye while sucking noisily, she stared back stone-faced.

This is what you wanted.

A regular job that would allow her to earn money—and not rely on the many millions her stepfather had in the bank. If she dropped her last name, slurpy ol' Christian would spit out his cold brew. But apart from Sergei, no one knew that Hannah was the legendary producer's daughter, and that's how she chose to keep it.

Stepdaughter, she mentally corrected herself.

A distinction she never would have bothered to make before last summer.

Had that trip to Westport six months ago really happened? The weeks she'd lived above the Pacific Northwest bar, restoring it lovingly with her sister in tribute to their birth father, seemed like a hazy dream. One she couldn't seem to shake. It rode her consciousness like dolphins outlined in a barrel wave, making her wistful at the oddest times. Like now, when Christian was bugging his heartthrob eyes out, letting her know he was ready for straw removal.

"Thanks," he huffed. "Now I'm going to have to pee."

"Look at the bright side," Hannah murmured, so as not to interrupt an effusive Sergei. "There are mirrors in the bathroom. Your favorite."

Christian snorted, allowing a grudging uptick to one side of his mouth. "God, you're such a bitch. I love you."

". . . is what you say into the mirrors?"

They traded a lip-twitching glare.

"I think I speak for the production team when I say we've found our Lark," Sergei said, coming around the table to kiss both cheeks of the bouncing actress. "Are you available to begin shooting in late March?" Without waiting for the girl to answer, Sergei pressed a row of knuckles to his forehead. "I am seeing an entirely different location for the shoot now. The energy Christian and Maxine create together does not work against the backdrop of Los Angeles. I'm certain. It's so earthy. So original. They sanded the edges off each other. We need a softer location. The sharp corners of LA will only snag them, hold them back."

Hannah stilled, watched the table of producers trade nervous glances. The artistic temperament was real—and Sergei's tended to be more volatile than most. He'd once made the entire crew wear blindfolds on set so they wouldn't dilute the magic of a scene by viewing it. *Every set of eyes strips another layer of mystery!* But that temperament was one of the main reasons Hannah gravitated toward the director. He operated on chaos, bowing to the whims of creativity. He believed his choices and didn't have time for naysayers.

Real leading-man material.

What was that like? To be the star in the movie of your life?

Hannah had been playing second fiddle so long, she was getting arthritis in her fingers. Her sister, Piper, had demanded the spotlight since childhood, and Hannah was always comfortable waiting in the wings, anticipating her cue to walk on as best supporting actress, even providing bail money on more than one occasion. That was where she shined. Bolstering the heroine at her lowest point, stepping in to defend the leading lady when necessary, saying the right thing in a pivotal heart-to-heart.

Supporting actresses didn't want or need the glory. They were content to prop up the main character and be instrumental in their mission. And Hannah was content in that role, too. Wasn't she?

A memory trickled in without her consent.

A memory that made her jumpy for some reason.

That one afternoon six months ago at a vinyl convention in Seattle when she'd felt like the main character. Browsing through records with Fox Thornton, king crab fisherman and a lady-killer of the highest caliber. When they'd stood shoulder to shoulder and shared a pair of AirPods, listening to "Silver Springs," the world just kind of fading out around them.

Just an anomaly.

Just a fluke.

Restless, probably because of the nine cups of black coffee she'd drunk throughout the day, Hannah returned Christian's cold brew to the fridge and waited on the periphery to see what kind of curveball Sergei was about to throw the team. Honestly, she loved his left turns, even if no one else did. The tempest of his imagination could not be stopped. It was enviable. It was hot.

This guy was her type.

She just wasn't his, if the last two years were any indication.

"What do you mean you no longer see Los Angeles as the backdrop?" one of the producers asked. "We already have the permits."

"Am I the only one who saw the rain falling in this scene? The quiet melancholia unfolding around them?" Who didn't want to date a man who dropped that kind of terminology without batting an eyelash? "We cannot pit the raw volume of Los Angeles against them. It'll drown them out. We need to let the nuance thrive. We need to give it oxygen and space and sunlight."

"You just said you wanted to give it rain," the producer pointed out drily.

Sergei laughed in that way artists do when someone is too dense to grasp their vision. "A plant needs sunlight *and* water to grow, does it not?" His frustration was causing his normally light Russian accent to thicken. "We need a more subtle location for the shoot. A place that will lend focus to the actors."

Latrice, the new location scout, raised her hand slowly. "Like . . . Toluca Lake?"

"No! Outside of Los Angeles. Picture—"

"I know a place." Hannah said it without thinking. Her mouth was moving, and then the words were hanging in the air like a comic-strip quote bubble, too late to pop. Everyone turned to look at her at once. A very un–supporting actress position to be in, even if it was refreshing to have Sergei's eyes on her longer than the usual fleeting handful of seconds. It reminded Hannah, rather inconveniently, of the way someone else gave her his undivided attention, sometimes picking up on her moods simply via text message.

So she blurted the next part in an attempt to block out that useless thought. "Last summer, I spent some time in Washington. A small fishing town called Westport." She was only suggesting this for two reasons. One, she wanted to support Sergei's idea and possibly earn herself one of those fleeting smiles. And two, what if she could sneak a trip to see her sister in the name of work? Counting their brief visit at Christmas, she'd only seen Piper and her fiancé, Brendan, once in six months. Missing them was a constant ache in her stomach.

"Fishing village," Sergei mused, rubbing his chin and starting to pace, mentally rewriting the screenplay. "Tell me more about it."

"Well." Hannah unwrapped her hands from inside her sleeves. One did not pitch a genius director, a location scout, and a panel of producers with her fists balled in a UCLA sweatshirt. Already she was cursing her decision to pile her straw-colored hair into a baseball cap this morning. *Let us not add to the kid-sister vibe.* "It's moody and misty, set right on the water. Most residents have lived there since they were born, and they're very, um"—*set in their ways, unwelcoming, wonderful, protective*—"routine-oriented. Fishing is their livelihood, and I guess you could say there's an element of melancholy there. For the fishermen who've been lost."

Like her father, Henry Cross.

Hannah had to push past the lump in her throat to continue. "It's quaint. Has kind of a weathered feel. It's like"—she closed her eyes and searched through her mental catalogue of music—"you know that band Skinny Lister that does kind of a modern take on sea shanties?"

They stared back at her blankly.

"Never mind. You know what sea shanties sound like, don't you? Imagine a packed bar full of courageous men who fear and respect the sea. Imagine them singing odes to the water. The ocean is their mother. Their lover. She provides for them. And everything in this town reflects that love of the sea. The salt mist in the air. The scent of brine and storm clouds. The knowledge in the eyes of the residents when they look up at the sky to judge the oncoming weather. In fear. In reverence. Everywhere you go there's the sound of lapping water against the docks, cawing seagulls, the hum of danger . . ." Hannah trailed off when she realized Christian was staring at her like she'd swapped his cold brew for kitty litter.

"Anyway, that's Westport," she finished. "That's how it feels."

Sergei said nothing for long moments, and she forced herself not to fidget in the rare glow of his attention. "That's the place. That's where we need to go."

The producers were shooting flamethrowers at Hannah from their eyes. "We don't have it in the budget, Sergei. We'll have to apply for new permits. Travel expenses for an entire cast and crew. Lodging."

Latrice tapped her clipboard, seeming kind of eager for the challenge. "We could drive. It's a trek, but not out of the question . . . and skipping the plane would save on funds."

"Let me worry about the money," Sergei said, waving a hand. "I'll crowdsource. Put my own cash toward it. Whatever is necessary. Hannah and Latrice, you'll work out the permits and travel details?"

"Of course," she said, agreeing to a slew of sleepless nights.

Latrice nodded, shooting Hannah a wink.

More flamethrowers from the men who'd been silly enough to think they were in charge. "We haven't even scouted locations—"

"Hannah will take care of it. She obviously knows this place like the back of her hand. Did you hear that description?" Sergei gave her a once-over, as if seeing her for the first time, and her toes curled inside her red Converse. "Impressive."

Don't blush.

Too late.

She was a cherry tomato.

"Thank you." Sergei nodded and started collecting his things, draping a worn leather satchel over his slim shoulder, messing up his dark boyish locks in the process. "We'll be in touch," he called to Maxine, sailing out of the studio.

And that, as they say in the business, was a wrap.

Hannah escaped the collective glare of the producers and jogged from the room, already drawing the phone from her back pocket to call Piper. She ducked into the ladies' lounge for privacy, but before she could hit the call button, Latrice popped her head in through the door.

"Hey," she said, sticking a thumbs-up through the opening. "Good job in there. I've been dying to stretch my legs a little. Between us, we've got this."

Thank God they'd hired Latrice to take location-scout duties off Hannah's plate. She was a dynamo. "We've so got this. I'm starting an email to you as soon as I make this call."

"You better."

Latrice dipped out again, and, bolstered by the vote of confidence, Hannah dialed Piper. Her sister answered on the third ring sounding out of breath.

Followed by the very distinct groan of bedsprings.

"I don't even want to know what you were doing," Hannah drawled. "But say hi to Brendan for me."

"Hannah says hi," Piper purred to her sea captain fiancé, who'd obviously just rung her bell, which was a constant event in their household. A fact Hannah unfortunately knew all too well after living with them for a couple of weeks over the summer. "What's up, sis?"

Hannah hopped up onto the counter beside the end sink. "Is your guest room free?"

A rustle of sheets in the background. "Why? Oh my God. Why?" Hannah could almost see the wild flutter of her sister's hands in the vicinity of her throat. "Are you coming here? When?"

"Soon." Then she qualified: "If we can get permits to film."

A beat passed. "Permits to film in Westport?"

"Pretty sure I just convinced Sergei it's the only place on earth that will work for his vision." Hannah sniffed. "My powers of persuasion often go unrecognized."

"Like hell a film crew is coming here," Brendan said in the background.

Hannah's chest squeezed at the familiarity of her sister's ebullient nature set alongside her fiancé's growly, no-bullshit personality. She missed them so much.

"Tell the captain it will only be for a couple of weeks. I'll make sure to scrub the Hollywood stink off every precious cobblestone before we leave."

"Let me worry about him," Piper said playfully. "He's forgetting what a good mood I'll be in having my sister in town. And of course you can stay here, Hanns. Of course. Just . . . . I hope you're not planning for *this* month? Brendan's parents are coming to visit soon. They'll be using the guest room."

"Ooh." Hannah winced. "If we get a fast enough turnaround on the permits, it could be late March. Sergei is on a mission." Hannah turned on the counter to check her reflection, wincing at the hair sticking out of the sides of her ball cap. "But don't stress, I can just stay wherever they put up the crew. Getting to see you will be more than enough."

"Can't you stall Sergei? Maybe tell him Westport is extra moody in April?"

"How did you know he was going for a moody vibe?"

"His last film was called *Fragmented Joy*, wasn't it?"

"Valid point." Hannah laughed, pressing the phone tighter to her ear, trying to feel her sister's warmth over the phone. "Seriously, though. Don't worry about the guest-room thing. It's no big—"

"You know, there is one poss . . ." Piper trailed off. "Never mind."

Hannah's head tilted at her sister's hasty retreat. "What?"

"No, really. It was a bad idea."

"Then tell me. I want to pooh-pooh it, too."

Piper humphed. "I was going to say that Fox has that empty bedroom at his place. And as you know, he's out on the boat with Brendan for long stretches. But, like, he's also home for stretches, which is why it's a bad idea. Forget I said it."

Stupid, really. The way Hannah sprang off the counter at the mention of the devilish charmer's name and started shoving pieces of her hair back under the brim of her hat. "It's not a bad idea," she said, automatically defending Fox, even though they hadn't seen each other in six months.

There had only been the daily texts.

That she definitely wouldn't be mentioning to Piper.

"We're friendly." *Lower your voice.* "We're friends."

"I know that, Hanns," Piper said indulgently.

"And you know"—she dropped her volume even more—"I still have that thing for a certain someone." Why Hannah suddenly felt the need to prove to Piper—and possibly herself—that she was, indeed, only friends with a man who went through women like nickels in a slot machine, she had no idea. But there it was. "Staying with Fox isn't a terrible idea. Like you said, he'll only be there half the time. I'll be able to keep food in the fridge, which I won't in a hotel room. It will slice a little off the production's expenditures and earn me points with Sergei."

"Speaking of Sergei, are you finally going to ask him?"

Hannah took a deep breath, glancing toward the door of the bathroom. "Yeah, I think this might be my moment, since I just proved my worth in there. There is already a music coordinator on the payroll, but I'm going to ask to assist. It's a step in the right direction, at least, right?"

"Damn right," Piper said, clapping at the rate of a humming-bird's wings in the background. "You got this, bish."

Maybe.

Maybe not.

Hannah cleared her throat. "Will you talk to Fox for me about using the guest room? He might feel pressured if I ask him directly. It's just to put the idea out there, in case it's March for sure and the guest room will be taken."

Piper hesitated briefly. "Okay, Hanns. Love you."

"Love you, too. Hugs to the mean one."

Hannah hung up the phone on a giggle from Piper and tapped the device against her mouth. Why was her pulse racing? Surely not because there was a possibility she could occupy a room in Fox's apartment. There might have been an inescapable attraction toward the relief skipper the first time they met, but after his phone pinged for the thousandth time with blatant booty calls, it became woefully obvious that his incredible looks were used to his advantage with the opposite sex.

Fox Thornton has not her type. He was bad boyfriend material. But he *was* her friend.

Her thumb hovered over the screen of her phone momentarily before tapping on their text thread, reading the one he'd sent last night just before she drifted off to sleep.

FOX (11:32 PM): Today was a Hozier vibe for me.

HANNAH (11:33 PM): My day was so very Amy Winehouse.

There was nothing friendlier than sharing what kind of music defined their day. It didn't matter how much she looked forward to those nightly texts. Staying with Fox imposed no risk whatsoever. It was possible to be just friends with a man who exuded sex—and she would have no problem proving it.

Satisfied with her logic, Hannah got on the phone and started organizing.

Chapter Two

Fox settled back into his couch cushions and tipped a beer to his lips, taking a long sip to disguise the urge to laugh at the serious expression of the man sitting across from him. "What is this, Cap? An intervention?"

It wasn't that he'd never seen Brendan looking disgruntled before. God knows he had. Fox just hadn't seen the *Della Ray*'s captain anything but blissful for the last six months since meeting his fiancée, Piper. It was almost enough to make a man want to reevaluate his position on relationships.

Yeah. Right.

"No, it's not an intervention," Brendan said, adjusting the beanie on his head. Then taking it off altogether and resting it on his knee. "But if you keep putting off the conversation about taking over as captain, I might have to stage one."

This marked the eighth time Brendan had asked him to step up and lead the crew. At first, he'd been nothing short of baffled. Had he given the impression he could be responsible for the lives of five men? If so, it must have been an accident. He was content to take orders, do his job well, and skedaddle with his cut of the haul, whether his earnings came from crabs in the fall or fishing the rest of the year.

Thriving under pressure was in a king crab fisherman's blood. He'd stood beside Brendan on the *Della Ray* and stared death in the eye. More than once. But battling nature wasn't the same as taking charge of a crew. Making decisions. Owning up to the mistakes he would inevitably make. That was a different kind of pressure entirely—and he wasn't sure he was built for that. More specifically, he wasn't sure the crew *believed* he was built to lead them. Speaking from a lot of experience, a fishing vessel's team needed to have total trust in their captain. Any hesitation could cost a man his life. Those assholes barely took him seriously as a human being, let alone as the one giving orders.

Yeah. All he needed was a place to sleep and watch baseball, a couple of beers at the end of a hard day, and a willing, lush body in the dark.

Although the need for that last one hadn't been all that pressing lately.

Hadn't been pressing at all, really.

Fox popped his jaw and focused. "An intervention won't be necessary." He shrugged. "Told you, I'm honored you'd think of me, man. But I'm not interested." He wedged the beer bottle between his thighs and reached down to stroke the braided leather wrapped around his wrist. "I'm happy to relieve you when you're belowdecks, but I'm not looking for permanent."

"Yeah." Brendan eyed Fox's barren apartment pointedly. "No kidding."

That was fair enough. Anyone who walked into the two-bedroom overlooking Grays Harbor would assume Fox was in the process of moving in, when in reality he'd just passed his six-year anniversary in the place.

At thirty-one, he was back in Westport, with no plans to leave. Once upon a time, he'd purposely attended college in Minnesota, but that didn't turn out so well. Served him right for thinking this place wouldn't suck him back in. It always did eventually. Leaving the first time had cost him most of the ingenuity he possessed, and now? He channeled what was left into fishing.

And women. Or he used to, anyway.

"Have you considered asking Sanders?" Fox forced himself to stop messing with his bracelet. "He could use the extra cut with the baby on the way."

"He belongs on deck. Your place is in the wheelhouse— that's a gut feeling." Brendan didn't blink. "The second boat is almost finished. I'll be forming a new crew, expanding. I want to leave the *Della Ray* in good hands. Hands I trust."

"Jesus, you don't let up," Fox said on a laugh, pushing to his feet and crossing to the fridge for another beer, even though he'd only drunk half of the first. Just for something to do with his hands. "Part of me is almost enjoying this. Not every day I get to tell the captain no."

Brendan grunted. "I'm going to wear you down, you stubborn bastard."

Fox gave him a tight smile over his shoulder. "You won't. And you're one to call someone stubborn, dude who wore his wedding ring seven extra years."

"Well," Brendan rumbled. "I found a good reason to take it off."

There he went, looking blissful again.

Fox chuckled, uncapped his second beer with his teeth, and spat the cap into the sink. "Speaking of your reason for ending your self-imposed celibacy, shouldn't you be home having dinner with her?"

"She's keeping my spaghetti warm for me." Brendan shifted in his seat, pinned him with a laser look that was famous among the crew. It translated to *Sit down and shut the hell up.* "I had another reason for coming over here to talk."

"Do you need advice on women again? Because you're way out of my depth now. If you're here to ask me what your fiancée wants, ask me to recite the periodic table, instead. There's a better chance of me getting that right."

"I don't need advice." Brendan looked at him hard. Closely. On the hunt for bullshit. "Hannah is coming to town."

Fox's throat closed up. He was halfway to sitting down when Brendan said those five words, so he twisted at the last second, staying half turned, stuffing an unnecessary pillow behind his back so he wouldn't have to look his oldest friend in the eye. And, God, how absolutely pitiful was that? "Oh yeah? What for?"

Brendan sighed. Crossed his arms. "You know she's still working for that production company. Somehow she convinced them Westport would be a good place to film."

Fox's laughter cracked in the sparse living room. "You must be thrilled."

The captain was the unofficial mayor of Westport. He was notoriously a man of few words, but when he gave his opinion on something, everyone damn well listened. In some towns, football stars were revered. In this place, it was the fishermen—and that went double for the man behind the wheel. "I don't care what they do as long as they stay out of my hair."

"People from LA staying out of your hair," Fox mused, forcing himself to delay the conversation about Hannah. Like some kind of weird, self-inflicted punishment. "How did that work out last time?"

"That's different. It was Piper." *Well, I'll be damned.* The tips of the man's ears were red. "Anyway, my parents will be here visiting while this whole filming business is going on. That's why Hannah can't use our guest room."

He feigned annoyance. "So you offered mine."

It was hard to tell if Brendan was buying his act. "Piper had kind of nixed the idea, but Hannah seemed interested."

Fox's thumbnail dug into the beer label and ripped a clean strip down the side. "Really. Hannah wants to stay here?" Why were his palms turning damp? "How long are they going to be filming? How long would she stay?"

"Two weeks or so. Figured she'd have the place to herself half the time, when we're out on the boat."

"Right."

But the other half of the time, they would be there together.

How the hell was Fox supposed to feel about that?

More importantly—and this was a question he asked himself way too often—how the hell was he supposed to feel about Hannah? He'd never, not once, had a girl for a friend. Last summer, Hannah and her sister had crash-landed in Westport, two rich girls from LA who'd been stripped of their allowances by Daddy. Fox had only been trying to help Brendan nurse his crush on Piper by distracting the younger sibling with a walk to the record store.

Then they'd gone to the vinyl convention together. Spent the last six months texting each other about everything under the sun . . . and she'd had the nerve to crawl up under his skin in a way that made absolutely no sense to him.

Sex was a non-possibility between them.

That had been established early on, for a host of reasons.

Number one being that he didn't fish local waters.

If he needed the company of a woman—and he should really get back to doing that kind of thing sometime—he went to Seattle. No chance of accidentally sleeping with someone's sister or wife or cousin's cousin, and he could wash his hands of the whole encounter afterward. Return to Westport with no chance of bumping into a hookup. Easy. No muss, no fuss.

The second reason he couldn't sleep with Hannah was the very man sitting in his living room. Fox was read the riot act last summer. It was seared into his memory. Sleeping with Piper's little sister would spell disaster, because if she got attached, Fox would undoubtedly hurt her feelings. And that would make his captain and best friend's life hell, because the Bellinger sisters stuck together.

But Fox had a third, and most important, reason for keeping his hands off Hannah. She was his friend. She was a woman who genuinely liked him for something other than his dick. And it made him feel terrifyingly good to be around her. To talk to her.

They had fun. Made each other laugh.

The way she translated song lyrics out loud made him think. In the six months that she'd been gone, he'd noticed the sunrise more. He'd started paying attention to strangers, their actions. Listening to music. Even his job seemed to have more gravity to it. Hannah did that somehow. Made him look around and consider.

Brendan was staring at him, brows drawn. Uncomfortable.

"Of course Hannah can stay here. But are you sure it's a good idea?" His stomach drew in on itself. "People might notice she's staying here. With me."

The captain hedged. "I think certain speculation might be par for the course. As long as what folks are speculating on isn't really happening."

"Say it plainly." Fox made an impatient sound, growing increasingly aware of what was coming. "Tell me not to fuck her."

The captain rubbed the center of his forehead. "Look, I hate having to say this to you more than once. Feels like overkill and . . . Jesus, your sex life is your own business, but it could be different with her staying here. Close quarters and all that."

Fox refused to make the conversation easy for his friend. And he suspected Brendan had known that coming here. They were men who regularly took responsibility for each other's lives. They didn't lecture each other. It *was* overkill. Maybe that was why the conversation hit below the belt this time, when before it felt more like a minor slap.

When the silence extended without Fox saying anything, Brendan sighed. "She's my future sister-in-law. She's not temporary in any way, okay? Hands off." He made a decisive gesture. "That's the last time I'll bring it up."

"Are you sure? I can pencil you in for tomorrow—"

"Don't be a jackass." They both visibly shook off their irritation, adjusting shirt collars and pretending to be interested in the television. "We probably didn't even need to have this conversation, considering she's still got a crush on this director guy. Sergei." Brendan tapped his knee. "Am I supposed to do something about that situation, too? Go threaten to break his jaw if he takes advantage of Hannah?"

"No. Christ, it's not the guy's fault she likes him." Fox said the words in a burst to relieve the pressing weight on his chest. He'd known about this crush of Hannah's since summer and she'd still been pining for him in February, so it had probably been stupid of him to hope the infatuation had run its course. It wasn't his favorite subject to discuss. On account of any mention of the director making him want to kick a hole through his drywall. "You're going to be busy with your parents while Hannah is here. I'll keep an eye on it, if you want. This thing with the director."

Why on God's green earth did he offer to do that?

Not a damn clue.

But he'd be lying if Brendan's immediate gratitude didn't ease the sting of their prior conversation. Fox might be a manwhore, but he could be trusted to protect someone's back. He'd made a career out of it. "Yeah?"

Fox jerked a shoulder, took a sip of his beer. "Sure. If I think something is developing there, I'll . . ." Sabotage came to mind. "Make sure she's safe." He didn't even want to explore why those words spread like warm honey on his agitated nerve endings. Protecting Hannah. What a responsibility that would be. "Not that she isn't capable of that herself," he added quickly.

"Right, sure," Brendan said. Also quickly. "Even so . . ."

"Uh-huh. Watch him like a hawk."

Brendan filled up his barrel chest and let out a gusting exhale, slapping the arm of his chair. "Well. Thank God this is over."

Fox pointed his beer straight ahead. "Door's that way."

The captain grunted and took his leave. Fox didn't even pretend to be interested in his beer after that. Instead, he got up and crossed the room, stopping in front of the cabinet he'd picked up at a rummage sale. Buying furniture went against his grain, but he'd needed somewhere to store the vinyl records he'd started collecting. He'd bought his first on their trip to Seattle. The Rolling Stones. *Exile on Main St.* Even Hannah had approved when he'd picked it out at the record convention.

Anyway, the damn thing had started looking lonely, just sitting there all by itself, so he'd walked over to Disc N Dat and purchased a few more. Hendrix, Bowie, the Cranberries. Classics. The stack had grown so much, it felt almost accusatory in its silence, so—after trying to talk himself out of it for a couple of weeks—he'd ordered a record player.

Fox reached back behind the cabinet where he kept the key, sliding it out of the leather pouch. He unlocked the door and looked at the vertical rainbow of albums, only hesitating for a second before pulling out Madness. Dropping the needle on "Our House." After listening to it all the way through, he pulled out his phone and started the song again, recording an audio clip and firing it Hannah's way.

A few minutes later, she sent him back a clip of the *Golden Girls* theme song.

Through music, they'd just acknowledged she'd be staying in his guest room—and this was how it had been since she left. Fox waiting for the messages to stop, holding his breath at the end of every day, only releasing it when the text came.

Swallowing, he turned and looked at the guest room. Hannah was in LA. This was a friendship based on something more . . . pure than he was accustomed to. And it was safe. Texting was safe. A way of offering more to someone without giving up everything.

Would he be able to keep that up with her living in the same apartment?

Chapter Three

Ƒor two weeks, Hannah and Latrice had worked overtime to make the location swap from LA to Westport happen in the name of artistic vision. Westport business owners had been finessed, the chamber of commerce fluffed. Permits sealed and housing nailed down. Now they were T-minus ten minutes until the chartered bus reached the small Washington fishing village.

If Hannah was going to make professional strides during the filming of *Glory Daze*, it was now or never. She finally had to woman up and ask Sergei for the opportunity, because as soon as the bus pulled to a stop, he'd hit the ground running and she'd miss her chance.

Stalling shamefully, Hannah sunk down in the pleather seat and scrubbed her hands over her face. She yanked out her AirPods, cutting off Dylan's greatest hits, and shoved the devices into her pockets. Reaching up, she removed her ball cap, running nervous fingers through her hair several times, struggling to see her reflection in the window. Her movements stilled when she realized the impromptu primp session wasn't working. She still looked like a PA. The lowest woman on the food chain.

Definitely not someone Sergei would trust with an entire film soundtrack.

She flopped back in the seat, knee jiggling, and let the raucous sounds of the bus drown out her sigh. Over the top of the seat in front of her, she watched Sergei and Brinley, the music coordinator, lean their heads together to converse and then break apart laughing.

Now, Brinley?

She was leading-lady material. A tailored, tasteful, bobbed-brunette transplant from New York who had a different statement necklace for every outfit. A woman who walked into a room and got the job she applied for, because she dressed for it. Because she exuded confidence and expected her due.

And Brinley had Hannah's dream job.

Two years ago, Hannah had purposefully asked her stepfather to find her a low-level position at a production company, and he'd tapped Sergei at Storm Born. At Hannah's request, her stepfather had asked his casual acquaintance to be discreet about their connection, so she could be just Hannah, as opposed to famed producer Daniel Bellinger's stepkid. She had a bachelor's in music history from UCLA, but she knew nothing about film. If she'd leaned harder on her stepfather's name, she probably could have landed a producer position, but where was the fairness in that when she didn't know the industry? It had been a choice to learn from the sidelines.

And she had. Being in charge of boatloads of paperwork and record keeping meant she'd had a lot of opportunities to study Brinley's cue sheets, synchronization contracts, and notes. No one technically knew she'd taken a quiet interest in that side of the production company. Hannah still lacked hands-on training, but two years later, she was ready to move up the ranks.

She observed Sergei and Brinley with a hole in her stomach.

They were behind-the-scenes talent, but approaching them was just like walking up to the lead actors. Still, she was growing weary of holding Christian's straw and getting slurped on.

A salt-air breeze filtered in through the cracked bus window. While it jolted her with nostalgia, kissing her skin with welcome wherever it touched, it also told Hannah they were really close to Westport. If she wanted to make the slightest step toward progress, she needed to act now.

Hannah rolled her shoulders back and shoved the baseball cap into her tote bag, ignoring the curious looks from cast and crew as she picked her way up to the front of the bus. Her pulse ticked in the base of her neck, moisture fleeing from her mouth. When she drew even with Sergei and Brinley, they smiled expectantly. Kindly. As in, *Kindly explain why you're interrupting our conversation.*

Not for the first time, she wondered if Brinley and Sergei were secretly seeing each other, but the gap of pleather seat between them—and the rock on Brinley's finger from someone else—spoke to them being just friends.

Fact was, the two of them had to work closely. Coordinating music for movies was an intricate process, the score often crafted in postproduction. But Storm Born had their own way of compiling the track list that would play beneath the dialogue or during montages. They created it *while* the filming process took place, relying heavily on the mood of the moment (read:

Sergei's whims). And they tended to use music that already existed and trimmed it down accordingly, rather than creating music to fit the film.

Hannah couldn't dream of anything better than summing up a distinct moment with the right song. To help weave together the atmosphere. Music was the backbone of movies. Of everything. One line from a song could help Hannah define her own feelings, and the opportunity to put that passion to art was something she spent every day wanting.

Ask them. The bus is almost there.

"Um . . ."

Oh, good opener. A filler word.

Hannah dug deep for the girl who'd been brave enough to pitch Westport to a room full of producers and talent. She was starting to think her nostalgia for this place had spoken on her behalf. "Brinley. Sergei," Hannah said, making herself look them both in the eyes. "I was wondering if—"

Of course the bus chose that moment to stop.

And of course Hannah was too busy adjusting her clothing and twisting her rings and generally fidgeting to catch hold of anything that might prevent her from sprawling sideways down the center of the row. She landed hard on her shoulder and hip, her temple connecting with the floor. A truly humiliating *oof* launched from her mouth, followed by the most deafening silence that had ever occurred on planet Earth.

No one moved. Hannah debated the merits of crawling under one of the seats until the world had the decency to end, but thoughts of hiding vanished when Sergei hopped across Brinley and stepped over Hannah's legs, bending down to help her back to her feet.

"Hannah!" His eyes ran over her, top to bottom. "Are you okay?" Without waiting for an answer, Sergei directed an angry look toward the front of the bus where the driver sat watching them, unfazed. "Hey, man. How about making sure everyone is seated before hitting the brakes?"

Hannah didn't have a chance to rightfully claim the blame, because Sergei was already ushering her off the bus while everyone stared openmouthed at the PA with the growing knot on her head. Yup, she could already feel it forming. Good God. She'd finally mustered up the courage to ask if she could observe the soundtrack process. Now she might as well just quit and start looking for positions as a sandwich-board operator.

Although, there were worse consequences to stupidity than having the dreamy director's arm around her shoulders, helping her off the bus. This close, she could smell his aftershave, kind of an orangey clove scent. It was just like Sergei to pick something unique and unexpected. She looked up into his expressive face, at the black hair that met in the middle of his head in a subtle faux-hawk. His goatee was engineered to perfection.

If she wasn't careful, she'd read too much into his concern. She'd start to wonder if maybe Sergei could learn to love an accident-prone supporting actress instead of a leading lady, after all?

Realizing she was staring, Hannah tore her wistful eyes off the man she'd been crushing on for two years—and saw Fox crossing the parking lot in their direction, his striking face a mask of alarm. "Hannah?"

Her mind made a scratchy humming sound, like the one a record makes in between songs. Probably because she'd communicated with this man every day for six—no, nearly seven—months now but never heard his voice. Perhaps because his identity had been whittled down to words on a screen, she'd forgotten that he commanded attention like a grand finale of fireworks in the night sky.

Without turning around, she knew every straight woman had her face pressed up against the windows of the bus, watching the maestro of feminine wetness cross the road, his dark blond hair blowing around in the wind, the lower half of his face covered in unruly, unshaped stubble, darker than the hair on his head.

With that pretty-boy face, he really should have been soft. Used to getting his way. Maybe, possibly even short. *God, if you're listening?* But instead he looked like a troublemaker angel that got booted out of heaven, all tall and well-built and resilient and capable-looking. On top of everything else, he had to have the most dangerous job in the United States, the knowledge of fear and nature and consequences in his sea-blue eyes.

The relief of seeing Fox practically bowled her over, and she started to call out a greeting, until she realized the fisherman's gravitational-pull eyes were homing in on Sergei, setting off a tectonic shift of plates in his cheeks.

"What happened to her?" Fox barked, bringing everything back to regular speed. Wait. When did her surroundings go into slow motion to begin with?

"I just fell on the bus," Hannah explained, prodding her bumped head and wincing. Great, she'd split her skin slightly as well. "I'm fine."

"Come on," Fox said, still bird-dogging Sergei. "I'll patch you up."

She was about to raise a skeptical brow and ask to see his medical degree, but then she remembered a story Piper had told her. Fox had once given Brendan makeshift stitches for a bleeding forehead wound. All while keeping his balance during a hurricane.

Such was the life of a king crab fisherman.

Couldn't he just be super short? Was that so much to ask?

"I'm fine," she said, patting Sergei's arm, letting him know she was okay to stand on her own. "Unless you have a cure for pride in your first-aid kit?"

Fox licked the seam of his lips, brows still drawn, and his attention slid back toward the director. "We'll take a closer look when we get home. You have a bag I can carry or something?"

"I . . ." Sergei started, looking at Hannah as if there was something new about her and he wanted to figure out what it was. "I didn't realize you were . . . so close to anyone in town."

Close? To Fox? Seven months ago, she would have thought that a stretch. Now? It wasn't exactly a lie. Lately, she'd been talking to him more often than Piper. "Well—"

Fox cut her off. "We should get that bump looked at, Freckles."

"Freckles," Sergei echoed, checking her nose for spots.

Was something afoot here?

Both men were inching toward her subtly, like she was the last slice of pizza.

"Um. My bag is in the luggage compartment of the bus."

"I'll get it," they said at the same time.

Was her head wound releasing some kind of alpha pheromone?

Fox and Sergei sized each other up, clearly ready to argue about who was going to get her bag. The way her day was going, it would probably ensue in a tug-of-war, the zipper would break, and her underpants would rain down like confetti. "I'll grab it," Hannah said, before either one of them could speak, hotfooting it away from the masculinity maelstrom before it affected her brain.

She turned for the bus just as Brinley glided down the stairs, giving Fox a curious look that Hannah was amazed to see, thanks to the window's reflection, he didn't return. Those sea-blues were fastened on her bump, instead. Probably trying to decide which needle to use to mutilate her.

"Sergei," Brinley called, twisting her earring. "Is everything okay?"

"Yes, totally fine," Hannah answered, beelining for the luggage compartment and attempting to open it. Everyone watched as she jerked on the handle, laughed, yanked more forcefully. Laughed again, then slammed her hip into it. No luck.

Before she could try a third time, Fox reached past her and opened it with a flick of his tan wrist. "You're having a shit day, aren't you?" he said for her ears alone.

She exhaled. "Yeah."

He made a humming sound, tilted his head sympathetically. "Tell me which bag is yours and I'll bring you back to my place." Gently, he tugged on a strand of her hair. "Make it all better."

It was totally possible she'd hit her head and ended up in an erotic sex dream with Fox Thornton. It wouldn't be the first time—not that she would admit to that in a court of law. Or even to her sister. There was simply no way to combat the subtle transmissions he gave off that screamed, *I'm good at sex.*

Like, really, really good. She was powerless against it. Thing was, that went for every other woman he came into contact with, too. And she had no interest in being one of thousands. That's why they were friends. Hadn't that been established? Why was he hitting on her?

"How . . . ? What do you mean by that? That you'll make my day better. How are you going to do that?"

"I was thinking ice cream." He gave her a smile that could only belong to an irreverent rascal—and, Lord, she'd forgotten about the dimples. Dimples, for crying out loud. "Why? What were you thinking?"

Hannah had no idea what her reply was going to be. She started to stammer something, but the view of Sergei and Brinley strolling toward the harbor together made the words catch in her throat. He didn't glance back once. Obviously she'd imagined the new spark of interest she'd seen in the director's eyes. He was just being a good boss by making sure her head injury wasn't serious.

Tearing her attention off the pair, she found Fox watching her closely.

After falling and being escorted off the bus by Sergei, she must have been in a state of distraction. Now that it was just the two of them—although Angelenos were beginning to file off the bus—a bubble of gratitude and fondness rose up in her middle and burst. She'd missed this place. It held some of her most treasured memories. And Fox was a part of them. His text messages over the last seven months had allowed her to hold on to a piece of Westport without intruding on her sister's bliss. She appreciated him for that, so she didn't second-guess her decision to hug him. With a laugh, she simply walked into his arms and inhaled his ocean scent, smiling when he laughed as well, rubbing the crown of her head with his knuckles.

"Hey, Freckles."

She rubbed her cheek on the gray cotton of his long-sleeved shirt, stepped back, and shoved him playfully. "Hey, Peacock."

No one was hitting on anyone. Or pulling alpha moves.

Friends. That's what this relationship was.

She wasn't going to mess that up by objectifying him. There was more to Fox than a chiseled face, thick arms, and an air of danger. Just like there was a lot more to her than being a coffee holder and note taker.

Fox seemed to notice the glumness eclipse her joy, because he picked up the only black bag in the pile—correctly assuming it was hers—and threw his opposite arm around her shoulders, guiding her toward the apartment building where he lived, across from the docks. "You let me fix your noggin, I'll throw in a cookie with that ice cream."

She leaned into him and sighed. "Deal."

Chapter Four

You're off to a fine start, idiot.

After his intervention with Brendan, he'd had a few weeks to sit on the fact that Hannah was coming to stay with him. A lot of that time had been spent out on the water, the ultimate head clearer. It was going to be no problem. A girl would be sleeping in his guest room. He'd be in the other room. With no expectation of sex. Great.

Causal sex was easier than this.

Before Hannah, Fox had relied on his personality a grand total of once in his life when it came to a woman. His one and only serious relationship hadn't gone over well, mostly because it had only been serious to him. His college girlfriend's perspective had been entirely different. Yeah, Fox had learned the hard way that he couldn't escape the assumptions people made about him—that he was temporary entertainment. Growing up, he'd ached to escape this town and the role his face—and to be fair, his actions—had carved out for him. God, he'd tried. But those expectations followed him everywhere.

So he'd stopped trying.

If you're laughing with them, they can't laugh at you, right?

Looking down at the crown of Hannah's head, Fox swallowed hard. They were walking past Blow the Man Down, and he could practically hear every stool in the place swiveling to watch Fox escort Hannah toward his apartment. They would be making jokes. Chuckling into their beers. Speculating. And, shit, how could he even blame them? Most of the time, Fox was the one making jokes about himself.

How was Seattle? they would ask him, eager to be entertained by his exploits. Distracted from their fishing stories for a moment.

Filthy place, he'd say, winking at them. Filthy.

Now he had the nerve to put his arm around Hannah? Distractingly pretty, endlessly interesting, not-after-his-dick Hannah. They were the Big Bad Wolf and Little Red Riding Hood crossing the street in front of the docks, her no-nonsense bag dangling from his free hand. And when they stopped in front of his building so he could unlock the door, Fox was painfully aware of Hannah glancing back from where they'd come, hoping to catch a glimpse of her director.

He'd never been jealous over a girl in his life. Except for this one. When he'd caught sight of Sergei bundling Hannah down the stairs of the bus, his head ducked toward her in concern, that ugly green had splashed across his vision like a rogue wave across the deck, reminding him of the first time he'd heard the director's name. His first impulse had been to break the guy's nose—the opposite of what he should be doing. If Hannah was his friend, why would he want to mess up her budding romance?

Maybe he was jealous in a friendly way?

A total possibility.

People got jealous over their friends. Right? It stood to reason that Fox's first female friend would be the one to inspire the feeling. He did covet this relationship, even though it scared him. If he was a scale, hope would sit on one side, fear on the other. Hope that he could be more than a hookup to her. Fear that he'd fail at it and be exposed.

Again.

"Thank you for letting me crash," Hannah said, smiling up at him. "I hope you didn't take down all the *Baywatch* posters on my account."

"I hid them in my closet with my Farrah Fawcett centerfold." That got a laugh out of her, but Fox could see she was still distracted by something. It took him the entire walk up the stairs to convince himself he wouldn't make it worse by bringing it up. "So . . ." he said, opening his apartment door, tipping his head to indicate she should enter. The first girl he'd ever brought to his place. No big deal at all. "You want to tell me what's bothering you?"

She squinted an eye. "Did you miss the whole head-injury thing?"

"Definitely not." If he didn't get antiseptic on the cut soon, he was going to sweat through his shirt. "But that's not what's bugging you."

Hannah walked over his threshold, hesitated like she was going to come clean, then stopped. "I was promised ice cream and a cookie."

"And you'll get it. I wouldn't lie to you, Freckles." He set down her bag by his small, two-person kitchen table, searching her face for some indication of how she felt about his apartment. "Come on."

It was purely his nature to distract himself with something physical. One second Hannah's feet were planted on the ground, the next he'd plucked her up and settled her onto his kitchen counter. He'd performed the action without a thought. At least until her pretty lips popped open in surprise as her butt hit the surface of the counter. The feel of her waist lingered on his palms, and he was definitely thinking then about things he shouldn't.

Reeling his hands back, Fox cleared his throat hard. He stepped to the side to open a cabinet and removed his blue metal first-aid kit. "Talk."

She shook her head as if to clear it. Then opened her mouth, closed it again. "Remember how I told you I wanted to assert myself more at work?"

"Yeah. You want to make a shift to soundtracks."

She'd told Fox about her dreams of compiling song lists for films last summer, namely the day they'd gone to the record expo together. Fox remembered every single thing about that day. Everything she'd said and done. How good it felt to be with her.

Realizing he was staring into space, recalling the way her elegant fingers walked through a record stack, he wet a cotton ball with antiseptic and stepped close, hesitating only a second before pushing the hair back from her forehead. Their gazes met and danced away quickly. "Are you going to cry when this stings?"

"No."

"Good." He blotted the wound with cotton, his gut seizing up when she hissed a breath. "So? What happened with creating the soundtracks?" he blurted, to distract himself from the fact that he was causing her pain.

"Well . . ." She breathed a sigh of relief when he removed the soaked cotton ball. "I'm kind of a glorified serf at the production company. When a task arises and no one wants to do it, they summon me like Beetlejuice."

"I can't imagine you as anyone's serf, Hannah."

"It's by choice. I wanted to learn the industry, then work my way up on my own merit, you know?" She watched him sort through the bandage section of his kit. "We were almost to Westport. I thought this trip could be my chance to . . . flirt with a higher position. I was just about to ask Sergei and Brinley if I could observe the soundtrack process, and that's when Hannah went splat."

"Oh, Freckles."

"Yeah."

"So you didn't get to ask at all?"

"No. Maybe it was a sign that I'm not ready."

Fox snorted. "You were born ready for making soundtracks. I have seven months of text messages to prove it."

At the mention of the texts, their eyes clashed, splotches of pink waking up in her cheeks. Blushing. He had a friend's blushing little sister sitting on his kitchen counter. Jesus Christ. Before he could reach out and test the temperature of those splotches with his fingertips, he went back to sorting through bandages.

"All right," he said. "One missed opportunity. You'll have more, right?"

Hannah nodded but said nothing.

Kept right on saying nothing as he applied Neosporin to her cut and laid the small Band-Aid on top, smoothing it with his thumb.

Not leaning in to kiss her when they were inches away felt foreign. Had he ever gotten this close to a woman besides his mother without the intention of sealing their mouths together? Flipping through his memories, he couldn't pinpoint a single time. On the other hand, he couldn't recall all the times he *had* kissed women. Not with any clarity.

He'd remember kissing Hannah.

No the fuck you won't.

With grabby movements, Fox collected the Band-Aid wrapper and opened a lower cabinet so he could brush it into the trash. "Wanting to observe doesn't seem like a big ask, Hannah. I'm sure they'll say yes."

"Maybe." She chewed her lip a moment. "It's just . . . did you notice the woman who was walking with Sergei?"

"No," he answered honestly.

Hannah hummed, looking at him thoughtfully. "She's the music coordinator. Brinley." She picked up a hand and let it drop. "I can't see myself doing anything that woman does. She's . . ."

"What?"

"A leading lady," Hannah said on an exhale, looking almost relieved to have gotten that baffling statement off her chest.

Fox's confusion cleared. "You mean, she's one of the actresses?"

"No, I mean she's a leading lady in life. Like my sister."

Nope, still confused. "I'm lost, Hannah."

She fell forward slightly with a laugh. "Never mind."

Damn. She'd only been here for five minutes, and he already wasn't living up to the friend status. Did she not want to confide in him? It scared him how much he wanted to earn her trust.

Fox moved to the freezer and took out the ice cream. Chocolate-vanilla swirl had seemed like a surefire bet when he picked it out at the supermarket yesterday. Best of both worlds, right? Watching her reaction, he took a spoon out of the drawer and stabbed it into the top, handing her the entire pint. "Explain what you mean about Piper and this Betty chick being leading ladies."

"Brinley," she corrected him, laughing with her eyes.

Fox made a face. "An LA name if I've ever heard one."

"You sound like Brendan."

"Ouch," he complained, clutching his chest. Letting his hand drop away. "An explanation, please, Freckles."

She seemed to wrestle with her thoughts while taking a relishing bite of ice cream and drawing the spoon from between her lips slowly. Mesmerizingly.

Fox coughed and dragged his attention higher.

"I'm good at being . . . supportive. You know? Giving advice and doling out helpful suggestions. When it comes to my own stuff, though . . . not so much." She let that settle quietly in the kitchen before continuing. "Like I can pack up, put my job on hold, and move to Westport because Piper needs me. But I can't even ask my boss for a chance to observe? How crazy is that? I can't even"—she gave a dazed chuckle—"tell Sergei I've had this dumb crush on him for two years. I just kind of stand around waiting for things to happen, while other people seem to make them happen so easily. I can help others—I like doing that—but I'm a supporting actress, not a leading lady. That's what I meant by that."

Wow. Here she was. Confiding in him—in person. About her insecurities. About the guy she wanted to date. This was his first heart-to-heart with a girl. No flirting or pretense. Just honesty. Up until that moment, it was possible Fox hadn't fully grasped that Hannah really, actually, one hundred percent only thought of him as just a friend. That all those texts weren't a unique, platonic style of foreplay. After all, she had eyes. She'd seen him, right? But there was no unspoken interest on her part. This really *was* just friendship. She apparently liked whatever the hell Fox had lurking on the inside. And even though he felt like he'd been socked in the fucking stomach, he still wanted to meet her expectations. Although, he suspected his ego would be purple with bruises by the time this was over.

"Hey," he said, clearing the rust from his voice, putting another few inches of distance between them. "Look, I'll be honest, I've never heard such a load of bullshit in my life. You're supportive, yeah. The way you defended Piper to the captain? You are fierce and loyal. All those things, Hannah. But you're . . . Don't make me say it out loud."

"Say it," she whispered, lips twitching.

"You are leading-lady material."

Those twitching lips spread into a smile. "Thanks."

Fox could see he might have made Hannah smile, but the issues were far from solved. For one, she liked the director, and for some reason Fox couldn't fathom, the dumbass wasn't chasing after her with a bouquet of red roses. How could he help with that? Did he *want* to help her with that? It was a fisherman's nature to plug leaks, fix problems when they arose. For another, Hannah not feeling one hundred percent happy was a definite problem in his book. "The guy was jealous, you know. Back at the bus when I came to pick you up."

Her head came up, expression hopeful, but it faded just as quickly, unlike the knot tying tighter inside him. "No, he was just being nice," she said, digging back into the ice cream. Chocolate side only, he noted for next time.

Next time?

"Hannah, trust me. I know when I'm intimidating another guy."

She wrinkled her nose. "Is jealous the same thing as intimidated?"

"Yes. When men are intimidated by other men, especially ridiculously hot men like yours truly—"

She snort-laughed.

"—they assert themselves. Fight to get the upper hand back. It's a natural reaction. Law of the jungle. That's why he wanted to get your bag. That's why he kept his arm around you way too long." Fox grabbed at the sweaty, icy skin at the nape of his neck. "He didn't like that you were staying with me, and he especially didn't like me calling you Freckles. He was intimidated and, therefore, jealous."

Fox didn't add that he was speaking from experience.

Intimidated by some artsy goatee-sporting guy from LA. A Russian, no less. Russians were their main competition during crab season, as if he needed another reason to dislike the motherfucker.

God, he was jumpy. "Anyway, all I'm saying is . . . he's not *not* interested."

"This is all very fascinating," Hannah said around her spoon. "But if you're right, if Sergei was jealous, he'll eventually realize there is nothing happening between you and me, and he has no reason to . . . resort to jungle laws." Casually, she poked at the ice cream. "Unless we *let* him think we're sleeping together. Maybe he needs to be shaken up."

Alarm stole downward through Fox's fingertips. He'd walked straight into a trap. One he'd set himself. "You can't let him think that, Hannah."

"I was only brainstorming." Whatever she saw on Fox's face caused her to narrow her eyes. "But why are you *so* opposed?"

Trying to mask the panic, he let out a crack of laughter. "You don't . . . No. I'm not letting you associate your reputation with mine, all right? A couple of days in this town and he'll probably hear all about it. Trust me, if he's worth a damn, the fact that I got to bandage your bump will make him jealous enough."

Hannah blinked. "If he's worth a damn, he won't believe everything he hears. Especially about someone he doesn't know personally."

"Unless a lot of what he hears is true, right?" He smiled straight through that rhetorical question, trying to give the impression that the answer didn't bother him. When she only seemed to look deeper, curious, Fox said something he immediately regretted just to distract her. To bump her off the topic of his reputation. "Have you tried letting him know you're interested? You know, a little lip biting and arm squeezing . . ."

"Gross." She looked him up and down. "Does that do it for you?"

Nothing was doing it for him lately. Nothing but the three little dots popping up in their text thread. And now head wounds. How pathetic was that? "Don't worry about what does it for me. I'm talking about this guy. He's probably clueless, and a lot of men will remain that way without a little encouragement."

Visibly amused, she tilted her head. "Are you one of those men?"

Fox sighed, resisted the urge to scratch at the back of his neck. "Encouragement is kind of a given for me."

"Right," she said after a pause, something flickering in her eyes.

How did the conversation get here? First, he's giving her pointers on landing the director, and now he's inadvertently bragging about his luck with women? *Off to a great start, man.* "Look, I'm not in the relationship race and I never will be. Clearly you are. I was just trying to be helpful. Flirting with Sergei is one thing, but the bottom line is we're not letting anyone incorrectly assume"—he sawed a hand back and forth in between them—"this is happening. For your own good, okay?"

Hannah definitely wanted to discuss it further, pick it apart, but thankfully she let it drop. "You don't have to tell me you're not in the relationship race," she said, biting her lip. "I can see your apartment just fine."

Grateful for the subject change, he breathed a laugh. "What?" He chucked her chin. "You don't think women are into the waiting-room look?"

"No. Seriously, would an area rug and a scented candle kill you?"

Fox took the ice cream and spoon out of her hands and set them on the counter. "You're not getting that cookie now." He grabbed her by the waist and tossed her facedown over his shoulder, prompting a squeal as he stomped toward the spare room. "I'm not putting up with an ungrateful houseguest, Freckles."

"I'm grateful! I'm grateful!"

Her laughter cut off abruptly when they entered her room—as he'd already begun to think of it—no doubt noticing the row of scented candles, the folded towels, and the pink Himalayan salt lamp. He'd seen it in a tourist shop window and decided she definitely needed one, but at this juncture, the purchase made him feel utterly silly.

Shaking his head at himself, Fox eased Hannah off his shoulder and dropped her gently onto the queen-sized bed, his chest tugging at the way her hair flopped down to cover one eye. "Oh. Fox . . ." she murmured, scanning the row of supplies.

"It's no big deal," he said quickly, backing up to lean sideways against the doorjamb. Crossing his arms. Definitely not thinking about how easy it would be to prowl over her on that bed, tease her a little more, run his fingertips along that section of skin between her hip bones and waist, flirt until kissing turned into her idea, instead of his intention all along. He knew the dance moves well.

None of them were right for a friend.

"Listen." When his voice sounded gruff to his own ears, he forced some levity into it. "I'm heading down to the docks to load the *Della Ray*. We'll be on the water starting tomorrow. Coming back Friday. Don't burn the place down while I'm gone and make me regret my first candle purchase."

"I won't, Peacock," she said, lips lifting at the corners, her hand smoothing the bedspread he hoped she couldn't tell was new. "Thank you. For everything."

"Anytime, Freckles."

He started to leave but stopped when she said, "And just for the record, I would be honored to fake sleep with you. Sordid reputation and all."

With a stone blocking his windpipe, all he could do was nod, grabbing his keys on the way out of the apartment. "Cookies are in the cabinet," he called, walking out into the sunshine, welcoming the way it blinded him.

Chapter Five

Hannah came to a stop outside her grandmother's door and removed her AirPods, silencing her "Walking Through Westport" playlist. It mainly consisted of Modest Mouse, Creedence, and the Dropkick Murphys, all of which reminded her of the ocean, whether it be pirates or a hippie playing harmonica on the docks. As soon as the melody cut out, she knocked, pressing her lips together a moment later to stifle a laugh. Inside the apartment, Opal was muttering to herself about morons who let solicitors into the building, her footsteps ambling closer.

At what point would having a grandmother on her father's side begin to feel normal? Opal's existence had been kept from Hannah and Piper growing up, but they'd discovered her—by mistake—last summer. And the woman was a delight. Fierce and sweet and funny. Full of stories about Hannah and Piper's father, too. Was that the reason Hannah had taken four days to come for a visit?

Sure, she'd been kept very busy on the set of their first location. On top of Hannah's other duties, they'd needed her on set for the filming of the high school lovers' reunion scene between Christian and Maxine outside the lighthouse. Getting it right had taken the full four days—but during the night she'd gone home to Fox's empty apartment, instead of going to see Opal. Piper had been out of town those four days, having taken her in-laws for a side trip to Seattle, so Hannah decided she should just wait. That way they could all visit together. There was more to her stalling, though.

Hannah pressed a hand to her stomach to subdue the bubbles of guilt.

Now that her sister was back in town, she'd called and asked Piper to meet her at Opal's this afternoon. Where was she?

Hannah was still craning her neck to see the end of the hallway when Opal answered the door. The older woman blinked once, twice, her mouth falling open. "You're not selling magazine subscriptions at all. You're my granddaughter." Hannah leaned in, and Opal enveloped her in a back-patting hug. "When did you get into town? I don't believe this. All I can make you is a ham sandwich."

"Oh. No." Hannah drew back, shaking her head. "I already had lunch, I swear. I just came to see you!"

Her grandmother flushed with pleasure. "Well, then. Come in, come in."

The apartment had changed drastically since the last time Hannah was there. Gone was the outdated furniture, the combined scents of lemon cleaner and must that left a sense of solitude hanging in the air. Now it smelled fresh. Sunflowers sat in the center of a new dining-room table, and there was no longer a plastic protector on the couch. "Wow." Hannah set her tote bag on the floor and unzipped her Storm

Born windbreaker, shrugging it off to hang on the peg. "Let me guess. Piper had something to do with this?"

"You guessed it." Opal clasped her hands near her waist, her expression pleased and prideful as she scanned the new-and-improved living space. "I don't know what I'd do without her."

Affection for her sister wiggled its way in next to Hannah's guilt but did nothing to eclipse it. Over the last seven months, she'd spoken to Opal only a handful of times on the phone. She'd sent a card at Christmas. It wasn't that she didn't adore the woman. They got along very well. She'd made Opal a Woodstock-themed playlist last summer, and they'd totally bonded over it. Even now, the welcoming vibes of the apartment wrapped around Hannah and warmed her.

It was when the stories about her father—Opal's only son—inevitably started rolling that Hannah got uncomfortable.

Hannah flat out couldn't remember him. She'd been two years old when the king crab fisherman had been sucked to the bottom of the Bering Sea. Piper could remember his laugh, his energy, but Hannah's mind conjured nothing. No melancholia, no affection or nostalgia.

For Piper, restoring Henry's bar had been a journey of learning about herself and connecting with the memory of Henry.

For Hannah, it was about . . . supporting Piper on that journey.

Of course, seeing the finished product after weeks of manual labor had been satisfying, especially when they changed the name to Cross and Daughters, but the coming-full-circle feeling never happened for Hannah. So whenever she came to see Opal and her grandmother brought out pictures of Henry, or stories were told about him over the phone, Hannah started to wonder if her emotions were stunted. She could cry over a Heartless Bastards song, but her own father got nothing from her?

Hannah joined Opal on the new indigo-colored couch and cupped her knees through her jeans. "I'm actually in town because the production company I work for is shooting a short film. Kind of a heartbreaking art house piece."

"A movie?" Opal winced. "In Westport? I can't imagine people being too thrilled with the disruption."

"Oh, don't worry, I thought of that. We're giving as many background parts and walk-on roles as we can. Once the locals realized they might be in a movie, it was smooth sailing."

With a sound of delight, Opal slapped her thigh. "That was your idea?"

Hannah fluffed her ponytail. "Yes, ma'am. I made my director think it was his idea to add locals for authenticity. It's a good thing I don't use my powers for evil, or everyone would be in big trouble."

It would be fantastic if she could use her powers to move ahead in her career, too, wouldn't it? Greasing the production wheels was easy for her. There were no personal stakes. No risk. Applying herself to music coordinating was scarier. Because it mattered.

A great deal.

Opal laughed, reached over to squeeze Hannah's wrist. "Oh, sweetie, I've missed your spunk."

The sound of a key turning in the lock made Hannah whip around, and Opal clapped happily. Piper was only halfway through the door when Hannah launched herself over the back of the new couch and plowed into her sister, tension she'd hardly been aware of seeping from her pores. Hugging Piper was like walking into a room filled with your best memories. Her sheer-sleeved romper, impractical heels, and expensive perfume made Hannah feel like they were back in Bel-Air, sitting on the floor of Piper's room, sorting her jewelry collection.

They hopped in a happy circle, laughing, while Opal fumbled with her phone, trying and failing to open her camera app.

"You're here." Piper sniffed, squeezing Hannah tightly. "My perfect, beautiful, hippie-hearted little sister. How dare you make me miss you this much?"

"I could say the same to you," Hannah said, voice muffled by her sister's shoulder.

The sisters pulled back, wiping their faces in very different manners. Hannah swiped for efficiency, while Piper dragged a careful pinkie in a perfect U shape to repair her eyeliner. Arm in arm, they moved around the couch and sat down plastered up against each other. "So when are you moving here permanently?" Piper asked, her tone still slightly watery. "Like . . . tomorrow. Right?"

Hannah sighed, resting her head on the back of the couch. "Part of me doesn't hate that idea. Get my job back at Disc N Dat. Haunt the guest room at your house forever"—she poked at a sequin in Piper's bodice—"but LA is keeping me, I'm afraid. It's where my dream career awaits."

Piper stroked her hair. "Have you made any headway on that?"

"Imminently . . ." Hannah responded, chewing the inside of her cheek. "I think."

Opal leaned forward. "Dream career?"

"Yes." Hannah sat up straighter but kept her side pressed to Piper's. "Movie soundtracks. The making of them."

"Isn't that interesting." Opal beamed.

"Thank you." She moved some of her hair out of the way and performed a show-and-tell with the bandaged knot on her forehead. "Unfortunately, this is what happened the first time I tried to ask." Piper and Opal both looked at her wound with an appropriate level of concern. "It's fine. It doesn't hurt." She laughed lightly, letting her hair drop back into place. "Fox bandaged me up and gave me ice cream."

It was fleeting and subtle, but she felt Piper stiffen, giving off definite protective-older-sister vibes. "Oh, did he?"

Hannah rolled her eyes. "This is your one and only reminder that me staying with Fox was your idea."

"I took it back right away," Piper fretted. "Has he tried anything?"

"No!" Hannah squawked. Never mind that she could still feel the shape and exquisitely defined musculature of his shoulder on her midsection. "Stop talking about him like he's some kind of sexual predator. I'm adult enough to make these judgment calls by myself. And he's been a perfect gentleman."

"That's because he hasn't been in town," Piper grumbled, smoothing her romper.

"He decorated my room with a Himalayan salt lamp."

Piper sputtered, "He might as well be mauling you!"

"Someone explain to me what is going on here!" Opal scooted her chair closer. "I want to be involved in a conversation about men. It's been an age."

"There is no conversation to have," Hannah assured her grandmother. "I am friends with a man who happens to . . . appreciate women. Frequently. But it has been established that he won't be appreciating me."

"Tell her about the Fleetwood Mac album," Piper said, patting Hannah vigorously on the knee. "Go on and tell her."

Hannah released a gusting breath toward the ceiling. Mostly to hide the weird twist that happened inside her when she thought of the album and how she'd gotten it. "It's no big deal, really." *Liar.* "Last summer, we all went to Seattle. Me, Piper, Fox, Brendan. We broke off for a while, and Fox took me to this record convention. And I found an album that sang to me. Fleetwood Mac. *Rumours.*" A paltry description for a shock to the nervous system. "But it was expensive. At the time, me and Pipes were on a tight budget, so I didn't buy it . . ."

"And then the day Hannah left to return to LA, there it was. On my porch. Fox went back and bought it without her knowing."

Opal made an O shape with her lips. "Oh my. That is romantic."

"No. No, you have it all wrong, ladies. It was kind."

Piper and Opal traded a very superior look.

Part of her couldn't even blame them. Fox buying her that album was the one thing she couldn't seem to define as one hundred percent friendly. It sat in a place of honor back home, facing out on the hanging rack that displayed her albums. Every time she passed it, she replayed the moment at the convention when she'd gasped over the find, tracing the square edge of the album with her fingers. The warmth of his arm around her, the unsteady pound of his heart. How for the first time, she'd let someone into the music with her, instead of disappearing into it alone.

Hannah shook herself. "You're actually helping me prove my point, Pipes. If he wanted to . . . appreciate me, why would he wait until I was leaving to hand me his golden ticket like that?"

"She makes a good point."

"Thank you, Opal. Case closed."

Piper rearranged the perfectly curled ends of her hair, physically accepting the end of the subject. "So. How is LA? Does she miss me?"

"She does. The house feels even bigger without you in it. Too big."

Their mother, Maureen, had left Westport over two decades earlier in a cloud of grief after Henry Cross's death, relocating to Los Angeles where she'd worked as a seamstress for a movie studio. She'd met and married their stepfather at the pinnacle of his success as a producer. Seemingly overnight, the three of them had gone from residing in a tiny apartment to a Bel-Air mansion, where Hannah still lived to this day.

With Piper in residence, the mansion never failed to feel like home. But ever since Piper moved to Westport, Hannah felt more like a visitor. Out of place and disconnected in the gigantic palace. It had become obvious that their parents led a separate life, and lately, she'd started to feel like an observer of it. Instead of someone who was happily off living her own.

"I'm thinking of moving out," Hannah blurted. "I'm thinking of a lot of things."

Piper angled her body to face Hannah, head tilted. "Such as?"

Being the focus of the conversation was unusual, to say the least. It wasn't that it embarrassed her to be the center of attention. There was simply no use involving everyone in problems she could fix herself, right? Like finagling a trip to Westport because loneliness and a sense of missing something had started getting to her. "Never mind." She waved a hand. "How are things going with Brendan's parents?"

"She's changing the subject," Opal pointed out.

"Yeah. Don't do that." Piper poked her with the tip of a red fingernail. "You're going to move out of Bel-Air?"

Hannah shrugged a shoulder. "It's time. It's time for me to . . . grow up the whole way. I got stuck halfway through the process." She thought of Brinley. "No one is going to consider a promotion for a girl who lives with her parents. Or they'll consider me less, anyway. If I want adult responsibilities, I have to be one. I have to believe I am one first."

"Hanns, you're the most responsible person I know," Piper said, hedging. "Does your interest in Sergei have anything to do with this?"

"There's *another* man in the mix?" Opal split a glance between her two granddaughters and sighed. "Lordy, to be young again."

"He's my director. My boss—only. Nothing has changed on that front," Hannah explained. "What I want from a career and my love life are totally separate, but I'd be lying if I said I didn't want Sergei to look at me like I'm a woman, you know? Instead of the scruffy PA."

The guy was jealous, you know. Back at the bus when I came to pick you up.

Fox's voice filtered in through her thoughts. She'd been busy over the last four days, getting everyone settled in their temporary housing, unpacking supplies in the trailers, meeting with the local business owners. But she hadn't been so busy that she wasn't aware of Sergei. Of course she was always aware of him on set. With his passion on full display, he was a magnet for attention. But if the director had really been jealous of Fox, he'd forgotten all about it and gone back to treating Hannah with polite distractedness.

Trust me, if he's worth a damn, the fact that I got to bandage your bump will make him jealous enough. There went Fox's deep rasp in her head again, when she should be thinking of Sergei. Still . . . she couldn't stop replaying what the fisherman said to her in the kitchen. About his reputation. About how he wouldn't want people assuming they were an item, because he thought it would be a bad look for Hannah. He didn't really believe that nonsense, right?

"Well." Piper broke into her thoughts. "As someone who has only recently embarked on adulthood herself, I can tell you it's scary but rewarding. There's also lots of making my own meals and wearing jeans." She pretended to cry, and Hannah laughed. "But I couldn't have done it without you, Hannah. You made me consider possibilities I never dreamed of. That's how I know you're capable of anything. Don't let a head injury and feeling scruffy stop you. My sister is dependable and creative and doesn't take anyone's shit. If this studio doesn't give you the opportunity, another one will. Dammit." Piper smiled prettily. "And I'm sorry for cursing, Opal. I'm just trying to get my point across."

"I'm a fisherman's mother, dear. Cursing is part of the vocabulary."

Piper was being Hannah's supporting actress for once, and that fact wasn't lost on her. The role reversal, coupled with the warm pressure behind her eyes, probably accounted for Hannah doing something totally out of character. "Can you help me out with the scruffiness? Just for tonight." She poked a finger through the thumb hole of her sweatshirt. "There's a cast party at one of the houses we're renting."

Her sister slowly laid a hand on her arm, nails digging in lightly. "Are you asking me to dress you up?"

"Just for tonight. I need all the professional confidence."

"Oh my God," Piper breathed, teary-eyed. "I know just the dress."

"Nothing flashy—"

"Zip. Zip it. Not another word. You're going to trust me."

Hannah swallowed a smile and did as she was told. There might have been a speck of vanity inside her that wanted to catch Sergei's attention at the crew party tonight, and she wondered if a Piper-style dress might do it. But that definitely wasn't her reason for dressing up. If she wanted to move to the next level in this industry, people had to start taking her seriously. Plain and simple? In Hollywood, image mattered, whether it should or not. Sparkle got attention and forced people to listen. To consider. No one would ever ask Piper or Brinley to hold their straw or stir their coffee counterclockwise, would they? *I'm looking at you, Christian.*

Nor would they expect Brinley to do all the heavy lifting at the studio without paying her properly. For a long time, Hannah had reasoned that it didn't matter what her paycheck looked like. She lived with her parents in Bel-Air, for crying out loud. They had an Olympic-sized swimming pool in the backyard and a full-time staff. Since getting back in her stepfather's good graces, money was available to her again, if she ever needed funds beyond her paycheck. But her meager earnings were becoming a matter of principle. They wouldn't have managed this location shoot without her—and Latrice—pulling several all-nighters. The difference being, Latrice got paid what she was worth.

Dressing for success seemed almost too easy compared to the hard work she'd been doing lately, but giving it a try wouldn't hurt.

"All this movie-soundtrack and Fleetwood Mac talk reminded me of something," Opal said, pulling Hannah from her ruminations. "I have something to show you girls."

Their grandmother got to her feet and power walked to the other side of the living room, taking a slim blue folder off the top of her bookcase. Knowing whatever was in that folder would pertain to her father, Hannah's stomach started to drop. This was the part of catching up with her grandmother she always dreaded: when Piper and Opal would be moved to tears over some piece of Henry's history, and she would feel like a statue, trying to relate.

"One of Henry's old shipmates brought these into Blow the Man Down over the weekend. I was out with the girls." Their grandmother said the last part with pride, winking at Piper. For a long time, Opal's grief over the passing of her son had kept her inside the apartment. At least until Piper came along, gave her a sassy haircut and some new clothes, reintroducing her to the town she'd been missing. Hannah liked to think her playlists had helped motivate Opal to get social again, too. "These were written by your father," she said, opening the folder.

Both sisters leaned in and squinted down at the small handwriting that took up several pages of stained and age-worn paper.

"Are they letters?" Piper asked.

"They're songs," Opal murmured, running a fingertip over a few sentences. "Sea shanties, to be exact. He used to sing them around the house in the early days. I didn't even know he'd written them down."

Hannah felt a tug of almost reluctant interest. She'd gotten her hopes up a few times that a photograph or a token of her father's might bring on some tide of emotion, but it never happened, and it wouldn't now. "Was he a good singer?"

"He had a deep voice. Powerful. Rich. A lot like his laugh, it could pass right through you."

Piper made a pleasurable sound, picking up the folder and leafing through. "Hannah, you should take these."

"Me?" Mentally, she recoiled but tried to soften her tone for Opal's sake. "Why me?"

"Because they're songs," Piper said, as if she'd been crazy to ask the question. "This is what you love."

Opal reached over and rubbed Hannah's knee. "Maybe Henry is where you got your love of music."

Why did she want to deny that so badly?

What was wrong with her?

It was right there on the tip of her tongue to say no. *No, my love for so many kinds of music is mine. I don't share it with anyone. It's a coincidence.* But, instead, she nodded. "Sure, I'd . . . love to take them for a while and give them a read."

Opal lit up. "Fantastic."

Hannah accepted the folder from Piper and closed it, a familiar desperation to change the subject from Henry settling over her. "Okay, Pipes. We've been in suspense long enough. Tell us about Brendan's parents. How is the visit with your future in-laws going?"

Her sister settled back into the seat, crossing long legs that had been buffed to a shine. "Well. As you know, I brought them down to Seattle this week, since Brendan is out on the boat. I planned all our time there, down to the second."

"And then?" Opal prompted.

"And then I realized all the plans were . . . shopping-related." Her voice fell to a scandalized whisper. "Brendan's mother hates shopping."

Opal and Hannah fell back in their seats laughing.

"Who hates shopping?" Piper whined, covering her face.

Hannah raised her hand. Piper smacked it down.

"Thank God Brendan is coming home tonight. I am running out of ways to entertain them. We've been on so many walks, Hanns. So many walks to nowhere."

The spread of anticipation in Hannah's belly had nothing to do with Fox coming home tonight along with Brendan. She was simply excited to see her friend again and not be alone in his oddly barren apartment.

Piper split a look between Opal and Hannah. "Give me some ideas?"

Hannah thought for a second, slipping into her supporting role as easily as a second skin. "Ask her to teach you how to make Brendan's favorite childhood meal. It'll make her feel useful, and it's not terrible knowledge to have, like for birthdays and special occasions, right?"

"That's genius," Piper squealed, wrapping her arms around Hannah's neck and wrestling her down to the couch while Opal laughed. "I'm totally going to bond it up with my future mother-in-law. What would I do without you, Hanns?"

Hannah pressed her nose to her sister's skin and inhaled, absorbing the hug, the moment, "Time After Time" by Cyndi Lauper playing in the back of her mind. It was tempting to stay there, to bask in the comfortable feeling of being the one to prop others up. There was nothing wrong with it, and she loved that role. But being comfortable had kept her in the second-fiddle position so long . . . and tonight she was finally going to conduct the orchestra herself.

Chapter Six

Hannah walked extra slowly down the sidewalk, a bottle of wine in hand. Her snail's pace had a lot to do with the three-inch heels, but it was mainly the dress delaying her progress. As soon as Piper unzipped the garment bag, she'd started to shake her head. Red? *Red?* Her wardrobe had been compiled for comfort and functionality. Lots of grays, blues, blacks, and whites so she wouldn't have to worry about matching. The only red items she owned were a baseball hat and a pair of Chucks. It was a color you used for a pop. Not the whole ensemble.

Then she'd put it on—and she'd never been more annoyed to have someone be right. There was something kind of nineties about the dress, and that spoke to the grunge-headed old soul inside Hannah. It reminded her of the red minidress Cher wore to the Valley party in *Clueless*. Piper had agreed, making Hannah say, "I totally paused," at least forty-eight times while they straightened her hair.

In most lines of work, this outfit would have been considered inappropriate, but entertainment was its own animal. At the end of the night, it wouldn't be unusual to catch crew members making out in the hallways. Or right out in the open. Often there were drugs, and always alcohol. But really, as long as everyone showed up the next morning and got their job done, pretty much anything went. While judgments and gossip were inevitable, being unprofessional after hours made you one of the gang as opposed to a pariah.

A block away from the rented house, Hannah could see the silhouettes of cast and crew in the dimly lit windows and hear the low thunder of music. The raucous laughter. Well aware of how rowdy industry parties could get, even on this small a scale, she'd booked a place on the semi-outskirts of town to avoid noise complaints. And it was a good thing she had, because someone was already passed out on the front lawn and it wasn't even ten P.M.

Hannah stepped over the intern with a low whistle, hiked up the steps in her admittedly gorgeous shoes—who knew she'd feel so fancy with sparkly little bows on her toes?—and walked into the house without knocking, since no one was going to hear it, anyway. Before leaving Fox's apartment, she'd given herself a pep talk in the mirror of his bathroom, which smelled like the collision of a minty glacier and something more interesting . . . like a ginger-laced essential oil.

Did he use essential oils?

Why was she so tempted to go into his bedroom and check for a diffuser so she could inhale directly from the source?

With an impatient tongue click, Hannah stepped into the house and immediately had to check her urge to find the person in charge of the playlist. If she let herself, she'd sit in the corner all night searching for the perfect next song—probably some Bon Iver to chill everyone out after the crazy week—and that wasn't the mission tonight.

Resigning herself to a night of ambient techno, Hannah took off her coat and draped it over the closest chair, waving to a couple sound engineers on her way down the hallway to the living room where everyone seemed to be congregated.

The song ended right as she walked into the room. Or it might have been all in her head, because everyone—and she meant everyone—turned to stare. If this was what a leading lady felt like, she'd rather be an extra.

Only, she wasn't happy with that anymore, right? So even though her palms were clammy and she kind of felt like an asshole for wearing a designer cocktail dress to a casual hang, she had no choice but to brazen it out and proceed with the plan.

"Am I the only one who got the formal dress memo?" She fake-cringed over the jeans and T-shirts worn by a group of hair and makeup artists. "Sad."

There was some laughter, but then mostly everyone went back to their drinks and conversation, allowing Hannah to exhale. Some liquid courage would not go amiss. One drink, and then she'd make the professional move of a lifetime. Hopefully.

Hannah spotted the liquor and mixers station on a bar cart in the corner of the room and headed that direction, reminding herself she was a certified lightweight and not to overdo it. She was still recovering from her foray into day drinking with Piper at the local winery last summer.

"Hey," Christian said in a bored tone, coming up beside her. "What are you drinking? Poison, I hope."

She pursed her lips and perused the various liquor bottles. "What can I drink to give you a personality?"

Looking pointedly at her dress, Christian gave an appreciative snort. "So, what are you, like, trying now?"

"Could you do the same, please? It took you sixteen takes to nail four lines of dialogue this morning."

"Can't rush perfection." He made an impatient sound and snatched up a red Solo cup. "What are you drinking, PA? I'll make it."

Hannah's mouth dropped open. "You're going to make my drink?"

"Don't let it go to your head." While pouring vodka, he gave her a once-over. "Or your hips. That dress is a little snug."

"You wish you had the hips for this dress."

He added some grapefruit juice and ice to the cup, all but shoving the prepared drink into her hands. "I hate that I like you."

"I like that I hate you."

It cost them both a visible effort not to laugh.

"Hannah?" Christian and Hannah turned at the same time to find Sergei, Brinley, and an assortment of on-camera talent approaching, including Maxine and her fictional best friend. For once, Sergei seemed at a loss for words, the drink in his hand lowering to the side of his thigh. "You . . . dressed up," he said, his attention straying briefly to Hannah's hemline. "If I didn't see you sparring with Christian, I wouldn't have recognized you."

"I do get a certain look of horror on my face when she's around," Christian drawled, giving her a lazy elbow in the side.

"Yes. You look fantastic," Brinley said, though she was scrolling on her phone.

"Thank you." Being the center of attention made it necessary to take a gulp of her (hopefully not poisoned) drink, the abundance of vodka burning her throat on the way down.

It might have been the dress and the liquor rapidly dulling her nerves that encouraged her to speak up. Or it could have been Piper's supportive words earlier in the day. All Hannah knew was that if she didn't ask for what she wanted now, she never would. "Brinley," she blurted, grabbing her own wrist so the ice in her cup would stop rattling. "I was wondering if I could assist you in any way with the score. Not that you need assistance," she rushed to qualify. "I was more just hoping to learn from you. From the process."

Silence descended on the circle.

It was not unusual for people to use parties as a chance to industry climb. But it was unusual for a personal assistant to address someone so much further up the ladder—in mixed company, no less. Maybe she should have waited. Or asked to speak to Brinley and Sergei alone? She hoped Brinley might find the request more palatable since it was posed casually instead of officially. Hannah didn't want the woman thinking she was trying to steal her job.

"Oh . . ." Brinley blinked slowly, sizing her up with new interest. "Are musical scores something you're thinking of pursuing long-term?"

"I haven't really gotten that far yet," Hannah said in a release of breath. "But I'd love to learn more about the process. To see if maybe it could be a good fit down the road."

Brinley rocked on her heels a moment, then shrugged, eyes zipping back to her phone. "I don't have a problem with you observing—if Sergei can spare you?"

It struck Hannah how long Sergei had remained uncharacteristically silent, his forehead lined as he studied her. When Brinley prompted him, he jolted, as if becoming aware of his own silence. "You're vital to me on set, Hannah. You know that." There was no help for the flush that rose in her cheeks over Sergei saying those words. *You're vital to me.* She stopped just short of pressing her drink to her cheeks to cool them down. Meanwhile, the silence stretched, the director running a finger around the inside of his black ribbed turtleneck. "But if you can manage both, I won't object."

Heat prickled the backs of Hannah's eyes, an unexpected jab of pride catching her in the breastbone. Relief—and the distinct fear of failure—traveled so swiftly through her limbs, she almost dropped her cup. But she forced a smile, nodding her thanks to Sergei and Brinley.

"Who's going to bring me coffee between takes?" Christian complained.

A collective laugh/groan from everyone in the group broke the tension, thankfully, and the subject was changed to Sunday morning's agenda. They'd been waiting for a good-weather day to film a kissing scene between Christian and Maxine on the harbor, and the next few days called for sunshine.

While Sergei engaged the small gathering with his vision of a wide, sweeping shot of the kiss, she flipped through her mental music catalogue for the right song, the right feeling . . . and she was surprised to find nothing landed. Nothing.

Not a single song came to mind.

That was odd.

What if she'd finally been given this opportunity only to lose her knack for plugging in the right sound for any occasion? What if she forgot how to weave together atmosphere, something she'd been doing since she was old enough to operate a turntable?

The thought troubled Hannah so much that she didn't notice Christian refreshing her drink. Twice. The electronic music started to match the tempo of her pulse, and when she got the urge to dance, she knew that was her cue to stop drinking. Although . . . it was a little late for that. A pleasurable buzz tickled her blood, and she lost all self-awareness, talking to anyone who would listen about any topic that popped into her head, from the running of the bulls in Pamplona to the fact that people's ears never stopped growing. And her brain told her it was interesting. Maybe it was? Everyone seemed to be laughing, one of the actresses eventually pulling her out onto the makeshift dance floor, where she closed her eyes, kicked her shoes off, and fell into a rhythm.

At one point, her neck tingled, and she opened her eyes to find Sergei watching her from across the room, though his attention was quickly diverted when Christian asked him a question. Hannah went back to dancing, unwisely accepting another drink from a makeup artist.

Her movements slowed when the air in the room changed.

It kind of just . . . lit up.

Hannah looked around and noticed everyone's eyes were glued to the entrance of the living room. Because Fox was standing there, one forearm propped high on the doorjamb, watching her with amusement.

"Holy mother," Hannah muttered, stopping to stare along with everyone else.

There was no other way to herald his arrival but to be rendered mute and immobile. Fox swaggering into the party was like a shark swimming slowly through a school of fish. He was freshly windblown from the ocean, his tan skin slightly weathered from salt, sunshine, and hard work. He towered over everyone and everything. Cocky. So cocky and confident and stupidly hot. Outrageously hot.

"That's him," one of the girls nearby said. "That guy we saw from the bus."

"God, he is like a walking spank bank."

"Dibs."

"Screw that. I already called dibs."

A twitch in Fox's cheek indicated he heard what was being said, but he didn't take his eyes off Hannah, and she started to . . . get kind of pissed. Yeah, no, she *was* pissed. Who called dibs on a human being? Or referred to him as a spank bank? How dare they assume it would be that easy to just . . . appreciate her friend?

What if it was that easy, though?

What if he liked one of them back?

That wasn't any of her business. Was it?

She watched as more whispers reached Fox, and his smile lost power. Not for the first time over the last four days, she replayed what he'd said her first day in town. *I'm not letting you associate your reputation with mine, all right?*

Now his step hesitated on the way to Hannah. Was he second-guessing approaching her? Because all these people were watching?

Without another thought, she set down her drink on a nearby windowsill and walked toward the man with purpose. The fizzy pop of alcohol in her bloodstream might have been contributing to her actions in that moment, but it was more indignation than anything else. These girls didn't even *know* him. Nor did it sound as if they'd learned anything about his actual character while in town. Where were these assumptions coming from?

She'd made them, too. Hadn't she?

Day one. She'd called him a pretty-boy sidekick. Assumed he was a player.

There were all those times she'd texted, asking if he was alone. Tongue in cheek. Like there was a very good chance he'd be with a girl. Hooking up.

So maybe the sudden, crushing need to apologize drove her forward. No one else was going to judge Fox on her watch, and no way was she going to let him hesitate to approach her at a party. He was in the middle of a room being objectified, and she wanted to be the anchor for him.

She wanted to comfort him.

Okay, maybe she was jealous, too. At the possibility someone else was calling dibs, but she didn't want to think about that too hard. Instead, she licked her lips, picking a landing spot for her mouth.

Hannah was approximately five feet from Fox when his expression changed, and he read her intention. His creeping insecurity vanished, and he rocketed to inferno status on a dime. Those blue eyes darkened, and that square, bristled jaw flexed. Ready. A man well used to being wanted and knowing what to do about it.

He whispered her name right before she pushed up on her toes, locking their mouths together, right there in the entrance to the living room. She was immediately bowled over by the hunger of his masculine lips, and then he turned her, pressing her back to the inside of the arched doorway, opening his mouth on top of hers and licking into the kiss with a choked sound.

With her thoughts muddling and a languid heat rendering her arms limp, Hannah realized she'd made a huge mistake. She was Eve in the Garden of Eden, and she'd just taken a bite from the apple.

Chapter Seven

$\mathcal{B}$ig mistake.

Huge.

Unfortunately, trying to stop kissing Hannah was a laughable endeavor.

Fox shouldn't have come here in the first place. But he'd walked into his apartment after four nights on the water expecting her to be there, only to find a note that she'd gone to a party. His apartment had smelled like summer, a garment bag hanging on the back of the guest-room door. And he'd paced while staring at it, wondering what the hell she owned that needed a special bag.

He'd tried showering and drinking a beer but found himself out walking through town, searching for this party for which she'd obviously dressed up. Wasn't that hard to locate a house full of outsiders in a place like this. He'd seen a dude staggering down one of the blocks and asked where he'd come from, reasoning that he would just check on Hannah, make sure she got home all right. Hadn't he promised Brendan he'd keep an eye on her?

That little red dress, though.

He loved it—and he hated it with every fiber of his being.

Because she didn't wear it for him. She wasn't even kissing him for him.

Before Fox left for the trip, Hannah had mused about a way to make the director jealous. Letting the man think she and Fox were more than friends. Fox had spotted the son of a bitch the second he walked into the room, not twenty yards from where Hannah was dancing so adorably. He was watching them kiss right now. She'd obviously ignored Fox's warning about comingling their reputations, and now . . . *Damn.*

He couldn't stop for the life of him. They were already kissing, and selling his authentic enjoyment wasn't exactly difficult. Not at all.

Jesus Christ, she tasted incredible. Fruity and feminine and grounding.

Even though he'd stepped off the *Della Ray* earlier, he was only now back on solid ground.

Did he push her up against the entryway too forcefully? He'd never needed to get his tongue inside a woman's mouth so badly. He'd never been gripped by urgency or jealousy or a thousand other unnamed emotions that had him pulling down her chin with his thumb to get deeper. God. God.

She's not temporary in any way, okay? Hands off.

Brendan's voice in his head forced Fox's eyes open, only to find Hannah's shut tightly. So tightly. He traced his thumb down to her throat and felt the moan building there, would have died to taste it. He could probably keep this up—bring her home from this party and take her to bed, orgasm her into a stupor—because seducing women was an effortless skill.

Yeah, a little more of this and she'd spend the night underneath him, but did she truly want that? No. No, she had her cap set at another man. They were giving the impression that sex was definitely happening, but actually sleeping with Fox when she wanted Sergei? That wasn't Hannah's style. She was too loyal. Too principled. And he wouldn't take that away from her, no matter how insane she tasted. No matter how hard she was making his cock with those committed strokes of her tongue, her hands pulling at his shirt.

Bottom line was, Brendan was right.

Hannah was the furthest thing from temporary, and Fox only did short-term. Very short-term. That personal rule kept him from getting his hopes up, from thinking he could be one half of a relationship again. Women didn't bring Fox home to meet their parents. He was more of the side-piece type. He'd been told his whole life that he'd turn out exactly like his father, and he'd confirmed a long time ago that he shared more than a pretty face with the man. He was perfect for making Hannah's director envious.

Yeah. A ruse was all this could be. A friend helping a friend. Unfortunately, he knew enough about women to know Hannah wasn't faking her enjoyment. Those breathy whimpers were for his ears alone. It was on Fox to make sure they didn't take this too far. As in, all the way back to his bed.

Despite the effort it cost him, Fox broke the kiss, pressing their foreheads together as they both struggled to catch their breath. "All right, Freckles," he said. "I think we convinced him."

Her eyes met his in a daze. "What? Who?"

For the first time, Fox felt his heart speed up into a sprint while off the water. Had Hannah just kissed him . . . to kiss him? Because she wanted to? He thought of the way she'd stopped dancing when he walked in, the way she'd moved in his direction as if drawn by a magnet. Had he misread everything? Was this not about making the director jealous? "Hannah, I . . . thought you were trying to show Sergei what he's missing?"

She blinked at him several times. "Oh. *Oh.* Yeah, I know," she said in a rushed whisper, shaking her head a couple of times. "I knew what you meant. S-sorry." Why wouldn't she look at him? "Thank you for . . . being so convincing."

Fox couldn't account for the ripple of pain in his stomach when she glanced sideways at Sergei to see if he'd been watching.

Oh yeah, the guy was looking, all right.

This plan was already working.

He suddenly ached to bury his fist in the wall.

When Hannah shifted, Fox realized he still had her flattened against the entryway and backed off before she felt his erection.

"How, um"—she cupped the base of her throat, as if to hide the pink skin there—"how did you know I was here?"

"I followed the trail of drunk people." He remembered the red cup in her hand when he'd arrived and concern drew his brows together. "You're not one of them, are you? I didn't realize—"

"Stop, I haven't had enough to drink that you took advantage of me, Fox. Only enough to dance to electronica." She puffed a laugh. "Anyway, I kissed you, remember?"

"I remember, Hannah," he assured her in a low voice, unable to keep his gaze from dropping to her swollen lips. "Do you want to stay awhile?"

She shook her head. Stopped. A smile bloomed across her face, and all he could do was watch it happen, dazed. "I did it," she murmured. "I asked to assist with the musical score and they said yes. And I didn't fall and nearly crack my head open this time."

Dumb heart. Dumb, pointless heart, please stop turning over.

The problem was, Hannah was extra cute after a few drinks and happy with her good news. All Fox could think about was kissing her again, and he couldn't. He'd done his job; now he needed to move back into friend territory fast. She seemed to have no problem putting him back there, right? He treasured this friendship, so he needed to follow suit. Pronto.

"Congratulations," he said, returning her smile. "That's amazing. You're going to be great at it."

"Yeah . . ." A little line formed between her brows. "Yeah. I will. I'll wake up tomorrow and the songs will be back."

Songs were the way she communicated her moods and feelings. How she interpreted everything. He'd known it last summer, and that knowledge of her had only grown over seven months of text messages. Knowing exactly what she meant made him feel . . . special. "Where did the songs go?"

"I don't know." Her lips twitched. "Maybe some ice cream would help?"

"We'll have to stop on the way home. Only the vanilla side is left."

"The not-chocolate side, you mean?" She surveyed the room. "I guess I should say good-bye. Or . . ." An odd look crossed her face. Something like reluctance, but he couldn't be sure. "Or I could introduce you to, um . . . There were some interested parties . . ."

It took him a minute to realize what she was getting at. "You mean the girls who called dibs on me when I walked into the room?" He kissed her forehead so she wouldn't see how much that bothered him. It shouldn't. He'd embraced the way people saw him. "Hard pass, Freckles. Let's go get ice cream."

The first three times Hannah teetered in her heels, Fox started to worry that she was, in fact, shit-faced. Had she really wanted that kiss? At the very least, if he'd known she'd had a lot to drink, he wouldn't have let it go on so long.

The clear quality of her speech put most of his fears to rest—all except the one about Hannah breaking her neck in those heels. So on their way out of the convenience store, he stepped in front of her, gesturing impatiently so she wouldn't suspect that he wanted to carry her. "This is not the kind of ride I usually offer women." He bent his knees a little to accommodate their height difference. "But the ice cream is going to melt if we have to take a trip to the ER, so hop on."

He loved that she simply jumped. Not a second's hesitation to read his intentions or tell him a piggyback ride was crazy. She just shoved the pint of chocolate ice cream under her arm and leapt, looping her free arm loosely around his neck. "You noticed my lack of high-heel game, did you? Know what's crazy? I actually like them. Piper wouldn't tell me how much they cost—I highly suspect because she never checked the price tag—but the astronomical price means they're kind of like walking on cotton balls." She yawned into his neck. "I've been judging her for wearing uncomfortable shoes for the sake of fashion, but they are cozy and they really do elongate the leg, Fox. I think I just need some practice."

Okay, she wasn't drunk, but she'd had enough alcohol to ramble, and he couldn't stop grinning as they passed beneath a streetlight. "They look nice on you."

"Thank you."

What a gigantic understatement. They made her legs look delicate and strong at the same time, flexing her calves. Making him acknowledge how perfectly they would fit into the palm of his hand. Making him want to stroke the contour of them with his thumbs. Fox swallowed, tightening his grip on her bare knees. *Don't go any lower or higher, asshole.* "So you got the green light to assist on the musical score. What does that mean?" His throat flexed. "Will you be spending more time with Sergei?"

If she heard the slightly strangled note in his voice, she chose to ignore it. "No. Just Brinley. You know, the leading-lady type?"

Some of the pressure crowding his chest dissipated. "I'm not on board with you calling other women that. As if you're not in the same category."

She dropped her chin onto his shoulder. "I felt like I was tonight. Got my big, dramatic movie kiss and everything."

"Yeah." His voice sounded like it was coming from the bottom of a barrel. Now that his shock from the kiss was wearing off, he could only worry about people in town finding out about it. *Did you hear Fox put the moves on the younger sister? It was only a matter of time.* "Was there any forward movement on the Sergei front while I was gone?" he forced out.

"Oh . . . no. No yards gained."

The quiet disappointment in her tone had Fox turning sharply, stomping up the stairs to his apartment, the crowded sensation back in his chest, along with that foreign smack of jealousy that he really didn't want to get used to. "That'll teach you to outright dismiss my lip-biting and arm-squeezing advice," he forced himself to say.

"Oh, come on, that wasn't real, usable advice. What else you got, Peacock?"

What was he supposed to do here? Refuse to give her advice and make his pointless envy obvious? For a split second, he considered giving her terrible suggestions. Like telling her that men love to diagnose strange skin rashes. Or be the sole male attendee at drunk karaoke nights with the girls. Hannah was too smart for that, though. He'd just have to hope she ignored this advice like the last time.

Why was he hoping that again? Wasn't he supposed to be her friend?

"Huh." He attempted to swallow the guilt, but only about half of it went down. "Men like to feel useful. It stirs up our precious alpha male pride. Find something heavy and tell him you need it lifted. You will have emphasized your physical differences and thus, the fact that he's a man and you're a woman. Men need way less prompting to think of . . ."

"Sex?"

Jesus, it was like he'd eaten something spicy. He couldn't stop clearing his throat. Or thinking of her with the director. "Right," he practically growled.

"Note to self," she said, pretending to write a note in the air, "find boulder. Ask for assistance. Manipulate the male psyche. By Jove, I think I've got it."

Fox doubted Pencil Arms could lift a pebble, let alone a boulder, but he kept that to himself. "You're a fast learner."

"Thank you." She smirked at him over his shoulder. So adorable, he couldn't help but give her one back. "How was the fishing trip?"

He blew out a breath while retrieving the keys from his pocket, using the moonlight to decipher which was the one for his apartment. "Fine. A little strained."

Fox probably never would have admitted that out loud if he wasn't thrown off by his jealousy. Damn, this was *not* a good look for him.

It wasn't as if he wanted Hannah to be *his* girlfriend, instead.

God, no. A girlfriend? Him? He doused the ridiculous flicker of hope before it could grow any larger. It was bad enough he'd allowed that kiss to go so long tonight. No way he'd drag her all the way into the mud with him.

As soon as they cleared the threshold of his apartment, Fox kicked the door closed behind them and Hannah slid off his back. He couldn't stop himself from observing the way she tugged the skirt of her dress down. It had ridden high, torturously so, on her legs. And, God, the skin on the inside of her thighs looked smooth. Lickable.

"Why was the trip strained?" she asked, following him into the kitchen with her pint of ice cream.

Strained, indeed.

Fox shook his head while taking two spoons out of the drawer. "No reason. Forget I said anything."

Wide-eyed and flushed, she leaned against his kitchen island. "Is it Brendan's fault? Because I can't talk trash about my sister's fiancé. Unless you really want to." A beat passed. "Okay, you convinced me. What's his problem? He can be so mean. And, like, what is with the beanie? Is it glued on?"

A laugh snuck out before he could catch it.

How did she do this? How could she rip him free of the jaws of envy and bring him back to a place of comfort and belonging? The fact that they were in his kitchen, with no one else around, made it a lot easier to relax. It was just them. Just Hannah, now barefoot, working off the top of the ice cream, giving him her undivided attention. He wanted to sink into it, into her. He was . . . selfish when it came to Hannah. Yeah. He wanted his friend all to himself. No directors allowed.

"I guess you could say it was tense because of Brendan," Fox said slowly, handing Hannah a spoon across the island. "But I'm equally to blame."

"Are you guys having a fight?"

He shook his head. "Not a fight. Just a difference of opinion." That was putting it mildly, considering he and his best friend had been like oil and water all week. Brendan continued to broach the uncomfortable subject of his intentions with Hannah, leading to Fox avoiding him, which was not easy to do in the middle of the ocean. They'd stormed off the boat in opposite directions as soon as it reached the dock in Grays. "You know Brendan is adding a second crabbing boat to the company? It's being built in Alaska. Almost finished at this point."

Hannah nodded around her first bite. "Piper mentioned it, yes."

It took him a deep breath to say the next part out loud. He'd told no one. "Last summer, around the time you and Piper showed up, Brendan asked me to take over as captain of the

Della Ray. So he could move to the new boat, focus on building a second crew so we can better compete during crab season."

He waited for the congratulations. Waited for her to gasp, come around the island, and hug him. Truthfully, he wouldn't have minded the hug.

Instead, she lowered the spoon and watched him solemnly, a wealth of thoughts dancing behind her eyes. "You don't want to be the captain of the *Della Ray*?"

"Of course I don't, Hannah." He laughed, a buzz saw turning against the back of his neck. "It's an honor to be asked. That boat—it's . . . a part of the history of this town. But, Jesus, I'm not interested in that level of responsibility. I don't want it. And he should know me well enough to realize that. You should know me well enough to realize it, too."

Hannah blinked. "I do know you well enough, Fox. The first conversation we ever had was about you being content to take orders and walk away whistling with a paycheck."

Why did he hate the first impression he'd given her when it was perfectly accurate? He was even perpetuating it now. Doubling down. Because it was the truth—he was content like this. Needed to be.

At eighteen, he'd had aspirations of being something other than a fisherman. He'd even formed a start-up with a college friend and fellow business major. Westport and his tomcat status were almost in the rearview when he realized he could never escape it. From thousands of miles away, his past and the expectations people had for him cast a shadow. Spoiled the business and partnership he'd tried to build. His reputation followed him, poisoning everything it touched. So, yeah, there was no sense trying to be something he wasn't.

Men didn't want a leader, a captain, they couldn't respect.

"That's right." He turned and took a beer out of the fridge, uncapping it with his teeth. "I'm fine right where I am. Not everyone has to strive for greatness. Sometimes getting by is just as rewarding."

"Okay." He faced Hannah again in time to see her nod, seeming like she wanted to stay silent but was unable to do it. "Have you let yourself visualize being captain, though?"

"Visualize it?" He raised an eyebrow. "You've never sounded more LA."

"If LA gets one thing right, Peacock, it's therapy."

"I don't need therapy, Hannah. And I don't need you to play the supporting actress, all right? That's not why I told you. So you could talk me through my problems."

She reared back, losing her grip on the spoon. It clattered onto the island, and she had to slap a hand down on it to stop the tinny noise. "You're right," she breathed. "That's exactly what I'm doing. I'm sorry."

Fox wished for quicksand to swallow him whole so he wouldn't have to see the dazed acceptance on her face. Had he really put it there? What the hell was wrong with him? "No, I'm sorry. That was a shitty thing for me to say. I'm sorry. I'm being . . . defensive."

Her mouth lifted at the corner, but her heart wasn't fully in the smile. "Being defensive? You've never sounded more LA."

God, he liked her.

"Look, I can't"—there was a pulsing squeeze in the dead center of his body, demanding he give her something, a pound of flesh, in exchange for snapping—"visualize it. Okay? When I visualize myself as the captain, I see an imposter. I'm not

Brendan. I don't take everything under the goddamn sun seriously. I'm just a good time, and everyone knows it."

He took a long sip of his beer, set it down with a clank. A few years back, Brendan had promoted him to relief skipper, and despite Fox's reservations, he'd grudgingly taken the position, knowing he'd seldom be required to take the wheel from steady-as-hell Brendan. Ever since then, the men liked to joke that Fox didn't mind sloppy seconds. When he took the wheel for a brief spell, they equated it to his one-night stands.

In and out. Just long enough to get your dick wet, right, man?

Fox laughed, pretended to let it roll off his back, but the comments dug under his skin, deeper each time. Especially since last summer. Now Brendan wanted him to be captain? To face even more skepticism and lack of respect? Not a fucking chance.

"Eventually he'd realize asking me was a mistake. I'm just trying to be considerate and save everyone some valuable time."

Hannah sat silent for a moment. "This is how you feel when I say I'm not a leading lady, I guess."

That gave him pause. The fact that she'd cast herself in some permanent benchwarmer role did drive him crazy. But no, they were coming from different places entirely. "The difference is, you want to be a leading lady. I don't want to be the hero of the story. I'm not interested."

She pressed her lips into a line.

Fox narrowed his eyes at her. "Are you doing that thing with your mouth because you're trying to trap all the psychological terms you want to throw at me?"

Her expression turned miserable. "Yes."

He forced a laugh. "I'm sorry to disappoint you, Freckles, but there's nothing here. Not everyone is fertile ground for fixing."

She lifted her shoulders and let them drop. "Okay, I won't try. If you tell me you don't want to be the captain, I'll believe you. I'll support that."

"Really?"

"Yes." A few seconds slid by. "After you visualize yourself being good at captaining. Put yourself in the wheelhouse and imagine yourself enjoying it. The crew thinks of you as a good time, but there is a time for fun and a time for responsibility. They see that you recognize the difference."

"Hannah . . ." Why was he panicking? He didn't want to visualize himself being taken seriously as Brendan's replacement. That would only lead to false hope. Didn't she realize that? Besides, it wasn't possible. Even if his imagination could conjure something so unlikely, he would never be able to realistically see himself in that leadership position. "I can't do it," he said, jerking a shoulder back. "I can't see it, Hannah, and I don't want to. All right? I appreciate you trying for me."

After a moment, she nodded. "Okay." A slow, playful smile. "I'm afraid our time together is up. We'll resume this discussion during next week's session."

"I'm sorry there weren't any breakthroughs."

She took her time enjoying another bite of chocolate ice cream, his suspicions rising when her mouth took on a cocky shape around the spoon. His bottle of beer remained poised an inch from his lips as he watched Hannah swagger around the counter, neatly placing her spoon in the dishwasher. "Oh, I think I sowed a few seeds."

And maybe she had.

Because when she looked up into his eyes, he pulled enough strength from her to visualize himself in the wheelhouse, just for the briefest moment. For the very first time since Brendan asked him to consider the job, he let himself grip the imaginary wheel, knowing he wouldn't have to give it up the second Brendan came back from taking a leak or fixing something in the engine room. He'd have it from the time they set sail, right up until docking again. He imagined hearing his voice over the radio, movement on the deck.

Returning home having done everything right, earning the respect of the crew—that's where he got stuck. He couldn't see that for the life of him.

Fox banished the image as quickly as possible, clearing his throat hard. "Good night, Freckles."

"Good night," Hannah said warmly, going up on her toes to kiss his cheek. "What kind of music day did you have?"

He let out a breath, happy to be back on familiar ground. "Coming home after four days on the water? Mmm. Something about home."

"'Home.' By Edward Sharpe and the Magnetic Zeros."

He barely kept his hand from lifting to brush back her hair. "I don't know that one," he managed.

"I'll text it to you before I go to sleep. It's perfect."

Fox nodded. "You?"

She waggled her eyebrows and backed away. "'Just One Kiss' by the Cure."

"Cute."

Watching her cross the apartment in her short red dress, smiling knowingly at him over her bare shoulder before disappearing into the guest room, Fox started to wonder if living with Hannah could be dangerous in more ways than one.

Put yourself in the wheelhouse and imagine yourself enjoying it. The crew thinks of you as a good time, but there is a time for fun and a time for responsibility. They see that you recognize the difference.

Hannah thought if she dug around a little, she'd find something interesting or worthwhile under his surface? She'd find his long-buried ambition?

Maybe he should show her exactly what he did best.

He could blur every thought in her beautiful head, leaving only the certainty that he lived up to the hype. That he was only good for one thing.

Fox pictured Hannah on the other side of the wall, that red dress slipping down to her ankles. How her skin would flush if he walked through the door.

Just one kiss, he'd say, exhaling against the nape of her neck. *Let's see about that.*

Don't. Don't fuck this up.

And he would. In a heartbeat. When the truth was . . . for the first time in a long, long time, he didn't want a girl thinking he was only good for one thing. Hannah was like a leaf blower aimed right at his undisturbed pile of possibilities, and damn, the hope felt kind of good. At the same time, he wanted them stuffed back under the tarp. Protected.

Fox took a step in the direction of her room, replaying that kiss, imagining the bump of the bed and her cries filling the apartment. It was only by the grace of God that he made it into his room without knocking on her door. But hell if he didn't spend the whole night thinking about it.

Chapter Eight

There was no filming on Saturday and most of the cast and crew headed to Seattle to take advantage of the time off. Hannah received a text from Christian at ten in the morning that read, **You coming to Seattle, yes or no? I don't care either way.** And while it was incredibly hard to pass up such a kind and generous invitation, Hannah was anxious to get some sister time with Piper. With Brendan back on terra firma to entertain his parents, the captain very wisely handed Piper his credit card, grunted at her to be careful, kissed her like the sky was falling, and nudged a dazed Piper toward Hannah, who waited in the driveway pretending to get sick over the public display of affection.

"Okay, but seriously," Hannah said, climbing into the passenger side of Brendan's truck, which they were borrowing for the day. "Does your vagina ever get tired?"

Piper snorted. "Sometimes I swear it is, but that's just my cue to hydrate." Hannah fell sideways onto the seat laughing, her sister ruffling her hair with an indulgent smile. "When he's doing it right, it never gets old." Piper checked her makeup in the rearview, smacked her lips together, and started the truck. "Someday you'll have a reason to agree."

Hannah didn't like where her mind went—and it went there immediately.

The way Fox stared at her last night as she'd walked into her bedroom.

He must not have expected her to glance back over her shoulder or he wouldn't have had that look in his eye. Honestly, the word "seductive" normally sounded ridiculous to her. A word that reminded her of old Sharon Stone movie trailers. Or maybe she'd hear it once in a while flipping through cable where the coffee commercials lived.

Seductive blends. Seductive aroma.

She'd never really considered the true meaning of the word until now. Fox was attractive. Like, insanely so. That was a given. But last night, that look in his eye had accidentally given her a peek behind the curtain, and it was like setting foot in a new country with a different currency and climate. She would even venture to call his expression smoldering. He'd been thinking about sex—no mistaking it. And while she'd be lying to say there wasn't always a current of physical tension running between them, she'd always assumed Fox just gave it off all by himself. It came with the territory of being in his vicinity.

Last night was different.

Last night, for that brief moment, all of that potent sexual energy had been concentrated on her, and she'd heated like an oven, the knobs on her awareness turned to the highest setting. Did he want to sleep with her? The fact that he'd given her advice on how to capture Sergei's attention made the possibility seem remote. But the mere thought of Fox wanting her was like skydiving. A free-falling, leave-her-stomach-in-the-air event.

At UCLA, she'd dated one of her fellow music history majors, that relationship lasting just over a year. It was serious enough to introduce him to her parents and take a vacation together in Maui. But her interest in him had mainly been based on convenience, since they had classes together, and he didn't make a fuss when Hannah retreated into her headphones. He'd just hop on the Xbox and zone out, too. After a while, the relationship turned into a competition of finding ways to ignore each other—definitely no reason to use the word "seductive."

Even while nursing her crush on Sergei, she'd dated. An extra she'd met on set, fresh from a farm in Illinois, following his dream in Los Angeles. A stunt coordinator who spent the entire date hitting her with classic movie trivia, which she didn't technically mind—they were social media friends now—but there'd been no viable connection.

In other words, she'd been playing in the minor leagues.

If that kiss at the party was any indication, Fox was in a major league all his own when it came to intimacy. Sure, she'd known that. In theory. He was a certified Casanova and didn't even bother trying to deny it. Experiencing those skills last night, putting that knowledge into practice, had been eye-opening to say the least.

She was pretty sure her brain and ovaries had briefly swapped locations during that kiss.

If he wanted to sleep with her—and come on, it was entirely possible she'd misread him—what would she do with all of that . . . seductive smolder? Why couldn't she stop thinking about it now? How he would move. How he would groan when the relief hit. What the fronts of his muscular thighs would feel like against the backs of hers.

He would do it right.

He'd dehydrate the shit out of her.

"Hannah."

"What?" she shouted.

Piper squeaked and swerved the truck, shooting Hannah a wide-eyed look. "I asked if you wanted to stop for coffee."

"Oh. Sorry." Was she sweating? "Of course I do."

Hannah shook herself, focused on counting the white lines painted in the middle of the road. Guilt settled into her stomach like sediment in a wineglass. No more thinking about Fox in those terms. Sex terms. The kiss, followed by that hungry look, had just thrown her for a loop. Now she needed to get back on track. Back to batting in the minors. Back to her harmless crush on the director. She'd probably misread Fox, anyway.

After they stopped for giant lattes smothered in caramel and whipped cream, Piper drove Hannah about forty minutes south to an outdoor shopping mall. They spent the day browsing racks but were too busy talking and catching up to buy much of anything, although Piper walked out of the lingerie store looking very superior with a little pink bag, and Hannah bought a new pair of round tortoiseshell sunglasses. They spent most of their time together lingering over lunch at a cozy French bistro, continuing to order more and more coffee so they wouldn't get kicked out.

The sky was darkening by the time they headed back to Westport, Hannah singing along to the radio, badly, but her sister was used to it.

"Hey," Piper said when the song had ended. "Brendan is bringing his parents into Cross and Daughters tonight. Come and meet them?"

"As if I would pass up a chance to meet those responsible for spawning the Mean One?" She tugged the phone out of her pocket. "Let me just text Fox."

Piper sniffed loudly.

"I'm staying with him. It's the polite thing to do." Hannah started to fire off a quick text, then hesitated. "Should I invite him?"

"It's Saturday night—he doesn't have"—her sister looked at her meaningfully—"plans?"

"Plans, like . . . oh." Her stomach had no right to drop. "I—I mean, he didn't mention anything. Like a date. But if I invite him, the worst he can say is no."

Why was she nervous he would turn her down? Tell her he was headed to Seattle for his usual recreational activities? What Fox did with his time was none of her business. Her fingers hovered over the screen for a few more seconds before she tapped out a text.

> **HANNAH (7:18 PM):** Heading to Cross & Daughters with Piper if you're interested.

A minute later, he answered.

> **FOX (7:19 PM):** See you there, Freckles.

Hannah let out a slow breath and tipped her head back against the seat. The speed with which her stomach calmed

was alarming. But it did. Like a raging sea turning into a tran-
quil lake in the space of four words. What was *that* about? Did
she simply covet the short length of time she had to spend with
a friend? That was totally possible, right?

They walked into Cross and Daughters a little while later,
the evening crowd only starting to trickle in. Hannah's heart
squeezed the moment she stepped over the threshold, bombarded by images of her and Piper sanding the old, neglected
bar, finding that photograph of Henry behind a piece of plywood, sprinting to the door with a flaming frying pan, getting
ready for the grand opening. So many memories packed into
such a small space. And there was a definite satisfaction that
came from looking up and knowing she was the one who hung
the gold, spray-painted fishing net from the ceiling.

Piper slipped behind the bar to consult with Anita and
Benny, the newly hired waitress and bartender Piper had told
her about over lunch. Her sister looked so confident, pointing
out things on the drink menu, answering a question about
how to operate the register. A year ago, Piper had never seen a
checkbook, let alone balanced one. Now she owned and operated a successful bar.

God, Hannah was proud of her.

"You okay over there?"

She turned at the sound of Fox's deep drawl, finding him
leaning back on a bar stool, one arm resting along the back of
the seat, the other steadying a beer bottle in his lap. There was
no help for the prickles that ran along her scalp, down her neck,
and around to the front, hardening her nipples into points. It
happened so fast, she didn't have time to think of something to
counter the effect, like slugs or snot or foot fungus.

Fox watched it happen knowingly, too, the blue of his eyes deepening a shade as they dipped to her breasts, the beer bottle lifting to his sculpted lips for a long, hard pull.

Get yourself together, Hannah.

This was simply the effect Fox had on women. But she didn't have to be like everyone else and let it become A Thing. She could acknowledge his attractiveness and remain objective, right?

"Hey. Yes. I was just, um . . ." Begging herself to stop being an idiot, Hannah hopped onto the stool beside him. "I was just remembering all the work that went into this place."

He nodded. "You girls brought it back to life."

She nudged him with an elbow, sighing inwardly when his firm muscle didn't budge in the slightest. "You helped."

"I was just here for the company," he said quietly, holding her gaze long enough to turn her stomach into a jungle gym. Then, as if forcing himself to switch gears, he reached over and tapped her nose. "What do you want to drink?"

"Hmmm. No liquor. I filled my yearly quota last night. Beer, maybe?"

"Beer it is."

Fox nodded at Benny and ordered something vaguely German-sounding. A moment later, Hannah was sipping on a cold pint glass full of a golden substance, an orange wedge stuck on the rim. "This is good. This is beer?"

He grinned. "Uh-oh. Someone is going to fill their yearly beer quota, too."

"Oh no. Not me. I have to be on set in the morning."

"We'll see." Cockily, he crossed his arms. "You haven't been here in a while."

Hannah paused midway through a sip. "What's that supposed to mean?"

She never got her answer, because at that same moment, Piper poked her in the shoulder, presenting Brendan's parents with a flourish. "Hannah, this is Mr. and Mrs. Taggart. Michael and Louise, this is my sister, Hannah."

Oh, these were Brendan's parents, all right. No mistaking it. They were stiff shouldered and serious, not at all comfortable in the bar setting. But they were trying, even if their smiles were distracted. Without looking at Piper, Hannah could feel her sister's nerves over having her future mother- and father-in-law in the bar, so Hannah did what she did best. She called forth her inner hype girl.

Putting on a broad smile, Hannah slipped back off the stool and leaned in to kiss the cheeks of the older couple, squeezing their hands at the same time, drawing their full attention. "It's so lovely to meet you. Are you enjoying your time back in Westport?"

Louise's tension unlocked slightly. "Yes, we are. Not much has changed about the town and I find that quite comforting."

Like mother, like son, huh?

"Piper has been telling me all afternoon how incredible it has been to have you visiting them. You should be worried about her locking you in the house and not letting you go."

Louise chuffed a little, her cheeks tinting with pink. "Oh. Well, isn't that sweet."

Hannah nodded. "She even created a signature cocktail for your visit. The . . . Taggart-tini. Right, Pipes?" Her sister stared back at her unblinking, a smile frozen on her face. "What are you waiting for? Get back there and make them one."

Piper turned and circled around to the other side at the pace of a sloth.

Wanting to buy her sister some time to actually create the Taggart-tini, Hannah laid a hand on Fox's arm. "You must know Fox, right? He grew up with Brendan."

It was impossible to mistake the slight cooling in Louise's temperature. Very subtle, but Hannah detected it in the pinch around the corners of her mouth. "Yes, of course we do. Hello, Fox."

Fox turned slightly and nodded at the couple. "Good to see you, Mr. and Mrs. Taggart." His smile seemed forced. "Hope you're having a nice visit."

"We are, thank you," Michael said, equally stiff.

Hannah frowned inwardly at the exchange, itching to address it with Fox, but Piper chose that moment to slide two cloudy red martinis across the bar. "Here it is!" Piper sang through her teeth. "The Taggart-tini."

"Oh, well, I couldn't possibly . . ." Louise started, clutching her collar.

"Oh, but you will, won't you?" Hannah passed the drinks to the couple, helping them clink their rims together. "One sip won't hurt."

Twenty minutes later, Louise had Piper's face in her hands, her words ever-so-slightly slurred. "I have never seen my son so happy. You are an angel. An absolute angel, isn't she, Michael? Our son smiles now! It's almost disconcerting how often he smiles, and you—you are going to give me grandbabies, aren't you? Oh please. You angel. My son is a lucky man."

Piper looked over at Hannah, blinking back grateful tears.

Thank you, she mouthed.

Hannah let out a satisfied exhale and went back to her beer, which was unfortunately warm now, realizing after several moments that Fox was staring at her. "Damn, Hannah. That was nothing short of masterful."

She gave a subtle bow. "The power of alcohol, Peacock."

"Uh-uh." Adamantly, he shook his head. "That was all you."

"Piper was having a hard time relating to Louise. They just needed a little push, that's all. Who doesn't love Piper?" She looked back over her shoulder to where Louise was now attempting to slow dance with Piper to a power ballad. "Let's see if my sister is still grateful tomorrow when she's got a hungover future mother-in-law on her hands."

Fox chuckled. "Nothing some greasy potatoes can't cure. The important thing is, the ice is broken."

Don't bring up the weird exchange between Fox and Louise. Don't. Why do you always have to address every little thing? "Speaking of ice . . ." *Nice segue, Barbara Walters.* "Did I imagine a little awkwardness between you and Brendan's mother?"

He took his time answering. "Nah, you didn't imagine it." His laugh crackled as he shifted in the chair. "Nothing serious. They were just protective of Brendan growing up, and I was, you know, the bad influence on her otherwise perfect kid."

There was no bitterness in the way he said it. Just making a statement.

"Do you think you were a bad influence?"

"No," he said slowly, after several seconds had ticked by. "I was, uh . . . promiscuous before the other guys my age were ready. But I'd never put pressure on anyone else to do . . . what I did. What I do," he amended quickly. "God, no. I'd never do that."

It seemed like he wanted to say more. A lot more.

Hannah wanted to hear it. That explanation masked something deeper, but he was already restlessly ordering them both another beer, changing the subject to what she'd done that day. The obviously sore topic was forgotten, and soon they were laughing. Other members of the *Della Ray* crew steadily made their way through the door and joined the group, until they were all crowded around two stools, telling stories, Hannah getting reacquainted with the locals who'd come to mean so much to her last summer.

She didn't have this in LA. And she'd missed it. A lot.

Back home, she went to work and went home. Every once in a while, she'd go out for a drink with her coworkers at Storm Born, but she never got *this* feeling. The one that said she was in the right place. That she was home and would be accepted here, no questions asked. Every time. During a particularly long-winded story from Deke, Hannah felt Fox watching her and looked back, the alcohol thrumming along in her veins, sending goose bumps riding in a slow wave up her arms and neck.

Right, it's the alcohol.

In a daze, she watched as he wet his lower lip, rubbing the moisture together with the top one, leaving his mouth looking fresh and male. His heavy-lidded blue eyes never leaving her.

Seductive blends. Seductive aromas.

Sharon Stone.

Go home, you're drunk.

"It's time for quarters!" Benny called out behind the bar, ringing a bell that was mounted above the register. "Who are tonight's victims?"

Fox took Hannah's wrist and raised her hand before she knew what was happening.

"How about sister versus sister?" Brendan shouted from the back of the bar.

Hannah and Piper locked eyes through the crowd like two western gunslingers.

"It's on!" Hannah cried.

The bar erupted in cheers.

So much for going home.

Fox tipped back on his stool to get a better view of Hannah where she was holding court in the middle of the bar, competing against her sister in the silliest game of quarters he'd ever witnessed.

The game had one rule.

Bounce the quarter off the table. Land it in the pint glass.

But in Cross and Daughters, there was a twist. Every time a player landed a quarter in the glass, they had to tell the entire bar an embarrassing fact about themselves. The tradition started one night when a sunburned tourist decided to play quarters and was somehow convinced this rule was the norm. What started as a way to razz an out-of-towner had become standard game play.

Hannah hadn't even flinched at the rules, just nodding as if they made perfect sense. Not for the first time, he marveled over how easily she fit into this place, like she'd always been there. She'd come here last summer and gotten a part-time job at Disc N Dat, melding seamlessly with the younger generation slowly making their mark on this old fishermen's town. What would life here be like if the pair of Bellingers hadn't shown up? Brendan would still be wearing his wedding ring, years passing as he turned harder, more closed off. Fox . . .

Nothing would be different on his end, he thought hastily.

He'd be exactly the same.

So, all right. Maybe he wouldn't be standing on the edge of the crowd, with a smile on his face a mile wide, watching Hannah laugh so hard she could barely stand up. There was no helping it. She felt like the sunrise coming up over the water after a bad storm. And she was terrible at quarters. Her only saving grace was that Piper was worse.

Both of their quarter rolls had run out before getting a single one in the glass. Now they were scooping quarters off the floor into their pockets and getting back in position, trying to compete while doubled over in laughter. Fox wasn't the only one held in complete thrall, either. The locals were enamored with both sisters, but he couldn't for the life of him take his eyes off Hannah. The entire place surrounded the girls, cheering them on—and finally, finally, Hannah got a quarter in the glass, sending the customers into a frenzy.

"What's your embarrassing fact?" Fox shouted over the noise.

Hannah cringed. "I failed my driver's test because I kept changing the radio station." She held up some fingers. "Three times."

"What she lacks in concentration behind the wheel, she makes up for in driving me home from jail," Piper added, laying a kiss on Hannah's cheek. "Just kidding, Louise!" she called to her gaping mother-in-law, sending her and Hannah into a fit of hysterics. She almost lost her balance completely, and Fox figured that was his cue to take her home.

He set his half-empty beer down on the closest table and approached Hannah, acutely aware of everyone within ear-shot, including Piper and Brendan. They were already wary of Hannah staying in his spare room. Every word out of his mouth, every action was being scrutinized to gauge his in-terest and intentions. The last thing Fox wanted was another "talk" from Brendan. He'd had enough of those on the boat.

So he tried to sound as casual as possible when he stopped in front of Hannah, ducking down a little to her level until their eyes met. "Hey, I'm heading home if you want to walk with me." Briefly, he met Brendan's eyes. "Or stay and get a ride. It's up to you."

Without a doubt, if she went with option number two, Fox knew he'd sit in his room and wait until she was safely inside.

"I should definitely go now if I don't want to be a zombie on set tomorrow," she said, turning and throwing her arms around Brendan and Piper. "I love you guys. See you soon."

"We love you, too," Brendan said, patting her on the head and earning heart eyes from his wife. Not that he saw it, be-cause he was busy giving Fox a death stare.

Right.

It was easy to see what his friend was trying to communi-cate to him.

Walking out of the bar with Hannah would send the wrong signal. A bad one. Get everyone's tongues wagging and ultimately make her look bad. God, that was the last thing he wanted. He needed to be more careful. As of now, they'd kept her temporary stay in his guest room pretty quiet, but leaving the bar together on a Saturday night would whip up any speculation that might already be brewing.

"I'll meet you outside," Fox said in a rush, turning and walking blindly through the crowd with a pit in his stomach. When he stepped out into the cool spring mist, he couldn't resist looking back through the window from where he'd just come, watching Hannah wave to everyone on the way out, getting caught up in long good-byes, until finally she joined him in the nighttime shadows.

Without a word, Hannah linked their arms together, laying her head against Fox's shoulder, the show of trust cementing right over the hole in his belly.

"Jesus, Freckles," Fox said, tracing the part running down the center of her head. "We need to work on your quarters game."

She gasped. "What do you mean? I won!"

"Ah, no. You were the least-worst loser."

Her laughter rang down the misty street. "What is the advantage of winning when you have to tell people something embarrassing about yourself? It's backward."

"Welcome to Westport."

She sighed, rubbed her cheek against his arm. "On nights like this, I think I could live here."

Fox's heart lurched so hard he had to wait a moment to speak. "Oh yeah?"

"Yeah. But then I remember what a crazy idea that is. I can't live in Westport and continue working in entertainment. And the bar . . ." She smiled. "The bar is Piper's."

Well, that's that. Right?

How the hell would he handle it if Hannah moved here, anyway? He'd see her constantly. Every Saturday night would be like this. Pretending to her and everyone watching that he didn't want to take her home. *Really* take her home. And once that happened, well. He'd be screwed. He'd have broken his own rule about not hooking up in Westport, fucked his relationship with Brendan, and potentially hurt Hannah's feelings. It was best for everyone if she stayed in LA.

But tell that to the disappointment so heavy that it almost dragged him down to the cobblestones.

They turned right on Westhaven and crossed the street, walking along the water without verbally agreeing to it. "Do you love the ocean as much as Brendan does?"

There she went, asking him questions that made him think. Questions that wouldn't allow him to skate by with a quip— and he didn't really like doing that with Hannah, anyway. He liked talking to her. Loved it, actually, even when it was hard. "I think we love it in different ways. He loves the tradition and structure of fishing. I love how wild nature can get. How it can be more than one thing. How it evolves. One year, the crabs are in one place, the next they're in another. No one can . . . define the ocean. It defines itself."

Hannah must have been holding her breath, because she blew it out in a rush. "Wow." She looked out over the water. "That's lovely."

He tried to ignore the satisfaction of being acknowledged and understood because of something that came out of his mouth. It wasn't often that happened to him. But he couldn't shrug it off, so he just let it settle in.

"Okay, I think you've convinced me. I want to hunt king crabs." Hannah nodded firmly. "I'm going to be your newest greentail."

He couldn't tell if she was joking or not.

She better be joking.

"A rookie is called a green*horn*—and that isn't happening, babe. You can't even keep your balance during quarters." An actual shiver blew through him thinking of Hannah on the deck, fifteen-story waves building in the background. "If you hear me screaming in the middle of the night, you're to blame for my nightmares."

"I can just be in charge of the music on the boat."

"No."

"You got me feeling all romantic about the ocean. It's your fault."

He looked down into her face and finally, thank God, was positive she was joking. And goddamn. In the moonlight, her amused features, her shining eyes . . . they were a masterpiece. His body thought so, too. It liked her mouth most of all, how she moistened the lush pillows of her lips, as if preparing for a kiss. Who wouldn't kiss this beautiful girl, so full of life, in the moonlight?

Fox lowered his head slightly. "Hannah . . ."

"Be careful of that one," someone shouted from across the street. "Run while you can, girl."

Laughter broke out, and Fox knew, before turning to look, that it would be the old-man regulars from Blow the Man Down, smoking outside in their usual spot. The same men he'd made jokes to hundreds of times about his exploits in Seattle. Because it was easier to give them what they wanted. Laugh with them, instead of being laughed at. Make the joke, instead of being the joke. And above all else, don't let them see how much it all bothered him.

Hannah blinked several times and stepped back from him, as if becoming aware of her surroundings and what had almost happened between them. They'd almost kissed. Or did he imagine that? It was hard to think with the warning signal going off in his head. Jesus, he didn't want Hannah to hear the kind of garbage that came out of these men's mouths.

"Who are those guys?" she asked, leaning slightly to look past him.

"No one." He took her wrist and started walking at a fast clip, glad she'd worn sneakers so she could easily keep up. "Just ignore them. They're drunk."

"Your mama didn't warn you about tomcats like this one? Make sure he shells out the cab fare—"

Hannah skidded to a stop beside Fox, yanking her arm free.

Before he could get ahold of her again, she'd marched halfway across the street.

"Hey, scumbag! How about you shut your mouth?" She jabbed a finger at the leader, and his cigarette froze on the way to his mouth. "Mamas don't bother warning girls about jerks like yourself, because no one would come within ten feet of you. Smelly old ball sac!"

"Now hold on. It's just a bit of fun," offered the man.

"At whose expense?" Hannah shouted, turning in a circle, searching the ground.

Fox, who'd been standing behind her completely dumbfounded, caught between awe and self-disgust, forced his throat to start working. "What are you doing?"

"Looking for something to throw at them," she explained patiently.

"Okay, how is Piper the one that ended up in jail?" He wrapped a forearm around her waist and shuttled her down the street toward his building, no idea what to say. None. He'd never had anyone stand up for him like that.

And he didn't want the breathless warmth winging its way into his chest. Would never be ready for the . . . dangerous hope that started to rise to the surface. Hope that if this girl believed he was worth a damn—enough to defend him in the street like this—maybe he was worth the effort?

No. Been there, done that whole dance with optimism. Wanted no part of it.

Right?

"Hannah, you didn't need to do that. In fact, I wish you hadn't."

He really didn't enjoy the flash of hurt in her eyes. "They were way out of line."

"No, they weren't." He laughed, even though it felt like razor blades. "They know it's okay to make those jokes to me, because I make them about myself. It's fine."

"Yeah, it really sounds fine," she murmured, allowing Fox to pull her up the stairs of his building, standing silently as he unlocked the door. Part of him, honest to God, wanted to throw his arms around her and say thank you, but no. No, he didn't need a defender. He'd earned that ridicule, fair and square, hadn't he?

The last seven months were nothing but an anomaly.

Even if his celibacy, even if the constant of Hannah's friendship, had made him feel better about himself than he had in years.

They walked into the apartment, and Fox turned on the one and only lamp.

He wanted to shut himself in his bedroom, before the shame of Hannah witnessing that ridicule on the walk home seeped out through his pores and turned visible, but he couldn't let her hurt expression be the last thing he saw that night. So Fox did what he did best and made light of it. "Have to admit, I'm pretty impressed by your creative use of the term 'ball sac.' Ten out of ten."

Her lips crept up into a smile on one end. "Are we okay?" She wet her lips. "Are you?"

"Everything is fine, Freckles." He laughed, the empty apartment mocking him. "Get some sleep, huh? See you in the A.M."

After a moment, she nodded. And that's where he left her, staring after him thoughtfully, halfway between the kitchen and the front door.

As soon as Fox was alone in his bedroom, he dropped his forehead to the cool door, barely resisting the urge to bash his head against it. Obviously he hadn't fooled Hannah into thinking he didn't give a shit about anything. That life was just a series of pleasures and amusements for him. This girl, she saw through it. Worse, she wanted to reach him. But he couldn't let that happen.

And he knew exactly how to prevent her from looking too deeply.

Chapter Nine

Hannah woke up at six A.M. with mice using her brain as a trampoline.

Her hand slapped down on the side table, fingers closing around her AirPods, shoving them into her ears. Next came her phone, her thumb locating the music app and selecting Zella Day from her library, letting the notes drift through the fog and wake her up slowly. Today was Sunday. Not an ideal day for working, but it was her first day on set as slightly more than a production assistant—she was an observer now, ooh, ahh—and she needed to set the right tone. Calm but focused.

Hannah, you didn't need to do that. In fact, I wish you hadn't.

Fox's reprimand from the night before came rushing back, and the mice ceased bouncing on her brain, creeping off to go hide in a hole somewhere. Oh man, she'd really yelled at those old men from the middle of the street, hadn't she? Not a dream? Truthfully, she was fine owning that reaction. Even if she *had* thrown something at them, they would have deserved the resulting concussion.

They'd deserved it for treating him—anyone, really—with so little respect.

Why didn't Fox think so?

He'd seemed fine before bed. Maybe the alcohol had amplified a situation that was really no big deal? What if fishermen simply spoke to each other that way and she'd misread the intention behind it?

But none of it sat right, so she resolved to ask Fox about it later and forced herself to focus on the upcoming day at work. She ran through the scenes in her mind, searching for inspiration to enrich the score, but an hour passed without anything feeling exactly right. Which was concerning. She'd never gone so far as to think scoring movies was her calling. That would have been putting the cart way before the horse. But she'd always been confident in her ability to pull songs from memory to perfect the mood of any situation. What if she'd been *too* confident?

The scent of ginger distracted Hannah from her troubling thoughts.

It wasn't an unpleasant smell at all. Quite the opposite. It was almost . . . stimulating in its richness? And she'd smelled it in the apartment before, but never so strong. What was that?

Hannah tossed aside the covers and climbed out of bed, leaving her AirPods in on the way to the bathroom, where she brushed her teeth and used the toilet, grudgingly removing the earbuds to shower. Fox had no reason to be awake this early, so she tried to be as quiet as possible, wrapping a towel tightly around her body and tiptoeing toward the guest room.

When the door to his bedroom opened and he breezed out, mid-yawn, in nothing but black briefs, Hannah ran smack into the side of the couch, sending a jolt of pain through her hip. It sent her stumbling back a couple of feet, her ass bumping into a floor lamp. Seriously, leave it to her to find two of the only pieces of furniture in the extremely sparse apartment and hit them . . . and now she was staring. Of course she was staring. What else was she supposed to do?

Fox was coming toward her with a lopsided grin and barely any clothes.

Dimples out. Ready to film a razor commercial.

And whoa. Until that moment, she hadn't even been aware of his tattoos.

The outline of an actual fox stretching across his right hip, a giant squid wrapped around an anchor on the left side of his rib cage, a series of different-sized stars on his pec, plus other ones she didn't have the wherewithal to decipher because his muscles were demanding attention. Were muscles supposed to be so thick? Yes. Yes, because he hadn't bought these in a gym. He'd come by them hauling giant steel pots out of the water, pulling in nets of fish, from balancing on a deck during rough weather.

"Whoa there, Freckles," he said in a raspy morning voice, tipping his head toward the teetering lamp. "Still getting your sea legs?"

"Um . . ." Resolutely, she looked down at the floor. "I guess I'm more hungover than I realized. Better lay low tonight."

The closer he came, the stronger the scent of ginger. And the harder it became not to look at Fox in all his nearly naked glory. Listen, Hannah got horny with the best of them. Once in a while, at least. Mostly when listening to Prince. But the times she'd felt slightly wanting and uncomfortable were a far cry from this cinching of muscles, this filtering of warmth to her private areas.

Guilt invaded her middle. Not quite enough to scare off her lady boner, but enough to mentally berate herself for being a bad friend. How was Hannah any better than the girls who'd called dibs on Fox at the party on Friday night?

"I, um . . ." She tipped her head down so the wet hair would curtain her face. *Must resist the call of those chisel-cut hip abductors.* "There's an early call time. I need to hurry up and get down there."

"Where are you filming today?"

Was his voice closer than before? The goose bumps racing up her skin made her wish dearly for something more substantial than a towel to cover herself. "We're shooting on the harbor. A kissing scene, actually. The big finale. We should have the lighting we've been waiting for."

"Finale?" he echoed quickly. "You just started."

"We don't always shoot the scenes in order. Sometimes it depends on the availability of the locations . . ." He stepped in front of Hannah, giving her no choice but to look up at the ceiling, where she pretended to search for cracks. Otherwise she wouldn't trust herself not to stare straight into the eye of the storm.

Also known as his crotch.

"You can't look at me, can you?" Fox said, amused. "I'm not used to having someone else in the house. You want me to put on sweatpants next time?"

Jesus, no, screamed the pervert who had rented space in her head.

"Yes, please. And I'll . . . use my robe, too. I didn't think you'd be awake."

The heat of his chest warmed her exposed shoulders, and everything down there turned soft and wet. She became acutely aware of the sound of his hands settling on his hips, skin rasping on skin. His height and strength compared to her.

It was shameful to be reacting to her friend this way.

She obviously wasn't going to sleep with him. At this juncture in her life, she wasn't interested in casual sex. Especially with Fox. He didn't merely eschew long-term, he was all about *no* term. Having her around afterward would make him uncomfortable, he'd regret getting physical, and that would ruin their friendship.

I'm just a good time, and everyone knows it.

His statement from Friday night drifted into her thoughts, and for some reason, the memory made her want to look him in the eye. He was scrutinizing her kind of expectantly, as if waiting for her to expire from arousal or attempt to climb him. Was he . . . trying to throw her off-balance for some reason? Why?

She couldn't work through it when that smell was muddling her brain. What kind of nuclear pheromones was this guy giving off?

Very discreetly, she hoped, Hannah inhaled his scent. "What is that?"

His brows drew together. "What is what?"

"That ginger smell. Is it like . . . lotion or aftershave or something?"

"No." He smirked. "None of those."

She waited for him to elaborate. He didn't. "What is it, then?"

He very briefly touched the tip of his tongue to the corner of his lips, his blue eyes twinkling. "Massage oil."

Of all the explanations, Hannah was not expecting that. "Massage oil." She laughed. "Were you, like, giving yourself a massage—" Flames climbed her face. "Oh. Wow. Walked right into that. I . . . Were you . . . d-doing that this morning?" She waved her hands frantically. "Never mind. Don't answer that."

His grin only widened. "Yeah, I was. First time I've had a chance since our last fishing trip. Had to blow off some steam. Should I have asked permission first?"

"No." Oh no. Now she was thinking about Fox asking for her permission to masturbate. It was like someone saying, "Don't think about pink elephants."

Except the pink elephant was Fox's penis.

"No, of course not. This is your apartment." And now she was reluctantly fascinated. "You use massage oil for that?"

He hummed in affirmation. "It doubles as a lubricant. You're welcome to borrow it." His attention dropped to the knot between her breasts, then lower, to the spot where the hem of the towel brushed her mid-thigh. "But only if you like to make yourself nice and sensitive first." He rubbed his knuckles over the breach of his belly button, through dark-blond hair and faded ink. "Kind of like foreplay with your own fingers."

A swallow got stuck in her throat.

A bead of sweat ran down the small of her back.

"I'll leave it in the bathroom cabinet." He winked at her as he backed away, eventually turning for his bedroom. "Orange bottle."

"Oo-kay," she said, tongue heavier than lead. "Thanks?"

Did friends share lube?

Maybe only people who were friends with *this* particular man?

"I'll be working on the boat all day," he said on his way into the bedroom, shutting the door behind him before calling through the crack, "See you down at the harbor, Freckles."

Oh.

Great.

She walked to her room in a daze.

Fox watched the film crew move like clockwork from his vantage point on the deck of the *Della Ray*. Three big white trailers were parked on the road, young people with headsets and clipboards scurrying around. Others congregated around a table of food and drinks. Large fluorescent-lamp-looking things surrounded two actors—a moody, skinny guy and a redhead who went from mooning over each other to checking their phones and not speaking in between takes.

For the last hour, he'd been replenishing supplies with Sanders and repairing the hydraulic launcher. They really only needed the piece of equipment for crab season, but apparently he was making every excuse to be out on deck.

Where he had a clear view of the film set.

Hopefully after this morning, Hannah wouldn't feel the need to defend his character anymore. She'd just disregard him with a knowing smirk, like everyone else, and he could get rid of this hope she inspired in him. He could stay where it was safe. Where his crewmates and fellow Westport residents chuckled and joked about him, but at least they weren't questioning his legitimacy as a leader.

Surely Hannah would laugh off a guy who had a favorite brand and scent of massage oil? Even though he'd never needed the shit until recently.

Usually, if he required relief and his hand was the only option, he just worked it out with a lathered palm in the shower. Now that he was seeing his five digits exclusively, he'd sprung for something with a little pizzazz. Sue him.

Brendan would kick his ass if he knew Fox had spoken to her like that. But he'd had to weigh the threat of his best friend's wrath against Hannah's growing expectations of him. Because he was definitely not a fucking captain. Not someone to be trusted with a valuable boat or the lives of five men. Definitely not someone Hannah offered her mouth to in the moonlight. Or berated strangers over.

Just a good time. Nothing more, nothing less.

Sanders walked out on deck beside Fox and greeted him with a grunt. He tossed down the wrench he'd been using to repair the oil pump and swiped a hand over his wealth of carrot-colored hair. "Fuck sake, it's hot down there. I'm thinking of installing a window in the hull. Do you think Brendan would mind?"

"If you sank the ship in hopes of a cross breeze? No, not at all," Fox answered drily, a stillness settling over him at the sight of Hannah and Sergei discussing something over a clipboard. His fingers gripped the rope he was coiling in his hand, letting the material bite into his skin, harder and harder until Hannah finally walked away. Was the director staring after her?

Yeah. He was.

That kiss the other night had worked its magic. Good.

Maybe she'd asked him to lift a heavy piece of filming equipment. Or employed some strategic lip biting. All thanks to his urgings.

It wouldn't be too long before they were both headed back to LA with a shiny new appreciation for each other.

Great.

Ignoring the acidic taste in his mouth, Fox went back to repairing the launcher and tried to focus. The sun beat down on the deck, unseasonably hot, until he and Sanders eventually gave up on shirts and shoes altogether.

Fox used to hate this kind of tedious work. He wanted to be out in the gale, warring with waves, battling their impact, witnessing nature at her angriest. Watching as she changed her mind in a matter of seconds. Maybe humans couldn't change, but nature could. Nature lived to change.

Lately, he hadn't minded the pedantic tasks as much. The repetition of bringing the *Della Ray* out to sea, docking it safely, and preparing it for the next run. Beneath his feet, the deck was warm, the vessel bobbing gently in the water, catching wakes from other boats taking tourists out to whale watch or on pleasure excursions. Salt flavored the air. Gulls floated on the breeze overhead.

In some other life, maybe, he would wrap his hands around the wheel of his own boat and greet nature on his own terms. Introduce himself as the one in charge, instead of the one who took orders and went home without the weight of responsibility. Growing up, occupying the wheelhouse had been the dream. A given. He'd learned to block it out, though. He'd blocked it so thoroughly, light couldn't even seep in around the edges.

A trill of notes in Fox's pocket had him swiping a forearm across his sweaty forehead and slipping out his cell.

Carmen.

He squinted an eye down at the name, trying to remember the face that belonged to it. No luck. Maybe the stewardess? If he answered the phone, her voice would probably jog a memory. Or he could ask for a reminder of her social media handle and figure it out that way. Most of the girls he met up with in Seattle didn't get bent out of shape over his blurry memory, anyway. They were just as interested in low commitment as Fox.

Staring down at the phone, he let it go to voicemail without answering, knowing damn well the box was full. He hadn't listened to the messages in months.

A minute after the phone stopped ringing, a text popped up on the screen.

Are you around tonight? —C

A vein started to throb in the middle of his forehead. Probably from the sun.

He tossed aside his phone, scrubbing at the itch on the back of his neck. He'd answer the message later. Or he wouldn't. There was something about the steady stream of hook-up calls that almost . . . panicked him lately. Had there always been so many?

Fox made no excuses for liking sex. The buildup and release of it. That race at the end when he didn't have to think, his body just doing the job.

Fox's phone dinged with another text message—not totally unusual for a Sunday, since his weekends were usually reserved for women, although his phone saw the most traffic on Friday nights. Lately he'd been going so far as to throw the goddamn thing into the refrigerator so he wouldn't have to hear or see any of the incoming messages. When was the last time he even answered one of them? Or left Westport to hook up?

You know exactly how long it has been.

After Hannah left last summer, he'd gone to Seattle. Once. Determined to rip out the twinge she'd left in his chest, the constant barrage of images of their days together.

He'd brought someone out for a drink, literally sweating over how shitty he'd felt the whole time, unable to focus on a single word she'd said or their surroundings. When the tab arrived, he'd dropped a fistful of cash on the bar, made an excuse, and bounced, the roiling in his stomach only settling when he'd pulled over to text Hannah.

Sanders cracked a can of Coke open to Fox's right.

"You going to answer those booty calls, man?" The deckhand took a gulping pull of his drink, balancing it on the edge of the boat. "How am I supposed to live vicariously through you if you're not even living?"

"Oh, I'm going to call them back." Fox flashed a smile that made the throb in his head worsen. "Maybe all of them at once."

Sanders's guffaw ran circles around the harbor.

On cue, Fox's phone started ringing again.

He yanked once, twice at the leather cuff around his wrist.

"Answer," Sanders said casually, tipping his head at the device. "We're almost done here."

In a high-pressure job full of ball-breaking adrenaline seekers, showing weakness was a bad idea, unless he wanted even more mockery. "You just want to listen in and steal my moves."

"You don't need moves, pretty boy. You just show up and take your pick. Me? I've got a face like a fucking walrus. I need moves." Sanders drained the rest of his soda in disgust. "I suffered through that live-action *Cats* movie last night trying to score points with the wife. One fart—one—and I lost all my progress."

Fox bit back a smile. "No luck, huh?"

"Had to sleep on the couch," grumbled the deckhand.

"Don't take it so hard, man." Fox shivered, despite the heat. "That movie could dry up the Pacific."

"I don't know, there's just something about Judi Dench . . ." Sanders mused.

Fox's phone beeped with another text, and he seriously considered throwing the damn thing in the ocean. He didn't even bother checking the name this time. He wouldn't be able to remember her face and that only made the taste in his mouth worse.

"What are you doing here? Playing hard to get?" Sanders chuckled, prodding Fox in the gut with an elbow. "That would be a first."

"Yeah." Fox laughed, his gaze straying back to where the movie was filming, finding Hannah in the group, surprised to find her looking back at him over her shoulder, her lip caught between her teeth. Thoughtful.

He saluted her.

She sent him back a half smile.

"Yeah . . ." Sanders was still going. "You've never been one to play hard to get. Remember senior year? Almost didn't graduate because you spent so much time getting busy in the parking lot."

Fox tore his eyes quickly off Hannah, feeling guilty for even looking at her while having this discussion. "Hey." He shrugged. "I still think it should have earned me extra credit toward my physical education grade."

Sanders laughed and went back to work.

So did Fox, but his movements weren't as fluid, cranks turning on either side of his forehead. Eventually he found himself braced on the edge of the boat, seeking out Hannah once again, watching as she talked to a sharp brunette. He could tell by Hannah's body language that something was off. Wrong.

Was that the soundtrack lady?

Had the songs come back for Hannah?

He could have asked her about it this morning instead of trying to divert her focus from his insecurities to something he was not insecure over in the slightest—sex. Too late for regrets now. Too late to worry about how his best friend would react if he knew Fox had talked to Piper's little sister about jacking off while he was wearing nothing but briefs and a smile.

Brendan was still clearly worried that Fox would make a move on Hannah. Despite the Talk. Despite common decency and the fact that touching her would almost definitely be unforgivable. But no one expected good behavior out of him. Not Brendan, not the people in town, the crew, anyone. Sanders had just neatly reminded Fox of that. Reminded him of it so well, he felt like a shower was in order.

No one trusted him. So the hell with it. Why try in the first place? A leopard couldn't change its spots.

A few minutes later when a visibly frustrated Hannah started speed walking to his apartment, Fox knew more than enough about women to recognize her problem. The flushed skin, the way she kept sneaking him covert looks. Lifting the hair off her neck to fan herself. She was turned on, frustrated. Horny. And that was one issue he damn well knew how to fix. What was the point of resisting?

Last night with the men outside Blow the Man Down, this morning with Sanders—hell, every day of his life—proved he couldn't outrun the notions about him. Giving in to his attraction to Hannah would serve him twofold. He could scratch this goddamn seven-month itch and cut off her bid to discover what really made him tick. One hookup with Hannah would bring everything back to surface level, where he was comfortable.

Hannah might still want the director. But hey, Fox's college girlfriend had used him as a hall pass—without his knowledge—for the better part of a year. No reason Hannah couldn't use him for the same purpose, right? Just a meaning-less good time.

Despite the fact that he was breathing through the hole of a straw, Fox didn't even bother putting on his shirt before he followed Hannah to his apartment.

Chapter Ten

There was no formal plan in regard to how she would be observing Brinley. That meant it was up to Hannah to create her own opportunities, in between wrangling actors, instructing the extras, and making sure lunch deliveries were going to arrive exactly right. Pickles on this one, no pickles on the other. Why was it always pickles? It was right there in the name—they can be picked off.

Christian was extra grouchy this morning thanks to his boyfriend's visit to Westport getting delayed, and the mood appeared to be contagious. It was clear from the dark circles under everyone's eyes that most of the crew had overindulged on Saturday night, and of course, a seagull shat on Maxine's head, delaying production by an hour while it was cleaned out, the actress restyled.

Hannah decided to use the lost hour to her advantage.

The moment there was a lull in her responsibilities, Hannah approached the music coordinator where she sat in a chair beside Sergei's vacant one.

"Morning, Brinley," she said, smiling.

A cool once-over. "Oh, hey." She scanned the notes in her lap. "Hannah, right?"

"Yes."

For no other reason than the boat was visible right over Brinley's shoulder, Hannah's gaze strayed to the *Della Ray*, where it sat docked in the harbor. It was not the first time she'd looked since arriving on set. In fact, everyone and their mother was staring at Fox and his godlike body glistening in the sunshine. His physique was the only thing saving the cranky cast and crew from turning to cannibalism this fine Sunday morning. Moreover, he didn't seem aware of the distraction he created, just casually sucking up everyone's already limited concentration.

Even Brinley lowered her sunglasses and threw a glance or two toward the boat before refocusing on Hannah . . . who was definitely not thinking about the fact that she'd been in the same apartment while Fox cleared his pipes.

First time I've had a chance since our last fishing trip.

Had to blow off some steam.

What did that mean exactly? Obviously that he was . . . jonesing for release. Was it a hardship for Fox to last four or five days without pleasure? Did he, like, light candles, get completely naked, and stroke himself really slowly, adding more oil as he went along? Biting his lip? Teasing himself? Just making a meal out of the whole affair?

Now, that was a disruptive piece of imagery.

Hannah could go months before it dawned on her that, hey! She had a vagina with a whole bunch of complicated nerve endings and she really ought to explore it more often.

Well, she could really go for exploring it right about now.

She'd worn a loose tunic dress and cardigan, though the latter had been discarded thanks to the heat. Sensibly dressed, yet at the moment, she felt almost naked. Fire tickled the back of her neck, her nipples chafing uncomfortably in her bra. Her thoughts refused to stay organized.

And her roommate parading around in all his tattooed seducer-of-women glory wasn't helping. That orange bottle of massage oil was calling her name. At this point, she might rip off the cap with her teeth to get it open.

But first. Work.

This chance with Brinley was months, if not years, in the making, and Hannah couldn't just blow an opportunity this huge because her body was misbehaving—and it was. *So* misbehaving. She wasn't supposed to lust after her friend. The only thing keeping Hannah from all-out guilt was the strange intuition that he'd done this to her on purpose.

Realizing she'd allowed the silence to stretch too long, Hannah cleared her throat and determinedly tore her attention off the muscle-strapped fisherman. "Um . . ." She angled her body toward the set where Christian and Maxine would have their big kiss, the water stretching out behind them, a couple of anchored vessels outlined in the horizon. "I was wondering if you could share your plans for the scene?"

"Sure," Brinley said without looking up. "I'm not straying from the original vision. I know the setting has changed drastically from LA to Westport. But I think the industrial sound is even edgier, given the small-town vibe. It's an interesting contrast."

"Oh. Yeah." Hannah nodded enthusiastically.

Did she agree, though? Contrast *was* interesting. There was definitely something to be said for bringing a modern spin to period dramas with the music. Putting hip-hop to ballet. Playing opera during a murder scene. An oddity like that could make a moment stand out. Could ramp up the drama. Familiar music could help an audience relate to something unfamiliar. And in this case, Sergei's art house viewership would appreciate a kiss set to industrial, because God forbid it was *too* romantic.

What music would she use in this scene, instead?

Her mind drew a big old blank.

As if sensing a moment of weakness, Brinley turned to her with an expectant smile. "What do you think?"

Mentally, Hannah browsed her album collection back home in Bel-Air, but she couldn't see a single cover, couldn't read any of the names. What was wrong with her? "Well . . ." she started, searching her mind for something useful to say. Anything that would make her worthy of this chance. "I've been reading about this technique. Giving the actors small earpieces and playing the music while rolling so they can emote at the appropriate times. Essentially act in tandem with the music—"

"Do you really think Christian would go for that?" Brinley cut in, going back to sorting through her notes. "He complains when we mic him. He stopped a take this morning because the tag in his T-shirt was too itchy."

"I could talk to him—"

"Thanks, but I think we'll leave that idea for another day."

After a moment, Hannah nodded, pretending to be absorbed by her clipboard so no one would see her red face. Why would she suggest a new technique with her first breath? Before they'd even built a rapport? She should have just agreed with

Brinley's choice and waited for a better chance to give input. Once she'd proven herself as helpful. Instead, she'd established herself as an upstart who thought she knew better than the veteran.

Sergei trundled down from one of the trailers, smiling broadly at Hannah. "Hey there." Reaching their twosome, he put a brief hand on Hannah's shoulder, squeezing, before letting it drop away. And whoa. What? He'd definitely never done anything like that before. Not unless she was bleeding from a head wound. Actually, if she wasn't mistaken, he was giving her sidelong glances while conferring with Brinley about the scene structure.

Hannah really should have been listening. Observing. As she'd asked to do.

But that was a difficult feat when something very important was occurring to her. The director's hand on her shoulder had elicited not a single tingle. There was far less gravitational pull in Sergei's direction than there had been on Friday. Normally, standing this close to him would have made her pulse tick along a little faster. At the very least she would be hoping she didn't have coffee breath.

Right now, all she wanted to do was be alone.

With that stupid orange bottle. Why couldn't she stop thinking about it?

Against her will, Hannah's attention strayed to the *Della Ray* where Fox was lifting a metal trap with very little effort, his trapezius muscles flexing, along with a lot of other ones she couldn't name. Once it had been secured, he scrubbed a forearm over his dark-blond hair, leaving it haphazard and sweaty. Suddenly it was becoming difficult to swallow. Very difficult.

She hated herself a little bit in that moment. Was she this easy to distract? The man standing not a foot away was a visionary director. A genius. He treated her with respect, and he was exceptionally good-looking, in a tortured artist kind of way. Sergei was her type. She'd never been one to get distracted by the hot guy passing through. Ever.

Yet she'd never been more turned on in her life, and it had everything to do with the man who was lending her his guest room. She just needed to handle it. Purge the desire. She hadn't *appreciated* herself in a really long time, and she'd been over-stimulated this morning. Once she got control of her hormones, appeased them, she could focus on this potential new facet of her job. Maybe even decide if she truly wanted to make it a career. She could also go back to having an appropriate interest in Sergei. This long-standing crush who was finally starting to show interest in her.

Yes. That was the plan.

"Lunch is here," one of the interns called from the other side of the trailers.

Thank God.

"I think I'll grab mine to go," Hannah murmured to no one, turning to leave. Stealthily. Looking right and left, whistling under her breath. *No one is going to know you're on a masturbation break. Relax.*

Hannah made it a few steps before Sergei caught up with her. "Hey. Hannah."

Oh no. Her body was already doing that hot-anticipation thing it did when she decided the mood was right. Wheels were in motion. Could Sergei tell just by looking at her? That she had plans that included gingery massage oil?

"Yes?" she croaked.

He traced the path of his goatee where it ran around his mouth, frankly looking kind of . . . shy? "Where are you running off to?"

Oh, nowhere. Just have a quick errand to run in Orgasm Village.

"I left something . . . at the apartment." She pointed to her face. "Sunscreen. I'm going to end up looking like Rudolph without it."

"Oh. No, you could never."

Why wasn't she exploding over that compliment?

A few weeks ago, at the mere suggestion from Sergei that he found her attractive, she would have found a private place to blast "For Once in My Life" by Stevie Wonder and dance (terribly) in place. Now all she could do was search for an excuse to get away. This was when she needed to reach out and brush her fingers against his arm. Locate his bicep and test for firmness, like an avocado at the farmer's market. Or remind him of their physical differences, as Fox had suggested. *You man, me woman. Science says we should do it!* But she didn't have the slightest desire to flirt or try to snag his interest.

What is happening to me?

"I could walk with you," he suggested.

Again, nothing. Not a spark of joy to be had.

No, she *did* like Sergei. The sparks would return. She just needed to eradicate this . . . temporary physical spell she was under. "No, that's okay." She waved him off. "Go eat your sprouts and hummus on wheat. I'll be back before you know it."

He nodded, looking disappointed, and she didn't even have the room to feel bad. There was only the selfish hunger that raked invisible hands down the front of her body, teasing erogenous zones wherever they touched.

Orange bottle. Orange bottle.

Hannah already had the key out by the time she got to Fox's building, and she slid it into the lock now, entering the dark, empty apartment and closing the door behind her. She was panting. Panting. It was ridiculous! But she beelined for the bathroom anyway, snatching the almighty bottle off the bathroom shelf and carrying it to the guest room like a running back protecting a football.

"Oh my God," she muttered, closing the bedroom door and leaning her forehead up against it. "Calm down."

Easier said than done, though.

Her hands were almost too unsteady to remove the bottle cap. Especially when she thought of the way Fox uncapped beer with his teeth. Why was that so stupidly hot? His dentist must be appalled.

Finally, Hannah got the top off the bottle, and the aroma filled the air, sensual and rich and heavy with sex. No wonder she'd been so determined to figure out the source. She wedged the container between her knees and stripped the dress off over her head, letting it drift to the ground—

The apartment door opened and closed.

What the . . . ? she mouthed.

"Hannah," came Fox's voice from the other side of the bedroom door. Like the immediate other side. It sounded like he was speaking right against the wood. *Don't think of wood.* "Are you okay in there? Looked like something was wrong."

"I'm fine," she lied—not very successfully, since her voice sounded like it had been sanded raw. "I just needed a minute."

Too much silence passed.

Then: "I can smell the oil, Hannah."

Fire blazed up her neck and cheeks. "Oh my God," she said, dropping her forehead to the door again. "This is so embarrassing."

"Stop that, Hannah." His voice had fallen another octave. "I wasn't embarrassed this morning when I admitted to doing the same thing."

"You didn't do it during business hours."

His low laugh made the tiny hairs on the nape of her neck stand up. "If you're done berating yourself for having natural impulses, you can open the door."

"What?" she breathed, staring at the barrier in shock. "Why?"

A slow exhale. "Hannah."

That was all he said.

What did he mean by that?

Hannah.

Narrowing her eyes, she tried to read between the lines, and meanwhile, none of the heat tickling her belly had dissipated. In fact, God help her, standing in her bra and thong with Fox right on the other side of the door was exciting her more.

And it shouldn't be.

For a lot of reasons.

One, he was unavailable. *I'm not in the relationship race and I never will be.* After he'd made that statement, he'd backed it up by trying to help her win another man. Never mind that she'd kissed him at that party because she couldn't seem to help it. She'd wanted to. Nothing to do with Sergei at all. But he'd made it clear he'd just been helping her out.

Right?

Another reason she shouldn't be considering throwing open the guest-room door? They were friends. She liked him. A lot. If she let him in and something happened, things would get awkward. Fox would probably regret hooking up with a houseguest immediately, because there would be no easy exit.

That brought her to the third reason she absolutely should not open the door.

The gut feeling that Fox had intentionally tried to put her off-balance this morning with his innate sexuality. That he'd wielded it like a weapon for some purpose she wasn't fully grasping.

So there she was, armed with her three reasons and gingery lube, when the knob of the bedroom turned, an inch of space appearing between the door and the jamb. And then another. Another. Until she was stepping back to allow it to swing open completely, her tummy muscles seizing at the sight of Fox outlined in the entrance to her room. Shirtless, filthy, rugged, and sweaty.

Uh-oh.

His gaze traveled down to the black triangle of her thong, a muscle popping in his jaw. "Don't move."

Frozen in place, she watched through the doorway as Fox crossed to the kitchen sink and washed his hands, drying them on a rag and tossing it away. And then he was prowling back in her direction through the unlit apartment, entering the room once more, and closing the door behind him. "Get over here, Hannah."

The rasped order almost made her moan. Did Fox washing his hands mean what she thought it did? That he was planning on . . . touching her? It was such a practical action. Like he was getting down to business. "I don't think that's a good idea."

"It's a great idea if you need to come." She took a step forward, and he caught her wrist, pulling her close, closer, until they were about to collide, then he moved at the last second and let her come up softly against the door, facing away from him. His fingers sunk into Hannah's hair, angling her head to the left, his breath fanning her neck, her vision doubling when he settled his hands on her waist and squeezed, his palms scraping slowly to the center of her belly, waking up a bunch of Jane Doe hormones, never before encountered and therefore never named. "Goddamn, Hannah. You are such a sexy little thing."

"Fox . . ."

"Uh-huh. Let's talk this out for a second," he said thickly against her neck, just grazing her skin with his teeth, his knuckles scrubbing side to side over her belly button. "You left the set like it was on fire to come over here and touch yourself."

She made an unintelligible noise that might have passed for a yes. Were they really discussing this out loud? Was this actually happening?

"I know it wasn't the director that made you need this." Ever so slightly, his fingertips brushed the waistband of her panties, the tip of his middle digit sneaking under, teasing right and left. "Maybe you'll go to him for stimulating conversation, but I'm where you come for the down and dirty."

What?

With an effort, Hannah tried to make sense of that. Not just the words coming out of his mouth, but the rebellion they provoked inside her. *Think.* Not so easy when slowly, so slowly, he crowded her closer to the door, and there . . . his erection met her bottom, his hips rolling as if he was doling out a treat. "Do you want my fingers between your legs?"

Yes.

Honestly, she almost screamed it.

There was something wrong with this picture, though. If her libido would stop wailing like a baby for a second, she'd be able to piece it together. "Fox . . ."

"This is what I do, Hannah. Let me do it." His tongue journeyed up the side of her neck with such blatant, animal sexuality, her eyes crossed. "It can just be a secret between friends in the dark."

Friends.

That word got through to her.

And then: *This is what I do.* A brag . . . but not. Because there was an edge just under the surface of his tone that didn't belong in a scenario like this. All day long, there had been a nettle under her skin regarding his behavior that morning, and now she understood what was happening. The why was still a mystery, but at least she had a starting point. "Fox, no."

His hands stilled immediately, lifted, and laid flat on the door. "No?"

It was painfully obvious he'd never heard that word before. Not from a woman. Hannah couldn't blame a single one of them, either. There was something about the way he spoke so frankly, touched with an aim toward arousing, moved so fluidly, that made inhibitions and insecurities seem irrelevant. They were only two people scratching an itch, and there was nothing wrong with that, right? He was a walking invitation to let loose.

But she wasn't falling for it.

Hannah didn't have a game plan. Couldn't formulate one when her brain and her vagina were at total odds. So she spoke honestly, without second-guessing herself.

"Okay . . ." She licked her lips, whispering into the dark. "Fine. You made me this way. You made me need to . . . do this. Talking about blowing off steam and . . . and the shirtlessness. Is that what you want to hear?"

"Yes," he growled beside her ear. "Let me finish you."

"No."

His hands curled into fists on the door, a humorless laugh pushing the hair at her temple around. "What are you worried about, Hannah? Making things weird between us? It won't. You know what is weird? The fact that I haven't fucked you. It's as easy as breathing for me."

"No, it's not."

As soon as she said it, the belief turned solid as concrete.

That was the edge she heard in his voice. That was why he'd seemed to almost be performing this morning. Acting. Overcompensating.

A pause ensued. "What?"

"It's not easy for you. Is it?" She turned between Fox and the door, looking up into his guarded expression, a heavy object tumbling end over end in her stomach. "Sex is what you do? Maybe. But it's not all you do. Stop trying to push that garbage on me. You did it this morning and you're doing it now."

His straight line of white teeth flashed in the darkness as he puffed a laugh. "Jesus, Hannah. Here we go with the psychology bullshit."

"Call it whatever you want."

All at once, his demeanor turned casually seductive. He dropped his mouth down, leaving it a millimeter away from hers. "You know," he rasped, his lips ghosting over hers. "I could talk you into it."

"You're welcome to try."

Okay, she really shouldn't have said that.

His ensuing smirk spelled disaster.

"Drop the oil, wet girl," he said. "We both know you don't need it."

God, that was such a cocky—and annoyingly true—statement. The line should have irked her. Not pushed her back toward that pinnacle of need, right where she'd been before she'd glimpsed the potential demons inside this man.

Her breath accelerated, heat licking at her buzzing nerve endings. She'd already admitted to Fox that he'd been the one to turn her on. But she needed to check the boxes of her own desire here. It couldn't be him that did it for her.

There was no denying that she wanted to share something with him, however. She'd called him out on using sex as a weapon, called his bluff on intimacy being so easy for him. His wall had come down briefly, unnerving him, and now Hannah wanted to be vulnerable in front of him. To give Fox a piece of herself in return.

An apology, maybe. Or an invitation to watch her be defenseless, as she'd seen him a few moments ago.

Exposure for exposure.

Hannah dropped the oil.

And he chuckled knowingly.

The sound cut off quickly when she slipped her fingers down the front of her panties, slowly parting her wet folds with her middle finger. Fox's innate sexuality allowed Hannah to keep eye contact while doing something so intimate. Something so out of character. Touching herself in front of a man, being the star of the show. She was stepping way outside her comfort zone to try to let him in.

The pad of her finger rode over her clit, nearly buckling her knees.

She made a sound, half moan, half stuttered breath.

"Hannah," he hissed between gritted teeth, those hands planted high above her head on the door, flexing thick laborer's muscles. Oh Lord. Having this man standing so close, exuding bucketloads of masculinity, smelling of sweat and massage oil, was going to end this pretty fast. "Let me take over."

All she could do was shake her head, a tightening sensation already beginning to occur deep in her core, some unreached place that she must only be tapping now. She would have remembered feeling this way before. This out of control and focused at the same time. Stroking herself to climax in front of this man was the ultimate rush, and yet, there was so much more happening. Communication passing between them that was way more important than physical relief.

Fox, obviously not giving up on throwing her off course, ran his nose up the slope of her neck, humming in her ear. "I was trying to keep this innocent, but maybe you're holding out for a better offer from me?" His breath filled her ear. "You want me to spread you out on the bed and use my tongue on that pussy, Hannah? Say the word and I'll do the rest. All you have to do is slide your fingers into my hair and hold on."

With that, Hannah lost the ability to breathe, her fingers moving faster on the sensitive pearl of flesh. It swelled along with the pressure inside her, and Fox's body heat, his scent, the way he watched her with salacious intention, his own breath turning shallow, made every inch of her more sensitive. Her hair follicles seemed to reach out to him, receiving an electrical charge in response, and she trembled, thighs squeezing tight around her hand. "You're enough when you're not touching me," she whispered, not even sure she said it out loud until Fox's expression went from lusting to dumbstruck, his chest starting to heave. "You're enough on your own."

She watched his face, watched the confusion give way to hunger and swing back again. "Hannah," he said raggedly, dropping his hands to rake them up and down her hips, twisting his fingers in the sides of her panties. "All right, I give in." The growl he let loose into her neck shook Hannah down to her toes. "You want to fuck, babe? Hop up here and let's get it done."

It was like he couldn't fathom a woman wanting nothing but his presence.

As if her turning him down only meant she wanted a different act.

A different favor from him.

Hannah didn't think there was a single thing under the sun that could turn her from hot to cold in that moment, but that glimpse past his exterior did it. The vulnerability shining through despite Fox's best efforts was like a desk fan blowing across her sweaty skin, turning it clammy. Something akin to indignation scaled the walls of her chest. Something was wrong here. Something was inside of Fox that shouldn't be, and she wanted to put a name to it.

Attempting to slow her breathing, Hannah removed her fingers from her underwear, letting them fall to her side. "Fox . . ."

He stepped back like he'd been shocked, nostrils flaring.

Opened his mouth to say something and snapped it shut again.

They stared at each other for long seconds. And then he reached for the doorknob, moving her gently but firmly out of the way so he could stride out, not stopping until he'd left the apartment.

Hannah stared at nothing, the opening riff of "Dazed and Confused" by Zeppelin playing in her head. What the heck just happened?

It wasn't totally clear, but suddenly she didn't feel so good about calling him Peacock—and in that moment, Hannah vowed she never would again.

Chapter Eleven

Fox would just pretend like it never happened.

That's all there was to it.

What had actually happened, anyway? Nothing.

Apart from seeing Hannah in a bra and panties, which was an image that would be burned into his brain for all eternity, he'd put his mouth on her neck, run his hands over her smooth skin. Dirty talked her a little bit. So what? Even though he'd almost slipped, no boundaries had been crossed.

There was nothing to be tense about.

No reason for this fissure in his gut.

Fox scrubbed a hand up and down the back of his neck forcefully, trying to rid himself of the tightness. He stood in the kitchen surrounded by ingredients for potato leek soup, vegetables finely chopped on the counter with no cutting board. He'd made a mess, and he could barely remember doing it. Or walking to the store to buy everything he needed. All he knew was that Hannah would be back from set any minute now, and he felt like he owed her an apology. She'd needed something from him, and he'd failed to give it.

He'd turned her off.

Not on. *Off.*

Hannah must like the director more than he thought. Otherwise she would have let Fox blow her mind, right? That had to be the reason she'd stopped before it was over. Couldn't be anything else. Couldn't be that Fox had exposed himself by accident, and she didn't like what she'd seen.

Could it?

He stirred a dash of thyme into the soup, watching cream swallow the green flecks, very aware of the pulse beating thickly in his throat. It wasn't as though rejection was a totally foreign concept to him. But after college, he'd kept himself out of situations where being denied was a possibility. He did his job well, went home. When he hooked up, the terms were already outlined with the woman ahead of time, no gray areas. No confusion about anyone's intentions. No chances were taken. No new horizons were embarked upon.

This thing with Hannah was nothing if not a new horizon.

It was friendship . . . and maybe that was another reason why he'd fucking pushed it earlier today. Because he didn't know how to be a friend. The possibility of failing at it, disappointing her, was daunting. Now, distracting her with sex? That was so much easier.

The sound of a key turning in the lock made Fox's insides seize up, but he stirred the soup casually, looking up with a quick smile when Hannah walked in. "Hey, Freckles. Hope you're hungry."

She visibly took his measure, hesitating before turning to close the door—and Fox couldn't help but take advantage of those few seconds she wasn't looking at him, absorbing as much as he could. The messy bun at the nape of her neck, strands of sandy-blond hair poking out on all sides. Classic Hannah. Her profile, especially her stubborn nose. The practical way she moved, pressing the door shut and locking it, her shoulder blades shifting beneath her T-shirt.

Jesus, she'd looked so hot in her underwear.

In street clothes, she was someone's little sister. The girl next door.

In a black bra-and-panties set, holding massage oil, eyes laden with lust, she was a certified sex kitten.

And she might have purred for him temporarily, but she wanted to get her claws into someone else. He needed to get on board with that. For real this time. Deep down, he'd believed that if he just put in a little effort, of a physical nature, she would fall at his feet and forget all about the director. Hadn't he? Well, he'd been mistaken. Hannah wasn't the type to genuinely like one man while hooking up with another, and it had been wrong, sickeningly wrong, to put her in that position.

Fox zipped his attention back to the stove when Hannah faced the kitchen once again. "That smells amazing." She stopped at the island behind him, and Fox could sense her working up to something. He should have known she couldn't just pretend this afternoon didn't happen. That wasn't her style. "About what happened today . . ."

"Hannah." He laughed, adding a forceful shake of pepper to the pot. "Nothing happened. It's not worth talking about."

"Okay." Without turning around, he knew she was chewing on her lip, trying to talk herself into dropping the subject. He also knew she wouldn't succeed. "I just wanted to say . . . I'm sorry. I should have stopped sooner. I—"

"No. I should have let you have your privacy." He tried to clear the pinch in his throat. "I assumed you would want me there, and I shouldn't have."

"It wasn't that I didn't want you there, Fox."

Christ. Now she was going to try to make him feel better over the rejection? He would rather turn the hot pot of soup upside down over his head than listen to her explain she was being true to her feelings for the director. "You know, it's totally possible to just eat this soup and talk about something else. I promise your urge to hash out every detail of what happened will pass."

"That's called suppression. It's very unhealthy."

"We'll survive just this once."

She moseyed around the far side of the island, dragging her finger along the surface. Then she reversed her course, filling one cheek with air and letting it seep out.

Man, it was wild that he could be frustrated with her inability to drop a sensitive subject while being grateful for it at the same time. He'd never met anyone in his life that gave a shit as hard as Hannah. For other people. She thought that compassion made her a supporting actress instead of a leading one, and didn't realize that her empathy, the fierce way she cared, made her something bigger. Hannah belonged in a category far more real than the credits of a movie. A category all her own.

And he wanted to give in to her. To rehash what happened in the bedroom earlier, his reaction to being made . . . useless. At least in that moment, he wanted to give in and let her sort through his shit, no matter how much this discussion scared him. Because every day that passed, she came a little closer to going back to LA, and Fox didn't know when he'd have her near him again. Maybe never. Not in his apartment. Not alone. This opportunity would be gone soon.

He used a ladle to fill two bowls with the thick soup, added spoons and slid one across the counter to Hannah. "Can we just work up to it a little?" he said gruffly, unable to look at her right away.

When he did, she was nodding slowly. "Of course." She visibly shook herself, picked up the spoon, and blew on a bite, inserting it between her lips in a way he couldn't help but watch hungrily, his abdomen knitting together and flexing beneath the island. "Should I distract us by telling you I had a terrible day? Not because of"—she jerked her head in the direction of the guest room—"not just because of that."

His vanity was in fucking shreds. "Okay. What else was terrible about it?"

"Well, we didn't get the shot we needed, because Christian wouldn't come out of his trailer after lunch. Might mean adding days to the schedule, if we're not careful." Fox shouldn't have been surprised when his pulse jumped happily at the possibility of Hannah staying longer, but he was.

How intensely did he feel for this girl and in what way? Everything, every feeling or non-feeling, was usually wrapped up in sex for him. Only sex. Even if the director wasn't in the picture, was he capable of going beyond that with Hannah?

"And I tried twice to approach Brinley, but she was pretty determined to blow me off. I'm not sure I'm going to get the experience I was hoping for and . . . don't tell anyone this part."

Fox raised an eyebrow. "Who am I going to tell?"

"Right." Her voice dropped to a whisper. "I don't love the direction she's going with the score on this film."

Containing his amusement was difficult. "Your shit-talking needs work."

"I'm not talking shit. I just . . . Sergei shifted gears by changing the location to Westport, and I don't think she shifted gears with him. There is grit in her choices. An LA club-scene vibe." He kept his smile in place when she mentioned the other man, but it took an effort. "The songs don't fit, but I can't make suggestions without looking like a know-it-all."

"What about talking to"—he tried to lick the acidic taste out of his mouth, gave up, took an extra-large bite of soup—"Sergei?"

"Go over her head?" Hannah drew an *X* onto the surface of her soup with the tip of her spoon. "No, I couldn't do that."

He scrutinized her for a second. "If you were in charge, what would you do differently?"

"That's the other terrible part of my day. I don't know. The songs aren't coming to me like they usually would. I guess . . . something that captured the timeless spirit of this place. The layers and generations . . ." She trailed off, quietly repeating that last word. "Generations."

When she didn't elaborate, Fox realized he was holding his breath, waiting to see what she said next. "Generations . . . ?"

"Yeah." She shook her head. "I was just remembering the sea shanties my grandmother gave me the other day. A whole folder of them she found. They were written by my father, apparently."

"Wow." He set down his spoon. Almost said, *Why didn't you tell me?* But thought it would sound presumptuous. "That's exciting, right?" He studied her features, noticing the tension around the corners of her mouth. "You're feeling some kind of way about the whole thing, yeah?"

She made a wishy-washy sound. "It's nothing."

"Oh no. Nope." He pushed his bowl aside, crossing his arms over his chest. "You want to bury my feet in cement and force me to talk about shit that makes me uncomfortable, Freckles, you're going to do the same."

"Uh, excuse me. Where do you get off being right?"

He cracked a smile, waved her on. "I'm waiting."

Glumly, she shoveled a final bite of soup into her mouth and made a whole show of mimicking him, pushing her bowl aside and crossing her arms. "Look. This is me stalling."

Why did he have to like her so fucking much, huh? "I can see that."

"This isn't going to distract me from the actual conversation we're going to have," she warned him.

His lips twitched. "Noted."

"Well. Fine." She dropped her hands and started to pace. "It's just that . . . you know, Piper, she really connected to the soul of Henry Cross. When we were here last summer? And me . . . I was kind of pretending to."

She stopped pacing to look at him, judging his expression, which he kept impassive. On the inside, he was curious as hell. "Okay. I get pretending."

Hannah studied his face thoughtfully before continuing. "I was two years old when we left Westport. I don't remember anything about Henry Cross or this place. No matter how much I dig, I can't . . . I can't feel anything for this . . . invisible past. Nothing but guilt, anyway."

"Why are you under pressure to feel something?"

"I'm not under pressure, really. It's just that I usually would. Feel something. I can watch a song play out in my head like a movie and bond with the words and sound, connect with something written about a situation I'm not even familiar with. I'm an emotional person, you know? But this . . . It's like zip. Like I've got a mental block on anything related to my father."

It was really bothering her. He could see that. And thus, it was bothering him. Not only that this lack of connection with Henry Cross was under her skin, but . . . what if he couldn't find the right words to make it better? Comforting women wasn't exactly his forte. "Do you want to forge some kind of bond with the past? With Henry?"

"I don't know."

"Why were you drawn back here?"

"I missed my sister. I missed this place. I even missed you a little," she said playfully, but sobered again quickly. "That's all."

"Is that all? Missing people? Or are you chewing on something you can't quite name?" Fox wished he had his shirt off, so he could feel less exposed. And what sense did that make? "Same way you came in here, poking at me until I gave in and agreed to have the damn talk . . . Maybe you're just doing the same with this place. Poking around until you find the way in. But you know what? If it doesn't happen, it doesn't make you guilty of anything, Hannah."

Slowly, gratitude spread across her features, and he let out a breath. "Thanks." She stared at something invisible in the distance. "Maybe you're right."

Desperate for some way to get the attention off himself, at least while he was attempting to dole out comfort, he coughed into his fist. "Want me to take a look at them? I might recognize one or two."

"Really? You still . . . sing shanties on the boat?"

"I mean, not very often. Sometimes Deke starts one off. Not joining in kind of makes you a dick. Case in point, Brendan never sings along."

That got a laugh out of her, and some weight left his shoulders. "Okay, I'll go grab them." She seemed nervous about the whole thing, so they might as well get comfortable. While Hannah was in the guest room, he put their bowls in the sink and moved to the living room, taking a spot on the couch. A minute later, she returned with a faded blue folder stuffed with papers and sat on the floor in front of the coffee table, pausing slightly before opening it. She ran a finger over a line of script, brows drawn in concentration, then handed him a stack.

Fox scanned a few lines on the first page, didn't recognize the lyrics, but the second one was very familiar. "Ah, yeah. I know this one well. The old-timers still sing it sometimes in Blow the Man Down." His chuckle betrayed his disbelief. "I didn't know Henry Cross wrote this. You always kind of assume these songs are a million years old."

Hannah shifted into a cross-legged position on the floor. "So you know that one. Can you sing it?"

"What? Like, right now?"

She gave him puppy-dog eyes, and his jugular stretched like the skin of a drum. *Sucker.* But knowing he could help, knowing he could do something to potentially make her happy? That was like holding the keys to a kingdom. Even if he had to sing to get to the other side. The desire to give Hannah what she needed had him adjusting the paper in his lap, clearing his throat.

There was a huge possibility this wouldn't mean much to her, either, but when she looked at him like that, he had to try. "I mean, if it means that much to you . . ."

In a voice that definitely wouldn't win him any contests, Fox started to sing "A Seafarer's Bounty."

Chapter Twelve

Born unto the fog
And ferried by the tide,
To the womb of his ship
Where he earns his pride,
A seafarer's bounty
Means coin in hand and no one at his side.

The hunt has no end.
It's a game, it's the fame.
A love to defend.
A treasure to claim.
Boots to the deck, men, come on now, let's ride.

Trade the glass
For my lass.
And the wild
For my child.
Trade the wind
For her.

Trade the mayhem
For them.
And it's anchors down. There's a life beyond the tide.

Treasure is not mere
Rubies and gold.
When a seafarer finds his warmth
From the cold.
No longer are the deep blue waves his only bride.

Home is the fortune,
Health is the prize.
To lie in her arms,
To look in their eyes,
By the laws of the land, a sailor will learn to abide.

Trade the glass
For my lass.
And the wild
For my child.
Trade the wind
For her.
Trade the mayhem
For them.
And it's anchors down. There's a life beyond the tide.

Soon, loves, soon.
Soon, loves, soon.
One last ride,
At the rise of the moon.

Then it's home to my bounty.
We'll write our family's tune.

Hannah was eleven when she got her first pair of headphones.

She'd always sung along loudly to whatever played on satellite radio. Always had a knack for remembering the words, knowing exactly where the tempo picked up. But when she got those headphones, when she could be alone with the music, that's when her enjoyment of it soared.

Since they were a gift from her stepfather, of course they were completely over the top. Pink noise-canceling ones that were almost too heavy for her neck to hold up. So she'd spent hours upon hours in her room lying down, head supported by a pillow, playing the music her mother had loaded onto her phone. Billie Holiday had transported her to the smoky jazz rooms of the past. The Metallica she'd downloaded, despite lacking her mother's permission, made her want to rage and kick things. When she got a little older, Pink Floyd made her curious about instruments and method and artistic experimentation.

Music could cut her straight down the middle. Nothing else in her life had the power to do that. She often wondered if something was wrong with her that a real-life event could have less of an impact than a song written fifty years ago. But those two parallel lines—real life and art—had never collided like this. And for the second time since she'd met Fox, he was inside the experience with her. This experience she'd always, always had alone. *Wanted* to have alone. The first time had been at the record expo in Seattle when they'd shared a pair of AirPods in the middle of a busy aisle, the world ceasing to exist around them. The second time was now. In his living room.

Fox sang her father's words, filling the unadorned living room with an echo from the past that wrapped right around her throat and squeezed.

His singing voice was slightly deeper than his speaking one, low and husky, like a lover whispering to someone in the dark, and that fit him so well, the intimate quality of it. Like he was passing on a secret. It racked her with a warm shiver and circled her in a hug she desperately needed, because, oh God, it was a beautiful song. Not just any song, though . . . It was about her family.

She knew from the first refrain.

An intuition rippled in her fingertips until she had to grasp them together in her lap, and as more and more lyrics about a fisherman's growing dedication to his family passed Fox's lips, his image begun to blur. But she couldn't blink to rid herself of the moisture, could only let it pool there, as if any movement might swipe the melody from the air, rob her of the growing burn in the center of her chest.

So many times she'd tried to bridge the gap between herself and this man who'd fathered her, and never succeeded. Not when she'd gone to visit the brass statue in his honor up at the harbor, not in looking at dozens of photographs with Opal. She'd felt a tremor of nostalgia upon opening Cross and Daughters with Piper, but . . . there had been nothing like this. Hearing the song was almost like having a conversation with Henry Cross. It was the closest she would ever come. This explanation of his conflicting loves—the sea and his family.

At one point, at least while writing this song, he'd wanted to quit fishing. He'd wanted to stay home more. With them. It just didn't happen in time. Or he kept being pulled back to the ocean. Whatever the reason may be, with his confession, he finally became real.

"Hannah."

Fox's worried voice brought her head up, and she found him rising from the couch, coming toward her. He let the paper float down to rest on the table, and she watched it happen through damp eyes, her heart flapping in her throat.

"Sorry, I didn't expect that. I didn't expect . . ."

She let the sentence trail off when her voice started to crack. And then Fox was scooping her up off the floor into his arms. He seemed almost stunned that he'd done it, circling for a moment as if he didn't know what to do with her now that he had her, but he finally turned and carried her from the room. With her forehead tucked into his neck—when did it get there?—she watched as they stopped in front of the door to his bedroom, his muscles tensing around her. "Just . . . I'm not suggesting anything by bringing you in here, okay? I just thought you'd want to get away from it."

Did that make any sense? Not really. But to her, it did. And he was right. She wanted to be removed from the moment before it ate her alive, and he'd sensed it. Fox shouldered open the door and brought her into his cool, dark bedroom, sitting them on the edge of the unmade bed, Hannah curled in his lap, tears creating twin rivers down her face. "Christ," he said, ducking his head to meet her eyes. "I had no idea my singing was this bad."

A watery laugh burst out of her. "It's actually kind of perfect."

He looked skeptical, but relieved she'd laughed. "I didn't remember what the song was about until I was halfway through it. I'm sorry."

"No." She leaned her temple against his shoulder. "It's good to know I'm not made of stone, you know?"

His fingers hovered just above her face momentarily, before he used his thumbs to brush away her tears. "You're the furthest thing from that, Hannah."

Several moments ticked by while she replayed the lyrics in her head, content to be held in an embrace that was unrushed and sturdy. "I think maybe . . . up until I heard the song, there was part of me that didn't really believe Henry could be my dad. Like it was all some mistake and I've been going along with it."

"And now?"

"Now I feel like . . . he's found a way to reassure me." She turned her face into his chest and sighed. "You helped with that."

His forearm muscles twitched beneath her knees. "I . . . No."

"Yeah," she insisted softly. "Opal thought Henry might be where I got my love for music. It's weird to think it came from somewhere. Like a little boop of DNA makes my spine tingle during the opening notes of 'Smoke on the Water.'"

Fox's chest rumbled. "It's 'Thunderstruck' for me. AC/DC." A beat passed. "All right, I'm lying. It's 'Here Comes the Sun.'"

His warm T-shirt absorbed her laugh. "There's no way to hear it without smiling."

"There really isn't." He stroked his fingertips down her right arm, then seemed to pull back, as if he'd done it without thinking and realized it was too much. "I always wonder why you don't play an instrument."

"Oh, do I have a story for you." Her arm still tingled from where he'd touched it. They were sitting in the dark, speaking in hushed tones on his bed. She was in his lap and wrapped in his arms, and there was nothing uncomfortable about it. None of the awkwardness that would normally come from blubbering in front of someone who wasn't Piper. Although Hannah couldn't deny there was an underlying tension in Fox. Like electricity that he didn't know how to turn off but was clearly trying to. "I went through such an obnoxious hipster phase when I was thirteen. Like I thought I was truly discovering all these classic songs for the first time and no one understood or appreciated them like me. I was terrible. And I wanted to be different, so I asked for harmonica lessons." She tilted her head back, found his eyes in the dark. "Word to the wise, don't ever learn the harmonica while you have braces."

"Hannah. Oh God. No." His head fell back briefly, a laugh puffing out of him. "What happened?"

"Our parents were in the Mediterranean, so we walked to our neighbor's house and they were in France—"

"Ah, yes. Typical neighborhood problems."

She snorted. "So their landscaper offered to drive me and Piper—who had actually peed her pants laughing—in the back of his truck." She could barely keep her voice even, the need to giggle was so great. "We were driven to the closest hospital in the back of a pickup truck while the harmonica was stuck to my face. Every time I exhaled, the harmonica would play a few notes. People were honking . . ."

His whole body was shaking with laughter, and Hannah could tell he'd finally, fully relaxed. The sexual tension didn't leave completely, but he'd shelved it for now. "What did they say at the hospital?"

"They asked if I was taking requests."

He was laughing before, but now he fell backward, the sound booming and unrestrained. Hannah yelped as the mattress dipped, causing her to roll without warning on top of him. She ended up sprawled with her hip against his stomach, her upper half twisted so their chests were pressed together.

Fox's laughter died when he realized their position.

Their mouths were only an inch apart—and Hannah wanted to kiss him. Terribly. His darkening eyes said he wanted the same. If she was being honest, she wanted to straddle his hips and do a lot more than kiss. But she listened to her instincts, the same ones she'd heeded that afternoon, and held back, scooting away so they were no longer touching and her head was resting on his pillow. Fox watched her from under his hooded eyelids, his chest rising and falling, then carefully arranged himself across from her, his head on the other pillow. As if following her lead.

They stayed like that for a while, several minutes passing without either of them saying a word. Almost as if they were getting used to being in a bed together. Being this up close and personal without the weight of expectations. It was enough to simply lie there with him, and Hannah needed him to know that. She couldn't shake the feeling that it was important for him to know that nothing needed to happen between them for this time together to be worthwhile.

"All right . . ." he started, watching her steadily. "I guess we've worked up to it."

Hannah didn't move. Didn't even swallow.

Fox shifted on the bed, held out the wrist on which he wore a leather bracelet. "This belonged to my father. He worked down the coast a ways. A fisherman, too. He married my mother after she got pregnant with me, but the marriage didn't last beyond a few pretty miserable years." He twisted his wrist, making the leather turn a little. "I wear this to remind myself I'm exactly like him and that will never change."

The way he said it dared her to recoil. Or issue a denial.

But she only held his gaze and waited patiently, her fist curled into his pillow, eyes and mouth puffy from crying. Cute and compassionate and singular. One of a kind. And she was interested in this sob story?

What the hell was this, anyway? A heart-to-heart in the dark with a girl? His headboard should be cracking off the wall right now. She should be screaming into his shoulder, drawing blood on his back. The cornered animal inside him bayed, begging him to distract. To reach over and fist her dress, drag her across the bed and roll right on top of her, make her dizzy with his tongue in her mouth.

His weapon had been taken away, though. She'd disarmed him this afternoon.

No armor. Nothing to deflect with.

And part of him seriously hated the vulnerable state in which she'd left him. The railing of his ship had disappeared, no barrier to block him from toppling into the turbulent sea. He didn't want this kind of intimacy. Didn't want sympathy or pity or understanding. He was just fine continuing to guard the wound. Pretending it wasn't there. Who the hell was she to come and rip off the bandage?

She was Hannah. That's who.

This girl who didn't want to have sex with him—and yet was still interested. Lying there in his bed wanting to know more about him. No sign of judgment. No impatience. No movements at all. And as much as he resented the intrusion into his inner hell, Jesus, he fucking adored her, wanted to give her anything she wanted. So badly that it burned.

I wear this to remind myself I'm exactly like him and that will never change.

With his words hanging in the atmosphere, he stuffed his hand under the pillow, putting the bracelet out of sight. "I never made a conscious choice to be like him, I just was. Even before I'd ever been with a girl, it was like . . . everyone treated me like being . . . experienced was inevitable. There is something in my personality, the way I look, I guess. The parents of my schoolmates were always saying, *Look out for that one. He's got the devil in his eyes.* Or, *He's the one your mama warns you about.* It didn't make sense when I was younger, but as I got older and started to recognize my father's behavior with women, I figured it out. My sixth-grade teacher used to say, *He's going to be a heartbreaker.* Everyone laughed and agreed and . . . Look, I don't remember exactly when it started, only that I eventually embraced that image once I was in high school until there was a blur. Just a fucking blur of bodies and faces and hands."

He breathed in and out through his nose, locating the courage to keep going. To completely unwrap himself in front of this girl whose opinion mattered so much to him.

"When I was a senior, my mom sent me to visit my father for a weekend. He'd been trying to reach out, sending cards and whatnot. They didn't have a formal arrangement, she just thought he deserved a shot. And . . . after a couple of days at his place, I knew. I knew I didn't want to be like him, Hannah."

Some details he kept to himself.

Already he felt like this whole seedy explanation of his lifestyle was corrupting Hannah. This sweetheart with all the fucking promise in the world and a head full of songs didn't need his past taking up space in her mind. They were on opposite ends of the bed, like two sides of the moon—one dark, one light—so he wouldn't tell her about the revolving door of women he'd witnessed coming in and out of his father's apartment that weekend. Or the sounds he'd heard. The flirting and fighting and cloying smell of pot.

Fox swallowed hard, begging the pace of his pulse to slow. "Anyway."

A full minute passed while he tried to get it together. He wasn't sure he could explain the rest until Hannah slid her hand across the bed and threaded their fingers together. He flinched, but she held on.

"Anyway," he continued, trying not to acknowledge the warmth spreading up his arm. "I always had decent grades, believe it or not. Probably have Brendan to thank for that. He was always roping me into study groups and forcing me to do flash cards with him."

"Flash cards are so Brendan," she murmured. "I bet they were color-coded."

"And alphabetized." He couldn't help pressing the pad of his thumb to her pulse, rubbing the sensitive spot once before forcing his touch back to platonic. There was no distracting her with sex—she didn't want it. As much as that disappointed him, he was starting to find there was something freeing in not having to perform physically. In not having to fulfill an expectation. "Most of my friends stayed close for college, but I got out of here. I wanted to get rid of this image. This . . . label as the local stud. I'd earned it, fine, but I didn't want it anymore. So I left. I went to Minnesota and I found new people. I was a new person. The first two years of college, I dated occasionally, but nothing like what I was doing in high school. Not even close. And then I met Melinda. We didn't go to the same school, but she lived close by and . . . I thought it was serious. I'd never been in a real relationship before, but it felt like one. We went to the movies, out of town. I stopped seeing other people. It was like, shit . . . I can do this. I don't have to fit into the mold anymore."

A sharp object slid between his ribs, preparing to skewer.

"At the same time, I had this friend, right? Kirk. He was the one who introduced me to Melinda. As his family friend. Kirk and I shared a dorm room, both of us majoring in business. Sophomore year, we decided to work together on a start-up. We had this idea for an online stock footage company that would specialize in aerial shots. From drones." He shook his head. "There are companies now that do this. Your production company has probably used one. But back then, there wasn't anything like it. And we worked on it hard. We were going to be business partners. I was, like, a million fucking miles from who and what I'd been in Westport, you know?"

Was he really going to tell her the next part and humiliate himself on purpose? It was bad enough that he had to live with the embarrassment of what happened back then, let alone watch Hannah register it. But her grip was firm on his hand, her eyes unwavering, and he just kept going, like he'd been given an invisible push, no idea where he would land but knowing he couldn't stop now.

"One holiday weekend, Melinda was home visiting her parents. I'd lied, saying I was going home, too. I didn't, though. I never went home back then. I wanted to pretend Westport didn't even exist. No one knew who I'd been, and I wanted to keep it that way." He let out a long breath. "That weekend, I came back from finishing a paper in the library, and they were in our dorm. Together. Watching a movie in Kirk's bed." He tried to pull his hand free of Hannah's, because he was starting to feel dirty over what was coming and he didn't want that filthiness touching her, but she held on, tightening her hold. "So I confronted them. Explained that Melinda and I had been seeing each other for months. Kirk was livid, but Melinda . . . she just laughed."

Hannah frowned. Her first visible reaction to the whole sordid story. For some reason, he absorbed that reaction like a sponge. Yeah, it was confusing, right? Yeah. She thought so, too. That was something. He'd have to explain in a minute, and her confusion would clear up, but for now, that frown provided him the push he needed to finish.

"Turns out, I was her hall pass." The sharpness in his sternum pulled back and lanced forward. "She reminded Kirk that I was her free pass, they'd established it on day one, so he couldn't be mad she'd cheated. I was just the side-door guy. Not a serious boyfriend." He shrugged jerkily. "I didn't know they were dating because he never brought her around me. Because of this. Because he was jealous over her finding me attractive. And spoiler, she'd definitely called his bluff on the hall pass. He was not okay with it at all. He walked away from the start-up, moved out of the dorm. Never wanted to speak to me again—and I couldn't blame him. I'd done the exact type of shit everyone expected me to do since grade school. Brought sex with me everywhere I went, intentional or not. It didn't matter how much I tried to be someone else, this manwhore label is welded onto me. Melinda knew it without any information about my past. My business partner wouldn't even bring his girlfriend around me. It's just what they saw in me."

Fox realized he was breathing fast and took a moment to slow down.

"I dropped out after that. Didn't see a point in trying to convince people to believe I'm something I'm not. I've been working on the *Della Ray* ever since."

They stayed very still, very quiet for several moments.

Panic ensued when Hannah started to scoot closer, her expression somber.

"I'm a good time. I'm easy. I'm fine with that."

"No."

"Hannah."

When she reached his side of the bed to stroke his face, he pushed their foreheads together, teased her lips with a brush of his own. Hannah couldn't disguise her reaction. Or the soft shudder that worked through her limbs and belly. Slowly, he dragged her tight to his body, locking their mouths together. It was fight-or-flight. Go on the offensive or risk further exposure, no matter that he was fighting the exact thing giving him comfort.

Distract. Distract.

"Come on, babe," he breathed against her lips, groaning at the rapid swell between his legs, his fingers gathering the hem of her dress higher, higher. "I'll make it so good for you. I want to."

"No." She wrapped her arms around his neck and hugged him, her smaller chest heaving against his larger one. "We're okay just like this." She nudged his jaw with her nose and settled closer, as if letting him know she wasn't afraid. "Just like this."

Even after what he'd just told her?

Wasn't she paying attention?

She could resist him all she wanted, hold his hand and be his friend, but nothing would change him. His identity was set in stone. What did she want from him?

This, apparently. Just this.

Wanted whatever he was, a blend of faults and ugly truths, wanted him just to lie there with her.

It took him some time to wade through the disbelief, but he finally managed to slide one arm beneath Hannah, cradling the back of her head in one hand. Carefully, he drew her into his neck, his eyes closing over the balm she spread inside him. Not quite healing his wounds, but definitely dulling the pain for a while.

Just for a while. He'd just hold her . . . for a while.

Seconds later, Fox fell asleep in Hannah's arms.

Chapter Thirteen

Hannah opened her eyes on Monday morning and absorbed the sight of Fox across the pillow they shared, morning light beginning to peek through the blinds behind him, outlining his bedhead in burnished gold. With his mouth slightly parted, beard growth shadowing his jaw and upper lip, he was startlingly gorgeous. Seriously? At six A.M., he could be shooting an advertising campaign for Emporio Armani.

After last night, however . . . she couldn't look at him without seeing past the packaging to the uncut gem beneath. Smooth and glorious on the outside. But on the inside, his light hit a jagged peak and refracted in a thousand different directions.

A dull ache spread down the middle of her chest, deepening so quickly that she had to press a palm to the spot, rubbing to alleviate the pressure. The pain he'd revealed last night had walked across the bed and burrowed into her breast, refusing to vacate—and she didn't want it to leave. She didn't want him to carry it alone. He'd clearly been doing that a long time, letting the damage fester.

What did it mean for Hannah to help him shoulder the burden of his past? Was she being a good friend—and a friend only? Or did her determination to stand with Fox come from somewhere else entirely?

Somewhere . . . romantic?

Because that wouldn't be a good idea.

That wouldn't be a good idea *at all*.

After last night, she would never consider him a player again. By selling himself short and doubling down on his irreverent image, he was playing himself more than anything. But he was still Fox Thornton, confirmed bachelor and connoisseur of women. He didn't want a relationship, period. He'd told her that.

So no matter what sticky, reckless feelings might be bubbling to the surface, the supportive buddy position was the only one available to her, wasn't it?

Hannah's thoughts scattered like the head of a dandelion when Fox's blue eyes opened, spearing her from the other side of the pillow. They were warm, a little relieved. And then he blinked and up went his guard.

"Hey," he said slowly, studying her closely. "You slept here all night."

Words crammed into her chest. Phrases she'd learned from her therapists over the years. Things she wanted to say to Fox that would explain why he felt so terrible over what happened in college. Suggestions for adjusting his outlook, and assurances that none of it was his fault.

For once, all the fancy supportive language in the world felt inadequate, though. Somehow, over the course of the night, she'd entered the fray with Fox without making a conscious decision. She was in it, this battle for his soul. Now that she was here, however, it was beginning to seem unlikely that she could remain too long without . . . falling for him.

God. She was. Falling fast.

"Yeah," she murmured finally, sitting up and brushing some static-charged strands of hair out of her face. "Sorry, I must have really passed out."

He pushed up onto an elbow. "Wasn't looking for a sorry. It's fine."

Hannah nodded. She looked over at him and . . . oh boy, there it was. An overwhelming urge to touch him. To push him down onto the mattress, climb on top, and tell him in between kisses that he was way more than a hall pass. Way more than he gave himself credit for. But that went beyond supportive friend. Those were the actions of a supportive girlfriend—and she couldn't be that for him.

"I have to be at work early," Hannah managed.

"Right." He pushed a hand through his hair, visibly at a loss. "Huh."

"What?"

His big shoulder shrugged, the laughter not quite reaching his eyes. "It feels like I'm sending you off with nothing."

The chasm that had formed down the center of her heart last night widened, and she barely managed to swallow a sound of distress. And then the anger flooded in. How dare his teachers and full-grown adults sexualize him at such a young age? How could his father bring women over while his eighteen-year-old son was visiting? Who were those *monsters* he'd befriended in college? They probably worked for the IRS now. And yes, a fair bit of rage was directed squarely at herself, because she'd definitely called him a pretty-boy sidekick the first time they'd met. Peacock after that. She wanted to bang her head against the wall now for being like everyone else.

Before Hannah could stop herself, she'd turned and walked on her knees across the bed, wrapping her arms around Fox's neck, hugging him in a manner that was freakishly tight, but she couldn't seem to make herself stop. Especially when his arms crept up and surrounded her, pulling Hannah to his chest, his face dropping into the slope of her neck.

"You sang for me last night," she said. "You brought me as close as I'll ever get to Henry. That wasn't nothing."

"Hannah . . ."

"And after what you told me last night, I could sit here for hours and rant about toxic masculinity and undervaluing yourself, but I'm not going to do that. I'm just going to tell you that . . . I'll be back tonight and that you're really important to me."

His swallow was audible. "We sail for five nights on Wednesday. Two days from now. Kind of a longer trip than usual. I just . . . If you were curious or wanted to know when I'd be gone."

"Of course I want to know." She pressed her lips together. "That means you'll come home the day we wrap on *Glory Daze*."

They looked at each other hard, neither of them seeming to know what to do with that information. Timelines, schedules, leaving, coming back. How it related to them as two people who'd just slept in the same bed.

So she kissed his coarse cheek and gave him a final squeeze, trying not to notice the way his hips shifted, his mouth breathing hard against her neck. "Just this, Hannah?" His long fingers slid up into her hair to cradle the back of her head, subtly tilting it to the left and brushing his lips along her pulse. "Just hugging for us?"

With one word of encouragement, Hannah knew she would be flat on her back and would love every second. But maybe . . . maybe her mission here wasn't to be the supportive friend, but to prove to Fox that *he* could be one. That his presence and personality were enough without any of the physical trappings. "Just like this."

Was she asking a lot of Fox to try seeing himself in a new light? Wasn't she in the process of doing that herself—and not finding it very easy? Maybe if she wanted this man to believe he could captain a ship and rely on his wit and humor and spirit alone, then she had to believe in herself first. She couldn't ask him to reach for a higher summit if she wasn't willing to reach herself.

The opening notes of "I Say a Little Prayer" by Aretha Franklin tumbled through Hannah's head, and her eyes flew open, a grateful smile curving her lips. Hallelujah. The songs were back. Sure, the lyrics were a little alarming, considering she was lying in Fox's bed, but maybe the whole song didn't have to pertain to their relationship. Just some of it? Just the prayer parts, maybe?

Hannah swallowed. Why had the songs returned now? Had listening to Fox sing Henry's shanties last night shaken them loose? The beckoning of a new direction for her career? Or did the return of her music-minded thinking mean something else?

Reluctant to examine the possibilities too closely, Hannah allowed herself a long inhale of Fox's scent, then unwound her arms from his neck, refusing to acknowledge the low pulse between her legs or the flapping in her chest. Not today. Probably not ever.

She climbed off the bed, her back warmed by his attention, left the room, and went into the bathroom. Once she'd showered, dressed, and blown out her hair, she stopped in the living room, hesitating a moment before picking up the folder full of original sea shanties and holding them to her chest. With Fox nowhere in sight, she left the apartment, returning once for an umbrella due to the clouds moving in overhead. But instead of heading down to today's shooting site, she let the hook in her gut pull her toward the record store, instead.

Hannah sighed when Disc N Dat came into view, nondescript and lacking in any signage, the blue Christmas lights adorning the window the only indication that it was open for business.

Last summer, she'd taken a part-time job at the record store. Mainly to add enough money to their budget that Piper wouldn't have to cook anymore and potentially burn the building down. But she'd also needed a way to occupy herself so Piper wouldn't feel terrible about spending more time with Brendan. Throw in the fact that Hannah lived for records, and it had been the perfect short-term gig.

A sense of familiarity settled over Hannah when her hand curled around the bronze handle and pulled, the smell of incense and coffee wafting out and beckoning her into the musty haven. She was relieved, especially today, to see that nothing had changed. Disc N Dat was still reliably dated and welcoming, the same posters that had been there over the summer still pinned to the wall, row after row of Christmas lights twinkling on the ceiling, Lana Del Rey rasping quietly from the recessed speaker.

The owner, Shauna, walked out from the tiny back room, face buried in a coffee mug, appearing almost startled to have a customer. "Hannah!" She brightened, setting her cup down on a console table that displayed her beaded jewelry and dream catchers. "I was wondering when you'd finally stop by."

"Sorry it took me so long." They embraced in the center of the aisle—the kind of hug one gives the person who talked them through their first typhoon. "I really don't have any excuse." Hannah turned in a circle, absorbing her surroundings. "I think I was worried if I came back in here, I would quit my job on the spot and beg to get this one back."

"Well, I'll save you the trouble. We're not hiring, seeing as how we've only had two customers since the last time you were here."

Hannah blew out a laugh. "I hope they were quality, at least?"

"Those who manage to find us usually are," Shauna said, grinning. "So what's new with you?"

Oh, not much. Just in the process of realizing I have feelings for a man who is the definition of unavailable.

"Mmmm. Work, mostly." She walked her fingers along the plastic record sleeves of the *B* section. B.B. King, the Beatles, Ben Folds, Black Sabbath. But her head came up when Lana's voice faded out and a series of notes opened the next song— were those fiddles? Followed by the ominous pound of a drum. Then came the voice. The gravelly female call to attention that made the hair on Hannah's arms stand up.

"Who is this?"

Shauna pointed to the speaker questioningly, and Hannah nodded. "This is the Unreliables. My cousin's girlfriend is the lead singer."

"They're local?"

"Seattle."

Now *this* music would be perfect for *Glory Daze*. Replacing the industrial sound with the dramatic pound of the drum, the rush of emotion in the singer's voice, the folk element of the fiddles. It would bring the small-town story to life. Give the film more than just texture—this sound would give it character.

Only when Shauna came up beside Hannah did she realize she'd been staring into space. "What's in the folder?"

"Huh?" In confusion, she looked down to find Henry's collection of shanties beneath her arm. She'd brought them along to show Brinley, one music lover to another, hoping it might be a way to bond with the music coordinator. "Oh. These are, um . . . sea shanties. Original ones that were written by my father when he was still alive. Most of them are just words on the page. I'd have to go digging with the locals to learn the tunes, but I'm guessing it would sound something like this." She pointed at the ceiling. "Like the Unreliables . . ."

Hannah murmured that last part, because a light bulb had started flashing in her brain. She looked down at the folder, flipping it open and leafing through page after page of lyrics with no music. But what if . . . music could be added? The lyrics were deep and heartfelt and poetic. Compelling. They'd made Henry feel real to Hannah. What if she could take it one step further and bring his music to life?

Was that a crazy idea?

"Weird question for you," she said to Shauna. "How well do you know the Unreliables? Would they be willing to"—what did she even call this?—"collaborate? I have these songs from my father, and I'd love to add music like theirs, add a voice—and they would be perfect. I only have the words, obviously, so they'd have a lot of creative input . . ."

Oh boy.

Now that one light bulb had gone off, her whole head looked like Hollywood Boulevard at night. She'd gone days without inspiration, and now it was pouring in, all because of the faded blue folder in her hands.

Glory Daze took place in Westport.

Westport was Henry Cross.

How many times had she been told that?

Currently, the music soundtrack was made up of songs that already existed and that never felt right to Hannah. Music for another time and place that dulled the magic of this location. It dulled the impact of Westport as the backdrop. But what if the score was made up of songs written by the man who defined this place?

"You want to record them? Intriguing," Shauna said, pursing her lips. "So you'd want them to add their own spin to the shanties. Lay down some tracks . . ."

"Yes. I mean, if they're in Seattle, I could meet with them myself. Compensate them." If there was ever a time to give in and use the family money available to her, this was it. And wow. All of this felt like leading-lady moves. But they felt good, so she took them one step further. "I'd like to have some input as well."

Shauna nodded, seeming kind of impressed. "Let me reach out to my cousin to see if they're available. But don't count on them. It could be a dead end. They're not called the Unreliables for nothing."

"Right," Hannah said wryly, closing the folder and running her hand over the front cover, getting more and more caught up in the idea, something telling her this was it. This was big. She'd only had the idea a minute ago and already ached to get started. To dive into the process she'd always watched from the wings. She could be a part of it. With her father. "Thanks."

Shauna shuffled across the ancient floor and plopped herself down on a stool behind the counter. "Where have you been staying while you're in town? With Brendan and Piper?"

"Not this time. Brendan's parents are in town, so"—she swallowed, thinking about her temporary roommate's face relaxed in sleep—"I'm staying with Fox up on the harbor."

Shauna slapped her thigh. "Oh! Wait, I take back what I said about only having two customers. Fox has been in here a bunch, too, lately."

Hannah did a double take. "Has he?"

"Uh-huh." Shauna got distracted by a smudge on the front counter, scratching at it with her thumbnail. "Surprised me, too, the first time he walked in. You know, he was a senior at the high school when I was a freshman. *The* Fox Thornton." She shook her head. "You don't just expect that face to breeze in off the street. Took me a few minutes to stop babbling. But he has pretty good taste. Last thing he bought was Thin Lizzy. Live."

Confusion settled over Hannah. "But he doesn't even own a record player." She took a mental tally of the sparse apartment. "Unless it's invisible."

"Weird," Shauna commented.

"Yeah . . ." Deep in thought, Hannah backed toward the exit, needing to make one more stop before heading to set. She'd have to deconstruct the riddle of Fox's record-buying habits later. "Weird. See you soon?"

"I better."

Chapter Fourteen

Hannah shifted in her sneakers, curling and uncurling the blue folder in her hands, waiting for Brinley to finish talking on her cell.

There was a good possibility this wasn't going to go well. But the more Hannah turned over the idea of recording Henry's shanties, the more it felt right. Inevitable. At the very least, she needed to voice the concept. To try. For Henry. For herself. And maybe she needed to try for Fox, too. Not because he expected or required her to make leading-lady moves, but because she couldn't encourage him to reach beyond his capabilities if she wasn't willing to do the same.

Speaking of Fox, she had a serious itch to hear his voice. Right now, while her nerves were trying to get the better of her. Normally her go-to person would be Piper if she needed a verbal chill pill, but she found herself pulling up her miles-long text thread with Fox, instead, her stomach calming simply from seeing his name on the screen. Keeping Brinley in her sights, she punched out a message.

HANNAH (1:45 PM): Hey there.

FOX (1:46 PM): Hey Freckles. What's up?

H (1:46 PM): Not much. Just saying hey.

F (1:47 PM): If you miss me so much, tell them ur sick and come home. I'll take you shoe shopping with me.

H (1:48 PM): Play hooky with a fisherman? Sounds dangerous.

F (1:48 PM): You won't feel a thing.

H (1:49 PM): Lies. Back up. Shoe shopping? Did I accidentally text my sister?

F (1:50 PM): I need some new XTRATUFs. Rubber boots for the boat. At the risk of diminishing my insane sex appeal, mine are starting to reek.

H (1:52 PM): Sex appeal maintained. Unbelievable. 🙄

F (1:54 PM): It's a curse.

F (1:55 PM): I can see you from the window. Turn.

Hannah's upper half twisted to find Fox looking back at her from his upstairs apartment, and an involuntary smile spread across her face. She waved. He waved back. And a powerful yearning to spend the day with Fox caught her so off guard, her arm dropped, a king-sized knot forming in her throat.

H (1:58 PM): Is it weird I want to sniff your boots to judge exactly how bad they are?

F (1:59 PM): It's your funeral.

F (2:00 PM): You're one of a kind, Hannah.

H (2:01 PM): So they say. See you later. Thanks. 😘

F (2:02 PM): For what?

Hannah started to respond, but up ahead Brinley ended her phone call.

No guts, no glory. And her guts didn't feel quite as liquified after texting with Fox. It helped to see him there in the window, a reassuring presence, there when she needed him.

Putting some starch in her spine, Hannah picked her way through the set in the other woman's direction, doing her best not to look queasy. When she reached the music coordinator, the woman took a full minute to look up from the note she was writing on a legal pad. "Yes?"

"Hi, Brinley." Hannah rolled her lips inward, turning the folder over in her hands. "So I brought something I thought you might be interested in—"

"Is this going to be quick? I have to make a call."

"Yes." Hannah resisted the impulse to blow off the whole thing, tell Brinley it was nothing and walk away. "Actually, I don't know if this will be quick? But I definitely think it's worth carving out a few minutes." Hannah exhaled and flipped open the folder. "These are original sea shanties. Written by my father, actually. And they're good. Really good. A lot of them are about Westport and family and love. Loss. They capture the themes of the movie, and after speaking to my grandmother this morning, we have permission to use them. I think . . . well, I was hoping you would consider approaching Sergei about using these original songs? I know it would be some extra legwork getting them professionally recorded, but—"

"Exactly. How much are you planning to pile on top of this budget, Hannah?" Brinley's laugh was exasperated. "Your last suggestion dragged us to the Capital of Fish. And now you want to record an original soundtrack? Maybe you want to hold the premier in Abu Dhabi—"

"I'd like to see the songs, please," Sergei said briskly, stepping out from behind the trailer to Hannah's right, almost startling her into dropping the folder. His gaze was hard on Brinley, who'd gone a ghostly shade of white, but his demeanor softened when he reached out to take the folder from Hannah. "May I?"

This kind of upstaging scenario was the last place Hannah wanted to end up. Brinley was good at her job, and she respected the woman. She'd been prepared to hand over the songs and let Brinley claim the original score as her idea.

That wasn't going to happen now.

Hannah tried to communicate a silent apology to Brinley, but the coordinator's attention was focused on Sergei as he read through the first couple of shanties. "It's hard to get anything from just the words," he said, sounding disappointed. "There is no way to hear them set to music?"

Brinley shot triumphant daggers at her.

"Well . . ." Hannah started, once again experiencing the urge to take back the folder, laugh, apologize for the bad idea. Instead, she took a deep breath and kicked down the door of her comfort zone. "I'm in the process of doing that. I've already arranged to have them recorded. It's just a matter of whether Storm Born wants them for this project or not."

That's right. Hannah lied. Just a little.

She was planning on finding a way to record the shanties, wasn't she? Sure, that ball had been set in motion only a matter of hours ago. There was also a strong chance the Unreliables wouldn't be interested, or they would be unavailable when Shauna got in touch. If so, eventually she'd find somebody else. But bottom line, she was making it sound as though having the end product was imminent—and it wasn't.

Sergei had a severely short attention span, though. And she had him semi-hooked on this idea she believed in with her heart, her soul, her gut. If she didn't feed the director something real, something substantial, right now, it would blow out of his consciousness like white fuzzies from a dandelion.

And this was entertainment, baby. Fake it till you make it.

Sergei eyeballed her, right on the verge of interest. One more push.

How?

"I can . . . you know," she mumbled into her chest. "I can sing one of them—"

"Yes, let's do that," Brinley said, beaming, resting her chin on her wrist. "Hey!" She leaned sideways and called to a group of crew members. "Hannah is going to sing us a sea shanty."

The way everyone swarmed, she might as well have been Hailey Bieber walking out of LAX, suddenly the focus of rabid paparazzi. "Uhh." She cleared her throat, reaching out to take the folder back from Sergei. This song had reduced her to tears last night. Was she really going to sing it in front of all her coworkers? Not only was she worried about having the same response in public, but her love for music didn't exactly extend to sterling vocal abilities. "So . . . this is called 'A Seafarer's Bounty.'"

For once on the boisterous set, a pin could have been heard dropping.

Even Christian looked interested in the proceedings.

The first line of the song came out flat, kind of hushed. And then she happened to lift her eyes and see the *Della Ray* bobbing in the water just ahead in the harbor. Something moved inside her. Something deep and unknown, a little scary. A bridge to the past, to some other time. Her father had made his livelihood on that exact boat. He'd met his death on it. And she was singing one of his songs, so maybe she'd just better do it justice. She'd been handed all his words and thoughts. She'd never meet him, but in this small way, wasn't she bringing him back to life?

Hannah didn't realize how much her voice had risen until the song was nearly over and still no one spoke or moved. In no way did she fool herself into thinking her talent kept them as still as statues. God, no. Their inaction was probably due to the fact that she'd put more effort into the song than she'd put into anything before, except maybe creating the perfect playlist.

Her voice traveled across the harbor, the wind seeming to carry it out to the water. When the song was over, Sergei started clapping and everyone joined in. It was so unexpected, the crack of sound firing her back into the present, that she recoiled and almost fell on her ass, earning her an eye roll from Christian. But she didn't have a chance to thank everyone or hear Sergei's opinion about Henry's song before Brinley tossed down her legal pad. "Look, I have been working on synchronization rights to our songs for weeks. Our sound-mixing team has already approved the sequence and outline. I hope you're not taking this seriously, Sergei, because it would mean starting from scratch, and we're already over budget and behind schedule. It's a terrible idea. From a kid."

A chorus of ooohs went up behind Hannah.

Hannah's face flamed. With embarrassment, yes, but mostly indignation. There was nothing terrible about this idea. About Henry's songs. And it was that anger that drove Hannah to double down. Why be nice and try to keep things smooth sailing with Brinley? Obviously that wasn't going to happen, so she needed to fight for what was important. What she could control.

Hopefully.

Hannah did all the paperwork for Storm Born. She knew the numbers, had been reading through Brinley's cue sheets and sync contracts for years. She used that knowledge to her advantage now.

"No. Actually, using the shanties would put us back *under* budget. And the rights would be exclusive."

Sergei liked the word "exclusive." A lot. He looked back down at the folder, that creative vein worming around in his temple.

"We could provide a flat fee of twenty thousand to the artists for the recording session. Currently, we're spending more than that on the rights to one song. I'm not taking a broker fee, but my grandmother will take fifteen percent off the top of any profit from the soundtrack over the next ten years. We'd be saving the producers money this way and possibly putting an indie band on the charts." From the corner of her mouth, she whispered, "Exclusive," for good measure.

"But the time it would take—" Brinley argued.

"At the very least, I would like to hear a demo. These songs give the film historical value, they enrich the backstory." Sergei executed a dramatic walk through the silent crew, fanning a hand out over the water. "I'm picturing a fast-motion sunrise while the haunted voice of a sailor calls from beyond the horizon. We open with purpose. With gravity. The audience is pulled into the time and place with the voices of the people who live here. The men who trod these waters."

One couldn't technically tread on water, unless one was Jesus, but Hannah didn't think now was a good time to point it out. Sergei was in full inspiration mode; everyone held their breath, and Brinley looked about two seconds from stabbing Hannah with a Bic.

Sergei turned on a heel and faced the group. "Brinley, let's continue in the direction we've been heading. But I'd like to pursue Hannah's angle, as well. We are already behind schedule and over budget. Brinley is right about that." He stroked his chin thoughtfully, a move that used to make Hannah swoon but that she now observed objectively. *Please don't be because of a certain emotionally complicated relief skipper.* "Hannah, if you can really have these songs recorded and make them digital on a smaller budget, I'm going to take the change of direction under advisement."

"Let me make it simple for you," Brinley said sweetly. "If you do that, I quit."

A hiss of collective breath went up in the crowd, and some of it came from Hannah. This was definitely not how she'd envisioned this going down when she woke up this morning. Instead of bonding with Brinley over the discovered shanties, she'd now been pitted against a woman whose work she actually admired.

Sergei let the threat hang in the air for a few beats. "Well." He brushed a hand over his dark hair, unbothered, possibly even appreciative of the drama. "Let's hope you don't have to put your money where your mouth is." He strode through the parted sea of gaping crew members. "Hannah, could I speak to you privately?"

Oh Lord.

Was he trying to get her killed?

Hannah thought of asking if they could speak later, like when she wasn't under intense—in one case, homicidal—scrutiny, but didn't want to seem ungrateful for the opportunity he'd just given her. Although, the word "opportunity" might be pushing it. He wanted her to record Henry's songs. To possibly end up on the film score. God, she didn't even have contact with the Unreliables yet. For all she knew, they'd broken up. Faking it until she made it had seemed like a great idea in the moment. But the making it part was going to be a challenge.

Was she able to do it?

Hannah increased her pace to catch up with the director. "Hi," she said, drawing even with him on his brisk walk along the water. "What did you want to speak to me about?"

"You've been very assertive lately," he said, slowing to a stop, tugging on the sleeves of his turtleneck. "I confess, I was going to be selfish and keep you as a production assistant forever, but I've . . . had my eyes opened recently. I've been paying closer attention, and I can see you're taking on responsibilities far beyond your pay grade."

She scratched the back of her ear. "I can't argue with you there."

He laughed, his eyes crinkling at the corners.

Come on, hormones. Last chance to get excited.

They remained obstinately dormant.

"I'm curious to see if you can deliver on these additions to the score. I wasn't lying when I said they could bring a lot of character to the piece. That . . . final aspect that has been missing."

It was gratifying and kind of a relief to know she wasn't the only one who noticed the lack of magic. "Thanks. I won't let you down."

Sergei nodded, pulled on his sleeves again. "Separate from that. Completely separate . . . Look, I don't want you to think I'm giving you this chance because I . . . like you. Or expect something from you . . ."

Hannah almost asked him to repeat himself. Did he just say he liked her? It didn't sound as though he'd meant that in a platonic way, either. In fact, he couldn't seem to make eye contact with her. Was this for real? She dug frantically for excitement, for the former version of herself that pined for the moody director all hours of the day and night, but . . . if she was being honest, she couldn't remember the last time she'd doodled his name on a napkin or stalked his Instagram. "Yes?" she prompted him slowly.

"It's probably not a very professional question, but I find myself"—he blew out a puff of breath—"extremely curious to know if your relationship with the fisherman is serious. Are you two doing the long-distance thing or . . . will you be available to see other people when we're back in LA and not so . . . distracted?"

Was her relationship with Fox serious?

That was a really good question. Hannah guessed neither of them would know which answer to give. Yes or no. And yet all signs pointed to yes. They'd kept up a ritual of texting each other every night for seven months. They knew each other's deepest insecurities. They'd slept in each other's arms, and hey, they talked freely about masturbation. So there was that.

When she thought about Sergei, her brain made muffled *beep-boop* sounds. She liked his drive and his creativity and vision. His turtlenecks flattered his slim physique. They would have mutual interests if they ever really engaged in a personal discussion. Fine. It would be just . . . fine.

But when she thought about Fox, her stomach turned into a bouncy ball. So many emotions rolling around at once—longing, protectiveness, confusion, lust—and on top of those humdingers, she was infinitely more excited to see him at home tonight than go on a date with Sergei upon returning to LA.

It was entirely possible her interest in the director had started fading around seven months ago, when a certain Fleetwood Mac album showed up on the doorstep, and now it was completely null and void.

Still, as far as an answer to the question, was her relationship with Fox serious? She didn't know.

But she found herself taking a deep breath and saying, "Yes, it's serious."

And somehow, saying it out loud felt entirely right.

Later that afternoon, Hannah walked slowly to Fox's apartment.

She'd rushed back to Disc N Dat after filming to impress upon Shauna the urgency of getting in touch with the Unreliables and stood there while her friend placed the call. She left copies of the shanties for Shauna to pass on, along with the exciting (and hopefully enticing) news that Storm Born would be able to pay the band.

It would be pretty crushing if they didn't come through, since they had the perfect sound, but worst-case scenario, she'd start hunting down other options bright and early tomorrow morning.

Toward the end of filming, the clouds overhead had darkened, settling a gloomy mood over Westport. Rainstorms always made Hannah want to go crawl into bed with her headphones, but after turning down Sergei—by telling him she was serious about Fox—she needed a minute before coming face-to-face with the fisherman. Would he know just by looking at her that she'd voiced such an impossibility out loud?

But maybe it wasn't *completely* impossible.

She couldn't stop replaying what Shauna told her. She supposed it wasn't crazy unusual that Fox would stop into Disc N Dat. It was a small town. He'd been the one to introduce Hannah to the shop in the first place.

The fact that he'd been buying records, though . . .

To the casual observer, Fox's purchases wouldn't be a big deal. Only he knew what they would mean to Hannah. It made no sense to keep it from her, unless there was some important reason. On set this afternoon, she'd scrolled back through their text messages and found the one that had tickled her memory, made her pulse click in her ears.

> **F (6:40 PM):** Apart from being dark and dramatic . . . what makes a man your type? What is eventually going to make a man The One?

> **H (6:43 PM):** I think . . . if they can find a reason to laugh with me on the worst day.

> **F (6:44 PM):** That sounds like the opposite of your type.

> **H (6:45 PM):** It does, doesn't it? Must be the wine.

> **H (6:48 PM):** He'll need to have a cabinet full of records and something to play them on, of course.

> **F (6:51 PM):** Well obviously.

Record collecting wasn't an interest he'd enjoyed before they met last summer. Him buying albums now was pertinent information. Where was he keeping them? And if he was hiding them from her . . . what *else* was he hiding?

Either he didn't want Hannah reading too much into his new collection or there was a lot to read into it and he needed more time before admitting that.

Unless, of course, she was completely nuts and he was just a dude who'd forgotten about buying a few albums. But for a man who never purchased anything for his apartment, wouldn't they have stood out? Been remarked on by now?

Lube had been a main topic of interest, but not a stack of vinyls?

Let's say, hypothetically, he'd started collecting records because he had a low-key interest in being Hannah's type. Never mind that her knees trembled over that possibility. How far did his interest go? She didn't know. But the same intuition that had led to calling their relationship "serious" was buzzing now. Telling her to wait, to be patient, to stay the course with Fox.

That if he was hiding records, he was hiding a desire to be . . . more.

Despite his assurances of the opposite.

Deep in thought, Hannah carefully wedged the new albums she hadn't been able to resist under one arm and let herself into the apartment. When she walked inside, she was immediately greeted by the spicy scent of aftershave—and when Fox walked out of his bedroom in dark jeans and a slate-colored button-down, she knew.

He was going on a date.

Hannah's stomach plummeted to the floor.

Chapter Fifteen

$\mathcal{F}$ox was going to see his mother.

He always found out on short notice when she was working in the vicinity of Westport. If Fox wasn't on the water, he always jumped, because he never knew when she'd be back again. He'd definitely been a little disappointed when Charlene called to say she'd be in Hoquiam for the night, because going to see his mother meant he wouldn't be home with Hannah.

Hannah, who had slept in his bed last night, her tight little butt in his lap for a good two hours somewhere in the middle of it all. She'd barely walked out his front door this morning before he rolled onto his back, gripped his cock, and came after six strokes. Six. It usually took him a good five minutes, at least. He'd thought of Hannah during every one of those six strokes. Same way he had every time since last summer. Only now, she wasn't just the girl he couldn't stop thinking about. She was the girl who flat-out refused to fuck him.

And goddammit. Now she walked into the apartment, clothes damp and clingy from the rain, and there he went, thinking about being inside her again. Picturing her bowed back, her mouth open on a cry of his name, the slap of flesh on flesh. *Stop it, you bastard.*

Until recently, Fox had never fantasized about anyone specific while beating off.

A body was just a body.

But in his fantasies with Hannah, their minds were in sync as well as their physical selves. They laughed as often as they moaned. Even thinking of their fingers gripped together, the trust in her eyes, added to the insane pleasure. Imagining himself inside Hannah felt great. *Better* than great. His orgasms were more satisfying by leaps and bounds.

And that scared the holy shit out of him.

Fox was distracted from his troubling thoughts when Hannah stopped short just inside the door, framed in the lazy rainstorm, her face going from thoughtful to dismayed. Sad, even? "Oh," she said, giving him a once-over. "Oh."

He tried valiantly to ignore the pounding in his chest. Jesus, it got louder and harder to manage every time they were in the same room. For the longest time, he'd thought if they just slept together, it would go away. This twisting, hot, melting, spearing sensation she inspired in him with a blink of her eyes. He'd feel shitty afterward for jeopardizing their friendship, but at least it would be over and he could stop obsessing about her so much. Now he was beginning to seriously doubt *anything* would work.

"Hello to you, too," he said, voice sounding strained.

"Sorry, I just didn't expect— I . . ." She dropped the bag she was holding underneath her arm, jolted, then stooped down to pick it up. "You're going on one."

Fox frowned. "Going on one what?"

"Going out." She stood slowly, holding the bag to her chest, eyes big and trained on him. "Going out on a date."

Understanding dawned.

And then he saw her demeanor for what it was. This assumption that he was going on a date had thrown her big-time. Honestly, part of him wanted to shake her and say, *Now you know how I feel sending you off to your director every morning.* But what would that argument make them? A couple?

They weren't. She lived in a different state and was actively pining for someone else. All he had to offer was a notched-up bedpost and the mockery that came along with it. Potentially for both of them. A relationship between them wasn't happening, despite her obvious disappointment that he could be going on a date. And so for a split second, Fox considered letting Hannah believe he *was* going to meet someone else. Maybe it would put an end to whatever was happening between them. They shouldn't be sleeping in the same bed, shouldn't be telling each other deep, dark secrets. Look where it led. Jealousy. Longing that made him want to carry her back into his bedroom, wrap himself in her goodness, and feel normal again. She was the only person who made him normal. Made him . . . okay.

In the end, Fox couldn't force himself to do it. He couldn't let her think for a second that he'd rather spend his time with anyone else. It would have haunted him. "My mother is in town," he said, relief coating his stomach when he saw hers. "Well, she's in Hoquiam—tonight only. About forty minutes from here. That's where I'm going. To see her."

Her shoulders relaxed. It took her a moment to respond. "Why tonight only?"

Fox's lips edged up into a half smile. "She's a traveling bingo caller. Goes up and down the coast running bingo nights at various churches and rest homes."

"Oh . . . wow. I did not expect you to say that." Amusement danced behind her features. "Are you going to play bingo?"

"Sometimes I do. But mostly I help with crowd control."

"You have to keep control of the bingo crowd?"

"Freckles, you have no idea."

Glancing down at the bag in her hand, her smile turned into a curious one, a line appearing between her brows. "Fox"—she seemed to scrutinize him—"do you have a record player?"

Too late, he recognized the brown paper bag stamped with the purple logo for Disc N Dat and his gut seized. Of course she'd gone there. Why wouldn't she visit at least once? It had been shortsighted of him to buy his records there when she could so easily find out he'd been to the shop. "Do I have a record player?"

Hannah raised an eyebrow. "That's what I just asked you."

"I heard."

Her chest rose and fell. "You do have one."

"I didn't say that."

"You don't have to."

"Hannah."

But she was already striding forward, on a mission, making panic sink like an anchor in his belly. Hiding the record player and albums from her had been selfish. He'd felt selfish so many times. But he'd bought the fucking thing for reasons he didn't know how to express out loud. A gut-born need to be what she wanted.

And Hannah . . . she would make him admit to it.

On her way past Fox, she set her paper bag down on the kitchen table and circled the room, her gaze finally landing on his locked cabinet. "Is she in there?"

Fox gulped. "Yes."

Hannah made a wounded sound, pressing a hand to the center of her chest.

This was it. No escaping what came next. With the discovery of the record player locked up in the cabinet, she was going to know how often he thought of her. She'd know the best parts of his days were her text messages before bed. She'd know his hands shook with the need to touch her when she was in the shower. That he could no longer look at other women, and his existence had become undeniably priestly. That all day long, her words from this morning had rung in his head, packing his chest tight with some unnamed emotion.

I'm just going to tell you that . . . I'll be back tonight and that you're really important to me.

Hannah remained silent so long, chewing on that full lower lip, he wondered if she was going to say anything at all. She seemed almost conflicted. What was she thinking?

"All this time, Fox? Really?" Her voice turned into a hushed whisper, and his pulse started to hammer against his eardrums. "I've been listening to music on my phone for no reason?"

Fox's breath released slowly, relief warring with . . . disappointment?

No. That couldn't be right.

Either she was letting him off the hook . . . or she didn't realize the significance of him buying the record player. To be close to her. To have a connection to that day they'd spent together in Seattle when he'd felt human and heard for the first time in as long as he could remember. To be the man she imagined herself with. "I was . . . saving it as a surprise," Fox said, reaching behind the cabinet for the leather pouch and removing the key, highly aware of how odd and telling it was that he'd hidden the damn thing. Beginning to sweat, he turned it in the lock. "Thought I'd break it out if you had a bad day at work, you know?"

His eyes closed when she hummed. From right behind him. She was so close he could almost feel the vibration on the back of his neck, his every hair follicle waking up. God, he wanted to touch and taste her so bad. Would get down on his knees if she batted her eyelashes. There was no denying the undercurrents between them—her distraught reaction to him going on a date spoke volumes. But he forced himself to accept what she was offering him, instead. Friendship.

Hannah knew it couldn't work between them. She knew it as well as he did, and she was saving them when he wasn't strong enough to do it. Maybe it would eventually get easier to keep his hands to himself. If he got friendship with Hannah out of the bargain, he had no choice but to be grateful.

Fox unlocked the cabinet and stepped back, absorbing her expression like a dry sponge dropped into the ocean.

When her face transformed with delight, he wanted to kick himself for not showing her sooner. "Oh. A Fluance." She ran her finger along the smooth edge. "Fox, she's beautiful. Are you taking good care of her?"

His lips twitched. "Yes, Hannah."

She stepped back and tilted her head, looking at it from a different angle. Released a happy sigh. "This is such a perfect choice for you, too. The wood chassis reminds me of the deck of a ship."

"That's exactly what I thought," he said, honestly. The validation she always seemed to give so effortlessly pushed him to open the cabinet beneath, revealing the neat row of records he'd collected over the last seven months. He laughed at her strangled gasp. "Go ahead. Play something."

She spoke with quiet reverence, bending forward to peruse the selection of everything from metal to blues to alternative. "Please. I'm going to be playing something all night while you're gone."

"No, you won't, because you're coming with me."

He didn't think there was anything that could compete with the records, but Hannah's eyes zipped to his with that pronouncement, and they stared at each other in the ensuing silence. Did he plan on inviting Hannah to come meet his mother? No. No, it shouldn't even have occurred to him. Introducing a girl to Charlene? Pigs must have been flying. But as soon as the words were out of his mouth, he couldn't imagine the night any other way. Of course she was coming with him. Of course.

"Who am I to turn down a bingo game so rowdy it needs crowd control?" she asked, breathless, her cheeks ever so slightly pink—and he had to restrain himself from kissing them. From tracing his lips down to her flushed neck and worshiping it until her panties were soaked. "Let me go change."

"Yeah," he said thickly, stuffing his fists into the pockets of his jeans.

Hannah was almost to her room when she stopped and jogged back to the turntable, pulling a Ray LaMontagne album out carefully and settling the needle on the first track, her lips curling happily at the first crackle. "For atmosphere," she explained, eyes twinkling.

Then she fluttered back to her room, leaving Fox staring after her with his heart clogging his throat.

Phew. That had been a close one.

Chapter Sixteen

Fox wasn't joking.

This bingo crowd came to win.

When they pulled into the church parking lot, there was already a line extending around the corner, and the (mostly) senior citizen players looked none too happy about being kept outside in a steady drizzle.

Fox turned off the engine and leaned back, tapping a finger in quick succession on the bottom of the steering wheel. Anxious. That's how he'd been on the second half of the ride, and although she didn't know why, she started to wonder if the jumpiness stemmed from seeing his mother.

Maybe she should be home searching for backup bands if the Unreliables didn't come through, but she didn't want to be anywhere else. The invitation to meet Fox's mother felt almost sacred. Like a glimpse behind the curtain. And she'd been unable to do anything but say yes.

Simply put, she wanted to be with him. Around him.

He'd bought a record player and hidden it.

She wasn't buying his excuse that he'd saved it for a rainy day. A surprise to pull out of the hat after a bad day on set. No, that was total baloney—and she was pretty sure both of them knew it. This man buying anything permanent for his bare-bones apartment had significance. And Hannah could admit to being a little scared to find out more. To peel back more layers and discover if her rapidly growing feelings for this man were returned. Because what then?

Apart from the obvious obstacle—they didn't live in the same state—a relationship between them would never work. Would it?

Fox claimed not to want a girlfriend or any commitments.

Hannah was the total opposite. When she decided to commit herself to someone or something, she went in one thousand percent. Loyalty to the people she cared about hummed in her blood. Loyalty made her Hannah.

She'd pretended the record player was cool. No big deal. A fun discovery. But her apparently self-destructive heart wanted to pounce all over the deeper meaning. Ignoring that desire burned, but she forced herself to focus on the here and now. Where Fox clearly needed a friend to distract him, to ground him, and that's who she'd be. Refusing to allow things between them to get physical had unlocked what felt like . . . trust between them. And it felt rare and precious, a lot like meeting his mother.

Hannah traced Fox's profile with her eyes, the strong planes of his face backlit by the rain-blurred driver's-side window. A line moved in his jaw, that finger still tapping away on the steering wheel. There was no denying she wanted to reach over, turn his head, and kiss him, finally let the fire burn out of

control between them, but . . . just this—being a true friend—
was more important.

"This is my favorite sound," she said, unhooking her seat
belt and getting more comfortable in the passenger seat. "It
doesn't rain very often in LA. When it does, I go driving just to
hear the drops land on the roof of the car."

"And what kind of music do you play?"

Hannah smiled, enjoying the fact that he knew her so well.
"The Doors, of course. 'Riders on the Storm.'" She sat forward
to fiddle with his satellite radio, searching for the classic rock
station. "It really lends itself to the whole main-character
moment."

"The main-character moment?"

"Yeah. You know, when you've got the perfect mood going,
soundtrack to match. And you're on a rainy road, feeling
dramatic. You're the star of your own movie. You're Rocky
training for the fight. Or Baby learning how to merengue
in *Dirty Dancing*. Or you're just crying over a lost love." She
turned slightly in the seat. "Everyone does it!"

Fox's expression was a mixture of amused and skeptical. "I
don't do it. I'm damn sure Brendan doesn't, either."

"You're never on the boat, hauling crab pots, and feel like
you're being watched by an audience?"

"Never."

"You're a filthy liar."

He tipped back his head and laughed. Quieted for a second.
"When I was a kid, I loved the movie *Jaws*. Watched it hundreds
of times." He shrugged a big shoulder. "Sometimes when our
crew is in the bunks talking, I think of that drinking scene
with Dreyfuss, Shaw, and Scheider."

Hannah smiled. "The part where they sing?"

"Yeah." He sent her a sideways squint. "I'm a total Scheider."

"Yeah, no, I have to disagree. You're definitely the shark."

His bark of laughter made Hannah turn more fully in the seat, leaning her cheek against the leather. Through the window, she could see the line of seniors eagerly moving inside, but Fox didn't seem in a rush to leave the car just yet, his tension still obvious in the lines of his body.

"What is your mom like?"

The subject change didn't seem to surprise him at all, and he reached for the leather bracelet resting in his lap, twisting it in a slow circle. "Loud. Loves an inappropriate joke. She's kind of a creature of habit. Always has her pack of cigarettes, her coffee, a story ready to go."

"Why are you nervous to see her?"

As if realizing he'd been transparent, his gaze zipped to her, then away, his Adam's apple lifting and falling slowly. "When she looks at me, she obviously sees my father. Right before she smiles, there's a little . . . I don't know, it's like a flinch."

A sharp-tipped spear traveled down her esophagus. "And you still come to see her. That's pretty brave."

He shrugged. "I should be used to it by now. One of these times I will be."

"No." Her voice was almost drowned out by the rain. "One of these times, she'll realize you're nothing like him and she'll stop flinching. That's more likely."

It was obvious that he didn't agree. In a clear effort to change the subject, he plowed his fingers through his dark-blond hair and shifted slightly to face her. "I didn't even ask you how filming went today."

Hannah blew out a breath, responsibility crashing down on her like a pile of bricks. "Oh, it was . . . interesting, I guess?"

His brow knit. "How?"

"Well." She dragged her bottom lip through her teeth, telling herself not to say the next part. It was selfish, wanting to see Fox's reaction. Secretly hoping it would give her some hint as to how he felt about her. What would she even do with that information? "Sergei hinted at wanting to go out. When we get back to LA."

An eye twitch was her only hint as to what was taking place in his head. "Oh yeah?" He cleared his throat hard, staring out through the windshield. "Great. That's . . . great, Hannah."

I turned him down.

I told him we were serious.

She wanted to make those confessions so badly, her stomach ached, but she could already see his incredulous expression. *I'm not in the relationship race and I never will be.* Fox might have been hiding a wealth of music and deeper meanings in a locked cabinet, but on the surface? Nothing about his confirmed bachelorhood status had changed in the space of a week, and if she pushed for too much too soon—or hinted at her deepening feelings—he could balk. And God, that would hurt.

"Um. But that's secondary to what else happened." She mentally regrouped, hemming in her disappointment. "It's kind of a long story, but bottom line? I have been tasked with recording a demo of Henry's sea shanties that could potentially replace the current movie score. And if that transpires, Brinley is threatening to quit, and the crew is taking bets on whether or not that day will come. Or if I can actually pull it off."

"Jesus," Fox muttered, visibly filling in the blanks. "How did that happen?"

She wet her lips. "Well, you know how the songs in my head went missing?" He nodded. "They came back this morning, with 'I Say a Little Prayer.' They started to flow back in. And then I was standing in Disc N Dat and it hit me: there are no better songs for the soundtrack than Henry's. It just makes sense. They were written about Westport." She paused. "Shauna is helping me get in contact with a Seattle band to maybe, possibly, record the shanties. I was going to get them recorded either way, but when I brought up the possibility of using them in the movie to Brinley—"

"She got her toes stepped on."

"I didn't mean to toe step," she groaned. "I was just going to float the option, but Sergei overheard the whole thing." Was she imagining the way every one of his muscles tightened at the mention of the director? "Anyway, it feels like a challenge has been issued. To show whether or not I'm ready for more responsibility with the company. Or maybe just . . . professionally. With myself."

"You are," he stated emphatically. Then: "Don't you think you're ready?"

Hannah turned her face into the seat and laughed. "My LA therapy-speak is beginning to rub off on you."

"Oh God. It is." He shook his head slowly, then went back to scrutinizing her. "That was a bold move, Freckles. Putting out feelers for a band. Approaching her with the songs. You don't want the challenge?"

"I don't know. I thought I wanted challenges. But now I'm just scared I won't deliver and I'll realize I was never meant to be a leading lady all along, you know? That feeling is just for driving alone in my car and listening to the Doors."

"Bullshit."

"I could say the same for your belief that you can't captain a ship," she pointed out quietly.

"The difference being I don't want to be a leader." There was far less conviction in his tone than the last time they'd spoken about him taking over the *Della Ray*, but he didn't appear to notice it. Hannah did, though. "You, Hannah? You can do this."

Gratitude welled in her chest, and she let him see it. Watched him absorb it with no small surprise. "Those songs would probably have remained meaningless in the folder if you hadn't sung for me." His chest rose and fell, but he could no longer look at her. "Thanks for that."

"Hey." He scrubbed his knuckles along the bristly shadow of his jaw. "Who am I to keep my minimal talent from the world?"

As if the cosmos had aligned perfectly, "You've Lost That Lovin' Feelin'" by the Righteous Brothers came on the radio and a blissful sigh escaped Hannah. "I'm glad you feel that way, because you're definitely singing this with me."

"Afraid not—"

She dropped her voice and sang the opening bars, making him laugh, the husky sound a low bass line in the rain-muffled car. For the second time that day, her lack of vocal skills made her want to stop, but when Fox glanced at the entrance to the church auditorium with renewed anxiousness, she turned up the volume and kept going, snatching a pen out of his cup holder to serve as a microphone. By the second verse, Fox shook his head and joined in. They sat in the rain, singing at the tops of their lungs, all the way until the final note.

When they finally walked into the church hall several minutes later, the stiffness was completely gone from Fox's shoulders.

Chapter Seventeen

Charlene Thornton was exactly as Fox described.

She wore big vintage eyeglasses with a rose tint, a long sweater wrapped around her slender body, and there were hints of gray springing out from her temples. The church hall was packed full of folding tables, and she walked through them, holding court, dropping witticisms on the bingo players as she passed, smoothing feathers that had been ruffled from their wait in the bad weather.

There was a pack of Marlboro Reds in her hand, though she didn't seem in a rush to do anything, let alone go outside and smoke one. She seemed more inclined to use the pack to gesture or possibly as a safety blanket.

Hannah wasn't prepared for the flinch Fox had warned her about, especially coming from his own mother. Or the fierce surge of protectiveness that permeated her, head to toe. It was so strong that she reached for Fox's hand and wound their fingers together without thinking, her heart leaping a little in her chest when he not only didn't pull away but tugged her closer to his side.

"Hey, Ma," he said, leaning down to kiss her cheek. "Good to see you. You look great."

"Likewise, of course." Before he could pull away, she caught his head in both hands, scanning him with a mother's eyes. "Would you look at these goddamn dimples on my son?" she called over her shoulder, turning several heads. "And who is this young lady? Isn't she just cute as hell?"

"Yeah, this is Hannah. She's pretty cute, but I wouldn't recommend messing with her." His lips jumped at one end. "I call her Freckles, but her other nickname is the Captain Killer. She's famous in Westport for going toe-to-toe with Brendan. And most recently for calling some of the locals ball sacs."

"Fox!" Hannah hissed.

Laughing, Charlene released her son's head and planted bent wrists on her hips. "Well, now, I'd say that deserves the best seat in the house." She turned and waved for them to follow. "Come on, come on. If I don't start soon, there is going to be a riot. Nice to meet you, Hannah. You're the first girl Fox has ever brought to meet me, but I don't have time to make a big deal out of it."

Dammit. Hannah liked her right away.

And she'd really wanted to hate her after that flinch.

Charlene pushed her and Fox toward some chairs at the top of the hall, right in front of the stage where her bingo equipment had been set up, pulling some bingo cards and blotters out of her apron and dropping them onto the table.

"Good luck, you two. Grand prize is a blender tonight."

"Thanks, Ma."

"Thanks, Mrs. Thornton," Hannah said grudgingly.

"Please! Let's not stand on ceremony." She squeezed Hannah's shoulders, guiding her into one of the metal chairs. "You'll call me Charlene and I'll hope my son has the good sense to bring you around again so you have the chance to call me any damn thing at all. How about that?"

Leaving that question hanging in the air, Charlene sailed off. Fox exhaled, looking chagrined. "She's a character."

"I really wanted to be mad at her," Hannah said glumly.

"I know exactly how you feel, Freckles," he responded, the words almost swallowed up completely in the shuffle of chairs and buzz of excitement around them. Across from Fox and Hannah sat two women who had erected a portable barrier between each other, ten cards spread out in front of them both, a rainbow selection of blotters at the ready.

"Keep your eye on Eleanor," said the woman on the right, closest to the stage. "She's an unrepentant cheat."

"You just shut your mouth, Paula," hissed Eleanor over the barrier. "You're still bitter about me winning that Dutch oven two weeks ago. Well, you can shove that high-and-mighty attitude where the sun doesn't shine. I won fair and square."

"Sure," Paula muttered. "If fair and square means cheating."

"Is it even possible to cheat at bingo?" Hannah asked Fox out of the side of her mouth.

"Stay neutral. Don't get involved."

"But—"

"Be Switzerland, Hannah. Trust me."

They were still holding hands under the table. So when Eleanor leaned across the table and smiled sweetly—bitter accusations apparently forgotten—and asked how long

Hannah and Fox had been dating, Hannah's answer sounded somehow fabricated. "Oh. No, we're just"—her gaze locked with Fox's fleetingly—"friends."

Paula was openly skeptical. "Oh, friends, huh?"

"This is what they do now, this younger generation," Eleanor said, straightening her cards unnecessarily. "They don't do labels and no one goes steady. I see it with my grandkids. They don't even go on dates, they do something called a group hang. That way there is no pressure on anyone, because God forbid."

Now Paula just looked disgusted with the both of them. "Youth is wasted on the young." She prodded the table with a bony finger. "If I was fifty years younger, I'd be labeling the heck out of anything that walked upright."

"Paula," Eleanor scolded through the barrier. "We're in a church."

"The good Lord already knows my thoughts."

Hannah looked at Fox, both of them practically shaking with unreleased laughter, their hands squeezing the blood out of each other under the table. They were saved from any further commentary about the downfalls of their generation when Charlene turned on the microphone, sending a peal of feedback through the church hall. "All right, you old buzzards. Let's play bingo."

It wasn't a date (or a group hang).

They were just two friends playing bingo.

Just two friends occasionally holding hands under the table, his knuckle brushing the inside of her thigh here and there. At some point Fox decided the hall was too noisy to hear Hannah properly and he'd yanked her chair closer, pretending not to notice her questioning look. What the hell was he doing?

Was he one of those idiots who wanted something twice as much because he couldn't have it? The director had asked her out. Pretty soon, they would be back in LA, and Sergei would have all the access to Hannah he wanted, while Fox was in the Pacific Northwest, probably staring at his phone waiting for her daily text message. Which is exactly how it needed to be.

And yet.

Every time Fox thought of Sergei holding her hand instead of him, he wanted to swipe an arm across the bingo table and upset everyone's cards. Scatter them all over the floor. Then maybe kick over the church bulletin board for good measure. Who the hell did this motherfucker think he was to ask out Hannah Bellinger?

A better man than him, probably. One who hadn't been cheapening himself since approximately one day after his balls dropped. Like father, like son. Wasn't that why he wore the bracelet that was currently resting on Hannah's thigh?

"Sweet Caroline. This is so addictive," Hannah whispered to him. And he heard it easily, because he was sitting way too close, trying not to stare at those little curly wisps of hair that the rain had created around her face. Or the way she sucked in a breath every time she got to blot out a square. Or her mouth. Dammit, yes, her insanely lush mouth. Maybe he should just lean over and kiss it, the hell with the consequences. He hadn't tasted her since that night of the cast party, and the need for another hit was unbearable.

"Addictive," he rasped. "Yeah."

Hannah's eyes shot to his, then down to his mouth, and the thoughts that ran through his mind were not appropriate to have in front of his mother. Anyone's mother, really.

This need for Hannah never went away, but it was especially heavy right now. Having her there was more comforting than Fox could have predicted. He forced himself to go see his mother occasionally, not only because he cared about her, but because that involuntary flinch validated his existence as a responsibility-free hedonist.

But Hannah . . . she was starting to pull him the opposite way. Like a gravitational force. And right now, stuck between Hannah and the reminder of his past, going in her direction seemed almost possible. She was here with him, wasn't she? Playing bingo, singing with him in the car, talking. Decidedly not fucking. If Hannah liked him for more than his potential to give her an orgasm . . . if someone so smart and incredible believed he was more . . . couldn't it possibly be true?

As if reading his mind, Hannah rubbed her thumb over the back of his knuckles, turning slightly and resting her head on his shoulder. Trustingly.

Like a friend. Just a friend.

God. Why couldn't he breathe?

"Bingo!" crowed one of the women sitting across from them.

"Oh hell. Did I hear Eleanor call bingo down there?" Charlene said, whistling into the microphone and banging the mini gong she kept perched on her station. "Eleanor, you have been on fire these past couple of weeks."

"That's because she's a filthy cheat!" Paula spat.

"Now, Paula, be a good sport," Charlene scolded lightly. "We all get a lucky run once in a while. Eleanor? My handsome son is going to bring me your card so I can check it over, okay?"

Eleanor handed the card to Fox with a flourish, baring her teeth in a triumphant smile entirely for Paula's benefit. Fox scooted his chair back, wishing the round had gone on longer so Hannah's head could have rested on his shoulder for another few minutes. Maybe if he played his cards right, she'd sleep in his bed again tonight? The prospect of holding her while she slept, waking up beside her, made him eager to get home and see how he could maneuver it . . .

Christ. Who am I anymore?

He was trying to come up with a way to get Hannah into bed so they could have an entirely platonic sleepover. Did he even own a dick anymore?

She'd probably be dreaming of another man the entire time.

Counting the minutes until she went back to LA.

Fox handed the card to his mother, realizing he'd nearly mangled the damn thing in his fist.

"Thank you, Fox," Charlene sang, leaning forward to cover the microphone. "You serious about that girl, son?"

He was caught off guard by the question. Probably because he'd never spoken to his mother about girls before. Not since he'd turned fourteen and she'd made him watch an online tutorial on how to apply a condom. After which she'd put an empty coffee can in the pantry and kept it full of singles and fives at all times. She'd told him it was there, pointedly, without explaining the exact purpose. But he'd known she was supplying him with condom money. Before he'd ever had sex, she'd predicted his behavior.

Or maybe he'd behaved a certain way because it had been expected.

Fox had never really considered that possibility. But over the course of the last week, there'd been a sense of emerging from a fog. Looking around and wondering how the hell he'd gotten to that exact spot. Empty hookups, no responsibilities, no roots digging into the earth. Had he been living this way too long to consider stopping?

You have stopped, idiot.

Temporarily.

Right.

With his mother's question still hanging in the air, Fox glanced back at Hannah. God, every cell in his body rebelled at the idea of meeting another woman—not Hannah—in Seattle. But he'd tried to escape himself before and it blew up in his fucking face. It left scars and taught him a painful lesson about the impression he gave people simply by existing. And he wasn't going to try it again, was he? For this girl who could decimate him by choosing someone else? In a sense, she *had* chosen someone else already.

"No," he finally answered his mother, sounding choked. "No, we're friends. That's it." He flashed her a grin that almost hurt. "You know how I am."

"I know you came home from school every day since freshman year smelling like Bath and Body Works." She chuckled. "Well, be careful with her, will you? There's something about her. Almost like she's protective of you even though she barely reaches your chin."

He caught the urge to tell Charlene that, yeah, that's exactly how she made him feel. Protected. Wanted. For reasons he couldn't have fathomed before meeting her. She liked him. Liked spending time with him.

"I'll be careful with her." His voice almost shook. "Of course I will."

"Good." She switched hands covering the microphone so she could reach up and cradle the side of his face. "My darling heartbreaker."

"I've never broken anyone's heart."

That was true. He'd never been close enough to anyone for that to be a possibility. Not even Melinda. He might have given his college girlfriend more of himself than anyone who came before, but they'd been nowhere near as close as Fox and Hannah.

Did he want to get even closer to Hannah?

If Sergei was out of the picture, what would closer look like?

A relationship? Hannah moving to Westport? Him moving to LA? What?

It all sounded completely ridiculous in the context of Fox's life.

"And, Jesus, I'm not going to start now," he added, shooting his mother a wink. "You want me to drop the blender off to Eleanor?"

Her smile dimmed slowly. "Are you sure?"

"I think I can handle it."

Charlene hesitated slightly before hefting up the small appliance, clearance sticker still attached to one side, handing it to her son. Fox stepped down off the stage and made his way back to the table. Everyone turned to watch him go by—or look at the blender, rather—like vipers in the grass. He set it down in front of Eleanor, pretending he didn't notice the tension at the table. Maybe if he ignored it, they would follow his lead.

Wishful thinking.

As soon as he set the blender down in front of Eleanor, Paula pounced.

Her bony fingers dug into the top of the box, but Eleanor was no rookie. She'd anticipated the move and started stabbing at Paula's hands with her blotter, leaving blue marks on the woman's skin. A hubbub ensued, bingo players shuffling around to get a better look at the action. Confident he could defuse the stressful situation—he was a king crab fisherman, after all—Fox inserted himself in between the women, giving them his best smile, in turn.

"Ladies. Let's end the night friends, huh? Let me get you both a soda from the snack bar and—"

Eleanor swung the blotter and got him right in the center of the forehead.

Hannah gasped, her hands flying up to cover her mouth.

And then her shoulders started to shake.

Could he really blame her for giggling? There was a giant blue dot in the middle of his forehead. He was a human bingo card. Weirdly, he was enjoying her happiness, even though it was at his expense. "Really, Hannah?" he drawled.

She dissolved into laughter, no longer trying to hide it. "Does anyone have a tissue?" she asked through her tears. "Or a wet wipe?"

"That's going to take some scrubbing," called someone from the cheap seats.

On her way around the table, someone pressed a pack of tissues into Hannah's hand, and she continued toward him, almost stumbling she was laughing so hard. And before Fox knew it, he was allowing Hannah to take his hand and pull him out the side door into the cool, misty night.

The rain had stopped, but moisture lingered in the air along with the distant smell of the ocean. Streetlamps cast yellow beams on puddles, turning them into pools of wavy, wind-blown light. Traffic moved in a hush on the nearby highway, the occasional big rig letting out a long-winded honk. It was a setting that, over the last seven months, might have made him feel lonely and exasperated with himself for missing Hannah. But there wasn't any loneliness now. There was only her. Opening the pack of tissues with her teeth, taking one of them out, and bringing the soft sheet to his forehead, her body still racked by laughter.

"Oh my God, Fox," she said, moving the tissue in circles. "Oh my God."

"What? You've never seen a geriatric hit job before?"

Her peal of renewed mirth rang through the quiet parking lot and shot his heart up into his mouth. "You tried to tell me bingo needed crowd control, but I didn't believe you. Lesson learned." She was giggling so hard, she could barely keep her arm up, the appendage repeatedly dropping to her side. "You were so confident, the way you stepped in between them." She dropped her voice to mimic him. "Ladies, ladies. Please."

"Yeah," he muttered. "Apparently you're not the only one who's immune to me, huh?"

He didn't mean to say it out loud, but it was too late to trap the words.

They were out there, and Hannah wasn't laughing anymore.

Wind blew through the scant space between them, whispering and damp in the silence, making more of those perfect curls at the sides of her forehead. And Fox realized he was holding his breath. Waiting for her to let him down gently.

He forced a chuckle. "Sorry, I meant—"

"I'm not immune," she breathed. "I'm far from immune to you."

The soft admission made his knees feel like fucking jelly, but right on the heels of that, he went hard. Everywhere. Each one of his muscles pulled taut, his cock turning thick in his briefs. "How far?"

Sandbags weighing down her eyelids, she let him see the answer. Her thirst for him. And in response, her name caught in his throat, his tone one of surprise. Relief.

Slowly, Hannah moved more thoroughly into the shadow of the building, turning and leaning back against the wall, reversing their positions in a deliberate dance, taking her time tracing the planes of his face. Wrecking him with her simple, perfect touch. The way she curled her fingertips into the collar of his shirt and drew him down, down, so they could exhale roughly against each other's mouths.

"Kiss me and find out."

He made a halting sound and moved, unable to stop himself now that he'd been given permission, catching her hips in his hands and gradually pinning her to the brick barrier, molding their lower bodies together until she whimpered.

"You're sure."

"Yes."

"Thank you, Jesus."

Where the hell to start? If he kissed her mouth first, he swore he might eat her whole, so he zeroed in on her neck, fisting her ponytail and tugging left, giving himself a clear path up to her ear and breathing a trail up that incredible softness, finishing his exhale just beneath her lobe. He savored her cry greedily, rejoicing in the way she went limp between him and the brick wall, her fingers twisting in the front of his shirt for purchase.

Still—still—worried he might implode if he actually allowed himself the singular flavor of Hannah's mouth, he nonetheless attacked those parted, waiting lips, groaning brokenly as her taste sank into his bones, made him light-headed.

God. Oh God.

He wrapped his tongue around hers and pulled hard, once, twice. He sensed her awareness, her anticipation, her hips squirming where he kept them stationary on the wall. Her movements rubbed against his erection, working him the hell up. So intensely worked up, so eager to fuck, he recognized immediately that he'd never, not once, wanted anyone like this.

Hannah was good. Hannah was right.

Being inside her would be a celebration, not merely part of a routine.

There was nothing typical about this. Or practiced. It was a spontaneous combustion of the urges he'd been suppressing where Hannah was concerned, both physical and emotional, and that implosion bred an urgency in him.

Now. He needed her now.

Fox dropped his hips down and lifted her slightly, creating friction against her sex, and her eyes rolled back, hands pulling him closer. Their mouths moved in a frantic rhythm, tongues meeting in long strokes, his hands traveling down her hips and up the valley of her sides, sensitizing the smooth skin beneath her shirt. Making her wet and pliant. He knew that truth like he knew the sea.

"You a virgin, Hannah?" Fox rasped, lightly scraping his teeth up her throat.

"No," she whispered, eyes dazed.

"Thank God," he growled, growing impossibly harder. Hungrier. "Once I'm good and deep, I don't think I'll be able to slow down."

He surged up with his hips again, watching her face closely, memorizing her tiny gasps of air, relishing the way her tits dragged up and down on his chest, nipples erect. God, this sweet, horny girl. He couldn't wait to get her out of that bra and panties. Get her splayed out, nothing in the way of his tongue, his fingers, his cock. She'd be screaming down the mother-fucking building tonight—

A shrill sound splintered his thoughts apart.

A phone ringing.

No. No, phones had no place here. Phones didn't matter.

They were part of reality, and this . . . this was way better than any reality he'd ever known. One where he didn't feel like an actor phoning in his part. But the sound kept up, over and over, vibrating where their hips met until, finally, they broke apart, foreheads pressing together as they looked down at the source of the noise. "M-my phone," Hannah stuttered, breathing hard.

"No."

"Fox . . ."

"No. God, I love your fucking mouth."

Their lips clashed again, battling to get the best taste, before she pulled her mouth away, neck losing power, eyes glazed over. "We can't just . . . here. We c-can't." She visibly struggled to form coherent thoughts, and Christ, could he relate. His head was overflowing, taking every particle of common sense with it. "Your mother is inside and there are things, like talking things, we have to do. I think?"

"Talking things," he exhaled gruffly, holding her chin steady, tipping it up so he could look at her beautiful face. "I talk to you more than I've ever talked to anyone, Hannah."

She blinked. Softened. "I want you to. I love that you do."

"Yeah?"

"Yeah. But . . ."

Her phone rang again, and he gritted his teeth, needing to hear what was going on in her head. Maybe it would help him figure out what was happening in his own. Because as far as he could tell, he was getting really damn close to either ruining his friendship with Hannah or being turned down again.

He loathed both of those options.

Sleeping together would mean potentially hurting her feelings when he couldn't give her any more than sex. And it would be a cold day in hell before he asked this girl to be friends with benefits. If another man suggested that to her, he would deck the asshole. How could he do the same?

Or she might not be immune, but didn't want him like this. Not enough, anyway. The lust might be there, but her willpower was strong enough to overcome it. Because ultimately she wanted someone else.

His chest lurched, a nerve starting to jump behind his eye.

"Go ahead and answer it," he rasped, easing her against the wall and backing off, turning to shove a handful of fingers through his hair.

Better to have her take the call than deliver him *that* blow, right?

"Shauna," Hannah said a second later into the phone, her breath still a touch labored. "Please tell me you have good news."

A long pause.

She sucked in a breath and turned in a circle, patting her pockets as if looking for a pen somewhere on the rain-soaked ground. Fox opened the notes application on his phone and handed it to her, nodding when she gave him a grateful look. Hannah stopped moving abruptly, both devices lighting up her face. "Tomorrow?" She shook her head. "No way they could pull that off. No way I can pull that off. Right?"

What? Fox mouthed.

She held up a finger. "Okay, could you send me their contact info and the address of the recording studio? Thank you! Thank you so much, Shauna. I owe you."

Hannah dropped the phone to her side, looking almost as dazed as when they were kissing. "What's happening, Freckles?"

"The band I want for Henry's shanties? They're leaving on tour in two days. For six months. They're going to be in the studio tomorrow recording some reels for Instagram and—"

"Reels. You lost me."

"It's not important." She waved the phones. "They like the material I sent and can work through the night on arrangements. Lay down a demo of the tracks tomorrow. The money I offered is a lot for an indie band to pass up. So is the opportunity to be on a film soundtrack. If Sergei likes what they do, they'll make time on tour to come back and record for real." A few seconds went by. "I mean, I could wait and try to find an LA band. But I know the way Sergei works and he'll lose interest in the whole idea if I don't move fast."

Hannah swiped her thumb over the screen of her phone, tapping. She closed her eyes when a woman's throaty growl filled the air outside the church hall, accompanied by twin fiddles and a snare drum—hand slowly lifting to her throat, the mouth he'd so recently kissed curling into a smile.

"This is them," she said. "I'm definitely going to Seattle."

Fox realized he was smiling back at her, because his heart wouldn't let him do anything else when she was happy. "No, Freckles. We're going to Seattle."

She brightened. Actually brightened at the news he'd be coming along. Did she really think he'd let her travel alone? "But your fishing trip . . ."

"Not until Wednesday morning. That gives us the entire day tomorrow."

"Okay," she breathed, shifting, then reaching out a hand for him to take. Leaving it there for a long moment, her expression vulnerable until he grabbed on, his throat in a manacle. Hannah hesitated to move back toward the bingo hall right away, and Fox sensed their earlier discussion was far from over. The same way a red sky meant rain was coming, Hannah needed every loose end tied together. And in this case, the loose ends were inside him. She wasn't going to stop digging until she found and identified them one by one.

Part of Fox was relieved as hell that she cared enough to try. But the rest of him, the man who guarded his wounds like a junkyard dog, had his back bunched up beneath the collar. She was either going to pour salt into those wounds by rejecting him . . . or force him to suture himself. Was he even close to prepared for either one?

No.

Since college, his defense mechanism had been to bail out before he could be patronized or reminded he was only good for one thing. But bailing wasn't going to be possible with Hannah. Not in the way he usually did it—by pulling a disappearing act. God no. He didn't *want* to disappear on her. But he could put a stop to this snowballing expectation of sex between them. Now. He could do that before she pulled the rug out from under his feet. Because with Hannah? He wouldn't survive the landing.

Chapter Eighteen

The ride home was quiet.

They returned to the church hall to say a quick good-bye to Charlene, and then Fox held Hannah's hand all the way to his car. He opened the door for her like they were on a proper date, a muscle flexing nonstop in his cheek. Charged silence followed as he got them back onto the highway. What was he thinking?

What was *she* thinking?

Her thoughts were in disarray, like a tornado had blown through.

That kiss.

Holy hell.

The one they'd shared at the cast party was the gentle opening notes of "The Great Gig in the Sky." But the one against the church wall was that wailing solo three-quarters of the way through the song. The one that never failed to make her want to wax poetic about the complexity of women and their turbulent hearts.

And speaking of turbulence, there was no better description for what Fox's skilled mouth had done to her. Her body had responded like a flower finally being given sunlight, desperate and starved. Even now, she could still feel the zap of electricity in her fingertips, the dampness on the seam of her jeans.

Once I'm good and deep, I don't think I'll be able to slow down.

At the memory of that blunt pronouncement, Hannah turned her head and moaned soundlessly into her shoulder, the intimate muscles below her waist catching and releasing. Were they going home to have sex? Was that what she wanted?

Yes.

Obviously.

There was little doubt that sex with Fox would be mind-blowing. She'd known that since meeting him last summer. But if he thought they didn't have a reason to talk first? To solve some things? He was out of his ever-loving mind. Their relationship was a complicated riddle that got more confusing every day. They were good friends, highly attracted to each other. They'd behaved like a couple tonight, no denying that. No denying how much she'd liked it, too. Holding his hand under the table, sharing private jokes with their eyes, no words necessary.

Her feelings for Fox were growing at an exponential rate, with no signs of slowing down, and she could only liken it to heading for a steep waterfall in a kayak. Hannah might mean more to Fox than the average girl, but that didn't mean he wanted to be more than friends.

Charlene's flinch popped into Hannah's head, and she traced her eyes over Fox's stiff jaw, his hair made messy by his own fingers. And not for the first time, she saw someone who was scared. His expression reminded her of the afternoon she'd turned him down in the guest room, stripped him of his sensual power. She saw that same trepidation now. Like maybe . . . maybe he did want to be the man who held her hand at bingo and drove her to Seattle, but flinches and leather bracelets and hang-ups from the past got in his way. Made him doubt he could do it.

Was she reaching?

Hannah dragged her eyes off his perfect profile, watching the windshield wipers move in their rhythmic pattern on the glass, catching the obscuring rain and smoothing out the view, making it clear so they could move ahead. Doing it over and over again until the rain finally stopped.

What if she could do the same with Fox?

Stay steady, unwavering until his view cleared?

Was she strong enough for that?

Forget strong. Trying to lure this man out of bachelorhood was flat-out self-destructive, and it could end with her heart in tatters. Although walking away, going back to Los Angeles, as if Fox wasn't claiming more and more acreage in her heart, seemed infinitely worse than trying.

Oh boy. A sign for Westport passed on the side of the road, but it might as well have said Trouble Ahead.

Hannah swallowed hard. "So, um"—she clutched the nylon of the seat belt—"are you sure about driving me to Seattle in the morning? I have no idea what to expect when I get to the studio. Could be a lot of waiting."

"I'm sure, Hannah." He cut her a sidelong glance. "Now ask me what you really want to ask me."

Her stomach flopped over at the continual proof that he knew her so well. "Okay." The pulse at the base of her neck sped up. "You, um . . . we . . . um . . . You know, that was definitely kind of foreplay back there, right? Like, you asked if I'm a virgin and that seems like, yeah, you were checking for a reason. A reason like sex."

His long fingers stretched on the steering wheel, then gripped it seemingly tighter. "That's accurate enough. Keep talking."

"Well. I guess I'm wondering what would happen after. After we did that. If we did that."

He rolled a shoulder. "Wait for me to get hard again. Hit a different position."

"Fox."

"Hannah. I can't answer what I don't know," he said through stiff lips. "What do you want me to say? Do I want to fuck you? Yes. Oh my God, I"—his eyes closed briefly, those fisherman's hands flexing on the steering wheel—"I want you underneath me so bad that I can't lie in bed without already feeling you there. I've never even had you, and your body haunts mine."

That took the breath right out of her lungs, leaving her winded. Thank God he kept going, because there was no chance of her speaking with that statement hanging in the air. *Your body haunts mine.*

"Look"—his chest rose and fell hard—"it's better if we don't. You wouldn't believe how much it kills me to say that. But the fact that you're already asking me what happens afterward is a good sign it's a bad idea. Because what happens afterward, Freckles, is I usually call a cab and get the hell out."

"Why?"

"I guess . . . so I can own the fact that I'm just about sex . . . before they do. All right?" he said in a burst. "I'd rather leave instead of seeing that look on anyone's face ever again. Almost like . . . *Wow, how cute. The pretty boy thought this was more than a quick fuck.* Owning who I am is easier than getting hit with the proof that I've been used. No one gets to make me feel shitty. And it's not just the women making me feel like a joke. It's . . ."

"Keeping talking," she said, forcing herself to take in the hard confession, to keep treading water for him so he could let it all out. "Who else makes you feel that way?"

It took him a moment to continue, his gaze pinned straight ahead on the road. "When I get a text or a phone call in front of the crew, if I even hint that I might not be interested in whatever empty hookup is being thrown into my lap, they treat me like something is wrong with me. It's always been like that. The male pressure to live up to this expectation—and I don't even know when the hell it was set."

Heat pressed in behind her eyes. This was not okay. None of it was okay. But she wanted, needed, to know the name of every ugly truth swimming around inside him. "It's wrong every time someone makes assumptions about what you feel or want. You set your own expectations for yourself and there's nothing . . . less masculine about saying no, if that's what they're putting on you. Jesus. Of course there isn't."

His throat worked long and hard. So long she wasn't sure he was going to respond. "If I'd met *you* in college, Hannah, I could have excused the shit I did before. Chalked it up to wild oats or something—and been your man. Through and through. But now I've just been doing this so damn *long*. I've . . . paved over whatever chance I had at a clean slate. I've become what people seemed to want me to be. I've earned my reputation, and as good as you are, as sweet and fucking wonderful as you are, Hannah, I don't want to be the one thing you fail at. Or the choice you question." He cursed under his breath, pushed restless fingers along the back of his neck. "I won't kiss you again. I shouldn't have done it tonight. I know better. If we weren't interrupted . . ."

When he threw the car into park, she realized they were already outside his building, the ocean whitecaps appearing and disappearing across the road.

Silence dropped like a knife in the car, nothing to fill it except the lap of waves on the rocks and their accelerated breathing.

"Even if we weren't interrupted tonight, we'd still be having this conversation," Hannah said.

He was already shaking his head. "Why? What are you trying to get out of this little chat?" His mouth twisted, and she saw something in his face she'd never seen before. Something she couldn't quite name. "Anyway, you've obviously got the director hooked now." His swallow was loud enough to drown out the waves. "Maybe . . . maybe you should focus on that. Him."

"I turned him down," Hannah said. "When he asked if we could go out once we're back in LA, I said no."

It was blatantly obvious how hard he tried to hide his relief, but she saw it. She saw it blare through him like a siren, tension melting from his muscles, his eyes, his jaw. And she knew that unnamed emotion she'd seen before had been jealousy. "Well," he said, stiffly, after a few seconds had ticked by. "Maybe you shouldn't have done that. Sex is the only satisfaction you can get from me."

"No. It's not." Her voice shook. "I get satisfaction from holding your hand. Hearing you sing. Being your friend—"

"Being my friend?" He scoffed. "Then it's a good thing we're not going to fuck, because you'd just be another hookup to me afterward."

Hannah recoiled like she'd been slapped, shock and hurt punching a hole in her throat. Blindly, she reached for the passenger-side door handle and pulled, throwing herself out of the car. Ignoring his panicked call of her name, she took the outside stairs leading to his second-floor apartment two at a time, accelerating when she heard his steps pounding behind her.

She reached his door, her hands shaking as she tried to locate the apartment key in her pocket. She found it but never got the chance to slide it into the lock, because Fox was behind her, wrapping her tightly in his arms, drawing her back against his chest. Hard. "I didn't mean that," he said into her hair, pressing his lips to the crown of her head. "Please, Freckles. You need to know I didn't mean that."

Thing was, she did know.

There was the pink Himalayan salt lamp, hidden record player, introducing her to his mother, singing the shanty for her, offering to drive her to Seattle. The Fleetwood Mac record. Seven months' worth of texts. Even the way he was holding her now, his breath racing in and out, like he'd break down if she stayed mad. She knew he didn't mean the hurtful thing he'd said. She knew. But that didn't mean his dismissive words didn't sting.

Hannah realized in that moment that she could run away from the potential hurt that would come from fighting for Fox. Or she could hold her ground. Refuse to back down. Which would it be?

Fight. Like a leading lady.

He was worth it.

Even if a relationship between them wasn't possible or couldn't work out, she wasn't going to let the hideous beliefs inside him fester forever. She refused.

There wasn't a label for what they were to each other. Friends who burned to sleep together didn't quite communicate the gravity of what existed between them, waiting to be unearthed. But she knew this wasn't about curing him or being the best supporting actress. She wasn't falling into a pattern. Being supportive, as she'd done so many times in the past, was easy. So easy. As was being on the periphery and not an active part of the narrative. But this time, the consequences of her actions in *this* story could determine her future. Not a friend's and not her sister's.

Hers. And Fox's.

Did they continue their story together or apart?

She couldn't imagine the latter. Not for the life of her. Unfortunately, that didn't mean he felt the same. Even if he did, a relationship could be too much to hope for at this stage. They could end up friends *only*—that was a real possibility. One that made her stomach sink to the floor. Making the decision to be the one who pushed for a future together was scary. Terrifying. It made failure and rejection a possibility. He was worth fighting for, though. If anything forced Hannah to dig in and remain strong, it was the need to prove that to Fox. To *make* him believe in himself.

Even if it benefitted some other girl someday—and not her. She was unselfish enough to show him what was possible. That letting someone else in didn't have to be scary. She could do that, couldn't she?

Hannah took a deep breath for courage and turned in Fox's arms. She only caught a fleeting glimpse of his tortured eyes before lifting up on her toes and molding their lips together. Kissing him.

Momentarily surprised, it took him a few seconds to participate, but when he did, it was with gusto. He let out a broken, surrendering moan into her mouth, stumbling forward and pressing Hannah against the door, his hands lifting to frame her face, their mouths moving together feverishly in promise and apology.

Breaking away before it went too far might have been the hardest thing Hannah had ever done in her life, but she managed it, ending the kiss and rubbing her forehead against Fox's, shaken by the throb of energy between them.

"I'll see you in the morning," she whispered against his mouth.

Turning from his dazed expression, she let herself into the apartment and beelined for the guest room. She closed herself inside and slid down the back of the door, ending in a pool of hormones and resolve on the floor.

Better get some sleep. Fox and his deeply rooted doubts would still be there when the sun came up. Maybe if she had more time in Westport, she could chisel away at them little by little. Hope he'd eventually realize he was capable of a healthy commitment. She was running short on time, though. Her only option was to work with the days she had remaining.

Tonight he'd told her his modus operandi was to leave before any woman could demean him. Well, Hannah wasn't going to allow that. She could show up after their argument, after the hurtful words and revelations, and prove their relationship was resilient. That he could be part of something stronger than the pull of the past. That she could look him in the eye and respect him and care. She could show up, period. That was what she'd been doing all along, perhaps subconsciously, and she wasn't getting off course now. Hopefully she would leave Fox with the belief, the possibility, of more.

The courage and confidence to try again.

Hannah's eyes landed on the folder of sea shanties resting on her bed.

Yes, tomorrow she'd fight, in more ways than one.

Chapter Nineteen

Fox stood at the stove, spatula in hand, his gaze fastened to the door of the guest room, every cell in his body on high alert. Who was going to walk out that door? Or, more importantly, what was her game?

He'd barely slept at all last night, replaying the drive home. Every word she'd said, the meaning behind that kiss outside the apartment. What the hell was she playing at? He'd told her, plain as day, that they weren't going to bed together. That she should stick with her director, because nothing more than friendship could come from this thing between them.

Why did all those statements seem so empty now?

Probably because if she walked out of the guest room at this moment and kissed him, he would drop to his knees and weep with gratitude.

I'm wrapped around her little finger.

He needed to unwrap himself. Fast.

Didn't he?

Here he was, making her pancakes, more apologies for the inexcusable thing he'd said to her last night crammed up tight behind his windpipe. *Then it's a good thing we're not going to fuck, because you'd just be another hookup to me afterward.*

Christ, he didn't deserve to live after lying like that.

Or better yet, he *did* deserve to live with the expression on her face afterward and the knowledge that he'd put it there. Scumbag. How dare he? How dare he say poisonous shit like that to this girl who, perhaps unwisely, gave a damn about him?

He'd spent a long time trying to avoid the belittling expression on a woman's face when she implied he was a hall pass or a meaningless diversion. The one Melinda had all those years ago while lying in bed with his best friend. He'd never thought about seeing that look on Hannah's face—not until last night. Not until he'd confessed everything to her and his past had nearly crowded him out of the car.

If Hannah ever looked at him like that, she might as well slice the heart right out of his chest. Melinda's betrayal would be laughable compared to what Hannah's disappointment or dismissal would do to him. Even the possibility had caused him to strike first. To say something to push her away and protect himself in the process.

God. He'd *hurt* her.

And she might have expressed that pain, but . . . she'd forgiven him with that kiss.

That purposeful, no-holding-back kiss.

Which brought him back to his current worry. Who would walk out of the guest-room door? His best girl Hannah? Or Hannah with a plan? Because that kiss last night, the one that turned his dick into a stone monument, had resolve behind it. She'd stroked his tongue without any hesitation. Like she wanted him to know she meant it. She was all in. And that terrified him as much as it . . .

Teased hope to life in his chest.

Dangerous, stupid hope that made him ask questions like *What if?*

What if he just put his head down and dealt with the lack of respect from his crew? Took on some of the responsibilities he tried so hard to avoid?

Because someone worthy of Hannah would need to be responsible. Not him. Right? Just . . . someone. Whoever it was. He couldn't have an apartment totally lacking in character or comforts. He would need to have upward mobility in his job. Like going from a relief skipper to the captain. But that was just an example, because he wasn't referring to himself.

He wasn't.

Fox nodded firmly and flipped the pancake on the griddle, approximately 4.8 seconds passing before his attention snuck back to the door to watch the shadows move underneath. How ridiculous to miss someone he'd only seen the night before. Starting tomorrow, he'd be on the boat for five days. If he missed her after one night apart, 120 hours were going to be pretty damn inconvenient. Maybe he should practice blocking the emotion now.

You don't miss her.

He examined the churning in his chest.

Well, that hadn't worked.

"Hannah," he called, his voice sounding unnatural. "Breakfast."

The shadows stopped moving briefly, started again. "Coming in a sec."

Fox let out a breath.

Great. They were going to pretend like last night never happened. They were going to act like he hadn't spilled the insecurities he'd harbored for the majority of his life. Like he never revealed the seemingly well-natured ridicule he received from the crew. They'd kissed before and gotten over it.

This would be no different.

Why was the churn in his chest getting worse?

Maybe . . . he didn't want them to get over it.

When Hannah walked out of the bedroom, Fox's spatula paused in midair and he sucked up the sight of her like a vacuum cleaner.

No bun today. Her hair was down. Smooth, like she'd used one of those irons on it. And she wore a short, loose olive-green dress instead of her usual jeans. Earrings. Suede black boots that reached all the way up to her knees, making those hints of visible thighs look like dessert.

I should have jacked off.

It was hard enough to be around Hannah ordinarily. Spending the day with her in Seattle dressed for easy access? Torture. He wouldn't be able to blink without seeing the ankles of those boots crossed at the small of his back.

The smell of burning blasted him back to the present. Great. He'd decimated the pancake. Turned it almost totally black while ogling the girl who was making him consider buying some throw pillows and window treatments.

"Hey," she said, tugging on one of her earrings.

"Hey," he returned, picking up the burned pancake with his fingers and throwing it in the trash, pouring fresh batter onto the pan. "You look nice."

And I'd like to throw you down on the couch and devour you.

"Thank you."

Fox hated the tension hanging between them. It didn't belong. So he searched for a way to dispel it. "How late did you stay up making a road-trip playlist?"

"Too late," she answered without hesitation, wincing. "You can't really blame me, though. We're going to a recording studio in the grunge capital of the world. I'm overstimulated." She slid onto one of the stools in front of the kitchen island and propped her chin on a fist. "Sorry, babe. You're going to be sick to death of Nirvana and Pearl Jam by this afternoon."

That "babe" hung in the air like napalm, and he almost burned a second pancake. She proceeded to scroll through her phone, as if the endearment had never left her mouth, while it kicked him in the stomach over and over again. He'd called her "babe" before, too, but never like this. Never just . . . across the kitchen island in the broad daylight with the smell of warm syrup in the air. It was homey. It made him feel like one half of a couple.

Was this her plan? To walk out here after his ugly behavior last night and . . . stay? Not just in his apartment, but *with* him. Their bond intact. Unwavering. Because the fact that she knew every part of him, inside and out, and she was still sitting there . . . it was having an effect. The relief and gratitude that hit him was huge. Welcoming. And it was causing him physical pain not to hold her right now. Call her "babe," too, and give her a good-morning snuggle. Ask to hear about her dreams. Last night at bingo, he'd slipped into the role of boy-friend, and it was kind of scary how good it had felt. To hold her hand and laugh and let his guard down.

The more he thought of that final kiss last night, the more it felt like a promise. That she wasn't giving up on him? Or . . . the possibility of them?

Had he actually said the words "I won't kiss you again"?

Like actually said them?

That promise sounded absolutely ridiculous to him in the light of day. Especially when she took a bite of the pancake he'd made, making a husky little sound of pleasure at the taste, her finger dragging a path through the syrup on her plate and dip-ping into her mouth. Sucking on it greedily.

Was it hazardous to operate a motor vehicle with a dick this hard?

"I see what you're doing, Hannah."

She glanced up, startled, the picture of innocence. "What do you mean?"

"The dress. Calling me 'babe.' The finger sucking. You're trying to seduce me into thinking . . . this kind of morning thing could be normal for me."

"Is it working?" she asked, eyes momentarily serious as she took another bite.

He couldn't answer. Couldn't do anything but picture Hannah sitting there every single morning. Indefinitely. Knowing she'd be there. Knowing she *wanted* to be there.

With him.

"Might be, yeah," he admitted hoarsely.

Obviously startled by his confession, she paused mid-chew, swallowing with visible difficulty. Taking a moment to recover while they stared at each other over the counter. "That's okay," she said quietly. "That's good."

He had the sudden, overwhelming urge to go lay his head down in her lap. To surrender his will, which was thinning by the moment, and let her do with him what she would. He'd woken up with the intention of staying strong, committed to remembering all the reasons that being one half of a couple with Hannah was not in the cards. They'd almost escaped this visit unscathed. Hannah, most importantly. Less than a week to go—and he would be fishing for most of it. Giving her false hope now could lead to her being hurt and he would rather tie an anchor to his foot and jump overboard.

His resolve was already weakening, though.

The what-ifs were becoming more and more frequent.

There was still a stubborn voice in the back of Fox's head, telling him she deserved better than some responsibility-free tramp who had been bed hopping since he was in high school. But it was growing more and more subdued in the face of her . . . commitment to him. Is that what it was? All his cards were on the table. He'd taken off a layer of skin last night and exposed himself. Yet here she sat, not budging. Just being there. Right alongside of him. Permanent. And he was starting to re-alize the commitment already ran both ways. He'd formed it long before now. For Hannah, hadn't he? Somewhere along the line, he'd started thinking of Hannah as *his*. Not just his friend or girlfriend or sexual fantasy. His . . . everything.

And as soon as he admitted that to himself he . . . burned another pancake. But most importantly, the sense that she belonged to him—that they belonged to *each other*—took root.

Which explained why, a few hours later when they walked into the recording studio and several band members looked Hannah over with interest, Fox wrapped an arm around her shoulders and almost growled, *Back off, she's taken.*

This man was fully overboard.

Hannah's girl-crush on Alana Wilder was instantaneous.

The lead singer of the Unreliables was in the recording booth when they entered Reflection Studio, the sound of her throaty purr electrifying the air and holding Hannah in thrall. She approached the glass as if hypnotized, skin prickling with excitement, already imagining Henry's words belted out to the masses from the curvy redhead's throat.

Before she could lift a hand to the glass, as if to touch the music, Fox's warmth surrounded her, his palm rubbing up and down her bare arm. Tingles speared down to her toes, hair follicles sighing in contentment. Oh dear. She'd been wrong before. Traveling to grunge heaven to record a demo wasn't overstimulating.

This was.

With awareness coiling in her belly, Hannah tilted her head back to look at Fox questioningly and found his irritated gaze focused on something besides the woman belting out lyrics like she was born into magic.

Hannah followed his line of sight and found a couch occupied by three musicians, one holding a guitar, the second with a bass resting sideways in his lap, the third with a fiddle that looked like it had seen better days.

"Are you the girl from the production company?" asked the fiddle player.

"Yes." She extended a hand and walked toward the trio, finding herself moving in tandem with Fox, whose touch now rested on the small of her back. "Er . . . I'm Hannah Bellinger. Nice to meet you."

She shook hands with the guitar and bass players, noting they looked kind of amused by the fact that Fox was towering behind her like a bodyguard.

"Wow," Hannah breathed, tipping her head at the recording booth. "She's incredible."

"Isn't she?" This from the bass player, whose voice held a hint of the Caribbean. "We're just here for decoration."

"Oh, I'm sure that's not true." She laughed.

"We'll lose that job, too, now that you're here." The fiddle player stood, taking her hand and kissing her knuckles. "You're definitely easier on the eyes than us ugly bastards."

Fox's comically forced laughter lasted five seconds longer than the rest of theirs.

Hannah turned and raised an eyebrow at him over her shoulder.

What is wrong with you?

Seeming to realize the spectacle he was making of himself, he coughed into a fist and crossed his arms, but remained close. Was he jealous?

If she wasn't so shocked, she might have been . . . thrilled? Last night, she'd done a lot more than work on the grunge playlist to end all grunge playlists. While selecting songs, her determination to fight to change Fox's mind about himself had only built. She wasn't going back to Los Angeles without him knowing he could be more than some beautiful joke. A man who everyone expected to fulfill some bullshit destiny simply because he could. Not happening.

And maybe the fact that he could feel jealous was an indirect sign of progress? Maybe being jealous over her would prove to him he could want to get serious with . . . someone else someday?

If, for instance, he and Hannah weren't meant to be.

Hannah ignored the horrible burning in her breast and turned back around. "Have you had a chance to look at the songs I sent over last night?"

"We have. Been burning the midnight oil working on arrangements."

"You'll be happy with them," the bass player said, definitively, a musician's arrogance on full display. "No question."

The fiddle player gave her a look that was half chagrin, half apology for his bandmate. "Soon as Alana is done in there, we'll run through the shanties, make sure it all works for you."

She smiled. "That would be great, thank you."

The trio went back to their conversation, and Hannah returned to the glass to watch Alana, Fox coming up beside her. "What was that?" she whispered at him.

"What was what?"

"You're being weird."

"I'm being helpful. They were looking at you like a ten-tier birthday cake just walked in the door." He wasn't quite succeeding in pulling off a casual tone, an agitated hand lifting to scrub at the bristle on his jaw. "Musicians are bad news—everyone knows that. Now they'll leave you alone. You're welcome."

Hannah nodded, pretending to take him seriously. "I see." A few seconds of silence passed. "Thanks for the consideration, but no thanks. I don't need you running interference. If one of them is interested, I'll deal with it myself."

Now his eye ticced. "Deal with it how?"

"By deciding yes or no. I'm capable of doing that on my own."

Fox studied her as if through a microscope. "Why are you doing this to me?"

Hannah exhaled a laugh. "Doing what? Calling your bluff?" His jaw looked ready to shatter, his eyes revealing a hint of misery. "If you're jealous, Fox," she said quietly, "just say you're jealous."

Conflicting emotions waged a war on his face. Caution. Frustration. And then he visibly gave up the battle, standing in front of her naked with honesty. "I'm jealous as fuck." He seemed to be having a hard time getting breath into his lungs. "You're . . . *my* Hannah, you know?"

She tried very hard not to tremble or make a show of what was happening inside her. But there was a Ferris wheel turning at max speed in her stomach. Did he really just say that out loud? Now that he had, now that it was out there, she couldn't disagree. She'd been his for months. *Don't freak out and put him back on guard.*

Instead, she went up on her toes. "Yeah. I know," she whispered against his mouth.

Fox let out a relieved breath, his color returning gradually. He looked like he was right on the edge of making another admission, saying even more, his chest rising and falling. He wet his lips, his gaze raking over her face. But before he could say a word, the door of the booth was kicked open and out

came Alana, stomping into the lounge area. "All right, folks."
She clapped her hands twice. "Let's talk shanties before these
two start making out, yeah?"

Dealing with her imposter syndrome on the heels of Fox's
admission was no small task. Hannah felt pulled in several directions, acutely aware of the man stationed like a pillar at her
side, his exposed energy vibrating like a raw nerve, while also
determined to watch her artistic vision come to life.

Who was she to give an opinion on musical arrangements?

But after the third take, there was something not working
about the refrain in "A Seafarer's Bounty." It fell horizontal in
the middle, and as a listener, her interest flatlined, too, when
it should have been absorbed. The band seemed satisfied with
their angle, and, man, they were *so good*. Way better than she
should have expected on short notice. Why not just be grateful
and move on?

She stood beside Fox in the corner of the control room,
listening to the song's playback over the speaker, while on
the other side of the glass, the band was visibly preparing to
start the next song. Running through the lines individually.

Could she just interrupt the process with an opinion that
might be totally wrong?

"Just tell them what's bothering you," Fox whispered in her
ear, laying a lingering kiss on her temple. "You'll regret it if you
don't."

"How can you tell something is bothering me?"

He studied her face, almost seeming like he was battling the weight of his affection, nearly making Hannah's legs liquify. "You get this expression on your face when you listen to music, like you're trying to climb inside it. Right now, it looks like the door is locked and you can't get in."

"Yeah," she whispered, an ache moving in her breast. Unable to say more.

Fox nodded at her, his own voice strained when he said, "Kick it down, Hannah."

Adrenaline rippled up through her fingertips, along with a white-capped wave of gratitude. Urgency rushed in and she didn't hesitate a second longer. Approaching the microphone that extended up from the mixing desk, she pressed the button to talk. "Alana. Guys. The refrain on 'A Seafarer's Bounty.' When we get to 'trade the wind for her,' can we pause and embellish a little? How do you feel about drawing out the word 'wind' on a four-part harmony?"

"Make it sound like the wind," Alana called back, forehead wrinkling in thought. "I like that. Let's run through it."

Hannah let go of the talk button and exhaled in a rush, exhilaration coasting down from the crown of her head, down to her feet. When she leaned back, she knew she would land against Fox's warm chest, their fingers weaving together just like the music, rivaling the thrill of the band's next version of "A Seafarer's Bounty."

She'd been right. That one addition and it soared.

After that, the day was nothing short of a fairy tale.

In no way did the Unreliables live up to their name. In Hannah's head, they would henceforth be called the Reliables, but she sensed they'd be offended if she legitimized them, so she kept it to herself.

Sitting beside Fox on an old love seat, she listened to the band sing her father's songs about the ocean, tradition, sailing, home. At one point, Fox left and came back with tissues and only then did she realize her eyes had gone misty.

It sounded like a cliché, but they brought the words to life, made them curl and dance on top of the page, infusing them with sorrow and optimism and strife.

Alana seemed to feel every note, as if she'd known Henry personally, and lived through the triumphs and tragedies of his songs with him. Her band anticipated her and adjusted on the fly, boosting her, supporting her as she wove. Magic. That was how it felt to take part in the creative process. As an obsessive listener of music, Hannah had benefitted from that kind of inventiveness since she could remember, tucked away in the worlds turning inside her headphones, but she'd always taken it for granted. She couldn't see herself doing that ever again.

They ordered lunch in to the studio, the band members telling Hannah and Fox stories from the road. At least until they found out Fox was a king crab fisherman and then all they wanted were his stories. And he delivered. Brushing his thumb up and down the base of Hannah's spine, he recounted the close calls, the worst storm he'd ever seen, and the pranks the crew played on each other.

On the next take, there was even more flavor to Alana's vocals. Hannah and Fox watched it happen from outside the booth, his arm settling around her shoulders and pulling her close. He performed the action as if testing it, testing them both, and then one corner of his mouth edged up, his hold tightening with more confidence.

"Your stories did that," Hannah managed, nodding at Alana, then looking up at Fox to find him staring back down at her. "Do you hear that note of danger in her voice? You inspired her. The song is richer now because of you."

Fox stared back at her stunned, then moved in slowly to lay a kiss on her lips. With the sides of their bodies pressed together, they let the music wash over them.

Hannah wanted to stay and listen to them record the entire demo, but Fox had to leave in the morning, so they parted ways with a round of hugs, well-wishes on their tour, and a promise to have the digital recording files to Hannah the next day. She didn't realize her fingers were intertwined with Fox's until they were halfway to his car. Overhead, clouds were beginning to thicken in the early evening sky, as they were wont to do in Seattle, passersby on the sidewalks carrying umbrellas in preparation for the moisture collecting in the atmosphere.

Their earlier conversation came back to her in stark clarity, and the thoughtful expression on Fox's face suggested he was thinking about it as well. Would they pick up where they left off?

Doubtful. He would pretend it never happened. Kind of like this morning when he'd tried to gloss over the gravity of the prior evening by making pancakes and greeting her oh-so-casually.

Fox hit the button on his key ring to unlock the car door, opening the passenger side for Hannah. Before she could let go of his hand and climb in, he held fast, keeping her upright.

"If you're up for a detour . . ." he said, twisting one of her flyaways around his fingers and tucking it behind her ear. "There's somewhere I want to bring you."

His face was so close, his eyes so breathtakingly blue, her body so attuned to his size and warmth and masculine scent, that if he asked her to swim to Russia with him, she'd have vowed to give it the old college try. "Okay," she murmured, trusting him a hundred percent. "Let's go."

Chapter Twenty

$\mathcal{F}$ox had always prided himself on not taking anything seriously.

The memory of his failed reinvention burned in the center of his chest like a cattle brand, so he'd spent years doubling down, leaning into an identity that perhaps burned him even worse, but at least he could be good at it. It was what everyone expected, and there wouldn't be any more painful surprises.

And now he was going to open up wide, expose himself to all manner of outcomes he couldn't control. Because he was in love with Hannah. Stupid, hot-under-the-collar, pulse-tripping love that crowded his chest and throbbed in his fingertips. Might as well face it, he'd started stumbling last summer, and now? Now he was flat on his ass with canaries taking laps around his head.

He loved her humor, her tenacity and bravery, the way she defended the people she loved like a soldier in battle. He loved the fact that she didn't shy away from the tough subjects, even though they scared him in the moment. Her iron will, the way she closed her eyes and mouthed song lyrics like they were baptizing her. Her face, her body, her scent. She'd infiltrated him, become a part of him before he'd realized what was happening, and now . . .

He didn't want her out. He wanted to stay locked in her goodness.

And Jesus Christ, he might as well be walking on a tightrope across the Grand Canyon. In his experience, the only thing that came from reaching past his capabilities was failure. Getting slapped down and sent back to the beginning. But as they'd sat in the recording studio, Hannah leaning into his side, as if she belonged to him—it had felt so damn good—he'd started to wonder again . . . what if. What if.

She was set to return to LA soon, so he needed to answer that question. Or he was going to wake up one morning and put her on a bus out of his life, and the very idea of that covered his skin in ice.

Driving up to the security gate and handing a twenty-dollar bill to the guard, he still didn't have an ending to the what-if question. But he did have absolute faith in Hannah's ability to draw it out of him, if he let her. If he truly dropped the last of his defenses, she'd guide him there. Because she was the most extraordinary, loving, intelligent being on earth, and he cared about her so much it sometimes stole his ability to think straight.

"Where are you taking me?" She split a look between him and the windshield, the greenery rolling past on either side, draped in twilight. "I love surprises. Piper threw me a surprise party when I turned twenty-one and I had to lock myself in the bathroom because my nonstop tears of joy were embarrassing everyone."

Fox, having an easy time picturing that, smiled. "What is it that you love so much about them?"

She tugged the hem of her dress down, drawing his eye. "The fact that someone thought about me, I guess. Wanted me to feel special." She bit her lip and glanced over at him from the corner of her eye. "I bet you hate them, don't you?"

"No." Normally he might have left it at that, but he wasn't being charming or elusive or easy tonight. He was taking the words in the back of his mind and letting them out of his mouth. Starting now. And every time he balked, he'd think of putting Hannah on a bus. He might not have a solution in mind, since keeping her in Westport—just for him?—seemed like a stretch, but when he let Hannah know his thoughts, he always felt closer to her afterward, always felt better, so he couldn't go wrong with that. "You're a surprise, Hannah. How could I hate them?" He cleared his throat hard. "Even familiar . . . you're a constant surprise."

Silence ticked by slowly. "That's a beautiful thing to say."

More words were pressing up against the inside of his throat, wanting to get out, but the actual surprise was coming into view up ahead and he wanted to see her reaction. "Anyway. We'll see if we can keep the crying to a minimum tonight." He put the car into park several yards from the art installation, circling around the back bumper to open her door, offering his hand. "Come on, Freckles."

Her smooth fingers slipped into his, a furrow forming between her brows as she took in the giant steel towers, Lake Washington spread out behind them. At this time of day, they were the only ones there, giving the attraction kind of a lonely, abandoned feeling. Ironic since he'd never felt less lonely in his life. Least of all while holding her hand. "What is this place?"

"It's the Sound Garden," said Fox, guiding her toward the water. "The towers were designed so that when the wind hits them, they play music."

Fox studied Hannah's face, watched it transform with wonder when she heard the first howling note travel through the towers, the haunting melody that somehow softened the air, thickening it like they were inside a snow globe, their surroundings moving slowly. The whitecaps, the clouds, even the shift of her hair all seemed to travel at a different, more languid pace.

Unlike Fox's heart, which was beating out of his chest.

"Oh my God." A fine sheen formed in her eyes. "I can't believe this is just . . . here. And I knew nothing about it? Fox, it's . . . incredible." A loud whistle of sound whipped in the air, and she closed her eyes, laughing. "Thank you. Wow."

He stared down at their linked fingers, and it gave him the strength he needed to leap. "I wanted to bring you here last summer. That weekend we went to the record convention. But I was afraid to suggest it."

She opened her eyes and studied him. "Afraid? Why?"

Fox shrugged a shoulder. "You'd come to Westport for your sister. Such a selfless thing to do, working on the bar and living in that dusty little apartment and . . . you deserved a day just for you. I'd already spent so much time searching for that convention, finding something you might enjoy, though. I got worried that showing you the Sound Garden on top of the expo might make how I felt obvious. Might tip my hand."

There was never a sight more beautiful than Hannah standing on the shore with the sunset making her glow, the wind teasing strands of hair across her mouth. "'Tip your hand,'" she repeated with a blink.

Keep going. Confess every last word.

Think of Hannah getting on a bus back to LA.

"I had it bad for you. If the convention didn't make it obvious, I thought for sure the Fleetwood Mac album would do it." His voice stumbled. "I've got it so bad for you, Hannah. Really"—he blew out a breath—"really bad. I tried to keep you out of here." He knocked his free fist against his chest. "But you won't go. You're never going to go. You just won't."

"Fox . . ." she murmured haltingly, her tone weaving in seamlessly with the howling of the towers. "Why is it bad?"

"God, Hannah. What if I'm not what you need? What if everyone knows it but you? What if you realize it's true and I have you . . . *then* lose you? That would fucking kill me. I don't know what to do—"

"I've got it really, really bad for you, too."

The oxygen in his lungs evacuated in a rush, leaving his thundering heart in its wake. "If you'd gone out with Sergei, I would have fucking lost it, Freckles. You know that? I'd have begged you on my hands and knees not to go anywhere with him. I've been going crazy waiting for you to call my bluff—"

"I wouldn't have gone." Her hold tightened on his hand. "It was only a meaningless crush, but even that . . . even that went away. And I just hung on to the idea of it, so I wouldn't have to admit that I knew. I knew exactly why you left that album for me."

His body almost buckled under the relief, but he clung to his caution. "And what it meant scared you. It should. I should scare you, Hannah. I don't know how to do this." He dug through the cobwebs in his chest to find the truth for her. "I've gotten used to the way everyone thinks of me as this . . . this fucking reprobate. Someone who lives to get their rocks off. A good time and nothing more. But if . . . Hannah, I swear to God, I can't handle them doubting my character when it comes to you. It would break me. Do you understand? To have people waiting and wondering when I'm going to screw it all up. That I couldn't handle. To have your name spoken with sympathy because you're with me. I can already hear them. *She's out of her mind. He'll never settle down. He's not a one-woman man.* I'll want to die hearing them say that shit. It's the one form of ridicule I can't take. When it's attached to *you*."

Her chest rose and fell like she'd just swum eight miles. "Fox, if we were together, my trust would be the only trust that matters. And you would have it. I know who you are. If other people haven't looked closely enough, that's their flaw. Their dilemma. Not ours."

He swallowed a fist-sized obstruction. "You'd trust me?"

"Yes."

The fact that she looked pissed at him for even asking made his throat close up, flooded him with so much adoration, he almost choked on it. "I don't know what trying looks like for us. I just know that I want to."

"Oh, Fox," she whispered, bringing them chest to chest and pressing close, laying a cool palm against his cheek. "We've been trying this whole time."

There was no way to keep himself from kissing her after that.

With his heart rupturing and repairing on repeat in his rib cage, Fox dropped his mouth down on top of hers and begged

her with his tongue and lips to save him from the middle of the
ocean where he'd been existing without her for so long.

Fox came on like a storm.

Hannah still hadn't quite managed to catch her breath after
all that was said, and she definitely wasn't going to get the
chance now. His lid was off, there was nothing left between
them, and, God, she was so glad she'd forced herself to wait
until the right time to let the dam break.

Their kiss was honest and raw and unquenchable, as real as
the rain starting to fall around them, soaking into the earth,
wind howling through the garden structures, trapping them
in the center of a force field.

Fox's hands were in her hair, tunneling through, as if desperate to touch every single strand while his mouth quite simply
fucked hers. He'd been holding himself at bay or maybe presenting his playboy facade to seem unaffected. But that was gone
now, dropped like a veil, and his hunger was brutally naked. And
she matched him, clinging to his dampening, sinewy shoulders,
plying herself on strokes of his tongue. His hands raked down
her spine, where they gathered the hem of her dress, exposing
her in degrees.

The kiss slowed momentarily, his eyes communicating the
question.

Can I?

Hannah was already nodding, skin enflamed, positive if
he didn't touch her, all of her, that very second, she was going
to melt into the ground along with the rain. But Fox didn't

give that a chance to happen, his big, capable hands plunging down the rear of her panties, taking hold of her bottom, claiming ownership with a rough squeeze. "Been dying to do this for months," he ground out against her lips, molding her buns in his hands. "Been wanting it in my hands, bent over in my lap . . ."

"Now seems like the ideal time," she gasped.

"Nah . . ." He proceeded to walk her backward, toward the car, his voice seductive, hypnotic. "Want to look at your beautiful face the first time I take you." He caught her mouth in a hard, wet kiss. "Am I going to take you now, Hannah?" Her back met the side of the car, and she moaned at the rough press of his muscular body, the drag of his hand around the curve of her hip where it wedged between their bodies, his fingertips on the verge of sinking down the front of her underwear now. "Are you going to let me touch it this time or tell me no again?" Those fingers pressed down on the swell of her mons. "If you want to say no, we'll stop. I've gotten pretty fucking good at waiting for you." His open mouth dipped to her throat, exhaling heat into the hollow. "Waiting for you is the best I've ever had."

"I don't want to wait. N-no. No waiting."

He chuckled, licked a path up to her ear, and bit down, almost buckling her knees. Were those her teeth chattering? She didn't have the chance to find out or be embarrassed, because Fox's mouth trapped her once again in a cyclone of sensation, those long, knowing fingers slowly, slowly traveling downward on her sex. Stopping right when they reached the good part and teasing with light side-to-side brushes that sent heat flaring down to her toes. When she was right on the verge of begging him to touch lower, Fox eased back from the kiss to watch her face, his middle finger parting her flesh, gently petting her clitoris. "Ah, babe." He dragged his bottom lip through his teeth. "This sweet little thing wet for me?"

"Yes," she managed, mentally coining a new phrase.

Death by Fox.

Hannah would never define him by his innate sexuality, but pretending he wasn't insanely skilled would be futile. Because God almighty. He wielded his abilities like a sword. He knew where to touch her, how to speak, understood the virtues of pacing, and her body appreciated that like nobody's business. Her intimate flesh grew damp so rapidly, she was actually shaking between Fox and the car. And he knew it. The knowledge was there in the total and utter confidence of the finger rubbing her clit, a second one joining it and pressing just that much harder, causing her head to fall back, a whimper racking her entire frame. "Oh . . . my God," she hiccupped.

He looked her square in the eye and ripped off her panties in one twist. "Haven't even started, Hannah." His knees landed on the soft earth in front of her, rain dripping off the ends of his dark-blond hair, moisture trickling down his cheeks. And he seemed to sense that she was about to float away on a cloud of never-before-encountered lust, because he barred his forearm across her hips, pinning her roughly to the car, and buried his mouth between her thighs, sinking, pushing, pulling his tongue through the split of her femininity.

Watching her the whole time. Observing her reaction to that first perfect, deliberate drag of friction. Fox groaned, his pupils dilating, forearm flexing against her belly.

That absolute, unabashed carnality gave her permission to palm her breasts through the bodice of the dress, chafing the heels of her hands over stiff nipples, enjoying the way he watched her through darkening eyes. She arched her back, allowing him to settle the instep of her foot on his shoulder and go deeper with every stroke of his eager tongue, his lips closing around her sensitive bud, sucking lightly, rhythmically until her muscles began to quicken, pulsing, her vision turning hazy, her head thrashing side to side on the car. "Oh my God. I'm already . . ." She panted, the sound ending on a moan, her fingers twisting in his wet hair. "It's already . . . I'm going to. It's coming. I'm coming."

As if he wasn't already doing enough, doing the most, he chose the moment of her confession to press his middle and index fingers inside her. Deep. Until he executed that move, she'd loved the light finesse of his touch, but unbeknownst to her, she'd been starving for that rough push. But Fox knew. He knew everything about everything, and God, oh God, he delivered it, standing halfway through her orgasm to thrust his fingers into her clenching heat. In and out, fast. No gentleness in sight. Just his open mouth groaning on top of hers, her moisture spreading down his thick fingers, the sky weeping around them.

"Fox," she gasped, holding on to his shoulders, almost alarmed by the intensity with which her legs trembled, her flesh constricting, releasing, his fingers entering and leaving her slowly, slowly with the ebbing of her orgasm.

And it wasn't enough, somehow. The best climax of her existence wasn't enough. Nothing physical would ever be enough without him—all of him—ever again. That unchangeable knowledge concreted itself inside her as their mouths connected, demolished, her fingers racing down his stomach to unfasten his belt.

"Need you. Need you."

He caught Hannah's wrist, dragging her palm up and down his erection, his teeth catching her bottom lip, pulling. "I'm ready for you. Been aching so long." He yanked down his zipper and planted both hands on the top of the car. "Touch me. Please. Get a fist around it and stroke me hard. Fuck me up."

How?

How was she continuing to get wet? She'd already hit the peak of all peaks.

The way he looked at her, that's how. The bald honesty of his words, the crude thrust of his hips when she circled him with a hand and pumped. Firmly, like he'd asked. Her breath growing choppy when his arousal swelled and stiffened more, impossibly, giving her fist even more ground to cover. "Oh. Jesus . . ." she exhaled before she could stop herself.

A glimmer of familiar cockiness in his eyes made her heart spin crazily. "Ah, come on, babe." He wet his lips, a groan building and breaking from his mouth, his attention fastened on the treatment of her hand, the way she choked him up and down, massaging him intimately. "You knew it had to be huge."

She breathed a laugh, and he did, too, though the husky sound quickly turned into hot, panting breaths against her forehead, gasped instructions for her to go faster. Faster, faster . . . until his breath began to labor, and he reached for the door handle leading to the backseat.

"In," he rasped, not waiting for her to comply, just ripping the door open, wrapping an arm around the small of Hannah's back and dragging her inside, not stopping until her back was flat on the seat, the crown of her head almost reaching the opposite door.

His body came down on top of her, their mouths connecting frantically, her fingertips searching for the hem of his T-shirt, ripping it off so she could feel his chest, touch it, kiss his bare skin. Levering up so he could do the same to her dress, her bra, all their clothes save his pants ending up on the floor in a matter of seconds, his remaining jeans pushed down to his knees by two pairs of eager hands, their mouths ravenous.

"I have to get a condom on or we're going to be in trouble," he said in between kisses, his hips moving between her thighs, mouth traveling up and down her neck. "For the record, I didn't plan on this happening in the backseat of my car."

"Oh, you just thought you'd bring me to the most romantic place in the world to someone like me and I wouldn't want to rip your clothes off?"

He panted a laugh and fumbled the wallet he'd just fished out of his jeans pocket. "I didn't think past telling you how I feel and hoping like hell it would mean something to you." He picked the wallet back up and ripped credit cards out one by one, his shaking hands dropping them everywhere. "Swear to God, the one time it counts and I can't be smooth to save my life."

Hannah had a playlist consisting of 308 love songs and not one of them could describe this moment accurately. Not even close. Realizing she loved this man while he ripped his wallet apart looking for protection, his hair falling into his eyes, muscles heaving under ink and a light layer of sweat. Sunset lit the car in a deep orange, and she felt that rich color spread inside her chest, too, where her heart battled to keep up with the love that bloomed freely and wildly, a lot like the spring storm creating warm, white noise around the car.

I love him. I love him.

But then. Fox ripped the condom wrapper open with his teeth and rolled it down his abundant length, forearms flexing in the golden glow of sunset, his jaw going slack while looking at the place between her legs with anticipation—and lust came roaring back to the forefront. As soon as he was covered, they dove for each other once more, not a hint of restraint in their kisses. They were skin to skin, weathered man of the sea pressing down on her softness, one hand separating them briefly to bring the thick head of his sex to the entrance of Hannah's.

And then he pushed inside her in one slow, smooth motion, rocking home.

Hannah hissed out a breath and dug her fingernails into his hips, blindsided by the ripple of unequaled pleasure that sped through her and pulled taut.

"Yes," she whimpered. "More."

As if the feel of her was unexpected, Fox heaved a curse and slapped his hand down on the rapidly fogging window above her head. "Jesus Christ, so hot and tight." He reared his hips back and punched forward, making a low sound of misery, a shudder passing through his frame. "No. Dammit." His body flexed with tension on top of her. "Stay still. Stay still. Wasn't kidding when I said I can't be smooth with you. Then you have to go and feel so fucking perfect . . ."

"You feel pretty smooth to me," she said on a jagged exhale, bearing down around him with her inner walls. Milking his thickness with her femininity. "Mmmm. Please. Fox."

"Please stop, Hannah, stop . . ." As if he couldn't control it, his lower body ebbed back and rolled forward sinuously, filling her slowly, touching all different spots along the way, and she cried out, drawing blood on his hips. "I've just needed you so fucking long," he gritted out.

"You don't think I love that?" She trailed her touch inward and gripped his flexed buttocks, slowly rocked him deeper, lifting her hips at the same time, earning a long, hoarse sound from his throat. "You don't think I love feeling the proof of how bad you need me?"

"You want it, I'll give it to you," he rasped, rolling their foreheads together, kissing her roughly, tangling their tongues. "You want anything, I'll give it to you."

"Show me how badly I make you need to come."

His nostrils flared, his eyes closing—and when he opened them back up, there was a trace of the devil in them. And she loved being trapped in the eye of that male determination. She loved the way his upper lip curled, his forearms crowding close on either side of her head, his mouth dropping to an inch above hers. "Knees up, Hannah." He pulsed inside her, pupils blocking out the blue of his eyes. "Let's see how deep I can get it before you scream."

Spoiler: it didn't take very long.

Dutifully, eagerly, she brought her knees up, grazing them along his rib cage and locking them high on his torso. His next thrust made her eyes roll back in her head, the second one making her squirm out of pure confusion. How and what was he reaching inside her that seemed to unlock some undiscovered force? Pressure rode low and threaded through her core, knitting her together so tightly, she couldn't think or breathe, the roof of the car looking more and more like the gates to heaven. With his open, grunting mouth on her neck, he rode her roughly, yet somehow cherishingly at the same time, his tongue and lips continuously worshiping her throat, his mouth finding hers to swallow her screams. Yes, she was screaming his name, and he was, indeed, as deep as possible, scooping her hips off the seat with hard drives that quickened, roughened, going faster and faster. His body flattened her, using the flesh between her legs in the most deliciously frantic way, as if desperate for her to acknowledge his desire—and she did.

She had her proof. She had it and then some.

"Fox," she wailed between her teeth.

"I know you're close. I can feel it."

"Yes. Yes."

"Loving that cock, aren't you?" His teeth scraped her lobe and bit down. "Been craving it the way I've been craving this hot-ass pussy, day and night. On land and off. Now give it up, girl. Show me you love being on that back for me."

Her orgasm wound tight, tighter, and she dug her heels into his bucking ass, her mouth wide and gasping against his shoulder, her sex squeezing in one never-ending pulsation. "Ohhh God. Oh God."

He broke, moaning in fits and starts, the tempo of his drives stuttering, his mouth latching on to hers and holding, air rattling from his nose, his hands fisting in her hair. "Hannah." A rough, desperate kiss, another one, robbing the soul straight out of her body. "Hannah. Hannah."

The hard body that had just propelled her to a height of bliss she never knew existed collapsed on top of her, gathering her close and breathing heavily, his heart galloping against hers. Her legs were still locked around his waist, their bodies slick with sweat, and she didn't see herself moving in the foreseeable future. Maybe ever. Apparently being boneless *was* a thing.

"You make me feel like I'm in the exact right place." He exhaled into her neck, kissing it reverently. "Nothing to run or hide from. Nothing I want to avoid."

She turned her head and their mouths melted together. "It's okay to trust that feeling. I have it, too."

Fox studied her face with such intensity in his blue eyes, she didn't dare draw a breath. Then he swallowed heavily and turned them onto their sides, facing each other, his arm keeping her close. And they stayed there, breathing in the scent of each other's skin, until the storm stopped.

Chapter Twenty-One

Fox cracked open an eye that felt like it had been welded shut.

When he saw the explosion of sandy-blond hair draped across his chest, a smile spread across his face, his heart lifting into his throat like an elevator and lodging behind his jugular. Hannah.

He didn't move a muscle. Yes, because he didn't want to disturb her. But mainly because he wanted to savor every little detail, soak them into his memory bank. Like the slope of her bare back, the dusting of tiny freckles that popped up along that smooth column, like stars in the sky over the ocean. He'd look at those stars completely different now. He'd revere them.

Very slightly, he lifted his head so his gaze could traverse her spine, lower to the sexy backside she'd definitely begged him to spank last night in the middle of the third . . . fourth round? They'd barely made it in the door before he'd stripped her down and carried her over his shoulder to the bedroom, kicking the door shut behind them. And there they'd stayed, only emerging once for chocolate ice cream and a sleeve of graham crackers.

To call it the best night of his life would be an inexcusable understatement. He'd been right to tell her everything. Because if he thought she was perfection on legs before, she'd completely unlocked now. Gone was the hesitation in her eyes. Apparently, opening up meant getting more in return. Considering he'd never get enough of Hannah, being honest was definitely the way to go.

What else could he give her, though?

Permanence, whispered a voice in the back of his head.

A sharp object materialized in his gut, prodding, digging in.

This morning he left for five days on the water. When he came back, the movie would be wrapped. Sweat broke out on his skin when he thought of her boarding that bus, but what the hell could he do about it? Ask her to move in? He'd just gotten over the hurdle of admitting his feelings—and not even the extent of them. Not the part about being in love with her. Not yet.

She had a job back in LA. The career she wanted as a music coordinator would almost definitely have to be based there. So what was the plan? Ask her to move to his empty-walled bachelor pad and spend three to five days out of every week without him? Or did they do the long-distance thing?

That second option gave him fucking hives.

His cute, perfect, freckle-faced girlfriend running around LA being cute, perfect, and freckle-faced without him? He'd want to bang his head against the wall nonstop. It wasn't that he didn't trust her; it was the possibility of her finding a better, more local option. A long-distance relationship between them would incite the critics, too, no doubt. They didn't know he'd been faithful to Hannah. They wouldn't even believe it if he told them how easy it had been. How he couldn't fathom wanting anyone else. Like he'd told Hannah yesterday, having their ridicule connected to her? Whether it be the implications that he'd break her heart, use her, or turn out just like his father and cheat?

That he couldn't live with.

But what other option did he have but long-distance? For now, at least. Until they'd spent at least five seconds as boyfriend and girlfriend, right? Until she was positive that Fox was good for her. What she wanted. In a way, he'd been in a long-distance relationship with Hannah since last summer. Now that feelings had been acknowledged, being separated would be a lot harder, but he would do it. He'd get down to LA as much as possible and lure her to Westport any damn way he could.

And eventually, when they were both ready, there would be no luring necessary.

One of them would simply leave their life behind.

If Hannah was the one to do that, would she regret it, though? What would he need to do to ensure that didn't happen?

Hannah yawned into his chest and smiled up at him sleepily, sending his pulse sprinting in dizzying circles. And he should have known. He should have known that the second she was awake, looking at him, everything would be all right.

I'll just talk to her.

Problem solved.

"Morning," came her muffled greeting against his skin.

"Morning." He trailed his fingertips up and down her spine, eliciting a purr of appreciation. "How's your tush?" He cupped the buns in question. "Sore, I bet."

Her laughter vibrated through them both. "I knew you were going to bring up the spanking thing." She lightly wormed a finger between his ribs. "I'm never going to ask again."

"You won't have to." He grinned. "I know what you like now, freaky girl."

"I was caught up in the moment."

"Good. That's exactly where I want you." Fox caught Hannah under the arms and flipped her over, rolling on top of her, fitting their curves together with a groan and staring down at the most incredible sight imaginable. Hannah, naked. Tits decorated in love marks from his mouth. Blushing and giggling in his bed. How the hell was he supposed to leave for five days? Who could expect that of a man? "You're so damn beautiful, Hannah."

Her amusement died down. "Happiness does that to a person."

Talk to her. It always, always works.

She intertwined their fingers on the pillow, like she already knew. Of course she did. This was Hannah. The first and last girl he'd ever love.

"Your time here went so fast," he said thickly, looking her in the eye.

Her nod was slow. Understanding. "Now we're under the gun to figure it out."

The pressure of shouldering the worry alone dissipated like it was never there. Just like that. *The truth will set you free.* Apparently that wasn't just a generic phrase uttered by some politician three hundred years ago. "Yes."

"I know." She leaned up and kissed his chin. "It's going to be okay."

"How, Hannah?"

She wet her lips. "Do you . . . want me to be here when you get back?"

Pressure came spilling back in, caking his organs in cement. He scrutinized her eyes, finding nothing but earnest hope. "Was that . . ." He choked on the words. "Was it even a possibility that you wouldn't be here? Jesus Christ. Yes, I want you here." He swallowed a handful of spikes. "You better be here."

"I will. Okay, I will. I just wasn't sure if this was . . . if you expected me to know this was a one-time thing. Or casual, maybe. Like we could spend time together whenever I come to visit Piper . . ."

"It's not casual." Fuck. His throat had lit itself on fire. "How are you even asking me that?"

She inhaled and exhaled beneath him, seeming to mull something over.

"What's going on in your head?" he asked, getting right up close, pressing their foreheads together, as if he could extract her thoughts. "Talk to me."

"Well . . ." Her skin turned clammy against him. "It's just, you know, Seattle isn't far, and there are opportunities for me, for what I want to do . . . there. It's a creative job, not a nine to five. I probably wouldn't have to commute constantly. Just occasionally. I could think about relocating. To be closer to you."

The first emotion he experienced was utter relief. Euphoria, even.

They wouldn't have to do long-distance and he could see her every day.

The second was complete awe that he could make this girl want to uproot herself to be near him. How the hell had he managed to pull that off?

But the panic crept in, little by little, blanketing his awe.

She was talking about moving closer.

Now.

Living with him, really. Because that's what it would be, wouldn't it? When someone relocated to be closer to their boyfriend, they didn't live in separate apartments. Was she sure about him? *That* sure? Look how many times he'd come close to messing up this entire thing with Hannah already. Pushing her toward another man. Trying to sexualize himself so she'd do the convenient thing and disregard him as a player like everyone else. What hope did he have of giving her a reliable future?

They would laugh at her, too. Behind her back.

They'd think she was out of her goddamn mind, moving all the way north for a man who'd never been serious about a plate of fries, let alone a woman. He'd never even nurtured a houseplant. Would he be able to nurture an up-close-and-personal relationship with a live-in girlfriend? In a way that was worthy of Hannah? He refused to take the helm of the *Della Ray*. He was a walking innuendo among his friends and family. Now he had the audacity to believe he could be the right one for this girl?

Maybe she needed the long-distance time to be sure. He wouldn't be able to stand it if she dropped her life, her career for him, and then realized she'd acted impulsively.

"Hannah . . ."

"No, I know. I know. That was, like, really jumping the gun." She sounded winded. So was he. She reached for her phone on his side table, lighting it up. "What time does the boat leave this morning?"

"Seven," he responded hoarsely.

That was it? The conversation was over?

He'd had fifteen seconds to make a decision that would determine her future?

With an exaggerated wince, Hannah turned the screen so he could read it: 6:48.

"Christ," he groaned, forcing himself to roll off her deliciously bare body, dragging the duffel bag out from beneath his bed without taking his eyes off her once. He hated the indecision on her face, like she was suddenly feeling out of place in his bed, but hell if he knew what to do about it. What could he say? *Yes, move here. Yes, change your life for me—a man who just got the bravery to admit his feelings less than twenty-four hours ago.* A really huge part of him wanted to say those things. Felt ready for anything and everything with this girl. But that remaining niggle of doubt kept his mouth shut. "Hannah, please be here when I get back."

She sat up, shielding her body with the sheet. "I said I would. I will."

Talk to her.

Fox stood and crossed to his dresser, ripping out boxers, socks, thermals, shoving them into the bag. Heart in his throat, he stopped to look at her, cataloguing her patient features one by one. "I don't have enough confidence in myself to ask you to . . . change your life, Hannah. Not this fast."

"I have confidence in you," she whispered. "I have faith."

"Great. Would you mind sharing it?" God, why was he speaking to her so angrily, when all he wanted was to crawl back in the bed and bury his face in her neck? Thank her for having that faith, reward her for it with strokes of his body until she was delirious? "I'm sorry. I shouldn't be talking to you like that when you've done nothing wrong." He gestured between her and the duffel bag. "You think you could fit in here so I could bring you with me? Because an hour from now, I'm probably going to be sick over leaving like this."

"Then don't leave like this." She came up on her knees and shuffled to the edge of the bed, still clutching the sheet between her breasts. "Kiss me. I'll be here when you get back. We'll leave it at that."

Fox lunged for her like a dying man, dragging her body up against his and fusing their mouths together. Tunneling his fingers through her unbrushed hair, tilting her head, slanting his open mouth over hers, rubbing their tongues together until she moaned, her body sagging into him. He'd be leaving the harbor with a hard dick, but so be it. She was well worth the discomfort.

His fingers curled around the top of the sheet with the intention of ripping it off, giving her one more orgasm just to hear her call his name in that husky way of hers, and Fox knew he had no choice but to go. He'd never leave otherwise. He'd stay inside her all day, wrapped up in her scent, the sound of her laughter, the drag of skin on skin. And it would be the best. It would feed his fucking soul. But it didn't feel right to make love to her when he couldn't even commit to a course of action. Be confident in where they were headed, the way she was prepared to be.

He couldn't do that. Not to Hannah.

Fox broke the kiss with a curse, shoveling unsteady fingers through his hair. He held her tight for too-short seconds until, regretfully, he pressed her back into the pillows and tilted her chin up. Making eye contact but already missing her like hell. "Sleep here while I'm gone?"

After a second, she nodded, her expression unreadable.

"Be careful out there."

Her concern was like standing in front of a radiator, taking away the chill like only she could. "I will, Freckles."

Leaving her there, he dressed quickly, pulling on a long-sleeved thermal shirt, jeans, and a sweatshirt. Tugging thick socks onto his feet and shoving them into his boots. Fitting a cap onto his head. Restless now, he took one last look at her and walked out of the room.

Outside, morning mist enveloped him so that he couldn't see his building after a few hundred yards, and the pit in his stomach grew with every step he took toward the docks.

Go back.

Tell her to move here.

That seeing her on a daily basis would be your version of heaven.

God knew it was the truth. A few minutes away from her arms and he was already back to being cold.

He stopped halfway across the street, purpose beginning to settle over him. What if he *could* make her happy? What if they could prove everyone wrong? What if she just stayed and stayed and stayed, so he could wake up every morning and feel fucking substantial and alive, the way he'd done today? He would do everything in his power to give her that same feeling, so she'd never regret leaving LA—

"Fox!"

Brendan's voice beckoned him through the fog, and he took a few reluctant steps forward, the mist moving out of his way to reveal the harbor, the *Della Ray* in her usual slip in the distance. He nodded at his friend. They pounded fists.

Guilt he didn't want to feel tripped and fell in his belly.

He'd been so consumed with Hannah and the separate reality they'd created together that he'd all but forgotten Brendan's request that Fox keep his hands off his future sister-in-law. Realistically, nothing could have stopped him. His feelings for Hannah were too powerful to heed any kind of warning. That was obvious now. But the guilt wouldn't be pushed aside. Not when Fox knew Brendan's concern was warranted. After all, they'd been friends for a long time. While Brendan had been studying, learning the fishing business, Fox had been participating in very different extracurricular activities.

"What's up?" Fox asked, shouldering his duffel bag.

Brendan's gaze was unusually elusive. The captain was the type to look someone in the eye when speaking, impressing upon them his Very Important Words. "Something came up and I need to drive my parents home."

Fox processed that. "They're not flying?"

"No. There was some flooding in their basement while they were gone. Figured I'd drive them home and get it straightened out."

"All right," Fox said slowly. What was going on here? Brendan had never missed a job. Not once since Fox had known him. And surely if this was going to be the first time, he would have called and saved everyone the hassle of packing and hauling their asses down to the harbor. "So . . . the trip is canceled?"

The utter joy that blared through Fox almost knocked him over.

Five added days with Hannah.

He was going to be back inside her warmth in two minutes flat. And tonight he was going to take her to dinner. Wherever she wanted to go. A concert. She'd love a concert—

"No, it's not canceled. I'm just handing over the captain duties for the trip." Before Fox could react, Brendan was dropping the keys to the *Della Ray* into his palm. "She's all yours."

Fox's relief screeched to a halt. Brendan was now busy folding back the sleeve of his shirt with jerky movements. His friend had never been very good at deception, had he? Yeah, he'd even showed up at school on senior ditch day while everyone else had gone to the beach. This was a man who'd stayed faithful to his deceased wife for seven damn years. He was as honest as the ocean glimmering with the sunrise behind him, and there was no way he'd forgo a fishing trip for a flooded basement. His responsibilities and his customs were stitched into his very fabric.

For the first time, Fox was envious of that.

Even while annoyance nagged at the back of his neck.

Brendan had absolute conviction when it came to making decisions and sticking to them. He knew exactly what he wanted the future to look like, and he executed the steps to make it happen. Proposing to Piper. Commissioning a second boat to expand the business. The only place Brendan seemed to fall short was the absurd belief that Fox belonged in a wheelhouse. Believed it so much that he'd stand there and lie.

Fox nodded stiffly, flipping the keys over once in his hand. "Did you really think you could pull this off?"

Brendan squared up, firming his jaw. "Pull what off?"

"This. Lying to me about some imaginary flood so I'd be forced to captain the boat. What did you think? If I did it once, I'd realize it's meant to be?"

Brendan thought about holding on to his story, but visibly gave up after 2.8 seconds. "I hoped you'd realize the responsibility is nothing to be scared of." He shook his head. "You don't think you've earned the right? The trust that comes with it?"

"Oh, you trust me now? You trust me to captain the boat, but not with Hannah. Right?" His bitter laughter burned a path up his chest. "I'm all good to take the lives of five people in my hands. But I better keep my filthy hands off your future sister-in-law. I'll break her heart. I'll go behind her back. Which is it, Brendan? Do you trust me or not? Or is your trust just selective?"

Until Fox asked the question out loud, his voice absorbed by the mist around them, he didn't realize how heavy the weight of that worry, that distinction had been. Just perched on his shoulders like twin stacks of bibles.

For once, Brendan seemed at a total loss, some of the color leaving his face. "I don't . . . I never would have thought of it that way. I didn't realize how much it bothered you. The whole Hannah thing."

"The whole Hannah thing." He snorted. What a paltry description for being so in love with her, he didn't know what to do with himself. "Yeah, well. Maybe if you paid a little closer attention, you'd realize I haven't been to Seattle since last summer. There's been no one else. There will never be anyone else." He pointed back at his apartment. "I've been sitting there for months, thinking about her, buying records, and texting her like a lovesick asshole."

He closed his fist around the keys until they dug into his palm.

Was this what it would be like if he was with Hannah?

Constantly trying to convince everyone he wasn't the careless tramp he'd once been? Even the people who were supposed to love him—Brendan, Kirk and Melinda, his own mother—had looked at him and seen a character beyond repair.

Hannah has faith in you. Hannah believes in you.

Fox was caught off guard by the hesitant vote of confidence that came from within, but it made him think maybe . . . just maybe there was a chance he wasn't a lost cause.

Still, he allowed the thought to germinate. To grow.

If he could be a worthwhile friend to Hannah, if he could make *that* tremendous girl stick around and value him, his opinion and company, maybe he could do this, too. Be a leader. Captain a boat. Inspire the respect and consideration of the crew. After all, he had changed. He'd changed for the girl who was lying drowsy in his bed. In the beginning, she'd made some of the same assumptions about him that other people did. But he'd shifted her opinion, hadn't he?

Could he do it with the crew? Could he be the *more* that Hannah deserved?

He'd never know unless he tried.

And when he thought of Hannah in the recording studio the day before, bravely voicing her opinion—taking chances and succeeding—he found the courage to reach down and tap into an undiscovered reserve of strength. Strength he'd gotten from her.

Fox forced a patient smile onto his face, even though his insides had the consistency of jelly. "All right, Cap. You win. I guess . . . I've got the wheel on this trip."

Chapter Twenty-Two

𝓗annah stood outside Opal's apartment, waiting for her grandmother to reach the door. The last time she was here, just over a week ago, she'd been filled with dread over going inside. Talking about her father. Feeling totally disconnected from Opal and Piper in the process. Now, though, her shoulders were firm instead of slumped. She didn't feel like an imposter or like she was faking it until she made it. She belonged here.

She was Opal's granddaughter.

Finally the main character of her own life.

Youngest daughter of Henry Cross.

They'd come to an understanding through his music. Once, a long time ago, he'd loved her. He'd held her in his arms in a hospital room, taught her how to toddle, and gotten up with her in the middle of the night. He'd gone off to sea thinking he would see her again. And Hannah liked to think, maybe in a way that only she could understand, they'd had a nice, long visit through his songs, given each other a sense of closure. It was quite possible she'd even been given some fatherly advice in a roundabout way, because she'd woken up on Monday morning, the final day of shooting, with an idea. A place to go from here.

A place that would mean continuing to work in music . . . and be near Fox.

If that's what he wanted.

A knot that had grown familiar over the last five days grew taut in her belly, agitating the coffee she'd drunk this morning. If she went back to LA as originally planned, it would be with a heart broken beyond repair. Being without Fox since he'd left only cemented that belief. She missed him so much she ached with it. Missed the way he frowned and parted his lips slightly when she talked, like he was concentrating hard on what she was saying. She missed the way he tucked both hands under his armpits in the cold. Missed his devilish laugh, the stroke of his palm down her hair, the halting way he spoke when he was about to drop some honesty.

The fact that he'd learned how to be honest with her at all times.

Every time she closed her eyes, she envisioned him striding down the dock in her direction, opening his arms, the decision to put in the work, to build a relationship with Hannah right there on his face.

What if it wasn't, though? What if five days on the water made him realize it was too much too soon? Or too much work, period?

Maybe she'd been impulsive to suggest leaving LA to be closer to Fox. Maybe she should have just gone back home and tried to do the long-distance thing for a while. But she couldn't see herself being happy with that. Not now. Not when she knew how right it felt to have him at her side. At her back. All around her. Didn't he feel the same?

Yes. He did—and she'd have faith in his actions. She'd have faith in them.

The door opened and there stood Opal, a row of curlers down the center of her head. "Oh! Hannah. I was just in the middle of taking these rollers out and now you've caught me looking a fright. Come in, come in. It's just us girls. Who cares!"

Hannah entered on a laugh, tucking a finger into her jeans pocket to make sure the envelope was still there, as she'd done a hundred times on the walk from set to Opal's building.

"What brings you by, my dear? Not that you need a reason!"

She followed Opal into the bathroom and started helping her remove the final row of pink foam curlers. "I would have called first, but I was too excited." She wet her lips. "You remember when I asked for permission to use Henry's songs in the movie we're filming?"

"I surely do. But you said it was a long shot." Opal's hands dropped to the sink. "Don't tell me it's really going to happen, Hannah." She scrutinized Hannah's expression, and her own transformed with awe. "I don't believe it. I . . . How? How? They're not even recorded properly. They're just words on a page."

"Not anymore," Hannah murmured, relaying the events of the last week. "Come on, I have one cued up on my phone ready to play." She hooked an arm through Opal's, leading her from the bathroom to the couch. Once they were settled, she snuck out her phone and opened the sound file, exhaling roughly as the music filled the room. The opening dance of the fiddle and bass, followed by the purr of Alana Wilder's vocals, the muffled beat of the drum added in postproduction.

Hannah thought of the moment on set when she'd approached Sergei and wordlessly handed him a set of AirPods, hitting play and watching his eyes go wide, his fingers tapping on his knees. That sense of accomplishment. No matter what he decided, she'd created something magical. She'd moved the dials until it all came together and overcome the doubt to get it done.

Her first leading-lady move—and definitely not her last.

Opal covered her mouth with both hands, her knuckles going white. "Oh, Hannah. Oh, this does my soul good. It's the closest I've come to speaking with him in twenty-four years. It's extraordinary."

Warmth spread in her chest. "There are more. Three total. And I'm working on recording the rest." She took the envelope out of her pocket and handed it to Opal, her pulse beginning to tick faster. "In the meantime, the songs have been copyrighted in your name, Opal. You'll be getting a percentage of the income generated by the soundtrack, but I managed to negotiate a signing bonus, too. For the use of Henry's songs in *Glory Daze*. It doesn't include whatever the production company will have to pay you if they use the songs in advertisements—"

"Hannah!" Opal gaped at the check she'd pulled out of the envelope. The one Sergei had handed her this morning. "I get to keep this?"

"That's right."

"Oh, I couldn't," she said, flustered, trying to hand back the check.

Hannah pressed it back against her grandmother's chest. "You will. Henry would have wanted it." She swallowed around the sharp object in her throat. "I feel confident saying that now. Before . . . I wouldn't have. But his songs helped me know him, understand him better . . . and family was his life." She smiled. "This is a good thing, Opal."

Her grandmother sighed, and the last bit of resistance left her. "He would have been so damn proud of you."

"I hope so," Hannah said, pressing a wrist to her burning nose. "Now let's get the rest of those curlers out. You've got some cash to burn through."

Half an hour later, Hannah was back on set, still hugged by the warm glow.

She wrapped her arms around her trusty clipboard, enjoying the feel of it against her chest, knowing today would be her last day as a production assistant. She'd been right to start at the bottom and learn the ropes, but that time was coming to a definitive close. Propping other people up was something she'd always do naturally, because she loved being supportive. But career-wise? It was time to support herself, too, and go after what she wanted next. To chase the high she'd gotten by creating art on her own terms.

The entire crew crowded into one half of Cross and Daughters. On the other side of the bar Hannah had renovated with Piper, lights beat down on Christian and Maxine, capturing their final scene in the movie. One that Sergei, true to form, had written into the script at the last second, wanting to maximize the new soundtrack. There had been no plan to shoot at Cross and Daughters, but thankfully, Hannah technically owned half the bar. She'd called Piper for permission, either way, and her sister would be stopping by shortly to serve drinks to the celebrating crew.

In the scene building to a crescendo in front of Hannah, Christian and Maxine were dancing palm to palm, happiness and hope slowly transforming their features. Their movements grew more joyful. Less restrained. It would be in slow motion, Hannah knew, and it would be a perfect way to leave the audience.

After two more takes, Sergei yelled, "Cut!" He hopped out of his director's chair and high-fived the closest boom mic guy. "That's a wrap."

Everyone cheered.

Christian dropped character faster than a speeding bullet. "Who has my coffee? Hannah?"

She waved at him. Waited until he looked relieved, then gave him the finger.

His laughter filled the bar.

Still, she was in the process of taking pity on the actor and delivering his cold brew once more for old time's sake when Sergei stepped into her path. "Hannah. Hey." Did he seem almost . . . nervous? "I just wanted to say again how much grain the new score is adding to the film. It wouldn't have been the same without the songs. Or this place." He laughed. "You almost had as much to do with the movie as I did—and I'm the one who wrote and directed it."

A nostalgic fondness for the director made her smile. "And you did a great job, Sergei. It's going to be your best work yet."

"Yes, thank you." He hesitated. "You've already given notice, and I respect that. It's obvious you're ready for bigger and better things, but I'll regret not asking one more time if you'll accept a higher position. Since Brinley appears to be keeping her word about quitting, someone has to step in as music coordinator."

A month ago, she would have had to pinch herself, thinking she'd been hit by a bus and was approaching the pearly gates. A huge part of her was thrilled beyond belief that she'd proven herself enough to warrant this kind of offer. She just couldn't take it. Not only because she wanted to make things work with Fox, but because she'd loved working for herself. Discovering a band, being part of the process, coming up with a vision, and seeing it through. She planned to continue in her newfound leading-lady role.

"Thank you, but this is going to be my last project," she said. "I don't think I would have discovered what I really wanted to do without Storm Born. The experience has been invaluable, but I'm moving on."

"And moving out of LA, too, I'm guessing." His chagrin turned down the corners of his mouth. "For the fisherman."

"Yes." Once again, she had to suppress the scary doubt that marched into her stomach like stormtroopers. "Yes, for Fox."

Sergei made an unhappy sound. "You'll let me know if anything changes. Career-wise or personally?"

She wouldn't.

Even if the worst happened and things didn't work out with Fox, she knew what it felt like to love someone now. In that wild, brutal way that couldn't be fenced in or reasoned with. The crush she'd had on the director seemed like a sad, wet noodle in comparison. "Of course," she said, squeezing his arm.

"Okay, beauties. Who is ready to party?"

Hannah snorted at the sound of Piper's voice and the resulting gasps as everyone recognized her. Hannah turned around just in time to receive a smacking kiss on her cheek—which definitely left a Piper-sized lipstick mark—and watched everyone marvel as the former party princess of Los Angeles neatly stowed her purse behind the bar and smiled at the closest crew member. "Get you a drink?"

Christian came up beside Hannah, jaw in the vicinity of his knees. "Is that . . . Piper Bellinger?"

"The very one," Hannah answered, love rushing through her veins. "She moved here last summer after she fell in love with a sea captain. Isn't that romantic?"

"I guess. How do you know her?"

"She's my sister. We own this place." She tipped her head in the direction of the bar. "How about something a little stiffer than coffee?"

His mouth opened and closed until eventually he sputtered, "Yeah, I think I need it."

Hannah and Christian had just managed to wade through the buzzing crew to the bar when Hannah stopped dead in her tracks. Outlined in the door of Cross and Daughters was Brendan. But . . . it was only late afternoon. The *Della Ray* wasn't scheduled to be back in the harbor until tonight. Did they get back early? Nerves and anticipation warred in her stomach at the possibility of seeing Fox earlier than expected. But something in Brendan's expression caused the nerves to win.

"Hey," she murmured when her future brother-in-law reached her. "Aren't you supposed to be out on the boat right now? Are you back early?"

Brendan doffed his beanie and turned it over in his hands. "Not back early. I put Fox in charge of this run."

Hannah started, replaying that explanation six times in her head, some unwanted trepidation turning over in her gut. "You did? Was that a last-minute decision?"

"It was. Didn't want to give him a chance to back out." Brendan hesitated, trading a glance with Piper. "It seemed like a good idea. And it might work out exactly like I hoped it would. The man has great instincts, knowledge, and respect for the ocean—he just needs to believe in himself." He cleared his throat. "It didn't occur to me until after the boat left that it might have been bad timing. With everything . . . going on between you two. He was game for the challenge, but it's a lot at once."

"Wait . . ." Hannah swallowed a robin's-egg-sized lump, pleasure and shock turning her very still. "He told you about us?"

"Some."

Hannah made an exasperated sound. "What does that mean?"

"He told Brendan he hasn't been to Seattle since last summer," Piper supplied, leaning forward on the bar to join the conversation. "He's been waiting for you, Hanns. Like a 'lovesick asshole'—and that's a direct quote."

She barely had time to process the immense weight of that revelation when she noticed Brendan still looked nervous. And she knew there was more.

"I put the rest together without him telling me. I figured with him feeling like that, and you two in close quarters, something was . . . probably happening. Even though I went and spoke to him before you arrived. Asked him to keep things platonic—"

"You did *what*?"

"And," Brendan continued, "I may have reminded him to keep things friendly a couple of times since." He cleared his throat. "A couple . . . dozen."

"I take partial blame," Piper called, wincing. "We were trying to look out for you. But I think maybe . . . No, I *know* we underestimated him in the process. We've been doing it for a long time."

"Yeah. He had every right to throw that back in my face before he left." Brendan replaced the beanie on his head and accepted the pint Piper placed on the bar in front of him, drinking from it deeply as if the whole conversation had made him thirsty. When he set it down again, he took his time looking at Hannah. "I kept crowing about how much I trust him, wanting him to take my spot behind the wheel, but I didn't put my money where my mouth is. I regret that."

Heat tingled in the tip of Hannah's nose. Fox had told her his worst fear was someone questioning his intentions toward her, but it had already happened. His own best friend had done it. Had he been hurting over it all this time?

God, she was so proud of him for taking the keys to the boat. For trying.

She couldn't help but worry, though. Brendan was right. It was a lot at once.

They were right on the verge of carving out a unique place for themselves. A place to try to be together. To build on what was already a treasured friendship and make it into so much more. But a lot of Fox's insecurities were wrapped up in how people saw him. The town. The crew. What if his turn as captain didn't go as planned? What if he came home too discouraged to pick up where they'd left off?

It wasn't that she didn't believe in him. She did. But they'd left things unsettled, and this unexpected change of plans might have thrown off the balance even more.

Two weeks ago, she'd wanted to be a leading lady. For the sake of her career, not her love life. But tonight she'd have to gather up her newfound sense of self-purpose and be prepared to go to war if necessary, wouldn't she? Because she was no longer the type to watch from the sidelines or live vicariously through others, bolstering them when required. No, this was her story line, and she had to write it herself. Scary, sure. But if she'd learned anything since coming to Westport a second time, it was that she was capable of so much more than she realized.

Hannah signaled Piper for a drink. "Some liquid courage, please."

"Coming right up." A moment later, Piper shook something in a metal tumbler and poured it into a martini glass, sliding it in front of her sister. "You know"—Piper twisted an earring— "alcohol doesn't hurt, but I find some ice-pick heels and great hair lend the most courage of all."

"Let's do it." Hannah tossed back the drink. "I'm slightly ticked at both of you for warning Fox away from me, a capable adult human, but I need all the help I can get."

"That's fair," Brendan rumbled.

"Totally fair. I'm about to make it up to you." Piper threw back her shoulders with a sense of purpose. "Brendan, watch the bar. We have work to do."

Fox checked the final item off his clipboard and hung it back on the nail, letting out the breath he'd been holding for the last five days. He took the hat off his head and dropped into the captain's chair, staring out at the harbor. Letting the tension seep out.

Below, on the deck of the *Della Ray*, he watched the last of the haul get loaded by Deke, Sanders, and the rest of the crew. Normally he would be down there helping them, but he'd been on the phone with the market, preparing them for the arrival of fresh swordfish. He'd been inspecting the boat from top to bottom, making sure everything in the engine room was running properly, the equipment sound, the numbers recorded.

He'd done it.

A successful five-day trip.

He'd given orders and they'd been followed. It helped that he'd been insulated by the wheelhouse, instead of down on the deck where most of the ball breaking took place. Moreover, when the men retired to their bunks at night, exhausted, Fox had stayed up late mapping their course for the following morning, refusing to disappoint Brendan.

Or Hannah.

There hadn't been much of a chance to determine how the men felt about him taking over—and maybe that was for the best. Maybe if he kept his head down and completed a few more jobs without incident, he could ease back into the group slowly, having built the beginnings of a new reputation. Hard to believe such a thing was possible after years of the lifestyle he'd been living. Then again, he never thought he'd give up sex for half a year in exchange for witty text messages and record collecting. But here he was.

Dying. Fucking *dying* to get home to his girl.

He missed her so much, he was full of cracks.

She'd fill all of them in. And he was starting to think . . .

Yeah. That he could eventually do the same for her.

"Hey, man," Deke said, slapping the side of the wheelhouse and ducking his head in. "All set. I'm leaving for the market."

"Great," Fox said, fitting his hat back on. "Call me when you have a number." At the market, an attendant would test the fish for a grade of quality and decide on the price paid for each one. The process was important, because it determined the amount of everyone's paycheck. "I'll pass it on to Brendan, and he can contact them for payment."

"Sounds good." Deke nodded at him, followed by a playful look of disgust. "Look at you in the captain's chair. All large and in charge and making extra bank. Like you needed any help getting laid, huh?"

Sanders swung into the wheelhouse beside Deke, elbowing his friend. "Right? Why don't we just roll out a red carpet to the end of the dock? Make it even easier for the ladies to find you."

Fox was frozen to the seat.

Jesus. Really?

He hadn't expected their attitudes toward him to change overnight, but there wasn't even a hint of respect in how they spoke to him. Not even the slightest change in their demeanors or judgment of him. If they spoke to Brendan like that, they would have been fired before they finished a sentence.

Fox felt like he'd been hollowed out by a shovel, but he summoned a half smile, knowing better than to let his annoyance show. Or the ribbing would probably only get worse. "Seriously, I'm flattered by how obsessed you are with my sex life. Spend a little more time thinking of yours and we wouldn't have this problem." He pushed to his feet and faced them, his next words coming out involuntarily. They just sailed right past his better judgment, because his mind was occupied with thoughts of one person. "Anyway, I'm not going to Seattle. Or anywhere else. I'm going to see Hannah."

Their twin expressions of disbelief made his gut bubble with dread.

"Hannah," Sanders repeated slowly. "The little sister? Are you *serious*?"

Sensing he'd made a huge mistake bringing her up like this—it was *way* too soon, when he'd clearly earned none of the esteem that a man should have in order to be Hannah's boyfriend—Fox brushed past them out of the wheelhouse, seeing nothing in his path. But they followed. "Heard a rumor about you two at Blow the Man Down, but even I didn't think you were *that* much of a dog," Sanders said, some of his amusement fading. "Come on, man. She's a sweetheart. What are you thinking?"

"Yeah," Deke chimed in, crossing his arms. "You couldn't pick one of the thousand other women at your beck and call?"

"That ain't right, Fox." Sanders's expression was transforming to disgust. "You're supposed to wife a girl like that—you don't chew her up and spit her out."

"You don't think I *know* that?" Fox growled, taking a lunging step in their direction, his sanity going up in flames, along with the stupid, shortsighted hope that had been building. "You don't think I know she deserves the best of fucking everything? It's *all* I think about."

I kiss the ground she walks on.

I love her.

They were momentarily shocked into silence by his outburst, studying him with subdued curiosity, but instead of asking Fox about his intentions, Deke said, "Does Brendan know about this?"

And Fox could only turn and walk away laughing, the sound painfully humorless.

God, the way they'd looked at him. None of the respect afforded to the captain of a boat. He'd been an idiot to think they could ever see him in a new light. They'd treated him like the scum of the earth for even breathing the same air as Hannah, let alone being in a relationship with her. Fox could only imagine Hannah getting the same talk from her sister, their mutual friends, everyone in her life—and the idea made him nauseous, a dagger slipping through his ribs and twisting.

His worst nightmare was coming to fruition. Even earlier than expected.

But he could stop it now. Before it got worse for Hannah. Before she moved all the way to Westport and realized what a mistake she'd made.

Before *she* was forced to make this hard decision.

No, he'd make it for them both, even if it killed him.

There was an invisible match in his hand, lit and ready. He didn't seem to have much choice but to douse the best thing in his life in kerosene and toss the matchstick right on top.

Chapter Twenty-Three

An hour later, Fox stood in the shadows, leaning against the fish-and-chips shop across the street from Cross and Daughters. He should have stayed home. He shouldn't be out here trying to catch a glimpse of Hannah through the front window, his very existence seeming to hinge on just *seeing* her. At least one more time before he explained that he'd been wrong. Wrong to even consider that he could be good for her.

Someone walked out of the bar to light up a smoke, and in that brief second the door was open, Hannah's laughter drifted out through the opening. His body jolted off the wall, muscles tightening like bolts.

All right, look, he was still responsible for her safety until she went back to Los Angeles, so he'd just . . . make sure she got home okay.

Was he insane? If he had one ounce of self-preservation running in his blood, he'd have gone back to his apartment and changed the locks. Drunk a fifth of whiskey, blacked out, and woken up when she'd gone.

What had he done instead?

With the words of Sanders and Deke ringing in his head, he'd gone through the motions of a shower. Put on cologne. She was in town, and there was no earthly way he could stay away. Him needing to be near Hannah was just a fact of life. But once he saw her, he had to do the right thing.

Get your head in the game.

You are breaking it off with her.

A screwdriver slid into his gut at the thought of that. Breaking it off. It sounded so harsh, when his actions were the opposite of harsh. He was preventing her from making a mistake by wasting her time on him. Signing herself up for the same lack of respect that had become a normal part of his life. He couldn't let her move a thousand miles to be with someone who people—people who *knew* him—assumed would *chew her up and spit her out.* If his own crew thought so little of him, what would the whole town think? Her family?

So go in there and tell her.

He would . . . soon.

He'd gotten on the boat Wednesday morning on an upswing of hope. During the trip, the captain's wheel felt good sliding through his hands, the grain rasping against his palms. For a brief moment in time, the dreams of his youth had reappeared and sunk their hooks in, but that feeling was long gone right now. With Hannah believing in him, Fox thought he could earn the same honor from the men of the *Della Ray*, but that obviously wasn't going to happen. He was stuck in this place of no forward movement, boxed in by his reputation, and he wouldn't get her caught there alongside him. No fucking way.

Fox paced a few steps on the sidewalk, still unable to see Hannah through the window. Maybe he'd go to Blow the Man

Down, have a drink to settle his nerves, and come back. He started walking in that direction—and that's when he saw her.

Standing at the bar inside Cross and Daughters.

First, he saw her face, and his heart dropped into his stomach, a ripe tomato hurtling down a hundred-foot well and splattering at the bottom. God. God, she was beautiful. Hair down, curling in places he'd never seen it curled before.

He knew that expression on her face well, that mixture of earnestness and distraction, because she probably couldn't help listening to the music, repeating the lyrics in her head, the words derailing the course of whatever conversation she was having. In this case, a conversation with a man.

Not Sergei, but an attractive, actor-looking type.

Fox ran his tongue along the front of his teeth, his throat drying up.

Don't you dare be jealous when you're about to end things. She'd be back in LA soon talking to millions of men. There would probably be a whole herd of them waiting on the highway off-ramp, full of the right words and good intentions and—

And that's when he noticed the little turquoise dress.

"Ah, Jesus," he muttered, changing directions again. Moving at a much quicker pace this time. Even before he walked through the door of the bar, Fox wanted a lot more than a closer look. He'd spent five lonely nights on the ship with a hard-on, his dick stiff and aching for Hannah and Hannah only. So when he started to weave through the crowd, focused solely on her, his hands were already itching, and that was not a good sign. If this hard discussion was going to be successful, those hands needed to stay off her.

Be strong.

She turned, and their eyes met—and thank God the music was loud, because he made a sound midway between agony and relief. There she was. Safe and alive. Gorgeous and all-knowing and merciful and perfect. Any man with half a brain in his head would get down on his knees and crawl toward her, but he . . . couldn't be that man. It was especially hard to acknowledge that when her face brightened, the hazel color of her eyes deepening to a mossy copper, that heart-shaped mouth spreading into a smile.

"Fox. You're back."

"Yeah," he managed, sounding like a garrote was tightening around his throat. And it was a good thing Piper was behind the bar, or he might have kissed Hannah then and there. Two seconds in her presence, and he almost ruined his plans. Would have been worth it, though. "How . . . are you?"

A glimmer of sadness ran a lap around her face—because he hadn't kissed her?—and she set her drink down on the bar. "Good. I'm fine." Why did she seem to be measuring her breaths so carefully? Was something wrong? "Fox, this is Christian." She gestured to the man to his right. "He's the lead actor in the film. He's an absolute nightmare."

"She speaks the truth," purred the actor through his teeth, holding out a hand to Fox. "And you must be the one taking her away from us."

Just when Fox thought his stomach couldn't knot any tighter, it twisted into a pretzel. She'd already made plans. She'd made plans that would make it easier for them to be together. With Hannah standing in front of him, so familiar and sweet and soft, the word "plans" didn't sound quite as daunting. It was when they were apart that he started to doubt his ability to execute any kind of plan. It was the doubt of *others* that shook him.

The leather cuff around his wrist turned into molten metal, branding his skin.

"Oh. No," Hannah rushed to say, her face rapidly turning pink. "I mean, I . . . I'm leaving the production company. But that's a decision that I made . . . for me. Separate from Fox. Or anything."

Until that news came out of her mouth, Fox hadn't truly processed the weight of it. What it meant for her. "You quit your job?"

She nodded. Breathed, "They're going to use the songs. In the film."

"Aw, Hannah." His voice sounded like sandpaper, and he had to rub at the center of his sternum, the rush of feeling there was so intense. "Damn. Damn, that's amazing. You did it."

Her eyes sparkled up at him, communicating a million things. Her nerves, her excitement, her pleasure to be sharing the news with him. Fox sucked it down like a glass of cool water placed in front of a thirsty man.

"Yes . . ." Christian swirled his drink lazily, his attention moving back and forth between Hannah and Fox with unabashed interest. "Now she's off to go discover more new bands and plug them into indie soundtracks. Hannah Bellinger, music broker. She's going to be too good for me soon."

She placed a solemn hand on the actor's shoulder. "I'm already too good for you."

The guy tossed back his head and laughed.

The caveman part of Fox's brain relaxed.

There was nothing to be jealous over here. Hannah and Christian were obviously just friends. But there was still a lot to worry about. It couldn't be a coincidence that Hannah quit her job on the heels of them discussing potential logistics of a relationship, right? Had she made the move in anticipation of them trying?

Despite his worry over that, he wanted to hear more about this new job. Music broker. What did that mean exactly? Would she be traveling a lot? Was it Seattle-based? How excited was she on a scale from one to ten?

"You've definitely made a lot of decisions since I left," he said, keeping his questions to himself. Very soon, they wouldn't be any of his business.

Hannah studied his face. "Looks like you've made a lot of decisions, too."

"Lord, the undercurrents are a-flowing," Christian muttered, regarding them. "I'm going to go make fun of the interns. You folks have fun working this out."

Silence landed hard as soon as they were alone.

His brain repeated the speech he'd practiced on the walk through town. *I'm sorry. You are amazing. My best friend. But I can't ask you to move here. I can't make this work.*

His mouth said, "You look incredible."

"Thanks." She forced a smile, a fake one, and he wanted to kiss it right off her mouth. *You don't fake anything with me.* "Are you going to break up with me here or somewhere a little more private?"

"Hannah." Shock made her name sound ravaged, and he tuned his face away, unable to look at her. "Don't say 'break up.' I don't like how that sounds."

"Why?"

"It sounds like I'm . . ."

Pushing you away. Severing our connection.

Oh God, he couldn't do that. Might as well ram an ice pick into his heart.

"Can we mutually agree on this, please?" Fox asked, his lower body coiling tight when someone in the crowd nudged her closer, bringing the tips of her breasts up against his chest. Momentarily, he lost his train of thought. Was she even wearing a bra with that dress?

What had he been saying?

"If we both agree on this"—he swallowed the word "breakup"—"change of status, then we can stay friends. I need to stay friends with you, Hannah."

"Mmmm." The hurt she was trying so desperately to hide— chin lifted, gaze unwavering—gutted him slowly. "So when I come to Westport for a visit, we'll hang out like nothing ever happened. Maybe listen to my Fleetwood Mac album?"

It took him a moment to speak. To form a response. Because what could he say to that? He'd confessed the truth to her at the Sound Garden.

I had it bad for you. If the convention didn't make it obvious, I thought for sure the Fleetwood Mac album would do it. I've got it so bad for you, Hannah.

Really . . . really bad.

Was she remembering those words, too? Is that why she raised her chin another notch and delivered yet another blow to his resolve? "Look, I'm not going to fight you on this, Fox." She rolled a delicate shoulder. "You're ending whatever this was developing into and that's fine. It's your right."

He watched helplessly and miserably as she wet her lips.

What happened now? They just walked away from each other?

Was he really strong enough to do that?

"Could you do one last thing for me?" she asked, brushing their fingertips together ever so slightly.

"Yes," he said hoarsely, his temples beginning to pound.

Hannah tilted her head, and he eagerly memorized the curve of her neck.

"I want a good-bye kiss."

Fox's eyes flew to Hannah's, lust racking him, along with . . . panic. Flat-out panic. No way he could kiss her and leave it at that. Was she aware of how difficult that would be? How impossible? Was that her game? Her expression was so innocent, it didn't seem possible. Nor was it possible to deny her request. To deny her anything.

He'd kiss her here. In public, where it was safe.

Right.

Like anything about touching her was safe when he was on the verge of breaking. Shattering into a thousand tiny pieces.

Fox licked his lips and stepped closer to Hannah, his hand settling on her hip as if magnetized. His thumb encountered a very slight shape, almost like a . . . tiny strap, and he looked down, watching his fingers feel it out. "What panties are these?"

"I don't see how that matters. This is just a kiss."

It's a G-string. I know it's a fucking G-string.

Jesus, she'd look so hot in it.

"Right." He exhaled, pulse hammering at the base of his neck. "A good-bye kiss."

"That's right." She blinked at him slowly. "For closure."

Closure.

Case closed.

That was what he'd decided. That was what needed to happen.

She'd thank him someday.

Her mouth was so soft-looking, lips parted just a touch, waiting for him to place his own on top of them. One kiss. No tongue. No tasting or he'd be a goner, because no one on the planet had her perfect flavor, and he needed the memory of it to fade, not grow stronger.

Nice try.

The memory of her is never, ever going to fade.

Fox, apparently self-destructive, lowered his head anyway, desperate to get his fill of her one last time—

A bell started ringing behind the bar, Piper yelling, "Last call. Pay up and hit the bricks, kiddies."

Hannah tugged out of his arms, shrugging. "Oh well."

His mind struggled to play catch-up, the fly of his jeans infinitely tighter than it had been upon walking into the bar. "Wait. What?"

Despite her flushed complexion, her tone was casual. "Bad timing, I guess."

"Hannah," he growled, stepping into her space, twisting his hands in the sides of her dress. "You're getting the kiss."

She made a wishy-washy sound. "I mean, I guess I need to grab my bag from your apartment, anyway. The bus leaves at seven in the morning."

His head swam, stomach bottoming out, crashing straight down through the floorboards of Cross and Daughters. He'd known the bus would eventually depart, but somehow he'd blocked out that information. No staving it off now. She was going. Leaving. Her decision had been hinging on him, and they both knew he'd made it.

You're doing the right thing.

"I'm going to change out of this dress, too," she muttered, half to herself.

Oh, but he heard it. And definitely pictured her stepping out of the turquoise material in nothing but a G-string and heels. Definitely imagined his mouth on her skin and, Christ, that utterly perfect coming-home feeling only Hannah gave him.

Piper rang the bell again, and the bar lights flashed.

"I guess we better go," Hannah said, breezing past him.

Worried he might very well be walking to his doom, Fox was helpless to do anything but follow.

Chapter Twenty-Four

$\mathcal{H}$annah's heart was breaking.

He'd done it. He'd really done it.

She'd been concerned, of course. That Fox would return from his trip, having been duped by his best friend, and strain under the pressure of simultaneous shifts in his career and personal life. But she'd hung on to her faith, positive he wouldn't be able to look her in the eye and put a stop-work order on what they were building together. He'd done it, though. He'd really, actually done it, and as she clipped up the stairs to his apartment, her heart bumped along behind her, bruised and bloody.

God. The disobedient organ had almost burst free from her chest when he walked into Cross and Daughters, she'd been so happy to see him.

Stupid. So naive and stupid.

Get your bag and leave.

Just go.

Kissing him would only make the pain ten times worse, anyway. She'd kept the good-bye kiss in her back pocket as a last resort, knowing it would break down any defenses he'd built up over the last five days, but now . . . now she didn't want to fall back on last resorts. She wanted to find a dark place to crawl into and cry.

Part of her knew that wasn't fair. If Fox didn't want to be in a relationship, she should respect that, be a big girl, and wish him well. After all, she'd known about his cemented bachelor status since the beginning. This wasn't breaking news. But tell that to her heart.

Hannah unlocked the door and went inside, heels clicking as she traversed the apartment, Fox entering slowly behind her. The scent of his shower still hung in the air, and she breathed it in, making her way to the bedroom, where she'd left her suitcase packed and ready to go, some sixth sense telling her being prepared was wise. She'd hoped to unpack it again tomorrow, however. To stay in Westport. That he wouldn't let her leave without figuring out where they stood.

As was her routine, she tapped on the pink Himalayan salt lamp, forgoing the overhead light, casting the dark room in a blushing glow. Heaving the case up onto the bed and unzipping it, she took out a pair of cotton panties, jeans, and a Johnny Cash T-shirt. Laid the outfit on the bed and went to close the guest-room door so she could change. But she drew up short when she found Fox standing in the doorway, outlined in pink, watching her with a forearm propped high on the jamb, expression torn and tortured.

"I need to change."

He didn't move.

Frustrated with him, with everything, she marched over and shoved at the center of his chest to try to get him out of the room, her annoyance only increasing when his sturdy fisher-man frame didn't budge an inch. "Let me change so I can go."

"I don't want you to leave like this."

"We don't always get what we want."

Still, he stayed put, grinding glass with that square jaw.

And she'd had enough.

Hannah couldn't remember a single time in her life she'd wanted to lash out so badly. By nature, she was not a lasher. She was a helper. A mediator. A solver. He didn't want her to stay but wouldn't let her change so she could leave, either? Who the hell did he think he was? Her hands itched to push him again. Harder. She had a more effective weapon, though, and she'd learned from the best how to use it. She'd be hurting herself in the process, sure, but at least she'd have her pride.

Show him what he'll be missing.

On her way back to the bed, she stripped the turquoise dress over her head, getting an immense amount of satisfaction from his shaky hiss of breath. Slowly, she folded the borrowed gar-ment, bending forward slightly to tuck it into her suitcase, and Fox's guttural curse filled the room.

"Christ, Hannah. You look hot as fuck."

Every last one of her nerve endings popped like cham-pagne corks as his warmth materialized behind her. When she straightened and her bare back landed flush against his heav-ing chest, she could only compare it to that breathless moment on a Ferris wheel when you hit the top the first time and the world spreads out in front of you, huge and wondrous. Hot shivers traveled up her arms, starting at her fingertips, her nipples tingling and tightening—and he hadn't even touched her yet.

A notch in Hannah's throat made her want to turn around, press her face into his chest, and beg him not to walk away from them. She almost did it. Until he placed his open mouth beneath her ear and murmured, "Time for that good-bye kiss yet?"

And her determination to show him what he was giving up renewed itself.

Not only that, but she wanted to take a sledgehammer to his walls and walk away while the rubble smoked. Those desires belonged to a stranger. Then again, so did the love and heartbreak she'd experienced with this man. None of it was familiar and all of it hurt, so she'd indulge her impulses and deal with the fallout later. It was going to be painful no matter what, right?

Hannah turned, the smooth movement of her hands climbing his chest derailed by the tortured look on his face. She recovered quickly, however, taking tight hold of his collar and turning them, urging Fox into a sitting position on the edge of the bed. His eager blue eyes landed everywhere, her pouting breasts, her mouth, the place between her legs, his hands raking up and down the thighs of his jeans, throat muscles working roughly.

"Just one kiss," Hannah whispered against his mouth. "Our last."

He made a jagged sound that shifted a spike inside her. Made her want to hold him, but the hurt urged her on. Overrode the impulse.

Slowly, she straddled his lap and sat down, scooting until she met the proof of what he really wanted, the stiffness, the generous length of it. And she pressed down with her hips, letting her tongue tease into his mouth at the same time, soft lips writhing gently on top of hard ones, his stubble grazing her chin. Just as the pace started to pick up, his hands closing around her butt cheeks to draw her closer, closer, Hannah pulled her mouth away, both of them breathing erratically.

Fox's fist wound in her hair, his hips shifting beneath her. "You didn't strip for me just to be kissed, Hannah."

He yanked her lower body tighter against his lap, dragging the valley of her sex over the ridge of his erection, rocking her once, twice, making her whimper loudly. "What else were y-you thinking?"

Fox huffed a pained laugh. "Whatever act you're putting on, please knock it off," he growled, grinding their foreheads together. "Just be my Hannah."

The spike in her chest dug deeper. "I'm not your Hannah."

A possessive light came on in his eyes, though conflicted. As if he knew he'd forfeited the right to call her that but wasn't ready to relinquish the claim on his novelty just yet. Because that's what she'd been to him, right? A novelty. A temporary diversion. As badly as she'd wanted to be different, she'd gotten the same outcome as everyone else.

Not special.

"Maybe I planted a seed at least?" she half whispered. "Maybe one day you'll meet someone and this won't be as scary."

His eyes widened as she spoke. "*Meet* someone? Someone . . . else? Are you serious? You think this could happen *twice*?"

Hurt struck her. He wasn't hiding his feelings. He wanted her, needed her, but was still choosing to send her away? Goddamn him. Hannah tried to climb off his lap, but Fox—looking panicked—surged forward and caught her mouth in a kiss. A soul sucker that put every cell in her body on high alert. Warned them they were being invaded. She struggled to keep her thoughts clear, to remember her plan to make him regret sending her away, but there was only the magic of his mouth, his strong, welcoming body, and the hedonistic rock of their hips.

Her own barriers came crashing down, releasing a sob in her throat, her hands coming up to frame his face, holding him, running her fingers through his hair as they kissed desperately, so very aware it was the last time. It soon became obvious they weren't going to stop at kissing. A significant part of Hannah had known that when she took off the turquoise dress. His middle finger traveled down the crack of her backside to pet her flesh from behind, making sex that much more inevitable, because God, she was so wet. Instantly.

Their mouths moved at a frenzied pace, only breaking apart briefly to whip off Fox's shirt and then dive back in, her palms climbing over muscle and tangling back into his hair. He added a second finger against her dampening panties, then a third, massaging her from the back, his tongue sinking in and out of her mouth. Oh God, oh God, she wasn't in control anymore. Her body begged, pleaded for that full sensation, that stretch of him inside her . . . and she was fumbling with the button and zipper of his jeans before she'd even made up her mind to do so, ruled simply by need, need, need.

Time stopped when she drew him out through the opening, stroking him up and down in a loving fist. The kiss suspended itself, but their mouths remained right on top of each other, breaths firing in and out.

"Go on, babe, slip it in," he rasped, his eyes glazed with hunger and something else, something deeper she couldn't name. "It missed you. I . . . fuck. I missed you. I missed you so much. Hannah, please."

He'd struck her down, hurt her, made her vulnerable, so she closed her eyes and didn't respond in kind, though the words ached to escape her throat. *I missed you, too. I love you.* Instead, she guided his shaft between her thighs, Fox grunting and tugging the G-string to the side, allowing her to position his tip just inside her entrance and slowly, slowly, take him deep, both of them watching it happen, voyeurs of their own lust.

"Shit, shit, shit," Fox ground out, his head falling back. "No condom. I didn't put on a condom, Hannah."

He groped blindly for his wallet, but he gave up quickly, gasping and clutching Hannah's hips when she bucked involuntarily, moaning on his lap, digging her nails into his shoulders. "I . . . don't. I can't."

A shudder racked him. "You can't what? Stop?"

Was she nodding or shaking her head? She had no idea. The deep press of his hardness robbed her of rational thought, sensation rushing to her core, quickening those intimate muscles, turning them into throbbing little pulse points.

"Hannah," Fox said, forcing her to look him in the eye, his breath pelting her lips. "Are you on something?"

"Yes," she sobbed, the importance of the conversation finally making it through the sex static in her brain. "Yes, I get the shot. I get it."

She rode him with a circle of her hips, and his eyes rolled back in his head. "Oh. Jesus. That feels so fucking good." He visibly struggled to remain coherent. "I'm clean. Got checked last time you were here."

That confession made her quake. "And there's been no one since, has there."

It wasn't a question. She already knew the answer.

Eyes clenching shut, he shook his head. "No," he whispered. "God no, Freckles. I only want to be touched by you."

His mouth was back on hers, kissing her into a state of desperation, his hands holding her buttocks tight to rake her up and back in his lap, his thickness entering and leaving her in smooth strokes that rubbed that place, oh Lord, that spot. Right there. It was already swollen from his fingers, and now he exploited it, moving just right. Exactly how she needed, delivering friction that engulfed her entire body in heat. Made her feel sexual and powerful and feminine and uninhibited. So much so that she broke the kiss to lean back, offering her breasts to his mouth with unsteady hands, whining his name when he sucked her nipples eagerly, hungrily, left then right, their flesh now beginning to smack wetly.

And then Fox brought a hand down, roughly slapping her bottom, his teeth capturing the lobe of her ear. "Touch your clit." He spanked her again. Harder. Twice. "Help me get you there, Hannah. Now. Jesus, you've got me so fucking thick, I don't even know when the end is coming. I just know if I touch you there, it's over. Play with it."

Breath rattling in and out of her parted lips, Hannah dragged her shaking right hand downward from his shoulder and found that sensitive bud, biting her lip as she rubbed it up and down, up and down, switching to quick, quick circles, her moan mingling with Fox's as he jerked her up and back, faster, faster.

"Look at me while you do it." A bead of sweat rolled down the side of his head. "Look at me while we get you off."

"Not just me," she managed on an exhale.

He shook his head, the movement jerky. "Inside this tight thing without a rubber watching you ride dick like you've never had it so good?" He leaned back on his elbows and started to upthrust, abdomen flexing, bouncing her on his lap, breaking the dam of her pleasure wide open. "Nothing in this world could stop me getting off."

Hannah crested, lungs seizing, muscles locking tight as the orgasm took control, keeping her body prisoner while it wreaked havoc, clenching her sex around Fox and taking him past the breaking point, too. They ground out the pleasure, hips pushing down and pressing up, fingers digging into skin, teeth scraping flesh, loud groans rending the air of the glowing pink bedroom, his moisture streaking down her inner thighs, his dirty speech echoing in her head, prolonging the pleasure.

Inside this tight thing without a rubber . . .

Watching you ride dick . . .

Fox went flat on his back, taking Hannah with him, both of them spent but remaining locked together, her head resting on his shoulder. Their harsh inhales and exhales filled the room, his fingertips stroking up and down her back through the cooling sweat, mouth moving in her hair. A priceless embrace that was everything right in the world. Everything honest and perfect. And . . .

She wasn't giving this up.

God help her, she'd ridden the tide of more emotions tonight than she'd ever experienced in her life. Hopefulness, denial, devastation, anger. When he'd walked into Cross and Daughters obviously determined to break up with her, she'd lost her courage. Her resolve. The heartache had been so immense, there'd been no room for positivity. There was only survival. But before he'd returned from the ocean, she'd decided to fight, hadn't she? And now here she was, at the final round, weaving on her feet, closing in on unconsciousness, ready to quit just to mitigate the pain. Isn't this when she needed to be at her strongest?

Isn't this when being a leading lady really counted? When she wanted to quit?

And after what she'd accomplished over the last two weeks, she didn't have any excuses. She could do anything. She could be brave. Lying in the fetal position with a pint of ice cream wasn't going to salvage a relationship she knew damn well could be amazing and lasting. Fox needed her to believe in him right now, when his self-doubt was blinding him—and she needed to believe in herself, too.

Hannah kissed Fox's shoulder and rolled to the side, climbing off the bed.

Outwardly, she appeared calm, but on the inside her pulse was going a thousand miles an hour, a trench digging itself in her stomach. Fox sat up and watched her through bloodshot eyes as she dressed in jeans and her Johnny Cash T-shirt, eventually dropping his head into his hands, fingers tearing at his hair.

She zipped her suitcase again and stood in front of him, working to keep her voice even, though the effort didn't quite pay off. "I'm not giving up on us."

His head came up fast, eyes searching her face. With what? Hope? Shock?

"Yeah, um"—she swallowed, gathered her courage—"I'm not. Giving up on you. On us. You're just going to have to deal with it, all right?"

He was a man afraid to swim toward a life raft. She could see it.

"What happened since you left me?" she whispered, fighting the urge to stroke his face. His beautiful face that looked torn and haggard for once.

Fox pressed his lips together, looked away. Spoke in a raw voice. "It didn't matter. It was never going to matter how qualified I am for the captain's chair. How well I can manage the boat under pressure. No matter what I do, I'll just be someone they mock and doubt and criticize. Someone they can't respect or take seriously. A hall pass. The backdoor guy. And that will extend to you, Hannah. Your waters are clear and I'll muddy them." He massaged the center of his forehead. "You should have heard how horrified they were. Over us. I knew it would happen eventually, but goddamn, it was worse."

With every fiber of her being, she wanted to cradle his head to her breast and be gentle. Be supportive. If he'd been pushed into breaking up with her, whatever his crewmates said must have been bad. Really bad. But he didn't need sweet and cautious encouragement right now.

He needed a good, hard wake-up call.

"Fox, listen to me. I don't care how many different beds you've been in. I know you belong in mine. And I belong in yours, and *that's* what matters. You're taking something that happened in college out on us. You're taking the stupidity and shortsightedness of others out on us. The hurt they caused you . . . it's valid. It's meaningful. But you can't take the bad lessons you learned and apply them to every good thing that comes your way. Because there's nothing bad about what we have. It's really, really good." Her voice grew choppy. "You're wonderful, and I love you. Okay, you stupid idiot? So when you've done some thinking and pulled your head out of your stubborn ass, come and find me. You're worth the wait."

Eyes heavy with moisture, chest thundering up and down, Fox stood and tried to wrap his arms around her, but she moved out of his reach. "Hannah. Come here, please. Let me hold you. Let's talk about this—"

"No." Her body ached from the touch she denied herself, but she could be strong. She could do what needed to be done. "I meant what I said. Take some time and think. Because next time you tell me good-bye, I'll believe you."

On unsteady legs, she turned and wheeled her suitcase out of the apartment, leaving a ravaged Fox in her wake.

Chapter Twenty-Five

𝕱ox had never been overboard, but that possibility struck fear in the heart of every fisherman. The chances of being sucked down into the icy cold drink, the air drawn straight out of his lungs, the hull of the ship becoming smaller and smaller above, land a distant memory. Yet he knew with dead certainty that meeting his demise at the bottom of the ocean would be favorable compared to watching Hannah walk out his front door, her shoulders shaking with silent tears.

He'd been so sure he was doing the right thing.

But how could the right thing make that sweet girl cry?

Oh Jesus, he'd made her cry. And she loved him.

She fucking loved him?

His feet wouldn't move, his eyes burned, his body ached. He should go after her, but he knew Hannah. None of the words in his head right now were the correct ones, and she wasn't going to accept anything less. Christ, he couldn't help but be proud of the way she'd looked him in the eye and read him the riot act, even as she tore the heart clean out of his chest. That was some real leading-lady shit.

I love you more than life. Don't go.

Those were the words he wanted to shout at her retreating back. They wouldn't penetrate, though. He could see that. She didn't want impulsive, emotional statements from him. She wanted him to . . . pull his head out of his stubborn ass.

The door clicked shut behind Hannah, and his knees gave out, dropping him down to the bed, not a stitch of clothing on. With his pounding head clutched in his hands, he shouted a vile curse into the silent room that smelled like her, a fishhook impaling his gullet and ripping downward, all the way to his belly. He needed her back in his arms so badly, his entire body shook in bereavement.

But as terribly as he wanted her back, Fox didn't know how to do it the right way. He had no earthly clue how to make his head healthy for her. For them.

He only knew one thing. The answers weren't in this empty apartment, and the lack of Hannah's presence mocked him everywhere. In his bedroom where they'd spent nights wrapped around each other, the kitchen where he'd fed her soup and ice cream, the living room where she'd cried over her father. As quickly as he could, he dragged his jeans and T-shirt back on, grabbed his car keys, and left.

The change of scenery didn't help.

It wasn't the apartment Hannah was haunting so beautifully.

It was him.

Didn't matter how hard he applied the gas pedal, she came with him, as if her mussed dirty-blond head was resting on his shoulder, her fingers lazily playing with the radio. The image struck so deep, he had to breathe through it.

Fox had no idea where he was going. No clue at all.

Not until he pulled up outside his mother's apartment.

He cut the engine and sat there dumbfounded. Why here?

And had he really been driving a full two hours?

Charlene had sold his childhood home a long time ago and bought a condo in what amounted to a retirement complex. His mother grew up next door to the old folks' home where her parents worked, and she'd always been most comfortable around the blue-haired crowd, hence her living situation and job as a bingo caller. Fox's father had always made fun of her for that, telling her she would get old before her time, but Fox didn't see it that way. Charlene just stuck to what she knew.

Fox stared through the windshield at the complex, the empty pool visible through the side gate. He could count on one hand the number of times he'd been here. A birthday or two. Christmas morning. He'd have come more often if he didn't know it was difficult for his mother to look at him.

On top of tonight's catastrophe, did he really want to see his mother and encounter the flinch? Maybe he did. Maybe he'd come here to punish himself for hurting Hannah. For making her cry. For failing to be the man she stubbornly believed him to be.

Take some time and think.

Because next time you tell me good-bye, I'll believe you.

Did that mean she didn't believe him tonight?

Did she know he wouldn't have made it a day without texting her? Did she know he'd melt at the sight of her for the rest of his life, every single time she visited Westport? Did she suspect he'd fly to LA and beg for forgiveness?

He probably would have done all those things.

But he'd still be the same person, with all the same hang-ups.

And he didn't want them anymore.

Admitting that to himself untangled the fishing line in his gut, gave him the impetus to climb out of the car. All the apartments were identical, so he had to double-check his mother's address in his phone contacts. Then he was standing in front of her door, fist poised to knock, when Charlene opened it.

Winced at the sight of him.

Fox took it on the chin, like he always did. Smiled. Leaned in and kissed her cheek. "Hey, Ma."

She folded her arms behind his neck, squeezing him tight. "Well! Caroline from 1A called and said there was a handsome man lurking in the parking lot, and I was going to inspect. Turns out it was my son!"

Fox attempted a chuckle, but his throat only sounded like a garbage disposal. God, he felt like he'd been run over, the aches and pains stemming from the middle of his chest. "Next time, don't go check it out yourself. Call the police."

"Oh, I was just going to look through Caroline's binoculars and have a gab about it. Don't worry about me, boy. I'm indestructible." She stepped back and looked at him. "Not sure I can say the same for you. Never seen you look so green around the gills."

"Yeah." Finally, she took his elbow and ushered him inside, pointing him toward the small dining-room table, where he took a seat. The round piece of furniture was painted powder blue, covered in knickknacks, but the misshapen frog ashtray was what caught his attention. "Did I make this?"

"Sure did. Ceramics class your sophomore year of high school. Coffee?"

"No, thanks."

Charlene sat down across from him with a steaming mug in her hand. "Well, go on." She paused to take a sip. "Tell me what happened with Hannah."

Fox's chest wanted to cave in just hearing her name. "How did you know?"

"It's like I always say, a man doesn't bring a woman to bingo unless he's serious about her." She tapped a nail against her mug. "Nah. But in truth, I could tell by the way you looked at her, she was something real special."

"How did I look at her?" He was afraid to find out.

"Ah, son. Like a summer day showing up after a hundred years of winter."

Fox couldn't speak for long moments. Could only stare down at the table, trying to get rid of the painful squeeze in his throat, seventeen incarnations of Hannah's smile playing in his head. "Yeah, well. I told her it was over tonight. She disagreed."

Charlene had to set her coffee down, she was laughing so hard. "Hold on to that one." She used her wrist to swipe at her eyes. "She's a keeper."

"You don't really think I could, though." He twisted the ceramic frog on the table. "Hold on to her. Hold on to anyone."

His mother's laughter cut off abruptly. "And why not?"

"You know why."

"I surely do not."

Fox laughed without humor. "You know, Ma. The way I kept Dad's legacy alive. The way I've carried on more than half my life now. That's what I know. That's what I'm used to. It's no use trying to be something I'm not. And, Jesus, I'm definitely not one half of a couple."

Charlene fell silent, looking almost pained. Proof that she agreed. Maybe she didn't want to say it out loud, but she knew he spoke the truth.

It was too hard to witness her disappointment, but when Fox stood to leave, Charlene spoke and he lowered back into the seat.

"You never had the chance to try . . . to be anything else. 'He's going to be a heartbreaker, just like his father.' That's what everyone used to say, and I laughed. I laughed, but it stuck. And then . . ."

"What?"

"This is hard to talk about," she said quietly, standing to top off her coffee, eventually sitting back down and visibly gathering her poise. "I'd spent years of my life trying to change your father. Make him a home, make him happy with me and me alone. Us alone. Well, you know how that worked out. He came home smelling like a perfume factory five nights out of seven." She paused to huff a breath. "When you got older and started looking like him, I guess . . . I guess I was too scared to try. To teach you how to be different from him and have my heart broken all over again if you resisted. So I just . . . I didn't resist. In fact, I joined in with the chorus and encouraged you to break hearts and . . . and the coffee tin . . ." She covered her face with her hands. "I want to die just thinking about it."

On reflex, Fox glanced at the cabinet, as if he might find it there, stuffed full of condom money. Even though he wouldn't. Even though it wasn't the same house. "It's okay, Ma."

"No, it's not." She shook her head. "I needed to explain to you, Fox, that you're nothing like him. To correct the damaging things you believed about yourself. These misconceptions. But you'd already started doing exactly what we encouraged you to do from the start. When you came back from college, you'd retreated into a hard shell. There was no talking to you then. And here we are now, years later. Here we are."

Fox ran back through everything she'd said, his deepest insecurities exposed like a raw nerve, but so what. Nothing hurt like Hannah leaving hurt. Not even this. "If you don't think I'm anything like him, why do you flinch every time you see me?"

Charlene paled. "I'm sorry. I didn't realize I was doing that." A beat passed. "Some of the time, I can live with the guilt of failing you. When I see you, though, that guilt hits me like a backhand to the cheek. That flinch is for me, not you."

An unexpected burn started behind his eyes.

Something hard began to erode in the vicinity of his heart.

"I remember some of the things he said to you, all the way back to fourth grade, fifth grade. Which one in the class was your girlfriend? When were you going to start going on dates? Boy, you'll have your pick of the litter! And I thought it was funny. I even said those things myself once in a while." She reached for her pack of cigarettes, tapped one out and lit it, blowing the smoke out of the side of her mouth. "Should have been encouraging you to do well in class. Or join clubs. Instead, we made life about . . . intimacy for you. From the damn jump. And I don't have any excuse except to say, your father's life was women. By default, so was mine. The affairs surrounded us at the time, took up all the air. We let it hurt our son, too. Let it turn into a shadow to follow you around. That's the real tragedy. Not the marriage."

Fox had to stand up. Had to move.

He remembered his parents saying those things to him. Of course he did. However, all the way up until this moment, it never once occurred to him that *all* parents weren't saying those things to their kids. Never occurred to him that he'd effectively been brainwashed into believing his identity was the sum of his success with women. And . . .

And his mother didn't wince when she saw him because he reminded her of his father. It was guilt. Fox didn't like that, either. He owned his actions and didn't want his mother claiming responsibility for them, because that would be cowardly. But, God, it was a relief. To know his mother didn't dread seeing his face. To know he wasn't broken, but maybe, just maybe, he'd been wedged into a category before he even knew what was happening.

More than anything in that moment, he wished for Hannah.

He wished to burrow his face into her neck and tell her everything Charlene had said, so she could sum it up perfectly for him in her Hannah way. So she could kiss the salt from his skin and save him. But Hannah wasn't there. She'd gone. He'd sent her away. So he had to rescue himself. Had to work this out for himself.

"People will think she's crazy to take a chance on me. People will assume I'm going to do to her what Dad did to you."

When no response was forthcoming, Fox looked back over his shoulder to find Charlene aggressively stubbing out her cigarette. "Let me tell you a story. Earl and Georgette have been coming to bingo for over a decade, sitting on opposite sides of the hall. As far away from each other as they can get. They might look like sweet little seniors, but let me tell you, they are stubborn as shit." Charlene lit another cigarette, comfortable in the middle of her storytelling. "Earl used to be married to Georgette's sister, right up until she passed. Young. Maybe in her fifties. And, well, through comforting each other, Earl and Georgette got to falling in love, right? Both of them worried about people judging them, so they stopped seeing each other. Cut each other right off. But hell if they didn't stare at each other across the bingo hall like two lovesick puppies for years."

"What happened?"

"I'm going to tell you, aren't I?" She puffed her smoke. "Then Georgette got sick. Same illness as her sister. And there was Earl, not only left to realize he'd missed out on creating a life with the woman he loved, but having no right to help her through the rough time. No right to care for her. Did it matter what other people thought at that point? No. It did not."

"Christ, Ma. You couldn't have picked something a little more uplifting?"

"I haven't finished yet," she said patiently, enjoying herself. "Earl professed his love to Georgette and moved in, nursed her back to health. Now they sit in the front row every time I host bingo in Aberdeen. Can't pry them apart with a butter knife. And you know what? Everyone is happy for them. You can't live life worrying about what people will think. You'll wake up one day, look at a calendar, and count the days you could have spent being happy. With her. And no one else, especially the ones wagging their tongues, are going to be there to console you."

Fox thought of waking up in fifteen years and having spent none of it with Hannah, and he got dizzy, his mother's kitchen spinning around him, his lungs on fire. Crossing to the living room, he fell back on the couch and counted off his breaths, trying to fight through the sudden nausea.

Exhaustion crashed down on him unexpectedly, and he wasn't sure why. Maybe it was having his long-standing issues unraveled, explained, and the subsequent weightless feeling in his stomach. Maybe it was the emotional excess or the utter depression of losing Hannah and making her cry, plus knowing his mother didn't secretly hate him. All of it wrapping around his head like a thick, fuzzy bandage, blurring his thoughts until they were nothing more than a fading echo. His head dropped back against the cushion, and his roundabout worries eventually sent him into a deep sleep. The last thing he remembered was his mother laying a blanket over him and the promise he made to himself. As soon as he woke up, he'd go get her.

Hang on. I'll be right there, Freckles.

Fox woke up in the sunlight to the chatter of voices.

He sat up and looked around, piecing together the night before, trying to clear the cobwebs that clung harder than usual. Tchotchkes on every surface, the lingering smell of Marlboro Reds. This was his mother's living room. He knew that much. And then their conversation came back in precise detail, followed by a sinking feeling in his stomach.

It was morning. Eight in the morning.

The bus . . . the bus back to LA left at seven.

"No." Fox almost got sick. "No, no, no."

He was off the couch like a shot, his stomach pitching violently. Several pairs of eyes stared back at him from the kitchen, belonging to the senior ladies who'd apparently congregated in Charlene's kitchen for coffee and donuts.

"Morning, honey," his mother sang from the table, in the same place she'd sat last night. Same mug in her hands. "Got a bear claw over here with your name on it. Come meet the lady gang."

"I can't. I . . . She's leaving. She's . . . left?" He patted the pocket of his jeans and found his phone, the battery at 6 percent, and quickly tapped Hannah's number, raking a hand through his hair and pacing while it rang. No way. No way he let her get on a bus back to California. He didn't have a plan yet, didn't have a strategy for keeping Hannah. He only knew that the fear of God was rattling his bones. That—the reality of her actually being gone—along with what his mother had said to him last night, had damn well put Fox's priorities in order.

My head is out of my ass, Hannah. Answer the phone.

Voicemail.

Of course it was the opening bars to "Me and Bobby McGee," followed by the husky efficiency of her greeting.

Fox stopped pacing, the sound of her voice against his ear washing over him like warmth from a fireplace. Oh God, oh

God, he'd been such a jackass. This girl, this one-in-a-billion angel of a girl, loved him. He loved her back in a wild, desperate, uncontrollable way. And he didn't know how to build a home with her, but they would figure it out together. That he was positive about.

Hannah gave him faith. She *was* his faith.

The beep sounded in his ear. "Hannah, it's me. Please, please, get off the bus. I'm coming home right now. I'm . . ." His voice lost power. "Just get off the bus somewhere safe and wait for me, all right? I fucking love you. I love you. And I'm sorry you fell in love with an idiot. I'm . . ." *Find the words. Find the right words.* "Remember in Seattle, you said we've been trying this whole time. Since last summer. To be in a relationship. I didn't fully understand at the time, but I do now. There was never going to be a life away from you, because, Jesus, that's no life at all. You, Hannah. Are my life. I love you and I'm coming home, so please, babe. Please. Will you just wait for me? I'm sorry."

Fox stopped and listened, as if she might somehow answer and reassure him like she always did, then hung up with dread curdling in his stomach. Looked up to find the women in various states of crying, from dabbing away tears to openly weeping.

"I have to go."

No one tried to stop Fox as he ran out the door and sprinted to his truck, throwing himself into the driver's seat and peeling out. He hit a stoplight on the way to the highway and cursed, slamming on the brakes. Restless without being in motion, he took out his phone again and called Brendan.

"Fox," the captain said, answering on the first ring. "I've been meaning to call you, actually. I want to apologize again—"

"Good. Do it another time, though." The light turned green, and he floored it, merging onto the highway, thanking God there didn't seem to be any rush hour traffic. "Is Hannah with you guys? Did she stay there last night?"

A brief pause. "No. She didn't stay with you?"

"No." Knowing he could have spent the night with Hannah—and didn't—was a bitter pill to swallow. It was a world that didn't make sense, and he never wanted to live in it again. Where would she have gone? There were a couple of inns in Westport, but she wouldn't check in somewhere, would she? Maybe she'd gone to the house where the crew was staying. All of them would have gotten on the bus an hour ago. She went with them. *She's gone.* "No, she's not with me," he rasped, misery washing over him. "Look. It's complicated. Predictably, I fucked everything up. I need a chance to fix it."

"Hey. Whatever you did, I'm sure you can repair it."

No accusations. No knowing sighs or disappointment.

Just faith.

Fox ached just above his collarbone. Maybe, like the ocean, he could evolve.

Maybe the crew would realize they were wrong about him after some time passed. After all, they were just following his lead, treating him like he asked them to. Like the cheap version of himself he'd presented. Demanding respect from Brendan one time was all it took to change his best friend's tune. What if that was all it took to do the same with everyone else?

And if it didn't work? The hell with them. His relationship with Hannah belonged to him and her. No one else.

Either way, he was going to do everything in his power to keep Hannah.

That was a given.

Imagining a future without her had his hands shaking on the wheel.

For the first time since he'd left for college, he was eager to find out how far his potential could reach. He was ready to take chances again. Maybe because he now knew, after speaking frankly with Charlene, that he'd been guided incorrectly. Or maybe because he was no longer so afraid of being judged. He was driving blindly, pretty sure Hannah had gone back to LA. *This* was pain. This was self-loathing. Losing the love of his life—his future—because he'd let the past win. He could endure and overcome anything but this.

Cradling the phone between his cheek and shoulder, he ripped off the leather bracelet and threw it out the window of his car. "I want the boat, Brendan."

Even without seeing his best friend's face, he could imagine the raised eyebrow, the thoughtful stroking of his jaw. "You sure?"

"Positive. And I'm putting in a new chair. Your ass grooves are in the old one." He waited for his friend to stop chuckling. "Is Piper there? Has she spoken to Hannah?"

"She's out on her run. I can call her—"

Fox's phone died.

The breath hissed out of him, and he threw the device onto the dashboard, heart slamming in his ears as he wove in and out of traffic. She couldn't be gone. All right, they hadn't agreed on a timeline for him to come and find her. Perhaps she thought she'd go back to LA and he'd take a few weeks or even months to figure out he'd die without her? Maybe he should have assumed she would leave this morning? Well, he hadn't.

He'd been thinking about it for weeks, and when the moment finally came, his heart had blocked the painful possibility.

Too late. He was too late.

God, she could have changed her mind. Maybe she wasn't giving him time to pull his head out of his stubborn ass at all. That would explain why she wasn't answering her phone. She'd deemed Fox more trouble than he was worth. If that was the case, it wouldn't matter if he flew to LA. Or drove like a bat out of hell and caught up with the bus. If she was done with him . . .

No.

No, please. He couldn't think like that.

With his skin somehow icy and sweating at the same time, Fox took the exit to Westport an hour and a half later, searching the streets for members of the cast or crew. Would he even recognize any of them? At that moment, he would have been grateful to see the fucking director and his yuppie turtleneck. None of the people waving as he passed were non-locals, though. None of them. No bus idling on the harbor.

Gone.

"No, Hannah," he said hoarsely. "No."

He parked haphazardly outside his apartment, prepared to go inside and pack a bag. He'd get on the highway and catch up with the bus. Wait for it to stop and beg her to listen. If he couldn't find the bus, he'd get on a plane. Bottom line, he wasn't coming back here until they were unequivocally committed. With a plan.

A plan.

He might have laughed if he wasn't on the verge of splitting straight down the middle. Suddenly, he could think of a million plans. Because he was capable of anything. They were. Together.

As long as she hadn't given up on him—

Fox walked into his apartment and stopped dead in his tracks.

Hannah sat cross-legged on the floor in front of his record player, giant can headphones over her ears, humming along to the music.

If she'd heard him or turned around in that moment, she would have seen him slump back against the door, shaking. Seen him use the hem of his T-shirt to wipe the scalding moisture from his eyes. Would have seen the prayers he mouthed at the ceiling. But, oblivious, she didn't turn. Didn't witness him devouring the tilt of her neck with his gaze, the line of her shoulders. Inhaling the breathiness of her voice singing along to Soundgarden.

As soon as he could walk straight, he went toward her, picking up her phone where it rested on the counter, his voicemail not yet played.

He dug for the right words.

Ones that could possibly express how much he loved her.

But in the end, all he had to do was listen to his heart and trust himself.

He came to a stop beside her, and she jolted and looked up at him.

They stared for long moments, searching each other for answers.

He gave her one by changing the record. Putting on "Let's Stay Together" by Al Green. Watching her expression soften with each word. Lyrics that couldn't have been more appropriate. When tears started to fill her beautiful eyes, Fox pulled Hannah to her feet and they slow danced to the music in her ears and the music in his heart, the headphones only coming off when the song ended.

"I love you," Fox said thickly, still rocking her side to side. Holding on to her like a life preserver in the middle of the Bering. "Oh my God, I love you so much, Hannah." He burrowed his face into her hair, starved for closeness to her, this incredible person who somehow loved him. "I thought you left," he said, lifting her off the floor and walking toward the bedroom. "I thought you left."

"No. I couldn't. I wouldn't." Her arms tightened around his neck. "I love you too much."

As he laid her down on the bed, tears leaked from his eyes, and Hannah reached up, wiped them away, along with her own. "What happened to you giving me time to pull my head out of my ass?"

"Six hours seemed like more than enough," she whispered up at him.

Happiness rushed in, crowding him from all sides. And he let it. Let himself accept it and think of all the ways he could give happiness to her in return. For the rest of his life. Every hour, every day.

Fox covered her with his body, both of them groaning against each other's mouth, sliding and writhing muscle on curves. "We can find a place in between here and Seattle. That way if you get a job in the city, we cut the commute in half for us both." He unfastened her jeans and pushed a hand inside, watching her eyes go blind when his fingers tucked into her panties and found her. There. Pressing between her seam of flesh and rubbing with increasing pressure. "Does that work for you?"

"Yes," she gasped when he slowly worked his middle finger inside, drawing it in and out. "Mmmm. I like that idea. W-we can find out who we'll become together. Without everyone around all the t-time."

Fox nodded, took his time tugging off her jeans and panties, eventually rendering her naked while he remained fully clothed on top of her, pressing her down into the bedclothes. "Whoever we become together, Hannah," he said, mouth roaming over hers, fingers reaching down to lower his zipper. "I'm yours and you're mine. So it's always going to be right." His throat started to close as he pushed inside her, those thighs of hers jerking up into the perfect position. "I didn't know what right felt like until you," he choked out. "I'm holding on to the good you give me. I'm holding on to you."

"I'm hanging on to you, too, Fox Thornton," she murmured unevenly, her body propelled up the bed on his first drive, eyes glazing. "Never letting go."

"I'm in for the good, bad, and everything in between, Hannah." He pressed his open mouth to the side of her neck and pushed deeper, deep enough, close enough to feel her breathe, and rejoiced in it. "Decades. A lifetime. I'm in."

Epilogue

Ten Years Later

The smooth voice of Nat King Cole filled the interior of Hannah's Jeep as it bumped along the snowy road. Her headlights caught the falling flakes, twilight giving the sky a purplish-gray glow, towering pines creating a now-familiar pathway on either side of her—a pathway home to her family.

After ten years of residing in Puyallup, it was hard to believe she'd ever lived in sunny Los Angeles at all. And she wouldn't trade it for all the records in Washington.

Her eyes drifted to the rearview mirror, where she could see shopping bags filled to overflowing with elaborately wrapped presents in the backseat, and contentment swept through her chest, so intense it brought tears to her eyes. There would never be anything better than this. Coming home to her family on Christmas Eve after four days on the road. She missed them so terribly, it cost her quite an effort to drive slowly, carefully on the winter road.

When her house came into view a minute later and her tires crunched to a stop in the driveway, her heart started to beat faster. Smoke curled lazily from the chimney of their log-cabin-style home, sleds—man-sized and child-sized— leaned up against the wall by the front entrance. A Christmas tree twinkled in one of the many windows. And when her husband walked into view with one of their daughters slung casually over his brawny shoulder, a laugh filled with yearning and love and gratitude puffed out of her in the quiet car.

They'd more than made it work, hadn't they? They'd made a life happier and filled with more joy than either of them could have expected.

A decade earlier, Fox and Hannah went to Bel-Air to pack her things. She could still remember the zero-gravity feeling of that trip. The lack of restraint that came with their commitment to each other, every touch, every whisper heightened, given new meaning. And yet, on the verge of what felt like true adulthood, they'd both been scared. But they'd been scared together, honest with each other every step of the way, and they'd become a formidable team.

Initially, they'd signed an apartment lease in town, this midway point between Westport and Seattle. She still missed that apartment sometimes, itched to walk the creaky floor and remember all the lessons they'd learned within those walls. How fiercely they'd loved, how loudly they'd fought and made up, the music they'd danced to, how Fox had gotten down on one knee on a night just like this and asked Hannah to be his wife, how they'd panicked when she got pregnant a year later. How they'd sat on the floor and eaten cake straight out of the box with forks—Fox in a suit, her in a dress—on the morning they bought this house.

Since then, they'd made a million memories, each day with a different soundtrack, and she cherished every single one.

Unable to wait another second to see Fox and the girls, Hannah opened the driver's-side door, careful not to slip on the driveway in her fancy wedge boots. Not practical in this weather, but she'd gone straight to LAX after her final client meeting. Thank God she wouldn't have to see the inside of another airport until mid-January, well after the holidays. Her travel schedule had definitely lightened over the years, the process more streamlined and virtual, but every once in a while, she discovered a band worth seeing in person, as she'd done this week.

Garden of Sound Inc. had started as Hannah's baby, a way of connecting up-and-coming bands with film production companies seeking fresh voices for their scores—and years later, she'd found herself a staple in the industry. After *Glory Daze* released and the Unreliables blew up, her name got passed around more and more. She'd built a reputation for giving films their signature sound, adding an entirely new layer of creativity to the process, and she couldn't imagine doing anything else.

Hannah opened the back door of the Jeep and considered calling Fox to help her carry the bags, but decided she'd rather walk through the front door and surprise the three of them. And she'd better get her butt moving, because Piper, Brendan, and their two kids would be arriving soon to stay through New Year's. Not to mention, Charlene—aka Grams—would be here in the morning.

Draping a heavy bag over each arm, Hannah bumped the car door shut with a hip and headed up the path, her cheeks already aching from smiling. She set down the presents just outside the front door and dug in her coat pocket for her keys. They jingled only slightly, but that was all it took to set off their pair of yellow labs barking.

Shaking her head and laughing, distracted by trying to get the key into the lock, Hannah almost didn't see the moose. But when the giant shadow moved in her periphery, she froze, slowly turning her head, mouth falling open in shock as the granddaddy of all moose moseyed toward her like they were going to have a casual chat in the supermarket. Moose were not especially dangerous animals, but they'd lived in this area long enough to hear about attacks. Usually the animals only reacted poorly when provoked, but she wasn't taking any chances. That thing could mow her down like a semitruck.

"Fox . . ." Hannah called, way too quietly to be detected by human ears. And then she dropped her keys in the snow. Come on. No way she was bending down to pick those up. She'd have to take her eyes off the beast. Abandoning the presents and sidestepping off the porch slowly, she backed in the direction of the car. The moose watched from its height of at least thirteen, maybe twenty-nine feet while Hannah slipped the cell from her pocket and dialed HOME.

"You must be outside, since the dogs are acting like maniacs," Fox answered, voice warm in her ear. "Thank God, babe. I missed you like hell. You need some help carrying in your suitcase? I'll be right—"

"Moose," she said in a strangled whisper. "There's a moose right outside the door. Keep the girls inside. It's eight hundred feet tall, I'm not even kidding."

"A moose?" Concern hardened his voice. "Hannah, get inside."

"I dropped my keys." She turned and ran, squealing in her throat the whole way. "I'm hiding behind the car."

He was breathing hard. "I'm coming."

No less than ten seconds later, her husband skidded out onto the porch, barefoot in sweatpants and a hoodie, banging pots together and shouting obscenities at the moose, backing the animal up several paces. In the front window of the house, their girls—six-year-old Abigail and four-year-old Stevie—screamed bloody murder, their little palms slapping against the window hard enough to rattle it. The dogs howled. And crouching down behind the back bumper of the Jeep, Hannah absolutely lost it. She laughed hard enough to slip on the drive-way and land on her backside, which only made her laugh harder. By the time she got control of herself, she was looking up at Fox through tears of mirth.

Oh, but then, there was just . . . a long, wobbly sigh of appre-ciation for the man holding out his rope-worn hand to help her up. Age had done him so good. Now forty-one, the *Della Ray*'s captain had a full beard and dark blond hair, just beginning to show threads of gray, that almost reached his shoulders. He'd cut it once, last year, and the girls cried when they saw the shorter length, so he vowed to keep it long forever. They had their father wrapped around their pinkie fingers, and he would admit it to anyone who listened. Hannah estimated the devotion to his daughters made him around 400 percent more attractive.

And as always, his devotion to Hannah shone in his blue eyes, which were twinkling over the chaos, just like hers.

"He's gone," Fox said gruffly, wrapping their fingers together. "Come inside now and make up for scaring ten years off my life."

"Should be easy since I brought presents—"

She lost her balance, slipping on the ice, and Fox, his balance normally perfect thanks to his profession, went down with his wife. He tried to cushion her fall, but they just ended up sprawled on their asses in the driveway, snow falling around them, their howls of laughter bringing their daughters running from the house in flannel nightgowns and hastily shoved-on boots. While Abby and Stevie started an impromptu snowball fight, Fox pulled Hannah into his arms, tipping up her chin so he could look at her face, his heart knocking heavily against her shoulder.

"Jesus, Hannah," he whispered in a rough voice. "Do you ever get so happy, you can barely stand it?"

"Yes." She reached up and cradled his jaw. "With you? All the time."

He made a sound in his throat, brushed some snowflakes from her cheek. "Doesn't feel like enough to say I love you at this point."

"Our love is always enough. It's always more than enough."

Throat flexing, he nodded. Looked into her eyes for long moments, before lowering his lips and kissing her slowly, sweeping his tongue through her mouth enough times and with enough promise to make her squirm, breathless. One kiss only ignited their appetite, and with the dogs happily chasing the girls through the front yard, they were in no rush to stop. Not until minutes later when another car pulled up and Piper's giggle sailed out into the evening air, followed by Brendan's exasperated sigh.

"Hey, Aunt Hannah and Uncle Fox!" their nine-year-old nephew, Henry, called. "Get a room."

"We've got a whole house of them," Fox said, finally standing and pulling Hannah to her feet, tucking her against his side. "We've got everything we could ever want," he added, for her ears alone. And together, aunts, uncles, cousins, and dogs walked up the path to share Christmas Eve, same as they would every single Christmas, forever and always.

Have you read Piper's story? Find out how she
hooked a surly, sexy sea captain in . . .

IT HAPPENED
ONE SUMMER

Available now!

Read on for a peek at the first few chapters.

Chapter One

The unthinkable was happening.

Her longest relationship on record . . . over in the blink of an eye.

Three weeks of her life *wasted*.

Piper Bellinger looked down at her lipstick-red, one-shoulder Valentino cocktail dress and tried to find the flaw but came up with nothing. Her tastefully tanned legs were polished to such a shine, she'd checked her teeth in them earlier. Nothing appeared amiss up top, either. She'd swiped the tape holding up her boobs while backstage at a runway show in Milan during fashion week—we're talking the holy grail of tit tape—and those puppies were on point. Big enough to draw a man's eye, small enough to achieve an athletic vibe in every fourth Instagram post. Versatility kept people interested.

Satisfied that nothing concerning her appearance was glaringly out of place, Piper trailed her gaze up the pleated leg of Adrian's classic Tom Ford suit made of the finest sharkskin wool, unable to quell a sigh over the luxurious peak lapels and monogrammed buttons. The way her boyfriend impatiently checked his Chopard watch and scanned the crowd over her shoulder only added to the bored-playboy effect.

Hadn't his cold unattainability attracted her to him in the first place?

God, the night of their first meeting seemed like a hundred years ago. She'd had at least two facials since then, right? What *was* time anymore? Piper could remember their introduction like it was yesterday. Adrian had saved her from stepping in vomit at Rumer Willis's birthday party. As she'd stared up at his chiseled chin from her place in his arms, she'd been transported to Old Hollywood. A time of smoking jackets and women traipsing around in long, feathered robes. It was the beginning of her own classic love story.

And now the credits were rolling.

"I can't believe you're throwing it all away like this," Piper whispered, pressing her champagne flute between her breasts. Maybe drawing his attention there would change his mind? "We've been through so much."

"Yeah, tons, right?"

Adrian waved at someone across the rooftop, his expression letting whoever it was know that he'd be right with them. They'd come to the black, white, and red party together. A minor soiree to raise money for an indie movie project called *Lifestyles of the Oppressed and Famous*. The writer-director was a friend of Adrian's, meaning most of the people at this gathering of Los Angeles elite were his acquaintances. Her girls weren't even there to console her or facilitate a graceful exit.

Adrian's attention settled back on her reluctantly. "Wait, what were you saying?"

Piper's smile felt brittle, so she turned it up another watt, careful to keep it one crucial notch below manic. *Chin up, woman.* This wasn't her first breakup, right? She'd done a lot of the dumping, often unexpectedly. This was a town of whims, after all.

She'd never really noticed the pace of how things changed. Not until lately.

At twenty-eight, Piper was not old. But she *was* one of the oldest women at this party. At every party she'd been to recently, come to think of it. Leaning on the glass railing that overlooked Melrose was an up-and-coming pop star who couldn't be a day older than nineteen. She didn't need tape from Milan to hold up her tits. They were light and springy with nipples that reminded Piper of the bottom of an ice cream cone.

The host himself was twenty-two and embarking on a film career.

This was Piper's career. Partying. Being seen. Holding up the occasional teeth-whitening product and getting a few dollars for it.

Not that she needed the money. At least, she didn't think so. Everything she owned came from the swipe of a credit card, and it was a mystery what happened after that. She assumed the bill went to her stepfather's email or something? Hopefully he wouldn't be weird about the crotchless panties she'd ordered from Paris.

"Piper? *Hello?*" Adrian swiped a hand in front of her face, and she realized how long she'd been staring at the pop star. Long enough that the songstress was glaring back.

Piper smiled and waved at the girl, pointing sheepishly to her glass of champagne, before tuning back in to the conversation with Adrian. "Is this because I casually brought you up to my therapist? We didn't go in depth or anything, I promise. Most of the time we just nap during my appointments."

He stared at her for several seconds. Honestly, it was kind of nice. It was the most attention she'd gotten from him since almost slipping in puke. "I've dated some airheads, Piper." He sighed. "But you put them all to shame."

She kept her smile in place, though it took more determination than usual. People were watching. At that very moment, she was in the background of at least five selfies being captured around the roof, including one of Ansel Elgort. It would be a disaster if she let her sinking heart show on her face, especially when news of the breakup got out. "I don't understand," she said with a laugh, sweeping rose-gold hair over her shoulder.

"Shocking," he returned drily. "Look, babe. It was a fun three weeks. You're a smoke show in a bikini." He shrugged an elegant Tom Ford–clad shoulder. "I'm just trying to end this before it gets boring, you know?"

Boring. Getting older. Not a director or a pop star.

Just a pretty girl with a millionaire stepfather.

Piper couldn't think about that now, though. She just wanted to exit the party as inconspicuously as possible and go have a good cry. After she popped a Xanax and posted an inspirational quote on her IG feed, of course. It would confirm the breakup, but also allow her to control the narrative. Something about growth and loving herself, maybe?

Her sister, Hannah, would have the perfect song lyric to include. She was always sitting around in a pile of vinyls, those giant, ugly headphones wrapped around her head. Damn, she wished she'd put more stock in Hannah's opinion of Adrian.

What had she said? Oh yeah.

He's like if someone drew eyes on a turnip.

Once again, Piper had zoned out, and Adrian checked his watch for the second time. "Are we done here? I have to mingle."

"Oh. *Yeah*," she rushed to say, her voice horrifyingly unnatural. "You couldn't be more right about breaking things off before the boring blues strike. I didn't think about it like that." She clinked her champagne glass against his. "We're consciously uncoupling. *Très* mature."

"Right. Call it whatever you want." Adrian forced a wan smile. "Thanks for everything."

"No, thank *you*." She pursed her lips, trying to appear as non-airhead-like as possible. "I've learned a lot about myself over the last three weeks."

"Come on, Piper." Adrian laughed, scrutinizing her head to toe. "You play dress-up and spend your daddy's money. You don't have a reason to learn anything."

"Do I need a reason?" she asked lightly, lips still tilted at the corners.

Annoyed at being waylaid, Adrian huffed a breath. "I guess not. But you definitely need a brain that functions beyond how many likes you can get on a picture of your rack. There's more to life than that, Piper."

"Yes, I know," she said, prodded by irritation—and more than a little bit of reluctant shame. "Life is what I'm documenting through photos. I—"

"God." He half groaned, half laughed. "Why are you *forcing* me to be an asshole?" Someone called his name from inside the penthouse, and he held up a finger, keeping his gaze locked on Piper. "There's just nothing to you, okay? There are thousands of Piper Bellingers in this city. You're just a way to pass the time." He shrugged. "And your time has passed."

It was a miracle Piper kept her winning smile intact as Adrian sailed away, already calling out to his friends. Everyone on the roof deck was staring at her, whispering behind their hands, feeling sorry for her—of all the horrors. She saluted them with her glass, then realized it was empty. Setting it down on the tray of a passing waiter, she collected her Bottega Veneta satin knot clutch with all the dignity she could muster and glided through the throng of onlookers, blinking back the moisture in her eyes to bring the elevator call button into focus.

When the doors finally hid her from view, she slumped back against the metal wall, taking deep breaths in through her nose, out through her mouth. Already the news that she'd been dumped by Adrian would be blasted across all the socials, maybe even with video included. Not even C-list celebrities would invite her to parties after this.

She had a reputation as a good time. Someone to covet. An "it girl."

If she didn't have her social status, what *did* she have?

Piper pulled her phone out of her clutch and absently requested a luxury Uber, connecting her with a driver who was only five minutes away. Then she closed the app and pulled up her favorites list. Her thumb hovered over the name "Hannah" momentarily, but landed on "Kirby," instead. Her friend answered on the first ring.

"Oh my God, is it true you begged Adrian not to break up with you in front of Ansel Elgort?"

It was worse than she thought. How many people had already tipped off TMZ? Tomorrow night at six thirty, they would be tossing her name around the newsroom while Harvey sipped from his reusable cup. "I didn't beg Adrian to keep me. Come on, Kirby, you know me better than that."

"Bitch, I do. But I'm not everyone else. You need to do damage control. Do you have a publicist on retainer?"

"Not anymore. Daniel said me going shopping doesn't need a press release."

Kirby snorted. "Okay, boomer."

"But you're right. I do need damage control." The elevator doors opened, and Piper stepped off, clicking through the lobby in her red-soled pumps, eventually stepping out onto Wilshire, the warm July air drying the dampness in her eyes. The tall buildings of downtown Los Angeles reached up into the smoggy summer night sky, and she craned her neck to find the tops. "How late is the rooftop pool open at the Mondrian?"

"You're asking about hours of operation at a time like this?" Kirby griped, followed by the sound of her vape crackling in the background. "I don't know, but it's past midnight. If it's not already closed, it will be soon."

A black Lincoln pulled up along the curb. After double-checking the license plate number, Piper climbed inside and shut the door. "Wouldn't breaking into the pool and having the time of our lives be, like, *the* best way to fight fire with fire? Adrian would be the guy who broke up with a legend."

"Oh shit," Kirby breathed. "You're resurrecting Piper twenty fourteen."

This was the answer, wasn't it? There was no better time in her life than the year she turned twenty-one and ran absolutely buck wild through Los Angeles, making herself famous for being famous in the process. She was just in a rut, that was all. Maybe it was time to reclaim her crown. Maybe then she wouldn't hear Adrian's words looping over and over again in the back of her head, forcing her to consider that he might be right.

Am I just one of thousands?

Or am I the girl who breaks into a pool for a swim at one o'clock in the morning?

Piper nodded resolutely and leaned forward. "Can you take me to the Mondrian, instead, please?"

Kirby hooted down the line. "I'll meet you there."

"I've got a better idea." Piper crossed her legs and fell back in the leather seat. "How about we have *everyone* meet us there?"

Chapter Two

*J*ail was a cold, dark place.

Piper stood in the very center of the cell shivering and hugging her elbows so she wouldn't accidentally touch anything that might require a tetanus shot. Until this moment, the word "torture" had only been a vague description of something she'd never understand. But trying to *not pee* in the moldy toilet after roughly six mixed drinks was a torment no woman should ever know. The late-night Coachella bathroom situation had nothing on this grimy metal throne that mocked her from the corner of the cell.

"Excuse me?" Piper called, wobbling to the bars in her heels. There were no guards in sight, but she could hear the distinctive sounds of *Candy Crush* coming from nearby. "Hi, it's me, Piper. Is there another bathroom I could use?"

"No, princess," a woman's voice called back, sounding very bored. "There isn't."

She bounced side to side, her bladder demanding to be evacuated. "Where do *you* go to the bathroom?"

A snort. "Where the *other* non-criminals go."

Piper whined in her throat, although the lady guard went up a notch in her book for delivering such a savage response without hesitation. "I'm not a criminal," Piper tried again. "This is all a misunderstanding."

A trill of laughter echoed down the drab hallway of the police station. How many times had she passed the station on North Wilcox? Now she was an inmate.

But seriously, it had been one hell of a party.

The guard slowly appeared in front of Piper's cell, fingers tucked into her beige uniform pants. *Beige.* Whoever was at the helm of law enforcement fashion should be sentenced for cruel and unusual punishment. "You call two hundred people breaking into a hotel pool after hours a misunderstanding?"

Piper crossed her legs and sucked in a breath through her nose. If she peed herself in Valentino, she would voluntarily remain in jail. "Would you believe the pool hours weren't prominently posted?"

"Is that the argument your expensive lawyer is going to use?" The guard shook her head, visibly amused. "Someone had to shatter the glass door to get inside and let all the other rich kids in. Who did that? The invisible man?"

"I don't know, but I'm going to find out," Piper vowed solemnly.

The guard sighed through a smile. "It's too late for that, sweetheart. Your friend with the purple tips already named you as the ringleader."

Kirby.

Had to be.

No one else at the party had purple tips. At least, Piper didn't think so. Somewhere between the chicken fights in the pool and the illegal firecrackers being set off, she'd kind of lost track of the incoming guests. She should have known better than to trust Kirby, though. She and Piper were friends, but not good enough for her to lie to the police. The foundation of their relationship was commenting on each other's social media posts and enabling each other to make ridiculous purchases, like a four-thousand-dollar purse shaped like a tube of lipstick. Most times, those kinds of surface-level friendships were valuable, but not tonight.

That's why her one phone call had gone to Hannah.

Speaking of whom, where *was* her little sister? She'd made that call an hour ago.

Piper hopped side to side, dangerously close to using her hands to keep the urine contained. "Who is forcing you to wear beige pants?" she gasped. "Why aren't they in here with me?"

"Fine." The guard flashed a palm. "On this we can agree."

"Literally any other color would be better. *No* pants would be better." Trying to distract herself from the Chernobyl happening in her lower body, she rambled, as she was wont to do in uncomfortable situations. "You have a really cute figure, Officer, but it's, like, a commandment that no one shall pull off nude khaki."

The other woman's eyebrow arched. "You could."

"You're right," Piper sobbed. "I totally could."

The guard's laugh faded into a sigh. "What were you thinking, inciting that chaos tonight?"

Piper slumped a little. "My boyfriend dumped me. And he . . . didn't even look me in the eye the whole time. I guess I just wanted to be seen. Acknowledged. Celebrated instead of . . . disregarded. You know?"

"Scorned and acting like a fool. Can't say I haven't been there."

"Really?" Piper asked hopefully.

"Sure. Who hasn't put all their boyfriend's clothes in the bathtub and poured bleach on top?"

Piper thought of the Tom Ford suit turning splotchy, and shivered. "That's cold," she whispered. "Maybe I should have just slashed his tires. At least that's legal."

"That's . . . not legal."

"Oh." Piper sent the guard an exaggerated wink. "*Riiiight.*"

The woman shook her head, glancing up and down the hallway. "All right, look. It's a quiet night. If you don't give me any trouble, I'll let you use the slightly less shitty bathroom."

"Oh, thank you, thank you, thank you."

With her keys poised over the keyhole, the guard hit her with serious eyes. "I have a Taser."

Piper followed her savior down the hall to the bathroom, where she meticulously gathered the skirt of her Valentino and eased the unholy pressure in her bladder, moaning until the final drop fell. As she washed her hands in the small sink, her attention caught on the reflection in the mirror. Raccoon eyes looked back at her. Smeared lipstick, limp hair. Definitely a long way from where she'd begun the evening, but she couldn't help but feel like a soldier returning from battle. She'd set out to divert attention from her breakup, hadn't she?

An LAPD helicopter circling overhead while she led a conga line had definitely reaffirmed her status as the reigning party queen of Los Angeles. Probably. They'd confiscated her phone during the whole mug shot/fingerprint thing, so she didn't know what was happening on the internet. Her fingers were itching to tap some apps, and that's exactly what she would do as soon as Hannah arrived to bail her out.

She looked at her reflection, surprised to find the prospect of breaking the internet didn't set her heart into a thrilling pitter-patter the way it did before. Was she broken?

Piper snorted and pushed away from the sink, using an elbow to pull down the door handle upon leaving. Obviously the night had taken its toll—after all, it was nearly five o'clock in the morning. As soon as she got some sleep, she'd spend the day reveling in congratulatory texts and an inundation of new followers. All would be well.

The guard cuffed Piper again and started to walk her back to the cell, just as another guard called down to them from the opposite end. "Yo, Lina. Bellinger made bail. Bring her down to processing."

Her arms flew up in victory. *"Yes!"*

Lina laughed. "Come on, beauty queen."

Vigor restored, Piper skipped alongside the other woman. "Lina, huh? I owe you big-time." She clutched her hands beneath her chin and gave her a winning pout. "Thank you for being so nice to me."

"Don't read too much into it," drawled the guard, though her expression was pleased. "I just wasn't in the mood to clean up piss."

Piper laughed, allowing Lina to unlock the door at the end of the gray hallway. And there was Hannah in the processing area, wearing pajamas and a ball cap, filling out paperwork with her eyes half closed.

Warmth wiggled into Piper's chest at the sight of her younger sister. They were nothing alike, had even less in common, but there was no one else Piper would call in a pinch. Of the two sisters, Hannah was the dependable one, even though she had a lazy hippie side.

Where Piper was taller, Hannah had been called a shrimp growing up and never quite hit the middle school growth spurt. At the moment, she kept her petite figure buried under a UCLA sweatshirt, her sandy-blond hair poking out around the blank red hat.

"She clear?" Lina asked a thin-lipped man hunched behind the desk.

He waved a hand without looking up. "Money solves every-thing."

Lina unlocked her cuffs once again, and she shot forward. "*Hannnnns*," Piper whimpered, throwing her arms around her sister. "I'll pay you back for this. I'll do your chores for a week."

"We don't have chores, you radish." Hannah yawned, grinding a fist into her eye. "Why do you smell like incense?"

"Oh." Piper sniffed her shoulder. "I think the fortune-teller lit some." Straightening, she squinted her eyes. "Not sure how she found out about the party."

Hannah gaped, seeming to awaken at least marginally, her hazel eyes a total contrast to Piper's baby blues. "Did she happen to tell you there's an angry stepfather in your future?"

Piper winced. "Oof. I had a feeling I couldn't avoid the wrath of Daniel Q. Bellinger." She craned her neck to see if there was anyone retrieving her phone. "How did he find out?"

"The news, Pipes. The news."

"Right." She sighed, smoothing her hands down the rumpled skirt of her dress. "Nothing the lawyers can't handle, right?

Hopefully he'll let me get in a shower and some sleep before one of his famous lectures. I'm a walking *after* photo."

"Shut up, you look great," Hannah said, her lips twitching as she completed the paperwork with a flourish of her signature. "You always look great."

Piper did a little shimmy.

"Bye, Lina!" Piper called on the way out of the station, her beloved phone cradled in her arms like a newborn, fingers vibrating with the need to swipe. She'd been directed to the back exit where Hannah could pull the car around. *Protocol,* they'd said.

She took one step out the door and was surrounded by photographers. "Piper! Over here!"

Her vanity screeched like a pterodactyl.

Nerves swerved right and left in her belly, but she flashed them a quick smile and put her head down, clicking as fast as she could toward Hannah's waiting Jeep.

"Piper Bellinger!" one of the paparazzi shouted. "How was your night in jail?"

"Do you regret wasting taxpayer money?"

The toe of her high heel caught in a crack, and she almost sprawled face-first onto the asphalt but caught the edge of the door Hannah had pushed open, throwing herself into the passenger side. Closing the door helped cut off the shouted questions, but the last one she'd heard continued to blare in her mind.

Wasting taxpayer money? She'd just thrown a party, right?

Fine, it had taken a considerable amount of police officers to break it up, but like, this was Los Angeles. Weren't the police just waiting around for stuff like this to happen?

Okay, that sounded privileged and bratty even to her own ears.

Suddenly she wasn't so eager to check her social media.

She wiped her sweating palms on her dress. "I wasn't trying to put anyone out or waste money. I wasn't thinking that far ahead," Piper said quietly, twisting to face her sister as much as she could in a seat belt. "Is this bad, Hanns?"

Hannah's teeth were sunk into her lower lip, her hands on the wheel slowly navigating her way through the people frantically snapping Piper's picture. "It's not good," she answered after a pause. "But hey, you used to pull stunts like this all the time, remember? The lawyers always find a way to spin it, and tomorrow they'll be onto something else." She reached out and tapped the touch screen, and a low melody flooded the car. "Check it out. I have the perfect song cued up for this moment."

The somber notes of "Prison Women" by REO Speedwagon floated out from the speakers.

Piper's skull thudded against the headrest. "Very funny." She tapped her phone against her knee for a few seconds, before snapping her spine straight and opening Instagram.

There it was. The picture she'd posted early this morning, at 2:42, accused the time stamp. Kirby, the traitorous wench, had snapped it using Piper's phone. In the shot, Piper was perched on the shoulders of a man whose name she couldn't recall—though she had a vague recollection of him claiming to play second string for the Lakers?—stripped down to panties and boob tape, but like, in an artistic way. Her Valentino dress was draped over a lounge chair in the background. Firecrackers went off around her like the Fourth of July, swathing Piper in sparkles and smoke. She looked like a goddess rising from an electric mist—and the picture was nearing a million likes.

Telling herself not to, Piper tapped the highlighted section that would show her exactly *who* had liked the picture. Adrian wasn't one of them.

Which was fine. A million other people had, right?

But they hadn't spent three weeks with her.

To them, she was just a two-dimensional image. If they spent more than three weeks with Piper, would they scroll past, too? Letting her sink into the blur of the thousand other girls just like her?

"Hey," Hannah said, pausing the song. "It's going to be all right."

Piper's laugh sounded forced, so she cut it short. "I know. It always turns out all right." She pressed her lips together. "Want to hear about the wet boxers competition?"

Chapter Three

*I*t was *not* all right, as it turned out.

Nothing was.

Not according to their stepfather, Daniel Bellinger, revered Academy Award–winning movie producer, philanthropist, and competitive yachtsman.

Piper and Hannah had attempted to creep in through the catering entrance of their Bel-Air mansion. They'd moved in when Piper was four and Hannah two, after their mother married Daniel, and neither of them could remember living anywhere else. Every once in a while, when Piper caught a whiff of the ocean, her memory sent up a signal through the fog, reminding her of the Pacific Northwest town where she'd been born, but there was nothing substantial to cling to and it always drifted away before she could grasp on.

Now, her stepfather's wrath? She could fully grasp that.

It was etched into the tanned lines of his famous face, in the disappointed headshakes he gave the sisters as they sat, side by side, on a couch in his home office. Behind him, awards gleamed on shelves, framed movie posters hung on walls, and the phone on his L-shaped desk lit up every two seconds, although he'd silenced it for the upcoming lecture. Their mother was at Pilates, and out of everything? *That* made Piper the most nervous. Maureen tended to have a calming effect on her husband—and he was anything but calm right now.

"Um, Daniel?" Piper chanced brightly, tucking a piece of wilted hair behind her ear. "None of this is Hannah's fault. Is it okay if she heads to bed?"

"She stays." He pinned Hannah with a stern look. "You were forbidden to bail her out and did it anyway."

Piper turned her astonishment on her sister. "You did what?"

"What was I supposed to do?" Hannah whipped off her hat and wrung it between her knees. "Leave you there, Pipes?"

"Yeah," Piper said slowly, facing her stepfather with mounting horror. "What did you want her to do? *Leave* me there?"

Agitated, Daniel shoved his fingers through his hair. "I thought you learned your lesson a long time ago, Piper. Or *lessons*, plural, rather. You were still flitting around to every goddamn party between here and the Valley, but you weren't costing me money or making me look like a fucking idiot in the process."

"Ouch." Piper sunk back into the couch cushions. "You don't have to be mean."

"I don't have to be—" Daniel made an exasperated sound and pinched the bridge of his nose. "You are twenty-eight years old, Piper, and you have done nothing with your life. *Nothing.* You've been afforded every opportunity, given anything your little heart could ask for, and all you have to show for it is a . . . a digital existence. It means *nothing.*"

If that's true, then I mean nothing, too.

Piper snagged a pillow and held it over her roiling stomach, giving Hannah a grateful look when she reached over to rub her knee. "Daniel, I'm sorry. I had a bad breakup last night and I acted out. I won't do anything like that ever again."

Daniel seemed to deflate a little, retreating to his desk to lean on the edge. "No one handed me anything in this business. I started as a page on the Paramount lot. Filling sandwich orders, fetching coffee. I was an errand boy while I worked my way through film school." Piper nodded, doing her best to appear deeply interested, even though Daniel told this story at every dinner party and charity event. "I stayed ready, armed with knowledge and drive, just waiting for my opportunity, so I could seize it"—he snapped his fist closed—"and never look back."

"That's when you were asked to run lines with Corbin Kidder," Piper recited from memory.

"Yes." Her stepfather inclined his head, momentarily pleased to find out she'd been paying attention. "As the director looked on, I not only delivered the lines with passion and zeal, but I *improved* the tired text. Added my own flair."

"And you were brought on as a writer's assistant." Hannah sighed, winding her finger for him to wrap up the oft-repeated story. "For Kubrick himself."

He exhaled through his nose. "That's right. And it brings me back to my original point." A finger was wagged. "Piper, you're too comfortable. At least Hannah earned a degree and is gainfully employed. Even if I called in favors to get her the location scout gig, at least she's productive." Hannah hunched her shoulders but said nothing. "Would you even care if opportunity came knocking on your door, Piper? You have no drive to go anywhere. Or do anything. Why would you when this life I've provided you is always here, rewarding your lack of ambition with comfort and an excuse to remain blissfully stagnant?"

Piper stared up at the man she thought of as a father, stunned to find out he'd been seeing her in such a negative light. She'd grown up in Bel-Air. Vacationing and throwing pool parties and rubbing elbows with famous actors. This was the only life she knew. None of her friends worked. Only a handful of them had bothered with college. What was the point of a degree? To make money? They already had tons of it.

If Daniel or her mother had ever encouraged her to do something else, she couldn't remember any such conversation. Was motivation a thing that other people were simply born with? And when the time came to make their way in the world, they simply acted? Should she have been looking for a purpose this whole time?

Weirdly, none of the inspirational quotes she'd posted in the past held the answer.

"I love your mother very much," Daniel continued, as if reading her mind. "Or I don't think I would have been this patient for so long. But, Piper . . . you went too far this time."

Her eyes shot to his, her knees beginning to tremble. Had he ever used that resigned tone with her before? If so, she didn't recall. "I did?" she whispered.

Beside her, Hannah shifted, a sign she was picking up on the gravity of the moment, too.

Daniel bobbed his head. "The owner of the Mondrian is financing my next film." That news landed like a grenade in the center of the office. "He's not happy about last night, to put it quite mildly. You made his hotel seem like it lacks security. You made it a laughingstock. And worse, you could have burned the goddamn place down." He stared at her with hard eyes, letting it all sink in. "He's threatened to pull the budget, Piper. It's a very considerable amount. The movie will not get made without his contribution. At least not until I find another backer—and it could take me years in this economy."

"I'm sorry," Piper breathed, the magnitude of what she'd done sinking her even farther into the couch cushions. Had she really blown a business deal for Daniel in the name of posting a revenge snap that would make her triumphant in a breakup? Was she that frivolous and stupid?

Had Adrian been right?

"I didn't know. I . . . I had no idea who owned the hotel."

"No, of course not. Who cares who your actions affect, right, Piper?"

"All right." Hannah sat forward with a frown. "You don't have to be so hard on her. She obviously realizes she made a mistake."

Daniel remained unfazed. "Well, it's a mistake she's going to answer for."

Piper and Hannah traded a glance. "What do you mean by"— Piper wiggled her fingers in the shape of air quotes—"'answer for'?"

Their stepfather took his time rounding his desk and opening the bottom filing drawer, hesitating only a moment before removing a manila folder. He tapped it steadily on his desk calendar, considering the nervous sisters through narrowed eyes. "We don't talk a lot about your past. The time before I married your mother. I'll admit that's mostly because I'm selfish and I didn't want reminders that she loved someone before me."

"Awww," Piper said automatically.

He ignored her. "As you know, your father was a fisherman. He lived in Westport, Washington, the same town where your mother was born. Quaint little place."

Piper started at the mention of her birth father. A king crab fisherman named Henry who'd died a young man, sucked down into the icy depths of the Bering Sea. Her eyes drifted to the window, to the world beyond, trying to remember what came *before* this swanky life to which she'd grown so accustomed. The landscape and color of the first four years of her life were elusive, but she could remember the outline of her father's head. Could remember his cracking laugh, the smell of salt water on his skin.

Could remember her mother's laughter echoing in kind, warm and sweet.

There was no way to wrap her head around that other time and place—how different it was from her current situation— and she'd tried many times. If Maureen hadn't moved to Los Angeles as a grieving widow, armed with nothing more than good looks and being a dab hand at sewing, she never would have landed a job working in wardrobe on Daniel's first film. He wouldn't have fallen in love with her, and this lavish lifestyle of theirs would be nothing more than a dream, while Maureen existed in some other, unimaginable timeline.

"Westport," Hannah repeated, as if testing the word on her tongue. "Mom never told us the name."

"Yes, well. I can imagine everything that happened was painful for her." He sniffed, tapping the edge of the folder again. "Obviously she's fine now. Better than fine." A beat passed. "The men in Westport . . . they head to the Bering Sea during king crab season, in search of their annual payday. But it's not always reliable. Sometimes they catch very little and have to split a minor sum among a large crew. Because of this, your father also owned a small bar."

Piper's lips edged up into a smile. This was the most anyone had ever spoken to her about their birth father, and the details . . . they were like coins dropping into an empty jar inside of her, slowly filling it up. She wanted more. She wanted to know everything about this man whom she could only remember for his boisterous laugh.

Hannah cleared her throat, her thigh pressing against Piper's. "Why are you telling us all of this now?" She chewed her lip. "What's in the folder?"

"The deed to the bar. He left the building to you girls in his will." He set the folder down on his desk and flipped it open. "A long time ago, I put a custodian in place, to make sure it didn't fall into disrepair, but truthfully, I'd forgotten all about it until now."

"Oh my God . . ." Hannah said under her breath, obviously predicting some outcome to this conversation that Piper was not yet grasping. "A-are you . . . ?"

Daniel sighed in the wake of Hannah's trailed-off question. "My investor is demanding a show of contrition for what you did, Piper. He's a self-made man like me and would like nothing more than to stick it to me over my spoiled, rich-kid daughter." Piper flinched, but he didn't see it because he was scanning the contents of the file. "Normally I would tell anyone who demanded something from me to fuck off . . . but I can't ignore my gut feeling that you need to learn to fend for yourself for a while."

"What do you mean by"—Piper did air quotes again—"'fend'?"

"I *mean* you're getting out of your comfort zone. I *mean* you're going to Westport."

Hannah's mouth dropped open.

Piper shot forward. "Wait. What? For how long? What am I supposed to do there?" She turned her panicked gaze on Hannah. "Does Mom know about this?"

"Yes," Maureen said from the office doorway. "She knows."

Piper whimpered into her wrist.

"Three months, Pipes. You can make it that long. And I hope you would do it without hesitation, considering I'll maintain my film budget by making these amends." Daniel came around the desk and dropped the manila folder into Piper's lap. She stared at it like one might a scuttling cockroach. "There is a small apartment above the bar. I've called ahead to make sure it's cleaned. I'm setting up a debit account to get you started, but after that . . ." Oh, he looked way too pleased. "You're on your own."

Mentally listing all of the galas and fashion shows that would happen over the course of three whole months, Piper got to her feet and sent her mother a pleading look. "Mom, you're really going to let him send me away?" She was reeling. "What am I supposed to do? Like, fish for a living? I don't even know how to make toast."

"I'm confident you'll figure it out," Maureen said softly, her expression sympathetic but firm. "This will be good for you. You'll see. You might even learn something about yourself."

"No." Piper shook her head. Didn't last night yield the revelation that she was good for nothing but partying and looking hot? She didn't have the survival skills for a life outside of these gates. But she could cope with that as long as everything stayed familiar. Out there, her ineptitude, her uselessness, would be *glaring*. "I—I'm not going."

"Then I'm not paying your legal fees," Daniel said reluctantly.

"I'm shaking," Piper whispered, holding up a flat, quaking hand. "Look at me."

Hannah threw an arm around her sister. "I'm going with her."

Daniel did a double take. "What about your job? I pulled strings with Sergei to get you a coveted spot with the production company."

At the mention of Sergei, Hannah's long-standing crush, Piper felt her sister's split second of indecision. For the last year, the youngest Bellinger had been pining for the broody Hollywood upstart whose debut film, *Nobody's Baby*, had taken the Palme d'Or at Cannes. Most of the ballads constantly blaring from Hannah's room could be attributed to her deep infatuation.

Her sister's solidarity made Piper's throat feel tight, but there was no way she'd allow her sins to banish her favorite person to Westport, too. Piper herself wasn't even resigned to going yet. "Daniel will change his mind," she whispered out of the side of her mouth to Hannah. "It'll be fine."

"I will not," Daniel boomed, looking offended. "You leave at the end of July."

Piper did a mental count. "That's, like, only a few weeks from now!"

"I'd tell you to use the time to tie up your affairs, but you don't have any."

Maureen made a sound. "I think that's enough, Daniel." With a face full of censure, she corralled the stunned sisters out of the room. "Come on. Let's take some time to process."

The three Bellinger women ascended the stairs together, climbing up to the third floor where Hannah's and Piper's bedrooms waited on opposite sides of the carpeted hall. They drifted into Piper's room, settling her on the edge of the bed, and then stepped back to observe her as if they were medical students being asked to make a diagnosis.

Hands on knees, Hannah analyzed her face. "How are you doing, Piper?"

"Can you really not get him to change his mind, Mom?" Piper croaked.

Maureen shook her head. "I'm sorry, sweetie." Her mother fell onto the bed beside her, taking her limp hand. For long moments, she was quiet, clearly gearing up for something. "I think part of the reason I didn't fight Daniel very hard on sending you to Westport is . . . well, I have a lot of guilt for keeping so much of your real father to myself. I was in so much pain for a long time. Bitter, too. And I bottled it all up, neglecting his memory in the process. That wasn't right of me." Her eyelids drifted down. "To go to Westport . . . is to meet your father, Piper. He *is* Westport. There's so much more history . . . still living in that town than you know. That's why I couldn't stay after he died. He was surrounding me . . . and I was just so angry over the unfairness of it all. Not even my parents could get through to me."

"How long did they stay in Westport after you left?" Hannah asked, referring to the grandparents who visited them on occasion, though the visits had grown few and far between as the sisters got older. When Daniel officially adopted Piper and Hannah, their grandparents hadn't seemed comfortable with the whole process, and the contact between them and Maureen had faded in degrees, even if they still spoke on holidays and birthdays.

"Not long. They bought the ranch in Utah shortly after. Far from the water." Maureen looked down at her hands. "The magic had gone out of the town for all of us, I think."

Piper could understand her mother's reasoning. Could sympathize with the guilt. But her entire life was being uprooted for a man she didn't know. Twenty-four years had gone by without a single word about Henry Cross. Her mother couldn't expect her to jump all over the opportunity now because she'd decided it was time to dump the guilt.

"This isn't fair," Piper groaned, falling backward on her bed, upsetting her ecru Millesimo bedsheets. Hannah sprawled out beside her, throwing an arm over Piper's stomach.

"It's only three months," Maureen said, rising and floating from the room. Just before she walked out, she turned back, hand poised on the doorframe. "Word to the wise, Piper. The men in Westport . . . they're not what you're used to. They're unpolished and direct. Capable in a way the men of your acquaintance . . . aren't." Her gaze grew distant. "Their job is dangerous and they don't care how much it scares you, they go back to the sea every time. They'll always choose it over a woman. And they'd rather die doing what they love than be safe at home."

The uncharacteristic gravity in Maureen's tone glued Piper to the bed. "Why are you telling me this?"

Her mother lifted a delicate shoulder. "That danger in a man can be exciting to a woman. Until it's not anymore. Then it's shattering. Just keep that in mind if you feel . . . drawn in."

Maureen seemed like she wanted to say more, but she tapped the doorframe twice and went, leaving the two sisters staring after her.

Piper reached back for a pillow and handed it to Hannah. "Smother me with this. Please. It's the humane thing to do."

"I'm coming with you to Westport."

"No. What about your job? And Sergei?" Piper exhaled. "You have good things happening here, Hanns. I'll find a way to cope." She gave Hannah a mock serious face. "They must have sugar daddies in Westport, right?"

"I'm definitely going with you."

ABOUT THE AUTHOR

New York Times bestselling author Tessa Bailey aspires to three things: writing hot and unforgettable character-driven romance, being a good mother, and eventually sneaking onto the judging panel of a reality-show baking competition. She lives on Long Island, New York, with her husband and daughter, writing all day and rewarding herself with a cheese plate and Netflix binge in the evening. If you want sexy, heartfelt, humorous romance with a guaranteed happy ending, you've come to the right place.

MORE ROM-COMS BY TESSA BAILEY

Fix Her Up

A bad-boy professional baseball player falls for the girl next door . . . who also happens to be his best friend's little sister.

Love Her or Lose Her

A young married couple signs up for relationship boot camp in order to rehab their rocky romance and finds a second chance at love!

Tools of Engagement

Two enemies team up to flip a house . . . and the sparks between them might burn the place down or ignite a passion that neither can ignore!

It Happened One Summer

The *Schitt's Creek*-inspired TikTok sensation about a Hollywood "It Girl" who's cut off from her wealthy family and exiled to a small Pacific Northwest beach town . . . where she butts heads with a surly, sexy local who thinks she doesn't belong.

IT HAPPENED ONE SUMMER

Also by Tessa Bailey

HOT & HAMMERED
Fix Her Up • *Love Her or Lose Her* • *Tools of Engagement*

THE ACADEMY
Disorderly Conduct • *Indecent Exposure* • *Disturbing His Peace*

BROKE AND BEAUTIFUL
Chase Me • *Need Me* • *Make Me*

ROMANCING THE CLARKSONS
Too Hot to Handle • *Too Wild to Tame*
Too Hard to Forget • *Too Close to Call* (novella)
Too Beautiful to Break

MADE IN JERSEY
Crashed Out • *Rough Rhythm* (novella)
Thrown Down • *Worked Up* • *Wound Tight*

CROSSING THE LINE
Riskier Business (novella) • *Risking It All* • *Up in Smoke*
Boiling Point • *Raw Redemption*

LINE OF DUTY
Protecting What's His • *Protecting What's Theirs* (novella)
His Risk to Take • *Officer Off Limits*
Asking for Trouble • *Staking His Claim*

SERVE
Owned by Fate • *Exposed by Fate* • *Driven by Fate*

BEACH KINGDOM
Mouth to Mouth • *Heat Stroke* • *Sink or Swim*

STANDALONE BOOKS
Unfixable • *Baiting the Maid of Honor*
Off Base (with Sophie Jordan)
Captivated (with Eve Dangerfield)
Getaway Girl • *Runaway Girl*

IT HAPPENED ONE SUMMER

a novel

Tessa Bailey

AVON

An Imprint of HarperCollinsPublishers

IT HAPPENED ONE SUMMER. Copyright © 2021 by Tessa Bailey. All rights reserved. Printed in the United States of America. No part of this book may be used or reproduced in any manner whatsoever without written permission except in the case of brief quotations embodied in critical articles and reviews. For information, address HarperCollins Publishers, 195 Broadway, New York, NY 10007.

HarperCollins books may be purchased for educational, business, or sales promotional use. For information, please email the Special Markets Department at SPsales@harpercollins.com.

FIRST EDITION

Designed by Diahann Sturge

Library of Congress Cataloging-in-Publication Data has been applied for.

ISBN 978-0-06-304565-1 (paperback)
ISBN 978-0-06-308235-9 (hardcover library edition)

22 23 24 25 26 LBC 59 58 57 56 55

Acknowledgments

This book was my mental escape during the Great Quarantine of 2020 and will always have a special place in my heart. When everything got too overwhelming, I was able to close my office door and travel to Westport to help two people fall in love—and I'm very grateful for it. I couldn't have written this book without my husband, Patrick, who kept a confused nine-year-old occupied without the benefit of school or any sense of normalcy for months on end.

Thank you, as well, to my friends—Nisha, Bonnie, Patricia, Michelle, Jan, and Jill—who bolstered my spirits via text or socially distanced visits, from the curb, while I shouted from the porch in sketchy pajamas. Thank you to the character Alexis Rose from *Schitt's Creek*, whom I fell so madly in love with that I needed to give her a happily ever after via Piper. Thank you to the essential workers and medical personnel who worked tirelessly at the risk of their health throughout 2020 and beyond. You are heroes. As always, thank you to my fantastic editor, Nicole Fischer; my agent, Laura Bradford; and, of course, the readers who continue to read my stories. I treasure each and every one of you.

IT
HAPPENED
ONE
SUMMER

Chapter One

$\mathcal{T}$he unthinkable was happening.

Her longest relationship on record . . . over in the blink of an eye.

Three weeks of her life *wasted*.

Piper Bellinger looked down at her lipstick-red, one-shoulder Valentino cocktail dress and tried to find the flaw but came up with nothing. Her tastefully tanned legs were polished to such a shine, she'd checked her teeth in them earlier. Nothing appeared amiss up top, either. She'd swiped the tape holding up her boobs while backstage at a runway show in Milan during fashion week—we're talking the holy grail of tit tape—and those puppies were on point. Big enough to draw a man's eye, small enough to achieve an athletic vibe in every fourth Instagram post. Versatility kept people interested.

Satisfied that nothing concerning her appearance was glaringly out of place, Piper trailed her gaze up the pleated leg of Adrian's classic Tom Ford suit made of the finest sharkskin wool, unable to quell a sigh over the luxurious peak lapels and monogrammed buttons. The way her boyfriend impatiently checked his Chopard watch and scanned the crowd over her shoulder only added to the bored-playboy effect.

Hadn't his cold unattainability attracted her to him in the first place?

God, the night of their first meeting seemed like a hundred years ago. She'd had at least two facials since then, right? What *was* time anymore? Piper could remember their introduction like it was yesterday. Adrian had saved her from stepping in vomit at Rumer Willis's birthday party. As she'd stared up at his chiseled chin from her place in his arms, she'd been transported to Old Hollywood. A time of smoking jackets and women traipsing around in long, feathered robes. It was the beginning of her own classic love story.

And now the credits were rolling.

"I can't believe you're throwing it all away like this," Piper whispered, pressing her champagne flute between her breasts. Maybe drawing his attention there would change his mind? "We've been through so much."

"Yeah, tons, right?"

Adrian waved at someone across the rooftop, his expression letting whoever it was know that he'd be right with them. They'd come to the black, white, and red party together. A minor soiree to raise money for an indie movie project called *Lifestyles of the Oppressed and Famous*. The writer-director was a friend of Adrian's, meaning most of the people at this gathering of Los Angeles elite were his acquaintances. Her girls weren't even there to console her or facilitate a graceful exit.

Adrian's attention settled back on her reluctantly. "Wait, what were you saying?"

Piper's smile felt brittle, so she turned it up another watt, careful to keep it one crucial notch below manic. *Chin up, woman*. This wasn't her first breakup, right? She'd done a lot of the dumping, often unexpectedly. This was a town of whims, after all.

She'd never really noticed the pace of how things changed. Not until lately.

At twenty-eight, Piper was not old. But she *was* one of the oldest women at this party. At every party she'd been to recently, come to think of it. Leaning on the glass railing that overlooked Melrose was an up-and-coming pop star who couldn't be a day older than nineteen. She didn't need tape from Milan to hold up her tits. They were light and springy with nipples that reminded Piper of the bottom of an ice cream cone.

The host himself was twenty-two and embarking on a film career.

This was Piper's career. Partying. Being seen. Holding up the occasional teeth-whitening product and getting a few dollars for it.

Not that she needed the money. At least, she didn't think so. Everything she owned came from the swipe of a credit card, and it was a mystery what happened after that. She assumed the bill went to her stepfather's email or something? Hopefully he wouldn't be weird about the crotchless panties she'd ordered from Paris.

"Piper? *Hello?*" Adrian swiped a hand in front of her face, and she realized how long she'd been staring at the pop star. Long enough that the songstress was glaring back.

Piper smiled and waved at the girl, pointing sheepishly to her glass of champagne, before tuning back in to the conversation with Adrian. "Is this because I casually brought you up to my therapist? We didn't go in depth or anything, I promise. Most of the time we just nap during my appointments."

He stared at her for several seconds. Honestly, it was kind of nice. It was the most attention she'd gotten from him since almost slipping in puke. "I've dated some airheads, Piper." He sighed. "But you put them all to shame."

She kept her smile in place, though it took more determination than usual. People were watching. At that very moment, she was in the background of at least five selfies being captured around the roof, including one of Ansel Elgort. It would be a disaster if she let her sinking heart show on her face, especially when news of the breakup got out. "I don't understand," she said with a laugh, sweeping rose-gold hair over her shoulder.

"Shocking," he returned drily. "Look, babe. It was a fun three weeks. You're a smoke show in a bikini." He shrugged an elegant Tom Ford–clad shoulder. "I'm just trying to end this before it gets boring, you know?"

Boring. Getting older. Not a director or a pop star.

Just a pretty girl with a millionaire stepfather.

Piper couldn't think about that now, though. She just wanted to exit the party as inconspicuously as possible and go have a good cry. After she popped a Xanax and posted an inspirational quote on her IG feed, of course. It would confirm the breakup, but also allow her to control the narrative. Something about growth and loving herself, maybe?

Her sister, Hannah, would have the perfect song lyric to include. She was always sitting around in a pile of vinyls, those giant, ugly headphones wrapped around her head. Damn, she wished she'd put more stock in Hannah's opinion of Adrian.

What had she said? Oh yeah.

He's like if someone drew eyes on a turnip.

Once again, Piper had zoned out, and Adrian checked his watch for the second time. "Are we done here? I have to mingle."

"Oh. *Yeah*," she rushed to say, her voice horrifyingly unnatural. "You couldn't be more right about breaking things off before the boring blues strike. I didn't think about it like that." She clinked her champagne glass against his. "We're consciously uncoupling. *Très* mature."

"Right. Call it whatever you want." Adrian forced a wan smile. "Thanks for everything."

"No, thank *you*." She pursed her lips, trying to appear as non-airhead-like as possible. "I've learned a lot about myself over the last three weeks."

"Come on, Piper." Adrian laughed, scrutinizing her head to toe. "You play dress-up and spend your daddy's money. You don't have a reason to learn anything."

"Do I need a reason?" she asked lightly, lips still tilted at the corners.

Annoyed at being waylaid, Adrian huffed a breath. "I guess not. But you definitely need a brain that functions beyond how many likes you can get on a picture of your rack. There's more to life than that, Piper."

"Yes, I know," she said, prodded by irritation—and more than a little bit of reluctant shame. "Life is what I'm documenting through photos. I—"

"God." He half groaned, half laughed. "Why are you *forcing* me to be an asshole?" Someone called his name from inside the penthouse, and he held up a finger, keeping his gaze locked on Piper. "There's just nothing to you, okay? There are thousands of Piper Bellingers in this city. You're just a way to pass the time." He shrugged. "And your time has passed."

It was a miracle Piper kept her winning smile intact as Adrian sailed away, already calling out to his friends. Everyone on the roof deck was staring at her, whispering behind their hands, feeling sorry for her—of all the horrors. She saluted them with her glass, then realized it was empty. Setting it down on the tray of a passing waiter, she collected her Bottega Veneta satin knot clutch with all the dignity she could muster and glided through the throng of onlookers, blinking back the moisture in her eyes to bring the elevator call button into focus.

When the doors finally hid her from view, she slumped back against the metal wall, taking deep breaths in through her nose, out through her mouth. Already the news that she'd been dumped by Adrian would be blasted across all the socials, maybe even with video included. Not even C-list celebrities would invite her to parties after this.

She had a reputation as a good time. Someone to covet. An "it girl."

If she didn't have her social status, what *did* she have?

Piper pulled her phone out of her clutch and absently requested a luxury Uber, connecting her with a driver who was only five minutes away. Then she closed the app and pulled up her favorites list. Her thumb hovered over the name "Hannah" momentarily, but landed on "Kirby," instead. Her friend answered on the first ring.

"Oh my God, is it true you begged Adrian not to break up with you in front of Ansel Elgort?"

It was worse than she thought. How many people had already tipped off TMZ? Tomorrow night at six thirty, they would be tossing her name around the newsroom while Harvey sipped from his reusable cup. "I didn't beg Adrian to keep me. Come on, Kirby, you know me better than that."

"Bitch, I do. But I'm not everyone else. You need to do damage control. Do you have a publicist on retainer?"

"Not anymore. Daniel said me going shopping doesn't need a press release."

Kirby snorted. "Okay, boomer."

"But you're right. I do need damage control." The elevator doors opened, and Piper stepped off, clicking through the lobby in her red-soled pumps, eventually stepping out onto Wilshire, the warm July air drying the dampness in her eyes. The tall buildings of downtown Los Angeles reached up into the smoggy summer night sky, and she craned her neck to find the tops. "How late is the rooftop pool open at the Mondrian?"

"You're asking about hours of operation at a time like this?" Kirby griped, followed by the sound of her vape crackling in the background. "I don't know, but it's past midnight. If it's not already closed, it will be soon."

A black Lincoln pulled up along the curb. After double-checking the license plate number, Piper climbed inside and shut the door. "Wouldn't breaking into the pool and having the time of our lives be, like, *the* best way to fight fire with fire? Adrian would be the guy who broke up with a legend."

"Oh shit," Kirby breathed. "You're resurrecting Piper twenty fourteen."

This was the answer, wasn't it? There was no better time in her life than the year she turned twenty-one and ran absolutely buck wild through Los Angeles, making herself famous for being famous in the process. She was just in a rut, that was all. Maybe it was time to reclaim her crown. Maybe then she wouldn't hear Adrian's words looping over and over again in the back of her head, forcing her to consider that he might be right.

Am I just one of thousands?

Or am I the girl who breaks into a pool for a swim at one o'clock in the morning?

Piper nodded resolutely and leaned forward. "Can you take me to the Mondrian, instead, please?"

Kirby hooted down the line. "I'll meet you there."

"I've got a better idea." Piper crossed her legs and fell back in the leather seat. "How about we have *everyone* meet us there?"

Chapter Two

$\mathcal{J}$ail was a cold, dark place.

Piper stood in the very center of the cell shivering and hugging her elbows so she wouldn't accidentally touch anything that might require a tetanus shot. Until this moment, the word "torture" had only been a vague description of something she'd never understand. But trying to *not pee* in the moldy toilet after roughly six mixed drinks was a torment no woman should ever know. The late-night Coachella bathroom situation had nothing on this grimy metal throne that mocked her from the corner of the cell.

"Excuse me?" Piper called, wobbling to the bars in her heels. There were no guards in sight, but she could hear the distinctive sounds of *Candy Crush* coming from nearby. "Hi, it's me, Piper. Is there another bathroom I could use?"

"No, princess," a woman's voice called back, sounding very bored. "There isn't."

She bounced side to side, her bladder demanding to be evacuated. "Where do *you* go to the bathroom?"

A snort. "Where the *other* non-criminals go."

Piper whined in her throat, although the lady guard went up a notch in her book for delivering such a savage response without hesitation. "I'm not a criminal," Piper tried again. "This is all a misunderstanding."

A trill of laughter echoed down the drab hallway of the police station. How many times had she passed the station on North Wilcox? Now she was an inmate.

But seriously, it had been one hell of a party.

The guard slowly appeared in front of Piper's cell, fingers tucked into her beige uniform pants. *Beige.* Whoever was at the helm of law enforcement fashion should be sentenced for cruel and unusual punishment. "You call two hundred people breaking into a hotel pool after hours a misunderstanding?"

Piper crossed her legs and sucked in a breath through her nose. If she peed herself in Valentino, she would voluntarily remain in jail. "Would you believe the pool hours weren't prominently posted?"

"Is that the argument your expensive lawyer is going to use?" The guard shook her head, visibly amused. "Someone had to shatter the glass door to get inside and let all the other rich kids in. Who did that? The invisible man?"

"I don't know, but I'm going to find out," Piper vowed solemnly.

The guard sighed through a smile. "It's too late for that, sweetheart. Your friend with the purple tips already named you as the ringleader."

Kirby.

Had to be.

No one else at the party had purple tips. At least, Piper didn't think so. Somewhere between the chicken fights in the pool and the illegal firecrackers being set off, she'd kind of lost track of the incoming guests. She should have known better than to trust Kirby, though. She and Piper were friends, but not good enough for her to lie to the police. The foundation of their relationship was commenting on each other's social media posts and enabling each other to make ridiculous purchases, like a four-thousand-dollar purse shaped like a tube of lipstick. Most times, those kinds of surface-level friendships were valuable, but not tonight.

That's why her one phone call had gone to Hannah.

Speaking of whom, where *was* her little sister? She'd made that call an hour ago.

Piper hopped side to side, dangerously close to using her hands to keep the urine contained. "Who is forcing you to wear beige pants?" she gasped. "Why aren't they in here with me?"

"Fine." The guard flashed a palm. "On this we can agree."

"Literally any other color would be better. *No* pants would be better." Trying to distract herself from the Chernobyl happening in her lower body, she rambled, as she was wont to do in uncomfortable situations. "You have a really cute figure, Officer, but it's, like, a commandment that no one shall pull off nude khaki."

The other woman's eyebrow arched. "You could."

"You're right," Piper sobbed. "I totally could."

The guard's laugh faded into a sigh. "What were you thinking, inciting that chaos tonight?"

Piper slumped a little. "My boyfriend dumped me. And he . . . didn't even look me in the eye the whole time. I guess I just wanted to be seen. Acknowledged. Celebrated instead of . . . disregarded. You know?"

"Scorned and acting like a fool. Can't say I haven't been there."

"Really?" Piper asked hopefully.

"Sure. Who hasn't put all their boyfriend's clothes in the bathtub and poured bleach on top?"

Piper thought of the Tom Ford suit turning splotchy, and shivered. "That's cold," she whispered. "Maybe I should have just slashed his tires. At least that's legal."

"That's . . . not legal."

"Oh." Piper sent the guard an exaggerated wink. "*Riiiight.*"

The woman shook her head, glancing up and down the hallway. "All right, look. It's a quiet night. If you don't give me any trouble, I'll let you use the slightly less shitty bathroom."

"Oh, thank you, thank you, thank you."

With her keys poised over the keyhole, the guard hit her with serious eyes. "I have a Taser."

Piper followed her savior down the hall to the bathroom, where she meticulously gathered the skirt of her Valentino and eased the unholy pressure in her bladder, moaning until the final drop fell. As she washed her hands in the small sink, her attention caught on the reflection in the mirror. Raccoon eyes looked back at her. Smeared lipstick, limp hair. Definitely a long way from where she'd begun the evening, but she couldn't help but feel like a soldier returning from battle. She'd set out to divert attention from her breakup, hadn't she?

An LAPD helicopter circling overhead while she led a conga line had definitely reaffirmed her status as the reigning party queen of Los Angeles. Probably. They'd confiscated her phone during the whole mug shot/fingerprint thing, so she didn't know what was happening on the internet. Her fingers were itching to tap some apps, and that's exactly what she would do as soon as Hannah arrived to bail her out.

She looked at her reflection, surprised to find the prospect of breaking the internet didn't set her heart into a thrilling pitter-patter the way it did before. Was she broken?

Piper snorted and pushed away from the sink, using an elbow to pull down the door handle upon leaving. Obviously the night had taken its toll—after all, it was nearly five o'clock in the morning. As soon as she got some sleep, she'd spend the day reveling in congratulatory texts and an inundation of new followers. All would be well.

The guard cuffed Piper again and started to walk her back to the cell, just as another guard called down to them from the opposite end. "Yo, Lina. Bellinger made bail. Bring her down to processing."

Her arms flew up in victory. "*Yes!*"

Lina laughed. "Come on, beauty queen."

Vigor restored, Piper skipped alongside the other woman. "Lina, huh? I owe you big-time." She clutched her hands beneath her chin and gave her a winning pout. "Thank you for being so nice to me."

"Don't read too much into it," drawled the guard, though her expression was pleased. "I just wasn't in the mood to clean up piss."

Piper laughed, allowing Lina to unlock the door at the end of the gray hallway. And there was Hannah in the processing area, wearing pajamas and a ball cap, filling out paperwork with her eyes half closed.

Warmth wiggled into Piper's chest at the sight of her younger sister. They were nothing alike, had even less in common, but there was no one else Piper would call in a pinch. Of the two sisters, Hannah was the dependable one, even though she had a lazy hippie side.

Where Piper was taller, Hannah had been called a shrimp growing up and never quite hit the middle school growth spurt. At the moment, she kept her petite figure buried under a UCLA sweatshirt, her sandy-blond hair poking out around the blank red hat.

"She clear?" Lina asked a thin-lipped man hunched behind the desk.

He waved a hand without looking up. "Money solves everything."

Lina unlocked her cuffs once again, and she shot forward. "*Hannnnns*," Piper whimpered, throwing her arms around her sister. "I'll pay you back for this. I'll do your chores for a week."

"We don't have chores, you radish." Hannah yawned, grinding a fist into her eye. "Why do you smell like incense?"

"Oh." Piper sniffed her shoulder. "I think the fortune-teller lit some." Straightening, she squinted her eyes. "Not sure how she found out about the party."

Hannah gaped, seeming to awaken at least marginally, her hazel eyes a total contrast to Piper's baby blues. "Did she happen to tell you there's an angry stepfather in your future?"

Piper winced. "Oof. I had a feeling I couldn't avoid the wrath of Daniel Q. Bellinger." She craned her neck to see if there was anyone retrieving her phone. "How did he find out?"

"The news, Pipes. The news."

"Right." She sighed, smoothing her hands down the rumpled skirt of her dress. "Nothing the lawyers can't handle, right? Hopefully he'll let me get in a shower and some sleep before one of his famous lectures. I'm a walking *after* photo."

"Shut up, you look great," Hannah said, her lips twitching as she completed the paperwork with a flourish of her signature. "You always look great."

Piper did a little shimmy.

"Bye, Lina!" Piper called on the way out of the station, her beloved phone cradled in her arms like a newborn, fingers vibrating with the need to swipe. She'd been directed to the back exit where Hannah could pull the car around. *Protocol*, they'd said.

She took one step out the door and was surrounded by photographers. "Piper! Over here!"

Her vanity screeched like a pterodactyl.

Nerves swerved right and left in her belly, but she flashed them a quick smile and put her head down, clicking as fast as she could toward Hannah's waiting Jeep.

"Piper Bellinger!" one of the paparazzi shouted. "How was your night in jail?"

"Do you regret wasting taxpayer money?"

The toe of her high heel caught in a crack, and she almost sprawled face-first onto the asphalt but caught the edge of the door Hannah had pushed open, throwing herself into the passenger side. Closing the door helped cut off the shouted questions, but the last one she'd heard continued to blare in her mind.

Wasting taxpayer money? She'd just thrown a party, right?

Fine, it had taken a considerable amount of police officers to break it up, but like, this was Los Angeles. Weren't the police just waiting around for stuff like this to happen?

Okay, that sounded privileged and bratty even to her own ears.

Suddenly she wasn't so eager to check her social media.

She wiped her sweating palms on her dress. "I wasn't trying to put anyone out or waste money. I wasn't thinking that far ahead," Piper said quietly, twisting to face her sister as much as she could in a seat belt. "Is this bad, Hanns?"

Hannah's teeth were sunk into her lower lip, her hands on the wheel slowly navigating her way through the people frantically snapping Piper's picture. "It's not good," she answered after a pause. "But hey, you used to pull stunts like this all the time, remember? The lawyers always find a way to spin it, and tomorrow they'll be onto something else." She reached out and tapped the touch screen, and a low melody flooded the car. "Check it out. I have the perfect song cued up for this moment."

The somber notes of "Prison Women" by REO Speedwagon floated out from the speakers.

Piper's skull thudded against the headrest. "Very funny." She tapped her phone against her knee for a few seconds, before snapping her spine straight and opening Instagram.

There it was. The picture she'd posted early this morning, at 2:42, accused the time stamp. Kirby, the traitorous wench, had snapped it using Piper's phone. In the shot, Piper was perched on the shoulders of a man whose name she couldn't recall—though she had a vague recollection of him claiming to play second string for the Lakers?—stripped down to panties and boob tape, but like, in an artistic way. Her Valentino dress was draped over a lounge chair in the background. Firecrackers went off around her like the Fourth of July, swathing Piper in sparkles and smoke. She looked like a goddess rising from an electric mist—and the picture was nearing a million likes.

Telling herself not to, Piper tapped the highlighted section that would show her exactly *who* had liked the picture. Adrian wasn't one of them.

Which was fine. A million other people had, right?

But they hadn't spent three weeks with her.

To them, she was just a two-dimensional image. If they spent more than three weeks with Piper, would they scroll past, too? Letting her sink into the blur of the thousand other girls just like her?

"Hey," Hannah said, pausing the song. "It's going to be all right."

Piper's laugh sounded forced, so she cut it short. "I know. It always turns out all right." She pressed her lips together. "Want to hear about the wet boxers competition?"

Chapter Three

It was *not* all right, as it turned out.

Nothing was.

Not according to their stepfather, Daniel Bellinger, revered Academy Award–winning movie producer, philanthropist, and competitive yachtsman.

Piper and Hannah had attempted to creep in through the catering entrance of their Bel-Air mansion. They'd moved in when Piper was four and Hannah two, after their mother married Daniel, and neither of them could remember living anywhere else. Every once in a while, when Piper caught a whiff of the ocean, her memory sent up a signal through the fog, reminding her of the Pacific Northwest town where she'd been born, but there was nothing substantial to cling to and it always drifted away before she could grasp on.

Now, her stepfather's wrath? She could fully grasp that.

It was etched into the tanned lines of his famous face, in the disappointed headshakes he gave the sisters as they sat, side by side, on a couch in his home office. Behind him, awards gleamed on shelves, framed movie posters hung on walls, and the phone on his L-shaped desk lit up every two seconds, although he'd silenced it for the upcoming lecture. Their mother was at Pilates, and out of everything? *That* made Piper the most nervous. Maureen tended to have a calming effect on her husband—and he was anything but calm right now.

"Um, Daniel?" Piper chanced brightly, tucking a piece of wilted hair behind her ear. "None of this is Hannah's fault. Is it okay if she heads to bed?"

"She stays." He pinned Hannah with a stern look. "You were forbidden to bail her out and did it anyway."

Piper turned her astonishment on her sister. "You did what?"

"What was I supposed to do?" Hannah whipped off her hat and wrung it between her knees. "Leave you there, Pipes?"

"Yeah," Piper said slowly, facing her stepfather with mounting horror. "What did you want her to do? *Leave* me there?"

Agitated, Daniel shoved his fingers through his hair. "I thought you learned your lesson a long time ago, Piper. Or *lessons*, plural, rather. You were still flitting around to every goddamn party between here and the Valley, but you weren't costing me money or making me look like a fucking idiot in the process."

"Ouch." Piper sunk back into the couch cushions. "You don't have to be mean."

"I don't have to be—" Daniel made an exasperated sound and pinched the bridge of his nose. "You are twenty-eight years old, Piper, and you have done nothing with your life. *Nothing.* You've been afforded every opportunity, given anything your little heart could ask for, and all you have to show for it is a . . . a digital existence. It means *nothing.*"

If that's true, then I mean nothing, too.

Piper snagged a pillow and held it over her roiling stomach, giving Hannah a grateful look when she reached over to rub her knee. "Daniel, I'm sorry. I had a bad breakup last night and I acted out. I won't do anything like that ever again."

Daniel seemed to deflate a little, retreating to his desk to lean on the edge. "No one handed me anything in this business. I started as a page on the Paramount lot. Filling sandwich orders, fetching coffee. I was an errand boy while I worked my way through film school." Piper nodded, doing her best to appear deeply interested, even though Daniel told this story at every dinner party and charity event. "I stayed ready, armed with knowledge and drive, just waiting for my opportunity, so I could seize it"—he snapped his fist closed—"and never look back."

"That's when you were asked to run lines with Corbin Kidder," Piper recited from memory.

"Yes." Her stepfather inclined his head, momentarily pleased to find out she'd been paying attention. "As the director looked on, I not only delivered the lines with passion and zeal, but I *improved* the tired text. Added my own flair."

"And you were brought on as a writer's assistant." Hannah sighed, winding her finger for him to wrap up the oft-repeated story. "For Kubrick himself."

He exhaled through his nose. "That's right. And it brings me back to my original point." A finger was wagged. "Piper, you're too comfortable. At least Hannah earned a degree and is gainfully employed. Even if I called in favors to get her the location scout gig, at least she's productive." Hannah hunched her shoulders but said nothing. "Would you even care if opportunity came knocking on your door, Piper? You have no drive to go anywhere. Or do anything. Why would you when this life I've provided you is always here, rewarding your lack of ambition with comfort and an excuse to remain blissfully stagnant?"

Piper stared up at the man she thought of as a father, stunned to find out he'd been seeing her in such a negative light. She'd grown up in Bel-Air. Vacationing and throwing pool parties and rubbing elbows with famous actors. This was the only life she knew. None of her friends worked. Only a handful of them had bothered with college. What was the point of a degree? To make money? They already had tons of it.

If Daniel or her mother had ever encouraged her to do something else, she couldn't remember any such conversation. Was motivation a thing that other people were simply born with? And when the time came to make their way in the world, they simply acted? Should she have been looking for a purpose this whole time?

Weirdly, none of the inspirational quotes she'd posted in the past held the answer.

"I love your mother very much," Daniel continued, as if reading her mind. "Or I don't think I would have been this patient for so long. But, Piper . . . you went too far this time."

Her eyes shot to his, her knees beginning to tremble. Had he ever used that resigned tone with her before? If so, she didn't recall. "I did?" she whispered.

Beside her, Hannah shifted, a sign she was picking up on the gravity of the moment, too.

Daniel bobbed his head. "The owner of the Mondrian is financing my next film." That news landed like a grenade in the center of the office. "He's not happy about last night, to put it quite mildly. You made his hotel seem like it lacks security. You made it a laughingstock. And worse, you could have burned the goddamn place down." He stared at her with hard eyes, letting it all sink in. "He's threatened to pull the budget, Piper. It's a very considerable amount. The movie will not get made without his contribution. At least not until I find another backer—and it could take me years in this economy."

"I'm sorry," Piper breathed, the magnitude of what she'd done sinking her even farther into the couch cushions. Had she really blown a business deal for Daniel in the name of posting a revenge snap that would make her triumphant in a breakup? Was she that frivolous and stupid?

Had Adrian been right?

"I didn't know. I . . . I had no idea who owned the hotel."

"No, of course not. Who cares who your actions affect, right, Piper?"

"All right." Hannah sat forward with a frown. "You don't have to be so hard on her. She obviously realizes she made a mistake."

Daniel remained unfazed. "Well, it's a mistake she's going to answer for."

Piper and Hannah traded a glance. "What do you mean by"— Piper wiggled her fingers in the shape of air quotes—"'answer for'?"

Their stepfather took his time rounding his desk and opening the bottom filing drawer, hesitating only a moment before removing a manila folder. He tapped it steadily on his desk calendar, considering the nervous sisters through narrowed eyes. "We don't talk a lot about your past. The time before I married your mother. I'll admit that's mostly because I'm selfish and I didn't want reminders that she loved someone before me."

"Awww," Piper said automatically.

He ignored her. "As you know, your father was a fisherman. He lived in Westport, Washington, the same town where your mother was born. Quaint little place."

Piper started at the mention of her birth father. A king crab fisherman named Henry who'd died a young man, sucked down into the icy depths of the Bering Sea. Her eyes drifted to the window, to the world beyond, trying to remember what came *before* this swanky life to which she'd grown so accustomed. The landscape and color of the first four years of her life were elusive, but she could remember the outline of her father's head. Could remember his cracking laugh, the smell of salt water on his skin.

Could remember her mother's laughter echoing in kind, warm and sweet.

There was no way to wrap her head around that other time and place—how different it was from her current situation—and she'd tried many times. If Maureen hadn't moved to Los Angeles as a grieving widow, armed with nothing more than good looks and being a dab hand at sewing, she never would have landed a job working in wardrobe on Daniel's first film. He wouldn't have fallen in love with her, and this lavish life-style of theirs would be nothing more than a dream, while Maureen existed in some other, unimaginable timeline.

"Westport," Hannah repeated, as if testing the word on her tongue. "Mom never told us the name."

"Yes, well. I can imagine everything that happened was

painful for her." He sniffed, tapping the edge of the folder again. "Obviously she's fine now. Better than fine." A beat passed. "The men in Westport . . . they head to the Bering Sea during king crab season, in search of their annual payday. But it's not always reliable. Sometimes they catch very little and have to split a minor sum among a large crew. Because of this, your father also owned a small bar."

Piper's lips edged up into a smile. This was the most anyone had ever spoken to her about their birth father, and the details . . . they were like coins dropping into an empty jar inside of her, slowly filling it up. She wanted more. She wanted to know everything about this man whom she could only remember for his boisterous laugh.

Hannah cleared her throat, her thigh pressing against Piper's. "Why are you telling us all of this now?" She chewed her lip. "What's in the folder?"

"The deed to the bar. He left the building to you girls in his will." He set the folder down on his desk and flipped it open. "A long time ago, I put a custodian in place, to make sure it didn't fall into disrepair, but truthfully, I'd forgotten all about it until now."

"Oh my God . . ." Hannah said under her breath, obviously predicting some outcome to this conversation that Piper was not yet grasping. "A-are you . . . ?"

Daniel sighed in the wake of Hannah's trailed-off question. "My investor is demanding a show of contrition for what you did, Piper. He's a self-made man like me and would like nothing more than to stick it to me over my spoiled, rich-kid daughter." Piper flinched, but he didn't see it because he was scanning the contents of the file. "Normally I would tell anyone who demanded something from me to fuck off . . . but I can't ignore my gut feeling that you need to learn to fend for yourself for a while."

"What do you mean by"—Piper did air quotes again—"'fend'?"

"I *mean* you're getting out of your comfort zone. I *mean* you're going to Westport."

Hannah's mouth dropped open.

Piper shot forward. "Wait. What? For how long? What am I supposed to do there?" She turned her panicked gaze on Hannah. "Does Mom know about this?"

"Yes," Maureen said from the office doorway. "She knows."

Piper whimpered into her wrist.

"Three months, Pipes. You can make it that long. And I hope you would do it without hesitation, considering I'll maintain my film budget by making these amends." Daniel came around the desk and dropped the manila folder into Piper's lap. She stared at it like one might a scuttling cockroach. "There is a small apartment above the bar. I've called ahead to make sure it's cleaned. I'm setting up a debit account to get you started, but after that . . ." Oh, he looked way too pleased. "You're on your own."

Mentally listing all of the galas and fashion shows that would happen over the course of three whole months, Piper got to her feet and sent her mother a pleading look. "Mom, you're really going to let him send me away?" She was reeling. "What am I supposed to do? Like, fish for a living? I don't even know how to make toast."

"I'm confident you'll figure it out," Maureen said softly, her expression sympathetic but firm. "This will be good for you. You'll see. You might even learn something about yourself."

"No." Piper shook her head. Didn't last night yield the revelation that she was good for nothing but partying and looking hot? She didn't have the survival skills for a life outside of these gates. But she could cope with that as long as everything stayed familiar. Out there, her ineptitude, her uselessness, would be *glaring*. "I—I'm not going."

"Then I'm not paying your legal fees," Daniel said reluctantly.

"I'm shaking," Piper whispered, holding up a flat, quaking hand. "Look at me."

Hannah threw an arm around her sister. "I'm going with her."

Daniel did a double take. "What about your job? I pulled strings with Sergei to get you a coveted spot with the production company."

At the mention of Sergei, Hannah's long-standing crush, Piper felt her sister's split second of indecision. For the last year, the youngest Bellinger had been pining for the broody Hollywood upstart whose debut film, *Nobody's Baby*, had taken the Palme d'Or at Cannes. Most of the ballads constantly blaring from Hannah's room could be attributed to her deep infatuation.

Her sister's solidarity made Piper's throat feel tight, but there was no way she'd allow her sins to banish her favorite person to Westport, too. Piper herself wasn't even resigned to going yet. "Daniel will change his mind," she whispered out of the side of her mouth to Hannah. "It'll be fine."

"I will not," Daniel boomed, looking offended. "You leave at the end of July."

Piper did a mental count. "That's, like, only a few weeks from now!"

"I'd tell you to use the time to tie up your affairs, but you don't have any."

Maureen made a sound. "I think that's enough, Daniel." With a face full of censure, she corralled the stunned sisters out of the room. "Come on. Let's take some time to process."

The three Bellinger women ascended the stairs together, climbing up to the third floor where Hannah's and Piper's bedrooms waited on opposite sides of the carpeted hall. They drifted into Piper's room, settling her on the edge of the bed, and then stepped back to observe her as if they were medical students being asked to make a diagnosis.

Hands on knees, Hannah analyzed her face. "How are you doing, Piper?"

"Can you really not get him to change his mind, Mom?" Piper croaked.

Maureen shook her head. "I'm sorry, sweetie." Her mother fell onto the bed beside her, taking her limp hand. For long moments, she was quiet, clearly gearing up for something. "I think part of the reason I didn't fight Daniel very hard on sending you to Westport is . . . well, I have a lot of guilt for keeping so much of your real father to myself. I was in so much pain for a long time. Bitter, too. And I bottled it all up, neglecting his memory in the process. That wasn't right of me." Her eyelids drifted down. "To go to Westport . . . is to meet your father, Piper. He *is* Westport. There's so much more history . . . still living in that town than you know. That's why I couldn't stay after he died. He was surrounding me . . . and I was just so angry over the unfairness of it all. Not even my parents could get through to me."

"How long did they stay in Westport after you left?" Hannah asked, referring to the grandparents who visited them on occasion, though the visits had grown few and far between as the sisters got older. When Daniel officially adopted Piper and Hannah, their grandparents hadn't seemed comfortable with the whole process, and the contact between them and Maureen had faded in degrees, even if they still spoke on holidays and birthdays.

"Not long. They bought the ranch in Utah shortly after. Far from the water." Maureen looked down at her hands. "The magic had gone out of the town for all of us, I think."

Piper could understand her mother's reasoning. Could sympathize with the guilt. But her entire life was being uprooted for a man she didn't know. Twenty-four years had gone by without a single word about Henry Cross. Her mother couldn't expect her to jump all over the opportunity now because she'd decided it was time to dump the guilt.

"This isn't fair," Piper groaned, falling backward on her bed, upsetting her ecru Millesimo bedsheets. Hannah sprawled out beside her, throwing an arm over Piper's stomach.

"It's only three months," Maureen said, rising and floating from the room. Just before she walked out, she turned back, hand poised on the doorframe. "Word to the wise, Piper. The men in Westport . . . they're not what you're used to. They're unpolished and direct. Capable in a way the men of your acquaintance . . . aren't." Her gaze grew distant. "Their job is dangerous and they don't care how much it scares you, they go back to the sea every time. They'll always choose it over a woman. And they'd rather die doing what they love than be safe at home."

The uncharacteristic gravity in Maureen's tone glued Piper to the bed. "Why are you telling me this?"

Her mother lifted a delicate shoulder. "That danger in a man can be exciting to a woman. Until it's not anymore. Then it's shattering. Just keep that in mind if you feel . . . drawn in."

Maureen seemed like she wanted to say more, but she tapped the doorframe twice and went, leaving the two sisters staring after her.

Piper reached back for a pillow and handed it to Hannah. "Smother me with this. Please. It's the humane thing to do."

"I'm coming with you to Westport."

"No. What about your job? And Sergei?" Piper exhaled. "You have good things happening here, Hanns. I'll find a way to cope." She gave Hannah a mock serious face. "They must have sugar daddies in Westport, right?"

"I'm definitely going with you."

Chapter Four

$\mathcal{B}$rendan Taggart was the first Westport resident to spot the women.

He heard a car door slam out by the curb and slowly turned on the barrel that passed as a seat in No Name. His bottle of beer paused halfway to his mouth, the loud storytelling and music filling the bar fading away.

Through the grubby window, Brendan watched the pair exit on opposite sides of a taxi and immediately wrote them off as clueless tourists who obviously had the wrong address.

That is, until they started hauling suitcases out of the trunk. Seven, to be exact.

He grunted. Sipped his beer.

They were a ways off the beaten path. There wasn't an inn for several blocks. On top of misjudging their destination, they were dressed for the beach at night, during a late-summer rain, no umbrella to speak of—and visibly confounded by their surroundings.

It was the one in the floppy hat who caught his eye right away, purely because she looked the *most* ridiculous, a lipstick-shaped purse dangling from her forearm, wrists limp and drawn up to her shoulders, as if she was afraid to touch something. She tilted her head back and gazed up at the building and laughed. And that laugh turned into what looked like a sob, though he couldn't hear it through the music and pane of glass.

As soon as Brendan noticed the way the rain was molding the dress to Floppy Hat's tits, he glanced away quickly, going back to what he'd been doing before. Pretending to be interested in Randy's overboard story, even though he'd heard it eighty goddamn times.

"The sea was boiling that day," Randy said, in a voice equivalent to scrap metal being crushed. "We'd already hit our quota and then some, thanks to the captain over here." He saluted Brendan with his frothy pint. "And there I was, on a deck slipperier than a duck's ass, picturing the bathtub full of cash I'd be swimming in when we got home. We're hauling in the final pot, and there it was, the biggest crab in the damn sea, the motherfucking grandpappy of all crabs, and he tells me with his beady little eyes that he ain't going down without a fight. Noooo, sir."

Randy propped a leg up on the stool he'd been sitting on earlier, his craggy features arranged for maximum drama. He'd been working on Brendan's boat longer than Brendan had been captaining it. Had seen more seasons than most of the crew combined. At the end of each one, he threw himself a retirement party. And then he showed up for the next season like clockwork, having spent every last dime of last year's take.

"When I tell you that sucker wrapped a leg around the arm of my slicker, right through the pot, the mesh, all of it, I'm not lying. He was hell-bent for leather. Time froze, ladies and gentlemen. The captain is yelling at me to haul in the pot, but hear me now, I was *bamboozled*. That crab put a spell on me—I'm telling you. And that's when the wave hit, conjured by the crab himself. Nobody saw it coming, and just like that, I was tossed into the drink."

The man who was like a grandfather to Brendan took a pause to drain half his beer.

"When they pulled me in . . ." He exhaled. "That crab was nowhere to be found."

The two people in the crowded bar who hadn't already heard the legend laughed and applauded—and that was the moment Floppy Hat and the other one decided to make their entrance. Within seconds, it was quiet enough to hear a pin drop, and that didn't surprise Brendan one bit. Westport was a tourist stop to be sure, but they didn't get a lot of outsiders stumbling into No Name. It was an establishment that couldn't be found on Yelp.

Mainly because it was illegal.

But it wasn't only the shock of non-locals walking in and disrupting their Sunday-night bullshit session. No, it was the way they *looked*. Especially Floppy Hat, who walked in first, hitting the easy energy of the room with shock paddles. In her short, loose dress and sandals that wrapped around her calves, she could have stepped out of the pages of a fashion magazine for all those . . . tight lines and smooth curves.

Brendan could be objective about that.

His brain could point out an attractive woman without him caring one way or the other.

He set his beer down on the windowsill and crossed his

arms, feeling a flash of annoyance at everyone's stupefied expressions. Randy had rolled out the red carpet in the form of
his tongue lolling out of his mouth, and the rest of the men
were mentally preparing marriage proposals, by the look of it.

"Little help with the luggage, Pipes?" called the second girl
from the entrance, where she'd propped open the door with a
hip, struggling under the weight of a suitcase.

"Oh!" Floppy Hat whirled around, pink climbing the sides
of her face—and hell, that was some face. No denying it, now
that there wasn't a dirty windowpane distorting it. Those were
the kind of baby blues that made men sign their life away, to
say nothing of that wide, stubborn upper lip. The combination
rendered her guileless and seductive at the same time, and that
was trouble Brendan wanted *no* part of. "Sorry, Hanns." She
winced. "I'll go get the rest—"

"I'll get them," at least nine men said at once, tripping over
themselves to reach the door. One of them took the suitcase
from Floppy Hat's companion, while several others lunged
into the rain, getting stuck side by side in the doorway. Half
of those jackasses were on Brendan's crew, and he almost dis-
owned them right then and there.

Within seconds—although not without some familiar
bickering—all seven suitcases were piled in the middle of
the bar, everyone standing around them expectantly. "What
gentlemen! So polite and welcoming," Floppy Hat crooned,
hugging her bizarre handbag to her chest. "Thank you!"

"Yes, thanks," said the second girl quietly, drying the rain
off her face with the sleeve of a UCLA sweatshirt. *Los Angeles.
Of course.* "Uh, Pipes?" She turned in a circle, taking in their
surroundings. "Are you sure this is the right place?"

In response to her friend's question, she seemed to notice where she was standing for the first time. Those eyes grew even bigger as she catalogued the interior of No Name and the people occupying it. Brendan knew what she was seeing, and already he resented the way she recoiled at the dust on the mismatched seats, the broken floorboards, the ancient fishing nets hanging from the rafters. The disappointment in the downturned corners of her mouth spoke volumes. *Not good enough for you, baby? There's the door.*

With prim movements, *Pipes*—keeper of ridiculous names and purses—snapped the handbag open and drew out a jewel-crusted phone, tapping the screen with a square red nail. "Is this . . . sixty-two North Forrest Street?"

A chorus of yeses greeted the strangled question.

"Then . . ." She turned to her friend, chest expanding on quick breaths. "Yes."

"Oh," responded UCLA, before she cleared her throat, pasting a tense smile on a face that was pretty in a much subtler way than Pipes's. "Um . . . sorry about the awkward entrance. We didn't know anyone was going to be here." She shifted her weight in boots that wouldn't be good for anything but sitting down. "I'm Hannah Bellinger. This is my sister, Piper."

Piper. Not Pipes.

Not that it was much of an improvement.

The floppy hat came off, and Piper shook out her hair, as if they were in the middle of a photo shoot. She gave everyone a sheepish smile. "We own this place. Isn't that crazy?"

If Brendan thought their entrance had produced silence, it was nothing compared to this.

Owned this place?

No one owned No Name. It had been vacant since he was in grade school.

Originally, the locals had pooled their money to stock the place with liquor and beer, so they'd have a place to come to escape the tourists during a particularly hellish summer. A decade had passed since then, but they'd kept coming, the regulars taking turns collecting dues once a week to keep the booze flowing. Brendan didn't make it over too often, but he considered No Name to be theirs. *All* of theirs. These two out-of-towners walking in and claiming ownership didn't sit right at all.

Brendan liked routine. Liked things in their place. These two didn't belong, especially Piper, who noticed him glowering and had the nerve to send him a pinky wave.

Randy drew her attention away from Brendan with a baffled laugh. "How's that now? You own No Name?"

Hannah stepped up beside her sister. "That's what you call it?"

"Been calling it that for years," Randy confirmed.

One of Brendan's deckhands, Sanders, disentangled himself from his wife and came forward. "Last owner of this place was a Cross."

Brendan noticed the slight tremor that passed through Piper at the name.

"Yes," Hannah said hesitantly. "We're aware of that."

"Ooh!" Piper started scrolling through her phone again at the speed of light. "There's a custodian named Tanner. Our stepdad has been paying him to keep this place clean." Though her smile remained in place, her gaze crawled over the distinctly *not* clean bar. "Has he . . . been on vacation?"

Irritation snuck up the back of Brendan's neck. This was a

proud town of long-standing traditions. Where the hell did this rich girl get off waltzing in and insulting his lifelong friends? His crew?

Randy and Sanders traded a snort. "Tanner is over there," Sanders said. The crowd parted to reveal their "custodian" slumped over the bar, passed out. "He's been on vacation since two thousand and eight."

Everyone in the bar hoisted their beers and laughed at the joke, Brendan's own lips twitching in amusement, even though his annoyance hadn't ebbed. Not even a little bit. He retrieved his bottle of beer from the windowsill and took a pull, keeping his eyes on Piper. She seemed to feel his attention on her profile, because she turned with another one of those flirtatious smiles that *definitely* shouldn't have caused a hot nudge in his lower body, especially considering he'd already decided he didn't care for her.

But then her gaze snagged on the wedding band he still wore around his ring finger—and she promptly looked away, her posture losing its playfulness.

That's right. Take it somewhere else.

"I think I can clear up the confusion," Hannah said, rubbing at the back of her neck. "Our father . . . was Henry Cross."

Shock drew Brendan's eyebrows together. These girls were Henry Cross's daughters? Brendan was too young to remember the man personally, but the story of Henry's death was a legend, not unlike Randy's evil crab story. It was uttered far less often lest it produce bad luck, whispered between the fishermen of Westport after too much liquor or a particularly rough day on the sea when the fear had taken hold.

Henry Cross was the last man of the Westport crew to die

while hunting the almighty king crab on the Bering Sea. There was a memorial dedicated to him on the harbor, a wreath placed on the pedestal every year on the anniversary of the sea taking him.

It was not unusual for men to die during the season. King crab fishing was, by definition, the most dangerous job in the United States. Every fall, men lost their lives. But they hadn't lost a Westport man in over two decades.

Randy had dropped onto his stool, dumbfounded. "No. Are you . . . You ain't Maureen's girls, are you?"

"Yes," Piper said, her smile too engaged for Brendan's peace of mind. "We are."

"Holy mackerel. I see the resemblance now. She used to bring you girls down to the docks, and you'd leave with pockets full of candy." Randy's attention swung to Brendan. "Your father-in-law is going to shit himself. Henry's girls. Standing right here in his bar."

"Our bar," Brendan corrected him quietly.

Two words out of his mouth were all it took to drop a chill into the atmosphere. A couple of the locals shrunk back into their seats, drinks forgotten on the crates that served as tables.

Brendan finished his beer calmly, giving Piper a challenging eyebrow raise over the glass neck. To her credit, she didn't blanch like most people on the receiving end of one of his looks. A stony stare through the wheelhouse window could make a greenhorn shit himself. This girl only seemed to be evaluating him, that limp wrist once again drawn up against her shoulder, that long mane of golden-rosy-honey hair tossed back.

"Aw. The deed says otherwise," Piper said sweetly. "But

don't worry. We'll only be killing your weirdly hostile vibe for three months. Then it's back to LA."

If possible, everyone retreated farther into their seats.

Except for Randy. He was finding the whole exchange hilarious, his smile so wide Brendan could count his teeth, three of which were gold.

"Where are you staying?" Brendan asked.

The sisters both pointed up at the ceiling.

Brendan bit off a laugh. "Really?"

Several patrons exchanged anxious glances. Someone even hopped up and tried to rouse Tanner at the bar, but it was nothing doing.

This whole situation was absurd. If they thought the bar was in shambles, they hadn't seen anything yet. They—especially *her*—wouldn't last the night in Westport. At least not without checking in to one of the inns.

Satisfied with that conclusion, Brendan set his beer aside and pushed himself to his feet, kind of enjoying the way Piper's eyes widened when he reached his full height. For some reason, he was wary of getting too close to her. He sure as hell didn't want to know what she smelled like. But he called himself an idiot for hesitating and strode forward, picking up a suitcase in each hand. "Well, then. Allow me to show you the accommodations."

Chapter Five

Who the fuck. *Even. Was* this douche?

Piper forced her chin up and followed the beast to the back of the bar—the bar which was essentially the size of her closet back in Bel-Air—and up a narrow staircase, Hannah in tow. God, he was freakishly big. Just to make it up the stairs, he had to bend down slightly, so his beanie-covered head wouldn't hit the ceiling.

For a split second, she'd found the silver-green eyes under the band of that beanie kind of captivating. His black beard was decently groomed. Full and close cropped. Those shoulders would have been seriously valuable in the chicken-fight competition a couple of weeks ago, to say nothing of the rest of him. He was *large* all around, and not even his beat-up sweatshirt could conceal the beefy musculature of his chest, arms.

He'd been staring at her, so she'd done what she did best when a man seemed interested. She did a little stationary flossing.

It was as natural as breathing, the subtle hip shift. Finding the light with her cheekbones, drawing attention to her mouth and sucking his soul out with her eyes. It was a maneuver she normally performed with a high success rate. Instead, he'd only looked pissed off.

How was she supposed to know he was married? They'd walked into a crowd of two dozen people. Into her father's bar, which had apparently been commandeered by a group of townies. There'd been a lot to take in at once, or she might have noticed the gold band. He'd seemed to purposefully flash it at her, and as she was definitely not the type to go after someone who was taken, she'd shut down her come-hither glance immediately.

Piper rolled her shoulders back one by one and decided to try being friendly to the beast, at least one more time. It was kind of admirable of him, wasn't it? To be aggressively faithful to his wife? If she ever got married someday, she hoped her husband would do the same. Once he realized she wasn't trying to catch his eye, maybe he'd chill. She and Hannah would be living in Westport for ninety days. Making enemies right off the bat would suck.

"Don't we need to get an apartment key from Tanner?" Piper called up the stairs.

"Nope," he responded shortly. "No locks."

"Oh."

"The bar entrance has a lock," he said, kicking open the apartment door and disappearing inside. "But almost everyone downstairs has a copy."

Piper chewed her lip. "That doesn't seem very secure . . ."

His derision was palpable. "Are you worried someone is going to break in and steal your lipstick purse?"

Hannah sucked in a sharp breath. "He went there."

Tenaciously, Piper held on to her poise and joined him in the apartment. The light hadn't been turned on yet, so she stepped aside to let Hannah in and waited, more grateful than ever that her sister was stubborn and refused to let her be banished to Westport alone. "I think we might have gotten off on the wrong foot," Piper said to the man. Wherever he'd gone. "What did you say your name was?"

"I didn't," came that mocking baritone from the dark. "It's Brendan."

"Brendan—"

The light flipped on.

Piper gripped Hannah's arm to keep from collapsing.

Oh no.

No no no.

"Ohhhh fuuuuuck," Hannah whispered beside her.

There had to be some mistake.

She'd googled Westport and done some nosing around, if minimally. Everywhere else was simply *not* Los Angeles, so what did it matter? Her search told her Westport was quaint and eclectic, located right on the cusp of the Pacific Ocean. A surfing destination. A cute village. She'd imagined an ocean view in a rustic but livable apartment, with lots of photo ops of her roughing it, with the hashtag #PNWBarbie.

This was not that.

Everything was in *one room.* There was a paper-thin partition blocking off the bathroom, but if she went three steps to the left, she'd be in the miniature kitchen. Three to the right, and she'd ram into the bunk bed.

Bunk. Bed.

Had she ever even seen one of those in real life?

Brendan's boots scuffed to a stop in front of the sisters. He crossed his arms over his wide chest and surveyed the apartment, his disposition suddenly jovial. "Second thoughts?"

Piper's eyes tracked along the ceiling, and she lost count of the cobwebs. There had to be an inch of grime on every surface—and she hadn't even seen the bathroom yet. The one window looked directly at the brick wall of the building next door, so the musky odor couldn't even be aired out.

She started to tell Hannah they were leaving. They would take the pittance Daniel put in their debit accounts and use it to rent a car and drive back to Los Angeles. Depending on how much it cost to rent a car, that was. It could be a thousand dollars or fifty. She had no clue. Other people usually arranged these kinds of things for her.

Maybe if they called Daniel and told him his custodian had been cashing a check and doing none of the work, he would relent and allow her and Hannah to return home. How could he say no? This place was unlivable. At least until it was scoured clean—and who was going to do that for them?

Brendan's unwavering gaze remained on her, waiting for her to crack.

She *was* going to crack, right?

Multiple voices drifted back to her, tightening the nape of her neck.

You play dress-up and spend your daddy's money.

You don't have a reason to learn anything.

There's just nothing to you, okay?

You have no drive to go anywhere. Or do anything. Why would you when this life I've provided you is always here, rewarding your lack of ambition with comfort and an excuse to remain blissfully stagnant?

Brendan's smugness was suddenly cloying, like glue drying in her windpipe. How original. Another man who thought she was worthless? How positively breathtaking.

He didn't matter. His opinion was moot.

Everyone's low expectations of her were beginning to wear kind of thin, though.

One look at her and this prick had become as dismissive of her abilities as her stepfather and her ex-boyfriend. What was it about her that courted such harsh judgment?

Piper wasn't sure, but after being dumped and banished to this murder hostel, she didn't really feel like taking another lump, especially when it wasn't warranted.

One night. She could do one night. Couldn't she?

"We're good, aren't we, Hanns?" Piper said brightly. "We never got to do the whole summer-camp thing. It'll be fun."

Piper glanced over at Hannah, relieved when her face warmed into a smile. "We're good." She sashayed across the space like she was surveying a million-dollar penthouse. "Very versatile. Cozy. Just needs a splash of paint."

"Mmmm," Piper hummed in agreement, nodding and tapping a finger against her chin. "Form *and* function. That abandoned pallet in the corner will make a lovely display shelf for my shoe collection."

When she risked a look at Brendan, it stressed her out to find his superior smile hadn't slipped an iota. Which was when she heard the scratching. It reminded her of a newspaper being crumpled in a fist. "What is that?" she asked.

"Your other roommate." Brendan tucked his tongue into his cheek, sauntered toward the exit. "One of several, I'm guessing."

No sooner had the words left his mouth than a rodent scurried across the floor, darting one way, then the other, his itty-bitty nose twitching. What was it? A mouse? Weren't they supposed to be cute? Piper scrambled onto the top bunk with a yip, Hannah hot on her heels. They met in the middle and clung to each other, Piper trying not to gag.

"Enjoy your night, ladies." Brendan's arrogant chuckle followed him out the door, his boots making the stairs groan on his way back down to the bar. "See you around. Maybe."

"Wait!" Gingerly, Piper climbed down off the bunk and shuddered her way out onto the landing where Brendan had paused, keeping her voice low. "You wouldn't happen to know a good, um . . . exterminator slash housekeeper in the area, would you?"

His derision was palpable. "No. We clean our own houses and catch our own vermin here."

"Catchy." She checked around her ankles for hungry critters. "Put that on the town welcome sign and watch real estate prices soar."

"Real estate prices," he echoed. "That kind of talk belongs in LA. Not here."

Piper rolled her eyes. "What is it like having such an accurate sense of where things belong? And who belongs where?" Still scouting for critters, she said absently, "I can be in a room full of people that I *know* and still not feel like I belong."

As she played that statement back to herself, Piper's eyes snapped up to find Brendan frowning down at her. She started to smooth her blurted truth over with something light and di-verting, but her exhaustion made it too much of an effort.

"Anyway, thanks for the warm welcome, Mayor Doom and Gloom." She retreated a step back into the apartment. "You've sure put me in my place."

He squinted an eye. "Hold on." Weirdly, Piper held her breath, because it seemed like he was going to say something important. In fact, she kind of got the feeling he didn't say much *unless* it was significant. But at the last second, he seemed to change his mind, dropping the thoughtful expression. "You're not here to film a reality show or some shit, are you?"

She slammed the door in his face.

Chapter Six

$\mathcal{B}$rendan locked the door of his house and double-checked his watch. Eight fifteen, on the dot. As was a captain's habit, he took a moment to judge the sky, the temperature, and the fog density. Smelled like the sun would burn the mist off by ten o'clock, keeping the early August heat minimal until he could finish his errands. He pulled on his beanie and took a left on foot toward West Ocean Avenue, traveling the same route he always did. Timing could make all the difference to a fisherman, and he liked to stay in practice, even on his off days.

The shops were just opening, the squawking calls of hungry seagulls blending with bells tinkling as employees propped open doors. The drag of a chalkboard sign being hauled out to the curb advertising fresh catches, some of which Brendan's crew had caught themselves on their last outing. Shopkeepers called lazy good mornings to each other. A couple of young kids lit cigarettes in a huddle outside the brewery, already dressed for the beach.

Since they were nearing the end of tourist season, there were markdowns advertised everywhere. On fishing hats and postcards and lunch specials. He appreciated the cycle of things. Tradition. The reliability of weather changing, and the shifting seasons setting people about a routine. It was the consistency of this place. Enduring, just like the ocean he loved. He'd been born in Westport, and he never intended to leave.

A ripple of aggravation fanned out beneath his skin when he recalled the night before. The stone tossed into the calm waters of how things were done. Outsiders didn't simply show up and claim ownership of things here. In Westport, people worked for everything they had. Nothing was handed over without blood, sweat, and tears. The two girls didn't strike him as people who had an appreciation for the place, the people, the past it was built on. The hard work it took to sustain a community on the whims of a volatile ocean—and do it well.

Good thing they wouldn't be sticking around for long. He'd be shocked if Piper made it through the night without checking in to the closest five-star hotel.

I can be in a room full of people that I know and still not feel like I belong.

Why did his mind refuse to let that drop?

He'd gnawed it over for far too long last night, then again this morning. It didn't fit. And he didn't like things that didn't fit. A beautiful girl—with admittedly sharp humor—like Piper could belong anywhere she chose, couldn't she?

Just not here.

Brendan waited at a stoplight before crossing Montesano, breezing through the automatic door of the Shop'n Kart, the wrinkle of irritation smoothing itself out when he saw that everything was in its place. He waved at Carol, the usual register attendant. Paper gulls hung from the ceiling and blew around in the breeze he'd allowed inside. Not many people were in the store yet, which was why he liked to come early. No conversations or questions about the upcoming crab season. If he expected a big haul, the course he'd charted. If the crew of the *Della Ray* would beat out the Russians. Talking about his plans would only jinx them.

As a seaman, Brendan was all about luck. He knew he could only control so much. He could construct a tight schedule, guide the boat in a direction of his choosing. But it was up to the ocean how and when she gave up her treasures. With crab season quickly approaching, he could only hope fortune would favor them once again, as it had the last eight years since he'd taken over from his father-in-law as captain.

Brendan picked up a handcart and headed west, to the freezer aisle. He didn't have a list and didn't need one, since he got the same groceries every time. First things he'd grab were some frozen burger patties and then—

"Siri, what should I make for dinner?"

That voice, drifting over from the next aisle, made Brendan stop in his tracks.

"Here's what I found on the Web," came the electronic reply.

A whine followed. "Siri, what is an *easy* dinner?"

He ground a fist into his forehead, listening to Piper speak to her phone as if it were a living, breathing human being.

There was some frustrated muttering. "Siri, what is *tarragon*?"

Brendan dragged a hand down his face. Who had let this girl child out into the world on her own without supervision? Frankly, he was kind of shocked to find her in a supermarket at all. Not to mention this early in the morning. But he wasn't going to question her. He didn't *care* about her explanation. There was a schedule to adhere to.

He trudged on, ripping the burger patties out of the freezer and throwing them into the handcart. He turned to the other side of the lane and picked out his usual bread. No-frills wheat. He hesitated before turning down the next aisle, where Piper was still yacking at her phone . . . and couldn't help but draw up short, a frown gathering his brows together. Who the fuck wore a sequined jumpsuit to the grocery store?

At least, he thought it might be called a jumpsuit. It was one of those deals women wore in the summertime with the top attached to the bottom. Except this one had shorts that ended right below her tight ass and made her look like a goddamn disco ball.

"Siri . . ." Her shoulders sagged, her handcart dangling from limp fingers. "What is a meal with *two* ingredients?"

Brendan let out an inadvertent sigh, and with a toss of hair, she glanced up, blinking.

He ignored the stab of awe in his chest.

She'd gotten prettier overnight, damn her.

With a roll of his shoulders, he tried to ease the tension bracketed by his rib cage. This girl probably inspired the same reaction in every man she ever came across. Even in the harsh supermarket lighting, he couldn't pick out a single flaw. Didn't want to *look* that closely. But he'd have to be dead not to. Might as well admit it. Piper's body reminded him, for the first time in a long, long time, that he had needs that couldn't be satisfied forever by his own hand.

Add it to the list of reasons her stay in Westport couldn't be over fast enough.

"Still here?" Jaw bunched, Brendan tore his eyes away from her long, achingly smooth-looking legs and moved down the aisle, dropping pasta and a jar of sauce into his basket. "Thought you'd be long gone by now."

"Nope." He could sense how pleased she was with herself as she fell into step beside him. "Looks like you're stuck with me at least one more day."

He lobbed a box of rice into his basket. "Did you make peace with the mice horde?"

"Yes. They're making me a dress for the ball right now." She paused, seeming to study him to see if he got the *Cinderella* reference. But he gave away nothing. "Um . . ."

Did he just slow his step so she could keep up with him? Why? "Um, what?"

To her credit, she didn't bat an eyelash at his shitty tone. Her smile might have been a little brittle, but she kept it in place, chin up. "Look, I sense you're in a hurry, but . . ."

"I am."

That fire he'd seen in her eyes last night was back, flickering behind the baby blue. "Well, if you're late for an appointment to go roll around in fish . . ." She leaned forward and sniffed. "Might as well cancel. You're already nailing it."

"Welcome to Westport, honey. Everything smells like fish."

"Not me," she said, cocking a hip.

"Give it time." He reached for a can of peas. "Matter of fact, don't."

She threw the hand holding her phone, let it slap down against the outside of her thigh. "Wow. What is your problem with me?"

"Bet you're used to men falling all over themselves to make

you happy, huh?" He tossed the can up in the air, caught it. "Sorry, I'm not going to be one of them."

For some reason, his statement had Piper's head tipping back on a semi-hysterical laugh. "Yes. Men *salivate* to do my bidding." She used her phone to gesture between them. "Is that all this is? You're being rude to me because I'm spoiled?"

Brendan leaned close. Close enough to watch her incredible lips part, to catch the scent of something blatantly feminine—not flowers. Smoky and sensual, yet somehow light. The fact that he wanted to get closer and inhale more pissed him off further. "I saw your judgment of this place before anyone else last night. The way you looked up at the building and laughed, like it was some cruel joke being played on you." He paused. "It's like this. On my boat, I have a crew, and each member has a family. A history. Those roots run all through the town. They've lived a lot of it inside No Name. And on the deck of my boat. Remembering the importance of each member of my crew and the people waiting on shore for them is my job. That makes this town my job. You wouldn't understand the character it takes to make this place run. The persistence."

"No, I don't," she sputtered, losing some steam. "I've been here less than one day."

When sympathy—and a little regret over being so harsh—needled him in his middle, he knew it was time to move on. But when he turned the corner into the next aisle, she followed, trying to look like she knew what she was doing by putting apple cider vinegar and lima beans in her cart.

"Jesus Christ." He set his cart down and crossed his arms. "Just what the hell are you planning on making with that combination?"

"Something to poison you with would be nice." She gave him one last disgruntled look and stomped off, that work-of-art backside twitching all the way to the end of the aisle. "Thank you for being so neighborly. You know, you obviously love this place. Maybe you should try being a better representation of it."

All right. That got him.

Brendan had been raised by a community. A village. By the time he was ten years old, he'd seen the inside of every house in Westport. Each and every resident was a friend of his parents. They babysat him, his parents returned the favor, and so on. His mother always brought a dish to celebrations when the men came back from sea, did the same for acquaintances who were sick. Kindness and generosity could be counted on. It had been a damn long while since he'd wondered what his mother would think of his behavior, but he thought of it now and grimaced.

"Fuck," he muttered, snatching up his basket and following Piper. Spoiled rich girl or not, she'd been right. About this *one* thing. As a resident of Westport, he wasn't doing this place justice. But just like the rare times he got off course on the water, he could easily correct the path—and get the hell on with his day. "All right," he said, coming up behind Piper in the baking aisle and watching her shoulder blades stiffen. "Based on the conversation you were having with your phone, it sounds like you're looking for a quick meal. That right?"

"Yes," she mumbled without turning around.

He waited for Piper to look at him, but she didn't. And he definitely wasn't impatient to see her face. Or anything like that. This close, he judged that the top of her head just about reached his shoulder, and felt another minor pang of regret for being a dick. "Italian's easiest, if you don't need it to be fancy."

Finally, she faced him, mid–eye roll. "I don't need fancy. Anyway, it's mostly . . ." She shook her head. "Never mind."

"What?"

"It's mostly for Hannah." She fluttered her fingers to indicate the lined shelves. "The cooking. To thank her for coming with me. She didn't have to. You're not the only one with important people and roots. I have people who I want to look out for, too."

Brendan told himself he didn't want to know anything about Piper. Why exactly she'd come, what she planned to do here. None of it. But his mouth was already moving. "Why are you in Westport, anyway? To sell the building?"

She wrinkled her nose, considered his question. "I guess that's an option. We haven't really thought that far ahead."

"Think of all the giant hats you could buy."

"You know what, assho—" She turned on a heel and started to bail, but he caught her elbow to halt her progress. When she ripped out of his hold immediately and backed away with a censorious expression, it caught him off guard. At least until he noticed she was looking pointedly at his wedding ring.

The temptation to put her misconception to rest was sudden and . . . alarming.

"I'm not interested," she said flatly.

"I'm not, either." *Liar*, accused the tripping of his pulse. "What you said before, about your sister being your roots. I get that." He cleared his throat. "You've got other ones, too. Here in Westport. If you feel like bothering."

Her disapproval cleared slightly. "You mean my father."

"For a start, yes. I didn't know him, but he's part of this place. That means he's part of us all. We don't forget."

"There are barely any memories for me to forget," she said. "I was four when we left, and after that . . . it wasn't spoken about. Not because I wasn't curious, but because it hurt our mother." Her eyes flickered. "I remember his laugh, though. I . . . can hear it."

Brendan grunted, really beginning to wish he'd stepped back and considered her from more than one angle before going on the defensive. "There's a memorial for him. Across from the museum, up on the harbor."

She blinked. "There is?"

He nodded, surprised by the invitation to bring her there that nearly snuck out.

"I'm almost scared to go look at it," she said slowly to herself. "I've gotten so comfortable with what little memories I have. What if it triggers more?"

The more minutes ticked past in Piper's presence, the more he started to question his first impression of her. Was she actually an overindulged brat from the land of make-believe? He couldn't help but catalogue everything else he knew about her. Such as, she wouldn't pursue an unavailable man. Thought she couldn't belong in a room full of people she knew. And she was in the store at eight thirty in the morning to buy ingredients to make a meal for her sister. So. Maybe not as selfish as he'd originally thought.

Honestly, though. What the hell did his impression of her matter?

She'd be gone soon. He wasn't interested. End of.

"Then I guess you'll have to call your therapist. I'm sure you've got one."

"Two, if you count my backup," she responded, chin raised.

Brendan staved off his interest in inspecting the line of her throat by rooting around in his basket. "Look. Make your sister an easy Bolognese sauce." He transferred his jar of marinara into her basket, along with the flute of pasta. "Come on."

He turned to make sure she was following on the way to the meat aisle, where he picked up a pound of ground beef and wedged it in along with her other purchases, which still included the lima beans and apple cider vinegar. He was kind of curious if she'd buy those two items just to be stubborn.

Piper looked between him and the meat. "What do I do with that?"

"Put a little olive oil on the pan, brown it up. Add some onions, mushrooms if you want. When it's all cooked, add the sauce. Put it over pasta."

She stared at him like he'd just called a football play.

"So like . . . everything stays in layers?" Piper murmured slowly, as if envisioning the actions in her head and finding it mind-blowingly stressful. "Or do I mix it all up?"

Brendan took the sauce back out of her basket. "Here's a better idea. Walk up to West Ocean and grab some takeout menus."

"No, wait!" They started a tug-of-war with the sauce jar. "I can do it."

"Be honest, you've never used a stove, honey," he reminded her wryly. "And you can't sell the building if you burn it down."

"I won't." She gave a closed-mouth scream. "*God*, I feel sorry for your wife."

His grip loosened automatically on the jar, and he snatched his hand back like he'd been burned. He started to respond, but there was something caught in his throat. "You should," he said finally, his smile stiff. "She put up with a lot."

Piper paled, her eyes ticking to the center of his chest. "I didn't mean . . . Is she . . . ?"

"Yeah." His tone was flat. "Gone."

"I'm sorry." She closed her eyes, rocking back on her heels. "I want to curl up and die right now, if it makes you feel any better."

"Don't. It's fine." Brendan coughed into his fist and stepped around her, intending to grab a few more things and check out. But he stopped before he could get too far. For some stupid reason, he didn't want to leave her feeling guilty. There was no way she could have known. "Listen." He nodded at her basket. "Don't forget to have the fire department on speed dial."

After the briefest hesitation, Piper huffed at him. "Don't forget to buy soap," she said, waving a hand in front of her face. But he didn't miss the gratitude in those baby blues. "See you around. Maybe."

"Probably not."

She shrugged. "We'll see."

"Guess we will."

Fine.

Done.

Nothing more to say.

It took him another handful of seconds to get moving.

And hell if he didn't smile on his way back up West Ocean.

Chapter Seven

After the groceries had been purchased and organized in the mini-fridge, the Bellinger sisters decided to go exploring—and escape the grunge of the upstairs apartment. Now Piper sat perched on the wooden railing overlooking the harbor, head tilted to allow the early afternoon breeze to lift the hair from her neck, sunshine painting her cheek. She looked inspired and well rested, fashion-forward in a scoop-back bodysuit and skinny jeans. Chloe ankle booties that said, *I might go on one of these boats, but someone else will be doing the work.*

"Hanns," she said out of the side of her mouth. "Lift the phone and angle it down."

"My arms are getting tired."

"One more. Go stand on that bench."

"Piper, I've gotten no fewer than forty shots of you looking like a goddess. How many options do you need?"

She gave an exaggerated pout. "Please, Hannah. I'll buy you an ice cream."

"I'm not a seven-year-old," Hannah grumbled, climbing onto the stone bench. "I'm getting sprinkles."

"Ooh, that would be a cute picture of you!"

"Yes," her sister replied drily. "I'm sure all nineteen of my followers would love it."

"If you'd let me share just *once*—"

"No way. We talked about this. Tip your head back." Piper complied, and her sister snapped the pic. "I like being private. No sharing."

Piper swung herself off the rail, accepting her phone back from Hannah. "You're just so cute, and everyone should know it."

"Uh-uh. Too much pressure."

"How?"

"You're probably so used to it by now, you don't stop to think of how . . . all these strangers and their responses to your posts are determining your enjoyment. Like, are you even experiencing the harbor right now, or are you trying to come up with a caption?"

"Oof. Below the belt." She sniffed. "Is 'Feeling a little nauti' cute?"

"Yes." Hannah snorted. "But that doesn't mean you can tag me."

"Fine." Piper harrumphed and shoved her phone into her back pocket. "I'll wait to post it so I won't be checking for likes. I can't get any reception, anyway. What should I look at with my eyeballs? What does reality have to offer me? Guide me, O wise one."

With an indulgent grin, Hannah locked her arm through Piper's. They each got an ice cream from a small shop and headed toward the rows of moored fishing vessels. Seagulls circled ominously overhead, but after a while, the sight of them and their shrill calls became part of the scenery, and Piper stopped worrying about being shat on. It was a clammy August afternoon, and tourists in sandals and bucket hats shuffled past signs advertising whale watching and boarded boats that bobbed in the water. Others stood in circles on the edges of the docks dropping what looked like steel buckets into the blue.

Piper noticed up ahead the white building proclaiming itself the maritime museum and recalled what Brendan had said about Henry Cross's memorial. "Hey. Um . . . not to spring this on you, but apparently there's a memorial for our father up here. Do you want to go look?"

Hannah considered. "That's going to be weird."

"So weird," Piper agreed.

"It would be weirder for his daughters *not* to visit, though." She chewed her lip. "Let's do it. If we wait, we'll keep finding reasons to put it off."

"Would we?" Not for the first time today, it occurred to Piper how little they'd spoken about the weird elephant in the room. Also known as the blurry start of their lives. "Finding out about Henry is something you'd want to avoid?"

"Isn't it?" They traded a glance. "Maybe following Mom's lead on this is just natural."

"Yeah." Only it didn't feel natural. It kind of felt like a chunk was missing from her memory. Or like there was a loose string in a sweater that she couldn't ignore. Or like perhaps Brendan's judgment had gotten to her in the supermarket. Her mother and grandparents had kept important details about Henry from her, but she could have found out about him on her own, right? Maybe this was her chance. "I think I want to go."

"Okay." Her sister studied her. "Let's do it."

Piper and Hannah continued along the harbor, scanning for the memorial. They returned the wave of an elderly man who sat on the museum lawn reading the paper. Shortly after, they spotted a brass statue outlined by the sea. Their steps slowed a little, but they kept going until they stopped in front of it. Gulls screeched around them, boats hummed in the distance, and life continued as usual while they stood in front of an artist's rendering of their long-lost father.

There he was. Henry Cross. He'd been standing there, immortalized, the whole time. A larger-than-life brass version of him, anyway. Maybe that's why his frozen smile and the metal ripple of his fisherman's jacket seemed so impersonal, foreign. Piper searched for some kind of connection inside of her, but couldn't find it, and the guilt made her mouth dry.

A plaque positioned at his feet read: *Henry Cross. Deeply Missed, Forever Remembered.*

"He looks like a young Kevin Costner," Piper murmured.

Hannah huffed a sound. "Oh shit, he really does."

"You were right. This is weird."

Their hands met and clasped. "Let's go. I have that Zoom call with Sergei in ten minutes, anyway."

Hannah had agreed to do some remote administrative work while in Westport, and she needed time to brush her hair and find a good background.

Their pace brisk, the sisters turned down the street that would guide them back to No Name and their apartment, but neither spoke. Hannah seemed deep in thought, while Piper tried to contend with the guilt—and a mild sense of failure—

that she hadn't been . . . grabbed by her first encounter with Henry.

Was she too shallow to feel anything? Or was the beginning of her life so far removed from her reality, she couldn't reach it so many years later?

Piper took a deep breath, her lungs rejoicing from the lack of smog. They passed fishermen as they walked, most of the men on the older side, and every single one of them gave the sisters a tip of the cap. Piper and Hannah smiled back. Even if they stayed a year in Westport, she'd probably never get used to the friendly ease of the locals, as they went around acknowledging other humans for no reason. There was something kind of nice about it, though she definitely preferred the bored indifference of Los Angeles. Definitely.

There was also something to be said for not looking at her phone as she walked. If she'd been responding to comments on her post, she might have missed the woman putting fresh fish into the window of her shop, two seagulls fighting over a French fry, a toddler trundling out of a candy shop stuffing saltwater taffy into his mouth. Maybe she should try to put her phone down more often. Or at least take in the real moments when she could.

When they reached No Name, Piper was surprised to find a man leaning up against the door. He appeared to be in his sixties, slightly round at the middle, a newsboy cap resting on top of his head. He watched them approach through narrowed eyes, a slight curve to his mouth.

"Hi," Hannah called, getting out her keys. "Can we help you?"

The man pushed off the door, slapped a hand against his thigh. "Just came to see Henry and Maureen's girls for myself, and there you are. How about that?"

After living two decades without hearing her father's name at all, it was a jolt to hear it out loud, have it connected with them. And their mother. "I'm Piper," she said, smiling. "This is Hannah. And you're . . . ?"

"Mick Forrester," he said affably, putting out his hand for a shake, giving each sister a hearty one. "I remember when you were knee high."

"Oh! It's nice to meet you as adults." She glanced at Hannah. "My sister has a work thing. But if you'd like to come in, I think there's still some beer in one of the coolers."

"No, I couldn't. I'm on my way to lunch with the old-timers." He smoothed his thick-knuckled hands over his belly, as if pondering what he'd order to fill it. "Couldn't let a day pass before I stopped by to say hello, see if you girls ended up favoring Maureen or Henry." His eyes twinkled as he looked between them. "I'd have to say your mother, for sure. Lucky, that. No one wants to look like a weathered fisherman." He laughed. "Although, Henry might have had that ocean-worn look about him, but, boy, your dad had a great laugh. Sometimes I swear I still hear it shaking the rafters of this place."

"Yeah." Inwardly, Piper winced at this stranger having more substantial memories and feelings for her own father. "That's kind of the only thing I remember."

"Shoot." Hannah's smile was tight. "I'm going to be late to the meeting. Pipes, you'll fill me in?"

"Will do. Good luck." Piper waited until Hannah had disappeared, the sound of her running up the back stairs of No Name fading after a moment. "So, how did you know Henry?"

Mick settled into himself, arms crossing over his chest. A classic storytelling stance. "We fished together. Worked our way up the ranks, side by side, from greenhorns to deckhands to crew, until eventually I bought the *Della Ray* and became my own captain." Some of the luster dulled in his eyes. "Not to bring up a sad subject, Piper, but I was right there in the wheelhouse when we lost him. It was a dark day. I never had a better friend than Henry."

Piper laid a hand on his elbow. "I'm sorry."

"Hell, you're his daughter." He reared back. "I'm the one should be comforting you."

"I wish . . . Well, we don't remember much about him at all. And our mother . . ."

"She was hurting too much to fill in the blanks, I'm guessing. That's not unusual, you know. Wives of fishermen come from tough stock. They have nerves of steel. My wife has them, passed them on to my daughter, Desiree." He gave a nod. "You might have met her husband, Brendan, the other night when you arrived."

Desiree. That was Brendan's late wife's name? Just like that, she was real. Someone with a personality. Someone with a face, a voice, a presence.

Sadness had turned down the sides of his mouth at the mention of his daughter. "Wives of fishermen are taught to lock up their fears, get on with it. No crying or complaining. Your mother rebelled against the norm a little, I suppose. Couldn't find a way to cope with the loss, so she picked up and left. Started over in a place that wouldn't remind her of Westport.

Can't say I wasn't tempted a time or two to do the same after my daughter passed, but I found it was worth staying the course."

Piper's throat felt tight. "I'm sorry. About your daughter."

Mick nodded once, weariness walking across his face. "Listen, I've got a lot more to tell you. Since you're staying awhile, I figure we'll have chances. A lot of us locals remember your father, and we never miss a chance to reminisce." He took a piece of paper out of his back pocket, handed it over to Piper. An address was written on it, blunt but legible. "Speaking of locals, I figured there's one who'd be more eager to catch up than any of us. This here is the address for Opal. I wasn't sure if you'd had a chance to stop over and see her yet."

Was Opal a woman Piper was supposed to know?

No clue.

But after visiting Henry's memorial and not being moved the way she should have been, she wasn't up for admitting her cluelessness, on top of the lingering guilt. Plus, there was something else she'd been wondering about and didn't want to miss her chance to ask.

"Opal. Of course." Piper folded up the piece of paper, debating whether or not she should ask her next question. "Mick . . . how exactly did Henry . . . ?" She sighed and started over. "We know it happened at sea, but we don't know the details, really."

"Ah." He removed his hat, pressed it to the center of his chest. "Rogue wave is what did it. He was standing there one minute, gone the next. She just snatched him right off the deck. We always thought he must have hit his head before going into the drink, because no one was a stronger swimmer than Henry. He had to be out cold when he went overboard. And that Bering Sea water is so damn frigid, there's only a minute's window before it sucks the breath right out of a man's lungs."

A shudder caught her off guard, goose bumps lifting on every inch of her skin. "Oh my God," she whispered, imagining the robust man made of brass being pitched over the side of a boat, sinking to the bottom of the ocean all alone. Cold. Did he wake up or just drift off? She hoped it was the latter. Oddly, her thoughts strayed to Brendan. Was he safe when he ventured out on the water? Was all fishing this dangerous? Or just crab fishing? "That's terrible."

"Yeah." Mick sighed and replaced his hat, reaching out to pat her awkwardly on the shoulder. Until he touched her, Piper didn't realize her eyes were wet. "I promise I won't make you cry every time I see you," he said, obviously trying to lighten the mood.

"Just once in a while?" She laughed.

Amusement lit his eyes again. "Here now, listen. We're having a little party on Friday night. Just us locals having some drinks, a potluck. Sharing memories. Consider yourself and Hannah invited." He pointed toward the harbor. "Up that way, there's a bar called Blow the Man Down. We'll be in the party room downstairs, around eight in the evening. I hope we'll see you there."

"I do love a party." She winked at him, and he blushed.

"All right, then." He gave her the signature Westport hat tip. "Great meeting you, Piper. You have a good day now."

"You too, Mick."

"Henry Cross's daughter," he muttered, heading off. "Hell of a thing."

Piper stood and watched him walk for a little before going inside. She didn't want to interrupt Hannah's Zoom call, so she took a seat on one of the barrels, letting the quiet settle around her. And for the first time, No Name felt like a little more than four walls.

Chapter Eight

*L*ater that night, Piper stared down at the package of ground beef and tried to gather the courage to touch it with her bare hands. "I can't believe meat looks like brains before it's been cooked. Does everyone know about this?"

Hannah came up behind her sister, propping her chin on Piper's shoulder. "You don't have to do this, you know."

She thought of Brendan's smug face. "Oh, yes I do." She sighed, prodding the red blob with her index finger. "Even if we could find a way to stretch our budget to cover takeout for every night, you should have home-cooked meals." Shifting side to side, she shook out her wrists, took in a bracing breath. "I'm the big sister, and I'm going to see that you're properly nourished. Plus, you cleaned the toilet from hell. You've earned dinner and sainthood, as far as I'm concerned."

She sensed her sister's shiver. "I can't argue with that. There were stains in there dating back to the Carter administration."

After her work call, Hannah had tripped over to the hardware store for cleaning supplies. They'd found a broom, dustpan, and a few rags in a supply closet downstairs in the bar, but that was it. Meaning they'd been forced to spend a chunk of their budget on bleach, a mop, a bucket, paper towels, sponges, cleaning fluids, and steel wool to block the mouse holes. All eight of them. When they'd dragged the bunk bed away from the wall, the panel running along the bottom had resembled Swiss cheese.

They'd been cleaning since midafternoon, and the studio, while still irreversibly grungy, looked a whole lot better. And Piper could admit to a certain satisfaction that came along with making her own progress. Being part of a before and after that didn't involve makeup or working with a personal trainer.

Not that she wanted to get used to cleaning. But still.

It smelled like lemons now instead of rotting garbage, and the Bellinger sisters of Bel-Air were responsible. Nobody back home would believe it. Not to mention, her manicurist would shit a brick if she could see the chipped polish on Piper's nails. As soon as they were settled, finding a full-service salon that did hair, nails, and waxing was top of the agenda.

But first. Bolognese.

Looking at the lined-up ingredients forced her to recall her impromptu morning shopping trip with Brendan. God, he'd been smug. Right up until she'd brought up his deceased wife. He hadn't been smug then. More like distraught. How long had the woman been gone?

If Brendan was still wearing his wedding ring, the death had to be recent.

If so, he had a thundercloud attitude for a good reason.

Despite her dislike of the burly, bearded fisherman, she couldn't stave off a rush of sympathy for him. Maybe they could learn to wave and smile at each other on the street for the next three months. If growing up in Los Angeles had taught her anything, it was how to make a frenemy. Next time they crossed paths, she also wouldn't mind telling him she'd mastered Bolognese and had moved on to soufflés and coq au vin.

Who knew? Maybe cooking was her undiscovered calling.

Piper turned the stove burner on, holding her breath as it clicked. Clicked some more.

Flames shot out of the black wrought iron, and she yelped, stumbling backward into her sister, who thankfully steadied her.

"Maybe you should tie your hair back?" Hannah suggested. "Fingers might be sacrificed tonight, but let's not lose those effortless beach waves."

"Oh my God, you're so right." Piper exhaled, whipping the black band off her wrist and securing a neat ponytail. "Good looking out, Hanns."

"No problem."

"Okay, I'm just going to do it," Piper said, holding her spread fingers above the beef. "He said to cook it on the pan until it turned brown. That doesn't sound too hard."

"Who said?"

"Oh." She made a dismissive sound. "Brendan was in the supermarket this morning being a one-man asshole parade." Closing her eyes, she picked up the meat and dropped the whole thing into the pan, a little alarmed by the loud sizzle that followed. "He's a widower."

Hannah came around the side of the stove, propping an elbow on the wall that was much cleaner than it had been this morning. "How did you find that out?"

"We were arguing. I said I felt sorry for his wife."

"D'oh."

Piper groaned while poking the meat with a rusty spatula. Was she, like, supposed to turn it over at some point? "I know. He kind of let me get away with sticking my foot in it, though. Which was surprising. He could have really laid on the guilt." Piper chewed on her lip a moment. "Do I come across really spoiled?"

Her sister reached up under her red ball cap to scratch her temple. "We're both spoiled, Pipes, in the sense that we've been given everything we could want. But I don't like that word, because it implies you're . . . ruined. Like you have no good qualities. And you do." She frowned. "Did he call you spoiled?"

"It has been heavily implied."

Hannah sniffed. "I don't like him."

"Me either. Especially his muscles. Yuck."

"There were definitely muscles," Hannah agreed reluctantly. Then she hugged her middle and sighed, letting Piper know exactly whom she was thinking about. "He can't compete with Sergei, though. Nobody can."

Realizing her hands were greasy from the meat, Piper reached over to the sink, which was right there, thanks to the kitchen being all of four feet wide, and rinsed her hands. She dried them on a cloth and set it down, then went back to prodding the meat. It was getting pretty brown, so she tossed in the onion slices, congratulating herself on being the next Giada. "You've always gone for the starving-artist boys," she murmured to Hannah. "You like them tortured."

"Won't deny it." Hannah slipped off her hat and ran her fingers through her medium-length hair. Hair just as nice as Piper's, but worn down far less often. A crime, to Piper's way of thinking, but she'd realized a long time ago that Hannah was going to be Hannah—and she didn't want to change a single thing about her sister. "Sergei is different, though. He's not just pretending to be edgy, like the other directors I've worked with. His art is so bittersweet and moving and stark. Like an early Dylan song."

"Have you talked to him since we got here?"

"Only through the group Zoom meetings." Hannah went to the narrow refrigerator and took out a Diet Coke, twisting off the cap. "He was so understanding about the trip. I get to keep my job . . . and he gets to keep my heart," she said wistfully.

They traded a snort.

But the sound died in Piper's throat when flames leapt up from the counter.

The counter?

No, wait. The rag . . . the one she'd used to dry her hands.

It was on fire.

"Shit! Hannah!"

"Oh my God! *What the fuck?*"

"I don't know!" Operating on pure reflex, Piper threw the spatula at the fire. Not surprisingly, that did nothing to subdue the flames. The flaring orange fingers were only growing larger, and the counter's laminate was basically nonexistent. Could the counters themselves catch on fire, too? They were nothing more than brittle wood. "Is that the rag we used to clean?"

"Maybe . . . yeah, I think so. It was soaked in that lemon stuff." In Piper's periphery, Hannah danced on the balls of her feet. "I'm going to run downstairs and look for a fire extinguisher."

"I don't think there's time," Piper screeched—and it galled her that in this moment of certain death, she could almost hear Brendan laughing at her funeral. "Okay, okay. Water. We need water?"

"No, I think water makes it worse," Hannah returned anxiously.

The meat was now engulfed in flames, just like her short-lived cooking career. "Well, Jesus. I don't know what to do!" She spied a pair of tongs on the edge of the sink, grabbed them, hesitated a split second before pinching a corner of the flaming rag and dragging the whole burning mess into the pan, on top of the meat.

"What are you doing?" Hannah screamed.

"I don't know! We've established that! I'm just going to get it outside of this building before we burn the place down."

And then Piper was running down the stairs with a pan. A pan that held an inferno of meat and Pine-Sol-soaked cotton. She could hear Hannah sprinting down the stairs behind her but didn't catch a word of what her sister said, because she was one hundred percent focused on getting out of the building.

On her way through the bar, she found herself thinking of Mick Forrester's words from earlier that day. *Boy, your dad had a great laugh. Sometimes I swear I still hear it shaking the rafters of this place.* The remembrance slowed her step momentarily, had her glancing up at the ceiling, before she kicked open the front door and ran out onto the busy Westport street with a flaming frying pan, shouting for help.

Chapter Nine

Brendan went through the motions of looking over the chalkboard menu at the Red Buoy, even though he already knew damn well he'd be ordering the fish and chips. Every Monday night, he met Fox at the small Westport restaurant. An institution that had been standing since their grandfathers worked the fishing boats. Brendan had never failed to get the same thing. No sense in fixing something that wasn't broken, and the Red Buoy had the best damn fish in town.

Locals came and went, calling hellos to each other, most of them picking up takeout to bring home to their families, greasy bags tucked under their arms. Tonight, Brendan and Fox were making use of one of three tables in the place, waiting for their orders to be called. And if Fox noticed Brendan glancing too many times at No Name across the street, he hadn't mentioned it.

"You're even more quiet than usual," Fox remarked, leaning back so far in his chair, it was a wonder he didn't topple over. He wouldn't, though, Brendan knew. His best friend and relief skipper of the *Della Ray* rarely made a misstep. In that way, he lived up to his name. "You got crabs on the brain, Cap?"

Brendan grunted, looking across the street again.

If he didn't have crabs on the brain, he sure as shit needed to put them there. In a couple of weeks, they would be making the journey to the Bering Sea for the season. For two weeks after that, they'd be hunting in those frigid yet familiar waters, doing their best to fill the belly of the boat with enough crab to support their team of six until next year.

Every crew member and deckhand of the *Della Ray* had year-round fishing jobs working out of Westport Harbor in addition to participating in the season, but king crab was their payday, and Brendan's men counted on him to deliver.

"Been studying the maps," Brendan said finally, forcing himself to focus on the conversation and not the building across the way. "Got a feeling the Russians are going to set their pots where we dropped ours last year, figuring it's tried and true. But the season is earlier than ever this year, and the tides are more volatile. Nothing is surefire."

Fox considered that. "You're thinking of heading farther west?"

"North." They traded a knowing look, both of them aware of the rougher waters that lay in that direction. "Can't think of a crew that's had much luck up toward St. Lawrence Island in several years. But I've got a hunch."

"Hey. Your hunches have always made my bank account happy." He dropped forward, clinked his bottle of Bud against Brendan's. "Let's do the damn thing."

Brendan nodded, content to let the silence settle.

But he noticed that Fox seemed to be battling a smile. "You got something to say?" Brendan finally asked.

Fox's mouth spread into the smile that made him popular

with women. In fact, he hadn't been at No Name on Sunday night because he'd taken a trip to Seattle to see a woman he'd met online. Seeing as he'd spent two nights there, Brendan had to assume the date had been . . . successful, though he'd cut his tongue out before asking for details. That kind of thing was better off left private.

For some reason, the fact that his best friend was popular with women was annoying him today more than usual. He couldn't fathom why.

"I might have something to say," Fox answered, in a way that presumed he did. "Took a walk up to the harbor this morning. Heard we've got some LA transplants in old Westport. Word is you had a little battle of wills with one of them."

"Who said?"

His friend shrugged. "Don't worry about it."

"Someone on the crew, then. Sanders."

Fox was visibly enjoying himself. "You're staring a hole through the window of No Name, Cap." There was a stupid dimple in his relief skipper's cheek. Had it always been there? Did women like shit like that? "Heard she didn't back down from your death stare."

Brendan was disgusted. Mostly because he was right. Piper hadn't backed down from it. Not last night and not this morning. "You sound like a teenage girl gossiping at her first sleepover."

That got a laugh out of Fox. But his friend went back to drinking his beer for a moment, his smile losing some of its enthusiasm. "It's okay, you know," he said, keeping his voice low in deference to the other customers waiting for their orders. "It's been seven years, man."

"I know how long it's been."

"Okay." Fox relented, knowing him well enough to drop the subject. Not the subject of his wife. But the subject of . . . moving on. At some point, near or far. Even the glimmer of that conversation made him nervous. Like everything else in his life, he'd remained married in his mind since she'd passed, because it had become a habit. A routine. A comfort of sorts. So he wasn't welcoming the possibility.

Still, when they both rose to collect their orders a minute later and sat back down at the table, Brendan didn't start eating right away. Instead, he found his hand fisted on the table, to the right of his plate. Fox saw it, too, and waited.

"Don't go sniffing around the older one. Piper," Brendan muttered. "And don't ask me to explain why, either."

Fox dipped his chin, his mouth in a serious line but his eyes merry as fuck. "Not a single sniff. You've got my word . . ." Brendan's friend dropped the fork he'd just picked up, his attention riveted on something happening out in the street. "What in the sweet hell?"

Brendan's head jerked around and pieced the situation together in the space of a second, his captain's mind immediately searching for a solution. His life might run on schedules and routine, but that organized mentality was what made it easier for him to manage chaos. Problems arose, solutions presented themselves. Just another type of order.

But this . . .

He didn't feel like his usual self watching Piper barrel into the street wielding fire.

His body moved for him, though. He shot from the table and

shouted to the visor-wearing register girl, "Fire extinguisher. Now."

She turned as pale as a ghost, and dammit, he'd have to apologize for scaring her later, but right then, he was moving across the street at a fast clip, pulling the pin out of the fire extinguisher. For a few hellish seconds, he watched Piper turn in circles, looking for somewhere safe to set down the enflamed pan, before she had no choice but to throw it into the street.

"Move," Brendan ordered, aiming and dousing the flames in sodium bicarbonate. Left behind was a charred pan from the nineteenth century, by the look of it. He took a breath, realized his heart was sprinting in his chest. Without stopping to think, he dropped the extinguisher and grabbed Piper's wrists, turning her hands over to look for burn marks. "Did you get yourself?"

"No," she breathed, blinking up at him. "Thanks. Um . . . thanks for putting it out."

He dropped her hands, not sure he wanted to acknowledge the free fall of relief he felt over her being unharmed. Stepping back, he whipped off his beanie, letting a welcome rush of irritation snake its way into his belly. "Really, Piper?" Brendan shouted. "I was only joking about having the fire department on speed dial."

Until Hannah stepped between them, Brendan wasn't even aware the little sister had followed Piper out of the building. Oh, but she was there, she was pissed, and her anger was directed squarely at him. "Don't yell at her, you fucking bully."

Inwardly, he flinched. *Bully?*

Fox made a choking sound. Brendan turned to tell his friend

to keep his mouth shut and realized they were drawing a crowd. A curious one.

"Hannah, it's fine." Piper sighed, moving out from behind her sister. Face red from embarrassment, she used the hem of her shirt to pick up the frying pan. The move left almost her entire trim stomach exposed, and Brendan ground his molars together. If he couldn't help noticing the little mole to the right of her belly button, nobody else could, either. She wasn't wearing the sequined thing anymore, but in bike shorts, with loose hair and a dirt smudge on her nose, she wasn't any less beautiful. "Ignore him," Piper said, dismissing him with a flick of her hand. "Do you see a place I can throw this away?"

"*Ignore* him, the lady says," Fox said, amused.

"What are you, his pretty-boy sidekick?" Hannah waved off a stunned Fox with a suck of her teeth and refocused her wrath on Brendan. "The last thing she needs is another dude making her feel like garbage. Leave her alone."

"*Hannah,*" Piper hissed sharply, walking past. "It's not worth getting upset over. Come help me."

But her sister wasn't finished. "And it was *my* fault. I left the cleaning rag on the kitchen counter, all soaked in chemicals. She's the one that saved the building from burning down." Hannah poked him in the middle of his chest. "Leave. Her. Alone."

Brendan was feeling shittier by the second. Something funny was stuck in his throat, and the appetite he'd left the house with had deserted him. He'd still been reeling over Hannah calling him a *bully* when she'd said, *The last thing she needs is another dude making her feel like garbage,* and now something hot and dangerous was simmering in his belly.

None of this was familiar. Women, especially ones half his size, didn't yell at him in the street. Or scare the shit out of him by nearly catching on fire. Part of him wanted to swipe a hand across the chessboard of the day and start over tomorrow, hoping and praying everything would be back to normal. But instead he found he wanted to . . . fix this situation with Piper more than he wanted to cling to the status quo. Maybe he was coming down with the goddamn flu or something, because when Piper tossed the pan into a trash can and sailed back toward her building, it was clear she intended to go home without saying another word to him. And for some reason, he just couldn't allow that to happen.

Leave her alone, the sister had said, and his apology got stuck in his throat.

Like he was a prize asshole who went around hurting women's feelings.

No. Just this one.

Why just this one?

Brendan cleared his throat hard. "Piper."

The woman in question paused with her hand on the door, gave an impatient hair toss that was way too sexy for a Monday night in Westport. Her expression said, *You again?*

Meanwhile, Hannah frowned up at him. "I said to leave my sister—"

"Listen up," Brendan said to the younger one. "I heard what you said. I respect you for saying it. You've got a nice, solid backbone for someone from Los Angeles. But I don't follow orders, I give them." He let that sink in. "I yelled at her because that's what people do when there's a close call." Over the top of Hannah's head, he met Piper's gaze. "I won't do it again."

A wrinkle appeared between Piper's brows, and damn, he was relieved. At least she no longer seemed indifferent about him. "It's okay, Hannah," Piper said, her hand dropping away from the door. "If you want to head back upstairs, I can go grab some takeout for dinner."

Hannah still wasn't budging. Neither was the crowd surrounding them. Brendan couldn't really blame the locals for being curious, either. These two girls were totally out of place in their small-fishing-town surroundings. Like two explosions of color.

Piper came forward and laid her head on her sister's shoulder. "I appreciate you defending me, Hanns, but you're a lover, not a fighter." She dropped a kiss on her cheek. "Go decompress. Your Radiohead albums are hiding in the secret pocket of my red quilted Chanel suitcase."

The younger sister gasped, whirling on Piper. "They wouldn't fit in any of my suitcases. You snuck them for me?"

"I was saving them for a rainy day." She bumped her hip to Hannah's. "Go. Fire up the turntable and listen as loud as you want."

"You a vinyl fan?" Fox piped up, reminding Brendan he was standing there in the first place. Hannah looked at Brendan's friend dubiously, but it only served to deepen that stupid dimple. He jerked a thumb in the direction of the harbor. "You know, there's a record store within walking distance. I could show you."

The younger Bellinger's eyes had gone wide as saucers.

"Fox," Brendan warned, taking his arm and pulling him aside.

"Oh, come on," Fox threw back, before he could say anything. "She's a kid."

"I'm not a kid," Hannah called. "I'm twenty-six!"

Fox dropped his voice another octave, moved in closer. "Jesus, she's cute, but she couldn't be further from my type. I'm just trying to buy you some alone time with Piper." He raised an eyebrow. "And who wouldn't want alone time with Piper. Good Christ, man. Sanders didn't do her justice."

"Shut the fuck up."

His friend laughed. "You really know how to make up for lost time, don't you?"

"I said, don't make me explain," Brendan gritted out.

"All right. All right. Just vouch for me," Fox muttered. "I'll have her back in twenty minutes, and I might even say some nice things about your grouchy ass. Wouldn't hurt."

Brendan hated admitting that Fox had a point. This was his third encounter with Piper, and he'd been a dick all three times. At first because she'd judged his town. Then he'd landed on the conclusion that she was an overindulged rich girl. After that, he could only blame being painfully rusty with the opposite sex. And this . . . being alone with a woman. It was a huge step. He could give her a simple apology now, go home, try to stop thinking about her. Yeah, he *could* do that. Just avoid this part of town for three months and stay the course of his routine.

She glanced up at him through her eyelashes. Not in a flirtatious way. More . . . inquisitive. As if she was wondering about him. And he found himself regretting the bad impressions he'd made. "He's my relief skipper. If he doesn't have her back in twenty minutes, I could drown him and make it look like an accident."

A smile teased her lips, and he wondered—couldn't help himself—what kind of man would get a kiss from a woman like that. "Take a picture of his ID, Hanns," Piper said, still looking at Brendan like he was a puzzle she wasn't sure she wanted to solve. "Text it to me first."

Sliding his wallet from his back pocket, Fox nodded. "I guess they grow them smart as well as beautiful in LA."

"Wow." Piper smiled at Fox. "A compliment. I was starting to think those were against the law in Westport."

Brendan turned a death glare on Fox. "What'd I say?"

Fox slid his ID to Hannah. "Sorry, Captain. The charm comes naturally."

The younger Bellinger snapped a picture of Fox's driver's license. A moment later, there was a *bing*, and Piper confirmed that she had the man's vital information. Fox gestured for Hannah to precede him down the sidewalk, and she did, arms crossed. But not before she mouthed a warning to Brendan.

Good Lord, what happened to him being well respected in this town?

If these two girls had had the proper tools, he was pretty damn sure he'd be tarred and feathered right about now. Maybe hanging from his toes in the harbor like a prize catch.

Brendan closed the distance between them, feeling like he was walking a plank. But he needn't have worried about being alone with Piper, because he swore half the damn town was still standing around, leaning in to see how he'd get out of the doghouse. "That fire ruin your dinner?"

She nodded, playing with the hem of her shirt. "I guess the

universe just couldn't allow something so perfect. You should have seen it. The meat barely looked like brains anymore."

He was caught off guard by the urge to smile. "I, uh . . ." He replaced his beanie, tried to scare off a few locals with a loud sniff, gratified when they scattered in all directions. "It was rude to shout before. I apologize." Lord, she was even prettier with the sunset in her eyes. That was probably why he added, "For this time and the other times."

Piper's mouth twisted and she ducked her head somewhat, like she was trying to camouflage her own smile. "Thank you. I accept."

Brendan grunted, dipped his chin toward the Red Buoy. "They called my number right before you ran out on fire. Go in there and eat it." When she blinked, he played back his demand and realized that's exactly what it had been. A demand. "If you'd like," he tacked on.

She hummed and slipped past him, her perfume reaching up and apparently doing something to his brain, because he followed in her wake without sending the order to his feet. Everyone turned and stared when they walked inside and sat down at the same table. Hell, the customers waiting for their orders didn't even attempt to disguise their interest.

He didn't want any of them to overhear their conversation. It was none of their business. That was the only reason he took the seat next to Piper and tugged her chair a little closer.

Brendan pushed the plate of fish and chips in front of her, then picked up the fork and put it in her hand.

"So . . ." She forked the smallest fry on the plate, and he frowned. "Your friend is your relief skipper. That makes you . . . the captain?"

Thank Christ. Something he could talk about.

"That's right. I captain the *Della Ray*."

"Oh." She tilted her head. "Where does that name come from?"

"I took the wheel from my father-in-law, Mick. It's named after his wife."

"How romantic." If bringing up his in-laws made for awkward conversation, she didn't let it show. Instead, her interest seemed piqued. "Me and Hannah walked up to the harbor this afternoon. So many boats are named after women. Is there a reason for that?"

He thought of Piper strutting along his harbor and wondered how many car accidents she'd caused. "Women are protective. Nurturing. A boat is given the name of a woman in the hopes that she'll protect the crew. And hopefully put a good word in with the other important woman in our lives, the ocean."

She took a bite of fish, chewing around a smile. "Have you ever had a woman on your crew?"

"Jesus Christ, no." There went the smile. "I'm trying *not* to sink."

Amusement danced across her face. "So the idea of women is comforting, but their actual presence would be a disaster."

"Yes."

"Well, that makes perfect sense." Her sarcasm was delivered with a wink. "My stepfather told us a little bit about king crab fishing. It's only a few weeks out of the year?"

"Changes every season, depending on the supply, the overall haul from the prior year."

Piper nodded. "What do you do the rest of the year? Besides yell at harmless women in the street."

"You planning on holding that over me for long?"

"I haven't decided."

"Fair enough." He sighed, noticed she'd stopped eating, and nudged her fork hand into action. When she'd put a decent-sized bite into her mouth, he continued. "In the summer, we fish for tuna. Those are the longer jobs. Four, five days out. In between those long hauls, we do overnight trips to bring in salmon, trout, cod."

Her eyebrows went up, and she angled her fork toward the plate. "Did you catch this?"

"Maybe."

She covered her mouth. "That's so weird."

Was it? He kind of liked sitting there while she ate something he'd brought back on his boat. He liked knowing most of the town either made money off his catches or fed them to their families, but it had never quite felt like the masculine pride hardening his chest right now. "You want me to put in an order for your sister? Or they can box up Fox's dinner, and he can fend for himself."

"She'll be happy with the other half of yours." She pushed Fox's plate toward him. "You should eat his, though. I don't know what it is, but it looks good."

Brendan grunted. "It's a potpie."

"Ohh." She waited, but he made no move to pick up his fork. "You don't like potpie?"

"It's not fish and chips."

"And that's bad."

"It's not bad, it's just not what I order." He shifted in his chair, wondering if the seats had always been so uncomfortable. "I always order the fish and chips."

Piper studied him in that way again, from beneath her long eyelashes—and he wished she wouldn't. Every time she did that, the zipper of his jeans felt tight. "You've never eaten anything else on the menu?"

"Nope. I like what I like."

"That's so boring, though."

"I call it safe."

"Oh no." A serious expression dawned on her face. "Do you think there is a female fisherman hiding in this pie, Brendan?"

His bark of laughter made her jump. Hell, it made *him* jump. Had anyone ever caught him off guard like that? No, he didn't think so. He turned slightly to find the employees of the Red Buoy and a half-dozen customers staring at him. When he turned back, Piper was holding out the fork. "Try the pie. I dare you."

"I won't like it."

"So?"

So? "I don't *try* things. If I make the decision to eat the pie, I'll have to eat the whole thing. I don't just go around sampling shit and moving on. That's indecisive."

"If Hannah was here, she'd tell you your problem is psychological."

Brendan sighed up at the ceiling. "Well, I didn't seem to have any damn problems until you two showed up and started pointing them out."

A beat passed. "Brendan."

He dropped his chin. "What?"

She held out the fork. "Try the pie. It's not going to kill you."

"Christ. If it's that important to you." Brendan snatched the fork out of her hand, careful not to graze her with the tines. As he held the fork above the pastry shell, she pressed her knuckles to her mouth and squealed a little. He shook his head, but some part of him was relieved she didn't seem to be having a terrible time. Even if her entertainment came at his expense. He reckoned he kind of owed her after the scene in the street, though, didn't he?

Yeah.

He stabbed the fork into the pie, pulled it out with some chicken, vegetables, and gravy attached. Put it in his mouth and chewed. "I hate it." Someone behind the counter gasped. "No offense," he called without turning around. "It's just not fish and chips."

Piper's hands dropped away from her face. "Well, that was disappointing."

He kept eating, even though the runniness of the gravy curled his upper lip.

"You're really going to eat the whole thing," she murmured, "aren't you?"

Another large bite went in. "Said I would."

They ate in silence for a couple of minutes until he noticed her attention drifting to the window, and he could see she was thinking about the frying pan incident. Another stab of guilt caught him in his middle for yelling at her. "You planning on trying to cook again?"

She considered her plate of food, which she'd hardly made a dent in. "I don't know. The goal was to make it through one night and go from there." She squinted an eye at him. "Maybe I'll have better luck if I give our stove a woman's name."

Brendan thought for a second. "Eris." She gave him an inquisitive head tilt. "The goddess of chaos."

"Ha-ha."

Piper laid her fork down, signaling she'd finished eating, and Brendan felt a kick of urgency. They'd been sitting there a good ten minutes, and he still didn't know anything about her. Nothing important, anyway. And he wouldn't mind making sense of her, this girl who came across pampered one minute and vulnerable the next. Hell, there was something fascinating about how she glimmered in one direction, then the other, delivering hints of something deeper, before dancing away. Had he really talked about fishing for most of dinner?

He *wanted* to ask what Hannah had meant when she said men treat Piper like garbage. That statement had been stuck in his craw since he'd heard it. "You never answered me this morning. Why exactly are you in Westport?" was what he asked instead. She'd been running fingers through her hair, but paused when she heard his question. "You said three months," he continued. "That's a pretty specific amount of time."

Beneath the table, her leg started to jiggle. "It's kind of an awkward story."

"Do you need a beer before telling it?"

Her lips twitched. "No." She closed her eyes and shivered. "It's more than awkward, actually. It's humiliating. I don't know if I should give you that ammunition."

Man, he'd really been a bastard. "I won't use it against you, Piper."

She speared him with those baby blues and seemed satisfied with whatever she saw. "Okay. Just keep an open mind." She blew out a breath. "I had a bad breakup. A public one. And I didn't want to be labeled social media pathetic, right? So I mass texted hundreds of people and broke us into the rooftop pool at the Mondrian. It got out of control. Like, police helicopters and fireworks and nudity out of control. So I got arrested and almost cost my stepfather the production money for his next film. He sent me here with barely any money to teach me a lesson . . . and force me into being self-sufficient. Hannah wouldn't let me come alone."

Brendan's fork had been suspended in the air for a good minute. He tried to piece it all together, but everything about this world she'd described was so far from his, it almost sounded like make-believe. "When was this?"

"A few weeks ago," she said on an exhale. "Wow, it sounds a lot worse when it's all strung together like that." Chewing her bottom lip, she searched his face. "What are you thinking? That you were right and I'm just some rich, spoiled brat?"

"Don't put words in my mouth. You're already making me eat this goddamn pie."

"No, I'm not!"

He shoveled in another bite of crap, his mind circling back to the bad breakup she'd mentioned. Why did his spine feel like it was getting ready to snap? "I'm thinking a lot of things," he said. "Mostly, I can't imagine you in jail."

"It wasn't so bad. The guard, Lina, was a doll. She let me use the regular bathroom."

"How'd you pull that off?"

"People like me." She looked down her adorable nose at him. "Most of the time."

He snorted. "Yeah, I can see that. Flirt."

She gasped. Then shrugged. "Yeah." A couple of seconds ticked past. "You didn't let me flirt with you. And then I thought you were married. My whole pattern got thrown off, and now I don't know how to act. Trying to flirt again seems pointless."

The hell it was. "Try it."

"No. I can't!" she sputtered. "The third wall is already down."

Was he sweating under his clothes? What the hell was wrong with him? "What is the next stage after flirting? Once you've settled in?"

"*Settled in?* Ew." She shrugged. "Also, I don't know. I've never gotten that far." She crossed her legs, drawing his gaze to the slide of her shorts along that smooth underside of her thigh. And there went his zipper again, confining things. "We've gotten way off the topic of my whole sordid story."

"No, we haven't," he responded. "I'm still digesting it all. Along with—"

"Don't you dare bring up the pie again." They each offered up half a smile. "Anyway, unless I can finagle a way back to Los Angeles, me and Hannah will be here until Halloween. I think my best bet is to spend less time cooking, more time figuring out how to finagle." She tapped a fingernail on the table. "Maybe if there was a way to prove I've learned how to be responsible, Daniel would let me come home."

Brendan was brooding over Piper being at a party that involved nudity—in what capacity, exactly? Had *she* been naked?—so he spoke more harshly than intended. "Here's an idea. Why don't you try and actually enjoy your time outside the ninth circle of hell that is Los Angeles?"

"Who said I'm not enjoying myself? Look at me, getting snipped at over fish and chips. If this isn't living it up, I've been doing it wrong." Smirking, she popped a fry into her mouth, and he tried not to watch her chew. "But you're right. I could try harder. Maybe I'll charm one of those cute fishermen up on the harbor into taking me fishing."

Something acidic burbled in his windpipe at the prospect of her on another man's boat. "You could. If you wanted a subpar experience."

"Are you saying you could deliver a better one?"

"Damn right."

Were they still talking about fishing? Brendan didn't know. But he was turned on . . . and she appeared to be waiting for something. For him to ask her out on his boat?

A breeze of panic kept his mouth shut a moment too long. Piper gave him an assessing look and visibly moved on, rising to her feet when her sister and Fox appeared outside the restaurant. "There they are. I'll grab a to-go box for the rest of this." She leaned down and kissed both of his cheeks, like they were in goddamn Paris or something. "Thanks for dinner, Captain. I promise to stay out of your hair."

As she dumped the remaining fish and chips into a container and bounced off to join her sister, Brendan wasn't sure if he wanted Piper out of his hair. If he didn't, he'd just missed a clear opening to ask her out. In the morning, he'd be leaving for a three-day fishing trip, so—assuming he *wanted* the opportunity to see more of the girl from Los Angeles—he'd have to wait for another one. And it might never come.

Fox dropped into the chair beside him, grinning ear to ear. "How'd it go, Cap?"

"Shut up."

Chapter Ten

𝒫iper was stuck in a nightmare in which giant mice with twitchy little noses chased her through a maze while she wielded a flaming frying pan. So when she heard the knock on the door the following morning, her waking thought was *The mouse king has come for me.* She pinwheeled into a sitting position and soundly smacked her head on the top bunk.

"Ow," she complained, pushing her eye mask up to her forehead and testing the collision spot with a finger. Already sore.

A yawn came from above. "Did you hit your head again?"

"Yes," she grumbled, trying to piece together why she'd woken up in the first place. It wasn't like much sunlight *could* filter in through their window and the building next door. Not when a scant inch separated them and the neighboring wall. The apartment was all but black. It couldn't even be sunrise yet.

A fist rapped twice on the door, and she screamed, her hand flying to the center of her chest. "Mouse king," she gasped.

Hannah giggled. "What?"

"Nothing." Piper shook off the mental cobwebs and eyed the door warily. "Who's there?"

"It's Brendan."

"Oh." She glanced up and knew she was trading a frown with Hannah, even though they couldn't see each other. What did the grumpy boat captain need from her that couldn't wait until normal-people hours? Every time she thought they'd seen the last of each other, he seemed to be right there, front and center. Confusing her.

She hadn't been lying about not knowing how to act in his presence. It was usually easy to charm, flirt, flatter, and wrap men around her pinky. Until they got bored and moved on, which they seemed to do faster and faster these days. But that was beside the point. Brendan had robbed her deck of the pretty-girl trump card, and she couldn't get it back. He'd had too many peeks behind the curtain now. The first time they'd met, she'd been a drowned rat and offended his beloved Westport. Meeting two, she'd blasphemed his dead wife. Three, she'd almost burned this relic of a building down . . .

Although eating with him had been kind of . . . nice.

Maybe that wasn't the right word.

Different. Definitely different. She'd engaged in conversation with a man without constantly trying to present her best angle and laugh in just the right way. He'd *seemed* interested in what she had to say. Could he have been?

Obviously, he hadn't been instantly enraptured with her appearance. Her practiced come-hither glances only made him grumpier. So maybe he wanted to be friends! Like, based on her personality. Wouldn't that be something?

"Huh," she murmured through a yawn. "Friends."

Swinging her legs over the edge of the bed, she slipped her feet into her black velvet Dolce & Gabbana slippers and padded to the door. Before she opened it, she gave in to vanity and scrubbed away the sleep crusties in the corners of her eyes. She opened the door and craned her neck in order to look up into the face of the surly boat captain.

Piper started to say good morning, but Brendan cleared his throat hard and did a quarter turn, staring at the doorjamb. "I'll wait until you're dressed."

"Sorry . . . ?" Nose wrinkled, she looked down at her tank top and panties. "Oh."

"Here," Hannah called sleepily, tossing Piper a pillow.

"Thanks." She caught it, held it in front of herself like a puffy shield.

Hold on. Was this man she'd judged as little more than a bully . . . blushing?

"Oh, come on, Brendan," she chuckled. "There's a lot worse on my Instagram. Anyone's Instagram, really."

"Not mine," Hannah said, voice muffled. A second later, she was snoring softly.

For the first time, Piper noticed the tool kit at Brendan's feet. "What's all that for?"

Finally, Brendan allowed his attention to drift back to her, and a muscle wormed in his jaw. The pillow covered Piper from neck to upper thigh, but the curve of her panty-clad backside was still visible. Brendan's eyes traveled over that swell now, continuing up the line of her back, his Adam's apple bobbing in his throat. "I changed the lock on the door downstairs," he said hoarsely, his gaze ticking to hers. "Came to change this one, too. It'll only take a few minutes."

"Oh." Piper straightened. "Why?"

"We leave this morning for three nights. Last fishing trip

before crab season. I just . . ." He crouched down and started rooting through his box, metal clanging so she could barely hear him when he said, "Wanted to make sure this place was secure."

Piper's fingers tightened on the pillow. "That was really nice of you."

"Well." Tools in hand, he straightened once again to his full height. "I saw you hadn't done it. Even though you've had two days."

She shook her head. "You had to go and ruin the nice gesture, didn't you?"

Brendan grunted and set to work, apparently having decided to ignore her. Fine. Just to spite him, she let the pillow drop and went to make coffee. On her sister's trip to the record store with Fox, Hannah had found a mom-and-pop electronics shop, purchasing the kind of one-cup brewer you'd normally find in a hotel room. They'd been selling it for *ten dollars*. Who sold anything for ten dollars? They'd rejoiced over Hannah's bargain hunting the way Piper used to celebrate finding a four-thousand-dollar Balmain dress at a sample sale.

"Would you like a cup of coffee?" Piper asked Brendan.

"No, thanks. Already had one."

"Let me guess." After adding a mug of water, she lowered the lid on the maker and switched it on. "You never have more than a single cup."

Grunt. "Two on Sundays." His brows angled down and together. "What's that red mark on your head?"

"Oh." Her fingers lifted to prod the sore patch. "I'm not used to sleeping with another bed three feet above mine. I keep whacking my head on the top bunk."

He made a sound. Kept frowning.

His visible grumpiness made the corner of Piper's mouth edge up. "What are you going fishing for this time?"

"Halibut. Rockfish."

She rolled her eyes at his abrupt answer, leaned back against the chipped kitchen counter. "Well, Hannah and I talked it over and we're running with your suggestion." She picked up her finished coffee, stirring it with her finger and sipping. "We want to enjoy our time in Westport. Tell me where to go. What to do."

Brendan took another minute to finish up the lock. He tested it out and replaced his tools in the box before approaching her, digging something out of his back pocket. She caught a tingle on the soft inner flesh of her thighs and knew he was checking her out, but she pretended not to notice. Mostly because she didn't know how to feel about it. That familiar burn of a man's regard wasn't giving her the obligatory thrum of success. Brendan's attention made her kind of . . . fidgety. He'd have to be dead not to look. But actual interest was something else. She wasn't even sure what she would do if Brendan showed more than a passing notice of her hotness.

And he was still wearing his wedding ring.

Meaning, he was still hung up on his deceased wife.

So she and Brendan would be friends. Definitely *only* friends.

Brendan cleared his throat. "You're a five-minute walk to the lighthouse. And it's still warm enough for the beach. There's a small winery in town, too. My men are always complaining about having to go there on date nights. They have something called a selfie spot. So you should love it."

"That tracks."

"I also brought you some takeout menus," he said in a low voice, slapping them down on the counter, and with him standing so close, it was impossible not to register their major size difference. Or catch a whiff of his saltwater-and-no-nonsense deodorant.

Friends, she reminded herself.

A grieving widower was not fling material.

Swallowing, Piper looked down at the menus. He'd brought three of them.

She pursed her lips. "I guess it's too early to be insulted."

"This isn't me telling you not to cook. These are fallbacks." He opened the first folded menu, for a Chinese restaurant. "In each of them, I went ahead and circled what I order every time, so you'd know the best dish."

She hip-bumped him, although thanks to him being a foot taller, her hip landed somewhere near the top of his thigh. "You mean, the only one you've ever tried?"

A smile threatened to appear on his face. "They're one and the same."

"Bah."

"You have your phone handy?" Brendan asked.

Nodding, she turned on a heel, took two steps, and picked up the discarded pillow, holding it over her butt to end his suffering—and to let him know she'd gotten the friends-only message. She collected her cell from its place of honor beneath her pillow, then pivoted, transferring the pillow once again to block her front. When she turned around, Brendan was watching her curiously, but didn't comment on her sudden modesty.

"If you and your sister have any problems while I'm gone, call Mick." He dipped his chin. "That's my . . . my father-in-law."

"We met him yesterday," Piper said, smiling through the odd tension at the mention of Brendan having a father-in-law. "He's a sweetie."

Brendan seemed momentarily caught off guard. "Ah. Right. Well, he's not too far from here. Let me give you his contact info in case you need something."

"Yes, Captain." She clicked her bare heels together. "And after that, I'll swab the deck."

He snorted. "She uses a mop once . . ."

Piper beamed. "Oh, you noticed our spruce job, did you?"

"Yeah. Not bad," he commented, glancing around the apartment. "Ready?"

Piper humored him by programming Mick's number into her phone as he rattled it off. "Thanks—"

"Take mine, too," he said abruptly, suddenly fascinated by one of the menus. "I won't have reception on the water, but . . ."

"Take it in case I need cooking advice when you get back?"

He made an affirmative sound in his throat.

Piper pressed her lips together to hide a smile. She'd seen Brendan with his friend Fox. How they needled each other like brothers as a means of communication. It really shouldn't come as a surprise that making new friends didn't come naturally to him. "All right. Give me those digits, Captain."

He seemed relieved by her encouragement, reciting the number as she punched it into her phone. When she hit dial on his number, his head came up as if trying to figure out where the sound was coming from.

"That's your phone," she said, and laughed. "I'm calling you so you'll have my number, too."

"Oh." He nodded, the corner of his mouth tugging a little. "Right."

She cupped a hand around her mouth and whispered, "Should I be expecting nudes?"

"Jesus Christ, Piper," he grumped, straightening the takeout menus and signaling an end to the discussion. But he hesitated a second before striding for the door. "Now that I'm in your phone, does this mean next time you break into a rooftop pool, I'll be on the mass invite?"

Brendan winked to let her know he was joking. But she couldn't help grinning at the mental image of this earthy giant of a man walking through a sea of polished LA social climbers. "Oh yeah. You're in."

"Great."

After one more almost imperceptible sweep of her legs, Brendan coughed into his fist and turned again. He picked up his toolbox and started down the stairs. Just like that. His work was done and formalities were stupid. Piper followed, looking down at him from the top of the stairs. "Are we friends, Brendan?"

"No," he called back, without missing a beat.

Her mouth hung open, a laugh huffing out of her as she closed the door.

Hannah sat up and asked, "What the hell is going on there?"

Slowly, she shook her head. "I have no freaking idea."

Chapter Eleven

$\mathcal{B}$rendan sat in the wheelhouse of the *Della Ray* stabbing at the screen of his phone.

He should have been helping the crew load groceries and the ice they would need to keep the fish fresh in the hold. But they'd be pushing off in ten minutes, and he needed to take advantage of the last remaining minutes of internet access, spotty though it was in the harbor.

He'd downloaded Instagram; now they were asking him for personal information. Did he have to be a member of this stupid thing to look at pictures? Chrissakes. He shouldn't be doing this. Even if Piper had volunteered the information that she was apparently half-naked on this fucking app, he shouldn't be looking. In fact, if he expected to concentrate worth a damn on this trip, he absolutely should not be adding to the treasure trove of Piper imagery already floating around in his head.

First and foremost was the memory of Piper answering the door in those little white panties. White. He wouldn't have figured on that. Maybe sparkly pink or peacock blue. But hell if the white cotton cupping her pussy, a contrast of innocent and sexy, had him sporting a semi an hour later and downloading apps like a goddamn teenager. He'd been grinding his back teeth since he walked out of No Name, bereft over his palms not sliding down the supple curve of her ass—and God, he had no business thinking about that.

Why had she covered herself with the pillow the second time?

Had he been so obviously turned on it made her uncomfortable?

Considering that, he frowned. He didn't like the idea of her being nervous.

Not around him. Not at all.

"All loaded. Ready to go," Fox said, swinging into the wheelhouse, his Mariners cap pulled down low over his eyes. But not low enough that Brendan could miss them lighting up. "You downloading Instagram, Cap?"

"Who's downloading Instagram?" Sanders asked, ducking his red curly head under the doorframe. "Who doesn't already have Instagram?"

"People who have better shit to do," Brendan growled, snapping both of their mouths shut. "They're asking me to make a username."

In came a third member of the crew, Deke, his dark brown fingers wrapped around a bottle of Coke as he took a sip. "Username for what?"

Brendan tipped his head back. "Jesus Christ."

"Instagram," Sanders said, filling in Deke.

"You're doing a little Piper recon, aren't you?" Fox asked, his expression one of pure, everlasting enjoyment. "Downloading a few pictures to keep you warm on the trip?"

"You can do that?" Brendan half shouted. "Anyone can just download pictures of her?"

"Or me, or you, or anyone," Deke said. "It's the internet, man."

Brendan stared at his phone with renewed disgust. As far as he was concerned, this was even more reason to get on this dumb app and see what's what. "It won't let me just use my own name as my username."

"Yeah, probably because about nine hundred Brendan Taggarts joined before you."

"So what should I use?"

"CaptainCutie69," Fox spat out.

"IGotCrabs4U," Deke supplied.

"SlipperyWhenWet."

Brendan stared. "You're all fired. Go home."

"All right, all right, we'll be serious," Fox said, holding up his hands. "Did you try CaptainBrendanTaggart?"

He grunted, punched it in with one blunt digit. It took him forever, because his finger was so big, he kept hitting erroneous characters. "Accepted," he grumbled finally, shifting in the captain's chair. "Now what?"

Deke settled in next to Sanders, like they were in the middle of goddamn gossip hour. "Search her name," he said, pulling out his own phone.

Brendan pointed at him. "You better not be looking."

The man pocketed his phone again without another word.

"The captain is a little sensitive about Piper," Fox explained, still wearing that shit-eating grin. "He doesn't know what to do with his confusing man feelings."

Brendan ignored his friend in favor of typing Piper's name

into the search bar, sighing when a whole list of options came up. "Does the blue check mark mean it's her?"

"Ooh." Sanders perked up. "She's got a check mark?"

"Is that good or bad?"

Deke polished off his Coke, letting out a belch that no one reacted to. It was merely a component of the fishing-boat soundtrack. "It means she's got a big following. Means she's internet famous, boss."

Making a low sound in his throat, Brendan punched the check mark . . . and Piper exploded across the screen of his phone. And Christ, he didn't know where the hell to look first. One little square had a picture of her kneeling in the surf at the beach, her back on display, wearing nothing but a thong bikini bottom. He could have stared at her gorgeous ass all day—and he'd definitely be coming back to it later when he was alone—but there was more. So much more. *Thousands* of pictures of Piper.

In another one, she had on a red dress, with lips to match, a martini in her hand, her foot kicking up playfully. More beautiful than anyone had the right to be. He zeroed in on a recent one, from a few weeks ago, and found his mouth dropping open at the spectacle. When she'd told him that story about how she'd gotten arrested and sent to Westport, he'd assumed she'd embellished a little.

Nope.

There she was, among the rowdy crowd, wreathed in smoke and fireworks, arms thrown up. Happy and alive. And was that the number of people who'd clicked the heart?

Over *three million*?

Brendan dragged a hand down his face.

Piper Bellinger was from a different, flashier planet.

She's out of your league.

Way out.

Remembering how he'd fed her fish and chips last night when she was obviously used to caviar and champagne, he was embarrassed. If he could go back in time and not bring her those stupid takeout menus, he would do it in a heartbeat. God, she must have been laughing at him.

"Well?" Fox prompted.

Brendan cleared his throat hard. "What does 'follow' mean?"

"Don't," Deke rushed to say. "Don't press it."

His thumb was already on the way back up. "Too late."

All three of his crew members surged to their feet. "No. Brendan, don't tell me you just tapped the blue button," Sanders groaned, hands on his mop of red hair. "She's going to see you followed her. She's going to know you internet stalked her."

"Can't I just unfollow now?" Brendan started to tap again.

Fox lunged forward. "No! No, that's even worse. If she already noticed you followed her, she's just going to think you're playing games."

"Jesus. I'm deleting the whole thing," Brendan said, throwing the offending device onto the dashboard, where it bashed up against the windshield. His crew stared back expectantly, waiting for him to put his money where his mouth was. "Later," he growled, firing up the motor. "Get to work."

As soon as the three men were out of sight, he picked the phone back up slowly. Weighing it in his hand for a moment, he opened the app again and scrolled through Piper's feed until one image stopped him. She was sitting beside Hannah on a diving board, both of them wrapped in the same towel, water droplets all over her face. This looked like the Piper he'd had dinner with last night. Was she *that* girl? Or the daring jet-setter?

The sheer number of photos of her glittering at parties, balls, even awards shows suggested she loved the spotlight, the wealth and luxury. Shit he knew nothing about. More than that, she clearly liked polished, manicured men, probably with bank accounts that matched her own. And that meant his interest in her wasn't only annoying, it was laughable. He was a set-in-his-ways fisherman. She was a rich, adventurous socialite. He couldn't even order something new at a restaurant, and she dined with celebrities. *Dated* them.

He'd just have to spend the next few months keeping his admiration of her to himself, lest he make himself look like a fucking fool.

With one last glance at the picture of her smiling on the diving board, he determinedly shoved his phone into the front pocket of his jeans and focused on what he knew.

Fishing.

Chapter Twelve

Obviously they visited the winery first.

Brendan was right about Piper loving the selfie spot—damn him—a jewel-toned wall painted to look like stained glass, vines crawling up the sides and wrapping around a neon VINO sign. Essentially an altar at which to worship the social media gods.

Hannah was not a drinker. Thanks to four glasses of wine, many attempts were made to get a non-blurry picture of Piper before an adequate one was selected.

Piper applied a filter before swiping over to Instagram. Automatically, she tapped her notifications. "Oh, look at that." Her pulse stuttered. "Brendan followed me." She tapped his profile and choked. "Oh. I'm the *only* one he's following. He just joined."

Hannah squished her cheeks together. "Oh boy. Rookie move."

"Yeah . . ." But it was a really, really endearing move, too.

How did she feel about Brendan looking at her plethora of side boob and booty? Even her most modest pictures were kind of provocative. What if her lack of modesty turned him off? Did he really create a profile *just* to follow her?

Maybe Hannah had a point about social media having too much ownership over her thoughts and enjoyment. Now she was going to spend the next three days wondering which pictures Brendan looked at and what he thought about them. Would he laugh at her captions? If this Instagram feed was his glimpse into Piper Bellinger's life, would it override the real-life impression she'd given him?

"You should have seen this little record shop, Pipes," Hannah said around a sip of wine. Leave it to her sister to wax poetic about a record store after too much to drink, instead of an ex-boyfriend or a crush. As far back as she could remember, Hannah had been hunkered down in headphones, her face buried in song lyrics. When she turned sixteen, Piper brought Hannah to her first concert—Mumford & Sons—and the poor girl had almost passed out from stimuli. Her soul was made of musical notes. "They had a poster for a 1993 Alice in Chains concert. Just tacked to the wall! Because they haven't had a chance to take it down!"

Piper smiled at her sister's enthusiasm. "Why didn't you buy anything?"

"I wanted to. There was a really nice *Purple Rain* LP, but they had it way underpriced. It would have felt like stealing."

"You're a good apple, kid." Piper had the niggling urge to scroll her Instagram feed and see everything through Brendan's eyes, but she determinedly ignored it. "So. What's Fox like?"

Hannah set down her glass. "Uh-uh. Don't ask me like that."

"What? He's cute."

"He's not my type."

"Not depressed and bitter enough?"

Her sister snorted. "His phone dinged like a hundred times in twenty minutes. That's either one passionate girl or several admirers, and my money is on the latter."

"Yeah," Piper admitted. "He did have that playboy look about him."

Hannah swung her feet. "Besides, I think he was just doing the wingman thing. He wasted no time extolling Brendan's virtues."

"Oh?" Piper took a too-casual gulp of wine. "What did Fox have to say about him? Just out of curiosity."

Her sister narrowed her eyes. "Tell me you're not interested in him."

"Whoa. I'm not. His wedding ring is like, welded onto his finger."

"And he's mean to you." Hannah shifted her weight on her stool, looking as if she was working up to saying something. "You've been tread on by some mean guys lately, all right? There was Adrian. The one before him who produced that sci-fi HBO pilot, whose name I can't remember. I just want to make sure you're not falling into a bad pattern."

Piper reared back a little. "A pattern where I pick men who'll make me feel shitty?"

"Well . . . yeah."

She replayed her last three relationships. Which didn't take that long, since collectively they'd lasted six weeks. "Shit. You might be onto something."

"I am?" Hannah's eyebrows shot up. "I mean . . . I know."

"Okay, I'll be more aware of it," Piper said, rubbing at the dull ache in the center of her chest. If her sister was right, why was she picking bad apples on purpose? Did the idea of a *good* relationship scare her? Because she didn't think she could pull one off? It was not only possible, but probable. Still, putting Brendan in the "bad apple" category didn't quite sit right. "None of those other guys were the type to apologize. They definitely weren't the kind of guys who'd pine for their dead wife. I think maybe I'm just curious about Brendan more than anything else. We don't grow them like him in LA."

"That is true."

"We had an actual conversation without sexual overtones. Neither one of us checked our phones even *once*. It was fucking weird. I'm probably just . . . fascinated."

"Well, be careful." Tongue tucked in the corner of her mouth, Hannah started folding a bar napkin into an airplane. "Or have some fun with Fox instead. Bet it would be way less complicated."

Piper couldn't even remember the guy's face. Only that she'd classified it as attractive.

Now, *Brendan's* face. She could recall crow's-feet fanning out at the corners of his eyes. The silver flecks dotting the green of his irises. His gigantic, weathered hands and the breadth of his shoulders.

She shook herself. They'd had a meal together yesterday.

Of course she recalled those things.

Can you even remember Adrian's voice?

"I think maybe I'll just stick to myself on this trip," Piper murmured.

Two hours later, they weaved down the sidewalk on the way

home. It was well past time to put her little sister to bed. At four o'clock in the afternoon, but who was keeping track?

Crossing the street toward home, Piper's step slowed. It appeared they had a visitor. A little old man with a toolbox and a smile like sunshine.

"Ma'am."

"Um, hi." Piper nudged Hannah into alertness, nodding at the man waiting outside No Name. Come to think of it, returning home to find a local at their door was beginning to be a habit. "Hi. Can I help you?"

"Actually, I'm here to help you." With his free hand, he plucked a slip of paper from the pocket of his shirt. "I own the hardware store down on West Pacific. My sons have the run of the place now, but they have little ones, so they don't make it in until later in the morning. When I opened up today, there was a note taped to my door."

He held it out to Piper. How could this possibly pertain to her? With a mental shrug, she took the note and scanned the four blunt lines with a burgeoning clog in her throat.

NO NAME BAR. UPSTAIRS APARTMENT. PIPER BELLINGER.
NEEDS PADDING INSTALLED ON THE BASE OF THE TOP BUNK.
SHE KEEPS HITTING HER HEAD.
CAPTAIN TAGGART

"Oh my," she breathed, fanning herself with the note. *Am I levitating?*

She'd just decided to be friends-only with the sea captain. *This* definitely wasn't going to help divert her rather irritating attraction to him.

"He left some cash to cover it," the man said, reaching out to pat her arm. "You're going to have to help me up the stairs once we're inside, I'm afraid. My legs decided they'd had enough living when I turned seventy, but the rest of me is still here."

"Sure. Of course. Let me take the tools." Grateful for something to distract her from Brendan's gesture, Piper claimed the dusty box. "Um. Hannah?"

"What?" Owlish eyes blinked back. "Oh."

Yawning, Hannah transferred her drunken weight onto the side of the building so Piper would be free to unlock the door. They all went inside, traveling in a comically slow-moving pack toward the stairs. Piper hooked her right arm through the old man's left, and they followed Hannah's uneven gait up toward the apartment. "I'm Piper, by the way. The girl from the note."

"I probably should have checked. My wife would have had some questions if I'd let some stranger squire me up to her apartment." She laughed, helping him up the fifth stair and the sixth, their pace slow and steady. "I'm Abe. I saw you walking yesterday in the harbor. I'm usually sitting outside the maritime museum reading my newspaper."

"*Yes.* That's how I recognize you."

He seemed pleased that she remembered. "I used to read the paper outside every day, but it's getting harder to climb the stairs to the porch. I'm only able to get up them on Wednesdays and Thursdays now. Those are my daughter's days off from the supermarket. She walks me over and helps me climb them, so I can sit in the shade. The other days, I sit on the lawn and pray the sun isn't too bright."

Keeping hold of Abe, Piper unlocked the apartment door.

Once they were inside and she'd shoved a bottle of water into Hannah's hands, Piper gestured to the bunk. "This is the one. You might be able to see the outline of my head on those boards by now."

Abe nodded and crouched down *very* slowly to access his toolbox. "Now that we're in the light, I can see that bruise you're sporting, too. Good thing we're getting this fixed."

While Abe got to work nailing memory foam to the top bunk with a nail gun, Piper tried to avoid Hannah's teasing pokes in her side. "Brendan no like Piper boo-boo. Brendan fix."

"Oh, shut up," she whispered, for her sister's ears alone. "This is just what people do in small towns like this. Maybe he's trying to rub LA's awfulness in my face."

"Nope. First the lock. Now this." Wow. She'd really slurred that *s*. "He's a real champ."

"I thought you didn't even like him. What happened to 'Leave my sister alone, you bully'?"

"At the time, I meant it," Hannah grumbled.

"Look, I'm just biding time until I can get back to my natural habitat. No distractions need apply."

"But—"

"You wouldn't be encouraging me to make time with a crab fisherman, would you?" She gave Hannah a once-over, followed by a sniff. "I'm telling Mom."

Hannah rolled her eyes and opened her mouth to deliver a rejoinder, but Abe interrupted with a jolly "All finished!"

God, how loud had they been at the end of that conversation?

Abe must have interpreted her worried expression, because he laughed. "I hope you don't mind me saying, it was nice listening to some bickering between sisters. Ours have grown up, gotten hitched, and moved out, you know. I spend a lot of time with my sons at the shop, but they have the nerve to get along."

Piper stooped down to help Abe put everything back in his toolbox. "So . . . um." She lowered her voice several octaves. "Do you know Captain Taggart well?"

Her sister snorted.

"Everyone knows the captain, but he does like to keep to himself. Doesn't do a lot of jawing, just comes into the shop and buys what he needs. In and out." Abe slapped his knee and stood. "He's downright focused."

"He is," Piper agreed, thinking a little too long and hard about those green-and-silver eyes. How they tried so hard to stay above her neck. When Abe cleared his throat, she realized she'd been staring into space. "Sorry. Let me help you down the stairs."

"I'll be on my way," Abe said when they'd reached the first level, a smile wreathing his mouth. "Say, have you gone to see Opal yet?"

Opal. Opal.

Piper rooted around her memory bank for that name. Hadn't Mick Forrester mentioned an Opal and written down the woman's address? Why did everyone think she would visit this person? Obviously, she needed to get some answers. "Um, no. Not just yet."

He seemed a little disappointed, but hid it quickly. "Right. Well, it was nice to meet you, Piper. Don't forget to give me a wave when you see me outside the museum."

"I won't." She handed him the toolbox carefully, making sure he could take the weight. While watching him head for the door, his feet shuffling, the stiffness in his legs obvious, an idea occurred. "Hey, Abe. I've got a pretty flexible schedule here, and the museum is only a quick walk. So . . . like, I don't know, if you wanted to sit outside and read your paper more than twice a week, I could walk over and help you climb the porch."

Why was she nervous this little old man was going to turn her down?

Is this what a man felt when he asked for her number?

Her nerves settled when Abe turned to her with a hopeful expression. "You would do that?"

"Sure," she said, surprised by how nice it felt to be useful. "Friday morning? I could meet you outside the hardware store after my run."

He winked. "It's a date."

Hannah had sworn off booze, so they avoided any more trips to the winery. Instead, they cleaned. Even put up some green-and-white striped curtains in the apartment. On Brendan's suggestion, they visited the lighthouse and took a day trip to the beach, although the abundance of rocks and the need for a sweatshirt by three P.M. made it nothing like the coastline in California. Still, Piper found herself relaxing, enjoying herself, and the rest of the week went by faster than expected.

She went out on her run Friday morning, finishing up outside the hardware store where Abe waited, a rolled-up newspaper tucked under his arm. He peppered her with questions about life in Los Angeles on the walk over to the maritime museum—he was yet another man who'd rarely ventured outside of Westport—and she left him in the Adirondack chair with a promise to meet him again tomorrow morning.

Piper walked down to the end of one of the docks in the harbor and dangled her feet over the side, looking out at the wide mouth of the Pacific.

What was Brendan doing at that very moment?

She'd kind of hoped distance and time would rid her of the adamant tingle she felt every time she thought of him. But three days had passed, and his image still popped into her mind with annoying regularity. This morning, she'd woken up with a start, jerked into an upright position, and the memory foam had blocked her forehead from ramming into the upper bunk. And she'd drifted back down to her pillow with an enamored sigh.

Was he thinking about her?

"Ugh, Piper." She surged to her feet at the end of the dock. "Get your life together." She needed another distraction. Another way to absorb some time, so her thoughts wouldn't keep drifting back to Brendan.

Maybe now was a good time to solve the mystery of this Opal character.

Piper had taken a picture of the address Mick gave her outside No Name, and she scrolled to it now, tapping it with her thumb. Distraction achieved. She'd told Mick she'd visit the woman, and with a whole day in front of her, there was no time like the present.

She punched the address into her map app, snorting to herself when she arrived after a mere two minutes of walking. Opal lived in an apartment building overlooking Grays Harbor, and it was kind of weird, buzzing someone's apartment without calling ahead of time, but the vestibule door unlocked immediately. With a shrug, Piper took the elevator to the fifth floor and knocked on the door of apartment 5F.

The door swung open and a woman Piper estimated to be in her late sixties leapt back, a hand flying to her throat. "Oh God, I thought you were my hairdresser, Barbara."

"Oh! Sorry!" Piper's cheeks burned. "I wondered why you buzzed me up so fast. You are Opal, right?"

"Yes. And I'm not buying anything."

"No, I'm not selling anything. I'm Piper. Bellinger." She put out her hand for a shake. "Mick told me I should come see you. I'm . . . Henry Cross's daughter?"

A different kind of tension gripped Opal's shoulders. "Oh my Lord," she breathed.

Something charged the air, causing the hair on the back of Piper's neck to stand up. "Did you . . . know me when I was a baby, or . . . ?"

"Yes. Yes. I did." Opal pressed a hand to her mouth, dropped it. "I'm Opal Cross. I'm your grandmother."

I'm your grandmother.

Those words sounded like they were meant for someone else.

People who got ugly knitted sweaters on Christmas morning or fell asleep in the back of a station wagon after a road trip to Bakersfield. Her mother's parents were living in Utah and communicated through sporadic phone calls, but Henry's . . . well, she'd stopped wondering about any extended family on her biological father's side so long ago, the possibility had faded into nothing.

But the woman hadn't. She was standing right there in front of Piper, looking as if she'd seen a ghost.

"I'm sorry," Piper whispered finally, after an extended silence. "Mick told me to come here. He assumed I knew who you were. But I . . . I'm so sorry to say I didn't."

Opal gathered herself and nodded. "That isn't too surprising. Your mother and I didn't end on the best terms, I'm afraid." She ran her eyes over Piper once more, shaking her head slightly and seeming at a loss for words. "Please come in. I . . . Barbara should be here for coffee soon, so I've got the table set up."

"Thank you." Piper walked into the apartment in a daze, her fingers twisting in the hem of her running shirt. She was meeting her long-lost grandmother in sweaty running clothes. Classic.

"Well, I barely know where to start," Opal said, joining Piper in the small room just off the kitchen. "Sit down, please. Coffee?"

It was kind of disconcerting the way this woman looked at her as if she'd returned from the dead. It felt a little like she had. As if she'd walked into a play that was already in progress, and everyone knew the plot except her. "No, thank you." Piper gestured to the sliding glass door leading to a small balcony. "B-beautiful view."

"It is, isn't it?" Opal settled into her chair, picking up a half-finished mug of coffee. Setting it back down. "Originally, I wanted an apartment facing the harbor so I could feel close to Henry. But all these years later, it just seems like a sad reminder."

She winced. "I'm sorry. I don't mean to be so casual about it all. It helps me to be blunt."

"It's fine. You can be blunt," Piper assured her, even though she felt a little jarred. Not only by the sudden appearance of a grandmother, but by the way she spoke of Henry like he'd only passed yesterday, instead of twenty-four years ago. "I don't remember a lot about my father. Just small things. And I haven't been told much."

"Yes," Opal said, leaning back in her chair with a tightened jaw. "Your mother was determined to leave it all behind. Some of us find that harder to do." A beat passed. "I'd been a single mother since Henry was a little boy. His father was . . . well, a casual relationship that neither of us had a mind to pursue. Your father was all I had, besides my friends." She blew out a breath, visibly gathering herself. "What are you doing back in Westport?"

"My sister and I . . ." Piper trailed off before she could get to the part about confetti cannons and police helicopters. Apparently the need to make a good impression on one's grandmother was strong, even when meeting her as a fully grown adult. "We're just taking a vacation." For some reason, she added, "And doing a little digging into our roots while we're here."

Opal warmed, even appearing relieved. "It makes me very happy to hear that."

Piper shifted in her chair. Did she want her father to become a more . . . substantial presence in her life? A serious part of Piper didn't *want* sentimental attachment to Westport. It scared her to have this whole new aspect of her world, her existence opened up. What was she supposed to do with it?

She'd felt so little at the brass statue—what if the same happened now? What if her detachment from the past extended to Opal and she disappointed the woman? She had clearly been through enough already without Piper adding to it.

Still, it wouldn't exactly hurt to find out a *little* more about Henry Cross, this man who'd fathered her and Hannah. This man people spoke of with a hushed reverence. This man who'd been honored with a memorial up on the harbor. Would it? Just this morning during her run, she'd seen a wreath of flowers laid at its feet. Her mother had been right. He *was* Westport. And although she'd felt less emotion than expected the first time she visited the brass statue, she was definitely curious about him. "Do you . . . have anything of Henry's? Or maybe some pictures?"

"I was hoping you'd ask." Opal popped up, moving pretty damn quickly for a woman her age, crossed to the living room, and retrieved a box from a shelf under the television. She took her seat again and removed the top, leafing through a few pieces of paper before pulling out an envelope marked *Henry*. She slid it across the table to Piper. "Go ahead."

Piper turned the envelope over in her hands, hesitating momentarily before lifting the flap. Out spilled an old fisherman's license with a grainy picture of Henry in the laminated corner, most of his face obscured by water damage. There was a picture of Maureen, twenty-five years younger. And a small snapshot of Piper and Hannah, tape still attached to the back.

"Those were in his bunk on the *Della Ray*," Opal explained.

Pressure crowded into Piper's throat. "Oh," she managed, running her finger over the curled edges of the picture of her and Hannah. Henry Cross hadn't been some phantom; he'd been a flesh-and-blood man with a heart, and he'd loved them with it. Maureen, Piper, Hannah. Opal. Had they been a part of his final thoughts? Was it crazy to feel like they'd deserted him? Yes, he'd chosen to perform this dangerous job, but he still deserved to be remembered by the people he loved. He'd had Opal, but what about his immediate family?

"He was a determined man. Loved to debate. Loved to laugh when it was all over." Opal sighed. "Your father loved you to pieces. Called you his little first mate."

That feeling Piper had been missing at the memorial . . . it rode in now on a slow tide, and she had to blink back the sudden hot pressure behind her eyes.

"I'm sorry if this was too much," Opal said, laying a hesitant hand on Piper's wrist. "I don't get a lot of visitors, and most of my friends . . . Well, it's a complicated thing . . ."

Piper looked up from the picture of her and Hannah. "What is?"

"Well." Opal stared down into her coffee mug. "People tend to avoid the grieving. Grief, in general. And there's no one with more grief than a parent who has lost a child. At some point, I guess I decided to spare everyone my misery and started staying home. That's why I have my hair appointments here." She laughed. "Not that anyone gets to see the results."

"But . . . you're so lovely," Piper said, clearing her throat of the emotion wrought by the pictures. "There's no way people avoid you, Opal. You have to get out there. Go barhopping. Give the men in Westport hell."

Her grandmother's eyes sparkled with amusement. "I bet that's more your department."

Piper smiled. "You would be right."

Opal twisted her mug in a circle, seeming unsure. "I don't know. I've gotten used to being alone. This is the most I've talked to anyone besides Barbara in years. Maybe I've forgotten how to be social." She exhaled. "I'll think about it, though. I really will."

Offering a relationship to this woman wasn't a small thing. This was her grandmother. It wasn't just a passing acquaintance. It could be a lifelong commitment. A relationship with actual gravity. "Good. And when you're ready . . . I'm your wingwoman."

Opal swallowed hard and ducked her head. "It's a deal."

They sat in companionable silence for a moment, until Opal checked her watch and sighed. "I love Barbara to death, but the woman is flakier than a bowl of cereal."

Piper pursed her lips, studied the woman's close-cropped gray hair. "What were you planning on having her do?"

"Just a trim, like always."

"Or . . ." Piper stood, moving behind Opal. "May I?"

"Please!"

Piper slipped her fingers into Opal's hair and tested the texture. "You don't know this, Opal, but you're in the presence of a cosmetic genius." Her lips curved up. "Have you ever thought about rocking a faux hawk?"

Twenty minutes later, Piper had shaped Opal's hair into a slick, subtle hill down the center of her head, using the lack of a recent haircut to their advantage by twisting and spiking the gray strands. Then they'd broken out a Mary Kay makeup kit Opal had caved and purchased from a door-to-door saleslady—leading to her current suspicion of solicitors—and transformed her into a stunner.

Piper took a lot of pleasure in handing Opal the mirror. "So?"

Opal gasped. "Is that me?"

Piper scoffed. "Hell yes, it's you."

"Well." Her grandmother turned her head left and right. "Well, well, well."

"Considering that night out a little more seriously now, aren't we?"

"You bet I am." She looked at herself in the mirror again, then back to Piper. "Thank you for this." Opal took a long breath. "Will you . . . come back and see me again?"

"Of course. And I'll bring Hannah next time."

"Oh, I would just *love* that. She was so tiny last time I saw her."

Piper leaned down and kissed Opal on both cheeks, which she seemed to find inordinately funny, then left the small apartment, surprised to find herself feeling . . . light. Buoyant, even. She navigated the streets back to No Name without the use of her phone's map, recognizing landmarks as she went, no longer unfamiliar with the friendly smiles and circling seagulls.

The envelope holding Henry's possessions was tucked into her pocket, and that seemed to anchor her in this place. She stopped outside of No Name, taking a moment to look up at the faded building, and this time . . . she tried to really *see* it. To really think about the man who made his livelihood within its walls, once upon a time. To think about Maureen falling in love with that man, so much that she married and conceived two daughters with him.

She was one of those daughters. A product of that love. No matter what Piper felt for her past, it was real. And it wasn't something she could ignore or remain detached from. No matter how much it scared her.

Feeling thoughtful and a little restless, she went to find Hannah.

Piper and Hannah stared down at the phone, listening to their mother's voice through the speakerphone. "I reached out to Opal several times throughout the years," Maureen said. "She's as stubborn as your father was. She saw my leaving as a betrayal, and there was no fixing it. And . . . I was selfish. I just wanted to forget that whole life. The pain."

"You could have told me about her before I came," Piper intoned. "I was blindsided."

Maureen made a sound of distress. "I was right on the verge and . . ." Maureen sighed. "I guess I didn't want to see your faces when I told you I'd been holding on to something so important. I'm sorry."

Twenty minutes later, Piper paced the scuffed floor of No Name while Hannah sat cross-legged on a barrel eating French fries, a thousand-yard stare in her eyes. Her sister was still processing the news that they had a freaking grandmother, but she probably wouldn't reach full understanding until she could be alone with her records.

Reaching out to rub Hannah's shoulder comfortingly, Piper looked around and surveyed the space. Was she suffering an emotional upheaval from the shock of finding a long-lost family member . . . or was she starting to develop an interest in this place?

They'd been so young when Maureen moved them. It wasn't their fault they'd forgotten their father, but they couldn't very well ignore him now. Not with pieces of him everywhere. And this disheveled bar was the perfect representation of a forgotten legacy. Something that was once alive . . . and now corroded.

What if it could be brought back to life?

How would one even begin?

Piper caught her reflection in a section of broken glass peeking out from behind a piece of plywood. Her talent for finding the most flattering lighting could not be discounted, but there were only a couple of cobweb-covered bulbs, with no light fixtures. It was basically anyone over twenty-five's worst nightmare, because it highlighted every crevice in a person's face. The place had a certain speakeasy vibe that could really benefit from some soft, red lighting. Moody.

Hmm. She was no decorator. Maureen paid an interior designer to come in annually and refresh the house in Bel-Air, and that included their bedrooms. But Piper understood atmosphere. What inspired people to stay awhile.

Some men went to bars to watch sports. Or whatever. But what *packed* a bar full of men? Women. Appeal to the ladies, and men started coughing up cover charges just for a chance to shoot their shot.

Where would she even start with this place?

"Just for the sake of argument, let's say we wanted to pretty this place up. Considering we have limited funds, do you think we could make it worthwhile?"

Hannah appeared caught off guard. "Where is this coming from?"

"I don't know. When I was talking to Opal, I started thinking how unfair it is that Henry's own family never grieved him. Sure, it was mostly Mom's decision, but maybe this is a way to make amends. To . . . connect with him a little bit. To have a hand in the way he's remembered. Is that silly?"

"No." Hannah shook her head. "No, of course it's not. Just a lot to take in."

Piper tried a different tack. "At the very least, this could be a way to convince Daniel we're responsible and proactive citizens of the world. We could make over the bar, show him how dazzlingly capable we are, and get an early trip home to Los Angeles."

Hannah raised an eyebrow.

"That's not a bad idea. Not bad at all." With a blown-out breath, her younger sister hopped off the stool, wiping her hands on the seat of her jeans. "I mean, we'd need a DJ booth, obviously."

"Over there in the corner by the window?" Piper pointed. "I like it. People walking by would see MC Hannah spinning and trip over themselves to get inside."

The sisters had their backs to each other as they completed a revolution around the bar. "This place isn't big enough for a dance floor, but we could build a shelf along the wall for people to set their drinks. It could be standing room only."

"Ooh. That's totally an option for a new name. Standing Room Only."

"Love." Hannah pursed her lips. "We'd have to do a lot of cleaning."

They shared a groan.

"Do you think we could fix these chairs?" Piper asked, running her finger along the back of a lopsided seat. "Maybe polish the bar?"

Hannah snorted. "I mean, what the fuck else are we doing?"

"God, you're right. Can you believe it has only been *five days*?" Piper dug a knuckle into the corner of her eye. "What is the worst that can happen? We do a ton of work, spend all of our money, Daniel isn't impressed and forces us to finish out our sentence, which should really just be *my* sentence?"

"Don't split hairs. And the best that can happen is we go home early."

They traded a thoughtful yet noncommittal shrug.

In that moment, the final shard of sunset peeked in through the grimy window, illuminating the mirror behind the plywood. There was a white corner of something on the other side, and without thinking, Piper moved in that direction, stepping over empty bottles to scoot behind the bar and pinch the white protrusion between her fingers. She gave it a tug and out came a photograph. In it, two people she didn't recognize appeared to be singing in this very establishment, though a much cleaner version, their hair proclaiming them children of the eighties.

"Oh. A picture." Hannah craned her neck to get a better look at the area behind the plywood. "You think there's more?"

"We could pull this board down, but we're either going to end up with splinters or a herd of spiders is going to ride out on the backs of mice, holding pitchforks."

Hannah sighed. "After cleaning that upstairs toilet, I'm pretty desensitized to anything unpleasant. Let's do it."

Piper whimpered as she took hold of the plywood, Hannah's grip tightening alongside hers. "Okay. One, two, *three*!"

They threw the wood board on the ground and leapt back, waiting for the repercussions, but none came. Instead, they were left staring at a mirror covered in old pictures. They traded a frown and stepped closer at the same time, each of them peeling down a photograph and studying it. "This guy looks familiar . . ." Piper said quietly. "He's way younger in this shot, but I think he's the one who was in here Sunday night. He said he remembered Mom."

Hannah leaned over and looked. "Oh my gosh, that's totally him." Her laugh was disbelieving. "Damn, Gramps. He could get it back then."

Piper chuckled. "Recognize anyone in yours?"

"No." Hannah took down another. "Wait. Pipes."

She was busy scanning the faces looking back at her from the past, so she didn't immediately hear the hushed urgency in Hannah's tone. But when the silence stretched, she looked over to find Hannah's face pale, fingers shaking as she studied the photo. "What is it?" Piper asked, sidling up next to her sister. "Oh."

Her hand flew to her suddenly pumping heart.

Whereas the brass statue of Henry had been impersonal and the fishing license had been grainy, an unsmiling man making a standard pose, this photo had *life* in it. Henry was laughing, a white towel thrown over one shoulder, a mustache shadowing his upper lip. His eyes . . . they leapt right off the glossy photograph's surface, sparkling. So much like their own.

"That's our dad."

"Piper, he looks just like us."

"Yeah . . ." She was having trouble catching her breath. She took Hannah's hand, and they turned it over together. The handwriting was faded, but it was easy to make out the words, *Henry Cross.* And the year, *1991.*

Neither of them said anything for long moments.

And maybe Piper was just overwhelmed by the physical proof that their birth father had really existed, a picture discovered while standing in his bar, but she suddenly felt . . . as if fate had placed her in that very spot. Their life before Los Angeles had always been a fragmented, vague thing. But it felt real now. Something to explore. Something that maybe had even been missing, without her knowing enough to acknowledge it.

"We should pretty up the bar," Piper said. "We should do it. Not just so we can go home early, but . . . you know. Kind of a tribute."

"You read my mind, Pipes." Hannah laid her head on Piper's shoulder as they continued to stare down at the man who'd fathered them, his face smiling back from another time. "Let's do it."

Chapter Thirteen

Brendan watched through his binoculars as Westport formed, reassuring and familiar, on the horizon.

His love for the ocean always made returning home bittersweet. There was nowhere he was more at ease than the wheelhouse, the engine humming under his feet. A radio within reach so he could give orders. His certainty that those commands would always be carried out, no questions asked. The *Della Ray* was a second layer of skin, and he slipped into it as often as possible, anxious for the rise and fall of the water, the slap of waves on the hull, the smell of salt and fish and possibilities.

But this homecoming didn't have the same feel as it usually did. He wasn't calculating the hours until he could get back out on the water. Or trying to ignore the emotions that clung to the inside of his throat when he got his crew home safe. There were only nerves this time. Jumpy, anxious, sweaty nerves.

His mind hadn't been focused for the last three days. Oh, they'd filled the belly of the ship with fish, done their damn job, as always. But a girl from Los Angeles had been occupying way too much headspace for his comfort.

God only knew, tonight was *not* the night for exploring that headspace, either.

As soon as they moored the boat and loaded the catches to bring to market, he was expected at the annual memorial dinner for Desiree. Every year, like clockwork, Mick organized the get-together at Blow the Man Down, and Brendan never failed to work his fishing schedule around it. Hell, he usually helped organize. This time, though . . . he wondered how he'd make it through the night knowing he'd been thinking of Piper nonstop for three days.

Didn't matter how many times he lamented her glamorous internet presence. Didn't matter how many times he reminded himself they were from two different worlds and she didn't plan to be a part of his for long. Still, he thought of her. Worried about her well-being while he was on the water. Worried she wasn't eating the right items off the menus he'd left. Hoped the hardware store had gotten his note and she was no longer bumping her head.

He thought of her body.

Thought of it to the point of distraction.

How soft she'd be beneath him, how high maintenance she'd probably be in the sack and how he'd deliver. Again and again, until she wrecked his back with her fingernails.

A lot of the men on board started checking their phones for reception as soon as the harbor was in sight, and Brendan normally rolled his eyes at them. But he had his phone in hand now, kept swiping and entering his password, wanting a look at her fucking Instagram. He'd barely been aware of the damn app a few days ago; now he had his thumb hovering over the icon, ready to get his fill of her image. He'd never been so hard up for relief that he beat off while on the boat, but it had been necessary the first damn night. And the second.

Three bars popped into the upper left-hand corner of his screen, and he tapped, holding his breath. The first thing he saw was the white outline of a head. Pressed it.

Piper had followed him back?

He grunted and looked over his shoulder before smiling.

There was one new picture in her feed, and he enlarged it, the damn organ in his chest picking up speed. She'd taken his suggestion and gone to the winery, and Jesus, she looked beautiful.

Making grape decisions.

He was chuckling over that caption when a text message popped up from Mick.

Call me was all it said.

Brendan's smile dropped, and he pushed to his feet, pulse missing a few beats as the call to his father-in-law connected. Dammit, Piper had gotten herself in trouble again, hadn't she? She'd probably started another fire or broken her neck falling down the stairs while trying to escape a mouse. Or—

"Yeah, hey, Brendan."

"What's wrong?" he demanded. "What happened?"

"Whoa, there." Mick laughed, music playing in the background. "Nothing happened. I just wanted to remind you about tonight."

Guilt twisted like a corkscrew in his gut. Here was this man preparing for a party to memorialize seven years without his daughter, and Brendan was worried about Piper. Could think of nothing *but* her. That wasn't right. Wasn't he a better man than that?

Brendan looked down at the wedding band around his finger and swallowed. Seven years. He could barely remember Desiree's voice, her face, or her laugh anymore. He wasn't the type to make a vow and easily move on from it, however. When a promise came out of his mouth, it was kept to the letter. She'd been woven into the fabric of his life in Westport so thoroughly, it was almost like she'd never really died. Which might account for him getting stuck on the *till death* part of his promise.

Remnants of her surrounded him here. Her parents, her annual memorial, people who'd come to their wedding. Taking the ring off had struck him as disrespectful, but now . . . now it was starting to feel even more wrong to keep it on.

Tonight was not the night to make big decisions, though.

He had a duty to be at the memorial and be mentally present, so he would be.

"I'll be there," Brendan said. "Of course I will."

The first few years after Desiree passed, the memorial potlucks had been reenactments of her funeral. No one smiling, everyone speaking in hushed tones. Hard not to feel disrespectful being anything but grief-stricken when Mick and Della plastered pictures of their daughter everywhere, brought a cake with her name in bright blue frosting. But as the years went on, the mood had lightened somewhat. Not completely, but at least nobody was crying tonight.

The venue probably didn't do much to cultivate an easy atmosphere. The basement of Blow the Man Down hadn't seen renovations like the upstairs. It was a throwback to the days of wood paneling and low, frosted lighting, and it reminded Brendan of the hull of his ship, so much so that he could almost feel the swell and dip of the ocean beneath his feet.

A collapsible table and chairs had been set up against the far wall, laden with covered dishes and a candlelit shrine to Desiree, right there next to the pasta salad. High tops and stools filled out the rest of the space, along with a small bar used only for parties, which was where Brendan stood with his relief skipper, trying to avoid small talk.

Brendan felt Fox studying him from the corner of his eye and ignored him, instead signaling the bartender for another beer. It was no secret how Fox viewed the yearly event. "I know what you're going to say." Brendan sighed. "I don't need to hear it again."

"Too bad. You're going to hear it." Apparently Fox had taken enough orders over the last three days and was good and finished. "This isn't fair to you. Dragging you back through this . . . loss every goddamn year. You deserve to move on."

"Nobody is dragging anyone."

"Sure." Fox twisted his bottle of beer in a circle on the bar. "She wouldn't want this for you. She wouldn't want to be shackling you like this."

"Drop it, Fox." He massaged the bridge of his nose. "It's just one night."

"It's not just one night." He kept his voice low, his gaze averted, so no one would pick up on their argument. "See, I know you. I know how you think. It's a yearly nudge to stay the course. Stay steady. To do what you think is honorable. When the hell is it enough?"

Goddammit, there was a part of him that agreed with Fox. As long as this memorial had remained on the calendar, Brendan kept thinking, *I owe her one more year. I owe her one more.* Until that refrain had turned into *I owe it one more year.* Or *I owe Mick one more.* For everything his father-in-law had done for Brendan. Making him captain of the *Della Ray.* Would that faith and trust go away if Brendan moved on?

Whatever the reason, at some point the grieving had stopped being about his actual marriage, but he had no idea when. Life was a series of days on land, followed by days at sea, then repeat. There wasn't time to think about himself or how he "felt." And he wasn't some selfish, fickle bastard.

"Look," Fox tried again, after a long pull of his beer. "You know I love Mick, but as far as he's concerned, you're still married to his daughter and that's a lot of pressure on y—"

"Hey, everyone!"

Brendan's drink paused halfway to his mouth. That was Piper's voice.

Piper was here?

He gripped his pint carefully and looked over his shoulder at the door. There she was. In sequins, obviously. Loud pink ones. And he couldn't deny that the first emotion to hit him was pleasure. To see her. Then relief that she hadn't gone back to LA already. Eagerness to talk to her, be near her.

Right on the heels of that reaction, though, the blood drained from his face.

No. This wasn't right. She shouldn't be there.

On one arm, she had that ridiculous lipstick-shaped purse. And cradled in her other arm was a tray of shots she'd obviously brought from the bar upstairs. She clicked through a sea of dumbfounded and spellbound guests, offering them what looked like tequila.

"Why the long faces?" She flipped her hair and laughed, taking a shot of her own. Jesus. This was all happening in slow motion. "Turn the music up! Let's get this party started, right?"

"Oh fuck," Fox muttered.

Brendan saw the exact moment Piper realized she'd just crashed a memorial for a dead woman. Her runway strut slowed, those huge blue eyes widening at the makeshift shrine next to the pasta salad, the giant poster-board picture of Desiree's senior photo, her name in script at the bottom. *Desiree Taggart.* Her mouth opened on a choked sound, and she fumbled the tray of shots, recovering just in time to keep them from crashing onto the floor. "Oh," she breathed. "I—I didn't . . . I didn't know."

She dropped the shots onto the closest table like they offended her—and that was when her eyes locked on Brendan, and his stomach plummeted at the utter humiliation there. "Piper."

"Sorry. I'm . . . Wow." She backed toward the exit, her hip ramming into a chair and sending it several inches across the floor, making her wince. "I'm so sorry."

As quickly as she'd arrived, she was gone, like someone had muted all sound and color in the room. Before and after Piper. And Brendan didn't think, he just dropped his beer onto the bar with a slosh and went after her. When he started up the stairs, she'd already cleared the top, so he picked up his pace, weaving in and out of the Friday-night crowd, grateful for his height so he could look for pink sequins.

Why did he feel like he'd been socked in the stomach?

She didn't need to see that, he kept thinking. *She didn't need to see that.*

Out of the corner of his eye, he caught a flash of pink crossing the street. There was Piper, in what appeared to be ice-pick
heels, heading toward the harbor instead of back home. Someone called his name from the bar, but he ignored them, pushing outside and following in her wake. "Piper."

"Oh no. No no no." She reached the opposite sidewalk and
turned, waving her hands at him, palms out. "Please, you have
to go back. You cannot leave your wife's memorial to come after the idiot who ruined it."

Even if he wanted to, he couldn't go back. His body physically wouldn't allow it. Because as much as he hated her obvious embarrassment, he would rather be out there chasing her
in the street than in that basement. It was no contest. And yeah,
he couldn't deny anymore that his priorities were shifting. As a
creature of habit, that scared him, but he refused to simply let
her walk away. "You didn't ruin anything."

She scoffed and kept walking.

He followed. "You're not going to outrun me in those heels."

"Brendan, *please*. Let me cringe to death in peace."

"No."

Still facing away from him, she slowed to a stop, arms lifting
to hug her middle. "Pretty shortsighted of me to leave those
shots behind. I could use about six of them right now."

He heard her sniffle, and bolts tightened in his chest. Crying
women didn't necessarily scare him. That would make him
kind of a pansy ass, wouldn't it? But he'd encountered very few
of them in his lifetime, so he took a moment to consider the
best course of action. She was hugging herself. So maybe . . .
maybe one from him, too, wouldn't be a bad move?

Brendan came up behind Piper and cupped her smooth

shoulders with his hands, making sure she wasn't going to run if he touched her. Lord, they were so soft. What if he scratched her with his calluses? Her head turned slightly to look at his resting right hand, and he was pretty sure neither one of them breathed as he tugged her back against his chest, circling his arms around her slight frame. When she didn't tell him to fuck off, he took one more chance and propped his chin on top of her head.

A sound puffed out of her. "You really don't hate me?"

"Don't be ridiculous."

"I really didn't know. I'm so sorry."

"That's enough apologizing."

"They all must hate me, even if you don't. They have to." He started to tell her *that* assumption was silly, too, but she spoke over him, sounding so forlorn he had to tighten his hold. "God, I *am* an airhead, aren't I?"

He didn't like anything about that question. Not the question itself. And not the way it was phrased, as if someone had used that bullshit term to describe her. Brendan turned her in his arms and promptly forgot the process of breathing. She was gorgeous as hell with her damp eyes and cheeks pink with lingering embarrassment, all of her bathed in moonlight. He had to call on every iota of willpower not to lower his mouth to hers, but it wasn't the right time. There was a ghost between them and a ring on his finger, and all of it needed resolving first.

"Come on, let's sit down," Brendan said gruffly, taking her elbow and guiding her to one of the stone benches overlooking the nighttime harbor. She sat and crossed her legs in one fluid move, her expression bordering on lost. Lowering himself down beside her, Brendan took up the rest of the space on the bench, but she didn't seem to mind their hips and outer thighs together. "You aren't an airhead. Who said that to you?"

"It doesn't matter. It's true."

"It is *not* true," he barked.

"Oh yes, it is. I have left an endless trail of proof. I'm like a super-hot snail." She smacked her hands over her eyes. "Did I really say 'Why the long faces' at a memorial dinner? Oh my *God*."

Unbelievably, Brendan felt a rumble of laughter building in his sternum. "You did say that. Right before you took a shot."

She punched him in the thigh. "Don't you dare laugh."

"Sorry." He forced his lips to stop twitching. "If it makes you feel better . . . that dinner needed a little levity. You did everyone a favor."

Brendan felt her studying his profile. "Tonight must have been hard for you."

"It was hard seven years ago. Six. Even five. Now it's just . . ." He searched for the right word. "It's respect. It's duty."

Piper was silent so long, he had to glance over, finding her with an expression of wonder. "Seven years?" She held up the appropriate number of fingers. "That many?"

He nodded.

She faced the harbor, letting out a rush of breath, but not before he saw her attention dip to his ring. "Wow. I thought it might have been a year. Maybe even less. She must have been really special."

Of course that was true. Brendan didn't know how to explain the convenience and . . . the practicality of his past marriage without it sounding disrespectful to a woman who could no longer speak for herself. Today, especially, he wouldn't do that. But he couldn't deny an urge to expose himself somewhat. It only seemed fair when she was sitting there, so vulnerable. He didn't want her to go it alone.

"I was away fishing when it happened. An aneurysm. She'd been out for a walk on the beach. Alone." He let out a slow breath. "She always went alone, even when I was home. I wasn't, uh . . . the best at being married. I didn't mold myself to fit new routines or different patterns—I'm sure you're shocked." She stayed quiet. "They say even if I'd been there, I couldn't have done anything, but I could have tried. I never tried. So this . . . year after year, this is me trying, I guess. After the fact."

Piper didn't respond right away. "I don't know a lot about marriage, but I think people mature and get better at it over time. You would have. You just didn't get a chance." She sighed into the night breeze. "I'm sorry that happened to you."

He nodded, hoping she would change the subject. Maybe Fox was right and he'd been serving a penance long enough, because dwelling on the past now just made him restless.

"My longest relationship was three weeks." She held up the right number of fingers. "This many. But in weeks."

Brendan hid a smile. Why did he kind of love knowing that there wasn't a single man in Los Angeles who could lock Piper down? And . . . what *would* it take? "Is he the one who called you an airhead?"

"You're hyperfocused on this." She pulled her shoulders back. "Yes, he was the one who said it. And I proved him right in the next breath by assuming he was ending things because I'd discussed the compatibility of our astrological signs with my therapist. I couldn't have sounded more like an LA bimbo if I tried."

"It pisses me off when you call yourself names."

She gasped. "Pissed off? That's a real switch for you."

The corner of Brendan's lips tugged. "I deserve that."

"No, you don't," she said, and sighed, falling silent for a few moments. "Since we got here, it has never been more obvious that I don't know what I'm doing. I'm really good at going to parties and taking pictures, and there's nothing wrong with that. But what if that's it? What if that's just *it*?" She looked at him, seeming to piece her thoughts together. "And you keep witnessing these huge fails of mine, but I can't hide behind a drink and a flirty smile here. It's just me."

He couldn't hide his confusion. "*Just* you?"

Once again, he was seeing flashes of insecurity beneath the seemingly perfect outer layer of Piper Bellinger, and they roused his protective instincts. He'd ridiculed her at the outset. Now he wanted to fight off anything that made her sad. Fucking hell, it was confusing.

Piper hadn't responded, quietly dabbing at her damp eyes—and he'd been okay with the crying for a while, but he should have been able to dry her tears by now. What was he doing wrong here? Remembering how the hug had at least gotten her to stop running away, he put his left arm around her shoulders and tucked her into his side. Maybe a distraction was the way to go. "What did you do while I was gone?"

"You mean, besides enjoying harbor tours from all the local fishermen?"

Despite her teasing tone, something hot poked him in the jugular. "Funny."

Her lips twitched, but over the course of a few seconds, she sobered. "A lot has happened since you left, actually. I met my grandmother, Opal."

Brendan started a little. "You didn't know her at all before this trip? No phone calls, or—"

"No." Her cheeks colored slightly. "I *never* would have known about her, either, if we hadn't come here. She's just been sitting in her apartment all this time, grieving my father. Knowing that kind of makes my life in LA feel like make-believe. Blissful ignorance." A beat passed. "She had some differences of opinion with my mother. We didn't get into it too deeply, but I'm guessing my mother wanted to put it all behind her, and Opal wanted to . . ."

"Live in the fallout."

"'Fallout' is a nice way of saying 'the real world,' but you're right." She looked down at her lap. "Me and Hannah went to see the memorial for Henry, and I didn't know what I was supposed to feel, but I didn't think it would be just *nothing*. It stayed that way right up until today when we found a whole collage of pictures in the bar. Behind some plywood. He was laughing in one of the photos, and that's when . . . there was finally recognition."

Brendan studied her. This girl he'd pegged as a silly flirt on day one. And he found himself pulling her closer, needing to offer comfort. Wanting her to lean on him for it. "What does the recognition feel like?"

"Scary," she said on an exhale. "But I have some guilt over ignoring this place, the past, even if it's not entirely my fault. It's causing me to lean into the scary, I guess. In my own way. So I gave Opal a faux hawk, and we're giving Henry's bar a makeover, starting tomorrow. If there are two things I know, it's hair and partying."

When had his thumb started tracing the line of her shoulder? He ordered himself to quit it. Even if it felt so fucking good.

"You're dealing with a whole lot of new information in your own way," he said gruffly. "Nothing wrong with that. You're adjusting. I wish I had more of that mentality."

Piper looked up at him, her eyes soft and a little grateful, turning his pulse up to a higher setting. They stared at each other three beats too long, before both of them diverted their gaze quickly. Sensing they were in need of a distraction from the building tension between them, Brendan coughed. "Hey, remember that time you were the only one I followed on Instagram?"

She burst out laughing, such a bright, beautiful thing, that he could only marvel. "What were you thinking?"

"I was just hitting buttons, honey."

More laughter. This time she actually pressed her forehead into his shoulder. "It makes me feel better about the world that someone out there isn't playing games." She drummed her fingers on her bare knee. "So which pictures did you look at?"

He blew out a long breath. "A lot of them."

She bit her bottom lip and ducked her head.

They sat in silence for a few moments. "Which girl are you? The girl in the pictures or the one sitting next to me?"

"Both, I think," she said after a pause. "I like dressing to the nines and being admired. And I like shopping and dancing and being pampered and complimented. Does that make me a bad person?"

He'd never met anyone like her. These luxuries weren't part

of his world. He'd never had to think about anything but fishing, working hard, and meeting quotas, but he wanted to get the answer right because it was important to her. "I've been on a lot of boats with a lot of men that do too much talking about women. And it seems to me that most people like being admired and complimented, they're just not as honest about it. That doesn't make you a bad person, it makes you truthful."

She blinked up at him. "Huh."

"Let me finish." He palmed her head and tucked it back against his shoulder. "I didn't think you'd survive one night in that apartment. Piper, *I* wouldn't even have stayed there, and I've slept in bunks with unwashed men for weeks on end. But you stuck it out. And you smiled at me when I was being a bastard. You're a good sister, too. I figure all of that has to balance out your carrying around that ugly purse."

Piper sat straight up and sputtered through a laugh, "Do you have any idea how much this ugly purse cost?"

"Probably less than I'd pay to have it burned," he drawled.

"But I love it."

He sighed, pushed a hand through his hair. "I guess I wouldn't burn it, then."

She was looking at him with soft eyes and a lush mouth, and if it were any other night, if the timing was better, he'd have kissed her and done his best to bring her home. To his bed. But he couldn't yet. So even though it pained him, he stood and helped Piper to her feet. "Come on, I'll make sure you get home all right."

"Yes. Oh my gosh, yes." She let him help her up. "You should get back. And Hannah will be wondering where I am."

"Why didn't she come tonight?"

"My sister is not a party person. All those genes landed on me. Plus, she's still a little scarred from her winery hangover."

"Ah."

Side by side, they started back, taking a different side street to avoid Blow the Man Down. When she rubbed her arms, he cursed the fact that he didn't take the time to grab his jacket when coming after her, because he would have given anything to wrap her in it at that very moment. Collect it tomorrow with her scent on the collar.

"You did it," she murmured, after they'd been walking for two blocks. "I'm still embarrassed about crashing the party. But I feel . . . better." She squinted an eye up at him. "Brendan, I think this means we're friends."

They arrived at her door and he waited for her to unlock it. "Piper, I don't just go putting my arms around girls."

She paused in the doorway. Looked back. "What does that mean?"

He gave in to just a touch of temptation, tucking a wind-tangled strand of hair behind her ear. *Soft.* "It means I'll be around."

Knowing if he stood there a second longer, he'd try to taste her mouth, Brendan backed away a couple of steps, then turned, the image of her stunned—and definitely wary—expression burned into his mind the whole way back to Blow the Man Down.

Later that night, Brendan stood in front of his dresser, twisting the gold band around his finger. Wearing it had always felt right and good. Honorable. Once something was a part of him, once he made promises, they stuck. He stuck. A fisherman's life was rooted in tradition and he'd always taken comfort in that. Protocols might change, but the rhythm of the ocean didn't. The songs remained the same, sunsets were reliable and eternal, the tides would always shift and pull.

He'd given no thought to where his life would go next. Or if it *could* go in a different direction. There was only routine, maintaining an even keel, working, moving, keeping the customs he'd been taught alive. Ironically, it had been those same qualities that made him a distracted husband. An absent one. He'd never learned to shift. To allow for new things. New possibilities.

Now, though. For the first time since he could remember, Brendan felt a pull to deviate from his habits. He'd sat on the harbor tonight with his arm around Piper, and it wasn't where he was *supposed* to be.

But he hadn't wanted to be anywhere else. Not serving penance for being a shit husband. Not paying respect to his in-laws, who still lived as if their daughter had died yesterday. Not even plotting courses or hauling pots onto his boat.

No, he'd wanted to be sitting there with the girl from Los Angeles.

With that truth admitted to himself, wearing the ring was no longer right.

It made him fraudulent, and he couldn't allow that. Not for another day.

The tide had changed, and he wouldn't make the same mistakes twice. He wouldn't stay so firmly rooted in his practices and routines that a good thing would come along and slip away.

As he slid off the gold band and tucked it into a safe place in his sock drawer, he said good-bye and apologized a final time. Then he turned off the light.

Chapter Fourteen

Deciding to make over the bar and actually *doing* it were two very different things.

The sisters quickly decided there was no way to salvage the floor in the bar. But thanks to an abundance of foot-sized holes in the hardwood, they could see the concrete beneath, and thus, their industrial-meets-nautical-chic vision was born.

Ripping up floorboards was easier said than done. It was filthy, sweaty, nasty work, especially because neither one of them could manage to pry open the windows, adding stagnant air into the mix. They were making progress, though, and by noon on Saturday, they'd managed to fill an entire industrial-sized garbage bag with No Name's former flooring.

Piper tied up the end of the bag with a flourish, trying desperately not to shed tears over the abysmal state of her manicure, and dragged it toward the curb. Or she tried to drag it, anyway. The damn thing wouldn't budge. "Hey, Hanns, help me get this thing outside."

Her sister dropped the crowbar she'd bought that morning

at the hardware store, shouldered up beside Piper, and took hold. "One, two, *three*."

Nothing.

Piper stepped back, swiping her wrist across her forehead with a grimace. "I didn't stop to think about the part where we actually had to move it."

"Me either, but whatever. We can just disperse it among a few bags that won't be so hard to carry."

A whimper bubbled out of Piper's lips. "How did this happen? How am I spending my Saturday dividing up garbage?"

"Reckless behavior. A night in jail . . ."

"Rude." Piper sniffed.

"You know I love you." Hannah peeled off her gloves. "Want to break for lunch?"

"*Yes.*" They took two steps and slumped onto side-by-side stools. As exhausting and difficult as this bar makeover was shaping up to be, with a little distance, the amount of work they'd done in just a few hours was kind of . . . satisfying. "I wonder if we could paint the floor. Like a really deep ocean blue. Do they make paint for floors?"

"Don't ask me. I'm just the DJ."

Now that the idea was in Piper's head, she was interested in getting the answers. "Maybe I'll go with you to the hardware store next time. Sniff around."

Hannah smiled but didn't look over. "Okay."

A minute of silence passed. "Did I tell you I crashed a memorial party for Brendan's wife last night? Walked in with a tray of shots like it was spring break in Miami."

Her sister turned her head slowly. "Are you shitting me?"

"Nope." She pulled an imaginary conductor's wire. "The Piper train rolls on."

To Hannah's credit, it took her a full fifteen seconds to start laughing. "Oh my God, I'm not laughing at . . . I mean, it's a sad thing, the memorial. But, oh, Piper. Just, oh my God."

"Yeah." She smacked some dust off her yoga pants. "Do you think my lipstick purse is ugly?"

"Uhhh . . ."

Hannah was saved from having to answer when the front door of No Name opened. In walked Brendan with a tray of coffees in his hand, a white, rolled-up bakery bag in the other. There was something different about him this morning, but Piper couldn't figure it out. Not right away. He was wearing his signature sweatshirt, beanie, and jeans trifecta as usual, looking worn in and earthy and in charge, carrying in with him the scent of the ocean and coffee and sugar. His silver-green eyes found Piper's and held long enough to cause a disturbing flutter in her belly, before he scanned the room and their progress.

"Hey," he said, in that raspy baritone.

"Hey back," Piper murmured.

Piper, I don't just go putting my arms around girls.

She'd lain awake half the night dissecting that statement. Pulling it apart and coming at it from different angles, all of which had led to roughly the same conclusion. Brendan didn't put his arms around girls, so it meant something that he'd put them around her. Probably just that he wanted to have sex with her, right? And she was . . . interested in that, it seemed, based on how her nipples had turned to painful little points the second he ducked into No Name with his big gladiator thighs and thick black beard. Oh yeah. She was interested, all right. But not in the usual way she was interested in men.

Because Brendan came with a whole roll of caution tape around him.

He wasn't a casual-hookup guy. So what did that make him? What else even *was* there? Apart from her stepfather, she'd come across very few serious-relationship types. Was he one of them? What did he want with *her*?

There was a good chance she was reading him wrong, too. This could very well just be a friendship, and since she'd never had a genuine friendship with a man, platonic intentions might be unrecognizable to her. This was a small town. People were kind. They tipped hats.

She'd probably been in LA too long, and it had turned her cynical. He'd just put his arms around her last night to be decent. *Relax, Piper.*

"Is that coffee for us?" Hannah asked hopefully.

"Yeah." He crossed the scant distance and set the tray down on the barrel in front of the sisters. "There's some sugar and whatnot in the bag." He tossed the white sack down, rubbed at the back of his neck. "Didn't know how you took it."

"Our hero," Piper said, opening the bag and giving a dreamy sigh at the donuts inside. But first, caffeine. She plucked out a Splenda and one of the non-dairy creamers, doctoring the coffee. When she glanced up at Brendan, he was following her actions closely, a line between his brows. Memorizing how she took her coffee? No way.

She swallowed hard.

"Thank you. This was really thoughtful."

"Yes, thank you," Hannah chimed in after taking a sip of hers, black, then riffling through the white bag for a donut. "It's not even made out of cauliflower. We really aren't in LA anymore, Pipes."

"Cauliflower? Jesus Christ." Brendan pulled his own coffee out of the tray—and that's when Piper realized what was actually different about him this morning.

He'd taken off his wedding ring.

After seven years.

Piper's gaze traveled to Brendan's. He knew she'd seen. And there was some silent communication happening between them, but she didn't understand the language. Had never spoken it or been around a man who could convey so much without saying a single word. She couldn't translate what passed between them, or maybe she just wasn't ready to decipher his meaning.

A drop of sweat slid down her spine, and she could suddenly hear her own shallow breaths. No one had ever looked her in the eye this long. It was like he could read her mind, knew everything about her, and liked it all. Wanted some of it for himself.

And then she knew, by the determined set of his jaw and his confident energy, that Brendan Taggart did not think of her as a friend.

"This donut is incredible," Hannah said, her words muffled by the dough in her mouth. "There's caramel in this glaze. Pipes, you have to try—" She cut herself off, her gaze bouncing back and forth between Piper and Brendan. "What's happening here?"

"N-nothing," Piper said in a high-pitched voice. "I don't know. Um. Brendan, do you know if it's, like, possible to paint concrete?"

Her flustered state seemed to amuse him. "It is."

"Oh good, good, good." Exasperated with her own awkwardness, she hopped off the stool. Then she knocked into another one in an attempt to give Brendan a wide berth. "We've decided to go with an industrial-meets-nautical theme. Kind of a chic warehouse vibe, but with like, fisherman-y stuff."

"Fisherman-y stuff," he repeated, sipping his coffee. "Like what?"

"Well, we're going with darker colors, blacks and steels and grays and reds, but we're going to distress everything a little. Most of the boats in the harbor have those muted, weathered tones, right? Then I was kind of thinking we could integrate new and old by hanging nets from the ceiling, but I could spray-paint them gold or black, so it's cohesive. I'm just rattling all of this off, though. It might be . . ." Her hands fluttered at her waist. "Like, I might have to rethink everything . . ."

Brendan's expression had gone from amused to thoughtful. Or maybe . . . disapproving? She couldn't tell. It seemed like weeks had passed since the first night she'd walked through the doors and he'd made it clear No Name belonged to the locals. So he probably hated her ideas and the fact that she wanted to change anything in the first place.

"Right," he said, rolling the word around his mouth. "Well, if you want nautical, you're not going to overpay for anything in the tourist shops up at the harbor. There's a fishing supply store in Aberdeen where they throw in netting for free with most purchases and everything doesn't have a goddamn starfish glued onto it." His lips twisted around a sip of coffee. "I can't help you with gold spray paint."

"Oh." Piper let out a breath she wasn't aware she'd been holding. "Thanks. We're on a budget, especially after our little trip to the winery, so that's helpful."

He grunted and walked past her, stepping over the gap in the floorboards. It seemed like he was heading toward the back staircase, so Piper frowned when he continued past that, stopping in front of yet another piece of plywood that had been nailed over holes in the wall. Only, when he ripped off the wood with one hand and tossed it away, there was a door behind it instead.

Piper's mouth fell open. "Where does that lead?"

Brendan set down his coffee on the closest surface, then tried the rusted knob. It turned, but the door didn't open. Not until he put his big shoulder against it and shoved . . .

And Piper saw the sky.

A fallen tree and, of course, more spiderwebs, but there was sky. "An outdoor space?"

Hannah hopped up, mouth agape. "No way. Like a patio?"

Brendan nodded. "Boarded it up during a storm a few years ago. Wasn't getting much use anyway, with all the rain." He braced a hand on the doorjamb. "You want this cleared out."

The sisters nodded along. "Yeah. How do we do that?"

He didn't answer. "Once the tree is gone, you'll see the patio is a decent size. Dark gray pavers, so I guess that's in keeping with . . . What is it, your theme? There's a stone hearth back in the corner." He jerked his chin. "You want to put up a pergola, get a waterproof cover. Even in damp weather, you'll be able to use it with a fire going."

What he was describing sounded cozy and rustic and *way* outside their capabilities.

Piper laughed under her breath. "I mean, that sounds amazing, but . . ."

"We're not leaving for crab season until next Saturday. I'll work on it." He turned and strode for the exit, pausing beside the impossible-to-lift trash bag. "You want this on the curb?"

"Yes, please," Piper responded.

With seemingly zero effort, he tossed it over his right shoulder and walked out, taking the smell of salt water and unapologetic maleness with him. Piper and Hannah stared at the door for several long minutes, the wind coming in from the patio cooling their sweaty necks. "I think that was it," Hannah finally said on a laugh. "I don't think he's coming back."

Brendan *did* come back . . . the next day, with Fox, Sanders, and a man named Deke in tow. The four of them hauled the tree out through the front of the bar, and with an indecipherable look in Piper's direction, Brendan promptly left again.

Bright and early on Monday morning, he was back. Just strolled in like not a moment had passed since his last dramatic exit, this time with a toolbox.

Piper and Hannah, who were in the process of prying sheetrock off the perfectly good brick wall, glanced through the front door to see a pickup truck loaded with lumber. One trip at a time, Brendan brought the wood through the bar to the back patio, along with a table saw, while Piper and Hannah observed him with their heads on a swivel, as if watching a tennis match.

"Wait, I think . . ." Hannah whispered. "I think he's building you that freaking pergola."

"You mean *us*?" Piper whispered back.

"No. I mean *you*."

"That's crazy. If he liked me, why wouldn't he just ask me out?"

They traded a mystified look.

Hannah sucked in a breath. "Do you think he's, like, courting you?"

Piper laughed. "*What? No.*" She had to press a hand to her abdomen to keep a weird, gooey sensation at bay. "Okay, but if he is, what if it's working?"

"Is it?"

"I don't know. No one's ever built me anything!" They hopped back as Brendan stomped through the bar again, long wooden boards balanced on his wide shoulder. When he set the lumber down, he grabbed the rear neck of his sweatshirt and stripped it off, bringing the T-shirt underneath along with it, and sweet mother of God, Piper only caught a hint of a deep groove over his hip and a slice of packed stomach muscles before the shirt fell back into place, but it was enough to make her clench where it counted. "Oh yeah," Piper said throatily. "It's working." She sighed. "Shit."

"Why 'shit'?" Hannah gave her a knowing smirk. "Because Mom made that ominous warning about fishermen?" She made a spooky woo-woo sound. "It's not like you'd let it get serious. You'd keep it casual."

Yes. She would.

But would Brendan?

Builds a Pergola Guy didn't seem like the casual type. And his lack of a wedding ring was almost more a presence than the actual ring had been. Every time their eyes met, a hot shiver roared down her spine, because there was a promise there, but also . . . patience. Maturity.

Had she ever dated a real man before? Or had they all been boys?

It was Wednesday afternoon during their lunch break. Brendan, Deke, Fox, and Sanders ate sandwiches from paper wrappers, while Hannah and Piper mostly listened to the crew pitch theories about their upcoming crabbing haul—and that's when it hit Piper.

She pulled out her phone just to be sure, blowing sawdust off the screen.

And decided the oversight couldn't stand for another moment.

"Brendan," she called, during a break in the crab conversation. "You still haven't posted your first picture on Instagram."

His sandwich paused halfway to his mouth. "That's not required, is it?"

Fox gave her an exaggerated nod behind the captain's back, urging her to lie. "It's totally required. They'll delete your account otherwise." She studied her phone, pretending to scroll. "I'm shocked they haven't already."

"Can't look at pictures if your account is gone, boss," Deke said, so nonchalantly Piper could only imagine how accustomed these guys were to pranking each other. "Just saying."

Brendan flicked a look at Piper. If she wasn't mistaken, being called out for stalking her Instagram account had turned the very tips of his ears a little red. "I can put up a picture of anything, right? Even this sandwich?"

How far could they take this without him calling bullshit? Already it was an unspoken game. Get the captain to post a picture on the internet by any means necessary. "Has to be your face the first time," Hannah chimed in, scrubbing at the hair beneath her baseball cap. "You know, facial recognition technology."

"Yup." Sanders pointed his sandwich at Hannah. "What she said."

"The light is perfect right now." Piper stood and crossed the floor of No Name toward Brendan, wiggling her phone in the air. "Come on, I can pose you."

"*Pose* me?" He tugged on his beanie. "Uh-uh."

"Just give in. We all do it, man," Sanders said. "You know those engagement photos I took last year? Two hours of posing. On a goddamn *horse*."

"See? You only have to pose with a *saw*horse." Piper put a hand on Brendan's melon-sized bicep and squeezed, loosing an unmistakable flutter in her belly. "It'll be fun."

"Maybe we don't have the same idea of fun," he said dubiously.

"No?" Aware she was playing with fire but unable to stop herself, Piper leaned down and murmured in his ear, "I can think of a few fun things we'd both enjoy."

Brendan swallowed. A vein ticced in his temple. "One picture."

"Fabulous."

Piper pulled Brendan to his feet, tugging the reluctant giant outside, his boots crunching through the construction debris. A rapid shuffling of barrels told her Hannah and the crew were following them to the patio, eager to catch this rare, sparkling moment in time.

"Everyone is going to remember where they were when Brendan took his first picture for the gram," Deke said with mock gravity.

"First and last," corrected the captain.

"Who knows, you might form a habit," Piper said, coming up beside Brendan where he stood behind the sawhorse. "Okay, so shirt on? Or off?"

Brendan looked at her like she was insane. "On."

Piper wrinkled her nose at him. "Fine, but can I just . . ." She pinched the sleeve of his sweaty red T-shirt between her fingers and tugged it up, revealing the deep cut of his triceps. "Ooh. That'll work."

He grunted, seeming annoyed at himself for being flattered.

But he *definitely* flexed that tricep a little.

Piper hid her smile and moved to stand a short distance away, phone at the ready in portrait mode. "Okay, left hand on the sawhorse, pick up the drill in your right."

"Big tools!" Hannah called. "Yay, symbolism."

"This is ridiculous." He looked around. "It's obvious I'm not drilling anything."

"Distract them with your smile," Hannah said, in between long sips of her fountain soda. "Show them those pearly whites."

"Who is *them*?" Brendan wanted to know. "Piper is the only one following me."

Everyone ignored that.

"Post some content and I'll consider it." Sanders sniffed.

"Smile like we're hauling in a hundred crabs per pot," Fox suggested.

"We *have* done that. Do you remember me smiling then?"

"That's a valid point," said Deke. "Maybe Cap's just got resting asshole face."

Finally, Piper took pity on Brendan and approached the sawhorse. "I forgot to tell you something. It's kind of a secret." She crooked her finger at the man, gratified when he leaned down as if compelled. His sweaty warmth coasted over her, and she went up on her toes, eager to get closer. Maybe even requiring the added proximity. "I've been ordering your suggested dishes off the takeout menus, and you were right. They're the best ones."

She caught his smile up close with the tap of the screen.

"Look at that," she whispered, turning the phone in his direction. "You're a natural."

The corner of his lips tugged, taking his beard along with it. "Are you going to tap the heart on it?"

"Mmm-hmm." Oh, she was openly flirting with the captain now. Did that mean the third wall was back up? Or was she in some undiscovered flirting territory that lay on the other side of the rubble? "I'd tap it twice if I could."

He made a sound in his throat, leaned in a little closer. "I know they don't require a picture to keep your account active. This was about making you smile, not me." His gaze fell to her mouth, taking its time finding her eyes again. "Well worth it." With that, he set down the drill and pinned his crew with a look. "Back to work."

All Piper could do was stare at the spot he'd just vacated.

Goose bumps. He'd given her goose bumps.

Throughout the course of the week, as Brendan constructed the pergola over the back patio, it was impossible for Piper not to feel a growing sense of . . . importance. There was a warmth in her middle working its way outward with every whirr of the saw, every swing of his hammer. She'd thought nothing could make her feel sexier than a pair of Louboutins, but this man building her something by hand not only turned her on, it made her feel coveted. Wanted. In a way that wasn't superficial, but durable.

So. That was terrifying.

But it wasn't just Brendan's work making her feel positive, it was her own persistence. Piper and Hannah came down the stairs every morning and got started, hauling debris, hammering up the sagging crown molding, sanding the window frames and giving them fresh coats of paint, and organizing the storage spaces behind the bar. A warm glow of pride settled in and made itself at home with the completion of each new project.

On Thursday, in the late afternoon, the sounds of construction ceased on the back patio, the hammer and saw falling silent. Hannah had gone to spend the afternoon with Opal, so it was only Piper and Brendan in No Name. She was sanding down some shelves behind the bar when his boots scuffed over the threshold, the skin of her neck heating under his regard.

"It's finished," Brendan said in that low timbre. "You want to come look?"

Piper's nerves jangled, but she set down her sandpaper and

stood. He watched her approach, his height and breadth filling the doorway, his gaze only dipping to the neckline of her tank top briefly. But it was enough for his pupils to expand, his jaw to tighten.

She was a dusty mess. Had been for the last six days. And it hadn't seemed to matter at all. In dirty jogging pants or sequins, she was still pergola worthy. Had he busted his hump simply because he liked *her* and not just how she looked? The possibility that he'd shown up to see her, help her, without anything in return, made her comfortable in her own skin—ironically, without any of her usual beautifying trappings.

At the last second, he moved so she could slide through the doorway, and it took all of her self-control not to run her hands up Muscle Mountain. Or lean in and take a hearty drag of real, actual male exertion. God, with every passing day, she was growing less and less enamored of the groomed and coiffed men of her acquaintance. She'd like to see *them* try to operate a table saw.

Piper stepped outside and looked up, startled pleasure leaving her mouth in the form of a halting laugh. "What? You . . . Brendan, you just *built* this?" Face tipped back, she turned in a slow circle. "This is beautiful. Amazing. This patio was a jungle on Sunday. Now look at it." She clutched her hands together between her breasts. "Thank you."

Brendan cleaned the dirt off his hands with a rag, but he watched her steadily from beneath the dark band of his beanie. "Glad you like it."

"No. I *love* it."

He grunted. "You ready?"

"Ready for what?"

"For me to ask you to dinner yet."

Her pulse tripped all over itself. Got up. Tripped again. "Did you think you needed to build a pergola to convince me?"

"No. I, uh . . ." He tossed down the rag, shoved his hands into his pockets. "I needed something to keep me busy while I worked up the nerve to ask."

Oh.

Oh *no*. That worrisome little flurry in her belly went wild, flying in a dozen directions and careening into important inside parts. She needed to do something about this before . . . what? She didn't know what *happened* with serious men. Men who courted her and didn't just go putting their arms around women all willy-nilly. "Wow. I—I don't know what to say. Except . . . I will absolutely have dinner with you, Brendan. I'd love to."

He averted his gaze, nodded firmly, a smile teasing one corner of his mouth. "All right."

"But . . ." She swallowed hard when those intense green eyes zipped back in her direction. "Well. I like you, Brendan. But I just want to be up front and say, you know . . . that I'm going back to LA. Part of the reason we're fixing up the bar is to impress Daniel, our stepfather. We're hoping the display of ingenuity will be a ticket home early." She smiled. "So we both know this dinner is casual. Friendly, even. Right? We both know that." She laughed nervously, tucking some hair into her ponytail. "I'm just stating the obvious."

His cheek ticced. "Sure."

Piper pursed her lips. "So . . . we're agreeing on that."

A beat passed as he considered her. "Look, we both know I like to put things into neat little boxes, but I . . . haven't been able to do that with you. Let's just see what happens."

Panic tickled her throat. "But . . ."

He just went along packing up his tools. "I'll pick you up tomorrow night. Seven."

Without waiting for a response, he turned and walked into the bar, toward the exit.

She took a moment to internally sputter, then trotted along after him. "But, Brendan—"

One second he was holding the toolbox, the next it was on the ground and he was turning. Piper's momentum brought her up against Brendan's body, *hard*, and his boat captain forearm wrapped around her lower back, lifting her just enough that her toes brushed the concrete. And then he bowed her backward on that steel arm, stamping his mouth down onto hers in an epic kiss. It was like a movie poster, with the male lead curling his big, hunky body over the swooning, feminine lady and taking his fill.

What?

What was she thinking? Her brain was clearly compromised—and it was no wonder. The mouth that found hers was tender and hungry, all at once. Worshipful, but restraining an appetite like she'd never encountered. As soon as their lips connected and held, her fingers curled into the neck of his T-shirt, and that arm at the small of her back levered her upright, flattening the fronts of their bodies, and oh God, he just devoured her. His lips pushed hers wide, his workingman's fingers plowed into her hair, and his tongue snuck in deep, invading and setting off flares in her erogenous zones.

And he *moaned*.

This huge, gritty badass of a man moaned like he'd never tasted anything so good in all his life and he needed to get more. He brought them up for a simultaneous gasp of air, then he went right back to work, his tongue stroking over hers relentlessly until she was using her grip on his collar to climb him, her mouth just as eager, just as needy.

Oh God, oh God, oh God.

They were going to have sex, right then and there. That was the only place a kiss like this could lead. With him moaning for an entirely different reason, those sturdy hips of his holding her thighs apart to take his thrusts. How had they been orbiting each other for over a week without this happening? With every slant of his hard mouth, she was losing her mind—

The door to No Name opened, letting in the distant sounds of the harbor.

"Oh! I'm sorry . . ." Hannah said sheepishly. "Um, I'll just . . ."

Brendan had broken the kiss, his breathing harsh, eyes glittering. He stared at her mouth for a few long moments while Piper's brain struggled to play catch-up, his hand eventually dropping away from her hair. *No,* she almost whined. *Come back.* "Tomorrow night," he rasped. "Seven."

He kept his eyes on Piper until the last possible second before disappearing out the door. At which point, she staggered behind the bar and uncapped a beer from the cooler. Thank God they'd had the foresight to fill it with ice. Piper drank deeply, trying to get her libido back in check, but it was no dice. The seam of her panties was damp, her nipples stiff and achy, her fingers itching to be twisted once again in Brendan's shirt.

"I'm going to need your help, Hanns," she said finally. "Like, a lot of it."

Her sister stared back, wide-eyed, never having seen Piper knocked sideways by a man. "Help with what?"

"Remembering that whatever happens with Brendan . . . it's temporary."

"Will do, sis." Hannah came around the bar, opened her own beer, and stood shoulder to shoulder with Piper. "Jesus. I've never seen you this worked up. Who knew your kink was outdoor living spaces?"

Piper's snort turned into a full-fledged laugh. "We have a date in approximately twenty-four hours. You know what that means?"

"You have to start getting ready now?"

"Yup."

Hannah laughed. "Go. I'll clean up here."

Piper kissed her sister's temple and jogged up the back stairs, going straight to her closet. She pressed the mouth of the beer bottle to her lips and perused her choices, wondering which dress said *I'm not the settling-down type.*

Because she wasn't.

Especially not in Westport. She just needed to remind Brendan of that.

With a firm nod, she chose the emerald-green Alexander Wang fit-and-flare velvet minidress. If she was just here to have fun, she'd have the *most* fun. And try to forget how involved her heart had been in that kiss.

Chapter Fifteen

$\mathcal{B}$rendan adjusted the silverware on his dining room table, trying to remember the last time he'd had reason to use more than one set. If Fox or some of the crew came over, they ate with their hands or plastic forks. Piper would be used to better, but that couldn't be helped. Instead of dipping his toe back into dating after a seven-year hiatus from all things female, he'd plunged right into the deep end with a woman who might be impossible to impress.

Sure, he was intimidated by the level of luxury Piper was used to, but he couldn't let making an effort scare him.

Trying was the least he could do, because . . . Piper Bellinger got to him.

He'd soaked up every second watching her work in No Name all week—and he'd come to find the high-maintenance-socialite aspect of her personality . . . well, adorable. She owned it. Wasn't apologetic about hating manual labor or her love of overpriced shoes and selfies. And fuck, every time she cringed about the dirt under her fingernails, he wanted to lay her on a silk pillow and do all the work for her, so she wouldn't have to. *He* wanted to do the spoiling. Badly.

It was obvious that she hated construction, yet she showed up every day with a brave smile and got it done. Furthermore, she made time in the afternoons to bring Hannah to see Opal, and he witnessed her growing comfort, day in and day out, with the fact that she had a grandparent. Noticed the way she'd begun weaving Opal into conversations without sounding stilted or awkward. She was trying new things and succeeding.

If she could do it, so could he.

Brendan opened the fridge and checked the champagne again, hoping the high price meant it was halfway decent. He'd tasted her unbelievable mouth yesterday evening, and his pride demanded only the best on her tongue. He'd have to stretch beyond his normal capabilities for this woman. She wasn't going to be happy with beer and burgers and a ball game at Blow the Man Down. Not always. She'd make him work to keep her content, and he *wanted* that challenge.

It hadn't been like this the first and only other time he'd dated a woman. There'd been no urgency or anticipation or raw hunger that never let up. There had been acceptance, understanding. All of it quiet.

But the thump of his heart as he climbed into his truck was not quiet.

No Name was within walking distance, but Piper would probably be wearing some ridiculous shoes, so he'd drive her to and from his house. Leaving home at this hour was not part of his usual routine, and everyone who saw his truck raised their eyebrows, waving hesitantly. They knew he'd be leaving tomorrow morning for crab season and probably wondered why he wasn't heading to bed early with two weeks of treacherous sea in his future.

There was a woman to see to first. That was why.

Brendan parked at the curb outside of No Name. He tried the front entrance and found it unlocked, so he went in and climbed the stairs to her door. It wasn't the first time he'd seen her dressed to kill a man, so he shouldn't have been surprised when she answered with a flirty smile and smelling exotic, like smoke. In a dress so short, he'd see everything if he went down two steps.

He almost swallowed his fucking tongue.

"Hey there, sailor."

"Piper." Brendan exhaled hard, doing everything he could to prevent his instant hard-on from growing unmanageable. Jesus, the date hadn't even started yet, and he needed to adjust himself. "You know we're just going to my house, right?"

"Mmm-hmm." She pouted at him. "You don't like my dress?"

And in that moment, Brendan saw right through her. Saw what she was doing. Making tonight about sex. Trying to keep things casual. Categorizing him as a friend with benefits. With a less determined man, she would have succeeded, too. Easily. She was paradise on legs, and probably a lot of weak-willed bastards wouldn't be able to stop themselves from taking *anything* she was willing to give.

But he remembered their kiss. Would likely remember it for the rest of his life. She'd hidden nothing while their mouths were touching. She'd been scared, surprised, turned on, and scared again. He could relate. And while he had no idea if he could offer this woman enough to make her happy, he wasn't letting Piper classify him as a casual hookup. Because what she made him feel wasn't casual. Not one bit.

"You know I love it, Piper. You look beautiful."

Her cheeks flushed at the compliment. "And you're not wearing your beanie." She reached out and ran her fingers through his hair, her nails lightly grazing his scalp. "I can't believe you've been hiding all of this from me."

Christ. He was in danger of swallowing his tongue again.

It wasn't just that he hadn't been touched by a woman in seven years. It was that *this* woman was the one doing the touching. "There's a chill in the air. Do you have a jacket or do you want to borrow mine?"

Hannah appeared behind her sister in the doorway, head-phones looped around her neck. She dropped a black sweater over Piper's shoulders and sniffed. "Have her home at a rea-sonable hour, please."

Brendan shook his head at the younger one and offered his hand to Piper. "Not much choice. We leave for Alaska in the morning."

Hannah hummed for a second, singing a song under her breath about the bottom of the deep blue sea, but he didn't rec-ognize it. Seemingly caught up in the words, Hannah patted her sister on the shoulder and closed the door.

Sliding her hand into Brendan's, Piper made an amused sound. "She's probably already making you a sailing-themed playlist for the trip. She can't help herself."

"If we're not setting traps or pulling them up, we're trying to get a few hours of sleep. Not a lot of time for listening to music." He cleared his throat. "I won't tell her that, though."

He opened the front door, and Piper smiled at him as she

passed through. There were a few customers waiting outside the Red Buoy across the street. When they saw him helping Piper into his truck—and sure enough, she was wearing those ice-pick heels again—they elbowed each other, one of them even running inside to relay the gossip. He'd been prepared for a reaction. Didn't mind it at all, especially with him going out of town for two weeks. Right or wrong, it would ease his mind if the town knew she was spoken for.

Even if Piper wasn't aware of it yet.

They drove the three minutes to Brendan's house, and he pulled into the driveway, coming around the front bumper to help her out. He didn't have a hope in hell of keeping his eyes off her legs when she turned all ladylike in the seat, using his shoulders for balance as she descended from the passenger side of his truck.

"Thank you," she whispered, running a finger down the center of his chest. "Such a gentleman."

"That's right." He tipped her chin up. "That's exactly what I'm going to be, Piper."

Her bravado slipped a little. "I guess we'll see about that."

"I guess we will."

She took her chin out of his hand and strutted up the walkway, which was just playing dirty. The clingy green material of her dress stretched and shifted over her ass, immediately making him question whether being a gentleman was overrated.

Yeah, he wanted to take her to bed more than he could remember wanting anything. Every muscle in his body was strung tight at the sight of her gorgeous legs in the darkness outside his front door. But he couldn't shake the intuition that going too fast with Piper would be a mistake. Maybe she even wanted him to give in, just so she could put him in a box labeled *Fling*.

Worst part of it was . . . maybe he *was* only fling material for her. Tonight, she looked more suited to gliding around a Hollywood mansion than eating a homemade meal at his bachelor pad. He might be delusional trying to shoot his shot. If she was determined to go back to LA, there was no way he could stop her. But something inside him, some intuition, wouldn't allow him to give Piper anything but his best effort.

Brendan unlocked the door, flipped on the lights, and turned to watch her reaction. She'd be able to see most of it at first glance. The downstairs was an open concept, with the living room on the right, kitchen and dining room on the left. It wasn't full of knickknacks or cluttered with pictures. Everything was simple, modern, but what furniture he did have was handmade locally with driftwood—and he liked that. Liked that his home was a representation of what the people of his town could do with wood from the ocean.

"Oh." She let out a rush of breath, a dimple popping up in her cheek. "Brendan . . . you set the table already."

"Yeah." Remembering his manners, he went to the kitchen and took the bottle of champagne out of the fridge. She came to stand by the dining table, seeming a little dumbfounded as she watched him pop the cork and pour. "You'll have to tell me if this is any good. They only had two kinds at the liquor store, and the other one came in a can."

She laughed, set her purse down, and removed the sweater in a slow, sensual movement that nearly caused his composure to falter. "Why don't you have some with me?"

"I drink beer. No champagne."

Piper edged a hip up onto the table, and he almost overflowed the glass. "I bet I'll convince you to have some by the end of the night."

Jesus, she probably could convince him to do a lot of things if she put her mind to it, but he reckoned he should keep that to himself. He handed her the champagne flute he'd purchased that very afternoon, watched her take a sip, and the memory of their kiss rolled through him hard.

"It's fantastic," she said with a sigh.

Relief settled in next to need. He ignored the latter. For now. "Just going to put the fish in the oven, then I want to show you something."

"Okay."

Brendan opened the fridge and took out the foil-covered baking dish. He'd already prepared the sole, drizzled it with lemon juice, salt, and pepper. In Westport, you learned young how to make a fish dinner, even if you never honed another skill in the kitchen. It was necessary, and he thanked God for that knowledge now. As he turned on the oven and slid in the dish, he decided his kitchen would forever look boring without Piper standing in it. She was something out of another world, posed to seduce with her killer body angled just right, elbow on hip, wrist lazily swirling her champagne.

"Come on." Before he could give in to temptation and lift her onto the table, forget about dinner altogether, he snagged her free hand, guiding her through the living room toward the back of the house. He slapped on the light leading to his back patio and opened the door, gesturing for her to precede him. "Thought I'd show you what's possible with the outdoor space at the bar, if you wanted to add some greenery." It occurred to him then that maybe gardening wasn't exactly a sexy trait for a man to have. "I just needed something to do on my days off—"

Her gasp cut him off. "Wow. Oh my God, Brendan. It's magical out here." She walked through the roughly cut stone pathway, somehow not tripping in her heels. The ferns, which he really needed to get around to trimming, grazed her hips as she passed. The trickling sound from the stone water feature seemed to be calling her, and she stopped in front of it, trailing a finger along the surface. There was a single wrought-iron chair angled in the corner where he sat sometimes with a beer after a long trip, trying to get his equilibrium back. "I wouldn't have pegged you for a gardener, but now I can see it. You love your roots." She glanced back at him over her shoulder. "You've got everything carved out just the way you like it."

Do I?

He would have thought so until recently.

His going through the motions, doing the same thing over and over again, had become less . . . satisfying. No denying it.

"I do love this place," he said slowly. "Westport."

"You'd never think of leaving." A statement, not a question.

"No," he answered anyway, resisting the urge to qualify that definite *no* somehow.

She leaned down to smell one of the blooms on his purple aster bush. "What about a vacation? Do you ever take them?"

He rubbed at the back of his neck. "When I was a kid, my parents used to bring me camping on Whidbey Island. They moved down to Eugene, Oregon, a while back to be closer to my mother's family."

"No leisure trips since childhood? Nothing at all?"

Brendan shook his head, chuckling when Piper gave him a scandalized look. "People take trips to see the ocean. I don't need to go anywhere for that. She's right here in my backyard."

Piper came closer, amusement dancing in her eyes. "My mother warned me all about you king crab fishermen and your love affairs with the sea. I thought she was being dramatic, but you really can't resist the pull of the water, can you?" She searched his face. "You're in a serious relationship."

Something shifted in his stomach. "What do you mean, she warned you?"

Her shoulder lifted and dropped. "She loves her husband, Daniel. But . . . I think there was some unprocessed grief talking. Because of what happened to Henry." She stared off into the distance, as if trying to recall the conversation. "She told me and Hannah that fishermen always choose the sea. They go back over and over again, even if it scares their loved ones. Based on that, I'm guessing she wanted Henry to quit and . . . you know the rest."

This wasn't a conversation he'd planned on. Would he ever give up the more dangerous aspects of his job? No. No, battling the tides, the current, the waves was his life's work. There was salt water running through his veins. Making it clear that he would always choose the ocean, no matter what, put him at a deficit with Piper already—and they hadn't even eaten yet.

But when she turned her face up to the moonlight, and he saw only honest curiosity there, he felt compelled to make her understand.

"Every year, I get a couple of greenhorns on the boat. First-time crabbers. Most of them are young kids trying to make some quick cash, and they never make it longer than the first season. But once in a while, there's one . . . I can see it from the wheelhouse. The bond he's forming with the sea. And I know he'll never get away from her."

She smiled. "Like you."

A voice whispered in the back of his head, *You're screwing yourself.* He was an honest man, though, often to a fault. "Yeah. Like me." He searched her hairline. "That bruise on your head is finally gone."

She reached up and rubbed the spot. "It is. Did I ever thank you properly for sending Abe to pad the upper bunk?"

"No thanks necessary."

Piper eliminated the remaining distance between them, stopping just shy of her tits touching his chest. She was soft, graceful, feminine. So much smaller than him. With her this close, he felt like a tamed giant, holding his breath and waiting, waiting to see what the beautiful girl would do next. "You could have just kissed it and made it all better."

His exhale came out hard, thanks to all the blood in his body rushing south to his cock. "You told me your flirt was broken with me. It doesn't seem like that's the case tonight."

Her lips curved. "Maybe because I came dressed in body armor."

Brendan tilted his head and let his gaze sweep across her bare shoulders, legs, and back to her low, tight neckline. "That armor couldn't protect you from anything."

Something flickered in her eyes. "Couldn't it?"

She sailed into the house, leaving her seductive scent in her wake.

Brendan had always thought battling the ocean would forever be his biggest challenge. But that was before he met Piper. Maybe he didn't know the how or the what of this thing between them yet, but his gut never lied. He'd never lost a battle with the water when listening to his instincts, and he hoped like hell those same instincts wouldn't fail him now.

Chapter Sixteen

*P*iper watched Brendan take a seat on the opposite side of the table and frowned.

The boat captain didn't appear to be easily seduced. When she'd picked this dress out, she hadn't even expected them to make it through the front door, but here they were, sitting in his charmingly masculine dining room, preparing to eat food *he made himself.*

And he'd bought her champagne.

Men had bought her jewelry, taken her to nice restaurants— one eager beaver had even bought her a Rolls for her twenty- second birthday. She'd made no bones about liking nice things. But none of those gifts had ever made her feel as special as this homemade meal.

She didn't want to feel special around Brendan, though. Did she?

Since arriving in Westport, she'd had more frank conversa- tions with Brendan than anyone in her life, save Hannah. She wanted to know more about him, to reveal more of herself in return, and *that* was intensely scary.

Because what could come of this?

She was only in Westport for three months, almost two weeks down already. Tomorrow *he'd* leave for two weeks. Then back in and out to sea, three days at a time. This had all the makings of a temporary hookup. But his refusal to put a label on this thing between them left the door of possibilities swinging wide open.

She actually didn't even know how to *be* more than a temporary hookup.

That impossible-to-ignore white tan line around his ring finger and the fact that she was his first date since taking it off? It was overwhelming for someone whose longest relationship had only been three weeks and had ended with her confidence shot full of holes. Whatever he expected to happen between them . . . she couldn't deliver on that.

And maybe that was the real problem.

The burly sea captain waited in silence for her to take the first bite, his elbows on the table, totally unpracticed at being on a date. A muscle ticced in his cheek, telling her Brendan was nervous about her reaction to his cooking. But every thought in her head must have been showing on her face, because he raised an eyebrow at her. She rolled the tension out of her shoulders and dug her fork into the flaky white fish, adding a potato, too, and pushing it between her lips. Chewing. "Oh. Wow, this is great."

"Yeah?"

"Totally." She took another bite, and he finally started eating his own meal. "Do you cook for yourself a lot?"

"Yes." He ate the way he did everything else. No pussyfooting around. Insert fork, put food in mouth, repeat. No pausing. "Except for Monday nights."

"Oh, the Red Buoy is a scheduled weekly event. I should have known." She laughed. "I make fun of you for your routines, but they're probably what make you a good captain."

He made a sound. "Haven't been in my routines this week, have I?"

"No." She considered him. Even warned herself against delving too deeply into why he'd changed things up. But her curiosity got the best of her. "Why is that? I mean, what made you decide to"—*take off your ring?*—"rearrange your schedule?"

Brendan seemed to choose his words. "I'll never be impulsive. Consistency equals safety on the water, and I got comfortable abiding by rules at all times. It makes me worthy to have lives in my hands, you know? Or that was my reasoning in the beginning, and it just stuck. For a long time. But recently, here on land . . . someone kept throwing wrenches in my routines, and the world didn't end." He studied her, as if to judge her reaction and whether or not to continue. "It was kind of like I'd been waiting for a shoe to drop. Then it dropped, and instead of chaos, I just, uh . . ." A beat passed. "Saw the potential for a new course."

Piper swallowed hard. "The shoe dropped, but it was a peep-toe stiletto?"

"Something like that."

"I *can* harness my chaos for good. I might need you as a character witness at a future trial." Her words didn't quite convey the levity she was hoping for, mostly because she sounded breathless over his admission. Piper Bellinger had had a positive effect on someone. He'd admitted it out loud. "But it's not just me that forced the change," she said, and laughed, desperate to dull the throb in her chest. "There had to be other factors."

Brendan started to say something and stopped.

Since meeting this man, she'd suspected he never said anything without a reason. If he was holding back, she could only imagine how important it must be. She found herself setting down her fork, wanting to give him her undivided attention. "What is it?"

He cleared his throat. "I'm purchasing a second boat for next season. It's being built now. I'm going to check on the progress while I'm in Dutch Harbor—that's the port in Alaska where we'll wait a week after setting our traps."

"That's exciting." Her brow wrinkled. "How are you going to captain two ships?"

"I'm not. I'm going to put Fox in the wheelhouse of the *Della Ray*."

Piper smiled into a sip of champagne. "Does he know yet?"

"No. I can't give him time to talk himself out of it."

"Would he? He seems . . . confident."

"That's a nice way of saying he's a cocky asshole. And he is. But he's smarter than he thinks." Brendan paused, looking down with a knitted brow. "Maybe handing over the *Della Ray* is a good way to distance myself from the past."

Piper stayed very still. "Why do you want to distance yourself?"

"Apart from it being time? I think . . . a part of me feels obligated to remain in the past as long as I'm captaining Mick's boat." He scrubbed a hand down his face, laughing without humor. "I can't believe I'm saying it out loud when normally I'd just bury it. Maybe I *should* bury it."

"Don't." Her mouth was dry over this man opening up to her. Looking at her across the table with rare male vulnerability, as if he truly valued her response. "You don't have to feel guilty about wanting some space after seven years, Brendan," she said quietly. "That's a lot more than most people would give. The fact that you feel guilty at all just proves you're a quality human. Even if you wear a beanie at the dinner table."

The green of his eyes warmed. "Thank you. For not judging me."

Sensing his need to move on from the subject, Piper looked around the dining room. "Who am I to judge anyone? Especially someone who has a cool house his parents don't own. Two boats and a life plan. It's intimidating, actually."

He frowned. "You're intimidated by *me*?"

"Not so much you. More like your work ethic. I don't even know if I'm pronouncing that right. That's how *not* often I've said 'work ethic' out loud." She felt the need to even the playing field, to reward his honesty with some of her own. His confessions made it easy to confess her own sins. "My friend Kirby and I started a lipstick line called Pucker Up, maybe three years back. Once the launch party was over and we realized how much work we had to do, we gave away our inventory to friends and went to Saint-Tropez. Because we were tired."

"Maybe it wasn't the right career path."

"Yeah, well." Her lips twitched. "Professional napper was my fallback, and I nailed that. That's partially why I'm here. But *also* because my friend Kirby ratted me out to the cops."

"She didn't," he said, his expression darkening.

"She did! Fingered me as the ringleader from the shallow end of the pool. Appropriately." Piper waved a hand around. "It's fine, though. We're still friends. I just can't trust her or tell her anything important."

He seemed to be concentrating hard on what she was saying. "Do you have a lot of friends like that?"

"Yes." She drew a circle on the side of the champagne flute.
"It's more for image than anything, I guess. Influence. Being
seen. But it's weird, you know. I've only been out of Los Angeles for two weeks, and it's like I was never there. None of
my friends have texted or messaged me. They're on to bigger
and better things." She shook her head. "Meanwhile people
still leave flowers at Henry's memorial after twenty-four years.
So . . . how real or substantial is an image if everything it earns
someone can all go away in two weeks?"

"*You* haven't gone away, though. You're sitting right there."

"I am. I'm here. At this table. In Westport." She swallowed.
"Trying to figure out what to do when no one is watching. And
wondering if maybe that's the stuff that actually matters." Her
laugh came out a little unsteady. "That probably sounds ama-
teurish to someone who would build a freaking *boat* and not
tell a soul about it."

"No, it doesn't." He waited until she met his eyes. "It sounds
like you've been uprooted and dropped somewhere unfamiliar. Do you think I'd cope as well if I was shipped off some-
place where I knew no one, had no trade?"

She gasped. "How would you get your fish and chips on
Monday nights?"

A corner of his lips jumped. "You're doing just fine, honey."

It was the gruff *honey* that did it. Her legs snuck together
under the table and squeezed, her toes flexing in her shoes.
She wanted Brendan's hands on her. All over. But she was also
scared of going to him, because once again, the sexy smoke
screen she'd been hiding behind had dissipated, leaving only

her. Brendan was looking at her with a combination of heat and tenderness, and she needed to turn up the dial on the former.

This was all going too far, too fast, and she was starting to like him too much.

She might be having an existential crisis, but she still wanted Los Angeles back and all the glittery trappings that came with it. Didn't she? Sure, after weeks with no contact from her friends, the call of LA had quieted slightly. She'd actually started to enjoy not checking her notifications every ten seconds. But fame waxing and waning was part of the deal, right? That rush of recognition and adoration she'd stopped craving of late would come back. It always did. There was no other option but going home, and if anything, her time in Westport would make her appreciate her privilege this time around. Wasn't that the lesson she'd been sent to learn?

Yes.

Bottom line, she'd spent twenty-eight years building this image and couldn't just start over from scratch.

Could she have Brendan tonight and still keep her eye on that reality?

Of course she could.

Ignoring the notch in her throat, Piper pushed back from the table and stood, champagne in hand. She rounded the piece of furniture slowly, gratified when his throat worked in a heavy swallow. His eyes and chin were stubborn, though.

Well, if he was going to be obstinate, she'd have to play to win.

Piper slipped between Brendan and the table, scooting it back a little so she could stand comfortably in the V of his thighs. His eyes were all but black with hunger, lighting on her cleavage, her thighs and hips, her mouth. As soon as she raked the fingers of her free hand into his hair, that big chest started to heave, his eyelids drifting shut. "Piper," he said hoarsely. "This isn't why I invited you to dinner."

She took her hand back, set down the champagne being held in the other, and tucked her fingers under the straps of her dress. "Maybe it's not the only reason," she murmured, peeling down the green velvet bodice, leaving her breasts bare mere inches from his mouth. "But it's one of them, isn't it?"

Brendan opened his eyes, and a shudder racked him, his hands flying up to grip her hips. "Oh Jesus fucking Christ, they're so pretty, baby." He leaned in, pressing his open mouth to the smooth path of skin between her breasts, breathing heavily, using his hold on her hips to pull her closer, like he couldn't help it. "This is where you put that perfume, isn't it? Right here between your sexy little tits."

The desperation in his hands, the chafe of velvet on flesh, turned her nipples to points. "I put it there for you tonight," she whispered into his hair. "All for you."

He moaned, turned his head slightly so he could breathe against her nipple. "I know what you're doing. You want to make this about fucking."

Her pulse skittered in her ears. "Stop overthinking it and touch me."

Still, he hesitated, that jaw about to shatter.

Piper reached back and picked up the champagne flute, taking a slow sip. She swallowed most of the bubbly liquid, but left a trace of it on her tongue, bringing it to Brendan's lips. Licking the champagne into his mouth. "Told you I'd get you to try it," she murmured, teasing the tip of his tongue with her own. "Want more?"

That big body swayed closer, lines of strain appearing around his mouth. "Please . . ."

"You don't have to beg," Piper said, bringing the champagne flute to her breasts, tipping the glass and letting the champagne trickle out over one nipple, then the next, and Brendan started to pant. "Not for something we both want. Touch me, Brendan. Taste me. Please?"

"Christ, I have to." He traced his mouth to her left nipple, pressed his bared teeth against it, before rubbing his tongue against the stiff bud, yanking her hips forward, the move arching her back so she had to use his hair for balance, taking two big handfuls. Her mouth was in an O, watching him savor her, manhandle her body. No games. Just need.

His mouth raced down to her belly button, licking that hollow where some of the dripping champagne had ended up, before rising again to the opposite breast, suckling harder now. Devouring. She'd intended to be in control here, but his mouth was delivering the most incredible texture and suction, and her ass bumped back against the table clumsily, a sob ripping from her throat. "Brendan," she gasped. "*Brendan.*"

"I know, baby. Can I put my hands up your dress?" he rasped, his palms already kneading the backs of her thighs, his beard stroking back and forth over her distended nipple, and sending a rush of wet to the apex of her thighs. "*Piper.*"

"What?" she breathed, head spinning. "Whatever you said. Yes. Yes."

Those busy hands moved faster than lightning, clutching her ass so roughly, the air evacuated her lungs. He drew her forward so he could pant directly against her belly, his hands never ceasing to massage, squeeze, and lift the flesh of her bottom, his calloused fingers tangling in her thong in his haste to touch, to mold.

"Y-you're an ass man, I guess," she stammered.

He shook his head. "No, Piper. I'm a *this*-ass man."

"Oh," she simpered.

That was oddly romantic. And possessive. And she liked both of those qualities too much. She needed to regain control somehow, because she'd severely miscalculated how quickly Brendan could pull her under. This attraction was even more dangerous than she'd originally thought. "Brendan," she managed, taking hold of his broad shoulders and using every ounce of her strength to push him back into his chair. "W-wait, I . . ."

"I'm sorry," he said between breaths. "It's not just that it's been so long for me, it's that you had to be the sexiest woman on the fucking planet."

Had Piper heard him right? She shook her head to clear it, though most of the lust fog remained in place. "Wait, I know you wore the ring, but . . . no sex? At all? Knowing you, I should have assumed that, but . . ." Her gaze traveled down the front of his body, stopping when she reached the outline of his painful-looking erection. It protruded against the fly of his jeans, large and heavy. His own hand crept toward it, his sexual frustration obvious in every harsh line of his face.

There was a way to wrestle back control of this push and pull between them *and* make him feel good—and she suddenly couldn't help herself. "Oh, Brendan." She went down on her knees and pressed a kiss to the thick bulge. "We need to take care of this, don't we?"

His head fell back, chest lifting and plummeting. "Piper, you don't need to."

She cupped his big arousal, massaged him through his jeans, and he moaned through his teeth. "I want to," she whispered. "I want to make you feel so good."

She flicked open the button at the top of his fly and lowered the zipper carefully, sucking in a breath when his shaft grew impossibly larger inside his briefs in the absence of confinement. Brendan's knuckles were white on the arms of the chair, but he stopped breathing altogether as she drew down the waistband of his briefs and saw his erection up close. *Male.* There was no other way to describe the unapologetic weight and steel of him, the thick black hair at the base, the heavy sac. He was long and smooth and broad, veins wrapped around him like lines on a road map, and wow. Yes. She'd been telling the truth. She really did want to make him feel good. So badly, her inner thighs were turning slick with her own need. *Wanted* to be on her knees, giving pleasure to this man who'd been celibate so long. This man who'd treated her with care and respect and got nervous about her tasting his cooking.

Furthermore, she could establish up front that this was just sex.

Just sex.

"Look at you, Piper," Brendan said hoarsely. "Christ, I didn't stand a chance, did I?"

With a sympathetic pout, she gave his shaft a tight pump. And another one. Waited until his eyes started to glaze over, then she dragged her tongue up the meaty underside of him, closed her mouth over the velvet helmet on top. Making her tongue flat and stiff, she teased the salty slit, the sensitive ridges, before tunneling him in deep, deep, right up to the point where tears pricked her eyelids. God, he pulsed on her tongue, great, quick surges of life that her femininity started to echo, making her groan around his hard flesh.

"Goddamn, baby, that mouth," he groaned, one of his hands fisting her hair, urging her faster, even as he barked, "Stop. *Stop.* I'm going to come."

Piper let him slide from her mouth with a swirl of her tongue, her right hand working him, thickening him with every stroke of her fist. Yeah, he wasn't going to last much longer, and there was something so hot about it. How much he'd needed the relief. "Where do you want to give it to me?" she whispered, taking his sac in her hand and juggling him gently, leaning in to curl her tongue around the purpling tip. "Anywhere you want, Captain."

"*Fuck,*" he gritted out, his thighs starting to vibrate. Instead of answering her pretty, pressing question, he closed his eyes, nostrils flaring as he took in a drag of air. "No."

Then the unexpected happened.

Right on the verge of his well-deserved orgasm, Brendan surged forward, wrapping his hands around her waist and lifting her up onto the dining room table. She teetered, dizzy from the rapid ascent, but she snapped back to reality when Brendan dropped to his own knees and stripped off his shirt. "Ohhh," she said in slow motion. "Heyyy, looook aaaat thaaaat."

Dude was *yoked.*

She'd known, on some level, that Brendan was built like a motherfucker. His arms always tested the seams of his sweatshirts, his chest ridged with muscle, but she'd been unaware of the definition. The chiseled planes of his pecs ended in a tight drop-off; then it was a mountain range of abs. But not the obnoxious kind. They had meat on them. And hair. All of him did. He looked like a real man who worked in the wild, because that's exactly what he was. And not a single tattoo, which was so Brendan, it made her throat feel weird. Of course he wouldn't want to deal with the fuss of all that or waste his time getting one done.

Come back to earth, Piper.

"Wait, I was . . ." She pointed at his erection. "You were—"

"Don't worry about me," he rasped, dragging her to the edge of the table. "Open your thighs and let me see it, Piper."

Her inner walls clenched, delighting in his bluntness. "But—"

"You think I'm going to get sucked off and leave town for two weeks? Not going to happen. You're getting off, baby, or nobody is getting off."

As if on autopilot, her thighs squeaked wide on the table. Oh, this wasn't good. She didn't even know which part of her was in command. Her head, her heart, her lady business. Or maybe they all were, three bitches hitting the switches of her control panel. She only knew Brendan needed to stop revealing positive sides of himself.

Now they were adding *generous* to the mix?

The hem of her delicate dress in his boat captain's hands made her whimper. He lifted it, and God only knew what he was seeing. Her thong was sheer to begin with, but she'd never been this wet in her ever-loving life. Not to mention, his impatient hands on her butt had tugged it askew.

He stared hard at her juncture, the grip on her knees flexing, a curse issuing unsteadily from his mouth. "Yeah, I have to be an idiot leaving you without my attention for two weeks."

She panted. "Are you calling me high maintenance?"

"Are you denying it?" He tugged aside the strip of material shielding her core, which thankfully she'd waxed clean as a whistle right before leaving LA. "Fuck me. You can be as high maintenance as you want, honey. But I'm the only one who does the maintenance." He ran his thumb down the seam of her sex. "Understood?"

Piper nodded, as if in a trance.

What was the use of saying no? At least this one verbal agreement was about sex. Nothing emotional. And she wasn't going to pretend like someone in this town might come along and interest her even a fraction of the amount that Brendan did. She might have to travel pretty far to find that, come to think of it.

His lips ghosted up her inner thigh, blunt fingers hooking in the sides of her panties. "Lift up," he rumbled, nipping at her sensitive skin with his teeth. "Want them off."

Oh great. His voice could get even deeper? It resonated all the way up to her clit, and she fell back on her elbows, inching her hips up enough for Brendan to peel the thong down her legs. She watched this man, who grew more exciting by the moment, expecting him to drop the underwear on the floor. He wrapped the thin black material around his shaft instead, pressing his mouth and nose up against her wetness, groaning as he choked himself up and down in a tight fist.

"Holy . . ." Piper breathed, momentarily blacking out.

"See this, baby?" He rubbed his mouth side to side, parting the damp folds of her femininity, that hand jerking roughly between his thighs. "You're still getting me off, too."

When had her back hit the table?

One second she was looking down at Brendan's head, the

next she was staring wide-eyed up at the ceiling. Brendan's tongue snaked down slowly through the valley of her sex, and her fingers clawed their way into his hair, the move involuntary, but if he stopped, if he *stopped*, she was going to die.

"Good, Piper. Pull me in tight. Show me how bad you want my tongue."

No no no. His voice was like sandpaper now. Could she come from that baritone alone?

"Brendan." She lifted her legs, hooked them over his shoulders, earning a growl, another rough jerk of her hips to the edge of the table. "Please, please. *Please.*"

She'd never begged for anything sexual in her life. Especially not oral. Men always made it seem like they were doing a woman a favor. Or maybe she'd just been detached and projecting an explanation that would keep her that way. She couldn't remain detached now, and this . . . oh, it was definitely not a hardship for Brendan—and he let her know it. His forearm came down on her hips, pinning them to the table, and he growled into that second lick, dragging the tip over her clit, teasing it, the rippling flex of his shoulder telling Piper that his hand was moving feverishly just out of sight. With the use of her panties.

He was the most consistent man she'd ever met, and she thanked God for that now because he sealed his upper lip to the very top of her slit, his tongue never quitting or changing pace. It was perfect, perfect, lavishing her swelling clit with friction and pressure, and she was actually going to get there because of it. Oh my God, she was going to have an orgasm. Like a real, authentic orgasm. She wasn't going to fake it to stroke his ego. This was happening.

"Please don't stop, Brendan. It's perfect. It's . . . oh God, oh Jesus."

Her thighs started to tremor uncontrollably, and she could see nothing but sparks dancing in front of her eyes. The fingers she'd plowed into his hair drew him closer, legs wrapping around his head, her hips lifting, seeking, lower body twisting. And she still didn't dislodge him from that magical spot, and maybe he was Jesus. She didn't know. Knew nothing but the intense pleasure bearing down on her. But then he took his forearm off her hips and pressed the heel of his hand to her weeping entrance and rotated it—hard—and she screamed. She fucking screamed. And she didn't stop when he slid a thick finger inside of her, searched and found her G-spot, adding firm pressure.

She climaxed. Which was a pitiful word for traveling to a distant plane where fairies danced and gumdrops rained from the sky. When her back protested, she realized it had arched off the table involuntarily. She stared at her elevated hips in a daze, the endless relief coursing through her, tightening her muscles and letting them go. Wow. Oh wow.

Brendan moved over her slumped body, and his face, it was almost unrecognizable for the lust bracketing his mouth, the fever making his eyes bright. That huge part of him was still hard, his hand twisting up and down the length, one side of her panties wrapped around his shaft, the other around his fist. "Can I rub it here, baby?" Brendan rasped the question, his bare chest heaving, a fine sheen of sweat on those work-honed muscles. "Just want to rub it where I made you come."

"Yes."

He all but fell on her, his face landing in the crook of her neck, his fist positioning his stiffness between her thighs, right over that uber-sensitive flesh. "One day soon, Piper, I'm going to fuck you so goddamn hard." He alternated between dragging his swollen tip through her saturated folds and stroking himself. "Going to fuck the word 'friend' right out of your beautiful mouth. You'll forget how to say anything but my name. Real quick, honey."

Her clit hummed again, unbelievably, and that buzz of connection, of more promised pleasure had to be the reason she turned her head slightly, whispering in his ear, "Promise?"

With a strangled growl of her name, he hit his peak, shooting moisture onto her belly, his hand moving in a blur, his teeth bared against the side of her throat. "Piper. *Piper.*"

The power, the exhilaration of Brendan saying her name as he orgasmed was so incredible, she couldn't hold still. She raked her tongue up and down his straining neck, rubbed the insides of her thighs up and down his heaving rib cage, scraped her fingernails over his shoulders and down his back. When his heavy body collapsed on her, she kept going, some instinct she'd never had before urging her to soothe, to whisper words of praise that she actually, literally meant. She could have laid there straight through to tomorrow, just existing under the reassuring weight of him—and that complacency brought back her senses.

Okay, they gave good sex.

Or . . . *almost* sex, anyway.

Better than any actual intercourse she'd ever had, though. By leaps and bounds.

Because you like him. A lot. For who he is, not what he can do for you.

That realization smacked her hard in the face. *God.* She'd never thought of her past actions in those terms before, but they fit. Shallow. So shallow. Who was she to accept the sweet gestures this man offered? He should have waited to take his wedding ring off for some selfless local girl who would be content waving him off to sea for the rest of her life.

A pang caught Piper in the chest, and she tried to sit up but couldn't move because Brendan had her pinned to the table. His head lifted, eyes narrowing like he could already sense her building tension. "Piper."

"What?" she whispered, winded from her thoughts.

"Get out of your head."

With a sardonic smile, she rolled her eyes. "Aye, aye, Captain." With some effort, she tried to do as he asked. Tried to set aside her worries for later. He was leaving for two weeks tomorrow morning, after all. That would be plenty of time to pull her stupid head out of the clouds. "That was . . . wow." *Keep it light. Sexy.* "Really, really good."

Brendan grunted. He dropped his head and smiled into the valley between her breasts, making her heart flutter. "Good?" he snorted, kissing her breasts in turn and standing, visibly reluctant to leave her. After zipping his still semi-hard erection back into his jeans, he took some napkins out of the holder on the table and cleaned Piper of his spend, wiping efficiently like he did everything else, shaking his head slowly at her appearance. "I'm going to starve to death without the taste of you."

Despite the languidness of her muscles, she managed to sit up and fix her dress, blinking at the panties sitting in a wet heap on the floor, memories of the last half hour flooding in. Wow. She'd been so . . . present. Inside every second with him.

When she'd been intimate in the past, she spent the whole time obsessing about her appearance, what the guy was thinking, if she was meeting expectations. None of those anxieties had taken hold with Brendan. None. Because . . . he liked *her*. Not her image. Her actual personality and opinions. With Brendan's hands on her, she'd had no walls, no boundaries. Tonight had been all *about* boundaries, but instead of setting them, the line kept getting pushed further and further out.

She hopped off the table, landing on the heels she still wore, and gave him a flirty hip-check. "Maybe I'll give you another taste when you get back."

"Maybe, huh?" He caught her arm and spun her around, backing her up against the refrigerator, pinning her there with his rugged frame. Piper's traitorous body melted immediately, eager to be supported by his superior strength, her head lolling back. Brendan's hard mouth found hers with lips already opening, his tongue delving deep, carrying the light flavor of her climax, giving it to her with thorough strokes, a low growl of satisfaction simmering in his throat. When he pulled back, his silver-green eyes searched her face, one hand cradling her jaw. "Does that taste like 'maybe' to you?"

In other words, she'd be back for more.

"Somebody's cocky all of a sudden," Piper huffed.

"Not cocky, honey." He kissed her mouth again, softly this time. "Determined."

She sputtered. Determined to do what?

Oh man, she needed to get out of there.

"I have an early morning," she blurted. "And so do you, right? So."

"So." He seemed to be fighting a smile, and it was galling.

Still not wearing a shirt, he gathered Piper's cardigan and helped her put it on, before handing over her purse. At the very last second, he threw on his own shirt and picked up his car keys. "I'm going to have mercy on you this time, Piper, and drive you home." He threaded their fingers together and tugged her toward the door. "This just had to be the year crab season gets slotted early, didn't it? Otherwise I'd spend about a week getting inside your head—"

"It would take longer than that."

"But dammit." He jerked open the front door. "It'll have to wait until I'm back."

Ha. No way. There would be no getting in anyone's head. Two weeks was like, a million years. They wouldn't even remember each other's names by then. They'd pass each other on the street and vaguely recall a fish dinner and an oral-sex fest. *You're lying to yourself.*

And she kept right on doing it the whole ride home. Kept lying to reassure herself when Brendan walked her up the stairs to her apartment. But the pretense shattered at her feet when he kissed her like he'd never see her again, his mouth moving over hers with such tenderness, her knees turned to rubber and she had to hold on to his collar to stay upright.

"Here," he said, exhaling shakily and pulling the keys out of his pocket. "I'm giving you a spare key to my place, all right? Just in case you and your sister need somewhere to go while I'm out of town."

Piper stared at the object with dawning horror. "A *key*?"

"It's going to get cooler in the next couple of weeks, and the heat in this place probably isn't great." He folded her hand around it, kissed her forehead. "Stop freaking out."

She uttered a string of gibberish.

Did he think she would actually use this thing?

Because she wouldn't.

He chuckled at her expression and turned to go—and she panicked. A different kind of panic than the variety she felt at being handed the key. She thought of the brass statue on the harbor and Opal emptying the contents of an envelope onto the table.

"Brendan!"

Slowing, he turned with a raised eyebrow.

"Please be careful," she whispered.

Warmth fused into his eyes, and he checked her out, head to toe, before continuing on his way, the door downstairs closing behind him, followed by silence.

Much later, she realized what Brendan was really doing when he catalogued her features, her hands, her cocked hip.

Memorizing the sight of her.

Just in case?

Chapter Seventeen

The storm started thirteen days later.

Piper had fallen into a daily routine by then. Run along the harbor just after sunrise. Walk Abe to the maritime museum in the morning, visit Opal on her way home, often with Hannah in tow. Work on the bar until dinnertime, then collapse. They'd made a ton of progress on No Name and were going to start decorating next week, as soon as they installed the crisp white cornice and gave the concrete another coat of industrial paint.

They'd taken an Uber to the fishing supply store last week, thanks to Brendan's suggestion, and gotten most of what they needed to achieve the nautical theme, then ordered more accoutrements for cheap online. And to their utter astonishment, Abe's sons had shown up last week to drop off some hand-crafted bar stools and chairs as a thank-you for walking their father to the museum every morning. Piper told them it wasn't necessary, but they'd refused to take no for an answer, thank God, because they had actual furniture now!

Piper and Hannah were applying slow strokes of lacquer to

the antique bar when a boom of thunder outside made them both jump.

"Whoa," Hannah said, using the back of her wrist to wipe her forehead. "That sounded like cannon fire."

"Yeah." Piper tucked a stray piece of hair into her ponytail and crossed the bar to look out the window. A shudder went down her spine when she saw the Red Buoy closing early. Same with the bait shop two doors down. Was there going to be a really bad storm or something?

Brendan.

No, Westport was far enough from the Bering Sea that he wouldn't get hit with the same storm, right? She had no earthly idea. She was from Southern freaking California, where the sun shined and, other than fog, weather was just a vague entity people in other states had to worry about.

He'd be okay.

Piper pressed a hand to the center of her chest to find her heart racing. "Hey, can you call the record store and ask if they're closing early?"

Over the last two weeks, Hannah had become a regular fixture at the shop. Once she'd revealed her expertise in all things music related, they'd asked her to help give the place an update. While it had cut into Hannah's time working on the bar, Piper hadn't been able to deny her sister this most epic opportunity to flaunt her music snobbery. Hannah was now an unofficial employee of Disc N Dat and had even made some local friends who went and drank coffee together after hours.

"Yeah, sure," Hannah said, whipping her cell out of her back pocket. "I'll text Shauna."

"'Kay."

Piper took a deep breath, but the pressure in her chest wouldn't abate. Brendan was supposed to return the day after tomorrow, and she'd been mentally coaching herself to keep things between them strings-free. But with a storm darkening the sky, she couldn't seem to think straight, much less remember why her relationship with Brendan had to remain casual. She needed to, though, right? No Name was almost finished, and they were super close to nailing down a grand reopening date, at which time they would call Daniel and invite him. Providing this plan to impress Daniel worked, they could be in the homestretch. LA bound. She couldn't afford to get caught up with the boat captain, even if she missed him. Even if she looked for him around every street corner in Westport, just in case he'd gotten home earlier.

"I'm going to run over to the Red Buoy and see if they know what's going on."

Hannah saluted Piper on her way out the door. As soon as she stepped out onto the street, the wind knocked her sideways two steps, her hair blowing free of its ponytail and whipping around her face in a cloud, obscuring her vision. Quickly, she gathered the mane in a fist and looked up at the sky, finding big gray billowing clouds staring back at her. Her stomach dropped, and a wave of fear rolled through her belly.

This seemed like a big deal.

Unable to swallow, she jogged across the street, catching the girl who worked the register on her way out, her head buried in the hood of a rain slicker.

"Hey, um . . . is there going to be a pretty bad storm . . . or something?" Piper asked, clearly the most California girl who ever California'd.

The girl laughed like Piper was joking, sobered when she realized she wasn't. "We've got a typhoon closing in."

What the hell was a typhoon? She resisted the urge to get her phone out and google it. "Oh, but it's, like, contained to the Washington coast, right? Or is it bigger?"

"No, it's coming toward us from Alaska, actually. That's how we know it's going to be a bad motherfucker, excuse my language."

"Alaska," Piper croaked, her fingers turning numb. "Okay, thanks."

The girl scurried off, climbing into a waiting truck right as the first raindrops started to fall. Piper barely remembered walking back across the street and taking shelter in the doorway of No Name. She got her phone out and searched "typhoon" with trembling fingers.

The first two words that came up were "tropical cyclone."

Then, "a rotating, organized system of clouds and thunderstorms that originates over tropical or subtropical waters."

"Oh my God."

She had to breathe in and out slowly so she wouldn't throw up.

Brendan was very good at his job. Smart. The most capable, confident man she'd ever met. There was no way something could happen to him. Or Fox and Deke and Sanders. They were big, strong, God-fearing fishermen. There was no way, right?

Henry's laughing face sprung to her mind. Right on its heels, Mick's voice filtered through her thoughts. *And that Bering Sea water is so damn frigid, there's only a minute's window before it sucks the breath right out of a man's lungs.*

Not Brendan. It wouldn't happen to Brendan.

Getting her legs to carry her into No Name required effort,

but she made it, leaning back weakly against the wall. It took her a moment to realize Hannah was throwing on a sweatshirt. "Hey, Shauna asked if I could pop down really fast and help close up the shop. I should be back in ten minutes." She stopped short when she saw Piper's face. "Are you okay?"

"It's a typhoon. Coming in from Alaska."

Hannah laughed as she threw her messenger bag across her chest. "You sound like a meteorologist. What even is a typhoon?"

"A tropical cyclone," Piper said robotically. "A rotating, organized system of clouds and thunderstorms that originates over tropical or subtropical waters."

"Oh shit." Understanding dawned in Hannah's eyes. "Ohhh. Shit."

"He's going to be fine. They're going to be fine."

"Of course they will." Hannah hesitated, then started to take off her bag. "I'm going to stay here with you—"

"No. Go go go." Her laugh was high-pitched. "I think I can handle ten minutes."

Her sister was dubious. "Are you sure?"

"Totally."

Neither one of them had any idea how bad a storm could get in ten minutes.

Rain lashed the window so hard, Piper moved to the center of the bar for her own safety. The wind sounded like it was inside with her. With a growing sense of dread, she watched more and more people run for cover in the street, eventually clearing it completely. Thunder rocked the ground, followed closely by jagged twists of lightning in the sky.

Piper fumbled her phone in her hands, finding Hannah in

her favorites and dialing. "Hey," she said as soon as her sister picked up. "I think you should stay where you are, okay?"

"Shauna says the same. How'd it pick up so fast?"

"I don't know." She closed her eyes. Brendan had been in this same storm. Fast. Furious. "I'm fine here. Just stay in a safe place and don't move until it lightens up. All right, Hanns?"

"Okay."

Piper hung up and paced a moment, her stride hitching when the electricity went out.

She stood there in near darkness and acted on one of the most foolish instincts in her life—and Jesus *Christ*, that was saying something. But she couldn't stand there and think and worry and speculate. She had to move . . . and she wanted to be near Brendan the only way she could. So she locked the door of No Name behind her and started running in the direction of his house. It was only a three-minute drive. She'd be there in five if she sprinted. And then she'd be safe. And maybe being close to him would keep *him* safe, too, which was a ridiculous notion, but she clung to it hard and pounded the pavement.

Thunder boomed at her back, propelling her on, her sneakers sodden after only two blocks thanks to the rain coming down in torrents now. She turned two corners and ran down a narrow street that seemed semi-familiar? On the night of their date, she'd been too preoccupied to notice any of the street names. But then, there it was. Brendan's truck, parked in front of his house, looking as sturdy and dependable as its owner.

Relief swamped her, and she kicked into a fast sprint, the teeth of his house key biting into her palm. She ran up the path and unlocked the door with pale fingers, her teeth chattering, and fell over the threshold in a heap, kicking the door closed

behind her. And then the storm was nothing more than muffled rumblings, her own harsh pants drowning it out.

"Hello?" Piper sat up and called out, because it seemed like
the thing to do. Maybe he'd gotten back early and just hadn't
come to see her yet. "Brendan?"

There was no answer.

She used the hem of her shirt to dry the rain from her face
and stood, moving through the still, warm house while wind
whipped against the windowpanes, rattling them. Was this a
stalker move? That worry had her chewing her lip, but he'd
given her a key, right? Plus, there was something so inviting
about the house, almost as if it had been expecting her. His
scent lingered in the air of the living room, saltwater and man.

Piper kicked off her shoes and walked barefoot to the
kitchen and turned on his coffee machine, desperate to get rid
of the chill. When a mug had been prepared, she opened the
refrigerator to take out the milk—and an unopened bottle of
champagne rolled toward her in the crisper drawer. Her half-
drunk one was still wedged in the door, but . . . he'd bought
two? Just in case she stopped over while he was gone?

Her throat ached as she carried the mug of coffee up the
stairs, trying not to acknowledge how natural it felt to set her
coffee on the sink in his bathroom and strip off her soaked
clothes, hanging them over the towel rack. She brought the coffee into the shower and drank it while the water stole the chill
from her bones. She lathered herself in his body wash, and his
scent carried up to her on the wafting steam, making her nipples stiffen. Making her close her eyes, press her forehead to
the tile wall, and ask God, very politely, to bring the stubborn
man home safely.

Wrapped in a towel minutes later, she walked into Brendan's bedroom, turned on a lamp on his bedside table, and sighed. So practical. Navy blue and beiges everywhere, no-nonsense white walls, creaky floorboards that reminded her of the decks of ships she'd seen in the harbor. A window directly in front of his bed faced the harbor. The ocean beyond. The love of his life. As if he needed to see it first thing in the morning.

She sent a text to Hannah to make sure her sister was all right, then slumped sideways in the center of the bed, Brendan's pillow hugged to her chest, praying that when she woke up everything would be fine. That he'd walk through the door.

God must have been busy answering someone else's prayers.

Brendan tuned out the endless chatter coming in through the radio from the coast guard, his single-minded focus where it needed to be. Pulling pots. This wasn't their first typhoon, and it wouldn't be the last. They were par for the course this time of year in the Bering Sea and the neighboring Pacific. This job was dangerous for a reason, and they had no choice but to ride it out, finish retrieving this string, and make it back to Dutch. So he trained his eyes on the water ahead, searching for out-of-the-ordinary swells while keeping tabs on the busy deck below.

His crew moved like a well-oiled machine, although after a week of hauling pots, they were showing signs of fatigue. The next buoy appeared alongside the ship, and in a practiced movement, Sanders threw out his hook, dragging in the line and attaching it to the winch. Deke joined him on the other side to engage the hydraulic system, raising the pot. An exultant cheer went up from the men on the deck, though it was muffled by the storm raging around the boat, the burr of the engine below.

Half-full. If this pot didn't put them at their quota, it would bring them close, providing the crabs were male and they wouldn't be required to throw the lot of them back. It was against regulation to take females from the sea, as they kept the population growing.

He waited for Fox to signal a number through the window of the wheelhouse.

Seventy.

Brendan made a note of the number in his log, his mouth moving as he did the math. Their quota issued by the wildlife commission was eighty thousand pounds of crab for the season. They were at 99 percent with five pots left to collect. But with the storm howling outside and the men growing weary, it wasn't worth continuing. Especially not if he could beat the Russians to market and get a stronger price for what they'd caught.

He signaled Fox to wrap up the operation, secure the gear on deck, and get everyone below. They were heading back to Dutch early. And the fucking relief that gripped him around the throat was so much stronger than usual, he had to take several bracing breaths, his fingers flexing around the wheel as he waited for a break in the swells to start executing the turn.

Had this storm made landfall yet back home?

Where was she?

Would she be waiting for him?

Brendan braced his body against the side of the wheelhouse as the *Della Ray* carried over a three-story swell and slapped back down into a black pit of churning seawater. Goddamn this storm. It wasn't any fiercer than the ones they'd worked through in the past, but this time . . . the boat didn't seem quite as substantial under his feet. Was the wheel vibrating with too much force in his hands?

His life felt too easily snatched away.

These were worries he hadn't acknowledged since being a greenhorn, and it was because he'd never wanted to get home so badly. Not once in his fucking life.

A crew crabbing not too far from them had lost a member yesterday when his foot had gotten tangled in a rope, dragging him straight down to the bottom of the drink. Another boat had gone missing entirely, seven men on board. A bad season. More loss than usual. So easily, it could have been one of his crew. Could have been him.

Whitewater, high and downward-sloping, broke out of the corner of Brendan's eye, and he grabbed the radio, shouting down to the deck to brace for impact. *Rogue wave.* And for once, Brendan resented the wild rush he got from the danger. From taking on nature and winning. At that moment, it was just the thing keeping him from Piper.

The wave hit, and the boat groaned, tilting sideways. For long moments, the violent wave rained down on the wheelhouse and obscured his view of the deck. And with his world on its side, all he could hear was Piper's voice telling him to be careful.

The coast guard shouted through the radio, interspersed with static, and he prayed.

He prayed like he never had before.

Just let me go home and see her.

But the Bering Sea chose that moment to remind him exactly who was in control.

Chapter Eighteen

$\mathcal{P}$iper woke up to her phone ringing.

She blinked at the device, then at her surroundings. White walls, navy bedspread, beige chair angled in the corner by a lamp. No storm sounds. Was it over?

The world was almost eerily quiet around her, save the jangling notes of her ringtone, but she ignored the winding sensation in her stomach. There was a glow on the horizon that told her it was very early in the morning. Everything had to be fine now, right?

Taking one final inhale of Brendan's pillow, she answered her sister's call. "Hey, Hanns. Are you all right?"

"Yeah, I'm fine. I just got back to the building. Where are you?"

Piper's cheeks fused with heat. "Brendan's," she said sheepishly.

"Oh." There was a long pause. "Piper . . ."

Suddenly alert, she sat up, shoving the fall of hair out of her face. "What?"

"I don't know any of the details, okay? But I ran into one of the crew members' wives on the way back. Sanders? All she said was . . . there's been an accident."

Her lungs filled with ice. "What?" She pressed a hand between her breasts, pushing down, trying to slow the rollicking pace of her heart. "What kind of accident?"

"She didn't say. But she was upset. She was leaving for the hospital."

"Which . . . ? What?" Piper scrambled off the bed, naked, the towel having loosened overnight. "Did she say anything about Brendan?"

"Just that he's at the hospital."

"*What?*"

"I'm sure he's fine, Piper. Like . . . he's built like a semitruck."

"Yeah, but he's up against a body of fucking water and a cyclone. A *cyclone!*" She was screeching now, off the bed and turning in circles, trying to figure out what to do. Where to start. "Okay, okay, I'm not his girlfriend. I can't just go to the hospital, can I?"

"Pipes, I'd like to see someone try and stop you."

She was already nodding. As usual, her little sister was right. If she stayed there and waited for news, she would go absolutely insane. "Did she say which hospital?"

"Grays Harbor Community. I already mapped it and it's half an hour away. They were brought to a hospital in Alaska first, then flown back here."

Piper yanked open a middle drawer in Brendan's dresser and grabbed the first shirt she could find, then ran for the bathroom. "In a helicopter? Oh my God, this is bad." She met her own wild eyes in the mirror over the sink. "I have to go. I'll call you in a while."

"Wait! How are you going to get there?"

"I'm stealing Brendan's truck. There has to be a spare key around here somewhere. He's such a spare-key guy." Her hand shook around the phone. "I'll call you. Bye."

It took her five minutes to put on Brendan's shirt and her hang-dried yoga pants from the day before. She found a spare toothbrush under the sink, used it in record time, and ran down the stairs while finger-combing her hair. After shoving her feet into her still-soaked sneakers, she began her search for the truck's spare key. It wasn't in any of the junk drawers or hanging from any convenient pegs. Where would Brendan put it?

Trying desperately not to dwell on the image of him in a hospital bed somewhere, unconscious and gravely injured, she jogged to the kitchen and climbed up on the counter, running her hand along the top of the cabinets. Jackpot.

She was out the door a few seconds later, sitting in the driver's seat of Brendan's big-ass truck. And dammit, his scent was there, too. So strong that she had to concentrate on punching the hospital name into her map app, cursing autocorrect every time it swapped out right letters for the wrong ones. "Come on," she whined. "Not today, Satan."

Finally, she was on her way, flooring it down the quiet, empty, debris-strewn streets of Westport and onto an unfamiliar highway. There was no one on the roads, and she hated that. It made last night's storm seem even more serious. More likely to cause casualties.

Please, please, please. Not Brendan.

Okay, fine. She wasn't planning on getting serious with the man, but she really, *really* needed him to be alive. If someone that vital and enduring and stubborn could be wiped off the face of the earth, what hope did the rest of them have?

She used her shoulder to wipe away the moisture dripping down her cheeks.

Not getting serious about Brendan.

Right.

It took her twenty-five minutes to reach the hospital, and it was as quiet as the roads. There were a couple of cars parked outside and a sleepy administrator manning the front desk. "Sanders. Taggart," she blurted.

The woman didn't look up from her computer screen as she directed Piper to the fourth floor, nodding toward the elevator bank across the lobby. Upon entering the elevator, her fingers paused over the button.

The fourth floor was the ICU.

No. No. No.

After pressing the button, she closed her eyes and breathed, in and out, in and out, all but throwing herself through the doors when they opened. More lack of activity greeted her. Shouldn't doctors and nurses be rushing around trying to save Brendan? Her wet sneakers squelched on the linoleum floor of the dim hallway as she made her way to the information desk. There was nobody there. Should she wait or just start checking rooms?

A nurse left one room and ran to another, a clipboard in her hand.

Going to see Brendan? Was something wrong?

Heart in her throat, she crept toward the room where the nurse had gone—

"Piper?"

She whirled at the sound of Brendan's deep voice. And there he was in his signature jeans, beanie, and sweatshirt, the sleeves pushed up to his elbows. Above his head, the hallway light flickered, and briefly, she wondered if that meant he was a ghost. But no. No, there was his scent, the furrow of his dark brow, that baritone. He was there. Alive alive alive. Thank God. His eyes were so green. Had she ever noticed how beautiful a shade they were? They were ringed with dark circles, but they were incredible. "Oh good," she croaked, his image rapidly blurring. "Y-you're okay." She tried to be subtle about swiping the tears from her eyes. "They just said there'd been an accident, so I . . . I just thought I would come check. To be neighborly and all."

"Neighborly."

His raspy voice sent a hot shiver down her spine. "Yes. I even brought you your truck."

Brendan took a step closer, his eyes looking less and less tired by the moment. "You were at my house?"

She nodded, backed up, narrowly missing a supply cart.

His chest rose and fell, and he stepped forward again. "Is that my shirt, honey?"

Honey. Why'd he have to go and call her that? "No, I have one just like it."

"Piper."

"Mmm?"

"Please. Please come here."

Brendan's heart hammered, the tendons in his hands aching from the strain of not reaching for her. She'd come to the hospital. In his clothes. Did she realize tears were spilling down her cheeks and she was shaking, head to toe? No, she didn't. Based on her flirty shoulder shrugs and attempts to wink, she thought she was playing it cool, and it made his chest burn.

This girl. He'd be keeping her. There was no way around it.

There had been a moment last night when he'd thought his luck might have run out, and there'd just been images of her, flashing back to back, and he'd railed at the unfairness of meeting Piper but not being given enough time to be with her. If they weren't at the outset of something real here, his gut was a filthy liar. If he was honest with himself, it had been trying to tell him Piper would be important from the second he saw her in her floppy hat through the window of No Name.

"Piper."

"Mmm?"

"Please. Please come here."

She shook her head, stopped trying to put on a brave smile. "Why? So you can put me in the recharging station? You have the most dangerous job in the *country*, Brendan." Her lower lip wobbled. "I don't want your hugs."

His brow arched. "Recharging station?"

"That's what I call it . . ." Still backing away from him, she flipped her hair back, sniffed. "Never mind."

"When I hug you?" *Fuck.* His heart was turning over and over like a car engine. "My hugs are your recharging station?"

"Stop assigning meaning to my words."

An obstruction formed in his throat, and he had a feeling he'd never be able to swallow it. Not as long as she looked up at him, all beauty and strength and vulnerability and confusion and complications. "I should have called, but I left my phone on the boat and it's been hectic transporting him here on the helicopter. I didn't have time to find another phone, and then I worried you'd be sleeping." He paused. "Can you be mad at me while I kiss you, baby? It's all I've wanted to do for the last two weeks."

"Yeah, okay," she whispered, reversing directions and coming toward him. She jogged the final step and leapt. He made a gruff sound, wrapping his arms around her as tight as possible, and lifted her off the ground when her trembles increased.

"No, honey. No shaking." He planted kisses in hair that smelled suspiciously like his shampoo. "I'm fine. I'm right here."

Her face pressed into the crook of his neck. "What happened?"

"Sanders has a concussion. Bad one. A wave sent him sliding down the deck, and he clocked himself on one of the steel traps. We got back to Dutch and took him to the hospital." He rubbed circles on her back. "I left Fox in charge of bringing the crab to market and flew back with Sanders this morning."

"Is he going to be okay?"

"Yeah. He is."

She nodded, wrapped her arms tighter around his neck. "And the hydraulic system worked well the whole trip? No problems with the oil pressure?"

With an exhaled laugh, he angled his head back to meet her eyes. "Did you do a little googling while I was gone?"

"Maybe a little," she said, burying her face farther into his neck. "Are you sure you want to kiss me with my eyes all red and puffy?"

He fisted her hair gently, tugging until they were nose to nose. "I especially want to kiss you with your eyes all red and puffy."

The moment their mouths collided, Brendan knew he'd made a mistake. He should have waited to kiss her until they were home in his bed, because the uncertainty of the last eleven days reared back and punched him. It did the same to Piper—he could feel it.

She gave a broken moan and opened her sweet mouth for him, her breath coming in short pants almost immediately, just like his. He'd barely slid his tongue between her lips when she gripped his shoulders, drew herself high against his chest, and slung her legs around his waist. And Jesus, he'd already been halfway to hard, but his cock surged against his fly now, swelling like a motherfucker when she settled the warm give of her sex on top of him, the drag of friction making him curse. Making him wish they were anywhere but a hospital hallway, half an hour from his house.

Still, he couldn't keep from kissing her like he'd been dreaming of doing every night since he'd left, roughly, hungrily, using his hold on her hair to guide her left, right, meeting her lips with wide slants of his own, swallowing down her little whimpers like they were his last meal. God. God, she tasted so fucking good. Better than any port after a storm.

Home. He'd made it.

"Piper," he growled, taking two steps and flattening her against the closest wall, his mouth raking down her delicious neck, his left hand sliding up to cup her tits. "I can't fuck you here, baby. But that's exactly what I'm going to do if we keep at it like this."

Dazed blue eyes met his, her mouth wet from kissing. "I need you now," she said hoarsely, tugging on the collar of his shirt. "Now, now, Brendan. Please, I can't wait."

He learned something about himself in that moment. If this woman tacked the word "please" onto any request, he would find a way to fulfill it.

Build me a palace, please.

How many floors, baby?

Brendan was already carrying her to the darker end of the hospital corridor before she finished phrasing her demand. Thank Christ the floor was mostly empty, because nothing was going to stop him from getting inside her now. Not when she was scoring his neck with her teeth, her thighs clinging to his hips like ivy. He stopped in front of the farthest door from the mild action in Sanders's room, looked through the glass to make sure there was nobody occupying it, then brought her inside, capturing her mouth in a kiss as he walked them to the far side of the room. She rode her pussy up and down the rigid length of him, mewling into his mouth and pulling at his shirt, and Jesus, he was so turned on, their surroundings were inconsequential in comparison. Still, he wouldn't have someone walking in and seeing Piper in a private moment—that was for his eyes only—so he forced himself to focus. Just long enough to make it right.

He set Piper down on her feet and called on his willpower to tear himself away from her mouth. "Don't move," he said, propping her against the wall—yes, propped. Her legs didn't appear to be working, and hell if he wasn't gratified to know he wasn't so far out of practice that he couldn't get Piper hot and bothered. Thank God.

Wanting to get his hands back on her as soon as possible, he charged to the door and shoved a chair under the handle. On his return to the far side of the room, he yanked the curtain that would block them from view, in case anyone walked past. Then he was in front of Piper, framing her face in his hands, marveling over the feverish urgency in her eyes. For him. Less than twelve hours ago, he'd been sure his luck had run out, but he'd been wrong. It overflowed.

She ran her hands up under his sweatshirt, her fingernails dragging through his chest hair. "Will you take your shirt off for me?" she whispered, scrubbing the ridges of his abdomen with the heels of her hands. "Please? I love your body."

"That's my line," he said unevenly, rocked by her confession. Yeah, he took care of himself and the work kept his body strong and able, but he was a damn long way from perfect. Not like her. But as he'd already discovered, if Piper said please, he would comply, and he did so now, tugging off the sweatshirt in one quick move, finding her mouth as soon as his head was free of the collar.

Lips seeking and wet, their kiss escalated to the point of no return again. They both wrestled with the waistband of her yoga pants, shoving them down past her hips, lower until she could kick them away. And then she was back to climbing him, her lithe thighs skimming up to his waist, his hips punching forward to get his cock up against her softness, pinning her to the wall in the process.

"Noticed we didn't have to get any panties off," he said in between kisses, finding her incredible ass with both hands and kneading her buns almost angrily, because Jesus, this thing drove him fucking crazy. "You drive here in my truck with a bare pussy, Piper?"

She bit his bottom lip, tugged. "Slept in your bed with it, too."

"Christ." A rumble started in his chest, didn't stop until he'd drawn off the borrowed shirt she wore, dropping it to the ground, leaving her completely, blessedly naked. Naked and wrapped around him, all messy morning hair and eyes puffy from crying over him. If his cock wasn't throbbing with pain, he might have gotten down on his knees and worshiped her. All those moments on the boat, begging to see her one more time, had been well founded. If anything, he should have begged harder, because she was a siren, an angel of mercy, and a horny woman all rolled into one. A fucking dream.

And she was trying like hell to get the fly of his jeans open.

Brendan aided her, undoing the top snap, wincing as he lowered the zipper and his cock surged, filling with even more pressure now that it had room to breathe. It crowded into the notch between her legs, and she whimpered, digging her heels into his ass to bring him closer—and he came, grinding against her slippery flesh. One thrust and he'd be home.

That's when the worst possible thing occurred to him.

"Goddammit, Piper." His life flashed before his eyes. "I don't have a condom."

She paused in the act of laying kisses on his neck, her breath hitching. "You're lying. Please tell me you're lying."

"I'm not. I don't carry them." Her head fell back on a sob, and he couldn't stop himself from licking the sexy line of her throat, catching his teeth on her earlobe. "I didn't think I'd see you . . ."

Their heads turned at the same time, another kiss pulling them deep deep deep, and his hips pumped involuntarily, moving in the act of fucking, his shaft sliding up and back through the smooth lips of her sex without breaching her entrance.

"Brendan," she panted.

"Yes, baby."

"I had a physical. Right before I left." They breathed hard against each other's mouths. "I'm all clear and I'm on the shot and I just need you so bad. So bad."

He dropped his face into her neck and growled, reached between them to fist his erection. "I'm all clear, too. Piper, Jesus, are you going to let me fuck you bare?"

"Yes. Yes."

She purred that second "yes," and his balls cinched up painfully, making him grit his teeth, mentally ordering himself not to come too fast. But when he notched his first few inches inside of her wet heat, it became obvious what a challenge that would be. "God, baby. God." He rocked deeper, and she gasped. "You're tighter than sin."

By the time he filled her completely, she was shaking like a fucking leaf, and he had to focus, focus on staying still. Just long enough to organize his lust, garner some semblance of control, or he'd just take her in a frenzy. He just needed a minute. Just a minute.

"Rough," she sobbed, her back arching off the wall. "Want you rough."

There went his minute.

Brendan's first upward thrust drove her up the wall, and she choked on a scream, those beautiful blue eyes glazing over. He clapped a palm over her mouth and pumped again, harder, their eyes meeting over the curve of his hand. There was a coiling in the dead center of his chest, and it must have registered on his face because something flared in her gaze. A ripple of panic in the lake of her lust.

She pushed his hand away slowly, her expression changing. Her eyelids dropped to half-mast, and she looked up at him through the veil of them, biting her lip. "Does this feel good?" Rhythmically, she squeezed him with the walls of her pussy, humming in her throat, killing him slowly. "Are my thighs open wide enough for you, Captain?"

His legs almost gave out, but he held on. Held on, even though part of him was so starved for release that he was tempted to let her make this just about sex. Even though she'd slept in his bed, worried for him enough to show up at the hospital crying. But he would fight this battle with her as many times as it took. Until she realized he wasn't falling for it and there was more here. A hell of a lot more.

Brendan glued his mouth to her ear and started to fuck—hard—her legs jostling around his hips with every vicious thrust. "Came here to be neighborly, Piper? Is there anything neighborly about the way I'm giving you this cock?"

God, he loved the way she whined his name in response.

"I was out in the middle of a fucking storm thinking about you. Thinking about how pretty you look in my garden. Thinking about you waiting for me at the end of my dock, in my harbor. Standing there in the sunset so I can touch you before I even touch land." He opened his lips on the pulse at her neck, razing the spot with his teeth, his hips moving in hard punches. "I thought about your mouth and your eyes and your legs and your pussy. I never stopped. Now you knock that phony shit off, baby, and tell me you missed me."

She inhaled hard, her fingers curling on his shoulders. "I missed you."

A balm spread over his heart, even as his need, his urgency, wrenched higher, hotter. "You can wrap me as tight as you want around that little finger, but I won't play games about what this is. Get me, Piper?"

Their eyes locked just before their mouths did. They knew the battle of wills was far from over, but their hunger was going to eclipse it for now. He took hold of her ass and hefted her higher against the wall, jerking her knees up and propping them on his hips. He angled himself deep, inward and up, so he could hit that spot inside of her—and he went at her hard. Her throaty whimpers told him to stay right there, keep delivering, and he did. He put a lock on the hot seed inside of him dying to get loose and focused on the way her face changed every time he increased his pace. It went from optimistic to astonished to desperate.

"Oh my God, Brendan, don't s-stop." Her eyes lost focus, her nails digging into the skin of his shoulders. "Harder. Harder. You're going to . . . you're going to make me . . ."

"Every time, Piper." Out on the water, he'd replayed Piper having an orgasm while he licked her clit on his kitchen table about a thousand times, but feeling it happen around his cock flipped some primal switch inside of him, and he let loose, pressing their foreheads together and drilling into her sweet, snug channel that was already starting to convulse. "Come on, baby. Let's have it. Show me what I do to that high-maintenance pussy."

Her mouth formed an O, and she tightened up, her hands slapping at his shoulders—and then she crashed, her flesh rippling around him. She writhed between him and the wall, fighting the pleasure and requiring it at the same time, her eyes wide and seeing nothing. "Brendan. Jesus Christ. Jesus Christ. *Brendan*."

Hearing his name on her lips pushed him past his breaking point, and the seal ripped off his resistance. The bottom of his spine twisted, molten lust impacting him low, hard, more urgently than he'd ever felt anything. Piper's legs went limp right as he came, but she held on to him tight as he bucked. Lifting her feet off the floor until the last of the unbelievable pressure left him. And he collapsed against her.

"*Holy . . .*" she breathed into his neck. "Holy shit."

His heart pounded in his jugular. "Couldn't agree more."

She puffed a dazed laugh.

He kissed her temple, pulled back to search her eyes. "Don't tense up on me, Piper."

"I'm not sure I'll ever be tense again," she whispered, her lids falling.

With a chest full of pride, Brendan kissed her forehead, cheeks, mouth, then knelt down and kissed her belly, picking up her borrowed shirt before straightening. He dropped it over her head, helping her put both arms through the holes, and zipped himself back into his jeans. With Piper still leaning against the wall in a stupor that he definitely didn't mind, he found a box of tissues, plucked out a handful, and cleaned his spend off the insides of her thighs.

That last part woke her up. "I can do that," she said, reaching for the tissue box.

He caught her wrist. "I like doing it."

"Brendan . . ." Her swallow was audible. "Just because I missed you . . ."

There it was. "Yeah?"

"Well . . ." She stooped down and collected her pants, dragging them up her legs with trembling hands. "I—I'm worried I'm leading you on—"

"Jesus." He laughed without humor, took a moment to pull his sweatshirt over his head, and ignored the pinch in his chest. "I can only imagine what kind of idiots you've dated, Piper. But I'm not one of them. I'm a grown-ass man, and I know where we stand. I know you're going to make me work for you, and I'm not scared of it."

Her eyes went momentarily dreamy, but she snapped out of it fast. "Work for me? There's nothing to work for!"

"What the hell does that mean?" he barked.

"It means . . ." She wrung her hands. "I'm . . . I'm not available to be your girlfriend."

Brendan sighed. Was he annoyed? Yes. Did he want to be anywhere else in the world? No. And that was fucking confusing, but apparently it was what he enjoyed now. Being confused and charmed and pulled apart over this woman. "What do you want to call this, Piper? Let's compromise."

"Friends with benefits?"

"No."

"Why?"

He reached out, cupped her pussy roughly through the Lycra of her yoga pants, teasing the seam with his middle finger. "This is a hell of a lot more than a benefit."

Piper swayed.

He removed his hand quickly and caught her, gathering her up against his chest. "How about we call ourselves 'more than friends'?"

"That's too broad. It could mean anything." She rubbed absent circles on his chest while he counted her eyelashes. "Married people are more than friends."

It was too soon to examine why he liked the word "married" on her lips so much, right? "We'll go with 'more than friends,'" he rumbled, kissing her before she could protest. It took her a few seconds to participate, but their mouths quickly turned breathless. He backed her against the wall once more, Piper's palm molding to the front of his jeans where his cock rose again, ready, desperate for more of her—

"Brendan Taggart, please make your way to the fourth-floor information desk," came a tired voice over the PA system, repeating itself twice while they remained frozen mid-kiss.

"Fuck," he ground out, breathing through his nose and willing his hard-on to subside. There was no way it was happening, though, so he adjusted himself to be as inconspicuous as possible, then took Piper's hand and tugged her toward the door. "Come with me."

"Oh." He looked back over his shoulder to find Piper patting her haphazard hair in a way he found adorable. "Um. Okay."

Brendan moved the chair he'd braced under the door handle, and they walked side by side into the dim hospital hallway. He looked down at her, trying to puzzle together how she felt about the label "more than friends." This conversation, this war, was far from over, but he couldn't help but feel like he'd won a battle, just getting her to hold his hand as if it was the natural thing to do. *You're not getting rid of me, Piper.*

"Brendan?"

The sound of his father-in-law's voice caused a hitch in his stride. Brendan tore his attention off of Piper to find Mick loitering by the information desk. "Mick."

His father-in-law went still, dismay marring his features as he split a look between Brendan and Piper. Their joined hands. Piper's messy hair. And for a few seconds, Brendan couldn't stave off the guilt. Not completely. But only because he should have gone to Mick, told the man about his feelings for Piper. Blindsiding him like this was the last thing Brendan wanted to do. He'd never seen Brendan with anyone but his daughter, and the shock had to bite.

Distracted by his regrets, he didn't react quickly enough to Piper pulling her hand away.

He tried to get it back, but it was too late.

"Hey, Mick," she said quietly, wetting her lips.

Mick didn't respond. In fact, he blatantly ignored Piper, and Brendan felt a surge of anger. This was his fault, though. He'd missed a crucial step, and now here they were, in this awkward situation that could have been avoided. And dammit, the last thing he needed was to hand Piper another reason to keep distance between them.

"Oh good," said a smiling nurse, stepping behind the desk. "You found him."

"Just came to check on Sanders," Mick mumbled, jerking his thumb at nowhere in particular.

"Oh, um. I'm going to . . ." Piper started. "I, um . . . You can get a ride back with Mick, right?" She wouldn't look at him, was already edging toward the elevators. "Hannah is probably wondering where I am. I should head home."

Brendan followed Piper, catching her by the elbow before she could hit the call button. "Stay. We'll drive home together."

"Stop." She batted his chest playfully, falling back on flirting. "You totally have to stay here and make sure Sanders is okay. I'll just see you later!"

"Piper."

"Brendan," she echoed, mimicking his serious face while her finger desperately punched the elevator button. "It's fine, okay?" When he still hesitated to let go of her elbow, she lost her bravado and begged him with her eyes. "Please."

With a stiff nod, he watched her disappear behind the doors of the elevator, already missing the weight of her hand inside his. He wanted to go after her, at least kiss her before she drove home, but had a feeling she needed space. He just hoped the headway they'd made this morning on the journey to "more than friends" hadn't been erased in a matter of minutes.

Duty and respect pulled at him, so while he vowed to make things right with Piper later, he turned on a heel and went to face his father-in-law.

Mick put up a hand as Brendan reached him. "You don't have to explain, Brendan. I know you're a young man with oats to sow." He rubbed at the back of his neck. "Not a lot of fellas who'd be able to ignore a girl like that."

"No. She's . . . impossible to ignore." He'd made it all of one day, hadn't he? Less? Before she'd started feeling . . . inevitable. Brendan couldn't help glancing back at the elevator. When he turned around, Mick was fixated on his ring finger. The lack of hardware surrounding it, rather. The lines around Mick's eyes turned stark white and a sheen filled them.

Brendan hated the feeling of disloyalty that burrowed under

his skin. Logically, he knew there was nothing disloyal about him pursuing Piper. Not at all. But this man who'd taken Brendan under his wing, made him the captain of his boat, and been a damn good friend and father figure . . . shit, disappointing him burned. It was right there on the tip of his tongue to explain that he was serious about Piper, not sowing oats, but Mick seeing he'd finally taken off his wedding ring was enough for one day. He didn't need to hit the man over the head. Not when he probably saw the lack of Brendan's ring as one more piece of his daughter being chipped away.

He clapped Mick on the shoulder. "Let's go check on Sanders, all right?"

Mick, obviously grateful for the change of subject, nodded, and they walked side by side to the wing where Sanders was healing.

Chapter Nineteen

$\mathcal{P}$iper dragged herself up the steps to the apartment and unlocked the door. Out of concern for her growling stomach, she'd stopped for coffee and breakfast on the ride home, making it close to noon. She'd already texted Hannah to let her know Brendan and the crew were fine, then promptly ignored all the follow-up questions about how things went at the hospital. Because . . . how *did* things go at the hospital?

Still not in possession of concrete answers, she trudged into the apartment carrying a cinnamon dolce latte for Hannah, half expecting her sister to be working at the record shop, but Hannah was lying on the top bunk, obligatory headphones over her ears, wailing about a simple twist of fate.

Piper knocked on the frame of the bunk bed, and Hannah yelped, shooting up into a sitting position and knocking the headphones onto the cradle of her neck. Her startled expression turned quickly to delight. "Oooh. For me?"

Piper handed her sister the cup. "Hmm."

Hannah raised an eyebrow while taking a sip. "You look . . . different today."

"I took a shower last night and slept with wet hair," Piper murmured absently, sitting down on the bottom bunk. She stared at the far wall of the apartment—which was actually quite *near*—and tried to process the last few hours.

Her sister hopped down from the top bunk. "Piper." She snuggled close, nudging Piper in the ribs with an elbow. "You're too quiet. Talk to me."

Piper pressed her lips together and said nothing.

"Oh, come on."

Silence.

"Start small. Something innocuous. How was the drive?"

"I don't remember." Unable to keep a certain piece of news to herself any longer, though she would probably regret sharing at a later date, Piper reached over and clutched Hannah's knee. "Hannah, he . . . he gave me a vaginal orgasm."

Her sister almost dropped her coffee. "What? Like . . . you climaxed just from penetration?"

"Yes," Piper whispered, fanning her face. "It was like, I thought . . . maybe? And then . . . no way. But then, yes. Yes, yes, fucking *yes*. Against a wall. *A wall*, Hanns." She closed her eyes and added, "It was the most wonderful sex of my life. And he didn't even break a sweat."

"Oh, Piper." Hannah shook her head. "You are so fucked."

"No." Piper threw her shoulders back. "No, I escaped without too much damage. He got me to admit we're more than friends, but there was minimal cuddling and we have no plans to see each other again. I'll just avoid him for a while."

Hannah lunged to her feet and turned on Piper. "What are you scared of?"

Piper snorted. "I'm not scared."

And she wasn't. Was she? This constant weight in her belly was totally normal. As was the certainty that Brendan would eventually realize there were a thousand other girls just like Piper Bellinger; she was definitely not the kind of girl for whom a man kept a ring on for seven years, that's for sure!

She was just an exotic bird in this small, uneventful town, and he'd realize that eventually.

Or he wouldn't.

That was even *more* terrifying.

What if his feelings for her were actually genuine? She couldn't fight her own much longer. They were getting worse by the day. She'd driven like a bat out of hell to the hospital, already half in mourning. Sick with it. And the *joy* when he'd arrived, hale and hearty. My God, she was almost exhausted thinking about the gymnastics her heart had done.

If these feelings got deeper and deeper on both sides . . . then what?

She stayed in Westport?

"Ha!"

Hannah uncapped her coffee and took a long swig, swallowing. "You realize you're having a conversation inside your own head, right? I can't hear it."

"I'm not staying here," Piper breathed, her heart feathering in her throat. "He can't make me." She yanked her phone out of her pocket, tapping until she arrived at Instagram, scanning her colorful feed. These pictures and the effortless lifestyle they represented seemed almost foreign now—trite—and that was scary. Did it mean she was actually considering a *new* path? One she didn't document for the sake of adoration, albeit phony? Her daily life in Westport was fulfilling in a way she never expected, but she was still an outsider here. In LA, her fit was seamless, at least outwardly. She was good at being Piper Bellinger, socialite. Whether Piper could be a fixture in Westport remained to be seen.

She held up her phone, facing the stream of pictures toward Hannah. "For better or worse, this girl is who I am, right? I'm getting so far away from this Piper. So fast."

"Okay," Hannah said slowly. "Does Brendan make you feel like you need to change?"

Piper thought about it. "No. He even called my pussy high maintenance, like in a good way. I think he *likes* me like this. It's horrible."

"Yeah, it sounds like the worst. What is the real problem, Piper?"

Piper exploded. "Hannah, I was scared shitless last night!"

Her sister nodded, sobering. "I know."

"And he's not even my boyfriend."

"Yet."

"Rude." She brandished her phone. "This girl is not . . . strong enough. To worry like this all the time. To love someone and lose them, like Mom and Opal lost Henry. I'm not cut from that cloth, Hannah. I go to fucking parties and push bathing suit brands. I don't know who I *am* in Westport."

Hannah closed the distance between them, wrapping her arms around Piper. "Wow. A vaginal orgasm and a psychological breakthrough in the same day. You must be tapped."

"I am. I'm exhausted." She returned Hannah's hug, dropping her forehead unceremoniously into her sister's neck. She thought of Mick's face when he saw her holding Brendan's hand and cringed inwardly. Honestly, she wasn't even ready to tell Hannah about that moment. How low she'd felt. Not necessarily a home-wrecker, but . . . an interloper. An outsider. *Who does this LA party girl think she is, coming in here and trying to fill the shoes of a born-and-bred fisherman's wife?*

Piper's phone dinged.

Who was that?

It couldn't be Brendan. He'd left his phone on the boat. And none of her friends had reached out with so much as a hello since she'd left the Bel-Air zip code.

She held up the screen, and a smile bloomed across her face. "Oh, this is excellent news."

Hannah dropped her arms away from Piper's neck. "What is it?"

"It's Friday night and our grandmother is finally ready to party."

Never one to take partying lightly, Piper wasted no time.

She showered, coiffed until her hair looked presentable, carefully applied her makeup, and ventured purposefully toward the harbor with a garment bag containing a selection of dresses, including one for herself. Opal was petite, and with a little last-minute stitching, Piper would have her looking like a boss bitch in no time.

The second Opal opened the door—wearing a seriously cute lavender shortie robe—Piper could tell she was having second thoughts. "Nope." Piper cut her off with a kiss, right on the mouth. "Everyone gets pre-party jitters, Opal. You hear me? Everyone. But we don't let that stop us, do we? No. We persevere. And we get drunk until we feel nothing."

Visibly bolstered, Opal nodded, then went straight to shaking her head. "I'm a lightweight. I've been drinking nothing but coffee since the nineties."

"Sad. But that's why we use the Bellinger method. One glass of water between each alcoholic drink. Then a piece of toast and two Advil before bedtime. Soaks it right up. You'll be able to run a marathon tomorrow morning."

"I can't run one now."

"I know. That's how well it works."

Opal guffawed. "Since you started visiting me, Piper, I've laughed more than I have in decades. Hannah wasn't able to make it?"

"No, she had a shift at the record shop. But she sends a kiss."

Her grandmother nodded and transferred her attention to the garment bag, missing the unexpected moisture that danced in Piper's eyes. "Well, darling. Let's see what you got."

It only took three hours to transform Opal from grieving semi-hermit to a lady about town. After Piper added some styling mousse to the older woman's hair and did her makeup, Opal chose her dress.

Clearly, she had taste, because she went straight for the puff-sleeved Versace.

"The student has become the master, Grandma."

Opal started a little at the title, and Piper held her breath, too. It had slipped out unplanned, but felt oddly natural. Finally, Opal surged forward and wrapped Piper in a hug, holding tight a few moments before stepping back to study her. "Thank you."

Piper could only nod, thanks to the log jammed in her throat, watching Opal as she swept off to the bedroom to change. Surprised to find her fingers trembling, Piper sloughed off the leggings and sweater she'd worn for the trip over, zipping herself into a green-and-black zebra-striped minidress from Balmain. Muscle memory kicked in, and she lifted her phone to take a selfie, noticing with a start that she had a text from Brendan.

Want to see you tonight.

Wave after wave of flutters coursed through her midsection. God, she loved how he got right to the point. No games. No beating around the bush. Just *This is what I want, baby. Now it's your turn.*

Did she want to see Brendan? Yes. Undeniably yes. More than that, she wanted to be seen by him looking like this. Wanted to watch male appreciation draw his features tight and know with absolute conviction he was thinking about having sex with her. And it would be so much easier to play it cool in her battle armor, surrounded by witnesses in a bar. Westport's nightlife might not be *exactly* what Piper was used to, but it was closer to her environment than a bar under construction or a hospital with bad lighting.

She needed to feel like herself. Needed a reminder of her old life.

The life she was going back to. Sooner rather than later.

Too often lately she'd been thrown off-kilter by her feelings. Or the situation she found herself in, over a thousand miles from home. Friendless, a fish out of water.

Brendan, since she'd met him, had made it impossible for her to keep up a pretense. She'd never been able to be anything but honest with him. Scarily honest. But he wasn't standing in front of her now, brimming with all that intensity, was he? And LA Piper was rattling her hinges, demanding to be appeased. *That* Piper wouldn't text back that she wanted to see him tonight, too. Uh-uh. She'd leave a bread crumb and dance off in a flash of strobe lights.

Heading out for the night. Maybe catch you later in Blow the Man Down. xo

Three little dots popped up, letting her know Brendan was writing back.

Then they went away.

She pressed a hand to her stomach to counteract a kick of excitement.

Opal walked out of the bathroom looking like a certified snack.

"Well?"

"Well?" Piper gave a low whistle. "Look out, Westport. There's a stone-cold fox on the loose."

Piper's one and only experience in Blow the Man Down had been less than stellar and walking through the door again was nerve-racking. But tonight wasn't just about reminding herself of old Piper; it was about bringing this woman she'd really come to like out of her shell.

Opal had her arm linked through Piper's as they entered the noisy bar. Fishermen occupied the long row of stools near the entrance, toasting another week completed out on the water. And the survival of last night's storm seemed to give the atmosphere an added buoyancy. Bartenders dropped pints in front of mostly older men, their friends and wives. No one was smoking, but the scent of cigarettes drifted in from outside and clung to clothes. Neil Young's voice wove through the conversations and laughter.

Opal balked as soon as they stepped over the threshold, but Piper patted her arm, guiding her through the more boisterous section of the bar, toward the seating area in the back. Last time, she'd only stood at the bar long enough to order that fateful tray of shots, but it had been enough time to get the lay of the land. And she was relieved to see the tables in the rear of Blow the Man Down were occupied by women again tonight. Some of them were Opal's age, others were closer to Piper's, and they were all talking at once.

A couple of the older women nudged each other at Opal's appearance. One by one, the dozen or so ladies started to notice her. For long moments, they stared at her with mouths agape—and then they all ambushed her at once.

"Opal," said a kind-looking woman with a red bob, rising to her feet. "You're out!"

"And looking like hot shit!" inserted another.

Laughter rippled over the tables, and Piper could sense Opal's pleasure. "Well, I have a fancy stylist now," Opal told them, squeezing Piper's arm. "My granddaughter."

Westport was a small town, and it was obvious some of the women already knew the Bellinger sisters had taken up residence, as well as their familial connection to Opal, while others were visibly connecting the dots and marveling. Either way, the group as a whole seemed surprised to see them out together and looking so close.

"Is there . . . room for two more?" Opal asked.

Everyone shuffled at once, dragging chairs over from other tables. Opal's eyes held a suspicious luster when she looked up at Piper and let out a breath. "It's like I never left."

Piper leaned over and kissed her cheek. "Why don't you go sit down. I'll go grab us some drinks. Tequila for you, right?"

"Oh, stop." Opal tapped her arm playfully. "Stoli and Seven with two limes, please."

"Damn," Piper muttered with a smile, as Opal walked off. The older woman claimed a chair and was immediately heaped with well-deserved attention. "I have a feeling you'll be just fine."

Piper bought a round of drinks for her and Opal, taking a seat beside her. After half an hour of easy conversation, the evening appeared to be shaping up as a low-key lady hangout. Until one of the twentysomething girls bought Piper a drink in exchange for a beauty consultation. Really, the drink hadn't been necessary. She was happy to dole out advice based on the girl's skin tone and oval face shape . . . but then another girl slapped down a shot in front of Piper, wanting to know her beauty regimen. Another traded a lemon drop for tips on dressing sexy when it was always "balls-ass cold and raining" in the winter.

And then it all went downhill from there.

"It's all about swagger," Piper shouted over the music an hour later, an eye squinted so she would only see one set of people, instead of two.

Unless there were two sets? When did they get there?

She tried to remember what she'd been saying in the first place. Had all of it been a slurred mess? But no, the girls who'd pushed tables to the side to create a runway down the back of Blow the Man Down were listening to her with rapt focus. *Deliver, Piper.* "You, me, all of us, ladies. We wield the power." She threw out a finger aimed at the bar full of men. "They know it. They know we know it. The secret is to show them we know that they know that we know. Does that make sense?"

A chorus of yeses went up, followed by the clinking of glasses.

"Watch me walk," Piper said, pushing her hair back over her shoulders and strutting along the floorboards, turning on a dime at the end of her makeshift runway. Not her best work, but pretty decent after four, maybe eight drinks. "Look at my face. It's like, I don't have time for *your* shit. I'm busy. I'm living!"

"Is this going to get me laid?" one girl asked.

Piper grabbed the girl's face and stared into her soul. "Yes."

"I believe you."

"Hey, Piper." Another girl stumbled into view. Or was she twins? "Labor Day is coming up. We should have a party and try out the makeup tips."

"Oh my gosh," Piper breathed, the best/worst idea breaking through her delightful drunkenness. "I should throw the party. I own a *bar*."

"Hey, everyone! Piper is throwing a Labor Day party!"

The cheers were deafening.

"Show us the walk again!"

Piper took a shot someone offered her. "Screw that! Let's dance!"

Chapter Twenty

*B*rendan leaned against the wall of Blow the Man Down, arms crossed, a quiet smile on his face as he watched Piper weave her magic over everyone in her vicinity.

She was shit-faced—and adorable.

Everyone who spoke to Piper got her undivided attention and walked away like she'd just imparted the secrets of the universe. She forged connections to people, damn near instantaneously, and they loved her. Did she realize she was doing it?

Someone shouted at the bartender to play Beyoncé, and tables were shoved even farther out of the way, transforming the space from Piper's personal runway to a dance floor, and all he could do was stand there and watch her, his pulse thickening—along with another part of his anatomy—at the way she worked her hips, arms loose and careless over her head, eyes dreamy. She was drawing attention from a lot of men at the bar, and frankly, he didn't like it, but Piper was the girl he'd fallen for. Being jealous came with the territory.

Piper went still on the dance floor, a frown marring her forehead, and, as if she'd finally sensed his presence, turned to look directly at him. And when her face transformed with pure joy and she waved enthusiastically, Brendan knew he loved her.

God knew, it had happened fast, but he'd been incapable of putting the brakes on.

Not when she was the destination.

His mouth turned dry, but he managed to wave back.

This wasn't any emotion he'd experienced before. Not like the simple companionship of his marriage. Not like the love/hate bond he had with the ocean. What he felt for Piper turned him into a young man in the throes of his first infatuation, while also calling on the deepest roots of his maturity. In other words, to keep this woman, he'd step up and do whatever it took, but his fucking heart would be racing the whole time.

He could put every ounce of his effort into keeping Piper, and she still might leave. Could dance off into the sunset at a moment's notice and go back to her extravagant life, leaving him reeling. And that terrified him the most.

But Brendan determinedly set aside those dark thoughts. Because she was coming toward him now, all flushed from liquor and dancing, and he simply opened his arms, trusting she'd walk straight into them. His eyes closed automatically when she did, his mouth tracing her hairline, planting kisses. Christ, she fit against him in a way that made him feel protective, ready to act as her shield, while also making him hard, hungry.

"You're here," she murmured happily, going up on her toes to sniff his neck.

"Of course I'm here, baby."

"Sanders is okay? The crew made it back?"

"Sanders is home," he burred against her ear, warmed by

her worry for his men. "The rest of them, too. They reached the harbor just a little while ago."

"I'm so glad." She sent an accusatory look over her shoulder. "These unscrupulous local women made me drunk."

"I can see that." His lips twitched, his hand rubbing circles in the center of her back. "You want to dance some more, or can I bring you home?"

"Where is home?"

"With me."

"Mmmm." She looked up at him through one eye. "I don't have my wits about me, Brendan. You can't use anything I say tonight against me. It's all a wash."

"Okay, I promise."

"Good, because I missed you. Again." She kissed his chin, worked her way around to his ear, whined against it in a way that made his cock stiffen. "This morning with you was the best, best, best sex of my life."

She said it right as the music cut out.

Everyone at the bar heard it.

A couple of men saluted Brendan with their pints, but thankfully drunk Piper was none the wiser about her public confession. And hell, having Piper effectively tell everyone in Westport they were sleeping together—and that so far he'd been great at it—was one way to appease his jealousy.

The music started again, but she didn't seem compelled to do anything but stand there and hug him, which suited him down to the ground. "Here I am, once again, in the *recharg*-ing station!" Piper sang, giggling to herself. "I like it here. It's so warm. You're a big hard teddy bear from the sea. Like tuna from the sea, but with a bear."

Brendan's laugh turned heads. "I like drunk Piper."

"You should. I have zero inhibitions right now." She smelled his neck again, kissed it once, twice. "Or whatever number is less than zero."

He ran a hand down her hair. "All I'm doing to you tonight is putting you in bed."

"Ooh, do I get to sleep in the recharging station?"

His heart was living in his throat. "Yeah, honey. You can sleep in it every night."

She sighed contentedly.

"On my way over, I saw Hannah walking home and stopped off to grab you an overnight bag."

"That was nice of you." In an instant, her expression went from swoony to worried. "But Brendan, what if I'm potpie?"

"What?"

"You took a bite of me, and even if you decide you don't really like me, you're going to be noble and eat the whole thing. You can't do anything halfway. It's all or nothing. If I'm potpie, you have to tell me. You can't just keep eating and eating and . . . I'm drunker than I thought."

Yeah, she might be drunk, but her worry was genuine. Her forlorn tone of voice made that obvious, and it troubled him. Not because there was even a chance it might be valid—she was a woman, not a fucking pie. Her worry bothered him because she didn't feel secure. Yet. And he needed to find a way to fix it.

"Let's go home," he said.

"Okay. Let me just make sure Opal has a ride."

Piper trotted off to confer with a group of woman, hugging each of them multiple times before making her way back to his side. Brendan wrapped an arm around her shoulders and guided her out of the bar. He'd parked his truck near the entrance, and he unlocked it now, boosting Piper into the passenger side and buckling her in. When he climbed into the driver's side, her head was lolling on the seat, and she was studying him. "We're going to talk about what you said. In the morning. When you're clearheaded and you'll remember what I say back."

"That's probably a good idea. I'm feeling very share-y right now."

"I'm tempted to let you share, so I know what I'm up against. But I don't want you telling me things and regretting it tomorrow."

She was silent as he pulled onto the road and took the first right. "You talk about being with me like it's a battle."

"It is, in a way. But I'm grateful I'm the one fighting it."

He could feel her studying his profile. "You're worth fighting for, too. If you got banished to LA for three months, I would pull out all the stops to keep you there." She paused. "Nothing would work, though. It's not real enough for you. You'd hate it."

"'Hate' is a strong word, honey. You would be there."

"Eh." She waved a hand. "There are thousands of me there."

Brendan snorted at her joke. And then he realized she was serious.

"Piper, there is *nobody* like you."

She smiled like she was humoring him.

"*Piper.*"

She looked startled by his tone. "Whoa. What?"

He pulled the car onto the side of the road, slammed on the

brakes, and threw it into park. "Did you hear me?" He reached over to tilt up her chin. "There is nobody like you."

"Why are you getting so worked up?"

"Because I . . ." He raked a hand through his hair. "I thought I was an intuitive man. A smart man. But I keep finding out new ways I'm flying blind when it comes to something so important. You. *You* are important. And I thought you were just scared of commitment. Or didn't think you could belong in Westport. But it's more than that, isn't it? You think I have some kind of passing interest in you? Like it could just change like the wind?"

"Everyone else does!" Her eyes flashed. With pain, with irritation. "Not just guys. My friends, my stepfather. I'm this season's color, in demand today, on the sales rack in Marshalls tomorrow. I'm just . . . momentary."

"Not to me." God, he wanted to shake her, kiss her, shake her some more. "Not to me."

She jerked her chin out of his grip, flounced back against the seat. "Can we just talk about this tomorrow, like you said?"

Brendan slammed the car back into drive. "Oh, we're going to talk about it."

"Good! Maybe I'll put together some talking points."

"Me too, baby."

They drove past No Name, and she made a small sound. Sniffed.

"What?" he asked, softening his tone.

"I was remembering the time you sent Abe to nail the memory foam to the top bunk. You're actually really thoughtful and wonderful, and I don't want to argue with you."

He almost blurted out *I love you*, right then and there, but buttoned it up at the last second. The moment was too volatile to throw that confession into the mix, but he didn't think he'd be able to keep it inside much longer. "I don't want to argue with you either, Piper. All I want to do is bring you home, put you in one of my shirts, and find out if you snore."

She gasped, some of the humor returning to her eyes. "I don't."

"We'll see."

"Do you have toast and Advil?"

"Yes."

They pulled into his driveway a moment later. Brendan got out and rounded the front bumper to Piper's side, smiling when she melted out into his arms. He held her and swayed for a few beats in the darkness, in what he thought might be a silent, mutual apology for shouting at each other on the drive home. And he wanted to do this for the rest of his life. Collect her from a night out with the girls, have her soft and pliant against him, be her man.

"You're not even going to make out with me tonight, are you?" Piper said, her voice muffled by his shoulder. "You probably think you'd be taking advantage of me."

Brendan sighed. "You've got it right."

She pouted up at him. "That's romantic and I hate it."

"How about I promise to make up for it tomorrow?"

"Can we negotiate a kiss good night?"

"I think I can manage that."

Appeased, she let him bring her inside. While he made her toast, she sat perched on his kitchen counter with a glass of water, looking so beautiful, he had to keep glancing over his shoulder, checking to see if she was real. That he hadn't dreamed her up.

"What are you thinking about?" she asked after swallowing a bite.

"That I like you being here." He braced his hands on the counter, dropped his mouth to her bare knees, and kissed them, in turn. "That I liked going into my bedroom today and finding a Piper-sized indent on my comforter." A thought occurred to him. "When did you come over?"

She gulped. Didn't answer.

"Not with that storm going on." His right eye was beginning to tic. "Right?"

Piper set down her toast, laid the back of her hand against her forehead. Wobbled dramatically. "I feel kind of faint, Brendan. I think I'm fading."

With a growl, he drew her off the counter. And with her legs hooked around his waist, he left the kitchen and carried her up the stairs. "I'll add it to my list of talking points for tomorrow."

She groaned, her fingers playing with the ends of his hair. "Tomorrow sounds like it's going to be a super-sexy good time."

"We'll get to that after."

"Before."

"After."

"Before *and* after."

Brendan set Piper down on the end of his bed, rocked by the rightness of having her there. Emotion crammed into his chest, but he turned away before she could see it. "Take off that dress." He opened his drawer, took out one of his favorites—a white, worn-in T-shirt with GRAYS HARBOR written in script in the middle. "Speaking of which, do you even own a pair of jeans—" He turned back around to find Piper sprawled out on his bed in a neon-purple thong. And nothing else. "That can't be comfortable to sleep in," he said hoarsely, already regretting his vow to give her a good-night kiss and nothing more.

She raised her knees. "I guess you have to come over here and take it off."

"Christ." The flesh in his jeans swelled, curving against his zipper, and he blew out an uneven breath. "If the ocean doesn't kill me, you will."

Just like that, her knees dropped back down, her arms coming up to cross over her breasts. And maybe he shouldn't have been shocked when tears rushed into her eyes, but he was. They made his throat constrict.

"God," he said thickly. "That was a stupid thing to say."

"It's okay."

"No, it's not." He lifted her up and pulled the T-shirt down over her head, holding her tight to his chest. "It's not okay. I'm sorry."

"We can add it to the talking points for tomorrow," she said, looking him in the eye long enough to make his heart beat triple time, then tugging him down into the pillows. "Want my kiss," she murmured against his lips, pulling him under with a slow, wet complication of tongues, her smooth, bare legs winding through his, her fingers pulling him closer by the waistband of his jeans until their lower bodies were locked together, soft against hard, man against woman. "Maybe we're a little more than more than friends," she whispered, tucking her head under his chin. "Good night, Brendan."

His eyelids fell like shutters, his arms pulling her closer.

I love you, he mouthed over her head.

He didn't fall asleep for hours.

Chapter Twenty-One

Homey sounds came from somewhere. Drawers opening and thudding softly, bare feet on a floor, the sputtering of a coffee maker. Piper cracked an eye open but didn't move. She couldn't, because she'd lose the sweet spot of warmth and fluffy bedclothes and the scent of Brendan. Best sleep of her life, hands down. She'd woken up at some point during the night having to pee and found herself locked into the recharging station, Brendan's soft breaths against the back of her neck. And she'd decided to hold it.

What did she say last night?

Something about potpies.

She also remembered trying to seduce him and failing. Womp.

Some shouting on the ride home.

No sex.

She'd just have to gauge his mood to find out if she'd said or done anything irredeemably embarrassing. There was a good chance she had, because otherwise he would still be in bed, right? Like, hello. Horny lady. *Right* here.

Piper's bladder screamed at her, and she sat up, grateful the Bellinger Method had worked, and padded to the bathroom. She ignored the gooey, melting sensation in her belly when she found her toothbrush from the morning before waiting beside Brendan's in the medicine cabinet. Where else was he supposed to put it?

With the toothbrush in her mouth, she picked up an unused bottle of cologne and sniffed. But it wasn't him at all, and she couldn't imagine him using it. Other than that, there was only his razor, some shaving cream, and deodorant. Her medicine cabinet at home would probably make him break out in a rash, it was so jam-packed.

She finished brushing her teeth, splashed some water on her face, finger-combed her hair, and headed downstairs . . . and . . . and jackpot.

Brendan was standing in the kitchen in nothing but black boxer briefs.

Piper crowded against the wall so she could observe him without being discovered. He was hunched over the kitchen counter reading a newspaper, and good gravy, the thick, masculine ropes of back muscles were all she wanted for breakfast. How dare he with those thighs? Did he use them to anchor the boat? They were generous and ripped and—

"You want coffee?" he asked without looking up.

"Aherm?" Piper blurted loudly, coming the rest of the way down the stairs, very aware that he was in underwear while she wore nothing but his T-shirt and a thong. And then he pushed up from the counter and scratched his happy trail, and yes, she was very aware of that, too. "Um, yes? Coffee, sure. Sure."

He half grinned. "Okay."

She wrinkled her nose at him. "What is this extra cockiness you have going on?"

Brendan poured her a cup of coffee, preparing it exactly how she liked it. "You might have told me last night in the bar that I was the best, best, best sex of your life."

Heat climbed her cheeks. "I said 'best' three times, hmm?"

After handing her the coffee, he leaned back against the counter and crossed his ankles. "You sure did."

She hid her wan smile in a sip of coffee. "I think I might have also become a professional beauty consultant last night. One who gets paid in drinks." More and more memories knitted together. "And, oh God, I volunteered to throw a party on Labor Day at the bar."

"Whoops."

"I can't wait to tell Hannah." She cupped her hands around the mug, enjoying the warmth. Not just from the drink itself, but from Brendan's kitchen. The way he looked at her with affection, not a rush in the world to move or hurry. When had she started liking those things? The silence between them didn't need to be filled, but she was thinking too much, so she did it anyway. "Who would buy you cologne?"

His brow arched. "You mean the one in my cabinet? Birthday gift from Sanders. His wife picked it out. Obviously. He didn't even know what it was until I opened it—and the guys, they ragged on him for months. I probably just keep it because it makes me laugh."

"You're so close with them. Your crew."

"Have to be. Our lives—" He cut himself off, taking an abrupt sip of coffee.

"Are in one another's hands?" When she said it, the memory of her crying in his bed last night came rolling back in on a tide. This was probably it, then. No more smoke screens or hiding or flirting her way to safety with this man. Even if she couldn't recall every single second of last night, she could feel that the layers had been stripped away. By his hands. His words. His presence.

"Anyway, it's not the scent I would pick for you."

Interest lit his expression. "What would you pick?"

"Nothing. You already have the ocean on your skin. And it's not like you to embellish what's already working." Something heated in his eyes at her words. At the proof she'd been cataloguing his finer details? "But if I had to pick a scent . . . something, like, rainy and mossy. To remind me of your garden. How earthy you are. How substantial." Her attention meandered down the line of black hair disappearing into his briefs. "How male."

His chest rose and fell on a shudder. "You're really messing up my plans for the morning, Piper."

"What were your plans?"

"To take you out on the *Della Ray.*"

The smile blasted across her face. "*What?* Are you serious?"

"Uh-huh. Being out on the water is good for talking."

"Oh, right." She rocked back on her heels, her initial excitement tempered by the reminder that the reckoning had arrived. "Talking points."

"That's right." He raked her with a blistering look that turned her nipples to tingling peaks. "Now I just want to take you back to bed, though."

Her breathing went shallow. "Can't we do both?"

His regret was obvious when he shook his head. "Next time I fuck you, I want to be sure you're not going to pull away from me afterward."

"And I can't escape on a boat?"

"That might have crossed my mind."

She huffed a laugh. He was really serious about her. And she'd gone home with him last night knowing it. As natural as could be, like she did it all the time. That's how it felt being collected by Brendan and sleeping in his arms. Expected. Inevitable.

Damn him.

There was a chance she might be serious about Brendan, too. How had this happened?

"Just so we're clear," she said, setting down her coffee mug. "You are withholding sex."

"No, I'm not." His jaw flexed. "I'll fuck you facedown over that counter, Piper. If sex is all you want, I'll give it to you. But I want more." His voice brooked no nonsense. "You do, too, or you wouldn't have come here in the middle of a storm and slept in my bed. Don't *ever* do that again, by the way. I need to know you'll be safe when I'm not here."

"I'm a strong runner!"

He gave a dubious grunt.

"Fine," she said, voice irregular. "We'll talk!"

"Good. Whenever you're ready."

Lost in a sea of emotional vulnerability, she utilized her best physical weapon, stripping off his shirt and tossing it to him. Then she marched out of the kitchen and up the stairs in nothing but her thong, knowing full well he'd watch her the whole way. If he was going to demand she let him in completely, shed all of her defenses, she'd make sure it was a long day for them both.

As the *Della Ray* backed out of its slip into the mouth of the harbor, it became obvious to Piper that the boat was an extension of Brendan himself. And the time he spent on land was just filler. He sat in the captain's chair with easy command, confident in every movement, the wheel sliding through his ready hands, his eyes vigilant. Framed in the hazy sunlight, he could have been from past or present. A man and the ocean. Timeless.

Piper watched him from the relief skipper's seat, her cheek pressed to the wood paneling of the wheelhouse, never having felt safer in her life. Physically, anyway. The hum of the engine beneath posed an ominous warning to the trembling organ in her chest.

"How far out are we going to go?"

"Five or six miles," he said. "I'll drop the anchors and give you a tour. Sound good?"

She nodded, finding herself looking forward to it. Watching this man move in his natural habitat. It had the makings of capability porn all over it. And maybe if she asked enough questions, they could avoid having the talk of all talks.

Yeah, right. There was no getting out of this. The set of his jaw said a resolution was imminent, and he had way less of a hangover than she did. Also, he was in a sexy boat captain mode. It did not bode well.

"Hey," Brendan said, his bearded chin giving a persuasive jerk. "Come steer this thing."

"Me?" She stood slowly. "Are you sure? Based on my track record, I will find the one parking meter in the middle of the ocean and back into it."

Laugh lines appeared around his eyes—and then he patted his big, sturdy thigh. Oh yeah, like she was going to pass that up. "Get over here."

She feigned one more moment of indecision, then climbed onto his left thigh, mentally praising Hannah for packing her a skirt so she could feel the denim of Brendan's jeans against the backs of her legs. The shift of muscle.

Brendan took an old captain's hat off a peg on the wall and dropped it onto her head. Then he wrapped his left arm around her middle and tugged her back more securely against his chest. "See this dial? Just keep the arrow right about here. Northwest." He took her hands and placed them on the wheel, making sure they were steady before letting go. "How's that?"

"Cool." She laughed breathily, fascinated by the vibrations that started in her palms and traveled up to her elbows. "Really cool."

"Yeah. It is."

Feeling almost giddily light and kind of . . . unrestrained, she pointed out at the horizon. "Mermaid off the port bow!" He snorted in her ear. "Phew. I've gotten the *Little Mermaid* reference out of my system. I was going to explode."

"I don't know how I feel about my boat making you think of a Disney movie."

"Aw, don't be jealous of Prince Eric, we—" She turned her head and found him a breath away, those vivid green eyes trained on her mouth. Not on the water, where she expected them to be. The arm around her belly flexed, his palm molding to her rib cage. Heat slicked up the insides of her thighs, her skin sensitizing all over. "Don't you dare look at me like that," she said choppily. "You're the one who wanted to talk first."

He exhaled hard. "And then you ran up my stairs in a purple string. It had an impact."

"You live, you learn," she chirped.

A growl kindled in his throat. "You're going to punish me all day, aren't you?"

"Count on it. I bet you're second-guessing wanting a high-maintenance girlfri—" She cut herself off just in time. "I'm holding your livelihood in my hands, Brendan. Let me focus."

They drove the boat for another fifteen minutes before Brendan eased the throttle into an upright position. He pressed a series of buttons, and a steady rumble followed, which he explained was the anchors going down. And then it was quiet. Just the lapping of water against the side of the boat, and the gentle groans of the ship compensating for the rise and fall of the ocean. They sat in the captain's chair with her head leaned back against his shoulder, his fingers trailing up and down her bare arm.

"Come on," he said gruffly. "I'll bring you out on deck."

Nodding, she followed Brendan down the stairs of the wheelhouse and out onto the wide floating platform that made up the deck. The vessel bobbed beneath them, but he moved like it was stationary, his legs easily compensating for the dips and lifts. She tried to copy his effortlessness and thought she looked only slightly drunk.

"Last week, there were seventy steel traps stacked on this end." He gestured to the end of the deck nearest the wheelhouse, then stooped down to show her a covered portal. "When we're on the crab, this is where we put the keepers. Males over a certain weight. We send them below to processing, then on to the freezer hold."

"What if you're fishing?"

"Same hold. But we pack it full of ice. No water."

She squinted up at the large cranes overhead, the spotlights and antennas secured to the top, and a chill caught her off guard. "Those lights are to help you see in the dark? Or see if there's a wave coming?"

Brendan came to stand beside her, dropped a kiss onto her shoulder. "Yeah. I can see when they're coming, baby."

"Did you know . . . that's how Henry died?" Why was she whispering? "A rogue wave just knocked him right overboard. Mick told me."

"Yeah, I knew." He didn't say anything for a moment. "I'm not going to pretend things like that don't still happen, Piper, but it happens a hell of a lot less these days. Training to be on deck is more comprehensive, the machinery we have leaves less room for human error. Boats are better designed for safety now, and with all of the recent updates, mine is one of the safest."

Piper looked up at him. "Is this why you brought me out here?" she asked quietly. "To show me why I don't have to worry when you're gone?"

"It's one of the reasons. I don't like you crying."

She swallowed a sharp object in her throat. "When I heard there was an accident, I just kept thinking of the boat flipping over. Can that happen?"

"Rarely. Very rarely. Especially for one this large." Brendan studied her face for a beat, then moved behind her, wrapping his arms around her shoulders. "Close your eyes."

She forced herself to relax. "Okay."

"Just feel the way the boat moves like it's part of the water. That's how it's designed, to compensate for waves. Like an airplane going over turbulence. There are bumps, but they never stop you from moving." His hand snuck around the front to lift her chin. "You see how low the railings are on this boat? And those openings at the base? That's so the water can just pass right over and through. It can't hold water from a wave or make the weight uneven."

"But . . . because they're so low, isn't it easy for a man to go over the side?"

"It hasn't happened yet to anyone on my team." He let go of her chin and pulled her closer. "I can tell you when I worked on the crew, before I was a captain, my legs became part of the boat. You learn to balance. You learn to read the water, to brace, to loosen. I'm in the wheelhouse, so it's near impossible for me to go overboard, but I'm responsible for five men, not just myself anymore."

"Which is harder?"

"Responsibility."

Absently, she reached up and stroked his beard. "They're right to trust you."

She felt him swallow against the back of her head. "Do you . . . feel any better?"

"A little. Standing on the boat makes it seem more substantial."

It's a clear day, though. Not a rain cloud in sight. Storms are a different story.

He was making such a sweet effort to allay her fears that she kept silent.

"What else do you worry about?" Brendan asked against her ear.

Piper shrugged but didn't answer. One wrong move, and they could veer into dangerous territory. Maybe she should make another *Little Mermaid* reference—

"Piper."

"Oh yes?"

"What else do you worry about?"

Her sigh allowed the truth to sneak up her throat, but she played it off like her concern was minor. When it was definitely not. In fact, she was starting to think it was the kernel center of the whole piece of popcorn. "I'm not, um . . . built for this whole worrying business, Brendan. Keeping the home fires burning. Wrapping a cardigan around my shoulders and pacing the docks, clutching a locket or something? Does that sound like me? No. You *know* I'm too high maintenance for that. I'm . . ."

He stayed quiet, just held her.

Which was bad, because she started to ramble.

"You know. Just hypothetically speaking. Once a year, you go out to catch crab, sure. But all the time? Going to bed thinking you might not come back, night after night? Uh-uh. I'm not . . ." She squeezed her eyes closed. "I'm not strong enough for that."

"Yes, you are. I know it asks a lot, but yes, you are."

"No. I'm not. Not every woman can do this. She—" Ugh. Piper rolled her eyes at herself. How truly pathetic she was being, bringing up another woman. But as soon as the words started to flow, a pressure in her chest started to lessen, like a brick had been sitting on top of it. "You had a fisherman's wife. She was born here, and this was normal to her. You can't really expect *me* to live up to that. I will . . ." *Disappoint you. Disappoint myself. Disappoint Henry.* "A little less than a month ago, I had no responsibilities. No worries. And now, now . . . this huge one. It's huge. This guy I care about a lot, like, *a lot*, has the most dangerous job in the universe. And I don't have a job *at all*. I don't even live here. Not permanently. Like, we are *not* a fit, Brendan. It won't work, so stop—"

"Stop what, Piper? Thinking about you every second of the day? Missing you so much I climb the fucking walls? Stop being hungry for you? I can't turn any of that off and I don't want to." When he turned Piper around, she saw he was visibly concerned by what she'd revealed. *Well, welcome to the party, bucko.* "Okay, let's start from the beginning. We're going to talk about my marriage. Not how she died, but what it was like."

She took a breath. "I don't know if I want to."

"Can you trust me, honey? I'm just trying to get to the light. Get to *you*." He waited for her nod, then did that wide-stance, settling-in thing and crossed his arms. As if letting her know he was immovable. "I knew Desiree my whole life, but not well. She was a girl a year above me in school. Quiet. I didn't really get to know her until I started working for Mick. Right around the time my parents moved out of town, he took me under his wing and became kind of a . . . guide. He showed me this thing I love. Fishing. How to do it well. And over time, I guess she became family, too. I never felt . . ." He lowered his voice. "There wasn't an attraction like I have for you. I'm not just talking about sex. We were friends, in a way. She was always trying to meet her father's expectations, and so was I, after he gave me the *Della Ray*. He obviously thought we'd make a good match, so I asked her out, and I think . . . both of us just wanted to make Mick happy. That's what we had in common. So we just went through the motions, even when it didn't feel right. When she died, I kept the ring on, kept my vows, to keep him healed as much as possible. Then you showed up, Piper. Then you. And it felt wrong having *ever* given those vows to anyone else.

"Was she strong? Was she comfortable waving off me and Mick every time we left the harbor? Yeah. I guess she was. But she had decades to get there. It's been a month for you, Piper. Less, if you count the time we spent pretending we didn't want each other. So that comparison is unfair. You're unfair to yourself."

There was no doubt Brendan believed everything he was saying. And it was hard not to believe him, too, when he stood a foot above her, a sea captain in his domain with a voice full of conviction. He was huge in that moment. So intense she had to remind herself to breath. Was she happy his marriage hadn't been full of passion? No. This man deserved that. So had Desiree. But that part of his life had been a shadowy corner, and it helped to have the mysterious aspects of it gone. "Thank you for telling me."

"I'm not done."

"Wow. Once you get going, there's no slowing you down."

Brendan stepped closer, seized her by the elbows. "Last night, you said a couple of things that bothered me, and now we're going to work through those." He leaned down and kissed her forehead, her nose, her mouth. "Don't ever tell me again there are a thousand others like you, because that's the biggest pile of bullshit I've ever heard. And someday, trust me, I hope I meet the person who told you that. A person doesn't rebuild a legacy for a dead man unless they have character and can accept responsibilities." He kissed her temple hard. "Last night, I watched you in the bar, how you immediately made everyone your best friend. Made them count. And do you know what it meant to me having you show up at the hospital?" He didn't speak for a moment. "You have perseverance, character, and a huge heart. I think you might still be finding your way, but so am I. Me and my stupid routines. I thought I had it all figured out until you made me start breaking them. I want to keep breaking them with you."

As he'd been speaking, Piper had turned into a limp linguini noodle in his arms. The tip of her nose was red, and she had to blink up at the sky to keep from tearing up. Warmth and a sense of belonging reached all the way down to her toes, curling them in her ballet flats. "This is a lot to process," she whispered.

"I understand—"

"I mean, we're boyfriend and girlfriend now. I guess you got what you wanted."

A rush of his breath passed over the crown of her head. His arms were crushing her to that burly chest now. "Damn right I did." A beat passed. "About you going back to LA . . ."

"Can we put that one part off?" She pressed her nose to the collar of his shirt and inhaled his centering scent. "Just for now?"

He sighed, but she felt him nod. "Yeah. For now."

They stayed like that for a little while, Piper locked in the safety of his embrace while the boat carried high and low on the ocean, sunbeams warming her back.

He'd given her a lot to think about. Maybe it was time to

examine herself. Or, more importantly, how she viewed herself. But one thing she didn't have to overthink was making these moments with Brendan count.

She kissed his chin and eased back, lacing their fingers together and enjoying the way his gaze meandered down the front of her body. "Do I get the rest of the tour?"

"Yeah." He cleared his throat and pulled her back in the direction of the wheelhouse. "Come on."

Piper tilted her head while staring at Brendan's rippling back, wondering if he realized how hard he was about to get laid.

He'd woken up with a plan to try to slay her dragons . . . and he'd executed it. Nothing stood in his way. He'd even passed on sex so they could dig to the root of their issues, and God, that wasn't just commendable. It was hot.

Captain Brendan Taggart was a man. A real one.

Her first.

And she could admit now that staying with him would mean giving up Los Angeles and the life she knew. But there was one root he hadn't found despite all his digging: Who the hell would Piper Bellinger be if she stayed in Westport?

That was a problem for another time, though.

Hold her calls. Right now, she was one hundred percent sex brained.

First, Brendan showed her the engine room, and she nodded prettily while he explained what a thruster was for, commending herself for not giggling once. Then they went back upstairs to the crew room, the galley where they ate while on the water, and finally the bunk room. "Wow," she murmured, observing the narrow beds tucked in tight against the walls. "Close quarters." There were nine total, the majority of them stacked two beds high. Kind of like the bunk she shared with Hannah, but the boat's beds were attached to the wall. Most of them had snapshots taped up beside them. Kids, women, smiling men holding giant fish in their hands. One had a slightly inappropriate calendar that made her snort.

"Sorry about that," Brendan grumbled, rubbing at the back of his neck. "It's not mine."

She rolled her eyes at him. "Duh." She tapped her lips with a finger and did a revolution around the small room, stopping in front of a bunk along the far wall, as separate from the others as one could get in such tight quarters. It was the only one that didn't have a bed above it. "No, yours is this one. The bed without any pictures, isn't it?"

He grunted in the affirmative.

"Do you . . . want a picture of m—"

"Yes."

"Oh." Was she blushing? "Okay. That can be arranged."

"Thank you."

Piper approached her new boyfriend slowly, letting him see the intent in her eyes, and the green of his own deepened drastically, a muscle sliding vertically in his strong throat. She let just the tips of her breasts meet his chest. "Do you ever get alone time on the boat?"

"If I need time alone, I make it," he rasped. "I've needed a lot of it lately."

Which was as good as an admission that he'd masturbated on board while thinking of her. Feminine pleasure turned to slickness between her thighs. "Then, what about private pictures? Just for you." She rubbed her breasts side to side, and his breath stuttered. "Would you like some of those?"

His eyelids went to half-mast. "God, yes."

She bit her lip, stepped back. "Take out your phone."

Brendan reached back and removed his cell from his back pocket, not taking his eyes off Piper once while opening his camera. Then he nodded once to let her know he was ready.

She'd always liked being the center of attention, but having this man's undivided focus was thrilling in an entirely new way. Because her heart was involved.

Heavily, apparently.

It knocked impatiently against her ribs, echoing in her ears as she shrugged off the jacket she'd worn and hung it neatly on one corner of Brendan's bed. The boat groaned and sighed beneath their feet as she skimmed her palms up the front of her body, over her breasts, squeezing, then coasting back down to collect the hem, slowly easing the garment up and off, leaving her clad in just a red denim skirt and ballet flats. She stacked her hands behind her head, dropped a hip, dragged her lower lip through her teeth. Let it go with a pop.

He exhaled a pained laugh, shook his head. "*Fuck.*"

"We'll get to that."

Brendan's nostrils flared as he lifted the phone and set off the electronic shutter.

Click.

She unbuttoned her skirt next, turning around while lowering the zipper. With a flirty look over her shoulder, she let the red bottoms drop. Hannah had been pretty hilarious, not packing Piper underwear or a bra, but Brendan's reaction to her bare backside was definitely worth any chafing that had occurred. Yeah, it was all forgiven when he took an involuntary step forward, his chest heaving. *Click. Click. Click.*

She braced a hand on the wall and leaned forward slightly, arching her back and swinging her hips to pop that booty out—*CLICK*—and that was all she wrote.

Brendan dropped the phone and crossed to her in one lunge.

He stooped down and picked her up, tossing her with a bounce onto his bed, covering her naked body with his fully clothed one, and slamming his mouth down on top of hers. And oh Lord, oh Lord, that contrast fired off flamethrowers in her blood. She was vulnerable and coveted and lusted after, and it was everything. Everything.

"This bed isn't strong enough to survive what I'm going to do to you," Brendan growled against her mouth, capturing her lips again in a kiss fraught with male sexual frustration. It let her know in no uncertain terms that she was the source and he'd be exacting revenge.

Take it. Take it.

Without breaking contact with her mouth, Brendan's hand wedged down between them and wrestled his zipper down, the desperation of his jerky movements exciting her like nothing else, dampening the folds between her legs. "Hurry," she begged, biting at his lips. "Hurry."

"Goddammit, Piper, you make me so fucking hard." They both pushed down the waistband of his boxer briefs, hands colliding, tongues stroking into each other's mouths, Piper teasing, Brendan aggressing. Finally, his shaft was free, and he winced, sucked in a breath, wrapping a fist around the thickness of it. "Tell me you're wet. Tell me to put it in."

"I'm so wet," she moaned, lifting her hips, running the insides of her knees up and down his heaving rib cage. "I'm ready. I need you. Rough as you can."

That full, smooth dome pressed up against her entrance, and she braced, one hand flying to his shoulder, the other to the wooden bunk rail. And still she wasn't prepared for the savagery of that first thrust. With a hoarse roar, his hips drove Piper up the narrow bed, his thickness invading all available space within her, and without allowing her time to acclimate, he was already pumping feverishly, rocking the bed with staccato squeaks.

Piper's mouth was permanently wide open against his shoulder, her eyes watering with the force of pleasure. Pleasure from having his hard sex smacking through her wetness like it owned the joint, his calloused hands shoving her knees down, opening her wider for his convenience. Pleasure from having brought this vital man to his proverbial knees with need. God help her, she loved that. Knew he loved being challenged. Knew he loved that she loved challenging him. Perfect, perfect, perfect.

"Scream for it, baby," he panted, raking her ear with his open mouth. "Whine for my cock. No one can hear us."

A lid came off inside of her, whatever was left of her inhibitions hopping out and running wild on tiny legs. She choked on her first attempts to call his name, because the force he was exerting on top of her was so intense, his huge body surging between her legs without cease—and still fully clothed while she remained bare. Why was that so sinfully hot?

"Brendan," she gasped. Then louder, "Brendan. You're so good. It's *so good*."

"I'll never lie in this bed again without having to jerk off." His hand came up to frame her jaw, applying just enough pressure while looking her square in the eye that another rush of wetness coated her sex, aiding him in his destruction of her senses. "You love knowing that, don't you? You love making me fucking crazy."

She bit her lip and nodded. "Sure you want to be my boyfriend?"

"*Yes,*" he growled, and slammed into her, holding still, deep, his pained face dropping into the crook of her neck. "And don't call me that right now or I'm going to come."

Oh. Jesus. That confession sent a contracting ripple through Piper's core, and she let out a strangled sob, her hands flying to Brendan's ass inside his loosened jeans, fingernails sinking in and yanking him, scraping pathways into his flesh. "Oh my God. N-now. Now."

"*Fuck,*" he ground out, picking up his blistering pace again, the sound of wet slaps echoing in the tiny room. "Fuck it. I can't stop." She milked him with her intimate muscles, and he moaned, pumped harder, rattling the bed beneath them. "That make you hot, baby? Hearing how being your man is going to get me off? Get your boyfriend off? Say it again."

She ran her nails down his hard, flexing butt and dug them in, whispering, "My boyfriend fucks me so right, I let him come inside me whenever he wants." A smile, dazed and wicked, curved her lips when she snuck her middle finger down the split of his backside and cinched it inside the puckered entrance. "He knows just how to earn it."

Piper had been hovering right on the edge of her own orgasm when she purred those last three words, but Brendan's reaction pushed her even closer to oblivion. She watched through an opaque cloud of gathering bliss as he barked a shocked curse, his hips punching forward and back in desperation, neck tendons looking ready to snap. "Christ, I'm done. I'm done. And you better fucking come with me, Piper," he rasped, reaching down and fondling her clit with his thumb. "I satisfy my girlfriend's pussy every time."

And, oh God—*boom*—she fired out of the cannon. Her knees shot up and hugged his body, back arching as she screamed, shook, slapped at his shoulders, all while tears rolled down her temples. It wouldn't end. The hot, grinding pulsations wouldn't end, especially when Brendan drove deep, deep inside of her, stilled and then shuddered violently, his hips moving in disjointed patterns, the volume of his moans rivaling her scream that still lingered in the air. She writhed underneath him, trying to find the bottom of the pleasure well, but until his mouth landed on hers, anchoring her, she didn't realize . . . didn't realize the bottom of the well wasn't physical. She needed their emotional connection to calm herself down. Needed him, his heart, his Brendan-ness. As soon as their lips met, her heart sighed happily and rolled over, languidness traveling through her limbs and making her go boneless.

"Shhh, honey." He breathed hard, his fingers shaking as they stroked the side of her face. "I've got you. I've always got you."

She didn't look away. "I know."

Satisfaction filtered into his silver-green eyes. "Good."

Brendan eased off of Piper and disappeared into the bathroom, coming back with zipped jeans and paper towels, wiping off the insides of her thighs and kissing sensitive spots as he cleaned. Then he joined her in the bed, both of them turning onto their sides, her back up against his chest, a possessive arm wrapped around her waist.

Piper was slipping into a drowsy slumber when Brendan rumbled the question in her ear. "So are we going to just *not* talk about the finger thing?"

The boat rocked steadily in the sunshine as they laughed and laughed some more. And five miles from land, it was easy to pretend no hard decisions would have to be made.

Sooner rather than later.

Chapter Twenty-Two

They pulled into Grays Harbor that evening. Brendan had planned to be back earlier, but Piper had fallen asleep on his chest, and a bulldozer couldn't have moved him.

There she went again, changing his plans. Taking a red pen to his routines.

As he parked his truck in front of No Name and glanced across the console at Piper, he thought back to the conversation on the boat. They'd managed to clarify a lot of unspoken issues between them. His marriage, her fears about his profession, and most important, the way she viewed herself. All that talk, all that clearing the air, led to her staying in Westport, whether she was willing to discuss it yet or not. What would it take for her to consider it?

He was asking for a lot of sacrifice on Piper's part. She would have to leave her home, her friends, and everything she'd ever known.

Hannah, too, eventually, when she went back to LA.

Simply breaking free of his patterns didn't even come close to what he was asking of Piper. Compared to what—to *whom*—he would get in return, that was nothing.

And that bothered him. A lot.

Made him feel like a selfish bastard.

"Hey." Piper leaned across to the driver's seat and kissed his shoulder. "What's with the scary frown?"

He shook his head, debating whether or not to be honest. There had been a lot of honesty between them on the boat, and it had cleared their most pressing obstacles. Made the apprehension of what was to come feel mitigated. Manageable. But he couldn't bring himself to remind her of the unbalanced scales. Didn't want her thinking about it or considering the issue too closely. Not yet, when he hadn't been given enough time to find a solution.

Was there a fucking solution?

"I was just thinking about not having you in my bed tonight," Brendan said finally, glad he didn't need to lie. Not completely. "I want you there."

"Me too." She had the nerve to blush and avert her eyes after what they'd done on the boat? Goddamn. This woman. He wanted to spend decade upon decade deciphering all the little components that made her up. "But it's not fair to Hannah. She's in Westport because of me and I can't keep leaving her alone."

"I know," he grumbled.

"I'll text you," she coaxed. "And don't forget about your shiny new nudes."

"Piper, even when I'm dead I won't forget them."

She shimmied her shoulders, pleased. "Okay, well. Good. So, I guess this is where we do the big, dramatic boyfriend-girlfriend kiss and act like we won't see each other for a year."

Brendan sighed. "I always thought it was ridiculous, the way the guys can't peel themselves off their wives and girlfriends at the dock. Pissed they're making us late." He regarded his beautiful girlfriend stonily. "I'll be surprised if I don't try and carry you over my shoulder onto the boat next time. Take you with me."

"Really?" She sat up straighter. "Would you?"

"*Hell* no. What if there was a storm or you got hurt?" Why was he suddenly sweating? His pulse wasn't functioning the way it was supposed to, speeding up and tripping all over itself. "I'd lose my shit, Piper."

"Hannah would call this a double standard."

"She can call it whatever she wants," he said gruffly. "You stay on land unless it's a short trip like today. And *I'm* with you. Please."

Piper was battling a smile. "Well, since you said please, I guess I'll turn down all of my fishing boat invitations."

Even though she was being sarcastic, Brendan grunted, satisfied. "You said something about a big dramatic kiss," he reminded her, reaching over to unbuckle her seat belt, brushing a knuckle over her nipples, one at a time, as he took his hand back. They puckered under his gaze, her hips shifting on the seat. She cut off his miserable groan by leaning over, tugging his beard until he met her halfway, and kissing him. Lightly at first, then they surged together and sank into a long, wet sampling of lips and tongues, their breaths shuddering out between them.

They broke apart with reluctant sighs. "Mmmm." She blinked up at him, slid back into her seat, and pushed open the door. "Bye, Captain."

Brendan watched her disappear into the building and dragged a hand down his face.

If Piper Bellinger was going to kill him, he'd die a happy man.

He started to drive home but found himself turning toward Fox's place instead. His best friend lived in an apartment near the harbor, a stone's throw from the water, and where Brendan's house had an air of stability, Fox's was as temporary as it got. Cursory paint job, basic furniture, and a huge-ass television. In other words, a single man's dwelling. Brendan didn't tend to visit Fox at home very often, since they saw each other for days—often weeks—at a time on the boat. Not to mention, Brendan had his routines, and they didn't involve going to bars or meeting women or any of the things Fox did with his spare time.

But this whole business of Piper sacrificing everything while he gave very little? It was pushing up under his skin like tree roots. Turning the problem over and over in his mind wasn't solving it. Maybe he needed to address his worries out loud, just in case he was missing something. An easy solution. Hell, it was worth a shot. Better than going home and stewing about it alone.

Fox opened the door in sweatpants and bare feet, a bottle of beer in his hand. The sounds of a baseball game drifted into the breezeway from behind his skipper. "Cap." His brow was knitted. "What's up? Something wrong?"

"No. Move." He pushed past Fox into the apartment, tipping his head at the beer. "You got another one of those?"

"Got a dozen or so. Help yourself. Fridge."

Brendan grunted. He took a beer from the fridge and twisted the cap off with his hand, joining Fox in front of the baseball game, putting the men on opposite sides of the couch. He tried to focus on what was happening on the screen, but his problem-solver brain wasn't having it. Five or so minutes passed before Fox said anything.

"You going to tell me why you're chewing nails over there?" Fox held up a hand. "I mean, chewing nails is kind of your default, but you don't usually do it on my couch."

"You have company coming over or something?"

"Jesus, no." His friend snorted. "You know I don't date local."

"Yeah," Brendan said. "Speaking of which, you usually head to Seattle after a payday like the one we just had. What are you doing here?"

Fox shrugged, stared at the TV. "Don't know. Just wasn't feeling the trip this time."

Brendan waited for his friend to elaborate. When he didn't seem inclined to, Brendan guessed there was no point in putting off the reason for his visit anymore. "These women you meet in Seattle. You've never been . . . serious about any of them, right?"

"I think you're missing the point of leaving Westport to meet women." He saluted with his beer bottle. "Sorry, sweetheart. Just in town for the night. Take it or leave it." He tipped the drink to his mouth. "They always take it, in case that wasn't obvious."

"Congratulations."

"Thank you." Fox laughed. "Anyway, why are you asking me about—" He cut himself off with an expression of dawning comprehension. "Did you come here for advice on women?"

Brendan scoffed. "That's a stretch."

"You did, didn't you? Son of a bitch." Fox grinned. "Piper still giving you a problem?"

"Who ever said she was a problem?" Brendan shouted.

"Relax, Cap. I meant . . ." Fox searched the ceiling for the correct wording. "Have you gotten her out of your system?"

As though such a thing was possible? "No."

"You haven't slept with her?"

Fuck. He didn't like talking about this. What happened between him and Piper should be private. "I'm not answering that," he growled.

Fox looked impressed. "You have, then. So what is the problem?"

Brendan stared. "I think the problem might be that I came to you for advice."

His friend waved off the insult. "Just ask me what you want to know. I'm actually pretty fucking flattered that you came to me. I know two things: fishing and women. And those two things have a lot of similarities. When you're fishing, you use bait, right?" He pointed at his smile. "I've got your woman bait right here."

"Jesus Christ."

"Next you've got the hook. That's your opening line."

A hole opened in the center of Brendan's stomach. "My opening line to Piper was basically telling her to go home."

"Yeah, I'm pretty surprised that worked myself." He rubbed at the line between his brows. "Where was I with my analogy?"

"You were done."

"No, I wasn't. Once she's hooked, you just have to reel her in." He leaned forward and braced his forearms on his knees.

"Sounds like you've already done all that, though. Unless . . . Wait, the goal was just sex, right?"

"I didn't have a fucking goal. Not at the beginning. Or I probably wouldn't have shouted at her, called her purse ugly, and strongly suggested she go home." Suddenly sick to his stomach, Brendan slapped down the beer bottle and pushed to his feet. "God, I'm lucky she's giving me the time of day *at all*. Now I have the nerve to try and make her stay here for me? Am I insane?"

Fox gave a low whistle. "Okay, things have progressed a lot since the last time we talked." His friend's bemusement was alarming. "You want *that* girl to stay in *this* town?"

Brendan massaged the pressure in his chest. "Don't say it like that."

A beat of silence passed. "I'm out of my depth on this one, Cap. I don't have any advice on how to actually keep the fish *in* the boat. I usually just let them swim off again."

"Fuck sake. Stop with the analogy."

"It's a good one and you know it."

Brendan sat back down, clasped his hands between his knees. "If she went back to LA, I'd have no choice but to let her. My job is here. A crew who depends on me."

"Not to mention, you'd go crazy there. It's not you. You . . . *are* Westport."

"So that leaves Piper to give up everything." His voice sounded bleak. "How can I ask her to do that?"

Fox shook his head. "I don't know. But she'd be gaining you." He shrugged. "It's probably not a *total* shit trade."

"Thanks," Brendan said drily, before sobering. "If she's happy, she won't leave. That stands to reason, right? But what do women like? What makes them happy?"

Fox pointed to his crotch.

Brendan shook his head slowly. "You're an idiot."

The man chuckled. "What do women *like*?" This time, he seemed to actually consider the question. "I don't think there's any one thing. It depends on the woman." He jerked a shoulder, went back to looking at the ball game. "Take Piper's sister, for example. Hannah. She likes records, right? If I wanted to make her happy, I'd bring her to Seattle tomorrow. There's a vinyl expo happening at the convention center."

"How the hell do you know that?"

"It just popped up on the internet. I don't know," Fox explained, a little too quickly. "The point is, you have to think about the specific woman. They don't all like flowers and chocolate."

"Right."

Fox started to say something else, but a series of notes filled the room. It took Brendan a moment to realize his phone was ringing. He shifted on the couch and tugged it out of his back pocket. "Piper," he said, hitting the answer button immediately, trying not to be obvious that just the promise of hearing her voice sent his pulse into chaos. "Everything okay?"

"Yes. The building is still intact." She sounded breezy, relaxed, totally unaware that he was across town trying to unlock whatever magic would give them a chance for a future. "Um, would it be a lot to ask to borrow your truck tomorrow? There is this amazing, artsy chick on Marketplace selling a shabby chic chandelier that we need, like, absolutely need, for the bar. For *forty bucks*. But we have to pick it up. She's located between here and Seattle."

"About an hour drive," he heard Hannah call in the background.

"About an hour drive," Piper repeated. "We were trying to figure out the cost of an Uber, but then I remembered I have a hot boyfriend with a truck." She paused. "This wouldn't mess with any of your routines, would it?"

His gut kicked.

Routines.

Asking Piper to remain in Westport would require her to have a lot of faith in him. To take a major leap. Showing Piper how far he'd come in terms of bucking his habits might make a difference when it came time for her to decide whether or not to return to LA. If he could give her some of what she was missing in LA, he'd close the gap on that leap he'd eventually ask for.

Brendan could be spontaneous.

He could surprise her. Make her happy. Provide her with what she loved.

Couldn't he?

Yeah. He could. Actually, he was looking forward to it.

"Why don't we pick up your chandelier and keep driving to Seattle? We could stay the night and head back to Westport on Monday."

Brendan lifted an eyebrow at Fox. Fox nodded, impressed.

"Really?" Piper breathed a laugh. "What would we do in Seattle?"

No hesitation. "There's a vinyl expo at the convention center. Hannah might like it."

"A vinyl expo?" Hannah yelped in the background, followed by the sound of feet pounding closer on the wood floor. "Oh, um . . . yeah, safe to say she's interested." A beat passed. "How did you even know this expo was taking place?"

Piper's question must have been loud enough to hear through the receiver, because Fox was already shaking his head. "Fox mentioned it." Brendan gave him the finger. "He's going."

The look of betrayal on his friend's face was almost enough to shame Brendan. Almost. The chance to spend more time with his girlfriend trumped his own dishonor. God knew Piper was a distraction, and he didn't want Hannah to be un-safe in a strange city. Piper wouldn't, either.

"So we'd all go together?" Piper asked, sounding amused and excited all at once.

"Yeah."

She laughed. "Okay. It sounds fun! We'll see you tomorrow." Her voice dropped a few octaves, emerged sounding a little hesitant. "Brendan . . . I miss you."

His heart climbed up into his throat. "I miss you, too."

They hung up.

Fox jabbed the air with a finger. "You owe me. Big time."

"You're right. I do." Brendan headed for the door, ready for a night of planning. "How about I give you the *Della Ray*?"

He closed the door on his friend's stupefied expression.

Chapter Twenty-Three

$\mathcal{P}$iper had butterflies in her stomach.

Good ones.

She was going out of town today with her boyfriend. It didn't matter if she was a little suspicious of the circumstances. Nor did it matter that, by agreeing to be his girlfriend and traveling together, she was sinking deeper into a relationship. One that might not stand the test of time, depending on whether she went back to Los Angeles sooner or later. But none of that was happening today. Or tomorrow. So she was going to kick back, relax, and enjoy the ride. And Brendan would be enjoying a few rides himself.

Piper zipped her toothbrush into her overnight bag and snickered at her own innuendo, but she shut it down when Hannah gave her a questioning look. *Rein it in, horny toad.*

Seriously. It was damn near uncomfortable how sexually charged she'd become over the last couple of days. Vaginal orgasms were ruining her for regular life. Even the most casual mention of Brendan and her pussy started pumping out a slow jam.

Speaking of which. "I think I'll get waxed while we're in civilization," Piper said, trying to decide if she'd forgotten to pack anything. "You want to come with me?"

"Sure." Hannah slung her stuffed backpack over one shoulder. "Just in case we go to the hotel pool or something."

"As soon as I find out where we're staying, I'll schedule us." Piper clapped her hands together. "Sisters wax date!"

"It's all so thrilling," Hannah deadpanned, leaning a hip against the side of the bunk bed. "Hey, Fox isn't coming along to, like . . . babysit me. Right?"

Piper's nose wrinkled. "Brendan said he was already going."

"Yeah, except he didn't know the difference between a forty-five and a seventy-eight that day at the record shop." She narrowed her eyes. "I smell something fishy."

"Welcome to Westport. It's the official town aroma." Piper braced her hands on Hannah's shoulders. "He's not coming to babysit you. You're twenty-six. Anyway, why would you need a babysitter? Me and Brendan will be with you the whole time."

Hannah's mouth fell open. "Piper, you can't be this naive."

"What do you mean?"

"When I asked if Fox was coming to babysit me, I meant, is he coming to distract me so Brendan can have time alone with you and your freshly waxed box?" Now it was Piper's mouth's turn to fall open. "Because I definitely don't mind that. At all. I will be among my people, and I can browse records until the cows come home. But I don't want Fox to feel obligated to entertain me. That would kind of ruin the experience, you know?"

"I get what you're saying." Piper squeezed Hannah's shoulders. "Do you trust me?"

"Of course I do."

"Good. If one of us gets the sense they're trying to divide and conquer, we'll split. Okay? If both of us aren't having a good time, it's not worth it."

Hannah nodded, gave a small smile. "Deal."

"Sealed." Piper wet her lips. "Hey, before they get here, I have something to ask you." She blew out a slow breath. "How do you feel about having the grand opening of the new-and-improved bar on Labor Day?"

Her sister's lips moved, counting silently. "That's eight days from now! A week!"

Piper laughed prettily. "Doable, though?"

"You volunteered to throw a party, didn't you?"

Piper groaned, dropping her hands away from her sister's shoulders. "How did you know that?"

"I know *you*. Planning parties is what you do."

"I can't help it." Her voice dropped to a whisper. "They're so fun."

Hannah fought a smile and won. "Pipes, we haven't even invited Daniel yet." She studied Piper. "Are you even planning on inviting him anymore? Or do you want to stay the full three months?"

"Of course I plan on inviting him!" Piper said automatically. Something sharp twisted in her middle the moment she said those words. But she couldn't take them back.

It didn't hurt to have a fail-safe, though, right? Daniel could always agree to let Piper come home early, and she could turn down the offer. Even if their stepfather was lenient, she didn't have to get on a plane the same day. Her options just needed to stay open.

The more time she spent with Brendan, though, the less inclined she was going to be to give herself an out. And she was not even *close* to ready to make the decision to stay in Westport. How could she be? She might have made friends at Blow the Man Down. Might have started forging connections with people like Abe and Opal and the girls at the Red Buoy. And the hardware store owners and some of the locals who milled around all day at the harbor. So what if she liked stopping to chat with them? So what if she didn't feel as out of place now as she had upon arriving? That didn't spell forever.

She thought of Brendan stroking her hair while they napped in his bunk on the *Della Ray*. Thought of the gentle rocking of the water and the sound of his even breathing. And she had to force out her next words.

"I'll call and invite Daniel right now."

Just to be safe.

Hannah arched a brow. "Really?"

"Yeah." Piper reached for her phone, ignoring the weird stab of foreboding in her tummy, and dialed. Her stepfather answered on the second ring. "Hey, Daniel!"

"Piper." He sounded nervous. "Everything okay?"

She giggled, trying to dispel the coldness in her chest. "Why does everyone answer my calls this way? Am I that much of a disaster?"

"No." Liar. "No, it's just that you haven't called in a while. I expected you to be begging to come back to LA long before now."

Yeah, well. Who could have predicted a big bruiser of a sea captain who gave vaginal orgasms and made her forget how to breathe?

"Uh . . ." She tucked some hair behind her ear and gave

Hannah a reassuring look. "We've been a little distracted, actually. That's what I'm calling to talk to you about. Me and Hannah decided to give the bar a little face-lift."

Silence. "Really."

She couldn't tell if he was impressed or skeptical. "Really. And we're having the grand opening on Labor Day. Do you think . . . ? Would you come? Please?"

After a moment, Daniel sighed. "Piper, I'm busy as hell with this new project."

Was that relief she was feeling? God, if so, it was unnerving. "Oh. Well . . ."

"Labor Day, you said?" She heard him clicking a few buttons on his computer. Probably opening up his calendar. "I have to admit I'm a little curious to see what you call a face-lift." He sounded a little dry, but she tried not to get offended. She hadn't exactly given him a reason to suspect she would be DIY-gifted, unless she counted that bong she'd made out of an eggplant during her senior year of high school. "I could probably swing it. How far away is Seattle?"

A weight sunk low in her stomach. He was coming.

Piper forced a smile. This was a good thing. This was what she and Hannah needed.

Options. Just in case.

"Two hours, give or take. I'm sure I can find you a hotel near Westport—"

Daniel snorted. "No, thanks. I'll have my assistant find me something in Seattle." He sighed. "Well, it's on the calendar. I guess I'll see you girls soon."

"Great!" Piper's smile faltered. "What about Mom?"

He started to say something and changed track. "She isn't

interested in going back. But I'll represent us both. Sound good?" More key punching. "I have to go now. Good talking to you. Hugs to you and Hannah."

"Okay, bye, Daniel." Piper hung up and fused her features with optimism, staunchly ignoring the bonfire taking place in her stomach. God, why did she feel so guilty? Having her step-father come to Westport in the hopes of cutting their sabbatical short had been the plan all along. "All set!"

Hannah nodded slowly. "Okay."

"Okay! And he said to give you a hug." Piper crushed her sister to her chest, rocking her maniacally. "There you go." She picked up her bag. "Shall we?"

When the sisters walked outside, Brendan and Fox were leaning against the running truck wearing identical scowls, as if they'd been arguing. Upon seeing Piper, Brendan's face cleared, heat flaring in his eyes. "Good morning, Piper," he greeted her gruffly.

"Good morning, Brendan."

Piper couldn't help but notice that Fox looked almost . . . nervous when he saw Hannah, his rangy frame pushing off the truck to reach for her backpack.

"Morning," he said. "Take that for you?"

"No, thanks," Hannah said, skirting past him and throwing it through the open window of the truck's backseat. "I'll hang on to it."

Piper laughed. "My sister doesn't part with her headphones." She let Brendan take her bag and caught the lapel of his flannel, tugging him down for a kiss. He came eagerly, slanting their lips together and giving her the faint taste of his morning coffee. And in a move she found old school and endearing, he tugged off his beanie and used it to shield their faces from view. "Missed you," she whispered, pulling away and giving him a meaningful look.

Brendan's chest rumbled in response, and he damn near ripped the passenger-side door off the hinges, stepping back to help her inside. Fox and Hannah climbed into the rear cab, sitting as far apart as possible. Hannah's backpack rested on the seat between them, making Piper wonder if there was some tension there her sister hadn't told her about. Had she been so wrapped up in her own love life that she'd missed something important happening with Hannah? She vowed to remedy that at the earliest opportunity.

They were driving for five minutes before Piper noticed the address on the navigation screen. It included the name of a very upscale hotel. "Wait. That's not where we're staying, is it?"

Brendan grunted, turned onto the highway.

Marble bathtubs, Egyptian cotton, white fluffy robes, and flattering mood lighting danced in her head. "It is?" she breathed.

"Uh-oh. Someone is breaking out the big guns." Hannah chuckled in the backseat. "Well played, Brendan." Her voice changed. "Wait, but . . . how many rooms did you book?"

"I'm staying with Hannah," Piper said preemptively, passing her sister an I-got-you-bitch look over the cab divider.

"Of course you are," Brendan said easily. "I got three rooms. Fox and I will have our own. He gets enough of my snoring on the boat."

Three rooms? A month ago, she wouldn't even have considered the cost of staying the night at a luxury hotel. But she mentally calculated the price of *everything* now, right down to a cup of afternoon coffee. Three rooms at this hotel would be pricey. Well into the thousands. How much money did fishermen make, anyway? That hadn't been part of her research.

She'd worry about it later. Right now, she was too busy being turned on by the thought of a room service cheese plate and complimentary slippers.

The captain really did have her figured out, didn't he?

"I made a road-trip playlist," Hannah said, leaning forward and handing Piper her phone. "I named it 'Seattle Bound.' Just hit shuffle, Pipes."

"Yes, ma'am." She plugged it into Brendan's outlet. "I never question the DJ."

"The Passenger" by Iggy Pop came on first. "That's Bowie's voice joining in on the chorus," Hannah called over the music. "This song is about their friendship. Driving around together, taking journeys." She sighed wistfully. "Can you imagine them pulling up next to you at a stoplight?"

"Is that what you'll be shopping for at the expo?" Fox asked her. "Bowie?"

"Maybe. The beauty of record shopping is never knowing what you'll leave with." Animated by her favorite topic, Hannah sat forward, turning in the seat to face Fox. "They have to speak to you. More importantly, you have to listen."

From behind her sunglasses, Piper watched the conversation with interest via the rearview mirror.

"Records are kind of like fine wine. Some studios had better production years than others. It's not just the band, it's the pressing. You can be as sentimental as you want about an album, but there's a quality aspect, too." She grinned. "And if you get a perfect pressing of an album you love, there's nothing like that first note when the needle touches down."

"Have you had that?" Fox asked quietly after a moment.

Hannah nodded solemnly. "'A Case of You' by Joni Mitchell. It was the first song I played on her *Blue* album. I've never been the same."

"Fast Car" by Tracy Chapman came up next on the playlist.

Piper's sister hummed a few bars. "Mood is also a factor. If I'm happy, I might shop for Weezer. If I'm homesick, I'll look for Tom Petty . . ."

Fox's lips twitched. "Do you listen to anything from your own generation?"

"Sometimes. Mostly no."

"My Hannah is an old soul," Piper called back.

Brendan's friend nodded, regarding Hannah. "So you have songs for every mood."

"I have *hundreds* of songs for every mood," Hannah breathed, unzipping her backpack and yanking out her headphones and jam-packed iPod, pressing them to her chest. "What kind of mood are you in right now?"

"I don't know. Uh . . ." Fox exhaled up at the ceiling, that smile still playing around the edges of his lips. "Glad."

Glad, Hannah mouthed. "Why?"

Fox didn't respond right away. "Because I don't have to share a room with Brendan. Obviously." He nodded at Hannah's headphones. "What do you got for that?"

Looking superior, Hannah handed him the headset.

Fox put them on.

A moment later, he let out a crack of laughter.

Piper turned in the seat. "What song did you play him?"

"'No Scrubs.'"

Even Brendan laughed at that, his rusted-motor laugh making Piper want to crawl up into his lap and nuzzle his beard. Probably best to wait until they weren't driving for that.

Over the course of the two-hour trip, Fox and Hannah inched closer together in the backseat until they were eventually sharing the set of headphones, taking turns choosing songs to play each other and arguing over whose picks were better. And while Piper hadn't liked the tension between Fox and her sister, she wasn't sure she liked *this* any better. She'd gone on enough dates with players to spot one a mile away—and unless she was wildly mistaken, Fox had playboy royalty written all over him.

After a quick stop to pick up the chandelier and cover it with a tarp in the back of Brendan's truck, they arrived at the hotel before lunchtime. Piper was given precious few minutes to enjoy the lobby waterfall and soothing piano music before they were headed for the elevators.

"I asked them to put us as close as possible, so we're all on the sixteenth floor," Brendan said, passing out room keys, so casually in charge, Piper had to bite down on her lip. "The expo starts at noon. You want to meet in the lobby then and walk over?"

"Sounds good," said both sisters.

Although *I want to jump you* is what Piper was thinking.

They reached the sixteenth floor and headed in different directions—and Piper was grateful to have half an hour alone with her sister. "Hey, getting a little cozy with Fox there, eh?" she whispered, tapping the room key against the sensor, releasing the lock.

Hannah snorted. "What? No. We were just listening to music."

"Yeah, except music is like sex for you—" Piper broke off on a gasp, running the rest of the way into the room. It was magnificent. Muted sunlight. A view of the water. A white fluffy comforter on the king-sized bed, complete with mirrored headboard and mood lighting. Elegant creams and golds and marble. A seating area with a plush ottoman and tasseled throw pillows. Vintage *Vogue* covers even served as the artwork. "Oh, Hannah." Piper turned in a circle, arms outstretched. "I'm home."

"The captain done good."

"He done real good." Piper trailed her fingertips along a cloudlike pillow. "But we're still talking about Fox. What's going on there?"

Hannah plopped onto the love seat, backpack in her lap. "It's dumb."

"What is dumb?"

Her sister grumbled. "That day we walked to the record shop, I might have thought he was cute. We were having a good conversation—deeper than I expected, actually. And then . . . his phone just starts pinging nonstop. Multiple girl names coming up on the screen. Tina. Josie. Mika. It made me feel kind of stupid for looking at him that way. Like there was even . . . potential." She set aside her backpack with a shudder. "I think maybe the cleaning products we'd set on fire went to my head or something. But it was a momentary lapse. I'm all about Sergei. *All* about him. Even if he treats me like a kid sister."

"So . . . no gooey feelings for Fox?"

"No, actually." Hannah seemed pleased with herself. "I think

I like him as a friend, though. He's fun. Smart. It was natural for me to notice he's good-looking. I mean, who wouldn't? But it's all aboard the platonic train. Toot, toot. Friends only."

"You're sure, Hanns?" Piper eyeballed her sister. "Pretty obvious he's a lady's man. I wouldn't want you to get hurt or—"

"Pipes. I'm not interested." Hannah appeared to be telling the truth. "Swear to God."

"Okay."

"In fact, I'm cool hanging out with him today. There's no babysitting vibe." She made a shooing motion with her hand. "You and Brendan can go do couple-y things."

"What? No way! I want to browse vinyls, too."

"No, you don't. But you're cute for pretending."

Piper pouted, then brightened. "We will have our sisters wax date!" She gasped. "You know what? I booked it at a place closer to the convention center, because I assumed that's where we'd be staying. But I'm going to cancel it. I bet they have in-room waxing here. Let's splurge."

"Location doesn't matter to me. Hair is getting ripped out either way."

Piper lunged for the phone. "That's the spirit!"

Chapter Twenty-Four

$\mathcal{B}$rendan had been hoping to get a lot of time alone with Piper while in Seattle. He hadn't expected to get it so soon, but he sure as hell wasn't going to complain. As the four of them stood in the lavish hotel lobby getting ready to part ways, he did his best not to feel underdressed in jeans, flannel, and boots. He'd taken off the beanie as soon as he'd gotten to his room, kind of dumbfounded by the level of extravagance. The price of their stay had tipped him off that it would be fancy, but he was going to spend the whole time worried about leaving boot prints on the carpet.

This is what she's used to.

This is what you'll give her.

Piper was laughing at Hannah's disgruntled expression. "Is it that bad?"

"She didn't even warn me. Just *rip*."

"Who didn't warn you?" Fox asked, splitting a curious look between the women. "Jesus. What happened since we left you?"

"We got waxed," Piper explained breezily. "In the room."

Hannah poked her sister in the ribs. "*Piper.*"

Piper paused in the act of fluffing her hair. "What? It's like a basic human function."

"Not for everyone." Hannah laughed, red-faced. "Oh my God. I should go before my sister embarrasses me any more." She turned to Fox, raised an eyebrow. "Ready?"

For once, Brendan's best friend appeared to be at a loss for words. "Uh, yeah." He coughed into his fist. "Let's go record shopping."

"Meet back here at six for dinner," Brendan said.

Fox saluted lazily and followed Hannah toward the exit.

They were almost to the revolving door when Piper tugged on Brendan's shirt, making him look down. "They worry me a little. She says they're just friendly, but I don't want my sister to get her heart broken."

Brendan wouldn't say it out loud, but he'd been worried about the same thing. Fox didn't have female friends. He had one-night stands. "I'll talk to him."

Piper nodded, though she cast one more worried glance at her sister's and Fox's retreating backs. "So . . ." She turned on a heel and gave Brendan her full attention. "It's just the two of us. For the whole afternoon. Should we go sightseeing?"

"No."

"No?" Her eyes were playful. "What did you have in mind?"

She obviously thought he was going to throw her over his shoulder and bring her back up to the room. And goddamn, he was tempted to spend the whole day fucking a bare-naked Piper on that ridiculous bed, but being predictable wouldn't serve him. He needed to use his time with her wisely. "I'm taking you shopping."

Her smile collapsed. A sheen coated her eyes.

A trembling hand pressed to her throat. "Y-you are?" she whispered.

He tucked a fall of hair behind her ear. "Yes."

"But . . . really? Now?"

"Yes."

She fanned her face. "For what?"

"Whatever you want."

Those blue eyes blinked. Blinked again. A line formed between her brows. "I can't . . . I can't think of a single thing I want right now."

"Maybe once you start looking—"

"No." She wet her lips, seeming almost surprised by the words coming out of her mouth. "Brendan, I will always love shopping and fancy hotels. Like, *love* them. But I don't need them. I don't need you to do"—she encompassed the lobby with a sweeping gesture—"all of this in order to make me happy." Her cheek pressed to his chest. "Can you let me into the recharging station, please?"

Without delay, his arms were wrapped around Piper, his mouth pressed to the crown of her head. Until she said the words and relief settled over him, he didn't know how badly he needed to hear them. He might be able to afford places like this, but he couldn't deny the need to be enough on his own. Oddly, now that she'd erased that worry, he found himself wanting to treat her to a day of her favorite things even more. "I'm taking you shopping, honey."

"No."

"Yes, I am."

"No, Brendan. This isn't necessary. I'd be just as happy watching them throw fish at Pike Place Market with you, and oh my God, I really mean that." She snuggled in closer, her hand fisting in his flannel. "I really, actually do."

"Piper." He dropped his mouth to her ear. "Spoiling you makes my dick hard."

"Why didn't you say so?" She grabbed his hand and tugged him toward the exit. "Let's go shopping!"

"Jeans?"

Piper lifted her chin. "You said whatever I want."

Enjoying the hell out of himself, Brendan followed Piper through the aisles of the classy Pacific Place shop, watching her ass punch side to side in her pink skirt. She was so in her element among the mannequins and racks of clothes, he was glad as hell he'd pushed to go shopping. As soon as they'd walked through the doors, salesgirls had descended on his girlfriend and they were already on a first-name basis, running off to retrieve a stack of jeans in Piper's size.

"Of course, you can get whatever you want," he said, trying to keep from knocking over racks with his wide shoulders. "I just figured you'd go straight for the dresses."

"I might have." She sent him a haughty look over her shoulder. "If I didn't remember you sarcastically asking me if I owned a pair of jeans."

"The night you went dancing at Blow the Man Down?" He thought back. "I didn't think you recalled half that night."

"Oh, only the important parts," she said. "Like backhanded slights against my wardrobe."

"I like your . . . wardrobe." All right, then. He used the word "wardrobe" now. With a straight face, too, apparently. "In the beginning, I thought it was . . ."

"Ridiculous?"

"Impractical," he corrected her firmly. "But I've changed my mind."

"You just like my clothes now because you get to take them off."

"That doesn't hurt. But mainly, they're you. That's the real reason." He watched the salesgirl approach with an armload of jeans and just barely stopped himself from barking at her to go away. "I like the things that make you Piper. Don't go changing them now."

"I'm not changing anything, Brendan," she said, and laughed, pulling him into the dressing-room area. "But I can only get away with dresses for so long. It's going to be fall soon, in the Pacific Northwest."

The salesgirl breezed in behind them and ushered Piper away, putting her in the closest dressing room with a half-dozen pairs of jeans of various colors and styles. Then she pointed at a tiny, feminine chair, wordlessly implying that Brendan should sit—and he did, awkwardly, feeling a lot like Gulliver. "Is this what it's like when you go shopping in LA?" he asked Piper through the curtain.

"Mmmm. Not exactly." She peeked out at him and winked. "I typically don't have a six-foot-four sea captain along for the ride."

He made an amused sound. "Does that make it better or worse?"

"Better. Way better." She pushed back the curtain and walked out in a pair of light-blue painted-on jeans and a black see-through bra. "Ooh, not a fan." She turned and looked at her butt in the full-length mirror. "Thoughts?"

Brendan dragged his jaw up off the fucking floor. "I'm sorry. How are you not a fan?"

She made a face. "The stitching is weird."

"The . . . what?" He leaned in for a closer look and immediately got distracted by the ass. "Who gives a shit?"

The salesgirl walked in and tilted her head. "Oh yeah. No. Pass on those."

Piper nodded. "That's what I thought."

"Are you two playing a joke on me? They're perfect."

Both women laughed. Out went the salesgirl. Piper retreated to the changing room. And Brendan was left wondering if he'd taken crazy pills. "Yeah, safe to say this is definitely different than shopping with my friends back in LA. I'm pretty sure half the time they tell me something looks great even when it doesn't. There's always a sense of competition. Trying to get the edge." A zipper went up and he watched her feet turn right, left, right under the curtain, smiling at the sparkly polish on her toes. It was so Piper. "I think maybe shopping hasn't been fun for a while and I didn't even realize it. Don't get me wrong, I adore the clothes. But when I think of going dress hunting with Kirby now, I can't remember feeling anything. I spent all of that time trying to give myself that first euphoric rush. But . . . I was more excited to get a deal on a fishing net at the harbor supply shop than I was buying my last Chanel bag."

She gasped.

Alarm snapped Brendan's spine straight. "What?"

"I think Daniel's lesson worked." She pushed aside the curtain, revealing her shocked expression. "I think I might appreciate money now, Brendan."

If he wasn't supposed to find her utterly fucking adorable, he was failing miserably.

"That's great, Piper," he said gruffly, ordering himself not to smile.

"Yeah." She pointed down at a pair of dark jeans that molded indecently to her mouthwatering hips. "These are a no, right?"

"They're a *yes*."

She shook her head and closed the curtain again. "And they're a hundred dollars. I looked at the price tag!" Then she mumbled, "I *think* that's a lot?"

His head tipped back. "I make more than that on one crab, Piper."

"What? No. How many crabs do you catch?"

"In a season? If I hit the quota? Eighty thousand pounds."

When she opened the curtain again, she had the calculator pulled up on her phone. With her mouth in an O, she slowly turned the screen to show him all the zeroes. "Brendan, this is like, *millions* of dollars."

He just looked at her.

"Oh no," she said after a beat, shaking her head. "This is bad."

Brendan frowned. "How is this bad?"

"I just learned the value of money. Now I find out I have a rich boyfriend?" She sighed sadly, closed the curtain. "We have to break up, Brendan. For my own good."

"*What?*" Panic gave him immediate, searing heartburn. No. No, this wasn't happening. He'd heard her wrong. But if he hadn't misheard, they weren't leaving this fucking dressing room until she changed her mind. He lunged to his feet and ripped the curtain open, only to find Piper laughing into her cupped palm, her sides shaking. Relief washed through him, as if an overhead sprinkler system had been engaged. "That wasn't funny," he said raggedly.

"It was." She giggled. "You know it was."

"Do you see me laughing?"

She pressed her lips together to get rid of the smile, but her eyes were still sparkling with laughter. But he couldn't be mad at her, especially when she crossed her wrists behind his neck, pressed her soft body up against his hard one, and coaxed his mouth into a winding kiss. "I'm sorry." She licked gently at his tongue. "I didn't think you'd buy it so easily."

He grunted, annoyed at himself for enjoying the way Piper was trying to get back in his good graces. Her fingers twisted the ends of his hair, her eyes were contrite. All of it was oddly soothing. Christ, being in love was doing a number on him. He was a goner.

"Will you forgive me if I let you pick out my jeans?" she murmured against his lips.

Brendan smoothed his palms back and forth along her waist. "I'm not mad. I can't be. Not at you."

She dropped her hands away from his neck and handed him the next pair of jeans in the stack. As he watched, she unzipped the ones she was wearing and peeled them down her legs. Good God almighty, Piper was bent over in front of the mirror, her ass nearly brushing the glass—and looking down from above, he could see everything. The mint-green strip of fabric tucked up between her supple cheeks, the suggestion of a tan line peeking out.

By the time she straightened, her face was flushed, and Brendan's cock was straining against his zipper. "Put them on for me?"

Christ. It didn't matter that the salesgirl could come in at any minute. Arrested as he was by those big, blue bedroom eyes, nothing mattered but her. Hell, maybe that would always be the case. Brendan let out a shuddering breath and went down on his knees. He started to open the waistband so she could step into them, but the little triangle of her panties absorbed his attention when he remembered she'd gotten waxed that morning.

Truthfully, he'd never given a thought to women's . . . landscaping before. But ever since the first time he'd eaten Piper's pussy, he'd craved *hers*. The way it looked, felt, tasted, the smooth succulence of her.

"Can I see?"

Almost shyly, she nodded.

Brendan tucked a finger in the center of her thong's front waistband and tugged it down, revealing that teasing little split, the nub of flesh *just* pushing her lips apart. He swayed forward with a growl, pressing his face to the lush flesh and inhaling deeply. "This is mine."

Her stomach hollowed on an intake of breath. "Yes."

"Going to spoil you with my credit card now." He kissed the top of her slit. "Then have you sit on my face and spoil you fucking rotten with my tongue later."

"*Brendan.*"

He banded his arms around her knees when they dipped, using his upper body to lean her back against the dressing room wall. When he'd made sure she was stable, he urged her without words to step into the legs, one at a time. His hands scooted the denim up her calves, knees, and thighs, his mouth leaving kisses on the disappearing skin as he went. It hurt to drag the zipper up and hide her pussy away, but he did it, swirling his tongue around her belly button while engaging the snap.

He stood, turning Piper around so she was facing the mirror. He tugged her ass back into his lap so she could feel his hard-on, making her lips puff open, her neck go limp.

Through dazed eyes, she scanned her reflection, her attention on Brendan's hand as it traveled down her stomach, his long fingers delving into the front waistband to grip her pussy roughly, earning him a shocked whimper. "Keepers. Definitely."

"Y-yes, we'll get these," she said in a rush. Brendan tightened his grip again, lifted, and she went up on her toes, her lips falling open on a gasp. "Yes, yes, yes."

Brendan planted a kiss on the side of her neck, biting down on the spot and slowly sliding his hand out of her jeans. When she stopped swaying, he left her flushed in front of the mirror and edged out into the waiting area. "Good girl."

"You know," she panted through the curtain. "Shopping is more about the journey than the destination."

He gestured to the salesgirl as she walked in. "She'll take them all."

Chapter Twenty-Five

$\mathcal{P}$iper sniffed Brendan's neck and pursed her lips thought-fully. "Nope, it's not the right one yet. Too citrusy."

Brendan leaned an elbow on the glass counter, half amused, half impatient. "Piper, you're going to run out of places to spray me."

It was getting later in the afternoon, and after lunch downtown—during which Brendan tried his first tiramisu and *liked* it!—they were back at the hotel. Her boyfriend had seemed quite inclined to get her upstairs as fast as possible, but she'd dragged him into a men's shop just off the lobby to see if they could find him a signature scent.

Was she stalling? Maybe a little.

For some reason, her nerves were popping.

Which was crazy. So they were going upstairs to get it on. They'd done that twice before, right? There was no reason for the extra race of bubbles in her bloodstream. Except a new torrent of them was set loose every time Brendan kissed her knuckles or put an arm around her shoulder. And even in the air conditioning, the skin of her neck flamed, and she found herself taking deep, deep breaths, attempting to still her sprinting heart.

If she could just focus on finding him the perfect cologne, that would give her enough time to relax. Or at least figure out why she couldn't.

She leaned across the glass to pluck up a square, sage-colored bottle, and Brendan splayed a hand on the small of her back. Casually. But her pulse spiked like she was taking a lie detector test and being questioned about her past spending habits. Mentally shaking herself, she lifted the bottle and took a sniff. "Oh," she whispered, smelling it again to be sure. "This is it. This is your scent."

And maybe it was the craziest thing, but finding that elusive essence of Brendan, holding it right there in her hand and having it flood her senses . . . it dropped that final veil that had been obscuring her feelings. She was hopelessly, irrevocably in love with this man.

The change in their surroundings made it impossible not to acknowledge every little reason she gravitated toward him. His honor, his patience, his dependability and steadfast nature. How he could lead and be respected without being power hungry. His love of nature and tradition and *home*. The way he so delicately handled his father-in-law's feelings even got to her.

As soon as she acknowledged the depth of her feelings, those three little words threatened to trip out of her mouth. *That* was the source of her nerves. Because where would that leave her? In a relationship. A permanent one. Not *only* with this man but with Westport.

"Piper," Brendan said urgently. "Are you okay?"

"Of course I am," she responded, far too brightly. "I—I found it. It's perfect."

His eyebrow raise was skeptical as he turned the bottle around. "Splendid Wood?"

"See? You were made for each other." She stared into his eyes like a lovesick puppy for several too-long seconds, before breaking the spell. "Um, we have to smell it on you, though."

Brendan was regarding her with a puckered brow, practically confirming that her behavior was off. "You've already sprayed my wrists and both sides of my neck," he said. "There's nothing left."

"Your chest?" She looked around the small men's shop. The clerk was busy on the other side with another customer. "Just a quick sniff test. So we don't waste money." She beamed. "Oh, listen to me, Brendan! I'm practically cutting coupons here."

Affection flashed in his face. "Be quick," he growled, unbuttoning the top three buttons of his flannel. "I'm going to need three showers to get this stuff off."

Piper danced in place, excited by the imminent breakthrough. This was going to be perfect. She just knew it. With an effort, she held back her squeal and released a puff of mist into Brendan's chest hair while he held open the flannel. She leaned in, burying her nose there, inhaling the combination of the earthiness and Brendan's salt water . . . and oh Lord, yes, she was in love all right. Her brain sighed with total contentment and joy at having captured him, found a way to breathe him in anytime she wanted. She must have stayed there in a dreamlike state, exhaling gustily, for long moments, because Brendan finally chuckled, and she opened her eyes.

"What are you thinking about down there?"

That if I'm not careful, there are going to be little sea captain babies scampering around.

And how bad did that sound, anyway?

Not bad at all. Kind of amazing, actually.

"I was thinking that I'm proud of you," she finally answered, rebuttoning his shirt. "You tried tiramisu today. And . . . and you just plan trips to Seattle now. On a whim. You're like a new man. And I was thinking . . ."

How she'd changed a lot, too, since coming to Westport. Since meeting Brendan. What she'd thought before was living life to the fullest had actually been living life for other people to watch. To gawk at. She wouldn't lie to herself and pretend one month had completely cured her of her deeply rooted yen for attention. For praise. For what she'd once interpreted as love. Now, though? She was participating in her own life. Not just posing and pretending. The world was so much bigger than her, and she was really seeing it now. She was really looking.

In the dressing room while trying on jeans, it didn't even occur to her to snap a selfie in the mirror. She just wanted to be there, in the moment, with this man. Because the way he made her feel was three million times better than the way three million strangers made her feel.

Holy God. Was she going to tell Brendan she loved him?

Yeah.

Yeah, she was.

If she thought breaking into a rooftop pool and summoning the police department was crazy, this felt a million times riskier. This was like rappelling down the side of that LA hotel with sticks of dynamite poking out of her ears. Because she was new at this, and the road to finding out exactly where she fit into her new place was a long one.

What if, ultimately, she didn't fit at all?

The way she'd felt when Adrian cut her loose would be laughable compared to disappointing Brendan. He knew exactly who he was (commander of a vessel), what he wanted (a fleet of boats), and how to get it (apparently make millions of dollars and just have boats built??). Meanwhile, she'd spent a week trying to find a chandelier with the right vibe.

This could be a disaster.

But she looked into his eyes now and heard his words echo back from the deck of the *Della Ray. You have perseverance, character, and a huge heart.*

And she chose to believe him.

She chose to believe in herself.

"Brendan, I—"

Her phone went nuts in her purse. Loud, scattered notes that she didn't immediately place because it had been so long since hearing them.

"Oh." She reared back a little. "That's Kirby's ringtone."

"Kirby." His brows snuck together. "The girl who turned you in to the police?"

"The one and only. She hasn't called me since I left." Something told her not to, but she unzipped her purse and took out the phone anyway, weighing it in her hand. "I wonder if something is wrong. Maybe I should answer."

Brendan said nothing, just studied her face.

Her indecision lasted too long, and the phone stopped screaming.

She blew out a breath of relief, glad the decision had been

taken out of her hands—and then the phone started blowing up. It wasn't just Kirby calling again; it was text messages from names she vaguely recognized, email pings . . . and now another number with an LA area code was calling on the other line. What was going on?

"I guess I should take this," she muttered, frowning. "Can I meet you by the elevators?"

"Yeah," Brendan said after a moment, seeming like he wanted to say more.

"It's just a phone call."

When that statement came out sounding like she was trying to reassure herself, too, she cut her losses and left the shop. Was it just a phone call, though? Her finger hovered over the green answer button. This was the first time her LA life had touched her since coming to Washington. She hadn't even answered yet, but it felt like someone was shaking her in bed, trying to wake her up from a dream.

"You're being ridiculous," she scolded herself quietly, hitting talk. "Hey, Kirby. Really stretched that apology window, didn't you, babe?"

Piper frowned at her reflection in the steel elevator bank. Was it her imagination or did she sound completely different talking to her LA friends?

"Piper! I did apologize! Didn't I? Oh my God, if not, I am, like, down on my knees. Seriously. I was such a terrible friend. I just couldn't afford for my dad to cut me off."

Why, oh, why did she answer the call? "Yeah, neither could I." It might have something to do with the endless dings and vibrations happening against her ear. "Look, it's fine, Kirby. I don't hold it against you. What's up?"

"What's *up*? Are you serious?" A few honks fired off in the background, the sound of a bus motoring past. "Have you seen the cover of *LA Weekly*?"

"No," she said slowly.

"You are on it—and looking like a smoke show, bitch. Oh my God, *the headline*, Piper. 'A Party Princess's Vanishing Act.' Everyone is freaking out."

Her temples started to pound. "I don't understand."

"Go look at their Instagram. The post is blowing up." She squealed. "The gist of the article is that you threw the party of the decade and then disappeared. It's like a giant mystery, Piper. You're like, fucking *Banksy* or something. Everyone wants to know why you went from Wilshire Boulevard to some random harbor. You didn't even tag your location! People are dying for details."

"Really?" She found a bench and fell onto it, trying to puzzle through the unexpected news. "No one cared yesterday."

Kirby ignored that. "More importantly, they want to know when you'll come back and reclaim your throne! Which brings me to the main point of my phone call." She exhaled sharply. "Let me throw you a welcome back party. I've already got the venue lined up. Exclusive invites only. The Party Princess Returns. I might have leaked the idea to a few designers, some beverage companies, and they are offering to pay you, Piper. A whole lot of money to walk out in their dress, drink their shit on camera. I'm talking about six figures. Let's do this. Let's make you a fucking legend."

A prickle climbed Piper's arm, and she looked up to find Brendan standing a few yards away, holding her bag of jeans and a smaller one, which she assumed contained the cologne.

He wasn't close enough to hear the conversation, but his expression told her he sensed the gravity of the phone call.

Was the phone call that important, though? This rise in popularity would be fleeting, fast. She'd have to ride the wave as far as possible, then immediately start trying to find a fresh way to be relevant. Compared to the man she loved being out on a boat in a storm . . . or a wave coming out of nowhere and snatching someone off the deck . . . a trip back into the limelight didn't seem that significant.

A month ago, this unexpected windfall of notoriety would have been the greatest thing that ever happened in her life.

Now it mostly left her hollow.

Was there a nagging part of Piper that wanted to fall back into this lifestyle she was guaranteed to be good at? Yes, she'd be lying if she said there wasn't. It would be second nature to strut into a dark club to the perfect song and be applauded for accomplishing absolutely nothing but being pretty and rich and photogenic.

"Piper. Are you there?"

"Yeah," she croaked, her eyes still locked with Brendan's. "I can't commit."

"Yes, you can," Kirby said, exasperated. "Look, I heard Daniel slashed your funds, but if you do this party, you'll have enough cash to move out, do your own thing. Maybe we could even revamp Pucker Up now that you have some extra clout! I'll buy you the plane ticket back to LA, all right? You can stay in my guest room. Done and done. I booked the venue for September seventh. Everywhere was already taken for Labor Day."

"September seventh?" Piper massaged the center of her forehead. "Isn't that a Tuesday?"

"So? What are you, forty?"

God. This was her best friend? "Kirby, I have to go. I'll think about it."

"Are you insane? There is nothing to think about. Paris is on my short list to DJ this thing—and she's at the *bottom*. This is the one we'll be talking about for the rest of our lives."

Brendan was coming closer, his gaze laser-focused on her face.

I can't tell him.

She didn't want to tell him about any of this. *LA Weekly*. The party being planned in her honor. Her splashy new title. Any of it.

If she made a pro/con list of LA versus Westport, *Piper loves Brendan* would be in the pro-Westport column and that outweighed *any* con. They couldn't discuss a potential return to LA without Piper revealing her feelings, and then . . . how could she do anything but turn the opportunity down after telling him those three words? But she wasn't one hundred percent ready to say no to Kirby. Not just yet. If she said no to this triumphant return to the scene she'd lived for the last decade, she'd be saying yes to Westport. Yes to being with this man who endangered himself as a matter of course. Yes to starting over from scratch.

Kirby was rambling in her ear about a Burberry-inspired color scheme and a signature drink called the Horny Heiress.

"Okay, thanks, Kirby. I miss you, too. Have to go. Bye."

"Don't you dare hang—"

Piper hung up quickly and powered down her phone, hopping to her feet. "Hey." She directed her most winning and hopefully distracting smile at Brendan. "You bought the cologne? I wanted to get it for you as a gift."

"If it makes you want to smell me in public, I'll consider it an investment." He paused, nodding at her phone. "Everything okay?"

"What? Yes." *Stop fluttering your hands.* "Just some gossip that Kirby thought was urgent. Spoiler: it's not. Let's go upstairs, right?"

Piper sprung forward and hit the call button, praising the saints when an empty car to their immediate left opened. She took Brendan's thick wrist, grateful when he allowed himself to be dragged inside. And then she pushed him up against the elevator wall and utilized two of her favorite skills—avoidance and distraction—to keep him from asking any more questions.

Questions she didn't want to ask herself, either.

Chapter Twenty-Six

$\mathcal{B}$rendan couldn't shake the sense that Piper had just slipped out of his reach—and it fucking terrified him.

While cologne shopping, she'd looked up at him in a way she hadn't before. Like she was getting ready to lay down her weapons and surrender. He'd never had anyone look at him like that. Scared and hopeful all at once. Beautifully exposed. And he couldn't *wait* to reward that trust. To make her glad she'd taken the leap, because he'd catch her. Couldn't wait to tell her that life before she'd shown up in Westport had been lacking all color and light and optimism.

Her hands smoothed down his chest now. Lower, to his abdomen.

She leaned in and buried her nose in his chest, inhaling, moaning softly . . .

Tracing the outline of his cock with her knuckle.

That touch, obviously meant to distract, trapped him between need and irritation. He didn't want Piper when her mind was obviously elsewhere. He wanted those barriers gone. Wanted all of her, every fucking ounce. But there was a part of him that was nervous, too. Nervous as hell that he wasn't equipped to fight whatever unseen foe he was up against.

The latter accounted for his harshness when he caught her wrist, holding it away from his distended fly. "Tell me what the phone call was really about."

She flinched at his tone, pushed away from him. "I *did* tell you. It was nothing."

"Are you really going to lie to me?"

God, she looked literally and figuratively cornered, stuck in the elevator with nowhere to run. Not that she didn't look for an exit, even on the ceiling. "I don't have to tell you every single thing," she stammered finally, punching the OPEN DOOR button repeatedly, even though they were only midway to the sixteenth floor. "Are you planning on being this domineering all the time?" Her laugh was high-pitched, panicky, and it burned a hole in his chest. "Because it's a little much."

Nope. Not taking that bait. "Piper. Come here and look at me."

"No."

"Why not?"

She rolled her eyes. "I don't want to be interrogated."

"Good," he ground out. "I want the truth without having to ask you for it."

He caught her audible swallow just before the elevator door opened, and she was off like a shot, speed-walking in the opposite direction of his room, which was where the hell she was going to end up, if he had anything to say about it. Brendan caught up with her right before she could swipe into her own room, wrapping an arm around her middle and hauling her back up against his chest.

"*Enough.*"

"Don't talk to me like a child."

"You're acting like one."

She gasped. "*You're* the one—"

"Christ. If you tell me I'm the one who wanted a high-maintenance girlfriend, you're going to piss me off, Piper." He gripped her chin and tipped her head back until it met his shoulder. "I want *you*. However you are, whatever you are, I want *you*. And I'll fight to get inside that head as many times as it takes. Over and over and over. Don't you dare doubt me."

Her body heaved with two deep breaths.

"Kirby called to tell me I'm on the cover of *LA Weekly. Okay?* 'A Party Princess's Vanishing Act.' There's a whole story and . . . now I guess, ta-dah, I'm interesting again. After a month of silence, everyone suddenly wants to know where I've gone." She broke free of his grip and pushed away, her posture defensive. "Kirby wants to throw me a big, over-the-top coming-home party. And I didn't want to tell you because now you're going to bear down on me until I magically produce answers about what I want—and *I don't know!*"

Brendan's pulse ricocheted around his veins, his nerves escalating to full-on fear. *LA Weekly.* Over-the-top party. Did he stand a fucking chance against any of that? "What *do* you know, Piper?" he managed, hoarsely.

Her eyes closed. "I know I love you, Brendan. I know I love you and that's it."

The world went momentarily soundless, devoid of noise except for the sound of his heart tendons stretching, on the verge of snapping under the pressure of the wonder she'd just stuffed inside of it. She loved him. This woman loved *him*.

"How can you say 'that's it'?" He took a giant step and scooped her into his arms, rejoicing when she came easily, looping her legs around his waist, burying her face in his neck. "How can you say that's it when it's the best thing that's ever happened to me?" He kissed her hair, her cheek, pressed his mouth to her ear. "I love you, baby. Goddammit, I love you back. As long as that's the case, everything will be fine—and it will *always* be the case. We'll work on the details. Okay?"

"Okay." She lifted her head and nodded, laughed in a dazed way. "Yes. Okay."

"We love each other, Piper." He turned and strode toward his room, grateful he already had the key in his hand, because he wouldn't have been able to take his attention off her to search for it. "I won't let anything or anybody fuck with that."

Jesus. She'd been . . . unlocked. Her eyes were soft and trusting and beautiful and, most important, confident. In him. In them. He'd done the right thing pushing, hard as it had been to see her scared. But it was all right now, thank God. Thank *God*.

He slapped the room key over the sensor and kicked the door open, his sole mission in life to give this woman an orgasm. To see those softened blue eyes go blind and know his body was responsible. Would *always* be responsible for meeting her needs.

"I need you so bad," she sobbed, tugging at his collar, moving her hips in desperate little circles. "Oh my God, I'm *aching*."

"You know I'm going to handle it." He bit the side of her neck, thrust his hips up roughly, and listened to her breath catch. "Don't you?"

"Yes. *Yes*."

Brendan set Piper on her feet and spun her around, then

yanked her skirt up above her hips. "Maybe someday we'll be able to wait long enough to get undressed at the same time," he rasped, stripping her panties down to her ankles, before attacking his zipper with shaking hands. "But it's not going to be today. Get both knees on the edge of the bed."

God, he loved Piper when she was a shameless flirt. When she was pissed. When she was being a tease or making him work his ass off. But he loved her most as she was now. Honest. Hiding nothing. Hot and needy and real. Clambering onto the very edge of the bed and tilting her hips, begging. "Please, Brendan. Will you, please, will you, *please* . . ."

There was no way he couldn't take a moment to admire the work of art that was Piper. The lithe lines of her parted thighs, the ass that made his life heaven and hell. He gripped the cheeks now and kneaded them, spreading the flesh so he could see what was waiting for him in between. "Ah, baby. I should always be the one saying 'please,'" he said hoarsely, leaning down and stroking his tongue over the tight, gathered skin of her back entrance. She huffed his name, then moaned it hesitantly, hopefully, and yeah, he couldn't stop himself from yanking her sexy backside closer, burying his mouth in the valley between and tonguing her roughly.

"Oh wow," she breathed, pushing back against him. "What are you—*oh my God.*"

He brought his hand around her hip, trailing two fingers between her soft folds, and enjoyed the act of getting her pussy wet as hell by licking something else entirely. Enjoying her initial shyness and the way she eventually couldn't help but slide her knees even wider on the bed, her hips undulating in time with the hungry strokes of his tongue. By the time he let his tongue travel down and around to her sex, her clit was so swollen; he batted the nub with his tongue a few times, rubbed the sensitive button with his thumb, and she broke apart, hiccupping into the comforter, her delicious wetness coating her inner thighs, his mouth.

She was panting as he rose, dropped his chest down onto her back and pushed his cock inside of her still-contracting pussy. "*Mine,*" he gritted, the tightness of her cinching his balls up painfully, firing every ounce of his blood with possessiveness. "I'm taking what's mine now."

A movement ahead of them on the bed reminded Brendan of the mirrored headboard, and he almost came, caught off guard by the erotic sight of her slack jaw and tits that bounced along with every pump of his hips. His body loomed behind her, damn near twice her size, his lips peeled back from his teeth like he might very well devour her whole. Who wouldn't? Who wouldn't want to gather every part of this woman as close as possible? To consume her fire? Who wouldn't die trying to earn her loyalty?

"Christ, you're so beautiful," he groaned, falling on top of her, pinning her to the bed and bucking, filling her like she was filling his chest, his mind. All of him. Completing him just by breathing. He took her hair in a fist, using it to pull her head back, locking their gazes in the mirror. She gasped, jolted around his cock, her walls telling him she was as turned on by the movie they were starring in as he was. "Yeah, you like being admired and complimented, don't you, Piper? No better compliment than how hard you make my cock, is there? How rough you make me give it to you? Can't even get my goddamn jeans down." Her breath hitched, and she started to squirm underneath him, her fingers clawing at the comforter as she gave a closed-mouth scream of his name. "Go on. Give me that second one, baby. Want to turn you fucking limp."

Her blue eyes went blind, and she moaned hoarsely, her hips twitching beneath him, spasms racking her pussy and plunging him over the edge. He rocked into her hot channel one more time, spearing deep, looking her in the eyes as he growled her name, letting loose the excruciating pressure between his legs, panting against the side of her head.

"I love you," she gasped, the words seeming to catch her off guard, alarm her, and Brendan wondered if it was possible for his heart to explode out of his chest. How was he going to survive her? Every time he thought his feelings for her had finally reached their apex, she proved him wrong, and his chest grew another size. How could he continue at this rate for the next fifty, sixty years?

"Piper, I love you, too. *I love you.*" Still pressing her down into the bed, he left slow kisses on her temple, her shoulder, her neck, before finally rolling off her to one side, drawing her tight to the place she called the recharging station. And he'd laughed at that name, but when she found her place in his arms, her features relaxed and she sighed, as if being held by him truly made everything okay. Jesus Christ, that privilege humbled him.

"I've never said it to anyone before," she murmured, resting her head on his bicep. "It didn't feel like I always thought it would."

He ran his hand down her hair. "How did you think it would feel?"

She thought about it. "Getting it over with. Like ripping off a Band-Aid."

"And how did it feel instead?"

"The reverse. Like putting a bandage on. Wrapping it tight." She studied his chin a moment, then ticked her eyes up to his. "I think because I trust you. I completely trust you. That's a huge part of love, isn't it?"

"Yeah. I reckon it has to be." He swallowed around the lump in his throat. "But I'm not an expert, baby. I've never loved like this."

It took a moment for her to speak. "I'll never keep anything from you again." Her exhale was rocky. "Oh wow. Big post-coital declarations happening here. But I mean it. No more keeping things to myself. Not even for the length of an elevator ride. I won't make you fight to get into my head. I don't want that. I don't want to be constant work for you, Brendan. Not when you make it so easy to love you."

He crushed her against him, no other choice, unless he wanted to splinter apart from the sheer fucking emotion she produced inside of him. "Constant work, Piper? No. You mis-understand me." He tipped her chin up and kissed her mouth. "When the reward is as perfect as you, as perfect as this, the work is a fucking honor."

Brendan rolled Piper onto her back as their kisses escalated, his cock growing stiff again in a matter of seconds, swelling painfully when she begged him to take off his shirt. He com-plied, somehow finding a way to kick off his jeans and boxers before stripping her clean of any clothing, too. Satisfied sounds burst from their mouths when their naked bodies finally twined together, skin on skin, not a single barrier in sight.

Piper's lips curved with humor beneath his. "So are we just *not* going to talk about the tongue thing?"

Their laughter turned to sighs and eventually to moans, the bedsprings groaning beneath them. And it seemed like nothing could touch the perfection of them. Not after such hard-fought confessions. Not when they couldn't seem to breathe without each other.

But if Brendan had learned one thing as a captain, it was this: Just when it seemed like the storm was beginning to break and daylight spread across the calm waters? That's when the biggest wave hit.

And forgetting that lesson could very well cost him everything.

Chapter Twenty-Seven

The rest of their time in Seattle was a dream.

Hannah and Fox met them in the hotel lobby at the designated time, loaded down with secondhand records. And while Piper still wanted Brendan to speak to Fox about Hannah being off-limits, her fears were temporarily put to rest by the genuine friendship that seemed to have sprouted between the two. One afternoon together and they were finishing each other's sentences. They had inside jokes and everything. Not that it surprised Piper. Her sister was a goddess with a pure, romantic spirit, and it was about time people flocked to her.

As long as certain appendages remained in their pants.

At dinner, Brendan and Fox told them about life on the boat. Piper's favorite story was about a crab claw getting fastened to Deke's nipple, requiring Brendan to give him stitches. She made them tell it twice while she laughed herself into a wine-aided stupor. Halfway through the meal, Fox brought up last week's storm, and Piper watched Brendan stiffen, his gaze flying to hers, gauging if she could handle it. She was surprised to find that while her nerves bubbled up ominously, she was able to calm them with a few deep breaths. Apparently Brendan was so happy about Piper encouraging Fox to finish the story, he pulled her over onto his lap, and that's where she happily remained for the rest of the evening.

They slept in their assigned rooms that night, although some naughty texts had been exchanged between herself and Brendan, and the next morning they piled into the truck to head back to Westport.

With her hand clasped tightly in Brendan's on the console and Hannah's road-trip mix drifting from the speakers, Piper found herself . . . looking forward to going home. She'd called Abe this morning to let him know she would be late for their walk, followed by a quick call to Opal to arrange coffee later in the week.

There were over a hundred text messages and countless emails on her phone from LA acquaintances, club owners, and Kirby, but she was ignoring them for now, not wanting anything to steal the lingering beauty of the Seattle trip.

Apart from those increasingly urgent messages about September 7, Piper was delighted to have two texts from girls she'd met in Blow the Man Down. They wanted to meet up and help plan the Labor Day party. And how would she feel about a group makeup tutorial?

Good. She felt . . . *really* good about it. With her growing number of friends and the grand opening on the horizon, Piper suddenly had a packed schedule.

What if she could actually belong in Westport?

Yes, Brendan made her feel like she already did. But he had his livelihood here. A community he'd known since birth. The last thing she wanted was to be dependent on him. If she stayed in Westport, she needed to make her own way. To be a person independent of their relationship, as well as a member of it. And for the first time, that didn't seem like a far-fetched possibility.

When they arrived in Westport, Brendan dropped Fox off at his apartment first, then completed the five-minute drive to Piper and Hannah's. His expression could only be described as surly as he shoved the truck into park, visibly reluctant to say good-bye to her. She could relate. But there was no way she'd make it a habit to leave Hannah alone.

Her sister leaned over the front seat now, chin propped on her hands. "All right, Brendan," she said drily. "Piper was singing 'Natural Woman' at the top of her lungs in the shower this morning—"

"Hannah!" Piper sputtered.

"And since I like seeing her happy, I'm going to do you a solid."

Brendan turned his head slightly, his interest piqued. "What's that?"

"Okay. I'm assuming you have a guest room at your place," Hannah said.

Piper's boyfriend grunted in the affirmative.

"Well . . ." Hannah drew out. "I could come stay in it. That would alleviate Piper's sister guilt and she could stay in the captain's quarters."

"Go pack," Brendan responded, no hesitation. "I'll wait."

"Hold on. What?" Piper turned on the seat, splitting an incredulous look between these two crazy people she loved. "I'm not—we're not—just going to move into your house, Brendan. That requires a-a . . . at the very least, a serious conversation."

"I'll let you chat," Hannah said merrily, hopping out of the truck.

"Brendan . . ." Piper started.

"Piper." He reached over the console, brushed his thumb along her cheekbone. "You belong in my bed. There's nothing to discuss."

She puffed a laugh. "How can you say that? I've never lived with anyone, but I'm pretty sure a significant portion of time is spent with no makeup and . . . laundry! Have you taken dirty clothes into consideration? Where will I put mine? I've managed to maintain a certain air of mystique—"

"Mystique," he repeated, lips twitching.

"Yes, that's right." She batted away his touch. "What's going to happen when there is no more . . . mystery left?"

"I don't want any mysteries when it comes to you. And we have to leave on a fishing trip on Saturday. Two nights away." *Just a few days from now.* "I want every second I can get with you until I pull out of the harbor."

"Saturday." This was news to her, although she'd known at some point he would be going back out on the water. Usually the turnaround was even tighter, but they'd taken a full week off after crab season. "Do you think you'll be back for the grand opening on Labor Day?"

"Damn right I will. I wouldn't miss it." He raised a casual eyebrow, as if he hadn't just made her pulse thrum with undiluted joy. "Will separate laundry baskets sway you?"

"Maybe." She chewed her lip. "There would have to be a no-kissing-until-I've-brushed-my-teeth rule."

"Nah, fuck that." His gaze dropped to the hem of her skirt.

"I want to push right into sleepy Piper and make her legs shake first thing in the morning."

"Fine," she blurted. "I'll go pack, then."

His expression became a mixture of triumph and affection. "Good."

Frowning at her boyfriend, even though her heart was tap-dancing, she pushed open the door of the truck. Before she could close it behind her, she remembered her promise to meet Abe and walk him to the museum. "How about we come over around dinnertime?" she said to Brendan. "We'll get groceries on the way. Maybe you can give me a cooking lesson."

"I'll have my extinguisher handy."

"Har-har." Was it normal for one's face to actually ache from smiling? "I'll see you tonight, Captain."

His silver-green eyes smoked with promise. "Tonight."

Piper jogged to the hardware store and walked Abe to the maritime museum, chatting with him for a while before continuing her run to Opal's house for coffee. Walking back to No Name, she tapped out replies to her new friends, Patty and Val, arranging a time to plan for Labor Day. She and Hannah would have to kick their productivity into hyperdrive to have the bar ready in time—they didn't even have a new sign yet—but with some determination, they could do it.

That evening, the sisters packed enough clothes for a couple of nights and walked to the market with their backpacks, buying ingredients identical to the ones Brendan dropped into her handcart that first morning in Westport.

Butterfly wings swept her stomach when she knocked on his door, but the strokes turned languid and comforting the moment his extra-large frame appeared in the entrance . . . in gray sweatpants and a T-shirt.

And *o-kay*. Just like that, the advantages of this living arrangement were already making themselves known.

"Don't look at my boyfriend's dick print," Piper whispered to Hannah as they followed him into the house, sending her sister into doubled-over laughter.

Brendan cocked—ha—an eyebrow at them over his shoulder, but continued on until they reached the guest bedroom, carrying the groceries they'd brought in one hand. The room he led them to was small and just off the kitchen, but it had a nice view of the garden and the bed looked infinitely more comfortable than the bunk back at No Name.

"Thanks, this is perfect," Hannah said, dropping her backpack on the floor. She turned in a circle to observe the rest of the room and sucked in a breath, her hand flying up to cover her mouth. "What is . . . what is that?"

Puzzled by her sister's change in demeanor, Piper's gaze traveled from Brendan's sweatpants to the object that had elicited the reaction. There on the desk was a record player. Dusty and heavy-looking. "I remembered my parents gave me theirs before they moved," Brendan said, crossing his arms, nodding at it. "Went and got it out of the basement."

"This is a vintage Pioneer," Hannah breathed, running her finger along the glass top. She turned wide eyes on Brendan. "I can use it?"

He nodded once. "That's why I brought it up." As if he hadn't just made Hannah's life, he jerked his chin at the closet. "Put whatever records I could find in there. Might be nothing."

"Anything will sound like something on this." Hannah's knees dipped, and she leapt up, doing an excited dance. "I don't even care if you unearthed this specifically to drown out the sex noises. *Thank you.*"

Brendan's ears deepened slightly in color, and Piper somehow fell further in love with him. Doing something nice for her sister had earned her everlasting devotion. And when he said, in his gruff, reserved way, "No. Thanks for, uh . . . letting me have Piper here," she almost fainted dead away. "I'll take that."

He eased the backpack off Piper's shoulders, kissed her forehead, and abruptly left the room. They observed his departure like seagulls watching a full slice of bread sailing through the air—and thanks to her harbor jogs, Piper knew what that looked like now. Reverent.

You have to marry him, Hannah mouthed.

I know, Piper mouthed back. *What the fuck?*

Still no actual sound came out of Hannah's mouth. *Ask him first. Do it now.*

I might. Oh God. I might.

Hannah carefully draped herself over the record player. "You can go on double dates with me and my record player. Piper, *look* at it." She slumped into the desk chair. "At the expo, I had my eye on this perfect, perfect Fleetwood Mac forty-five. It was too expensive. But if I'd known I had this Pioneer to play it on, I would have splurged."

"Oh no. It spoke to you?"

"Loud and clear." Hannah sighed, waving off her sadness. "It's fine. If it was meant to be, I'll run into it again one day." She pushed to her feet. "Let's go make dinner. I'm starved."

The three of them fell into a happy pattern.

In the mornings, Brendan woke Piper up with fingertips trailing up and down her belly, which led to her backside teasing his lap. Sometimes he rolled her over facedown and yanked her up onto her knees, taking her fast and furiously, her hands clinging to the headboard for purchase. Other times, he tossed her knees up over his muscular shoulders and rocked into her slowly, whispering gruff praise into the crook of her neck, the thick push and pull of his shaft between her legs as reliable as the tide, never failing to leave her limp and trembling, her cries lingering in the cool, dim air of his bedroom.

After she'd floated back down to earth from their intense lovemaking, she dressed for her jog and went to meet Abe, helping him up the stairs of the museum before continuing on her way. She'd return home and shower, then have breakfast with Brendan and Hannah before heading to No Name for work in his truck. Apart from the sign, the bar just needed décor and a few final touches. Brendan hung the chandelier, laughing at the way Piper squealed in victory, declaring it perfect. They arranged high top tables and stools, hung strings of lights on the back patio, and cleaned sawdust off everything.

"I've been thinking about the name," Piper said one afternoon, waiting until her sister looked at her. "Um . . . how do you feel about Cross and Daughters?"

A sound rushed out of Hannah, her eyes taking on a sheen. "I love it, Pipes."

Brendan came up behind her, planting a hard kiss on her shoulder. "It's perfect."

"I wish we had a little more time," Hannah said. "That name deserves a great sign."

"It does. But I think . . . maybe what's perfect about this place is that it's not. It's personal, not flawless. Right?" Piper laughed. "Let's paint it ourselves. It'll mean more that way."

Hannah's phone rang, and she left the room to answer, leaving Piper and Brendan alone. She turned to find him scrutinizing her in this way he'd been doing often lately. With love. Attentiveness. But there was more happening behind those eyes, too. He said he wouldn't pressure her for a decision, but the longer she left him hanging, the more anxious he grew.

They painted the sign on Thursday with big, sloppy buckets of sky-blue paint. Brendan had spent the morning sanding down a long piece of plywood and trimming the edges into an oval shape with his table saw. Once Piper made a rough outline of the letters with a pencil, they were off to the races, applying the blue paint with playful curves and tilting lines. Some might've said it looked unprofessional, but all she saw was character. An addition to Westport that fit like an acorn in a squirrel's cheek. After the paint dried, Brendan stood by anxiously, prepared to catch them if they fell off the ladders they'd been loaned from the hardware store. Now they affixed it over the faded original sign with his nail gun, Brendan instructing them patiently from the ground. When the sign was nailed on all sides, the two sisters climbed down and hugged in the street.

She couldn't say for certain how Hannah felt about having the bar completed, but in that moment, something clicked into place inside Piper. Something that hadn't even existed before she landed in this northwest corner of the map. It was the welcome home Henry Cross had deserved but never got. It was a proper burial, an apology for deserting him, and it soothed the jagged edges that had appeared on her heart the more she'd learned about her father.

"Now all we need is beer," Hannah said, stepping back and wiping her eyes. "And ice."

"Yeah, time to call the wholesaler, I guess. Wow. That was fast." She peered up at the sign, warmed by the curlicue at the end of "Daughters." "If we want to serve spirits eventually, we'll need a liquor license."

"If *you* want to, Pipes," Hannah said softly, putting an arm around her shoulder. "Leaving you is going to suck, but I can't be here forever. I've got my job with Sergei waiting. If you decide to stay . . ."

"I know," Piper managed, the sign blurring.

"Are you? Staying for sure?"

Through the window, they watched Brendan inside the bar where he screwed a light bulb into the chandelier. So capable and reassuring and familiar now, her heart drew up tight, lodging in her throat. "Yeah. I'm staying."

"Shit," Hannah breathed. "I'm torn between happy and sad."

Piper swiped at her eyes, probably smearing blue paint all over her face but not caring one bit. "I swear to God, you better visit."

Her sister snorted. "Who else is going to bail you out when all this goes south?"

Chapter Twenty-Eight

Things were too good to be true.

On the water, that usually meant Brendan was missing something. That he'd forgotten to flush out a fuel line or replace a rusting winch. There was no such thing as smooth sailing on a boat, not for long. And since he'd long lived his life in the same manner he captained the *Della Ray*, he couldn't help but anticipate a time bomb going off.

He had this woman. This once-in-a-hundred-lifetimes woman who could walk into a room and rob him of fucking breath. She was courageous, sweet, clever, seductive, adventurous, kind, guileless one moment, mischievous the next. So beautiful that a smile from her could make him whisper a prayer. And she loved him. Showed him exactly how much in new ways every day—like when he'd caught her spraying his cologne onto her nighttime shirt, holding it to her nose like it could heal all ills. She whispered her love into his ear every morning and every night. She asked him about fishing and googled questions to fill in the blanks, which Brendan knew because she was always leaving her laptop browser open on the kitchen counter.

Too good to be true.

He was missing something.

A line was going to snap.

It was hard to imagine anything bad happening at the moment, however, while cooking in the kitchen with Piper. With her hair over her shoulder in a loose braid, she was barefoot in yoga pants and a clingy sweater, humming between him and the stove, absently stirring pasta sauce with one hand. They'd cooked it three nights in a row, and he didn't have the heart to tell her he was sick of Italian, because she was so proud of herself for learning to make sauce. He'd eat it for a decade straight as long as she held her breath for the first bite and clapped when he gave her a thumbs-up.

Brendan had his chin on top of Piper's head, arms looped around her waist, swaying side to side to the music drifting from Hannah's room. In these quiet moments, he continually had to stop himself from asking for a decision. Was she going back to LA for the party? Or at all?

This party in her honor made him nervous for a lot of reasons. What if she went home and was reminded of all the reasons she loved it there? What if she decided that being celebrated and revered by millions was preferable to being with a fisherman who left her on a weekly basis? Because, Jesus, that wouldn't be such a fucking stretch. If she would just tell him Westport was her home, he'd believe her. He'd let the fear drop. But every day came and went with them dancing around the elephant in the room.

Despite his refusal to pressure her, the unknown, the lack of a plan, was getting to him.

He'd never compare his relationship with Piper to his marriage, but after the typhoon and Piper's subsequent race to the hospital—not to mention the tears she'd shed in his bed afterward—a new anxiety had taken root.

Bad things happen when I leave. When I'm not here to do anything about them.

He'd returned home once to find himself a widower.

It felt like just yesterday that he'd scared the hell out of Piper. Sent her running through a dangerous storm and driving to reach him in a state of panic.

What if he came home next time to find her gone? Without an answer in regard to the future, the upcoming trip loomed ominously, impatience scraping at him.

"Who cooks when you're on the *Della Ray*?" she asked, leaning her head back against his chest.

Brendan shook off his unwanted thoughts, trying his best to be present. To take the perfection she was giving him and be grateful for every second. "We take turns, but it's usually Deke, since he likes doing it."

She sighed. "I'm sorry you'll never be able to enjoy anything as much as my sauce."

"You're right." He kissed her neck. "Nothing will ever compare."

"I'll have some ready when you get home. *Two* servings."

"Just have yourself ready," he rumbled, running a finger along the waistband of her pants.

Piper tipped her head back, and their mouths met in a slow kiss that made him anxious for later, when they could be alone in bed together. Anxious to hear those sobs of urgency in his ears. Anxious to memorize them so he could bring them on the boat tomorrow. "Brendan?"

"Yeah?"

She bit off a laugh. "How long are you going to eat this sauce before you admit you're sick of it? I'm going to lose my bet with Hannah."

He laughed so hard she dropped the spoon into the sauce.

"Oh!" Piper tried to fish the utensil out of the bubbling sauce with her fingers, but yanked them out with a yelp. "Oh crap! Ouch!"

His laughter died immediately, and he turned her around, swiftly using a kitchen towel to clean off her burned fingers and kissing them. "You okay, baby?"

"Yes," she gasped, her petite frame starting to shake with laughter against him. "I guess losing a couple of fingers is the price of winning the bet."

"I love the sauce." Curious, he shifted. "How long did Hannah think it would take to . . ."

"Admit you were sick of my sauce? Eternity."

"That's how long it should have taken," Brendan growled, pissed at himself. "You should have lost. And you should have assumed it would take an eternity, too."

Her lips twitched. "I'm not mad." She laid her cheek against the center of his chest. "I got to hear that big, beautiful laugh. I'm a double winner."

"I love the damn sauce," he grumbled into the crown of her head, deciding to give voice to another one of the worries that had been needling him. "Are you going to be all right when I leave tomorrow?"

"Yes." She looked up at him with a furrow between her brows. "Don't worry about me when you're out there, please. I need to know you're focused and safe."

"I am, Piper." He brushed her cheek with his knuckles. "I will be."

Her body relaxed a little more against him. "Brendan . . ." With his name lingering in the air, she seemed to come out of a trance, starting to turn away from him. "We should order pizza—"

He kept her from turning. "What were you going to say?"

Based on the way she squared her shoulders, she was remembering her promise not to keep anything locked in her head. Away from him. A mixture of dread and curiosity rippled in his stomach, but he stayed silent. This was good. The openness between them was coming easier and easier, because of trust. "I was going to ask if you wanted kids someday. And I realize that sounds like . . . like I'm asking if you want them with *me*, which . . ." Color suffused her cheeks. "Anyway. It's just that we never talked about it, and kids seem like something you'd have a firm plan on—"

Her phone started vibrating on the kitchen counter. "Leave it."

Piper nodded. Her phone had been unusually active since they returned from Seattle, which was another reason he'd been on edge. But just like when they'd been in the hotel lobby shopping for cologne, the phone wouldn't quiet, dancing and jangling on the counter. "Let me just silence it," she murmured, reaching for the device. Pausing. "Oh. It's Daniel." Her eyes widened a little, as if maybe she'd just remembered something. "I—I'll call him back later."

Brendan wanted nothing more than to get back to the conversation at hand, but when he told her that yes, he wanted kids, he didn't need her distracted. "It's fine. Answer it."

She shook her head vigorously and put the phone on silent, but the unsteadiness of her hands caused it to slip. When she caught it, the pad of her finger hit the answer button by mistake. "Piper?" came a man's voice over the speakerphone.

"Daniel," she choked out, holding the phone awkwardly between her chest and Brendan's. "Hey. Hi!"

"Hi, Piper," he said formally. "Before I book this flight, I just want to make sure the grand opening is still on. You're not exactly famous for your reliability."

Brendan stiffened, alarm and betrayal turning his blood cold.

Here it was. The other shoe dropping.

Piper closed her eyes. "Yes," she said quietly. "It's still on. Six o'clock."

"That'll do fine, then," her stepfather responded briskly. "There's a flight that gets in a few hours before. Is there anything I can bring you from home?"

"Just yourself," she said with false brightness.

Daniel hummed. "Very well. Have to run. Your mother sends her love."

"Same to her. Bye."

When she hung up the phone, she wouldn't look at him. And maybe that was a good thing, because he was too winded to hide any of the dread and anxiety that had taken hold of his system. "Daniel is coming." He swallowed the nails in his throat. "You're still planning on impressing him with the bar. So he'll let you come back to LA early."

"Well . . ." She threaded unsteady fingers through her hair.

"That was the original plan, yes. And then everything started moving so fast with us . . . and I forgot. I just forgot."

"You forgot?" Brendan's voice was flat, anger flickering to life in his chest. Anger and fear, the fear of her slipping away. Goddammit. Just when he thought they were being honest with each other. "We've been doing nothing but work on Cross and Daughters for the last week, and the reason you started renovating it in the first place slipped your mind? Do you expect me to believe that?"

"Yes," she whispered, extending a hand toward him.

Brendan moved out of her reach, immediately regretting the action when she flinched and dropped her hand. But he was too fucking worried and shot through with holes to apologize and reach for her. His arms were leaden anyway. Impossible to lift. "You didn't keep Daniel's visit as a safety net?"

Her color deepened, speaking volumes. "Well, I d-did, but that was—"

His laughter was humorless. "And your friend Kirby? Have you told her you're not planning on flying to LA for the party?"

Piper's mouth snapped into a straight line.

"No, I didn't think so," he rasped, a sharp object lancing through his ribs. "You've got all kinds of safety nets, don't you, Piper?"

"I wasn't going to go," she wheezed, hugging her middle. "Brendan, stop being like this."

But he was past hearing her. Past anything but weathering the battering waves. Trying to keep the whole ship from getting sucked down into the eddy. This was it. This was the storm he'd felt coming. Felt in his fucking bones. Had he ever really had a chance with Piper, or had he been a delusional idiot? "Jesus, what the hell is wrong with me?" he said, turning and leaving the kitchen. "You were never going to stay, were you?"

Piper jogged after him. "Oh my God. Would you just stop and *listen* to me?"

Brendan's legs took the stairs two at a time, seeing nothing in front of him. Just moving on autopilot. "I was right here, ready to listen this whole time, Piper."

She followed. "You're not being fair! Everything is new to me. This town. Being in a relationship. I'm . . . I'm sorry it took me longer than it should have to let it all go, but letting everything go is a lot to ask."

"I know that, goddammit. I do. But if you weren't even considering this, *us*, you shouldn't have kept stringing me along like one of your followers when you were just plotting your exit behind my back."

Reaching the bedroom, he glanced back over his shoulder to find her looking stricken. And his stomach bottomed out, his heart protesting anything and everything but making her happy. Soothing her. Keeping her in his arms at all times.

What the hell was wrong with him? He hated himself for the tears in her eyes, for the insecurity in her posture. God, he *loathed* himself. But the fear of losing her was winning out over common sense. Over his instinct to comfort Piper, tell her he loved her a thousand times. Making him want to rage, to protect himself from being gutted like a fish.

"Look, Piper," he said unevenly, pulling his packed gym bag out from beneath the bed. "You just need to think about what you actually want. Maybe you can't do that when I'm constantly in your face."

"Brendan." She sounded panicked. "Stop! You're being ridiculous. I wasn't going to leave. Put the bag away. Put it away."

His hands shook with the need to do as she pleaded. "You never told me you were staying. You wanted an out. A fail-safe. Whether you think so or not."

"It's a big decision," she breathed. "But I was—"

"You're right. It is a big decision." He swallowed the urge to rage some more. To rage against her potentially leaving. To rage at the awful possibility of coming home from the trip and finding her unhappy. Or gone. Or regretful. But all he could do was face it head-on and hope he'd done enough to make her stay. All he could do was hope his love was sufficient. "I'm going to spend the night on the boat," he managed, though his throat was closing. "Think about what you want to do. Really think. I can't handle this will-she-or-won't-she bullshit anymore, Piper. I can't handle it."

She stayed frozen as he went down the stairs, past a wide-eyed Hannah.

"I'll be at the dock in the morning," Piper shouted, coming down the stairs, her expression now determined—and he loved her so goddamn hard in that moment. Loved every layer, every facet, every mood, every complication. "I already know what I want, Brendan. I want you. And I'll be at the dock to kiss you good-bye in the morning. Okay? You want to storm out? Fine. Go. I'll be the strong one this time."

He couldn't speak for a moment. "And if you're not there in the morning?"

Piper threw out a belligerent hand. "Then I'm falling back on my safety nets. Is that what you want me to say? You have to have it in black and white?"

"That's who I am."

"I know and I love who you are." Temper crackled in her beautiful eyes. "Fine, if I'm not there tomorrow morning, I guess you'll know my decision. But I *will* be there." She blinked several times against the moisture in her eyes. "Please . . . don't doubt me, Brendan. Not you. Have faith in me. Okay?"

With his heart in his mouth, he turned to go. Before he reached for Piper and forgot the argument and lost himself in her. But the same problems would exist in the morning, and he needed them solved once and for all. He needed the mystery gone. Needed to know if he'd have a lifetime with her or a lifetime of emptiness. The suspense was eating him alive.

He took one last look at her through the windshield of his truck before backing out of the driveway—and he almost shut off the ignition and climbed out. Almost.

Chapter Twenty-Nine

$\mathcal{P}$iper went to sleep pissed and woke up even pissier.

She rocketed out of bed toward the dresser drawers Brendan had designated for her, snatching out a black sports bra and red (the color of anger) running pants, along with some ankle socks.

As soon as she completed a quick run and walked Abe over to the museum, she was going to strut down that dock like it was a fashion week runway and kiss the captain's stupid mouth. She'd leave him hard and panting and feeling like a massive jerk, then she'd sashay home.

Home. To Brendan's house.

She stomped down the stairs, bringing a sleepy-eyed Hannah out of her room. "Are you ready to talk yet?"

Piper shoved an AirPod into her ear. "No."

Hannah propped a hip against the couch and waited.

"I am laser-focused on burying him in regrets right now."

"Sounds like the start to a healthy relationship."

"He left." Piper fell onto her butt and started to lace up her running shoes. "He's not supposed to leave! He's supposed to be the patient and reasonable one!"

"You're the only one who is allowed to be irrational?"

"Yes!" Something got stuck in her throat. "And he's obviously already sick of my shit. It's all downhill from here. I don't even know why I'm bothering with going to the dock."

"Because you love him."

"Exactly. Look at what I've opened myself up to." She yanked her laces taut. "I would relive being dumped by Adrian a thousand times to avoid Brendan walking out *once*. The way he did last night. It *hurts*."

Hannah sat down cross-legged in front of her. "I think that means the good times are worth a little struggling, don't you?" She ducked her head to meet Piper's eyes. "Come on. Put yourself in his shoes. What if he walked out last night without the intention of ever coming back? That's what he's afraid you're going to do."

"If he'd just listened—"

"Yeah, I know. You're telling us you're going to stay. But, Pipes. He's a hard-proof guy. And you left the loopholes."

Piper fell back flat onto the hardwood floor. "I would have closed them. He's supposed to be understanding with me."

"Yeah, but you have to be understanding with him, too." Hannah chuckled, laid down beside her sister. "Piper, the man looks at you like . . . he's full of cracks and you're the glue. He just wanted to give you some space, you know? It's a big decision you're making." She turned on her side. "And also, let's account for the fact that he's a man and there are balls and pride and testosterone in the mix. It's a deadly concoction."

"Truth." Piper took in a deep breath and let it out. "Even if I forgive him, can I still march down there like a righteous bitch and make him rue?"

"I would be disappointed if you didn't."

"Okay." Piper sat up and climbed to her feet, helping Hannah up after. "Thanks for the talk, O wise one. Promise I can call you on the phone anytime I want for your sage advice?"

"Anytime."

Piper left for her run with more than enough time to squire Abe to the museum and make it down to the dock to wish Brendan bon voyage. Still, she was anxious to see Brendan and reassure both of them they were solid, so she set a quick pace. Abe was waiting in his usual spot outside the hardware store when she arrived, newspaper rolled up under his arm.

He waved warmly as she approached. "Morning, Miss Piper."

"Morning, Abe," she said, slowing to a stop beside him. "How are you today?"

"Well as can be expected."

They fell into an easy pace, and Piper lifted her face to the sky, grateful for the calm weather, the lack of storm clouds. "I've been meaning to tell you, we're throwing a grand opening party at Cross and Daughters on Labor Day."

He quirked a white brow. "Cross and Daughters? Is that what you decided to call it?"

"Yeah." She cut him a look. "What do you think?"

"I think it's perfect. A nod to the new and the old."

"That's what I thought—" Abe's toe caught on an uneven crack in the sidewalk, and he went down. Hard. Piper grabbed for him, but it was too late, and his temple landed on the pavement with an ominous thud. "Oh my God! Abe!" The sudden rapid fire of Piper's pulse buckled her knees, and she dropped to the ground beside him, hands fluttering over his prone form, no idea what to do. "Oh Jesus. *Jesus.* Are you okay?" She was already pulling out her phone with trembling hands. "I'm going to call an ambulance, and then I'll call your sons. It's going to be all right."

His hand came up and stopped her from dialing. "No ambulance," he said weakly. "It's not as bad as all that."

She leaned over and saw the blood trickling from his temple. Was it a lot? Too much? "I— Are you sure? I really think I should."

"Help me sit up." She did, carefully, swallowing a spike when the blood traveled down to his neck. "Just call my sons. No ambulance, kiddo. Please. I don't want to give everyone a scare by being taken to the hospital. My phone is in my pocket. Call Todd."

"Okay," she managed, scrolling through his phone. "Okay."

By the time Piper pulled up the contact and hit dial, a woman had rushed out of the deli with a wadded-up fistful of paper towels for Abe to press to his wound. He was still speaking in complete sentences and his eyes were clear, which had to be a good thing, right? *Oh God, please don't let anything happen to this sweet man.*

Todd answered on the fourth ring, but he was at school dropping off his kids and couldn't be there for fifteen minutes, and that . . . that was when Piper realized she was going to miss the *Della Ray* leaving. It was scheduled to leave two minutes ago. Her heartbeat slammed in her eardrums, and her movements turned sluggish. Brendan wouldn't leave, though. He would wait for her. He would know she was coming. And if she didn't show up, she had to believe he would come find her.

But she couldn't leave Abe. She couldn't. She had to make sure he was going to be all right.

She called Brendan, but it went straight to voicemail. Twice. The third time she called, the line disconnected. Fingers unsteady, she pounded out a text message, her panic increasing when he didn't answer immediately. God, this couldn't be happening. She'd found out early on how terrible cell reception was in certain parts of Westport, especially the harbor, but technology couldn't be failing her so completely right now. Not when it was this crucial.

Todd didn't make it there in fifteen minutes. It took him twenty.

By that time, they'd gotten Abe to his feet and moved him to a bench. He seemed tired and slightly embarrassed about the fall, so she told him about the time she'd tried to slide down a stripper pole after six shots of tequila and ended up with a sprained wrist. That made him laugh at least. Todd arrived in his truck looking concerned, and Piper helped Abe into the passenger side, wads of balled-up paper towels pressed to her chest. She made him promise to give her a call later, and off they went, disappearing around the corner of the block.

Piper was almost scared to look at her phone, but she gathered her courage and checked the time. Oh God. Half an hour. Half an hour late.

She started running.

She ran as fast as her feet would carry her toward the harbor, trying to hold on to the faith. Trying to ignore the voice whispering in the back of her head that Brendan kept a tight schedule. Or that he'd given up on her. *Please, please, don't let that be the case.*

At Westhaven Drive, she whipped a right and almost knocked over a restaurant's specials board set out on the sidewalk. But she kept running. Kept going until she saw the *Della Ray* in the distance, traveling out to sea, leaving a trail of white, sloshing wake, and she stopped like she'd hit an invisible wall.

A deafening buzz started in her ears.

He'd left.

He was gone.

She'd missed him and now . . .

Brendan thought she'd chosen LA.

A great hiccupping sob rose up in her chest. Her feet carried her toward the docks, even though going there was useless now. She just wanted to make it there. Making it was all she had, even if she would have nothing to show for it. No kiss. No reassurance. No Brendan.

Her eyes were overflowing with tears by the time she reached the slip of the *Della Ray*, her surroundings so blurry, she almost didn't notice the other women standing around, obviously fresh from waving off the boat. She vaguely recognized Sanders's wife from the first night she and Hannah had walked into No Name. Another woman's age hinted at her being the mother of one of the crew members, rather than a significant other.

Piper wanted to greet them in some way, but her hands were heavy at her sides, her vocal cords atrophied.

"It's Piper, right?" Sanders's wife approached but recoiled a little when she spotted the tears coursing down Piper's numb face. "Oh. Honey, no. You're going to have to be a lot tougher than that."

The older woman laughed. "It's a good thing you didn't show up here with that face, making your man feel guilty." She stepped over a rope and headed toward the street. "Distracted men make mistakes."

"She's right," Sanders's wife said, still looking uncomfortable around Piper's steady waterfall of tears. The boat was just a dot now. "Especially if you're going to be with the captain. You need to be reliable. Hardy. They don't like to admit it, but a lot of their confidence comes from us. Sending them off isn't an easy thing to do, week after week, but we do what's necessary, yeah?"

Piper didn't know how long she stood and stared out at the water, watching a buoy bob on the roll of waves, the wind drying the tears on her face and making it stiff. Fishermen wove their way around her, guiding tourists to their boats, but she couldn't bring her feet to move. There was a hollow ache in her stomach that felt like a living thing, the pain spreading until she worried it would swallow her whole.

But it wasn't the end of the world, right?

"It's not," she whispered to herself. "He'll be back. You'll explain."

Piper filled her lungs slowly and ambled off the dock on stiff legs, ignoring the questioning looks of the people she passed. Okay, fine. She'd missed the boat. That sucked. Really, really bad. It made her sick to think he'd be under the assumption that their relationship was over for two days. It wasn't, though. And if she had to scream and beg when Brendan got home, she would. He'd listen. He'd understand, wouldn't he?

She ended up outside of Cross and Daughters but didn't remember any part of the walk. It hurt to be there when so much of Brendan filled the space. His pergola. The chandelier he'd hung. His scent. It was still there from the day before.

Pressure crowded her throat again, but she swallowed it determinedly.

She had to call distributors and confirm deliveries for Monday's grand opening. She didn't even have an outfit yet, and then there was the meeting this afternoon with Patty and Val. To help plan the party. She was up for exactly none of it, but she'd soldier on. She could make it through the next two days. Her heart would just have to deal.

That afternoon, Piper and Hannah met Patty and Val in Blow the Man Down, and they divvied up responsibilities. Hannah was, of course, the DJ and already had an end-of-summer soundtrack ready to fire up. Patty offered to bring firework cupcakes and Val suggested raffling off prizes from local vendors. Mostly they day drank and talked about makeup, and that helped numb some of Piper's heaviest anxieties that Brendan was lost to her. That he'd already given up.

Have faith.

Have faith.

It was noon on Labor Day when Daniel called to cancel.

Piper was busy stocking the bins behind the bar with ice, so Hannah answered the phone—and one look at her sister's face told Piper everything she needed to know. Hannah put the call on speaker, and Piper listened with her hands unmoving in the ice.

"Girls, I can't make it. I'm so sorry. We're having some last-minute casting issues, and I have to fly to New York for a face-to-face with a talent rep and his client."

Piper should have been used to this. Should have been prepared for their stepfather to flake at the last possible second. In his line of work, there were always flights to New York or Miami or London at the eleventh hour. Until that moment, she hadn't realized how badly she was looking forward to showing Daniel what they'd accomplished with Cross and Daughters. For better or worse, Daniel was the man who'd raised her, given her everything. She'd just wanted to show him it hadn't been for nothing. That she could create something worthwhile if given the opportunity. But she wouldn't get that chance now.

After Brendan left without a good-bye, her stepfather's cancellation was another blow to the midsection. Neither one of them believed in her. Or had any faith.

She had faith in herself, though. Didn't she? Even if it was beginning to fray around the edges and unravel the closer it came to grand-opening time. But Brendan would be back tonight and the certainty of that calmed her. Maybe he'd return angry with her or disappointed, but he'd be back on solid ground and she'd fight to make him listen. She'd keep fighting until his belief in her returned.

That plan helped center Piper, and she worked, stocking beer and setting out coasters, napkins, straws, pint glasses, orange wedges for the wheat beer. She and Hannah did some last-minute cleaning and hung the GRAND OPENING banner they'd painted the previous night outside. And then they stood in the center of the bar and surveyed what they'd done, both of them kind of dumbstruck at the transformation. When they'd arrived over a month ago, the place had been nothing but dust bunnies and barrels. It was still kind of a dive, but hell if it wasn't chic and a lot more welcoming.

At least to them.

But by six thirty, no one had darkened the door of Cross and Daughters.

Hannah sat in the DJ booth shuffling through her summer mix, and Piper stood behind the bar wringing her hands and obsessively checking the time on her phone. She had nine new messages from Kirby, all since this morning, demanding she get her ass on a plane back to Los Angeles. Piper had let the invitation hang for way too long, and now she didn't know how to turn down the party. And *under duress*, she could admit . . . she'd peeked at some of Kirby's emails detailing the guest list and the designer dress options.

If she was going, she'd pick the black Monique Lhuillier with the plunging neckline.

She really did need to let Kirby know she couldn't make it tomorrow night, but for some reason, Piper couldn't bring herself to send the text. To sever that final tie when she was still so shaken up from Brendan walking out. From having that steady, dependable presence ripped away when she needed it most. And the thing about LA parties was, if she didn't show up, no one would *really* care. There would be five minutes of speculation and some fleeting disappointment before everyone went back to doing lines and guzzling vodka.

Still, she'd send the text soon.

Piper had worn one of the pairs of jeans Brendan bought her. The more time dragged on without a single customer, the more Piper felt like an imposter in the soft denim, so unlike her usual dresses or skirts. Seven o'clock came and went. Seven thirty. Patty and Val still weren't there. No Abe or Opal.

No Brendan.

She ignored the worried looks Hannah kept sending her from the DJ booth, her stomach starting to sink. The locals had liked No Name. They didn't want this place prettied up by two outsiders. This was their way of letting the sisters know it.

Finally, just before eight o'clock, the door creaked open.

Mick walked in with a hesitant smile on his face.

Piper's palms started to sweat at the appearance of Desiree's father. The last time she'd seen him was in the hospital, right after she'd been with Brendan for the first time. Before that, she'd crashed his daughter's memorial dinner. They might have gotten off on the right foot, but that footing wasn't so solid anymore. There was something about the way he looked at her, even now, that measured her up and found her lacking. Or, if not lacking, she was not his daughter. With Mick sauntering toward her to take a seat at the bar, Piper's stomach started to churn. Brendan had obliterated her insecurities over Desiree, but right now, standing in the painfully empty bar, they crept back in, making the back of her neck feel hot. The lack of customers was a judgment. Mick's gaze was a judgment. And she wasn't passing.

"Hi there," Mick muttered, shifting on his stool. "Guess I'm early."

It was a lie for her benefit, and the generosity of it made Piper relax a little bit.

Momentarily, anyway.

"Would you like a beer, Mick?"

"Sure would. Bud should do it."

"Oh, we have some local IPAs." She nodded at the chalkboard mounted overhead. "There's the list. If you're a Bud drinker, I recommend the—"

He laughed nervously, as if overwhelmed by the list of five beers, their descriptions painstakingly hand-lettered by Hannah. "Oh. I . . . I'll just sit awhile, then." He turned in his stool, surveyed the bar. "Not a lot of interest in flashy changes around here, looks like."

A weight sunk in Piper's belly.

He wasn't just talking about Cross and Daughters, that much was clear.

His daughter was the old. She was the new. The sorely lacking replacement.

Westport was small. By now, Mick had probably heard about Piper crying like a baby on the docks, watching the *Della Ray* blur into the horizon. And now this. Now no one had arrived at the grand opening, and she was standing there like a certified idiot. She'd been an *idiot*. Not only to believe she could win over everyone in this close-knit place by making over the bar, but by believing her stepfather would give a shit. She'd been an idiot to keep important things from Brendan, whether or not the omissions had been intentional, and he'd lost faith in her. Lost trust.

I don't belong here.

I never did.

Brendan wasn't coming tonight. Nobody was. Cross and Daughters was empty and hollow, and she felt the same way, standing there on two shaky legs, just wanting to disappear.

The universe was sending her a loud-and-clear message.

Piper jolted when Mick laid a hand on top of hers, patting it. "Now, Piper . . ." He sighed, seeming genuinely sympathetic. "Don't you go feeling bad or anything. It's a tough place to crack. You have to be strong to stay afloat."

Words from Sanders's wife came drifting back.

Oh. Honey, no. You're going to have to be a lot tougher than that.

Then her first conversation with Mick.

Wives of fishermen come from tough stock. They have nerves of steel. My wife has them, passed them on to my daughter, Desiree.

She thought of running into Brendan in the market on her first morning in Westport.

You wouldn't understand the character it takes to make this place run. The persistence.

In her heart, she knew his mind had changed since then, but maybe he'd been right.

Maybe she didn't understand how to make anything last. Not a relationship, not a bar, nothing. Henry Cross's legacy didn't belong to her, it belonged to this town. How ridiculous of her to swoop in and try to claim it.

Mick patted her hand again, seeming a little worried by whatever he saw in her expression. "I better get on," he said quickly. "Best of luck, Piper."

Piper stared down into the luminous wood of the bar, swiping the rag over it again and again in a pretense of cleaning, but she stopped when Hannah circled a hand around her wrist.

"You okay, Pipes? People probably just got the time wrong."

"They didn't get it wrong."

Her sister frowned, leaned across the bar to study Piper's face. "Hey . . . you're *not* okay."

"I'm fine."

"No, you're not," Hannah argued. "Your Piper sparkle is gone."

She laughed without humor. "My what?"

"Your Piper sparkle," her sister repeated, looking increasingly worried. "You always have it, no matter what. Even when you've been arrested or Daniel is being a jerk, you always have this, like, optimism lighting you up. Brightness. But it's gone now, and I don't like it. What did Mick say to you?"

Piper closed her eyes. "Who cares?"

Hannah huffed a sound at Piper's uncharacteristic response. "What is going to make you feel better right now? Tell me what it is and we'll do it. I don't like seeing you like this."

Brendan walking through the door and pulling her into the recharging station would cure a lot of ills, but that wasn't going to happen. She could feel it. How badly she'd messed up by keeping safety nets in place without telling Brendan. How badly she'd hurt him by doing so. Badly enough that even the most steadfast man on earth had reached the end of his patience with her. "I don't know. God, I just want to blink and be a million miles away."

More than that, she wanted to feel like her old self again.

The old Piper might have been lacking in direction, but she'd been happy, right? When people judged the old Piper, it was from the other side of an iPhone screen, not to her face. She didn't *have* to try and fail, because she'd never tried in the first place, and God, it had been easy. Just then, she wanted to slip back into that identity and drop out, so she wouldn't have to feel this uncomfortable disappointment in herself. Wouldn't have to acknowledge the proof that she wasn't tough. Wasn't capable. Didn't belong.

Her phone buzzed on the bar. Another message from Kirby.

Piper opened the text and sighed over the Tom Ford peep-toe pumps on her screen. White with gold chains to serve as the ankle strap. Kirby was playing hardball now. Putting on those shoes and a killer dress and walking into a sea of photo-snapping strangers would be like taking a painkiller right now. She wouldn't have to feel a thing.

"Go home, Pipes."

She looked up sharply. "What?"

Hannah seemed to be wrestling with something. "You know I think your LA friends are phonies and you're way too good for them, right?" She sighed. "But maybe you need to go to Kirby's party. I can see you want to."

Piper set down her phone firmly. "No. After all this work? No."

"You can always come back."

Would she, though? Once she walked back into that fog of dancing and selfies and sleeping until noon, was it realistic that she would return to Westport and face her shortcomings? Especially if she made enough money on endorsements tomorrow night to get her out of Daniel's pocket? "I can't. I can't just . . ."

But why couldn't she?

Look around. What was stopping her?

"Well . . ." A tremble of excitement coursed up her fingertips. "You'll come with me, right, Hanns? If I'm not here, you don't have to be either."

Her sister shook her head. "Shauna has me opening the record shop tomorrow and Wednesday. I can ask her to find a replacement, but until then, I have to stick around." Hannah reached out and took the sides of Piper's face in her hands. "I'll only be a couple of days behind you. Go. It's like you've flatlined and I hate it."

"Go right *now*? But . . ." She gestured weakly. "The bar. We did this for Henry."

Hannah shrugged. "Henry Cross belongs to this place. Maybe turning it back over to them is what he would have wanted. It was the spirit behind it that counted, Piper. I'm proud of us no matter what." She surveyed the line of empty stools. "And I think I can handle the rest of this shift alone. Text Kirby. Tell her you're coming."

"Hannah, are you sure? I really don't like leaving you here."

Her sister snorted. "Stop it. I'm fine. I'll go crash at Shauna's if it makes you feel better."

Piper's breath started to come faster. "Am I really doing this?"

"Go," Hannah ordered, pointing at the staircase. "I'll get you an Uber."

Oh wow, this was really happening. She was leaving Westport.

Returning to something she could do and do well.

Easy. Just easy.

Avoid this despair and disappointment. Just sink back in and never look back. Forget about this place that didn't want her and the man who didn't trust her.

Ignoring Brendan's clear, beloved image in her head, his deep voice telling her to stay, Piper ran up the stairs and started shoving her belongings into suitcases.

Chapter Thirty

𝔅rendan stood on the deck of the *Della Ray*, staring off in the direction of Westport. The direction they were headed now. He saw none of the seemingly endless water in front of him. Saw none of the men pulling lines and fixing lures around him, the low blare of Black Sabbath coming from the wheelhouse speakers. He'd been locked in a sedated state since Saturday morning when they'd left the harbor.

She didn't show up.

He'd given Piper time to think, and she'd realized that being with him required too much sacrifice, and she'd made her decision. He'd known it was too good to be real. That she would give up everything, her whole life, just for him. His jugular ached from supporting his heart. That's where it sat now, every minute of the day; having Piper in his life had been so painfully sweet. So much better than he knew life could be.

It just hadn't gone both ways.

Over a decade as a fisherman and he'd never once been seasick, but his stomach roiled now ominously. He'd been able to distract himself from the devastating blow, the memory of the empty dock, for the last two days, pushing the men and himself hard, poring over digital maps, and even working in the engine room while Fox manned the wheelhouse. If he stopped moving or thinking, there she was, and Jesus, he'd fucking lost her.

No. He'd never earned the right to her in the first place.

That was the problem.

It was Monday afternoon. Labor Day. Piper would be getting ready to open the bar. Did she still expect him there? Or would she assume he'd stay away now that she'd decided to move on? To leverage the new bar into a trip home. If he showed up at Cross and Daughters, he might be in her way. She may not want him there.

Brendan dug the knuckles of his index fingers into both eyes, images of Piper slaughtering him. Mussed-up, grumpy morning Piper. Confused in the grocery store Piper. Holding a flaming frying pan, crying over him in the hospital, moaning into his pillow Piper. Each and every incarnation of her was a stab to the chest, until he swore going overboard and sinking to the bottom of the icy fucking ocean sounded preferable to living with the memories . . . and not having the actual woman.

But she'd done the right thing for herself. Hadn't she?

Didn't he have to respect that?

Respect that this woman he wanted for his wife was leaving? Jesus Christ. He might never hold her again.

A drizzle started, but he made no move to go inside to grab his slicker. Getting soaked and dying from pneumonia sounded like a pretty good plan at present. A moment later, though, Sanders passed by and handed the rain jacket to Brendan. Simply to have something to do with his hands, he put it on and slid both hands into the pockets.

Something glossy slipped between his fingers.

He drew it out—and there was Piper smiling back at him.

A picture of them. One he hadn't been aware of her taking.

She'd taken a selfie behind his back while he held her in the recharging station. And her eyes were sex-drowsed and blissful. Happy. In love.

With an ax splitting his jugular in half, Brendan turned over the picture and saw she'd written a loopy, feminine message.

For your bunk, Captain.
Come back to me safely.
I love you so much, Piper.

The wind had been knocked out of him.

A wave rocked the boat, and he could barely make his legs compensate. All functioning power had deserted his body, because his heart required all of it to pound so furiously. He closed his eyes and clutched the picture to his chest, his mind picking through a million memories of Piper to find the one of her standing in his doorway. The last time he'd seen her.

Please . . . don't doubt me, Brendan. Not you. Have faith in me. Okay?

But hadn't he done exactly that by leaving?

He'd left her. After demanding over and over again she take a leap of faith, he'd walked out and ruined her tenuous trust. For God's sake, she'd only been in town for what? Five weeks? What did he want from her?

Everything, that's what. He'd asked for everything—and that hadn't been fair.

So she'd kept a few safety nets. *Good.* As the man who loved her, that's exactly what he should have been encouraging. Piper's safety. What the hell had he done instead?

Punished her for it.

No wonder she hadn't shown up at the dock. He hadn't deserved to see her there, much less stand there praying for her to show up, begging God to make her appear, when he now realized full well . . . that she *shouldn't* have come.

And now, when it was too late, the obvious solution to keeping her, to deserving her, bore down on him like a meteor. She didn't have to give up everything. He loved her enough to find solutions. That's what he did. There was no inconvenience or obstacle he wouldn't face if it meant having her in his life, so he'd fucking face them. He'd adapt, like Piper had.

"I made a mistake," he rasped, razor wire wrapping around his heart and pulling taut. "Jesus, I made a fucking mistake."

But if there was a chance he could fix it, he'd cling to that hope.

Otherwise he'd go insane.

Brendan whipped around on a heel and ran for the wheelhouse, only to find Fox looking concerned while he spoke to the coast guard over the radio.

"What is it?"

Fox ended the transmission and put the radio back in place. "Nothing too bad. They're just advising us to adjust our route south. Drilling rig caught fire about six miles ahead and there's some bad visibility, but it should only set us back about two hours."

Two hours.

Brendan checked the time. It was four o'clock. Originally,

they were scheduled to make it back at six thirty. By the time the boat was unloaded and they'd taken the fish to market, he was looking at goddamn ten or eleven o'clock before he'd make it to Cross and Daughters.

Now, on top of his inexcusable fuckup, he was going to break his promise to be at the grand opening.

Helplessness clawed at the inside of Brendan's throat. He looked down at the picture of Piper he still held, as if trying to communicate with her.

I'm sorry I failed you, baby.

Just give me one more chance.

The text message popped up on his phone the second they pulled into the harbor.

I'm coming. I had an emergency. Wait for me. I love you.

Those words almost dropped Brendan to his knees.

She'd tried to come? She'd wanted to see him off?

Oh God. What emergency? Had she hurt herself or needed him?

If so, if he'd left when she was in trouble, he would never recover.

After that, his ears roared and he saw nothing but his feet pounding the pavement.

When Brendan and Fox stormed into Cross and Daughters at eleven o'clock, it was packed to the gills. "Summer in the City" was playing at an earsplitting decibel, a tray of cupcakes crowd-surfed toward Brendan, and everyone had a drink in their hands. Momentarily, pride in Piper and Hannah, at what they'd accomplished, eclipsed everything else. But an intense urgency to see his girlfriend swarmed back in quickly.

She wasn't behind the bar.

It was just Hannah, uncapping beers as fast as she could, clearly flustered. She was shoving cash into her pockets and trying to make change, tossing bills across the bar and running to help the next customer.

"Christ. I'll go help her out," Fox said, already pushing his way through the crowd.

Where was Piper?

With a frown, Brendan moved in his friend's wake, nodding absently at the locals who called—or slurred, rather—his name. He went to the dance floor first, knowing it was a likely place to find Piper, although . . . that didn't track. She wouldn't leave her sister in the lurch behind the bar. And anyway, she was supposed to be bartending. Hannah was the DJ.

A hole started to open in his gut, acid gurgling out, but he tried to stay calm.

Maybe she was just in the bathroom.

No. Not there. A lady on the way out confirmed the stalls were empty.

Panic climbed Brendan's spine as he pushed his way to the bar. Fox's expression stopped him dead in his tracks before he could even get there.

"Where is she?" Brendan shouted over the noise.

Hannah's gaze danced over to him, then away just as fast.

She served another customer, and he could see her hands were unsteady, and that terrified him. He was going to explode. He was going to rip this place down with his bare hands if someone didn't produce his girlfriend right the hell now.

"*Hannah*. Where is your sister?"

The younger Bellinger stilled, took a breath. "She went back to LA. For Kirby's party. And maybe . . . to stay." She shook her head. "She's not coming back."

The world blurred around him, the music warping, slowing down. His chest caved in on itself, taking his heart down in the collapse. No. No, she couldn't be gone. She couldn't have left. But even as denial pounded the insides of his skull, he knew it was true. He couldn't feel her.

She was gone.

"I'm sorry," Hannah said, pulling out her phone and lowering the music with a few thumb strokes. People behind him protested, but shut up and quieted immediately, distracted by the man at the bar keeping himself upright with a stool and dying a slow, torturous death. "Look. There was no one here. *No one.* Until maybe half an hour ago. We thought it was a huge fail. And before that, our stepdad canceled, and you— well, you know what you did." Moisture leapt to Hannah's eyes. She swiped at her tears while Fox hesitantly began rubbing circles on her back. "She'd lost her Piper sparkle. It scared me. I thought if she went home, she'd get it back. But now she'll never know that everyone loves this place."

She'd lost her Piper sparkle.

It was girl language, and yet, he so thoroughly understood what Hannah meant, because Piper did have a singular sparkle. Whether they were arguing or laughing or fucking, it was always there, pulling him into her universe, making everything perfect. That sparkle was positivity and life and promise of better things, and she always, always had it, glowing within the blue of her irises, lighting up the room. The fact that it had gone out, and that he'd had something to do with it, gutted him where he stood.

"I should have gone and found her," Brendan said, more to himself than anyone else. "When she didn't show up at the dock. I should have gone to find her. What the hell did I leave for?"

"She did show up," a woman's voice said behind him. Sanders's wife approached, a half-drunk beer in her hand. "She was there, just late. Blubbering all over the place."

Brendan had to rely on the stool to hold his weight.

"Told her to toughen up," his crew member's wife said, but her tone changed when people around her started to mutter. "In a nice way," she added defensively. "I think."

Jesus. He could barely breathe for thinking of her crying while he sailed away.

He couldn't fucking stand it.

Brendan was still reeling from the news that Piper had come to see him off, that she'd shed tears over missing him, when an older man ambled toward the front of the crowd with a white bandage taped to his head.

Abe? The man who owned the hardware store in town with his sons?

"It was my fault Piper was late to the dock, Captain. She's been walking me to the museum every morning so I could read my paper. Can't get up the stairs alone these days." He fussed with his bandage. "Fell and smacked my noggin off the sidewalk. Piper had to stay with me until Todd came. It took a while because he was dropping my grandbaby off at school."

"She's been walking you to the museum every day?" Brendan asked, voice unnatural on account of the wrench twisting a permanent bolt into his throat. She hadn't said anything about Abe. She'd just picked up another best friend and made him important. It was what she did.

"Yes, sir. She's the sweetest girl you ever want to meet." His eyes flooded with humor. "If my sons weren't married and she hadn't gone and fallen in love with the captain here, I'd be playing matchmaker."

Stop, he almost shouted. Might have, if his vocal cords had been working.

He was going to die.

He was dying.

"Sweet doesn't even cover it," piped up Opal, where she stood near the back of the crowd. "I hadn't left my apartment in an age, since my son passed. Not for more than grocery shopping or a quick walk. Not until Piper fixed me right up, and Hannah showed me how to use iTunes. My granddaughters brought me back to the living." A few murmurings went up at the impassioned speech. "What is this nonsense about Piper going back to LA?"

"Yeah!" A girl Piper's age appeared at Opal's side. "We're supposed to have a makeup tutorial. She gave me a smoky eye last week, and two customers at work asked for my number." She slumped. "I love Piper. She's not really gone, is she?"

"Uh, yeah," Hannah shouted. "She is. Maybe try showing up on time, Westport."

"Sorry about that," Abe said, looking guilty along with everyone around him. "There was an oil rig fire off the coast. A young man from town works there, drilling. I reckon everyone was waiting for news, to make sure one of our own was all right, before heading to the party."

"We really need to get a television," Hannah muttered.

Brendan sat there bereft as more and more proof mounted that Piper had been putting down roots. Quietly, carefully, probably just to see if she could. Probably scared she wouldn't succeed. It had been his job to comfort her—and he'd blown it.

He'd lost the best thing that ever happened to him.

He could still hear her that night when they'd sat on a bench overlooking the harbor, moments after she'd waltzed into the memorial dinner with a tray of tequila shots.

Since we got here, it has never been more obvious that I don't know what I'm doing. I'm really good at going to parties and taking pictures, and there's nothing wrong with that. But what if that's it? What if that's just it?

And with those insecurities in tow, she'd proceeded to touch everyone in this room, in one way or another. Carving her way into everyone's hearts. Making herself indispensable. Did she even know how thoroughly she'd succeeded? Piper had once said Brendan was Westport, but now it was the other way around. This place was her.

Please . . . don't doubt me, Brendan. Not you. Have faith in me. Okay?

There was no way, no way in *hell*, he could let that be the last thing she said to him. Might as well lie down and die right there, because he wouldn't be able to live with it. And no way her last memory of him would be leaving his house, leaving her *crying*, for God sakes.

Brendan steadied himself, distributing his weight in a way that would allow him to move, to walk, without further rupturing the shredded heart in his chest. "It's my fault she's gone.

The responsibility is mine. *She* is mine." He swallowed glass. "And I'm going to get her."

Well aware he could fail, Brendan ignored the loud cheer that went up.

He started to turn from the bar, but Hannah waved a hand to catch his attention. She dug her phone out of her pocket, punched the screen, and slid it toward him across the wood Piper had spent a week sanding to perfection, applying the lacquer with careful concentration.

Brendan looked down at the screen and swallowed. There was Piper. Blowing a kiss beneath the words "The Party Princess's Triumphant Return," followed by an address for a club in Los Angeles. Tomorrow night at nine P.M.

Five-hundred-dollar cover.

People were going to pay five hundred dollars just to be in the same room with his girlfriend, and he couldn't fault them. He'd have given his life savings to be standing in front of her at that moment. Jesus, he missed her so much.

"Technically, she's not supposed to be back in LA yet or I'd tell you to try our house first. She's probably staying with Kirby, but I don't have her contact info." Hannah nodded at the phone. "You'll have to catch her at the club."

"Thanks," he managed, grateful she wasn't punishing him like he deserved. "I'd go anywhere."

"I know." Hannah squeezed his hand on the bar. "Go make it right."

Brendan paced toward the door, pulse ticking in his ears, but Mick stepped into his path before he could walk back out into the cold. "Brendan, I . . ." He bowed his head. "When you track her down, will you apologize for me? I wasn't too kind to her earlier tonight."

A dagger twisted between Brendan's eyes. Christ, how much heartache had his Piper been forced to deal with since he boarded the boat on Saturday? First he'd left, then her stepfather had canceled. No one showed up to her grand opening—or so she thought. And now he was finding out Mick had potentially hurt her feelings?

His hands formed fists at his sides, battling the fierce urge to break something. "I'm afraid to ask what you said, Mick," he whispered, closing his eyes.

"I might have implied that she couldn't replace my daughter," Mick said in a low voice, regret lacing every word.

Brendan exhaled roughly, his misery complete. Ravaging him where he stood. "Mick," he responded with forced calm. "Your daughter will always have a place in my heart. But Piper owns that heart. She came here and robbed me blind of it."

"I see that now."

"Good. Get right with it."

Unable to say another word, unable to do anything but get to her, get to her *by any means necessary*, Brendan strode to his truck and burned rubber out of Westport.

Chapter Thirty-One

Oh, she'd made a huge mistake.

Huge.

Piper sat astride a mechanical unicorn, preparing to be elevated through a trapdoor onto a stage. Kirby shoved a puffy princess wand into her hand, and Piper stared at the object, lamenting the fact that she couldn't magically wish herself out of this situation.

Her name was being chanted by hundreds of people overhead.

Their feet stomped on the floor of the club, shaking the ceiling. Behind the scenes, people kept coming over to her, snapping selfies without permission, and Piper imagined she looked shell-shocked in every single one of them.

This was exactly what she'd always wanted. Fame, recognition, parties thrown in her honor.

And all she wanted now was to go home.

Not to Bel-Air. No, she wanted to be in the recharging station. That was home.

Brendan was home.

The chanting grew louder along with the stomping, and Kirby danced in a circle around Piper, squealing. "Savor the anticipation, bitch! As soon as they start playing your song, the hydraulics are going to bring you up slowly. When you wave the wand, the lighting guy is going to make it look like you're sprinkling fairy dust. It looks so real. People are going to shit."

Okay, fine, that part was pretty cool.

"What song is it?"

"'Girls Just Want to Have Fun' remixed with 'Sexy and I Know It.' Obviously."

"Oh yeah. Obviously."

Kirby fanned her armpits. "Try and time your fairy flicks with the beat, you know?"

Piper swallowed, looking down at her Lhuillier dress, her black garters peeking out beneath the hem on either side of the unicorn. Getting dressed had been a fun distraction, as had primping and getting her hair professionally styled, but . . . now that the time had come to make her "triumphant" return, she felt kind of . . . counterfeit.

Her heart was in smithereens.

She didn't *want* to enter a club on a hydraulic unicorn.

She didn't want to have her picture taken and plastered all over social media. There would never be anything wrong with having a good time. Or dancing and dressing how she chose to dress. But when she'd gone to Westport and not one of these people had called or texted or been interested in the aftermath of the party they'd enjoyed, she'd gotten a glimpse at how phony it all was. How quickly the fanfare went away.

When the time came for her to rise up through the stage,

none of the applause would be for Piper. For the real Piper. It would be a celebration of her building a successful image. And that image didn't mean anything. It didn't count. She thought slipping back into this scene would be easy, that she'd just sink into it and revel, be numb for a little while. But all she could think about was . . . who would have coffee with Opal tomorrow? Who would walk Abe to the museum?

Those visits made her feel a million times better than the momentary bursts of internet stardom. Because it was just her, living in real moments, not fabricating them for the entertainment of others.

Making over the bar with her sister, standing on the deck of a boat with the love of her life's arms around her, running through the harbor mist, making friends who seemed interested in her and not what she could do for them. Those things counted.

This was all for show, and participating in it made Piper feel less true to herself. Like she was selling herself short.

This fame she'd always reached for was finally reaching back, and she wasn't interested.

Piper, Piper, Piper.

The chants were deafening now, but she only wanted to hear one voice saying her name. Why didn't she stay and fight for him? What was he doing now?

"Brendan," she whispered, the yearning for him so intense she almost doubled over. "I'm sorry, I miss you. I'm sorry."

"What?" Kirby shouted over the noise. "Okay, you're going up. Hold on, bitch!"

"No, wait." Piper swiped at her damp eyes. "I want to get off. Let me off."

Kirby looked at her like she was insane. "It's too late. You're already moving."

And she was. So much faster than she'd expected.

This unicorn really had some get-up-and-go.

Piper clung to the synthetic mane and held her breath, looking up to watch the stage doors slide open above her. *Dammit. Dammit.* There was no turning back. She could jump, but she'd almost certainly break an ankle in these shoes. She'd break these beautiful Tom Ford heels, too, and that went against her very religion.

Her head was about to clear the stage.

With a deep breath, Piper sat up straighter and smiled, waving at the crowd of people who were going wild. For her. It was an out-of-body experience, being suspended above their heads, and she didn't like it. Didn't want to be there, sitting like a jackass on this unicorn while hundreds of people captured her image on their phones.

I want to go home. I just want to go home.

The unicorn finally settled in on the stage. Great. She was already searching for the closest exit. But when she climbed off, she'd flash the entire club. There was no other way to stay modest than to block her crotch with the unicorn hair and awkwardly slide off, which she did now, people pressing in against the stage. She didn't just feel like a trapped animal. She was one. There was no way out.

Piper turned, searching for an avenue of escape—and there he was.

Brendan? No, it couldn't be. Her sea captain didn't belong in LA. They were two entities that didn't make sense in the same space.

She held up a hand to block the flashing strobe light, and God. *My God.* He really was there, standing a foot taller than everyone in the crowd, bearded and beautiful and steady and salt of the earth. They locked eyes, and he slowly pulled the beanie off his head, holding it to the center of his chest, almost a deferential move—and his expression was a terrible mixture of sadness and wonder. No. She had to get to him. Being this close and not being in his arms was positively torture. He was there. He was there.

"Brendan!" Piper screamed, her voice swallowed up by the noise.

But she saw his lips move. Knew he called her name back.

Unable to be parted from him any longer, she dropped to her butt and scooted off the stage, pushing through the tightly packed crowd, praying she was moving in the right direction, because she couldn't see him anymore. Not with the flashing lights and the phones in her face.

"Brendan!"

Hands grabbed at her, making it impossible for her to move. The arms of strangers slung around her neck, pulling her into selfies, hot breath glanced across her neck, her shoulders. No, no, no. She only wanted one touch. One perfect man's touch.

"Piper!"

She heard his deep, panicked voice and spun around in the kaleidoscope of color, flashes going off, disorienting her. Tears were rolling down her face, but she left them there in favor of trying to push through the crowd. "Brendan!"

Adrian appeared in front of her, momentarily distracting Piper from her maze run, because it was all so absurd. She was trying to get to the most wonderfully real human on earth, and this fake, hurtful man-child was blocking her path. Who did he think he was?

"Hey, Piper. I was hoping I'd run into you!" Adrian shouted over the music. "You look fucking amazing. We should get a drink—"

Brendan loomed behind her ex-boyfriend and, without hesitation, flicked him aside like a pesky ant, sending him flying, and Piper wasted no time in launching herself into the recharging station. A sense of rightness took hold in a split second, bringing her back to herself. Back to earth. Brendan lifted her up, locking his arms around her as tight as they would go, and she melted into the embrace like butter. Her legs wrapped around his hips, she buried her face in his neck and sobbed like a baby. "Brendan. Brendan."

"I've got you. I'm right here." Fiercely, he kissed the side of her face, her hair, her temple. "Stay or go, baby? What do you need?"

"Go, please. Please. Get me out of here."

Piper felt Brendan's surprise register—surprise that she wanted to leave?—followed by a tightening of his muscles. One hand cupped the back of her head protectively, and then he was moving through the crowd, ordering people out of his way, and she was positive she'd never, ever been safer in her entire life. She breathed in the scent of his cologne and clung to his shoulders, secure in her absolute trust of this man. He'd come. After everything, he'd come.

A moment later, they were out on the street, but Brendan didn't stop moving. He carried Piper past the line of gaping on-lookers, kept going until the pumping bass faded and relative quiet fell around them. And only then did he stop walking, but he didn't let her go. He walked her into the doorway of a bank and rocked her side to side, his arms like a vise.

"I'm sorry, baby," he grated against her forehead. "I'm so fucking sorry. I shouldn't have left. I should *never* have left or made you cry. Please forgive me."

Piper hiccupped into his neck and nodded; she would forgive him for anything in that moment if he just stayed. But before she could say anything, he continued.

"I *do* have faith in you, Piper. I will never doubt you again. You deserve so much better than what I gave, and it was wrong of me, so wrong, to get angry at you for protecting yourself. You were giving so much already. You give so much to everyone and everything you touch, you incredible fucking girl, and I love you. More than any goddamn ocean, do you hear me? I love you, and I'm falling deeper by the minute, so, baby, please stop crying. You looked so beautiful up there. God, you looked so beautiful and I couldn't *reach* you."

His words made her feel like she was floating. They were pure Brendan in their honesty and depth and gruffness and humility. And they were for her.

How wholly he gave himself, this man.

How wholly she wanted to give herself in return.

"I love you, too," she whispered tremulously, kissing his neck, his mouth, pulling deeply on his firm, welcoming lips. "I love you, too. I love you. I didn't want to be there tonight. I only wanted to be with you, Brendan. I just wanted to hear your voice so badly."

"Then I'll talk until my voice gives out," he rasped, slanting his lips over the top of hers, breathing into her mouth. Accepting her breath in return. "I'll love you until my heart gives out.

I'll be your man for a thousand years. Longer if I'm allowed." With a miserable sound, he kissed the tears off her cheeks. "I messed up so bad, Piper. I let my fear of losing you get between us. It blinded me." He drew back, waited until she looked at him. Up into all that intensity. "If you need Los Angeles to be happy, then we'll make it work. I can go up north for crab season and dock the new boat closer to LA the rest of the year. If you'll have me back, we'll make it happen. I won't let us fail. Just let me love you forever."

"If I'll have you back . . ." She exhaled her disbelief, his words taking a moment to actually sink in. Oh wow. Wow. Her knees started to tremble around his hips, love surging up inside of her and filling every part of her that had cracked over the last three days. "You would do that, wouldn't you? You would change your whole life for me."

"I'd be honored to. Just say the word."

"B-Brendan." Her chest ached almost too much to speak. "When I was falling in love with you, I was falling in love with Westport at the same time. That is my home. Our home. And I don't want to be anywhere else. I knew it as soon as I got here tonight. Nothing was right. Nothing was right without you."

"Piper," he rasped, their mouths heating, seeking. "Say you're mine again. Be clear. I need you to be clear. I've been fucking miserable thinking I lost you forever."

"I'm yours. Of course I'm yours. I'm sorry I ran. I'm sorry I doubted—"

He hushed her with a hard press of lips, his frame heaving with relief. "Thank Christ," he said hoarsely. "And no. You did nothing wrong. Nothing." His thumb brushed against the base of her spine, his body still rocking her side to side. "Everything is going to be okay now. We found our way back. I've got you back and I'm not letting you go ever again."

She clung to him. "Promise?"

"I'll make the promise every single day."

A blissful smile bloomed across her face. "I'll try again with Cross and Daughters. I'll be stronger next time at the docks. I can be—"

"Oh God, no. Piper." He ducked his head to make eye contact, his dark brows pulled together. "First of all, you don't have to be tough. Not all the time. I don't know who decided my perfect, kind, sweet, incredible girlfriend needed to fit some goddamn mold, but you don't. You just be Piper, okay? She's who I'm in love with. She's the only woman who was made for me. Cry if you want to cry. Dance if you want to dance. Hell, scream at me, if you need to. No one gets to tell you how to act or feel when I leave. *No one.* And, baby . . ." He puffed a laugh. "When I got to the bar, it was packed. Everyone *loves* it. People just move at a different pace in Westport. They're not all on a strict schedule like me."

"Wait. Really? It was packed?" She gasped. "Oh no. Hannah—"

"Is fine. Fox jumped in to help. And she helped me find you tonight."

"Oh! Oh. I'm so glad." Happiness bubbled up inside of her chest, and she gave a watery laugh. "We better get home, then. I guess I have a bar to run."

Brendan brought their mouths together and kissed her with painstaking affection that quickly started to burn. Her throaty moan met his urgent growl, their tongues winding deep, his hand scraping down to palm her backside. "We could go home tonight," he rumbled, tilting his hips so she could feel the firm rise of his need. "Or we could walk across the street to my hotel room and worry about getting home in the morning."

A sigh shuddered out. "Why aren't we already there?"

"Give me a minute." He jolted into a stride across the quiet avenue that turned into a jog, jostling her all over the place, sending her laughter ringing down the night-draped street, then a euphoric squeal when he threw her over his wide fisherman's shoulder. "So . . ." he said when they were halfway through the hotel lobby, scandalizing everyone in their wake. "Are we just *not* going to talk about the mechanical unicorn?"

"I love you," she gasped through mirthful tears. "So much."

"Ah, Piper." His voice shook with emotion. "I love you, too."

Epilogue

One week later

It was a sad day.

It was a happy day.

Brendan was coming home from a fishing trip, but Hannah was going back to LA.

Piper sat up in bed and pushed off her eye mask, marveling—not for the first time—over how much the room had changed. Before leaving LA, Brendan had driven her to Bel-Air for a quick visit with Maureen and Daniel. Halfway through the stopover, Brendan had disappeared.

She'd found him upstairs in her room, packing her things.

Not just her clothes, although it was nice to have her full wardrobe back. But her knickknacks. Her perfumes, her bed-spreads, her shoe display case and fashion scarves. And as soon as they'd gotten home to Westport—okay, fine, after a rough, sweaty quickie on the living room couch—he'd taken the items upstairs and made the room . . . theirs.

Her super-masculine sea captain now slept under a pink

comforter. His aftershave was sandwiched in between nail polish bottles and lipsticks, and he couldn't seem happier about the feminine clutter.

They'd only had a few days of officially living together before his trip, but they'd been the best days of her life. Watching Brendan brush his teeth with nothing but a towel wrapped around his waist, feeling his eyes on her as she bartended, pancakes in bed, shower sex, gardening together in their backyard, shower sex. And best of all, his whispered promise in her ear every morning and night that he would never, ever let her go again.

Piper flopped back against the pillows and sighed dreamily.

He'd be pulling into Grays Harbor in just a few hours, and she couldn't wait to tell him every shenanigan that had happened in Cross and Daughters since he'd been gone. Couldn't wait to smell the salt water on his skin and even continue their conversation about someday . . . *someday* having children.

He hadn't forgotten Piper's attempt to bring up the subject on the night of their argument. They'd tried to discuss it on four separate occasions since getting home, but as soon as the word "pregnant" was uttered, Piper always ended up on her back, Brendan bearing down on her like a freight train.

So. No complaints.

Fanning her face, Piper climbed out of bed and went through her morning routine of jogging and walking Abe to the museum. When she got home an hour later, Hannah was just zipping her packed suitcase, and Piper's stomach performed an uncomfortable somersault.

"I'm going to miss you," Piper whispered, leaning a shoulder against the doorjamb.

Hannah turned and dropped down onto the edge of the bed. "I'll miss you more."

Piper shook her head. "You know . . . you're my best friend."

Her sister seemed caught off guard by that, giving a jerky nod of her head. "You're mine. You've always been mine, too, Pipes."

"If you hadn't come . . ." Piper gestured to their surroundings. "None of this would have happened. I wouldn't have figured it all out on my own."

"Yes, you would have."

Piper blinked rapidly to keep the tears at bay. "You ready to head to the airport?"

Hannah nodded, and—after kissing the Pioneer record player good-bye—she wheeled her suitcase to the front of the house. Piper opened the door to let her sister through, frowning when Hannah pulled up short. "What's that?"

"What's what?"

Piper followed her sister's line of vision and found a brown parcel, in the shape of a square, leaning up against the porch. It definitely hadn't been there when she returned from her run. She stooped down and picked it up, inspecting the delivery label and handing the box to her sister. "It's for you."

Letting go of the handle of her suitcase, Hannah pried open the cardboard, revealing a cellophane-wrapped record. "It's . . . oh." Her throat worked. "It's that Fleetwood Mac album. The one that spoke to me at the expo." She tried to laugh, but it came out choked. "Fox must have tracked it down."

Piper gave a low whistle.

Hannah continued to stare down at the album. "That was so . . . friendly of him."

It was definitely something. But Piper wasn't sure "friendly" was the right word.

Several beats passed, and Piper reached over to tuck some hair behind her sister's ear. "Ready to go?" she asked softly.

"Um . . ." Hannah visibly shook herself. "Yeah. Yeah, of course. Let's go."

A couple of hours later, Piper stood on the dock and watched the *Della Ray* approach, her pulse going faster and faster the closer it came, white wake spreading out around the vessel like rippling wings. The crew's significant others, mothers, and fathers stood around sipping coffee in the cool fall weather, speculating on the trip's haul. They'd been kind to Piper this afternoon, but more important, she was learning to be kind to herself.

Learning to love herself, just as she was.

Frivolous and silly on occasion, determined and stubborn on others. When she was mad, she raged. When she was sad, she cried.

And when she was happy, like she was in that moment, she threw her arms open and ran right toward the main source, letting him sweep her away . . .

Keep an eye out for Hannah's story in . . .

HOOK, LINE, AND SINKER

Coming early 2022!

**Read on for a bonus scene featuring
Hannah and Fox!**

Bonus Scene

Damn.

This pint-sized girl with freckles had just gone toe-to-toe with the captain. Still looked spitting mad, too, underneath the brim of her red baseball cap.

It was a good thing Fox knew enough about women to wipe the amusement from his face. Hannah, the new girl in town, had briefly turned her wrath on him outside the Red Buoy, and he wasn't eager to revisit the moment. Neither was his dick, which had momentarily retreated into itself like a hermit crab at the rare display of displeasure in his company.

Just then, a blustery August wind caught Hannah's hat and knocked it off her head.

They went for it at the same time, his fingers wrapping around the brim before it could hit the ground. Still bent over—and with the most winning grin he could muster—Fox handed it back, his mouth widening further when she only peered at him suspiciously.

Hannah sniffed. "Thanks."

"Anytime."

With a skeptical hum, she pulled the hat back down over her eyes, but he'd already seen the evening sunlight travel over her face. *A cute face*, proclaimed the stubby nose located between two big hazel eyes and a dimple in her right cheek. Her toes peeked out of her flip-flops, showing off a musical note that ran the length of her second-largest toe.

Yup. Cute as hell.

But not so cute that she couldn't turn his manhood into a crustacean.

What are you, his pretty-boy sidekick?

Apparently in addition to being adorable and fearless, she was astute.

The pretty part was obvious. And now, here he was, squiring this spitfire to the record shop so his best friend could get some time alone with the first woman to rouse his interest since the passing of his wife seven years earlier. Thus Fox ticking the sidekick box.

Truthfully, though? He didn't mind not being taken seriously. Let Hannah put him in a neat little category. It saved him from having to try. Trying for anything worthwhile always led to disappointment.

Fox realized his smile had slipped and fixed it back in place, gesturing for Hannah to precede him along the sidewalk. "After you, sweetheart."

She studied him down the end of her stub nose, then breezed past. "You can turn down the wattage, peacock. Nothing I say to Piper about you will affect her decision."

Peacock? Brutal. "Her decision to what?"

"To embark on or decline an affair with the mean one."

The mean one. Savage. "You two seem close. She doesn't value your opinion?"

Hannah stopped short and turned, her expression that of a person jogging back their previous statement. "Oh no, she *does*. She does. But my sister, um . . ." Her fingers plucked at the air for the right words. "She is so desperate to see the good in people, she doesn't always heed a well-placed warning."

"Ah. Do you look for the *bad* in people?"

"Oh, my affliction is way worse than Piper's; I *like* the bad in people."

She showed him that dimple and kept sailing.

It took Fox a moment to regain his stride. Suddenly he was interested in a conversation. More than he'd been in a damn long time. Why? Apart from the fact that she'd gained his respect by refusing to back down from a man twice her size, there was no reason he should be picking up his pace to find out what Hannah was going to say next.

They weren't even going to sleep together.

Doing so could seriously mess things up for Brendan—and Jesus, she wasn't his type, anyway. For one thing, she'd be living in Westport for the foreseeable future. Way too close for comfort. Two, his charm was absolutely wasted on this out-of-towner. The way she speed-walked two yards ahead of him made that crystal clear.

Maybe that's why he wanted to continue talking to her.

He'd gotten the sex-is-a-no-no speech *and* she was immune to him. The pressure was off.

It surprised him how much that pressure was present in his chest when it started to abate, gradually, like the air coming out of a beach ball. "Want to slow down a little, Freckles?" he said, a little testier than he'd intended, because of the weird feeling. "I'm the only one who knows where we're going."

Hannah gave him an eyebrow raise over her shoulder but downgraded from a sprint to a jog. Maybe even seemed a little more curious about him—but what sense did that make? "Really? You think I'm a 'Freckles'?"

"It was that or Captain Killer."

Was that a hint of a smile?

Out of habit, he was about to compliment her on her smile when the phone in his pocket started to vibrate. He made the rookie mistake of taking it out, instead of ignoring it, but quickly put the device back when the name "Carla" blinked on the screen.

Not before Hannah saw it, though. Her gaze danced away quickly, her expression remaining neutral, but she definitely noticed a woman was calling him. There was no reason that should bother him. No reason for the stupid, sinking disappointment in his belly. None at all.

Fox coughed into his fist and they continued to walk, side by side. "What exactly do you mean by 'I like the bad in people'?"

Her dimple deepened while she thought about it. "It's like . . . the bad in someone is also the most honest part, right? When you meet someone new, you dig and dig until you get to the good stuff. Imagine how much time we would save if our biggest flaw was our opening line."

"You're pretty intense for someone nicknamed Freckles."

A laugh snuck out of her, and the weirdness that had been barrel-rolling in his chest stopped abruptly, slowed by satisfaction. Warmth. "Hey, I questioned your judgment. You were firm on Freckles." Her smile melted into a sigh. "And I know, I am a little intense. It's all the music I listen to. Everything is right on the surface in a song. Calamity, heartbreak, tension, hope. It's hard to dip back into normal life after a Courtney Barnett song." She snuck a glance at him. "I tend to overshare almost immediately after meeting someone. It's why I don't have a lot of friends back home. I come on stronger than cold brew."

That made him chuckle. "Hold on, now. I didn't say the intensity was a turnoff."

Her gaze cut to his, mouth in a flat line.

Whoops. Stepped on a land mine. Better backpedal. "'Turnoff' was the wrong expression. This isn't"—Fox seesawed a hand between them—"there's nothing to turn off or on."

She nodded her agreement and they went back to walking.

Shit, this was kind of nice. Having a mildly antagonistic interaction with a girl. *This* girl. There was something invigorating about passing the time with her without expectations attached. Not that a lot of effort went into seducing women. That talent was kind of a built-in mechanism. Trying to seduce Hannah would have been a lot more complicated, and the fact that he didn't have to . . .

The only remaining option was friendship.

Wow. What a turn the day had taken. When he woke up this morning, if someone had told him he'd be chumming around with a girl, he would have called them a damn liar. But here he was. Not even trying to have sex with her. It went against his nature not to check her out *a little,* just for posterity's sake, and she had the kind of twitchy buns that drove him crazy. But he was filing that away under *irrelevant.*

"What kinds of things do you normally overshare about?" he asked her.

She looked up at the sunset-streaked sky but quickly ducked back underneath the brim of her hat when a gull circled above. "My greatest fears, what movies make me cry, my relationship with my mother. Things like that. In Los Angeles, you're supposed to lead with what you do for a living."

"I've been meaning to ask, what do you do for a living?"

An honest-to-God giggle tumbled out of her. "I'm a location scout for an independent movie house."

Yeah, he could see her doing that. Clipboard, earpiece, chewing gum, watching some drama unfold on a movie set. "That sounds like it nurtures your intensity, sure enough. Is that what you want to do permanently?"

"No." She seemed hesitant to say more.

"Come on, oversharer. Don't let me down."

"It's just that I haven't told anyone yet." She dipped her cheek toward her shoulder. Her version of a shrug? "I want to craft movie soundtracks. Not scores. Just, selecting the perfect songs for a scene."

"That sounds pretty fucking cool."

She stuffed her hands in the pockets of her jeans. "Thanks." Was she biting that lip to subdue a smile? Damn. He kind of wanted to see it. "What about you? I gather you're a fisherman like the mean one?"

"That's right." He tapped his inner wrist. "Got salt water running in these veins."

"Does it scare you? When the ocean gets rough?"

"I'd be an idiot if it didn't scare me."

For some reason, that seemed to bring this interesting girl

over to his team. She nodded, examining him a little more closely. "I heard him call you the relief skipper. Do you ever want to captain your own vessel?"

"Hell no."

"Why not?"

"Too much responsibility." He dragged a hand through his hair. "I like things exactly the way they are now. Work a job, don't make any mistakes, come home with cash in my pocket, and end of the bargain fulfilled. Let someone else think about the big picture."

Hannah pursed her lips. "Are you lazy or afraid of messing up?"

Defensiveness stuck in his middle unexpectedly, and using the only weapon he had, Fox dropped his attention to her thighs. "I'm sure as hell not lazy, Freckles."

She gulped, hands balling in her pockets. "So you're . . . afraid, then?"

"Can't help digging, can you?" Laughing, Fox shook his head. "You're not going to find the bad in me that easily. It's sealed up tight."

"Famous last words," she murmured, and they regarded each other for a drawn-out beat. "Is there really a record shop, or are you luring me to a watery grave?"

"Don't be dark, Freckles." He pulled her to a stop outside Disc N Dat before she could walk past it. "This is it."

"Really?" She studied the low white-stucco building. "There's no sign."

"Don't you know that's what makes it cool? I thought you were from LA." Fox opened the door for Hannah before she could respond, grinning as she passed. And yeah, fine, he was a little gratified when her cheeks turned pink. He could be friends with a girl, but it wouldn't hurt for her to at least *recognize* his attractiveness. After all, he worked so hard to make sure it was the main thing people noticed about him.

Hannah set foot inside the record shop and came to a dead halt.

He wasn't a record enthusiast like this girl, but he'd been in Disc N Dat enough times growing up in Westport that he knew there was something magical about it. The fact that he'd been the one to present it to Hannah gave him a surprising sense of pride. Still standing in the doorway, he tried to see the shop through her eyes. The shelves had blue inset lighting, casting the rows of records in a dreamlike glow. Vintage bulbs hung down from the ceiling, amber and gold and silver, paper mobiles turning around them to cast shapes and shadows onto the walls and original flooring. The place smelled like coffee and dust and leather.

Hannah turned to him with wide eyes. She took off her hat, letting loose a tumble of dirty-blond hair, her face awash in jewel-toned lighting, drying up his mouth.

Cute.

Friend.

Fox repeated those words three times each, but he stopped thinking altogether when she took two steps and wrapped her arms around his neck. Hugging him. Snuggling her dips and peaks right up against his muscles and squeezing tight.

"Thank you for bringing me here."

Her breath was warm, her chin propped in that spot where his neck and shoulder met, and Jesus, it felt nice. Too nice. Way too nice. But that didn't stop him from leaning down slightly to compensate for their height difference and pull her closer to his chest.

Hannah shifted slowly, turning her head . . . and their eyes met.

"Fade Into You" played low and entrancing from the speakers. Nothing about this was expected or remotely resembled real life. Not for him. He didn't have moments like this. Not with anyone. But this . . . girl. This off-limits girl.

She was making him need to kiss her. How was she doing it?

Already mentally calling himself a moron, Fox lowered his head—and his phone vibrated in the front pocket of his jeans. This time, he didn't pull it out, but Hannah stepped back, visibly shaking herself free of the moment, because it seemed to hover unspoken between them that a woman was calling. Most likely it was. No sugar-coating it. Fox's hands didn't seem capable of doing anything but dropping heavily to his sides.

"I'm going to browse," Hannah said, hidden beneath her hat once more, already turning for the first aisle. "If you want to take your call."

"Yeah, thanks. I'll just . . . be outside."

But when Fox left the store, he let the call go to voicemail and watched Hannah moon over records through the window instead.

Nisha Ver Halen

ABOUT THE AUTHOR

New York Times bestselling author Tessa Bailey aspires to three things: writing hot and unforgettable character-driven romance, being a good mother, and eventually sneaking onto the judging panel of a reality-show baking competition. She lives on Long Island, New York, with her husband and daughter, writing all day and rewarding herself with a cheese plate and Netflix binge in the evening. If you want sexy, heartfelt, humorous romance with a guaranteed happy ending, you've come to the right place.

MORE BY TESSA BAILEY

Tools of Engagement

Two enemies team up to flip a house, but as the race to renovate heats up, sparks fly as Wes and Bethany are forced into close quarters, trading barbs and banter as they remodel the ugliest house on the block.

Love Her or Lose Her

A young married couple's rocky relationship needs a serious renovation. Never did Rosie believe her stoic, too-manly-to-emote husband would actually agree to relationship rehab, but she discovers Dom has a secret that could demolish everything.

Fix Her Up

Travis was baseball's hottest rookie. Now he's flipping houses and trying to forget his glory days. When Georgie, his best friend's sister, proposes a wild scheme that they pretend to date to help him land a new job, he agrees—but finds there's nothing fake about how much he wants her.

Disturbing His Peace

Danika can't stand Lt. Burns, her roommate's sexy-as-hell but cold, unfeeling older brother. She just wants to graduate the police academy and forget about her scowling superior, until a dangerous mistake lands her under his watch...

Indecent Exposure

Jack Garrett isn't a police officer yet, but there's already an emergency. His new firearms instructor, Katie McCoy, is the same sexy Irish stranger Jack locked lips with last night.

Disorderly Conduct

Tessa Bailey returns with a sexy and hilarious series about three hotshot rookie cops in the NYPD police academy.

Make Me

Construction worker Russell is head-over-work boots for Abby, but he knows a classy, uptown virgin like her could never be truly happy with a rough, blue-collar guy like him.

Need Me

Honey traded in her cowboy boots for stilettos and left her small town for school. She's completely focused on her medical degree—until she meets her newly minted professor, and her concentration is hijacked.

Chase Me

College drop-out Roxy signs up to perform singing telegrams to make some quick cash, but her first customer—a gorgeous, cocky Manhattan trust-funder—has more to his sexy surface and is determined to make Roxy see it.